Belle of the Ball

of the

Ball

Mari Costa

:01

First Second
New York

To all the gays who were obsessed with
High School Musical in middle school

First Second
Published by First Second
First Second is an imprint of Roaring Brook Press,
a division of Holtzbrinck Publishing Holdings Limited Partnership
120 Broadway, New York, NY 10271
firstsecondbooks.com

Library of Congress Cataloging-in-Publication Data is available.

Our books may be purchased in bulk for promotional, educational, or business use.
Please contact your local bookseller or the Macmillan Corporate and Premium Sales Department
at (800) 221-7945 ext. 5442 or by email at MacmillanSpecialMarkets@macmillan.com.

First edition, 2023
Edited by Calista Brill and Steve Foxe
Cover and interior book design by Molly Johanson
Production editing by Helen Seachrist

All artwork done in Clip Studio Paint Pro, with Frenden inking brushes for line art and effects.

Printed in China by 1010 Printing International Limited, Kwun Tong, Hong Kong

ISBN 978-1-250-78412-4 (paperback)
10 9 8 7 6 5 4 3 2 1

ISBN 978-1-250-78413-1 (hardcover)
10 9 8 7 6 5 4 3 2 1

Don't miss your next favorite book from First Second!
For the latest updates go to firstsecondnewsletter.com and sign up for our enewsletter.

CHAPTER

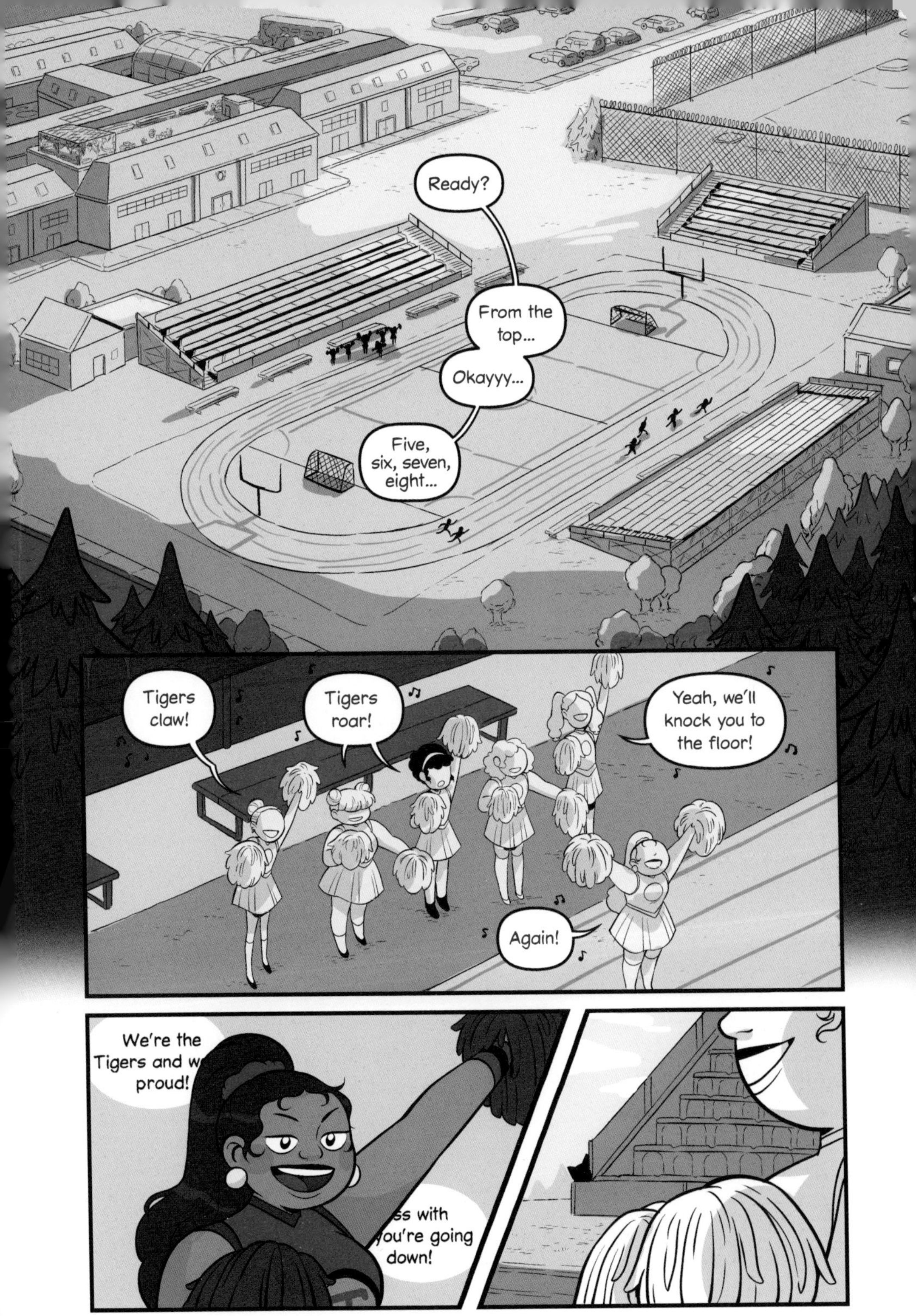
Ready?
From the top...
Okayyy...
Five, six, seven, eight...
Tigers claw!
Tigers roar!
Yeah, we'll knock you to the floor!
Again!
We're the Tigers and w proud!
ss with you're going down!

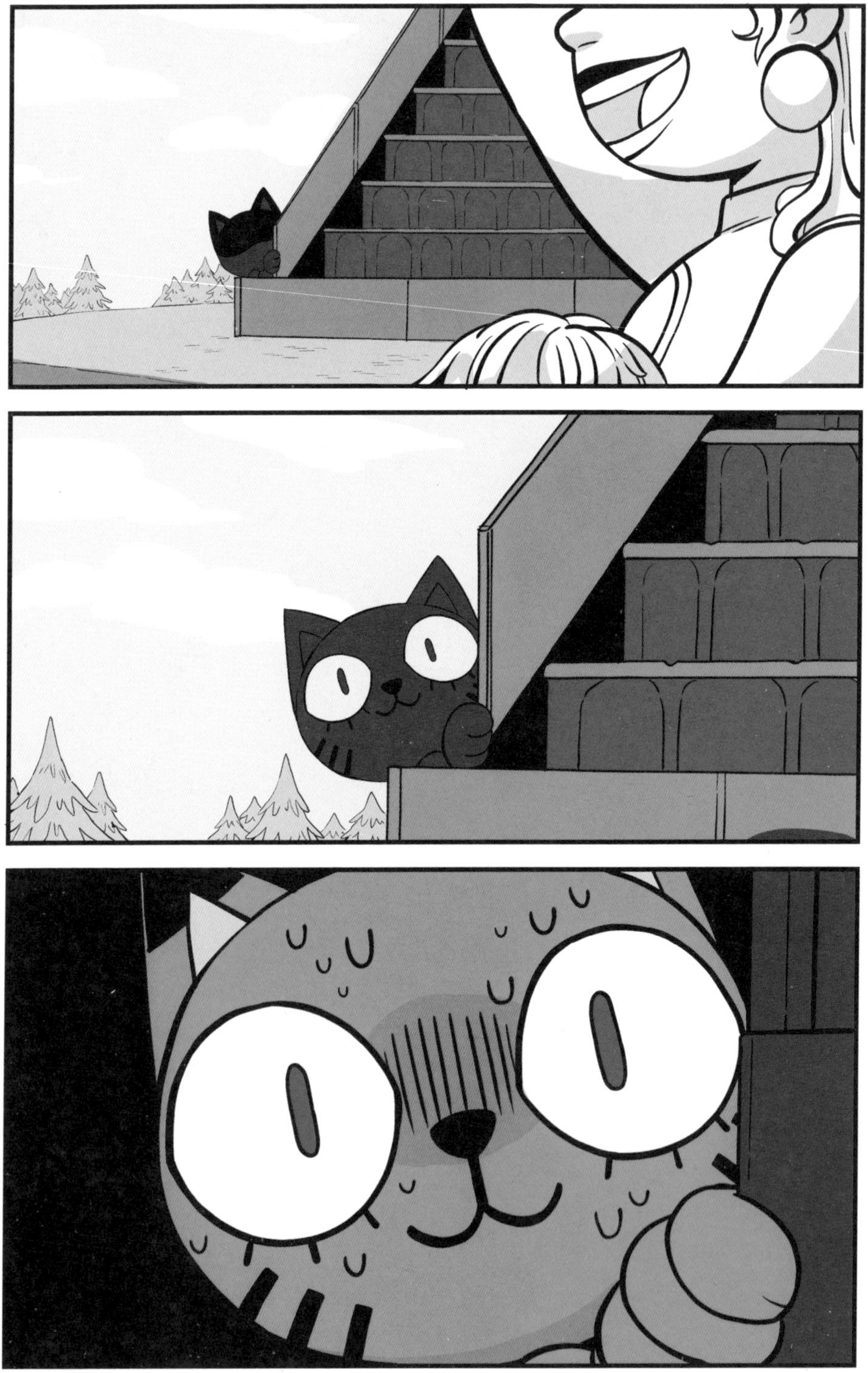

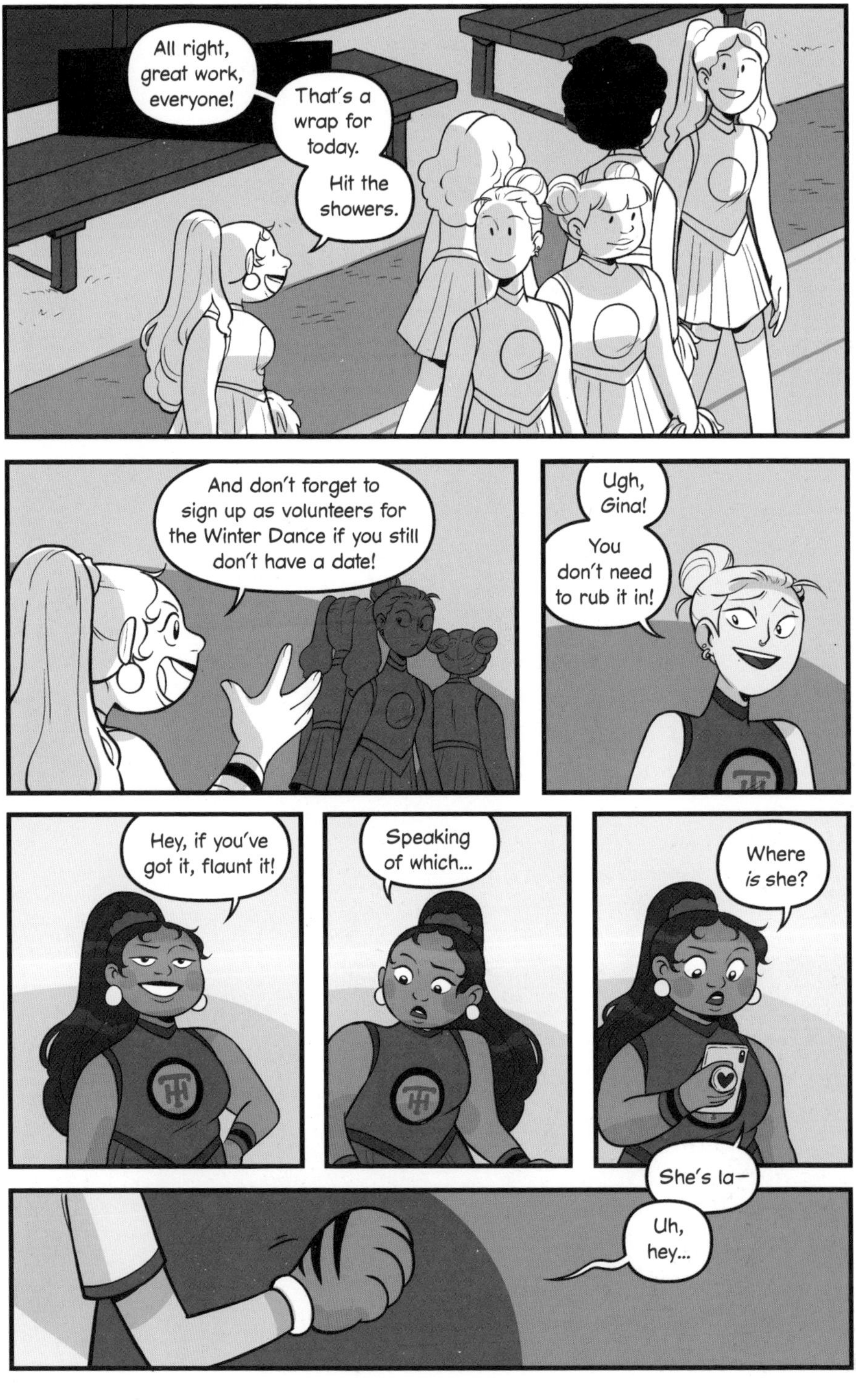
All right, great work, everyone!
That's a wrap for today.
Hit the showers.
And don't forget to sign up as volunteers for the Winter Dance if you still don't have a date!
Ugh, Gina!
You don't need to rub it in!
Hey, if you've got it, flaunt it!
Speaking of which...
Where *is* she?
She's la—
Uh, hey...

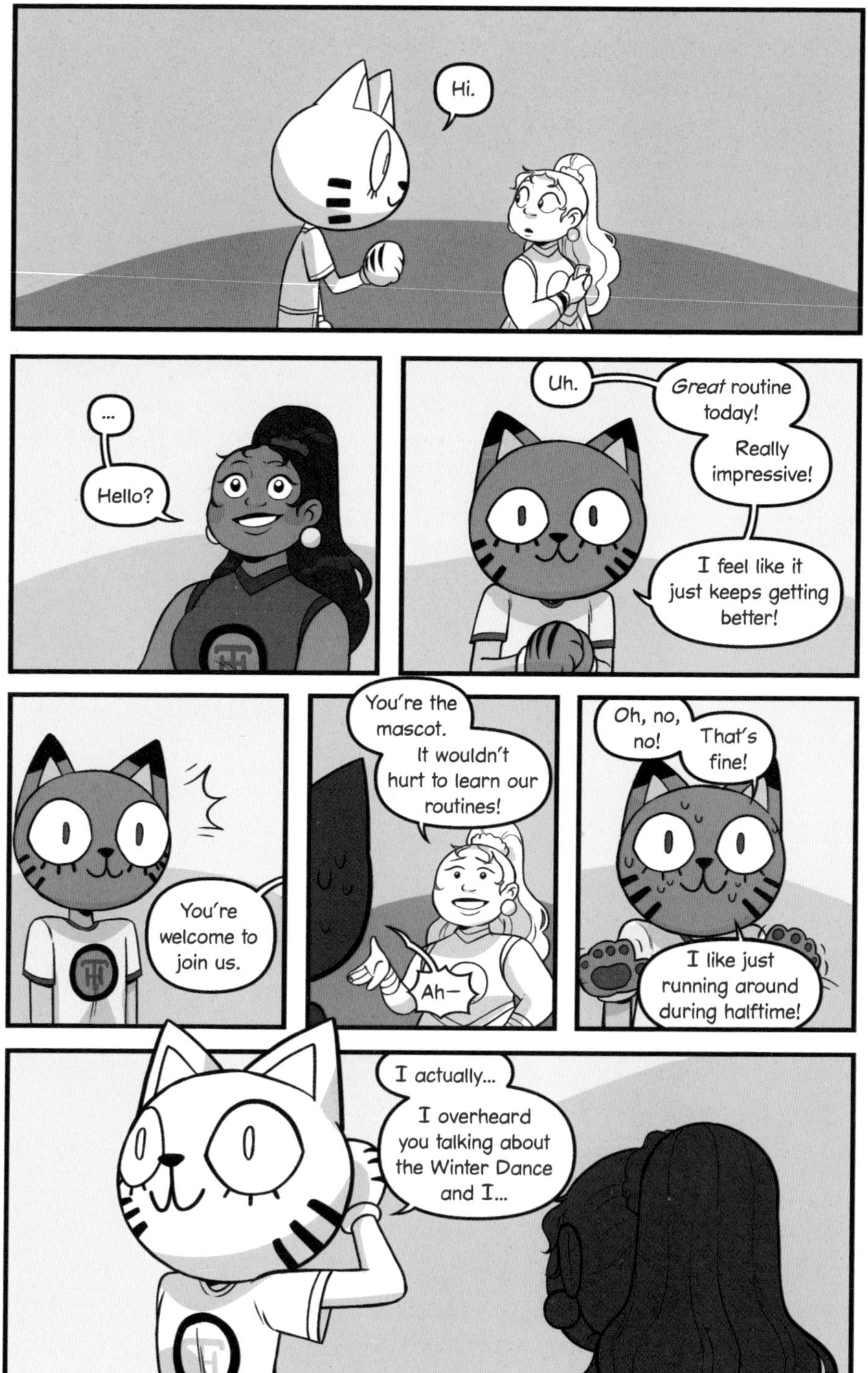

Hi.
...
Hello?
Uh.
Great routine today!
Really impressive!
I feel like it just keeps getting better!
You're welcome to join us.
You're the mascot.
It wouldn't hurt to learn our routines!
Ah—
Oh, no, no!
That's fine!
I like just running around during halftime!
I actually...
I overheard you talking about the Winter Dance and I...

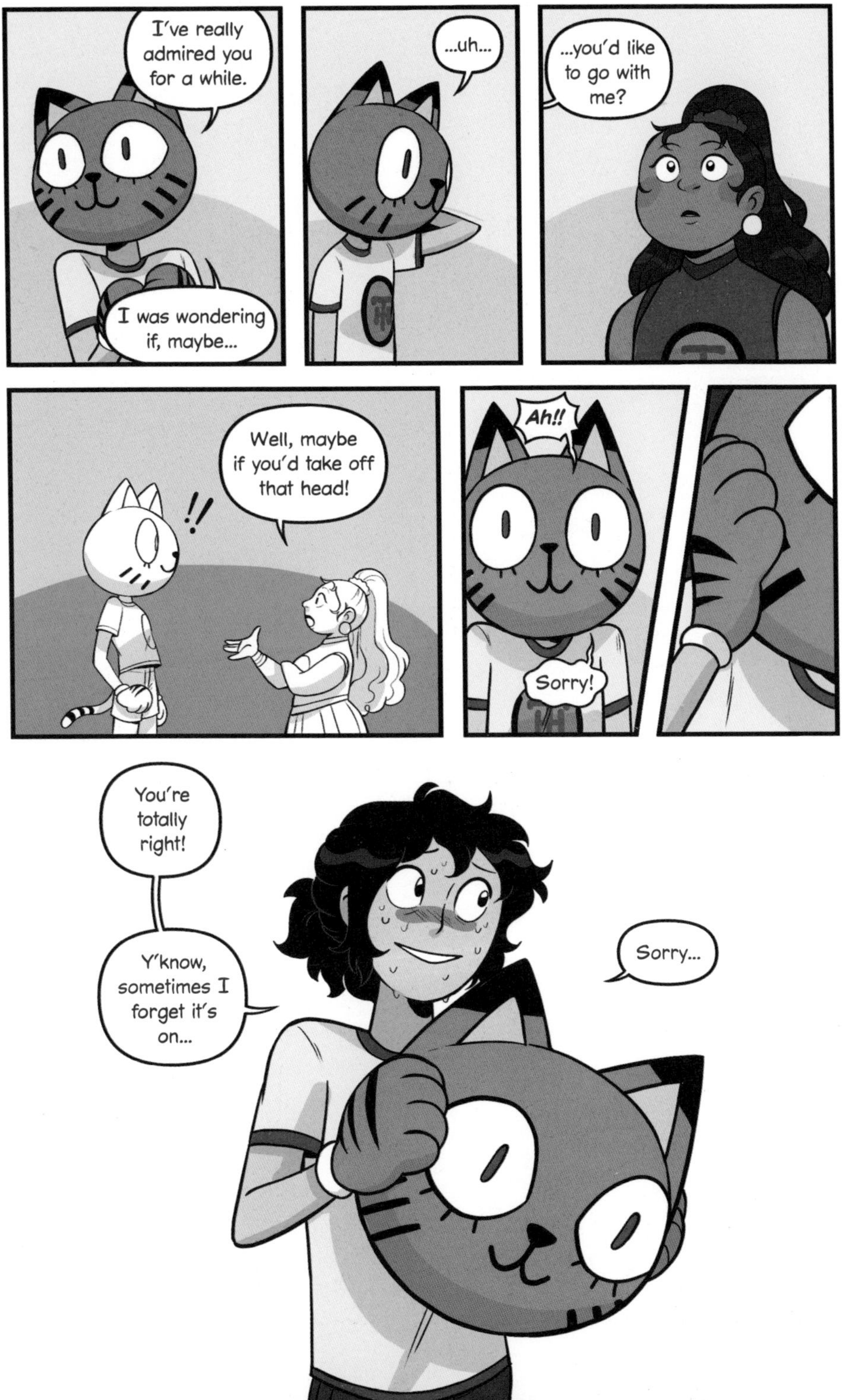
I've really admired you for a while.
I was wondering if, maybe...
...uh...
...you'd like to go with me?
Well, maybe if you'd take off that head!
!!
Ah!!
Sorry!
You're totally right!
Y'know, sometimes I forget it's on...
Sorry...

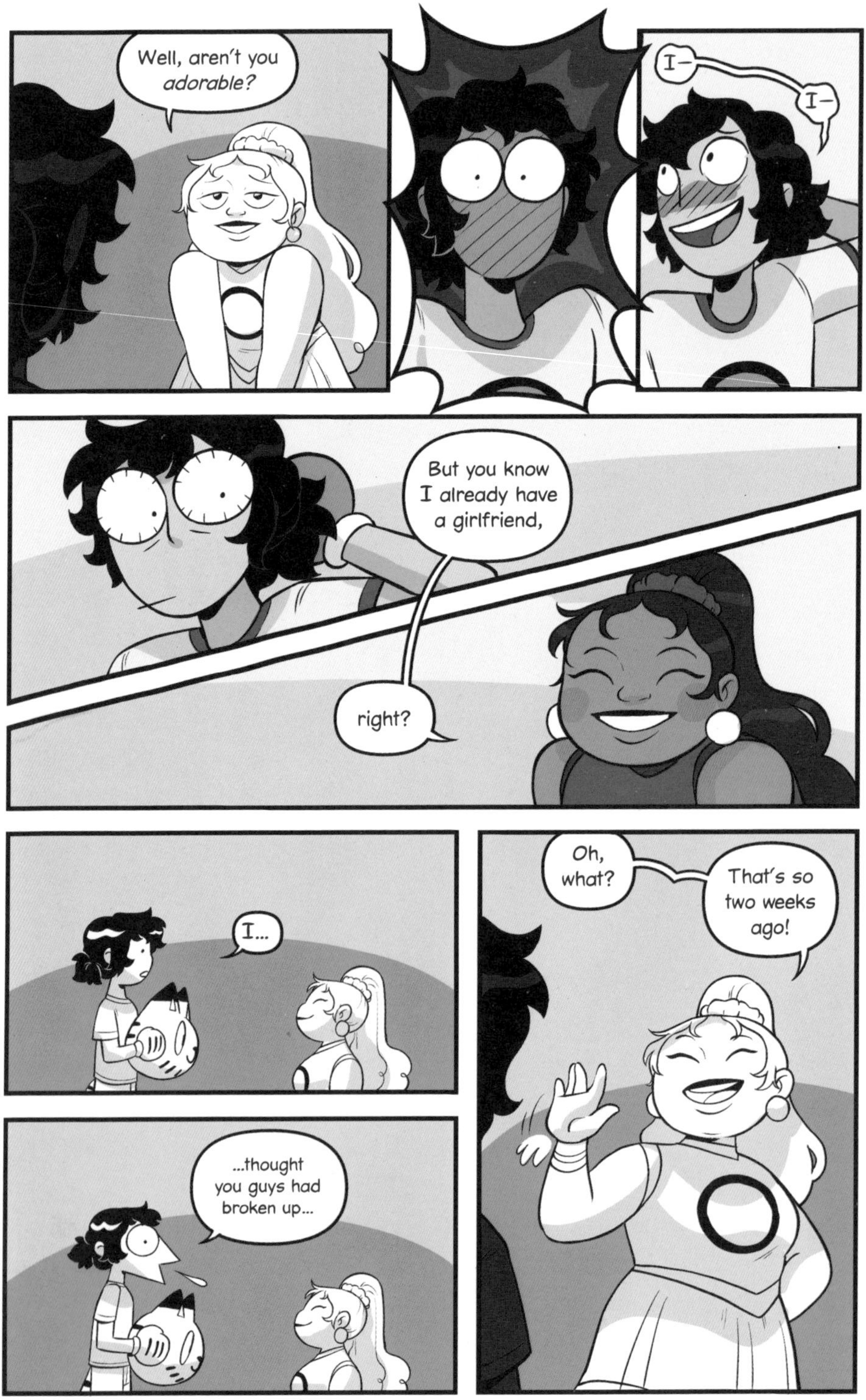
Well, aren't you *adorable?*
I—
I—
But you know I already have a girlfriend,
right?
I...
...thought you guys had broken up...
Oh, what?
That's so two weeks ago!

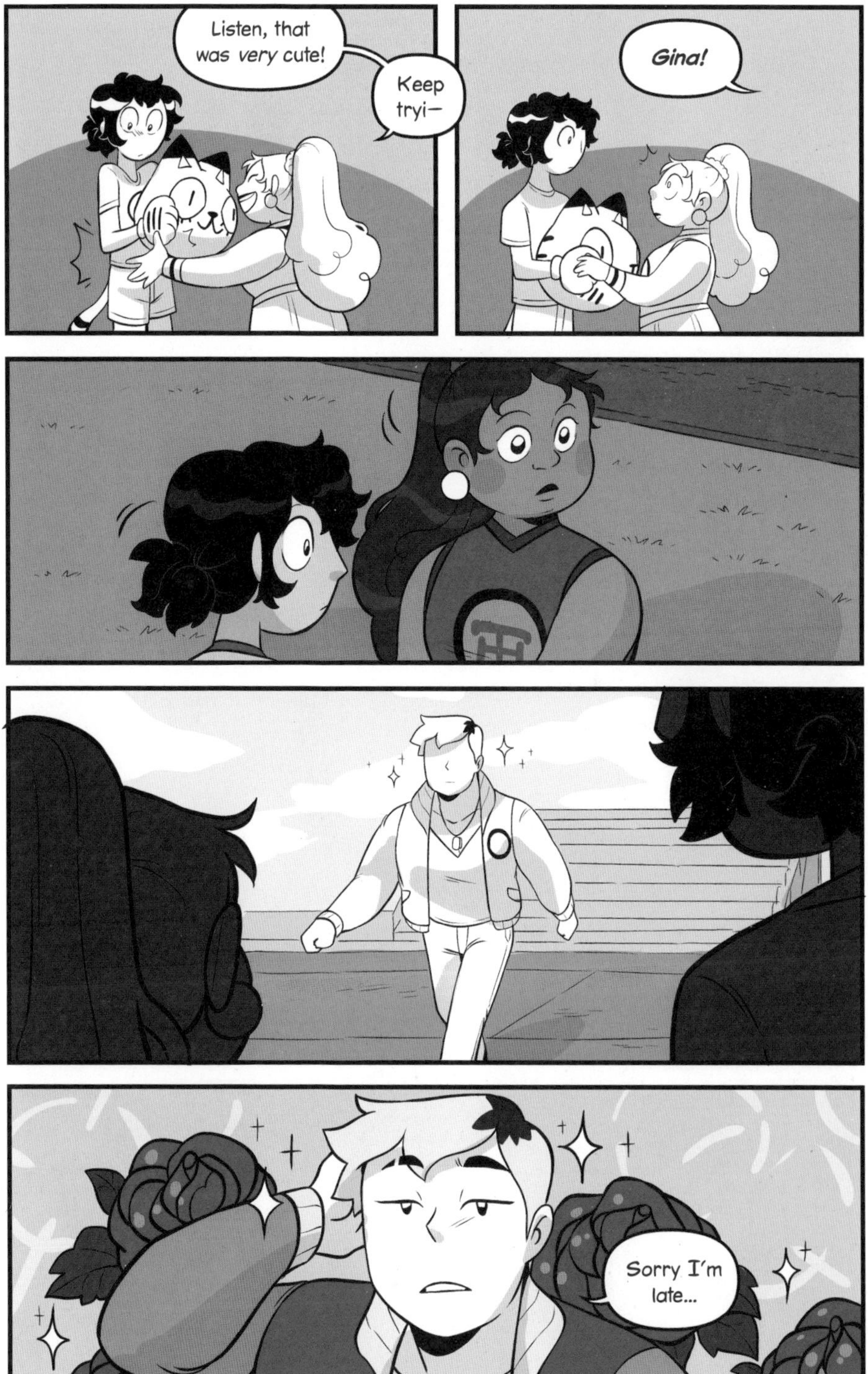
Listen, that was *very* cute!
Keep tryi—
Gina!
Sorry I'm late...

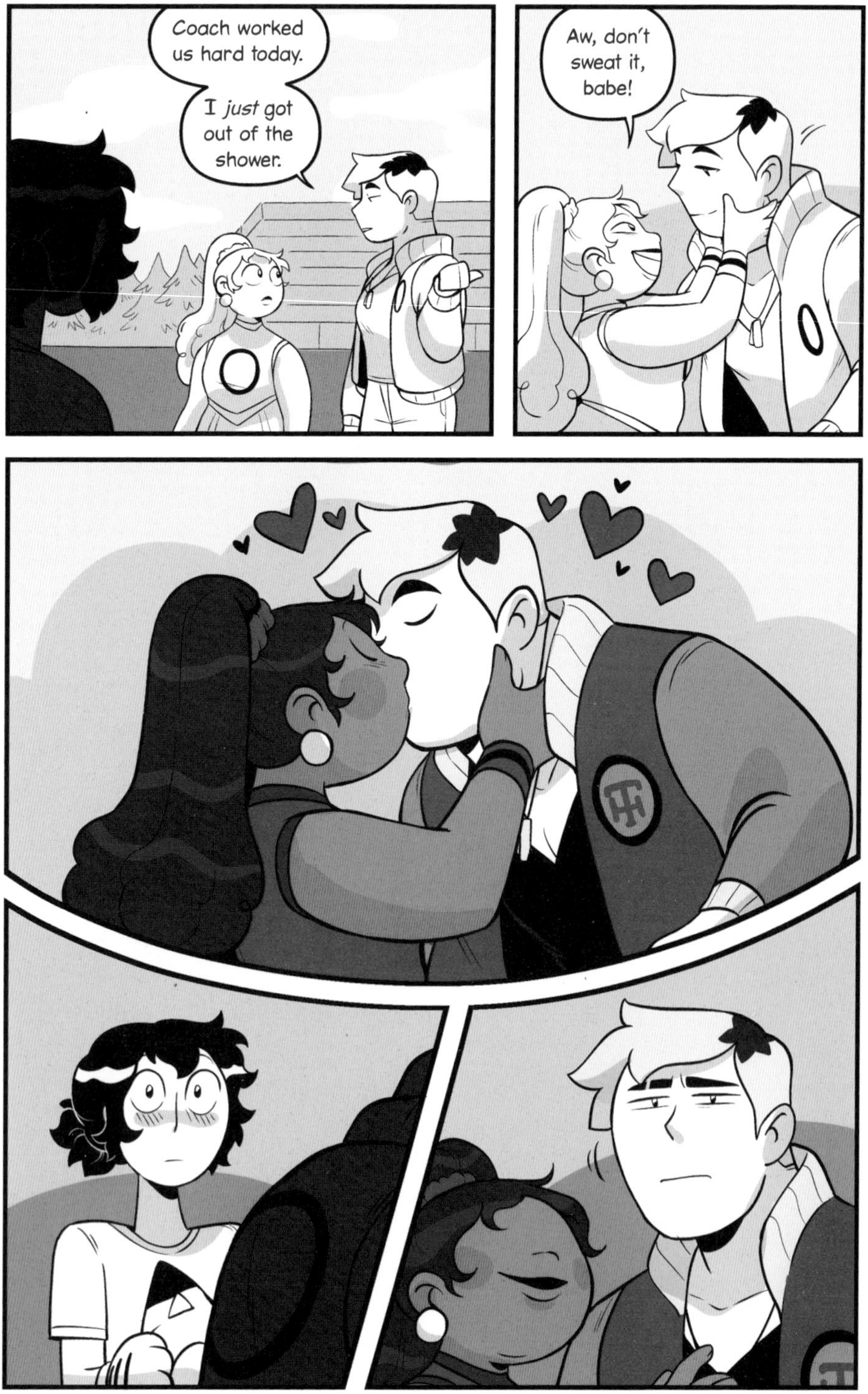
Coach worked us hard today.
I *just* got out of the shower.
Aw, don't sweat it, babe!

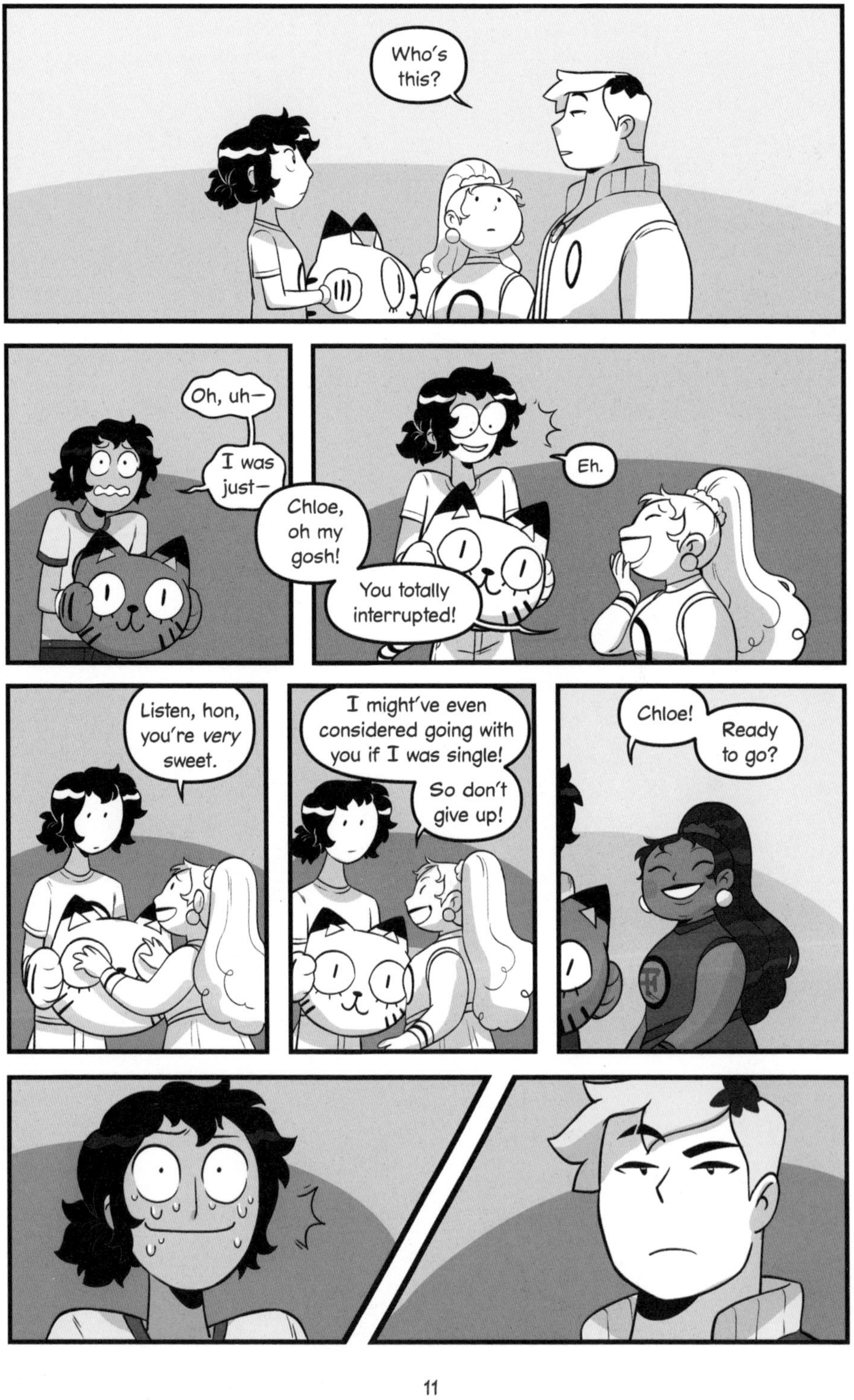
Who's this?
Oh, uh—
I was just—
Eh.
Chloe, oh my gosh!
You totally interrupted!
Listen, hon, you're *very* sweet.
I might've even considered going with you if I was single!
So don't give up!
Chloe!
Ready to go?

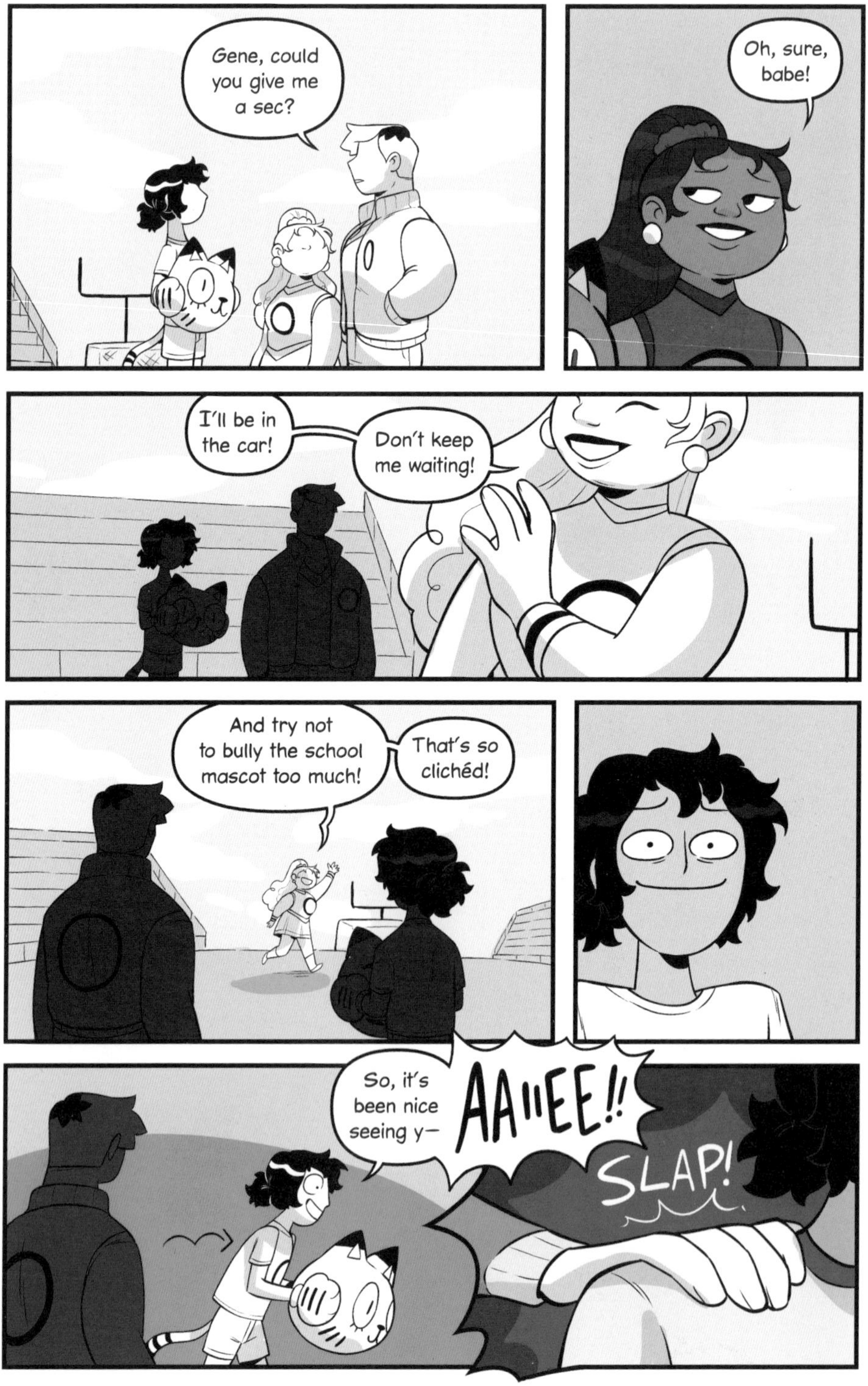
Gene, could you give me a sec?
Oh, sure, babe!
I'll be in the car!
Don't keep me waiting!
And try not to bully the school mascot too much!
That's so clichéd!
So, it's been nice seeing y—
AAIIEE!!
SLAP!

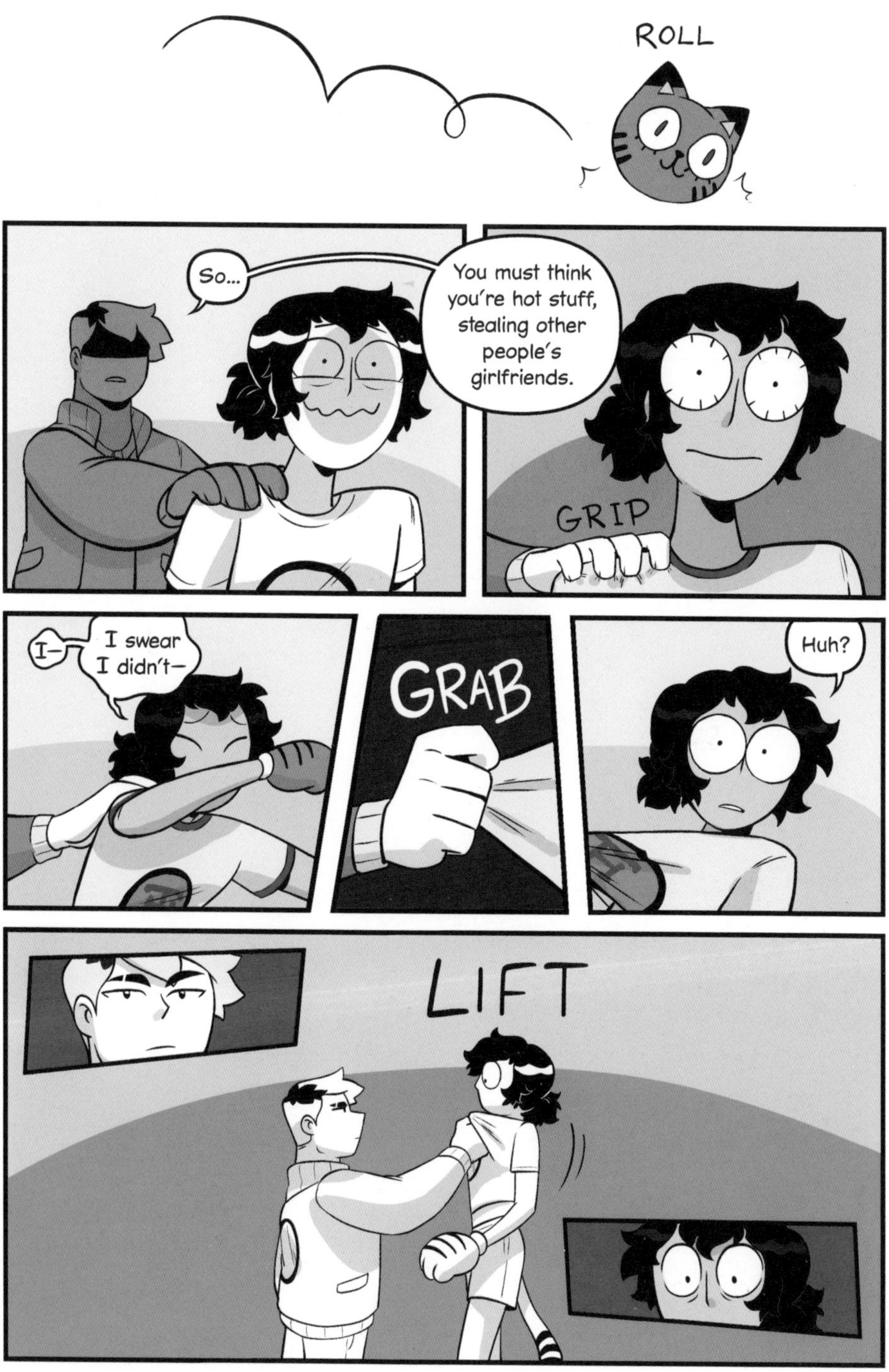
ROLL
So...
You must think you're hot stuff, stealing other people's girlfriends.
GRIP
I—
I swear I didn't—
GRAB
Huh?
LIFT

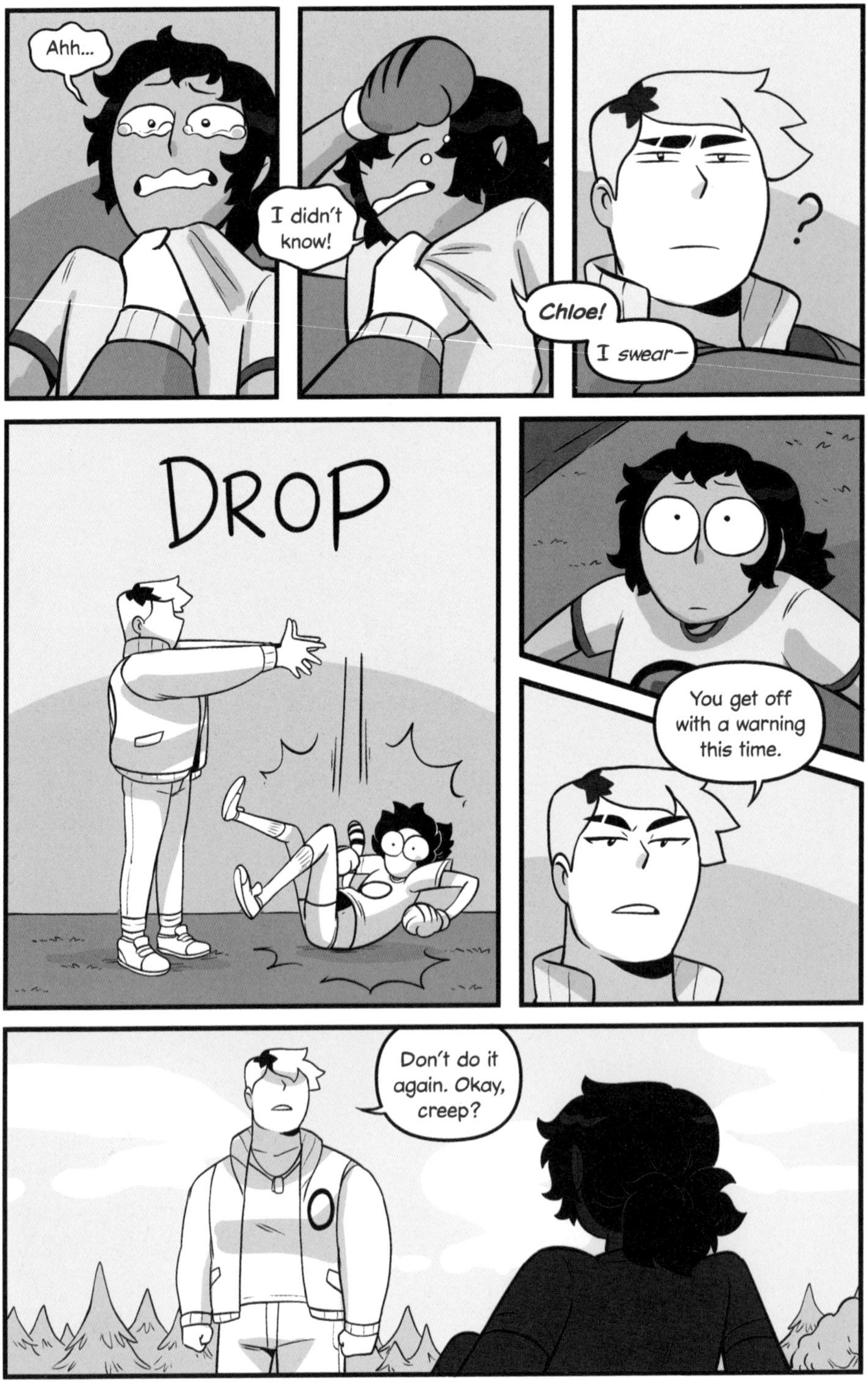
Ahh...
I didn't know!
Chloe!
I swear—
?
DROP
You get off with a warning this time.
Don't do it again. Okay, creep?

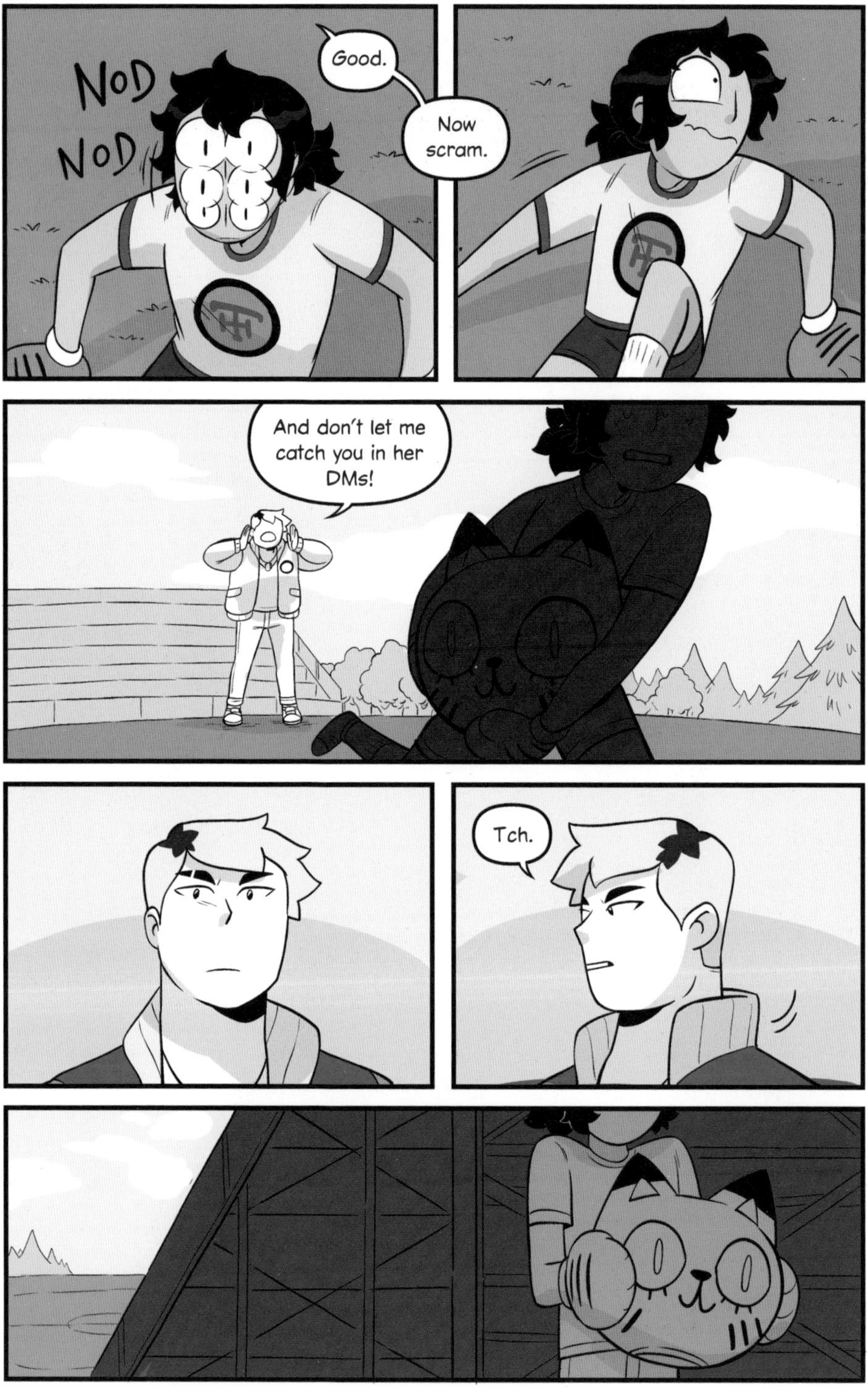
NOD
NOD
Good.
Now scram.
And don't let me catch you in her DMs!
Tch.

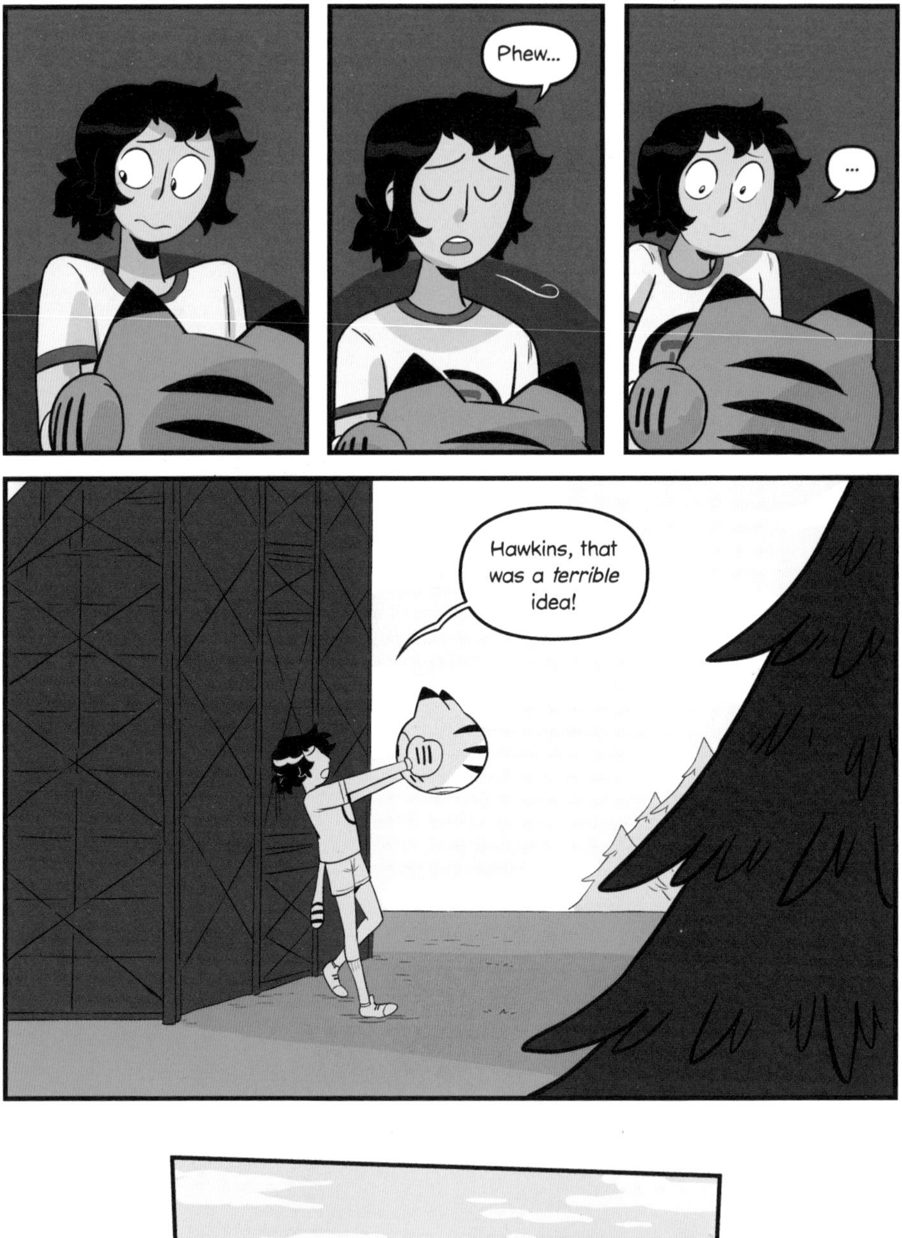
Phew...
...
Hawkins, that was a *terrible* idea!

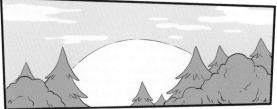

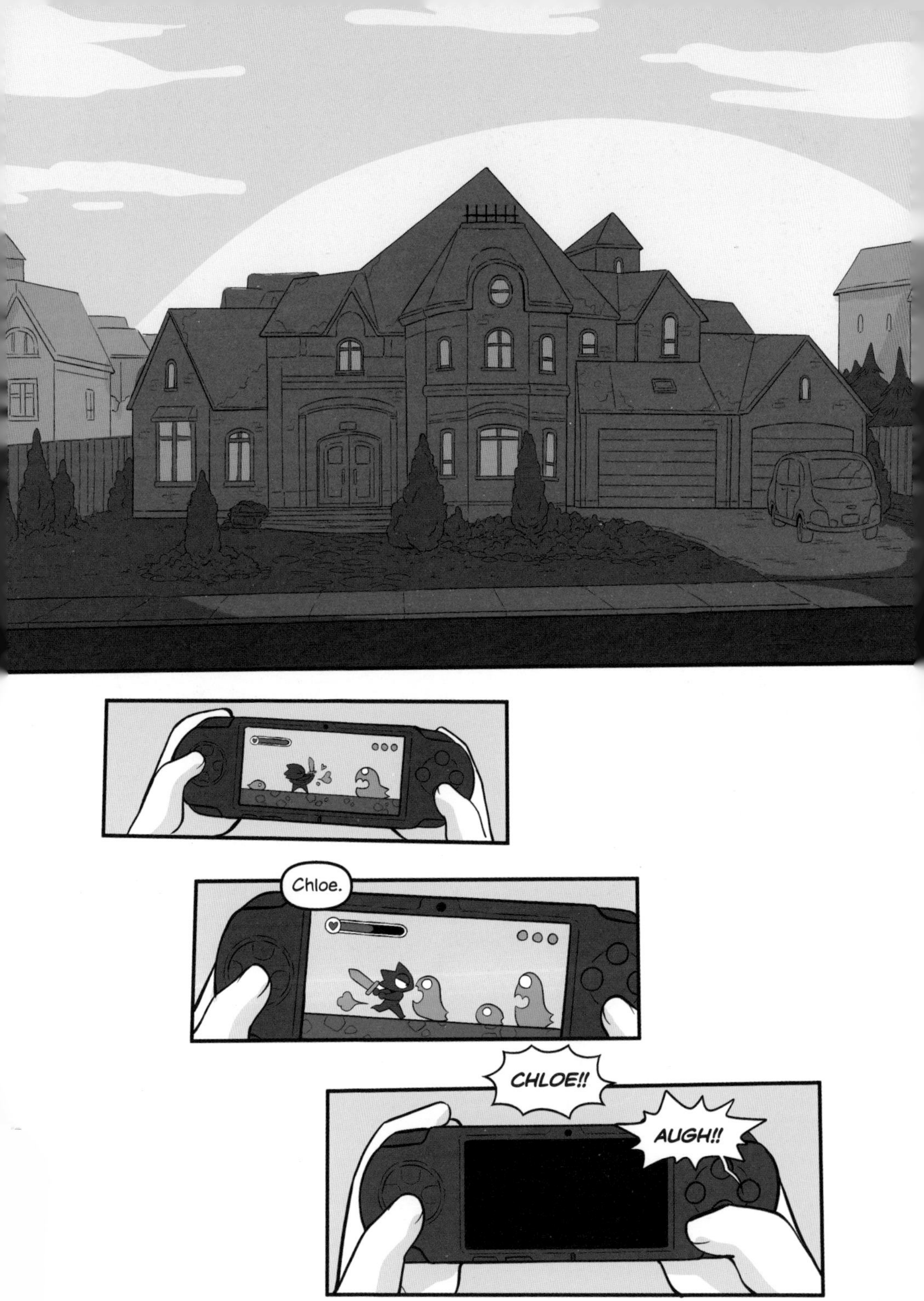
Chloe.
CHLOE!!
AUGH!!

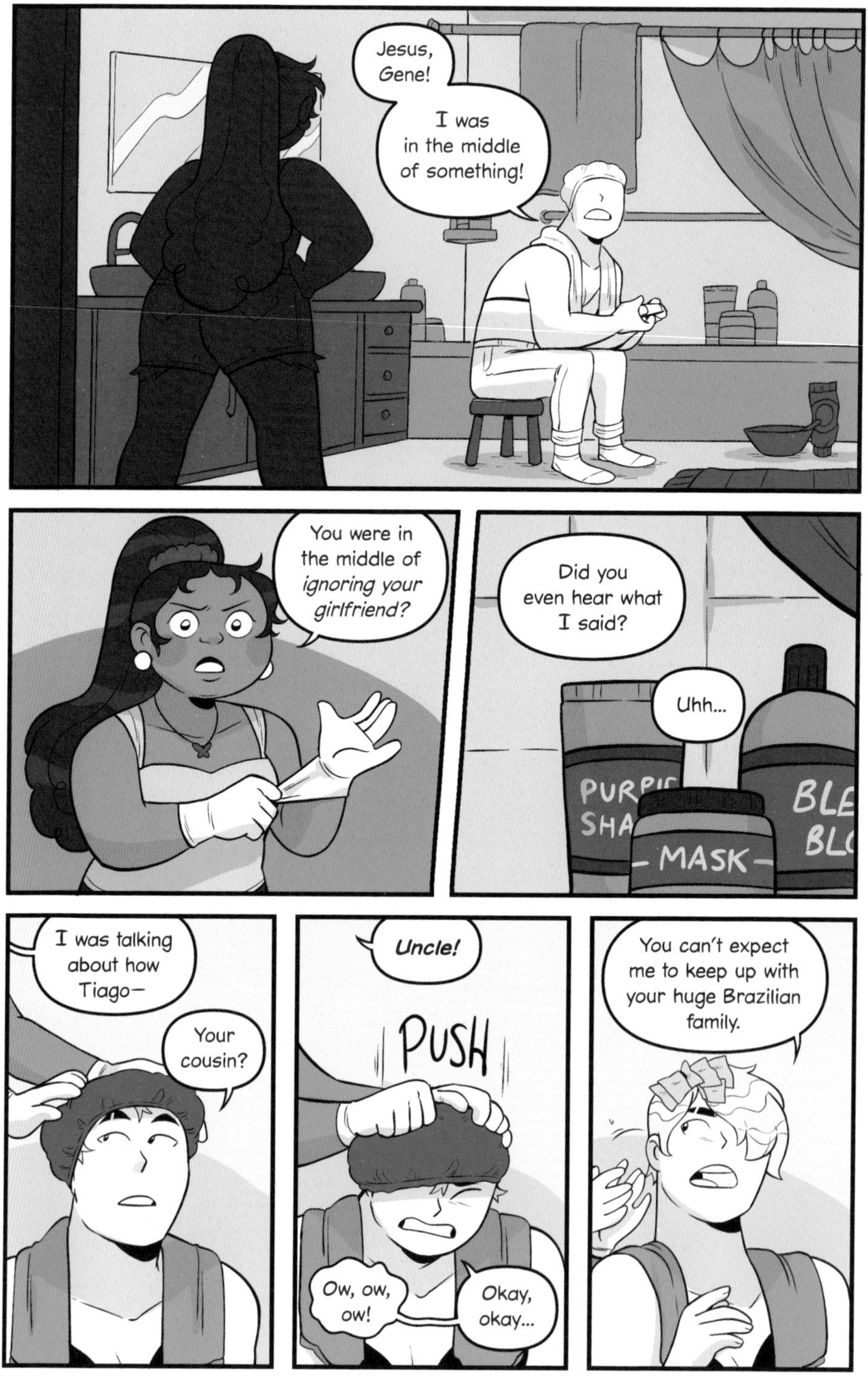

Jesus, Gene!
I was in the middle of something!
You were in the middle of *ignoring your girlfriend?*
Did you even hear what I said?
Uhh...
PURPLE SHA
MASK
BLE BLO
I was talking about how Tiago—
Your cousin?
Uncle!
PUSH
Ow, ow, ow!
Okay, okay...
You can't expect me to keep up with your huge Brazilian family.

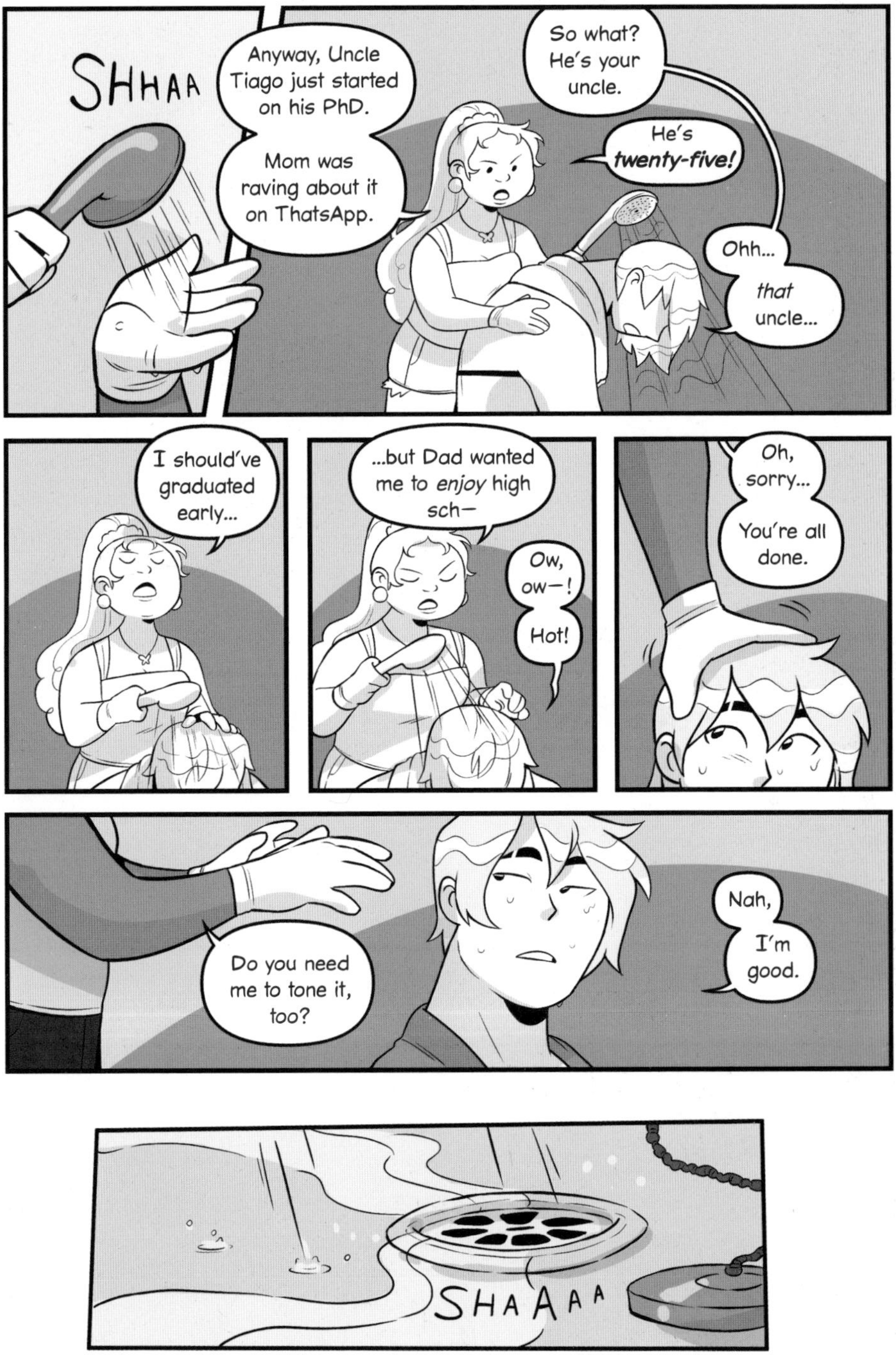
SHHAA
Anyway, Uncle Tiago just started on his PhD.
Mom was raving about it on ThatsApp.
So what? He's your uncle.
He's *twenty-five!*
Ohh...
that uncle...
I should've graduated early...
...but Dad wanted me to *enjoy* high sch—
Ow, ow—!
Hot!
Oh, sorry...
You're all done.
Do you need me to tone it, too?
Nah,
I'm good.
SHAAAA

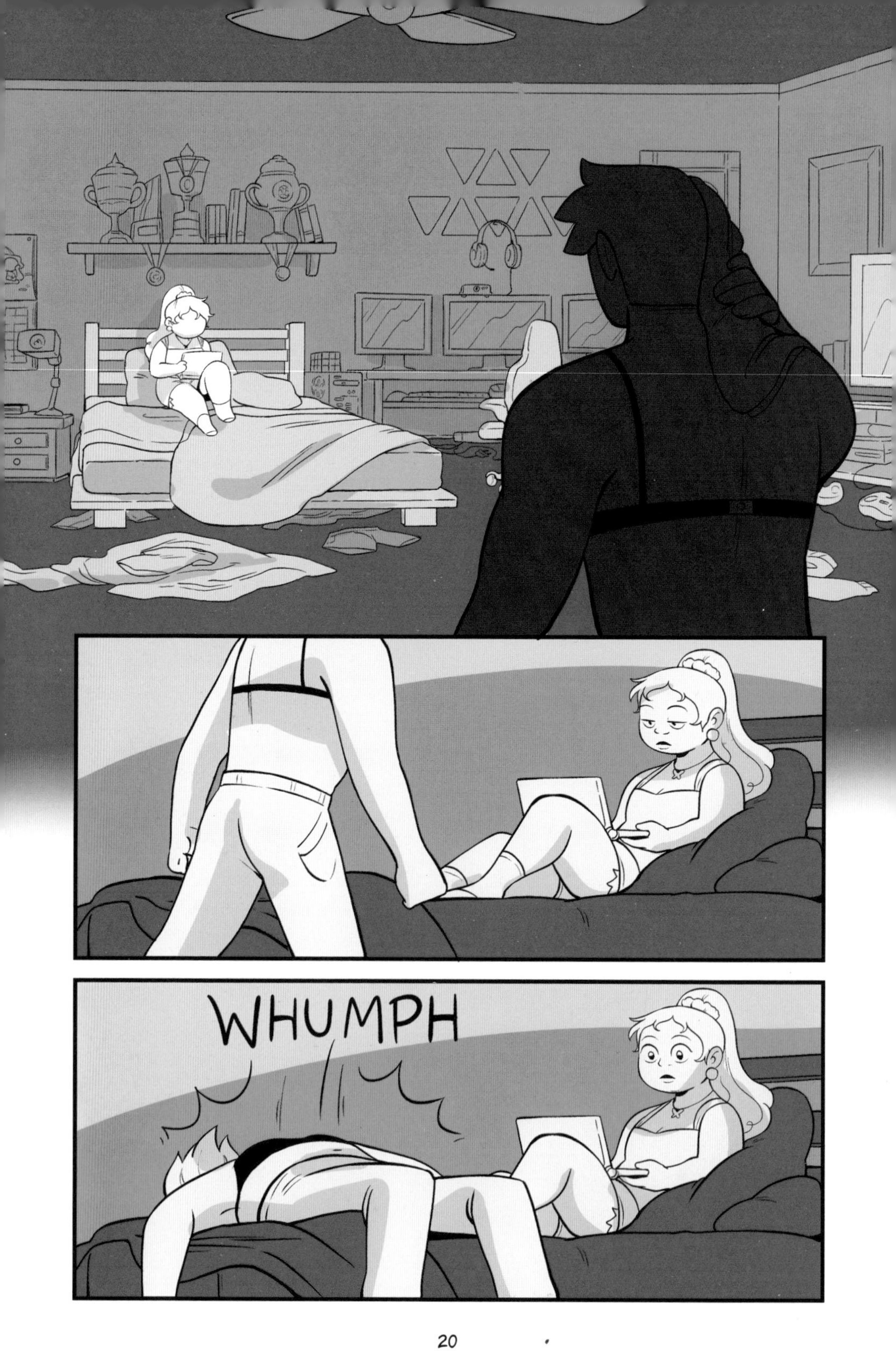
WHUMPH

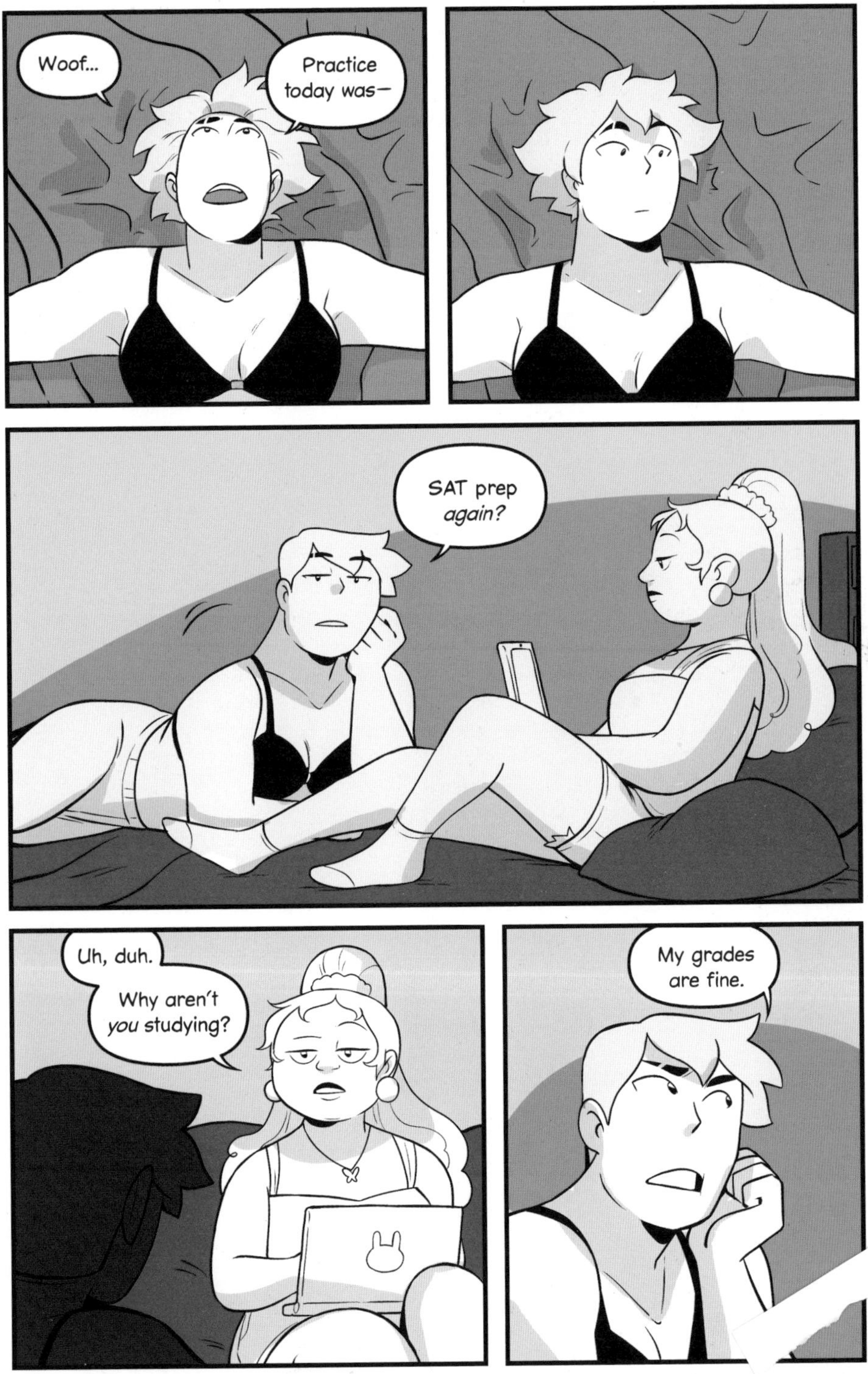
Woof...
Practice today was—
SAT prep *again?*
Uh, duh.
Why aren't *you* studying?
My grades are fine.

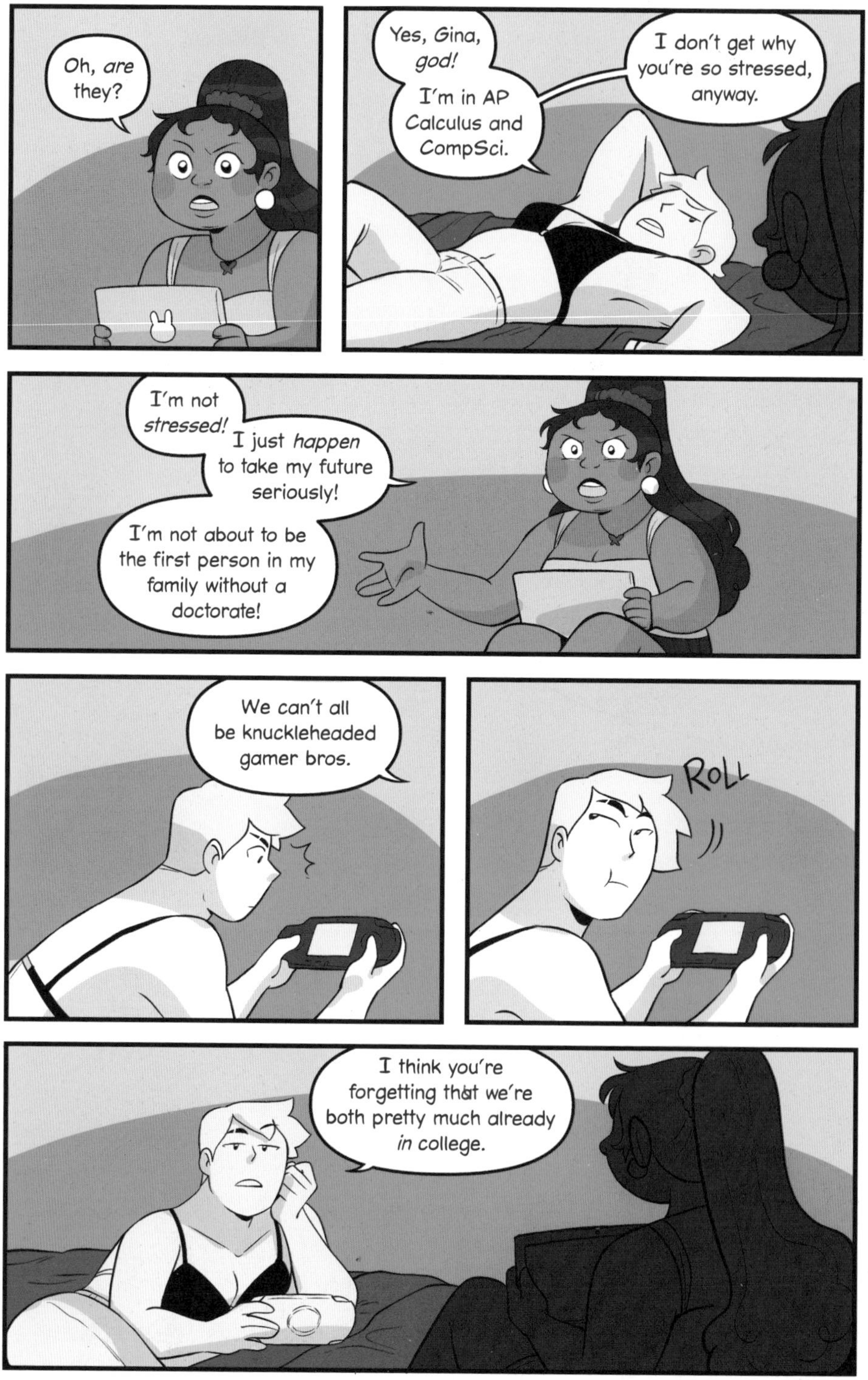
Oh, *are* they?
Yes, Gina, *god!*
I'm in AP Calculus and CompSci.
I don't get why you're so stressed, anyway.
I'm not *stressed!*
I just *happen* to take my future seriously!
I'm not about to be the first person in my family without a doctorate!
We can't all be knuckleheaded gamer bros.
ROLL
I think you're forgetting that we're both pretty much already *in* college.

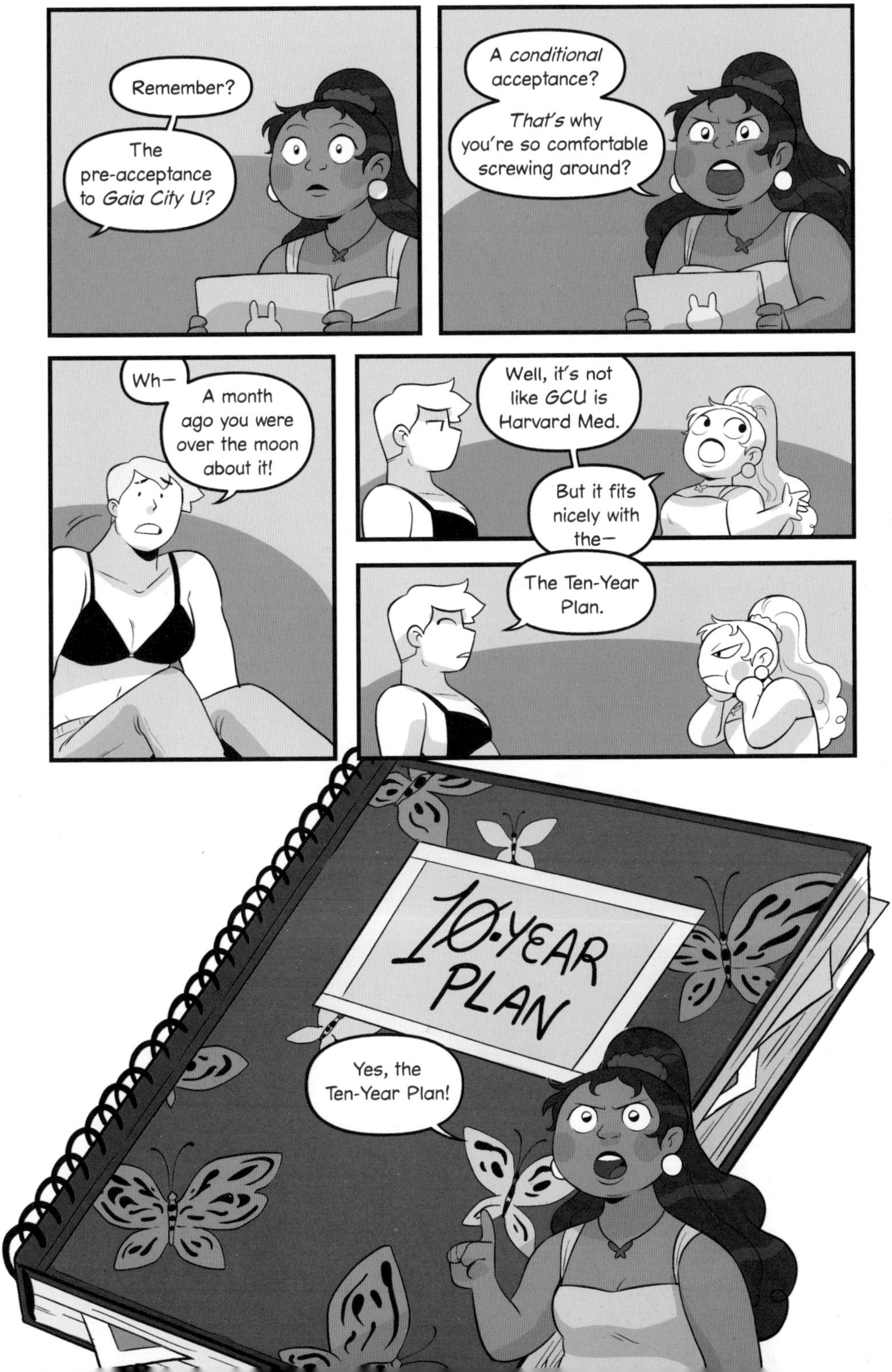
Remember?
The pre-acceptance to *Gaia City U?*
A *conditional* acceptance?
That's why you're so comfortable screwing around?
Wh—
A month ago you were over the moon about it!
Well, it's not like GCU is Harvard Med.
But it fits nicely with the—
The Ten-Year Plan.
10-YEAR PLAN
Yes, the Ten-Year Plan!

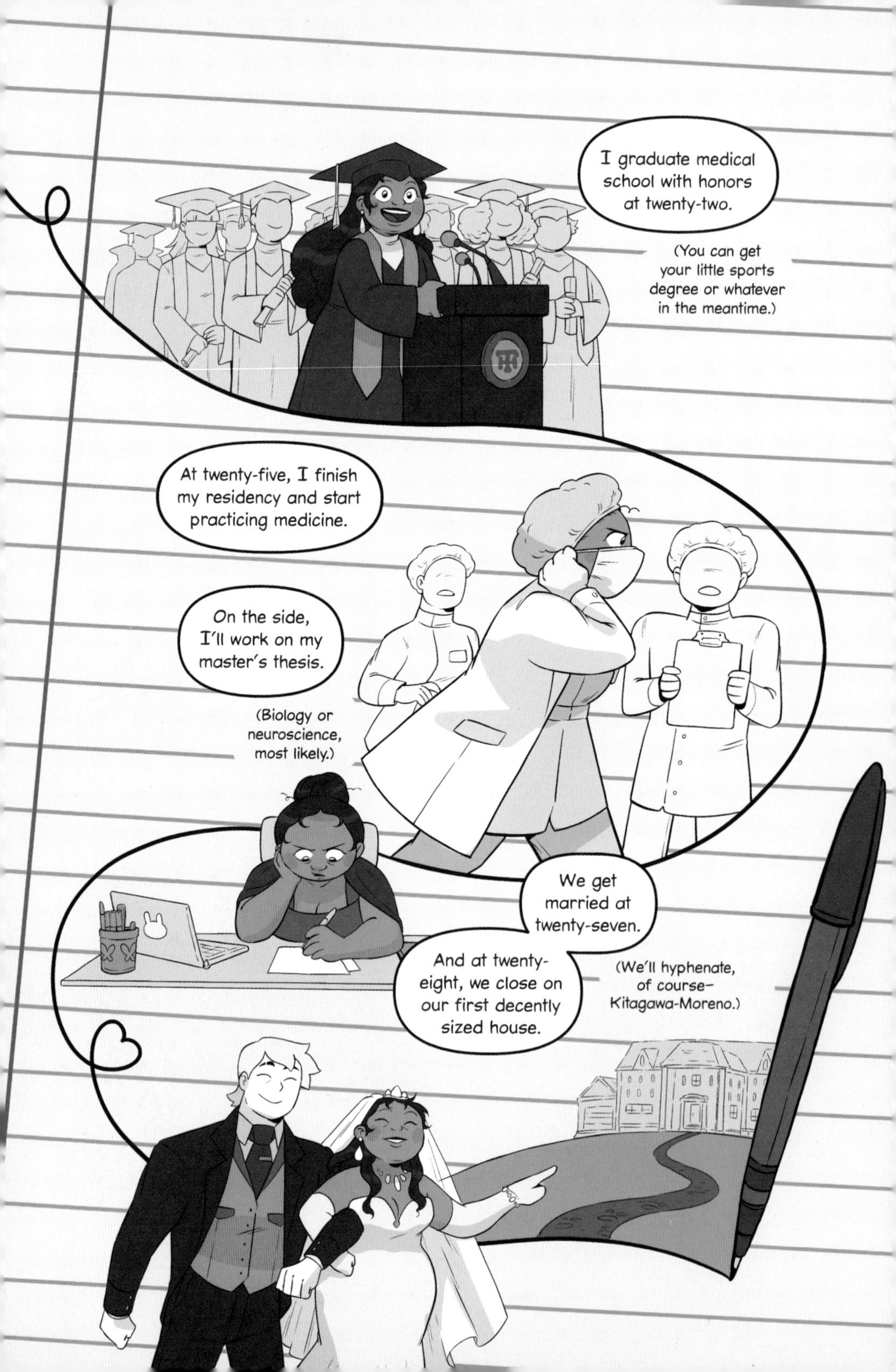
I graduate medical school with honors at twenty-two.
(You can get your little sports degree or whatever in the meantime.)
At twenty-five, I finish my residency and start practicing medicine.
On the side, I'll work on my master's thesis.
(Biology or neuroscience, most likely.)
We get married at twenty-seven.
And at twenty-eight, we close on our first decently sized house.
(We'll hyphenate, of course–Kitagawa-Moreno.)

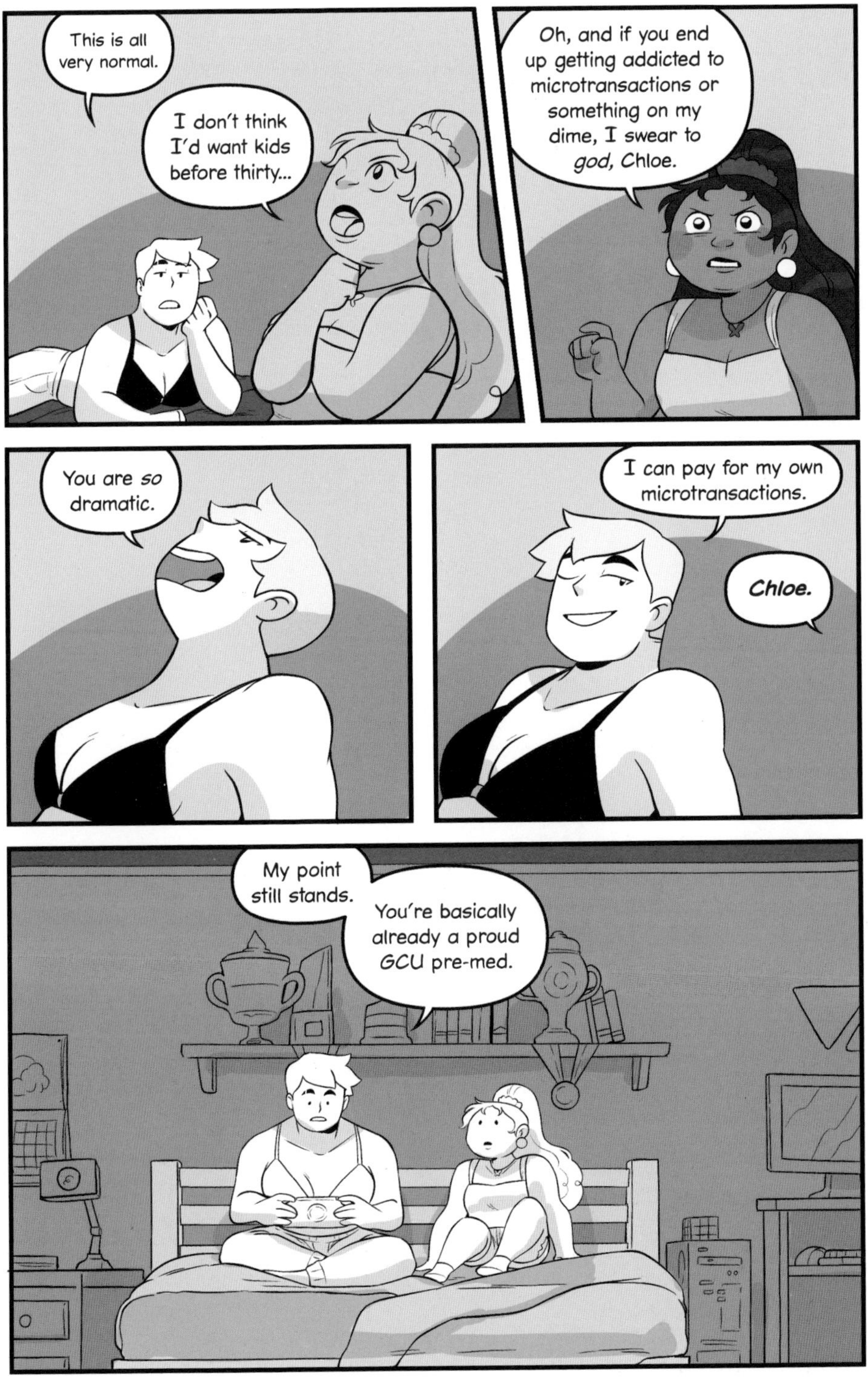
This is all very normal.
I don't think I'd want kids before thirty...
Oh, and if you end up getting addicted to microtransactions or something on my dime, I swear to *god,* Chloe.
You are *so* dramatic.
I can pay for my own microtransactions.
Chloe.
My point still stands.
You're basically already a proud GCU pre-med.

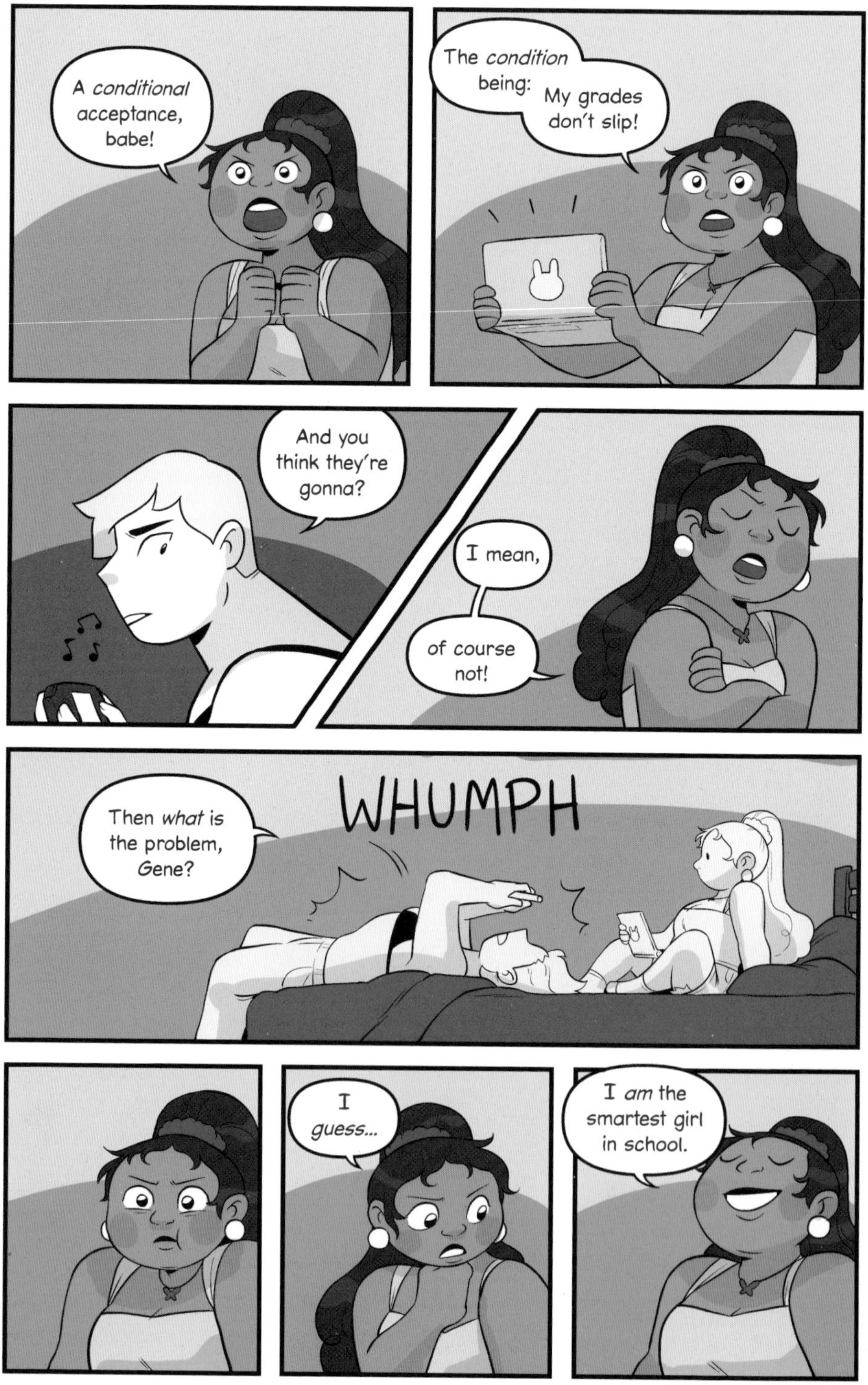
A *conditional* acceptance, babe!
The *condition* being:
My grades don't slip!
And you think they're gonna?
I mean,
of course not!
Then *what* is the problem, Gene?
WHUMPH
I *guess...*
I *am* the smartest girl in school.

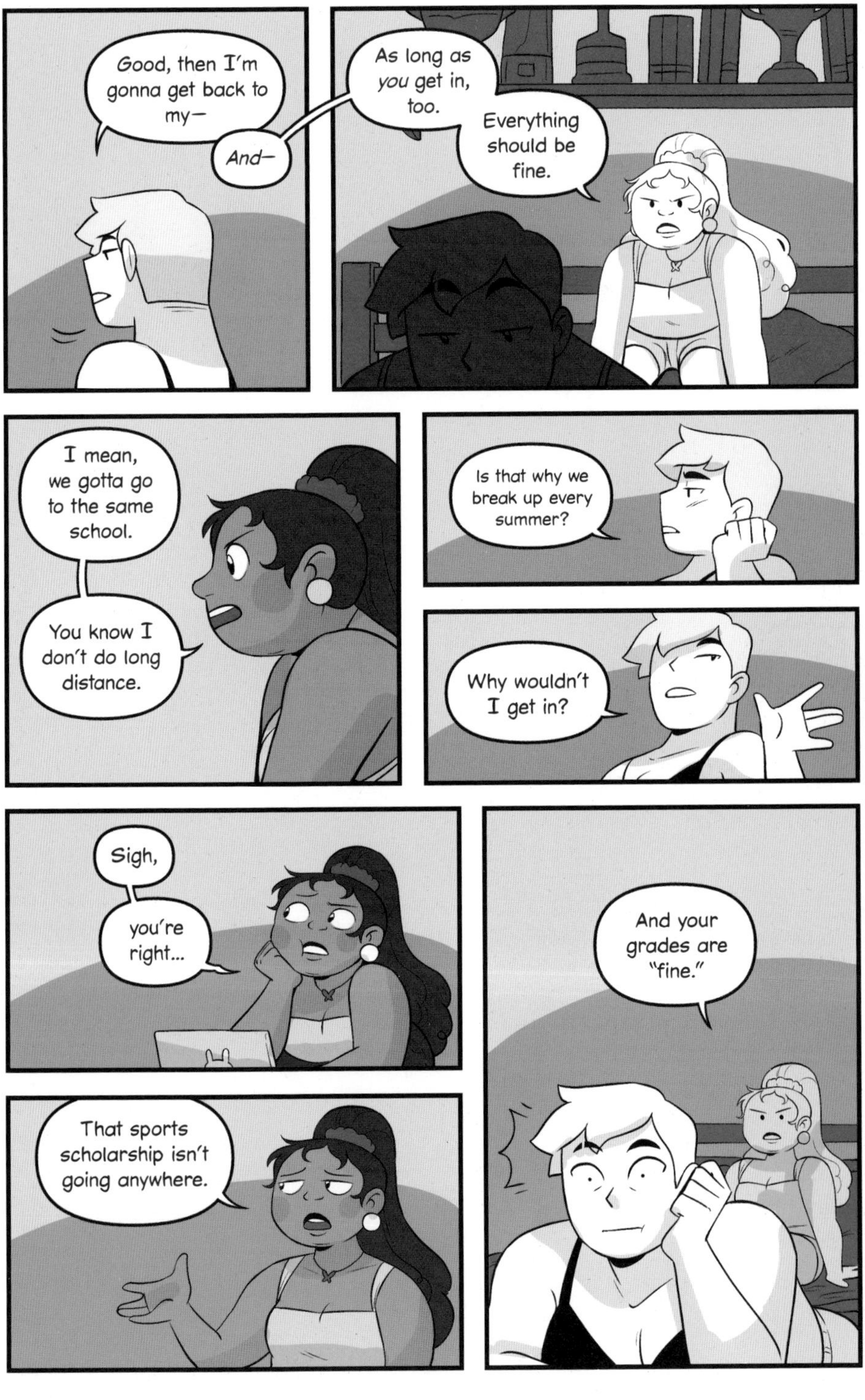
Good, then I'm gonna get back to my—
And—
As long as *you* get in, too.
Everything should be fine.
I mean, we gotta go to the same school.
You know I don't do long distance.
Is that why we break up every summer?
Why wouldn't I get in?
Sigh,
you're right...
That sports scholarship isn't going anywhere.
And your grades are "fine."

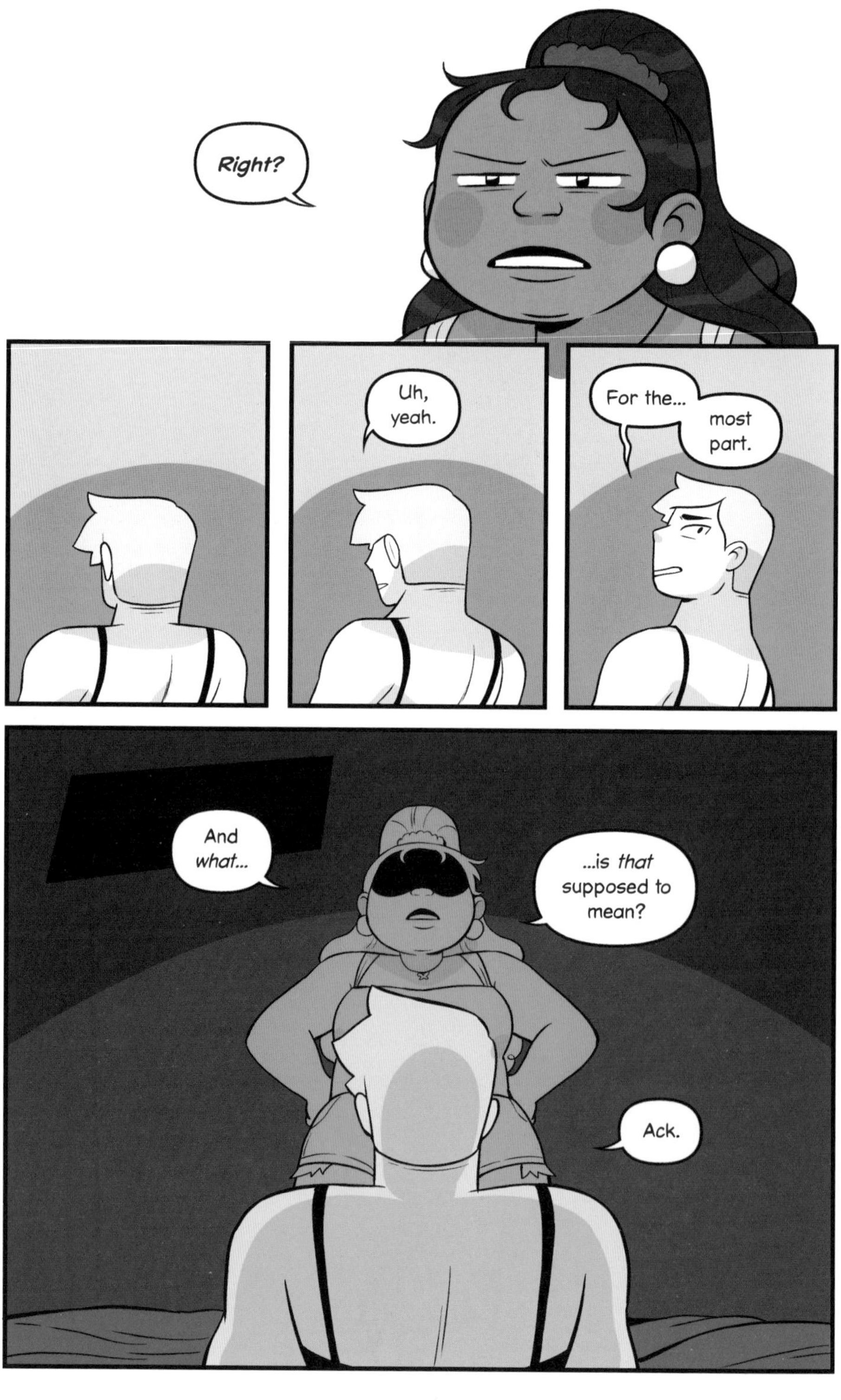
Right?
Uh, yeah.
For the...
most part.
And what...
...is *that* supposed to mean?
Ack.

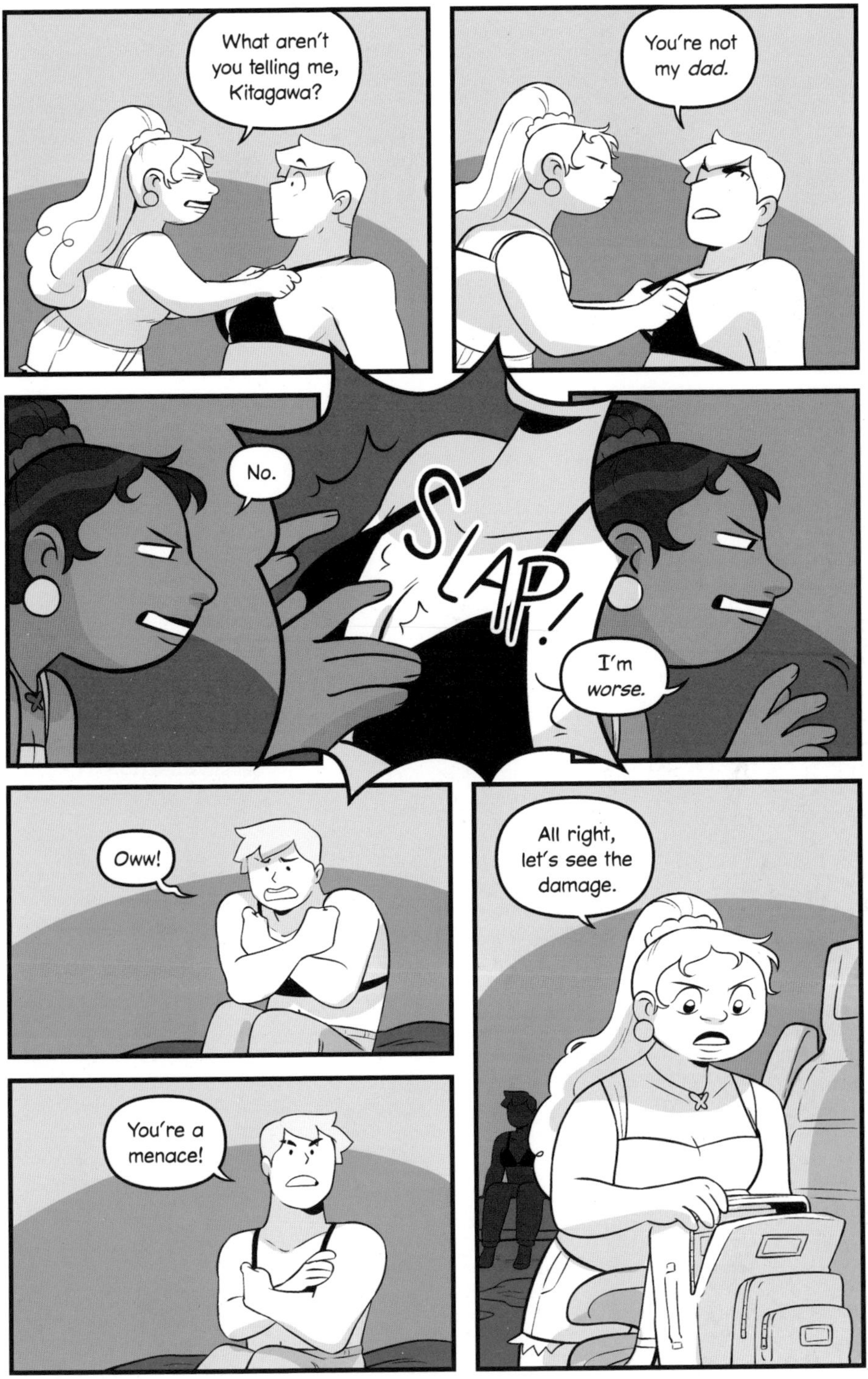

What aren't you telling me, Kitagawa?
You're not my *dad.*
No.
SLAP!
I'm *worse.*
Oww!
You're a menace!
All right, let's see the damage.

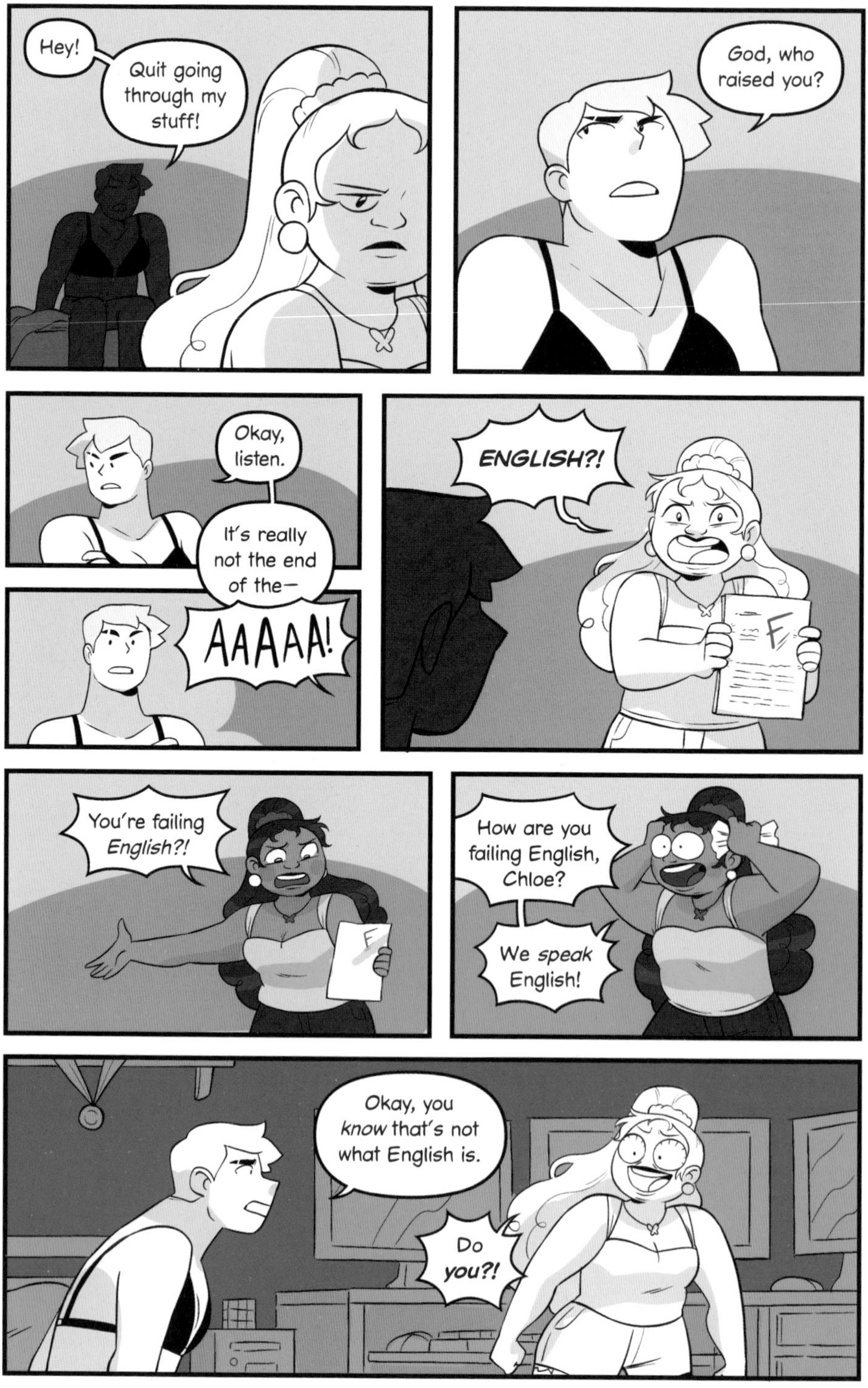
Hey!
Quit going through my stuff!
God, who raised you?
Okay, listen.
It's really not the end of the—
AAAAA!
ENGLISH?!
You're failing *English?!*
How are you failing English, Chloe?
We *speak* English!
Okay, you *know* that's not what English is.
Do *you?!*

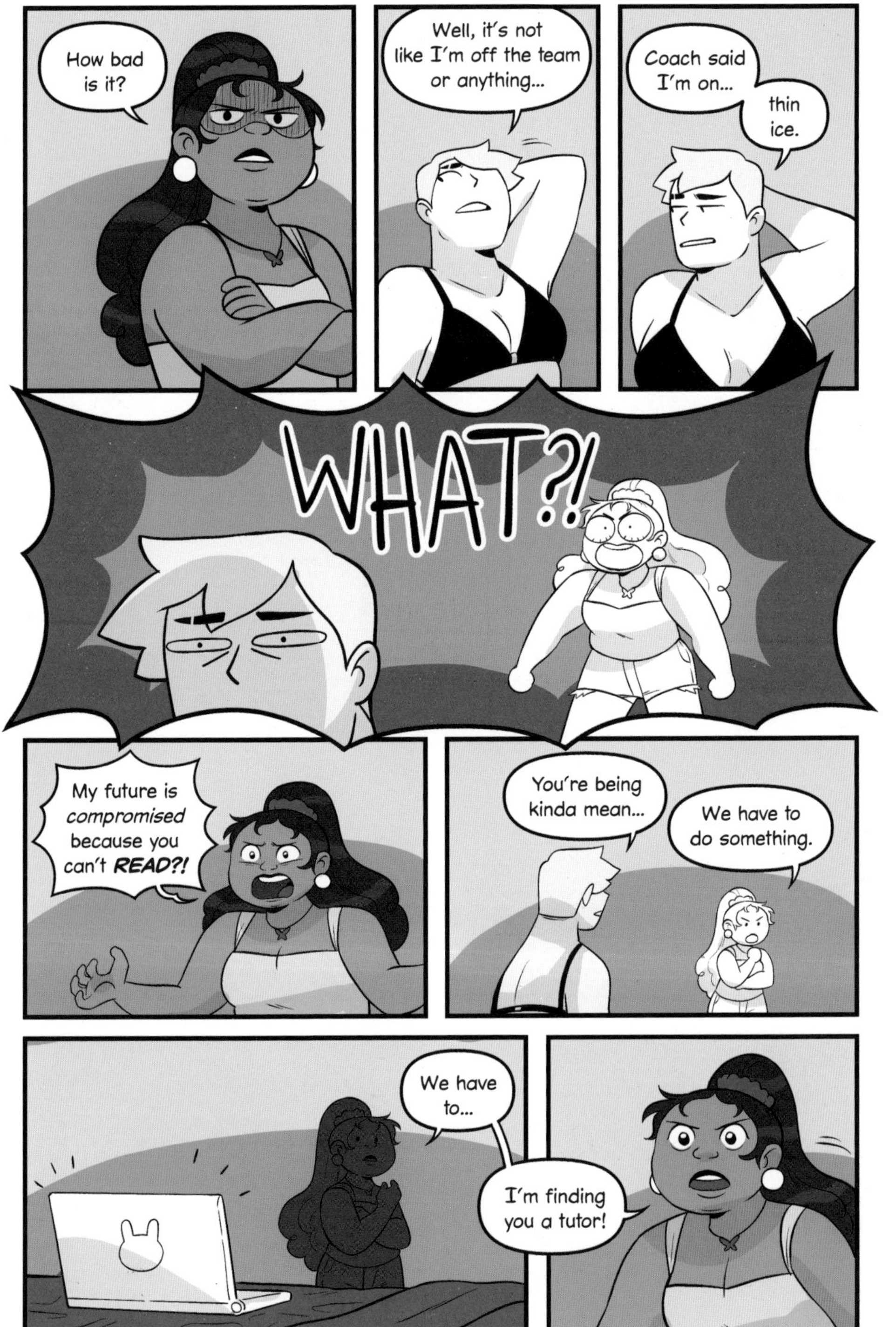
How bad is it?
Well, it's not like I'm off the team or anything...
Coach said I'm on...
thin ice.
WHAT?!
My future is *compromised* because you can't ***READ?!***
You're being kinda mean...
We have to do something.
We have to...
I'm finding you a tutor!

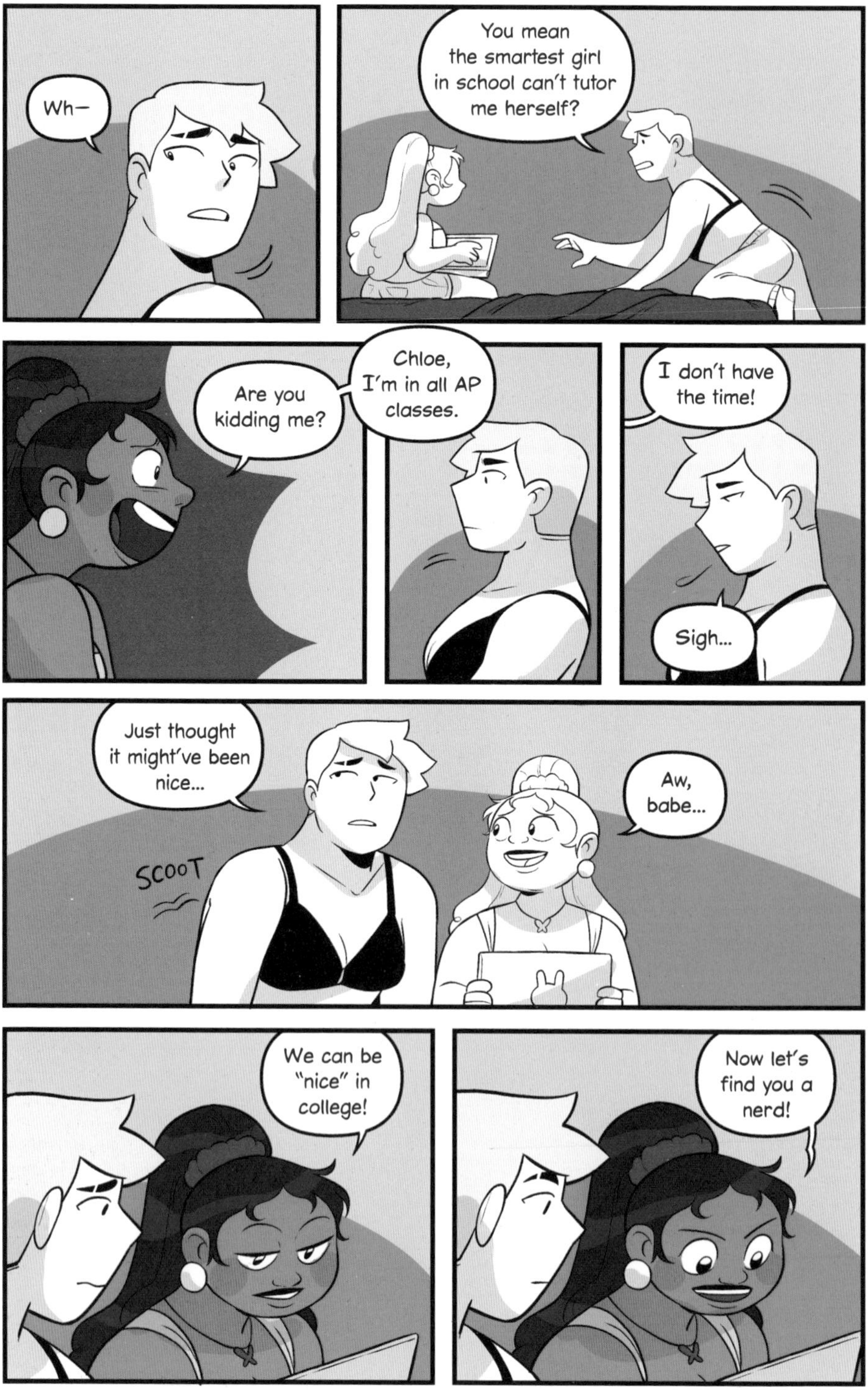
Wh—
You mean the smartest girl in school can't tutor me herself?
Are you kidding me?
Chloe, I'm in all AP classes.
I don't have the time!
Sigh...
Just thought it might've been nice...
Aw, babe...
SCOOT
We can be "nice" in college!
Now let's find you a nerd!

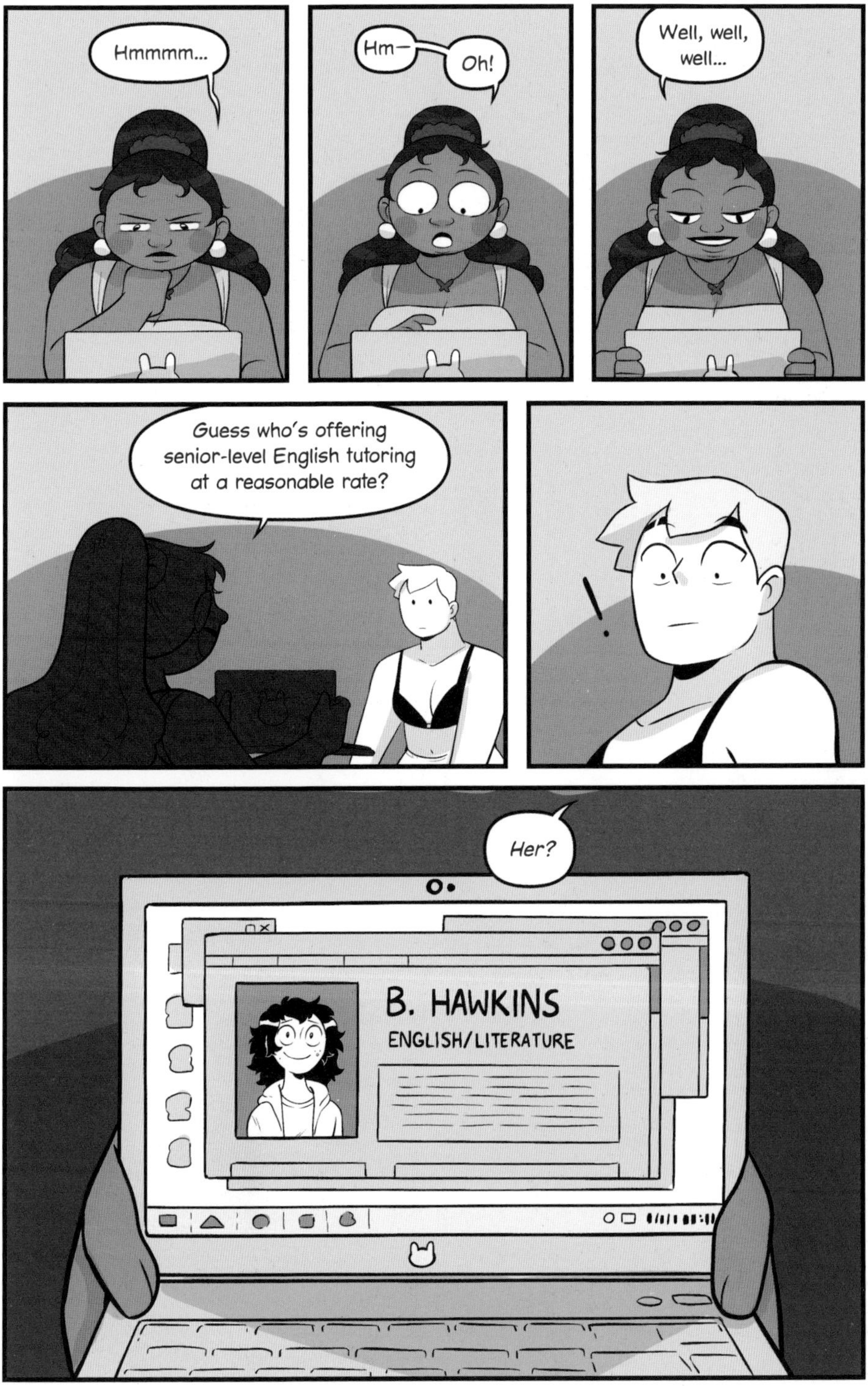
Hmmmm...
Hm—
Oh!
Well, well, well...
Guess who's offering senior-level English tutoring at a reasonable rate?
!
Her?
B. HAWKINS
ENGLISH/LITERATURE

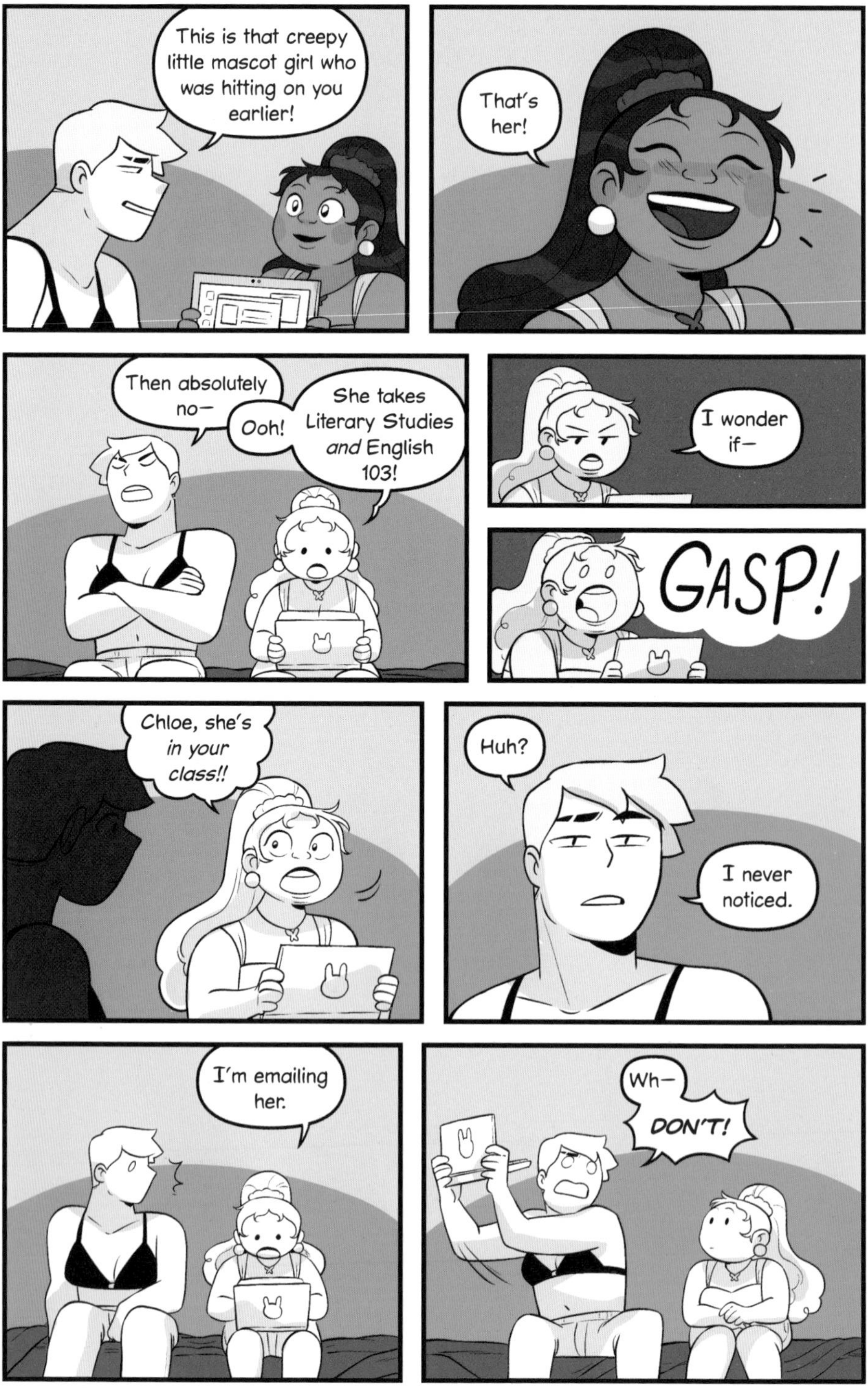
This is that creepy little mascot girl who was hitting on you earlier!
That's her!
Then absolutely no—
Ooh!
She takes Literary Studies *and* English 103!
I wonder if—
GASP!
Chloe, she's *in your class!!*
Huh?
I never noticed.
I'm emailing her.
Wh—
DON'T!

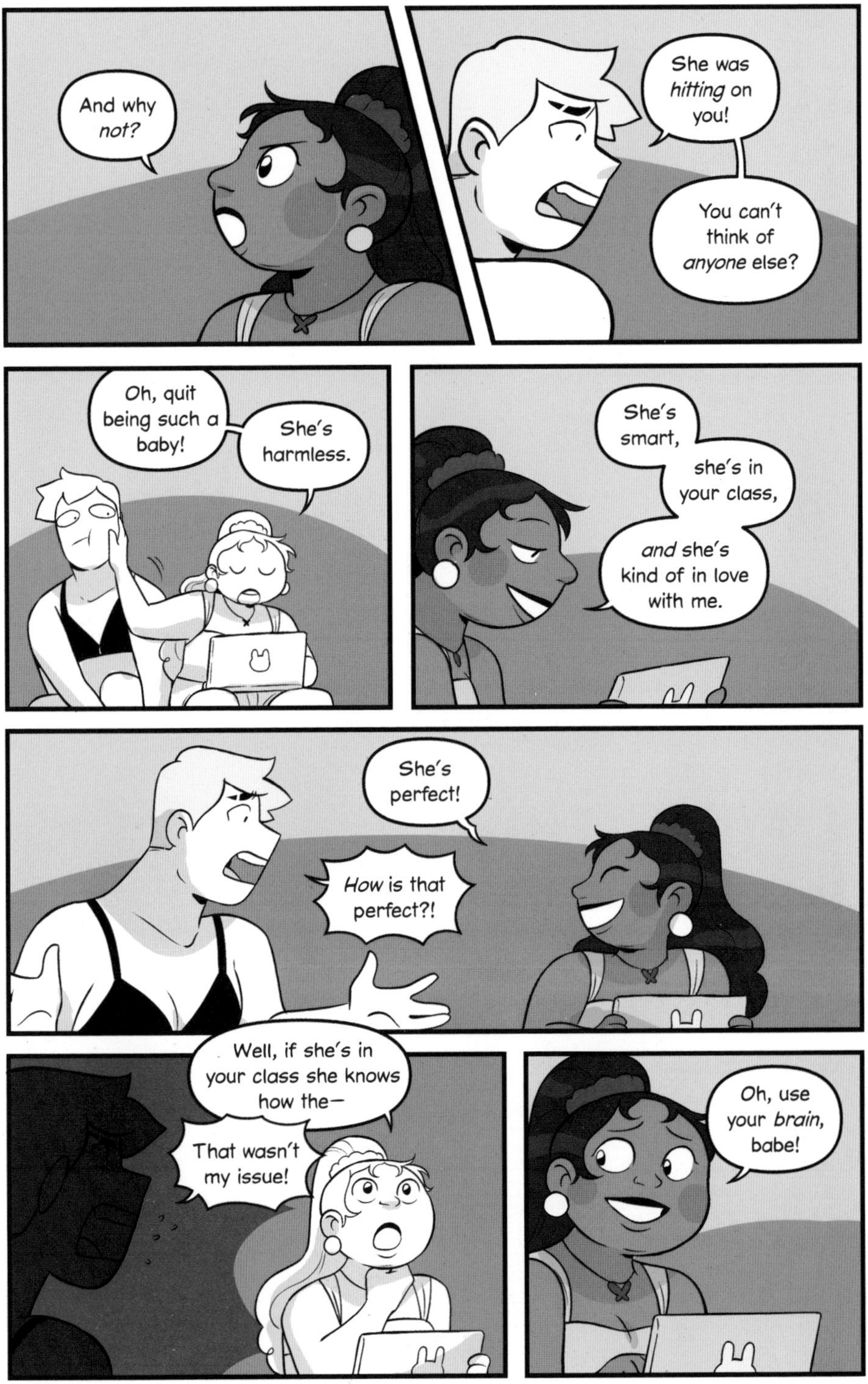
And why *not?*
She was *hitting* on you!
You can't think of *anyone* else?
Oh, quit being such a baby!
She's harmless.
She's smart,
she's in your class,
and she's kind of in love with me.
She's perfect!
How is that perfect?!
Well, if she's in your class she knows how the–
That wasn't my issue!
Oh, use your *brain,* babe!

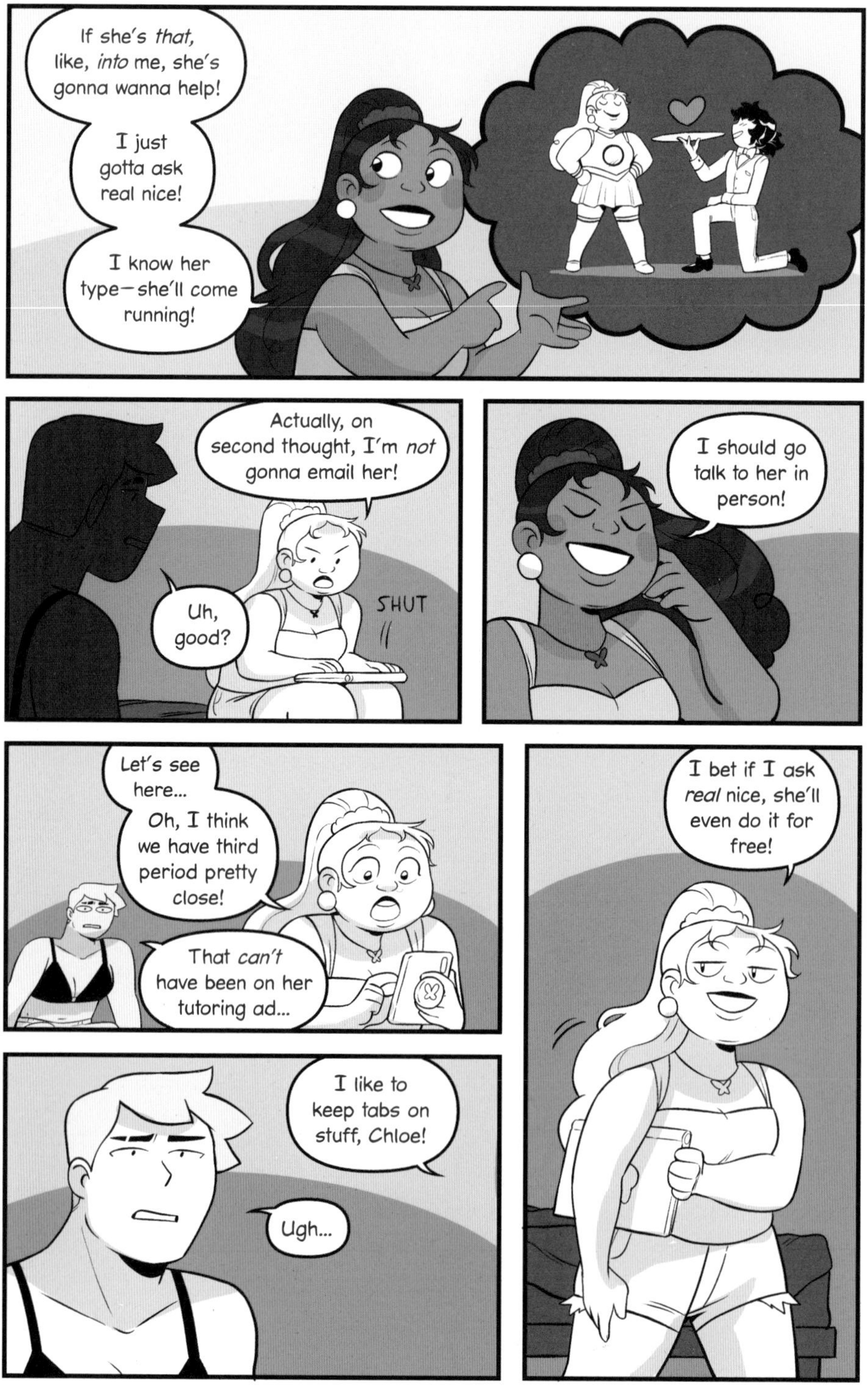
If she's *that,* like, *into* me, she's gonna wanna help!
I just gotta ask real nice!
I know her type—she'll come running!
Actually, on second thought, I'm *not* gonna email her!
Uh, good?
SHUT
I should go talk to her in person!
Let's see here...
Oh, I think we have third period pretty close!
That *can't* have been on her tutoring ad...
I like to keep tabs on stuff, Chloe!
Ugh...
I bet if I ask *real* nice, she'll even do it for free!

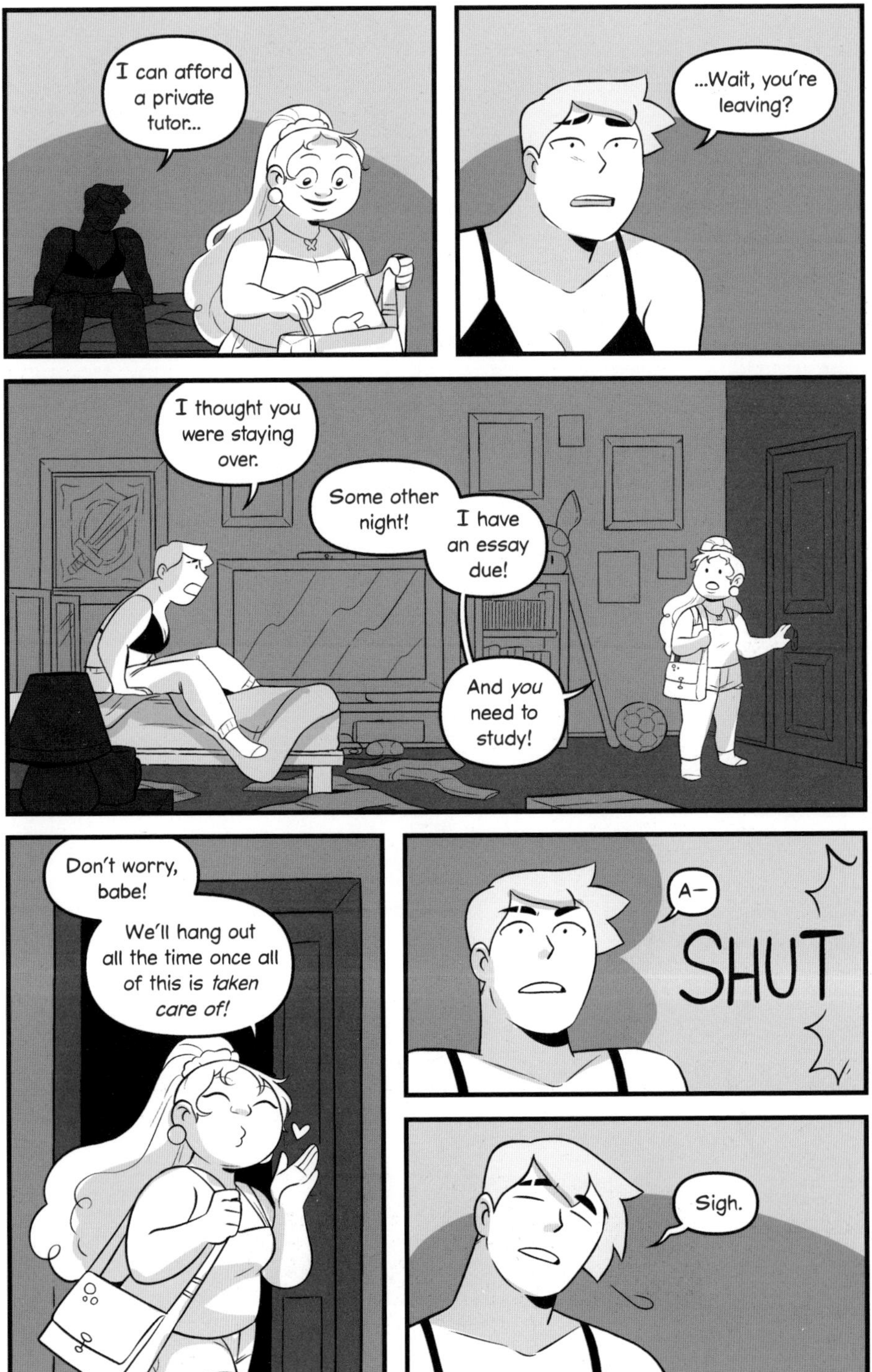
I can afford a private tutor...
...Wait, you're leaving?
I thought you were staying over.
Some other night!
I have an essay due!
And *you* need to study!
Don't worry, babe!
We'll hang out all the time once all of this is *taken care of!*
A—
SHUT
Sigh.

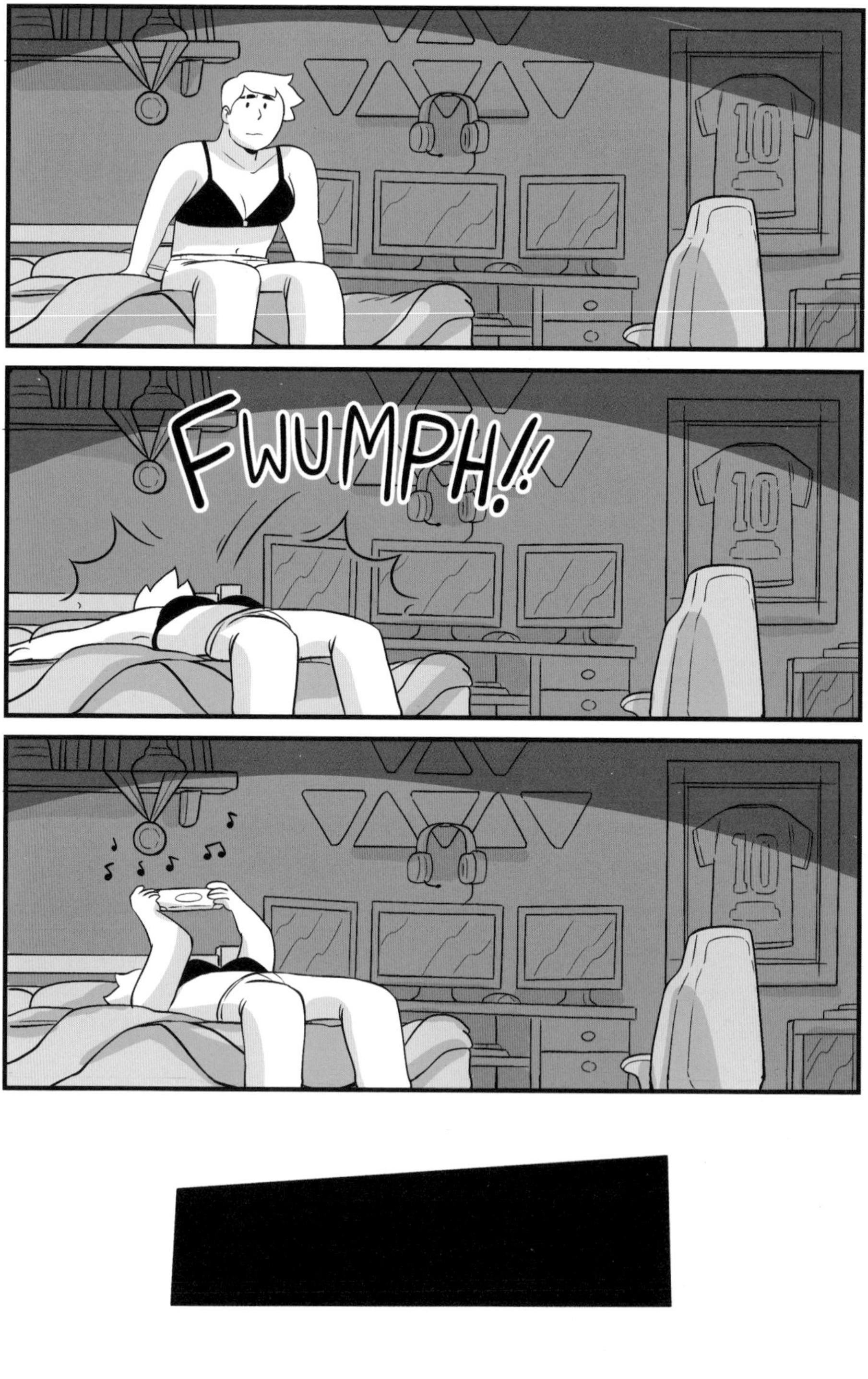
FWUMPH!!

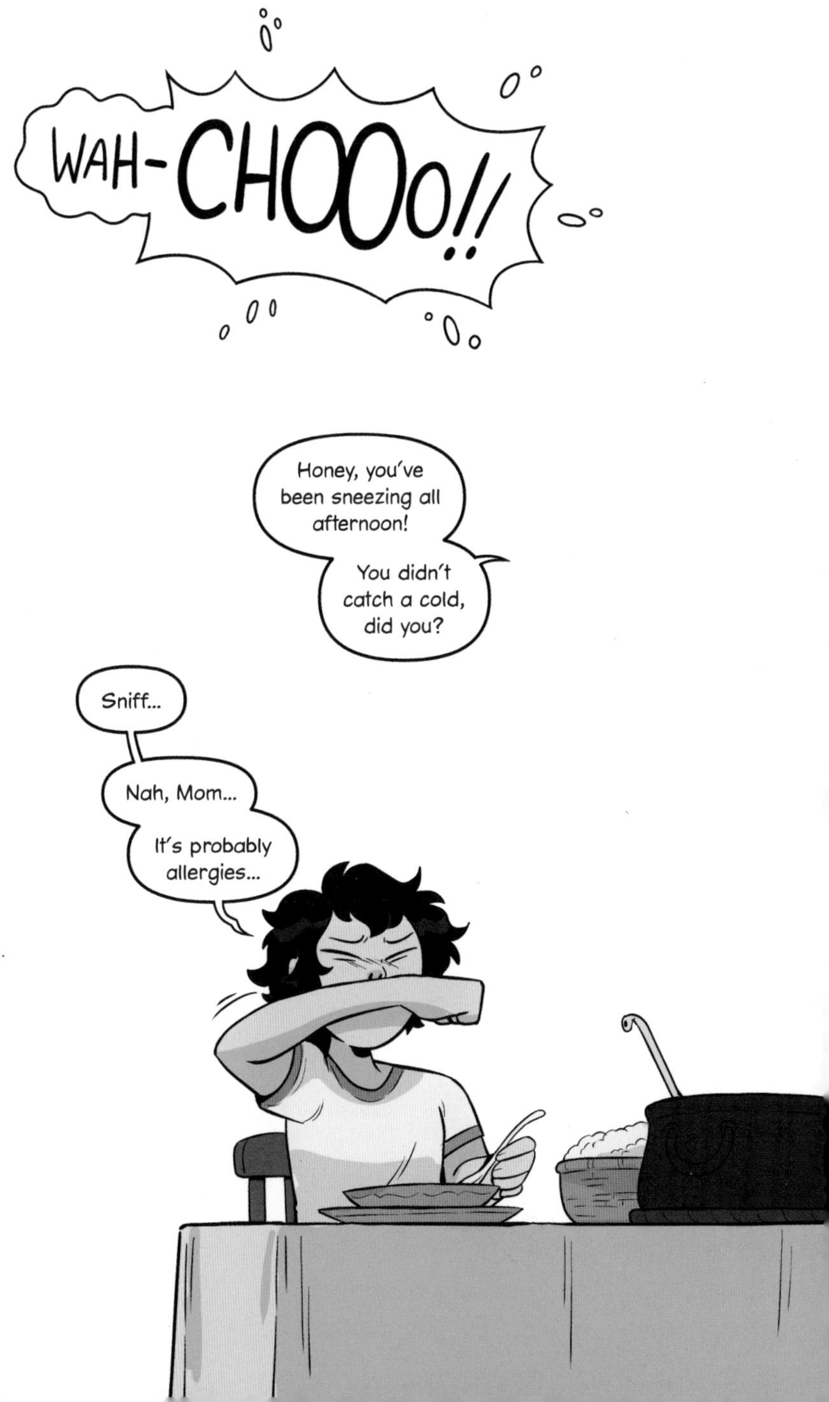
WAH-CHOOOo!!
Honey, you've been sneezing all afternoon!
You didn't catch a cold, did you?
Sniff...
Nah, Mom...
It's probably allergies...

CHAPTER

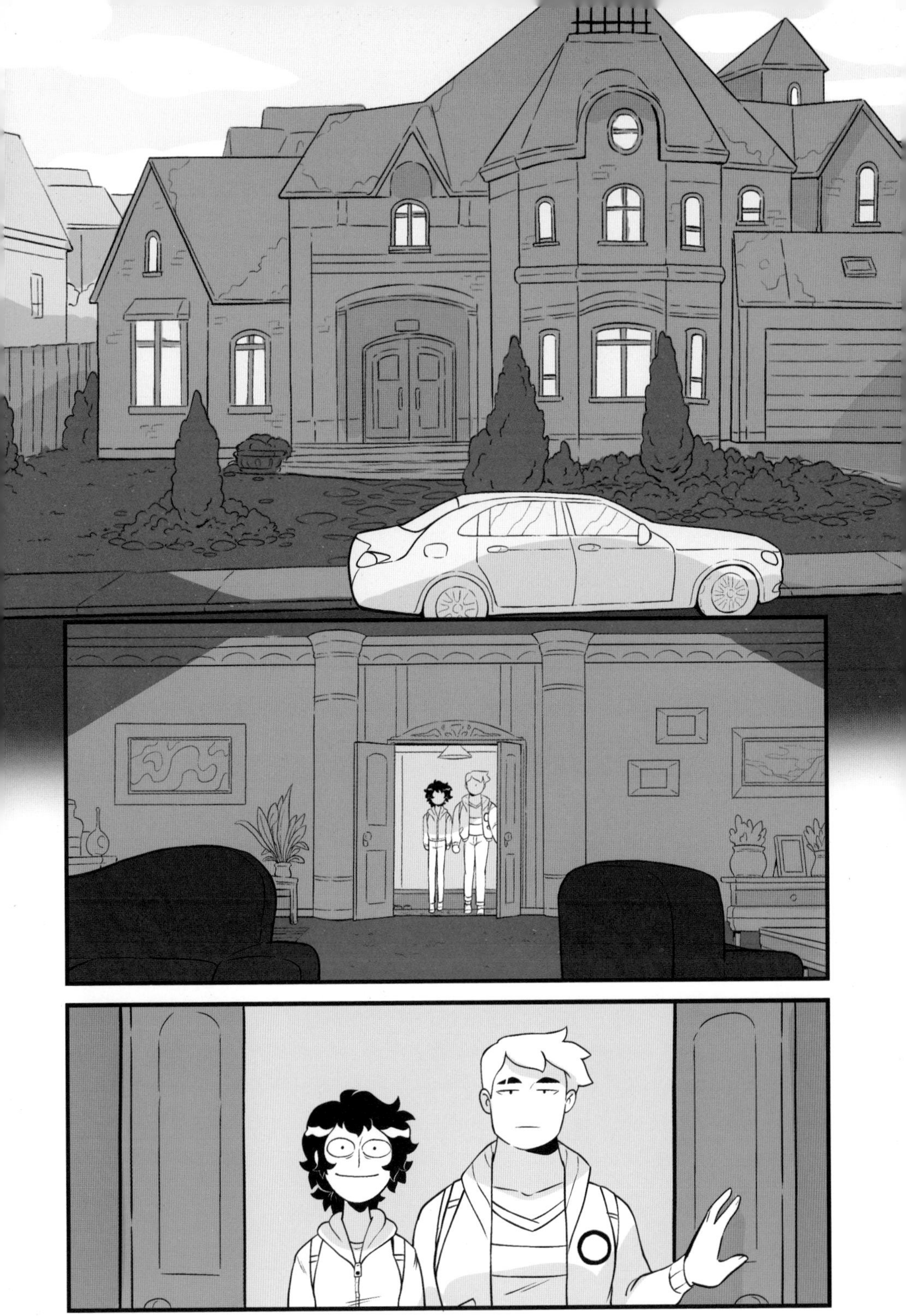

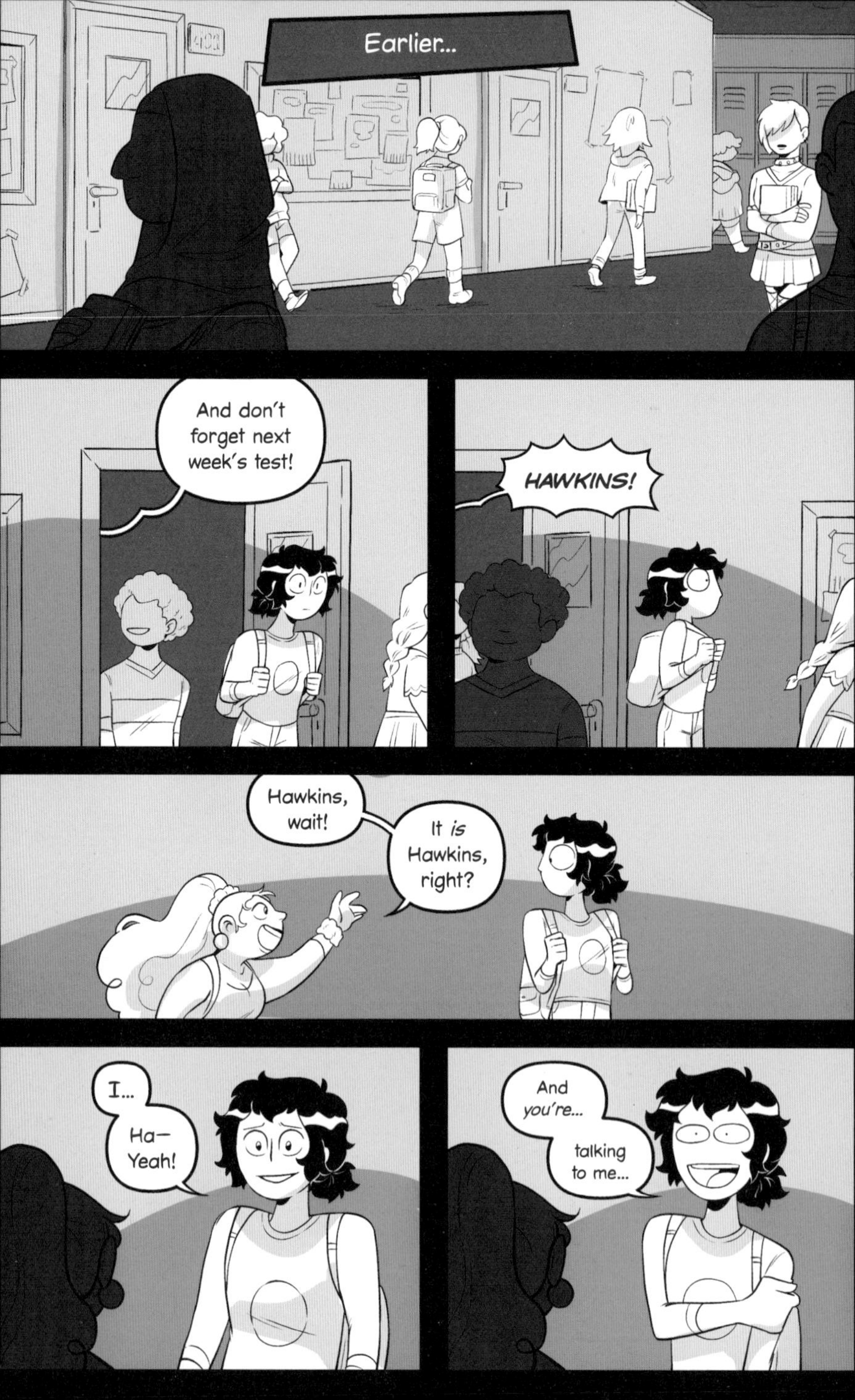
Earlier...
And don't forget next week's test!
HAWKINS!
Hawkins, wait!
It *is* Hawkins, right?
I...
Ha— Yeah!
And *you're*...
talking to me...

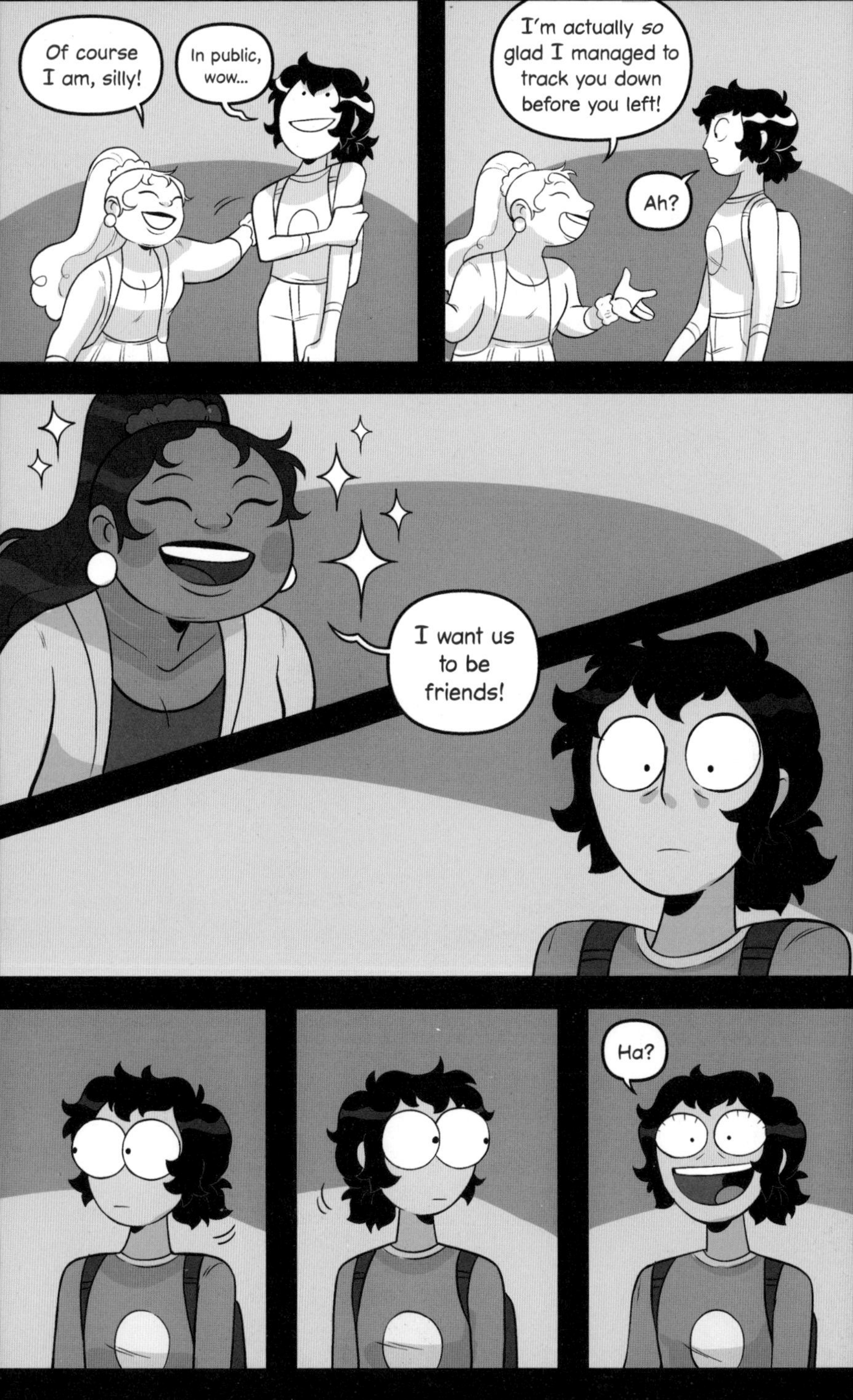
Of course I am, silly!
In public, wow...
I'm actually *so* glad I managed to track you down before you left!
Ah?
I want us to be friends!
Ha?

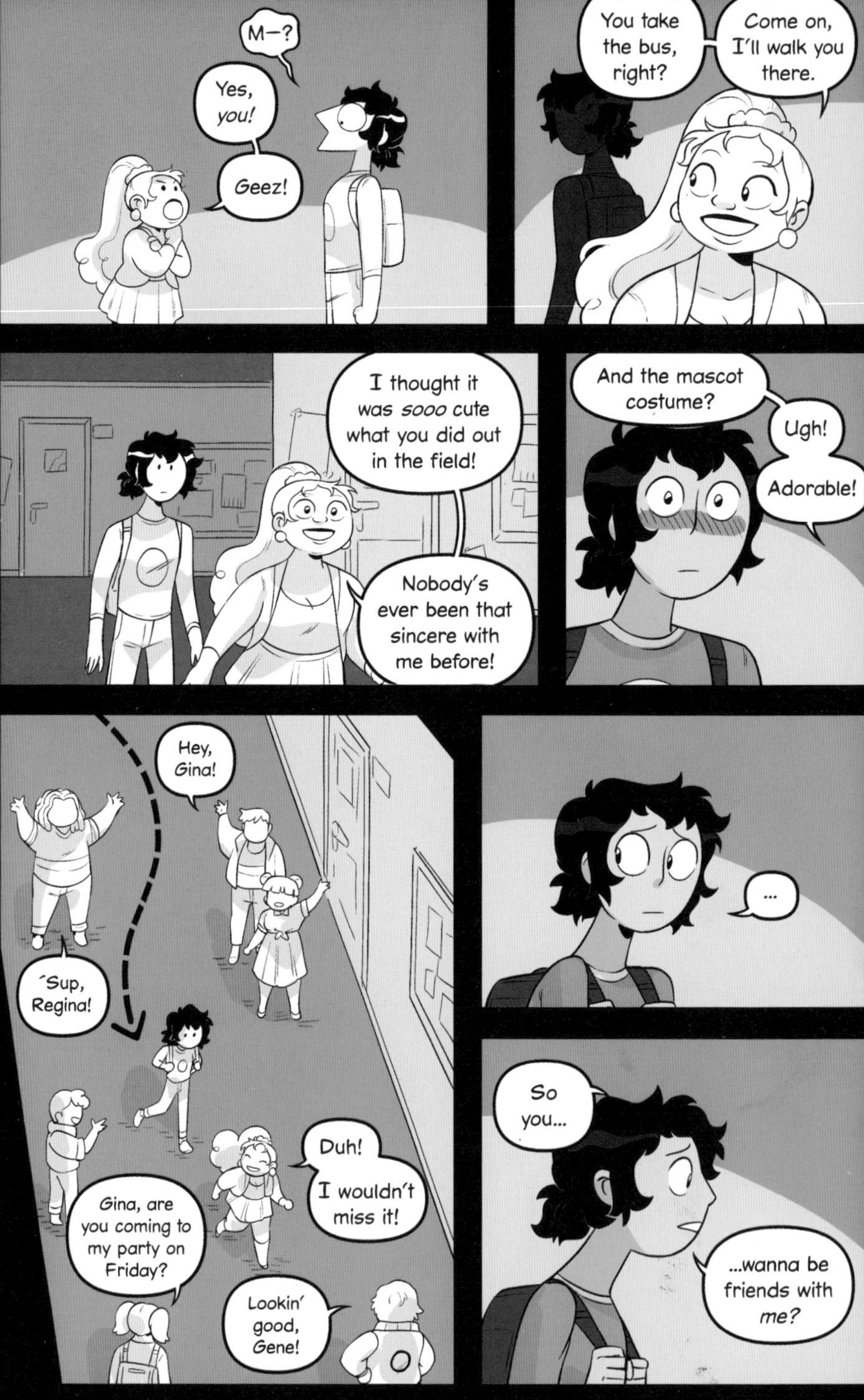
M—?
Yes, *you!*
Geez!
You take the bus, right?
Come on, I'll walk you there.
I thought it was *sooo* cute what you did out in the field!
Nobody's ever been that sincere with me before!
And the mascot costume?
Ugh!
Adorable!
Hey, Gina!
´Sup, Regina!
Gina, are you coming to my party on Friday?
Duh!
I wouldn't miss it!
Lookin' good, Gene!
...
So you...
...wanna be friends with *me?*

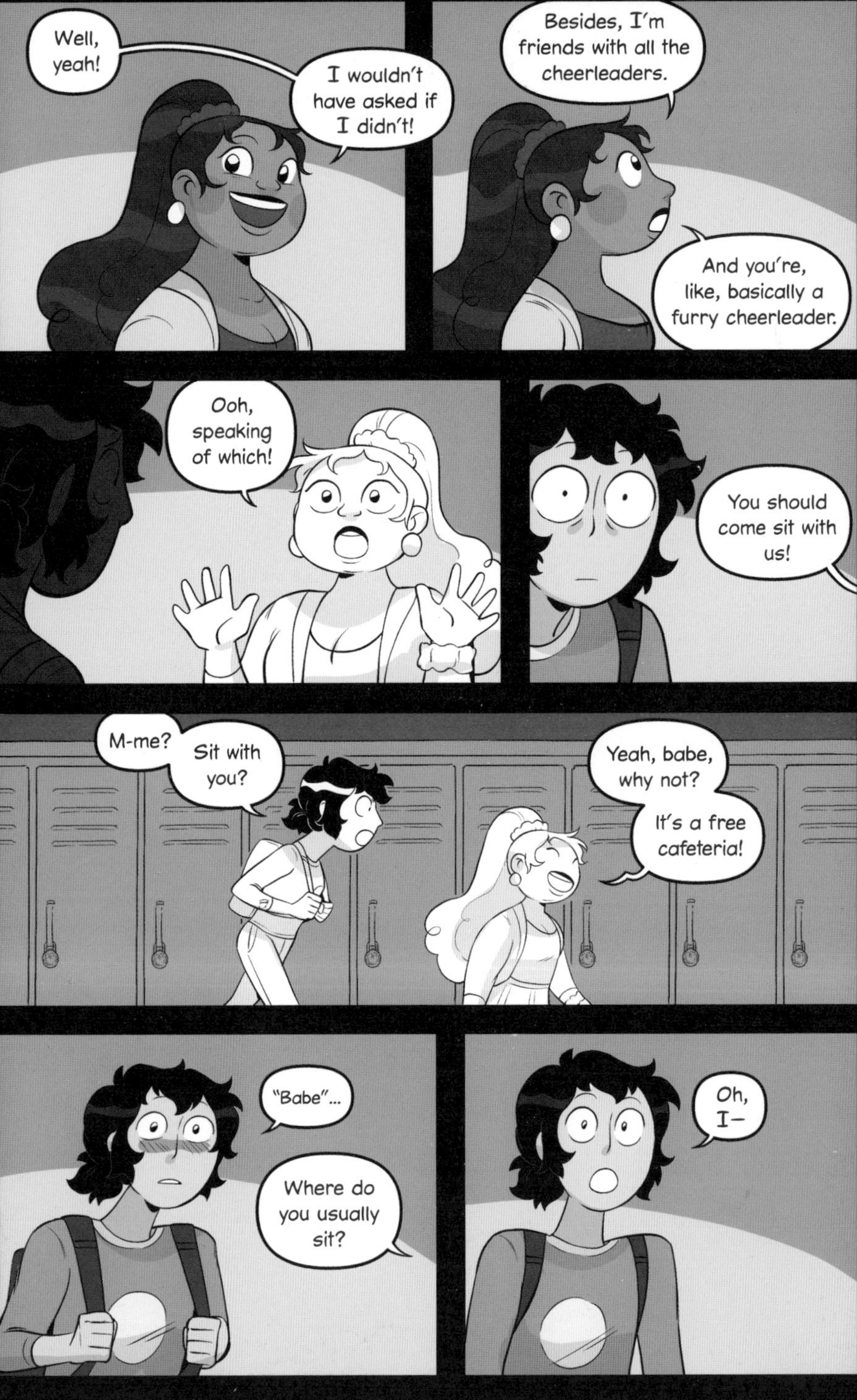
Well, yeah!
I wouldn't have asked if I didn't!
Besides, I'm friends with all the cheerleaders.
And you're, like, basically a furry cheerleader.
Ooh, speaking of which!
You should come sit with us!
M-me?
Sit with you?
Yeah, babe, why not?
It's a free cafeteria!
"Babe"...
Where do you usually sit?
Oh, I–

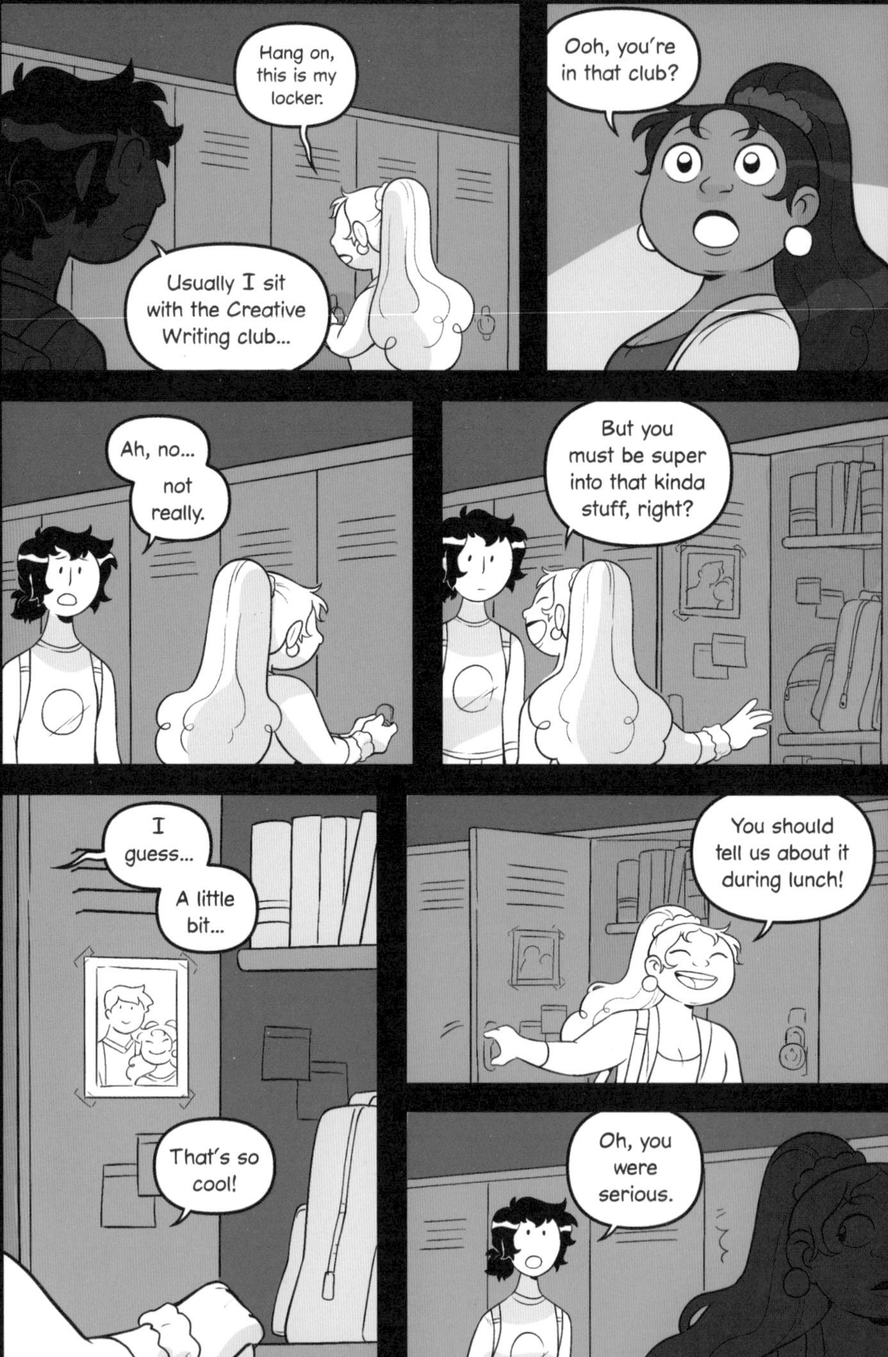
Hang on, this is my locker.
Usually I sit with the Creative Writing club...
Ooh, you're in that club?
Ah, no...
not really.
But you must be super into that kinda stuff, right?
I guess...
A little bit...
That's so cool!
You should tell us about it during lunch!
Oh, you were serious.

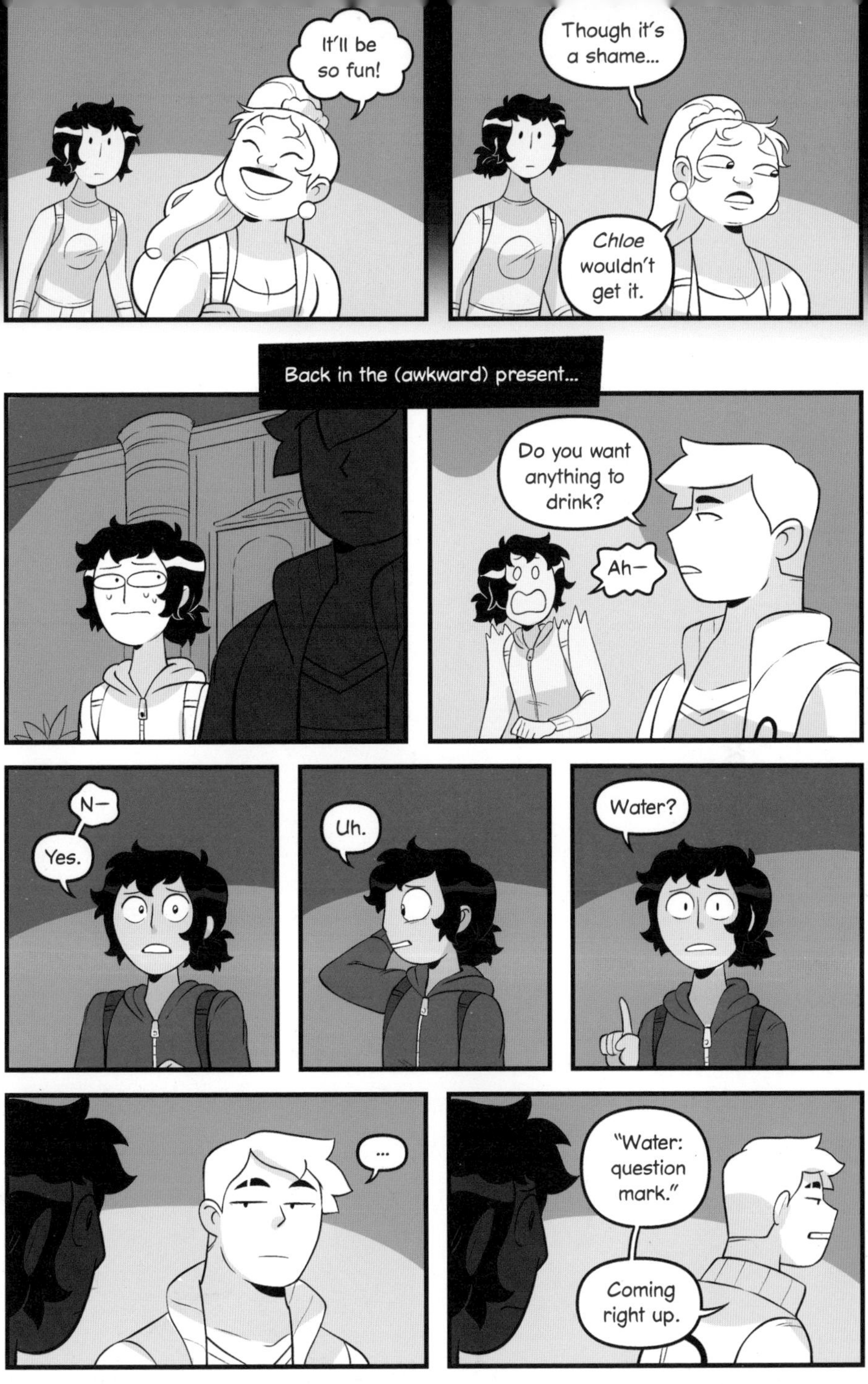

It'll be so fun!
Though it's a shame...
Chloe wouldn't get it.
Back in the (awkward) present...
Do you want anything to drink?
Ah—
N—
Yes.
Uh.
Water?
...
"Water: question mark."
Coming right up.

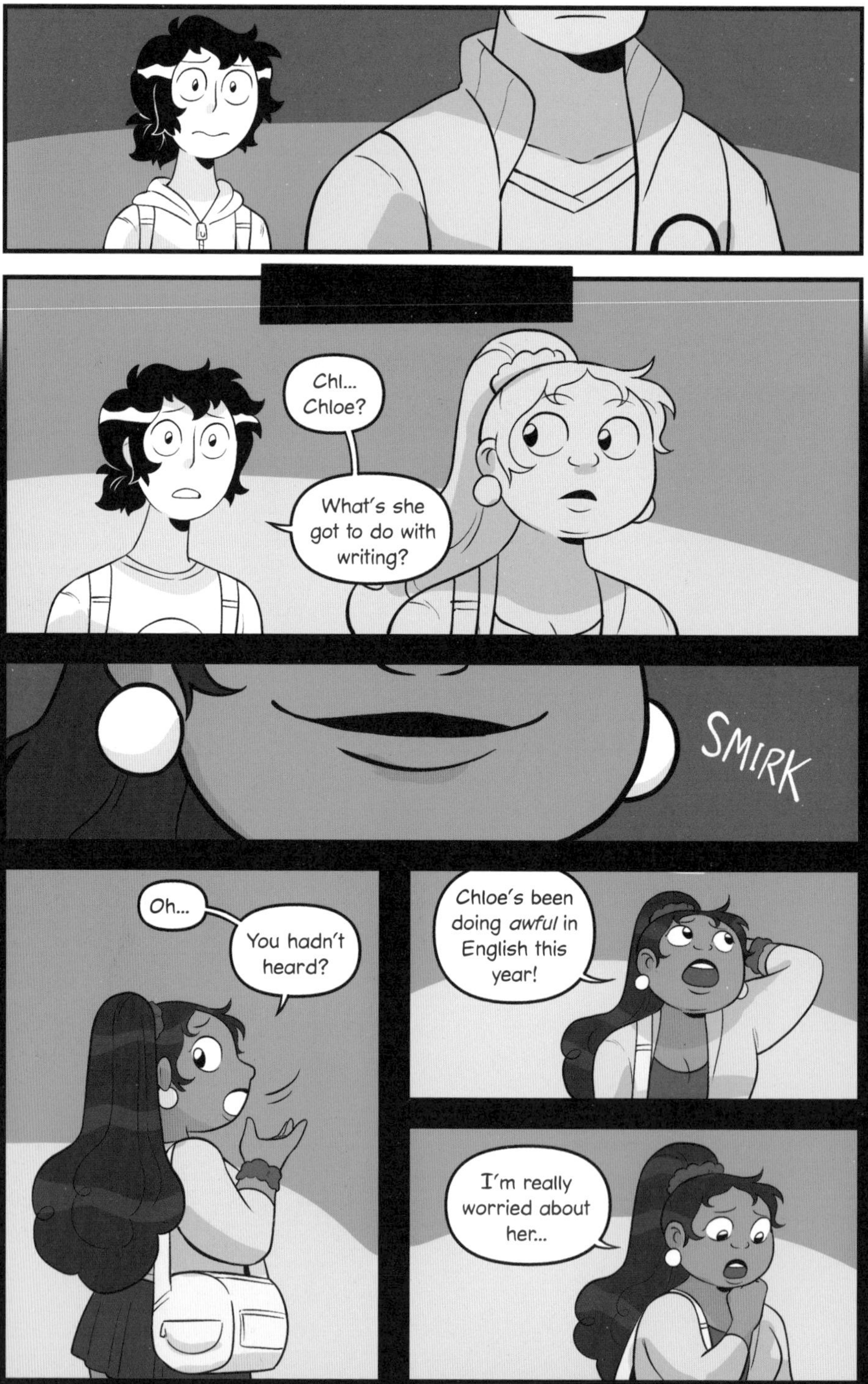

[redacted]
Chl... Chloe?
What's she got to do with writing?
SMIRK
Oh...
You hadn't heard?
Chloe's been doing *awful* in English this year!
I'm really worried about her...

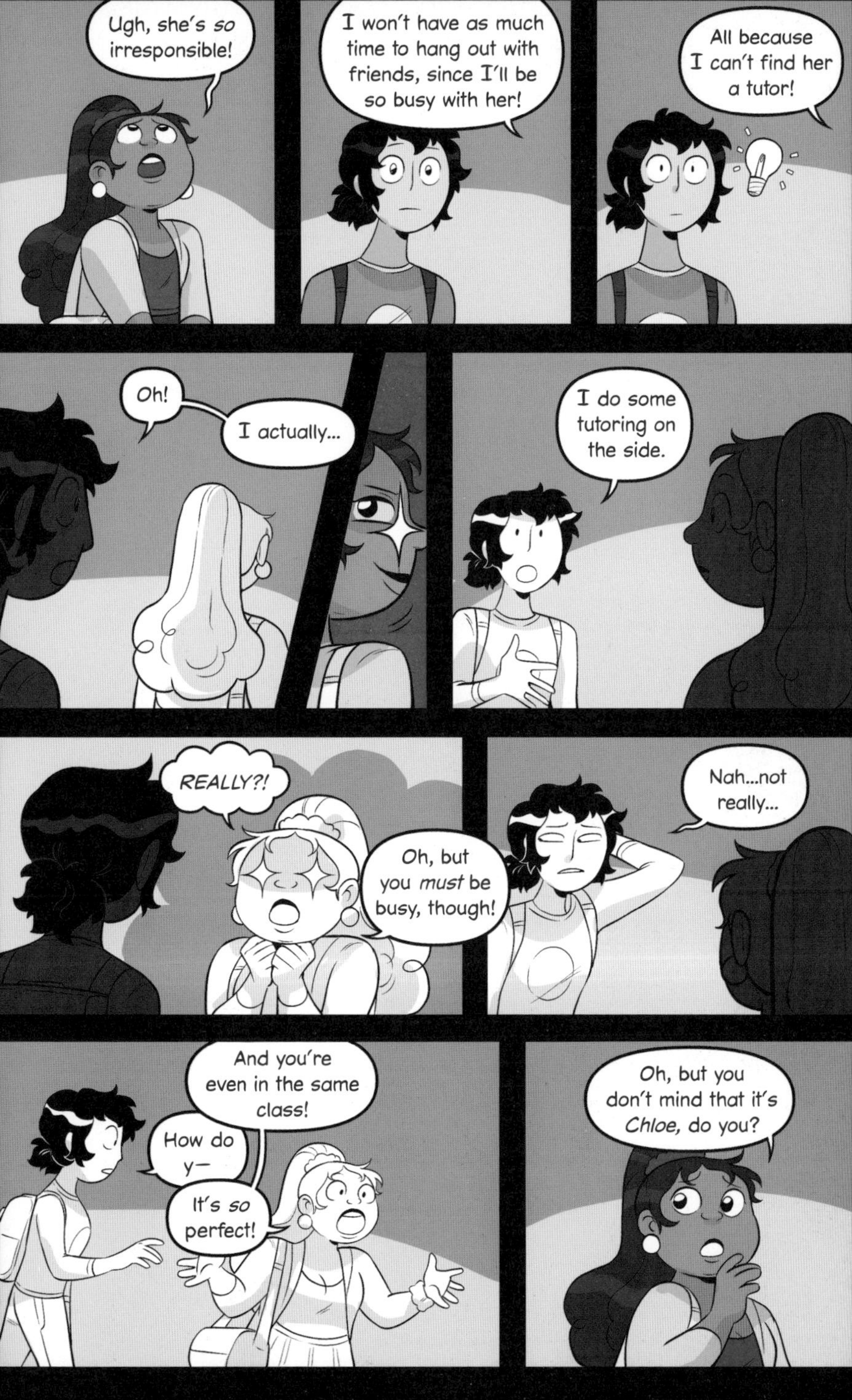

Ugh, she's *so* irresponsible!
I won't have as much time to hang out with friends, since I'll be so busy with her!
All because I can't find her a tutor!
Oh!
I actually...
I do some tutoring on the side.
REALLY?!
Oh, but you *must* be busy, though!
Nah...not really...
And you're even in the same class!
How do y—
It's *so* perfect!
Oh, but you don't mind that it's *Chloe,* do you?

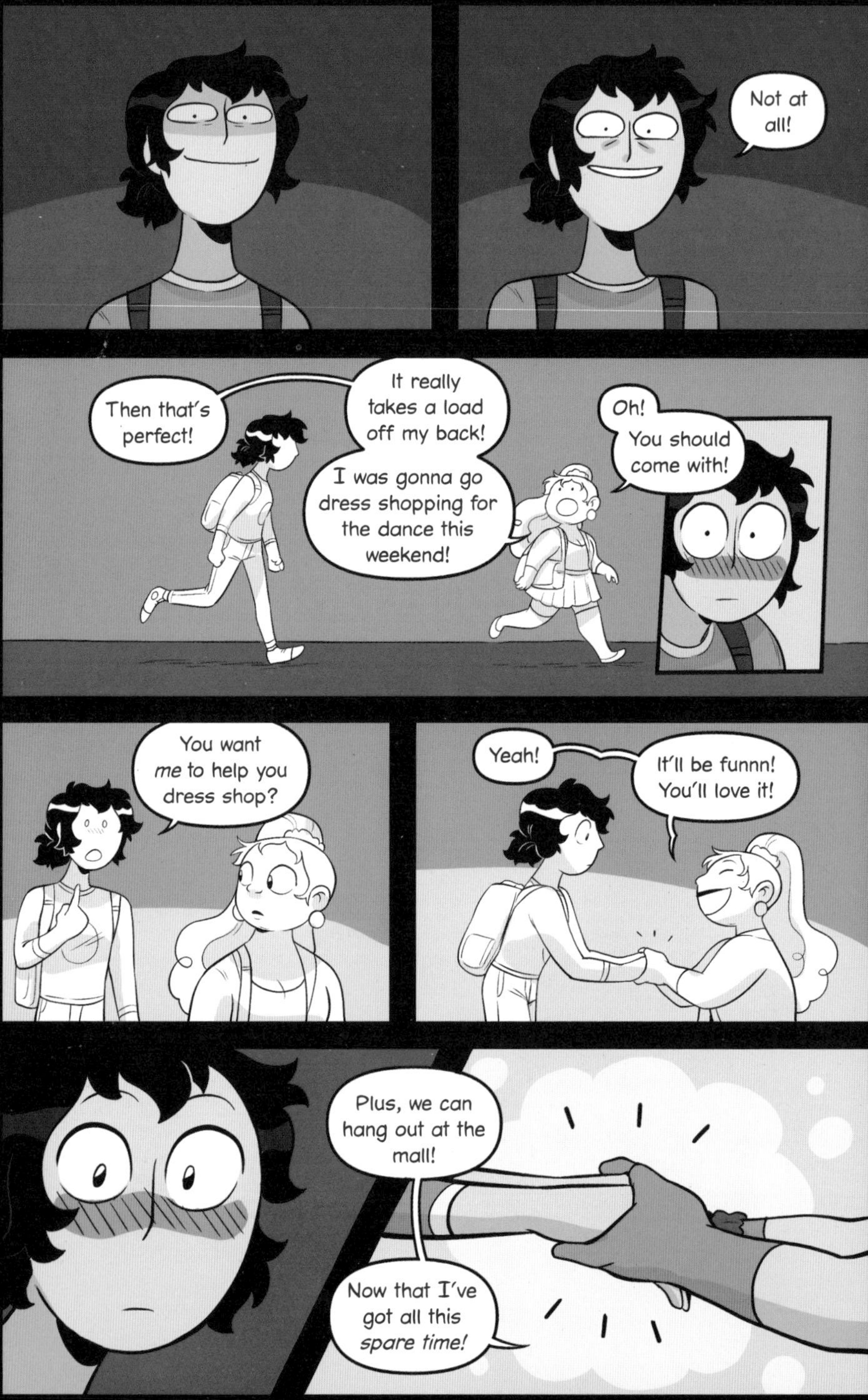
Not at all!
Then that's perfect!
It really takes a load off my back!
I was gonna go dress shopping for the dance this weekend!
Oh!
You should come with!
You want *me* to help you dress shop?
Yeah!
It'll be funnn! You'll love it!
Plus, we can hang out at the mall!
Now that I've got all this *spare time!*

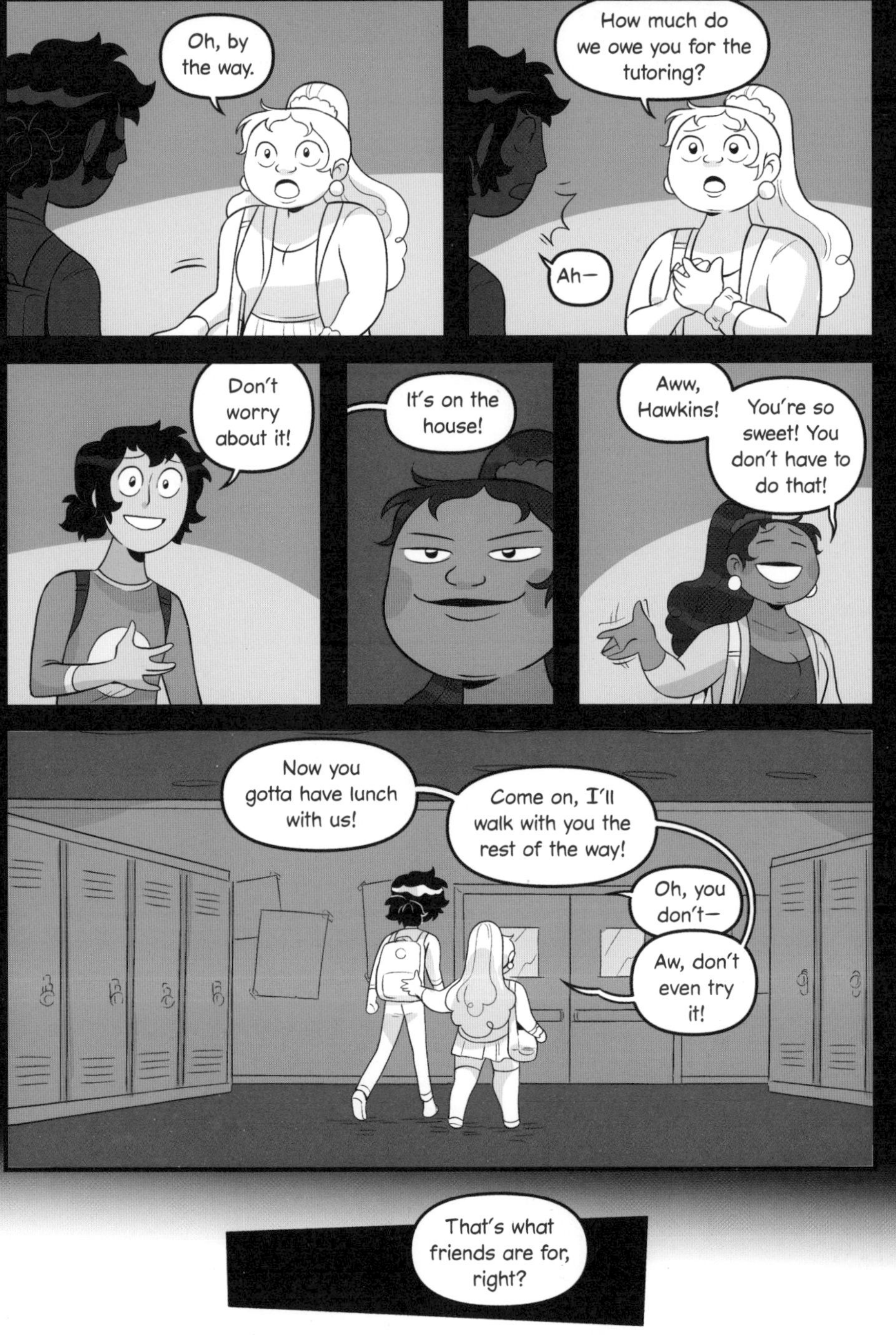
Oh, by the way.
How much do we owe you for the tutoring?
Ah—
Don't worry about it!
It's on the house!
Aww, Hawkins!
You're so sweet! You don't have to do that!
Now you gotta have lunch with us!
Come on, I'll walk with you the rest of the way!
Oh, you don't—
Aw, don't even try it!
That's what friends are for, right?

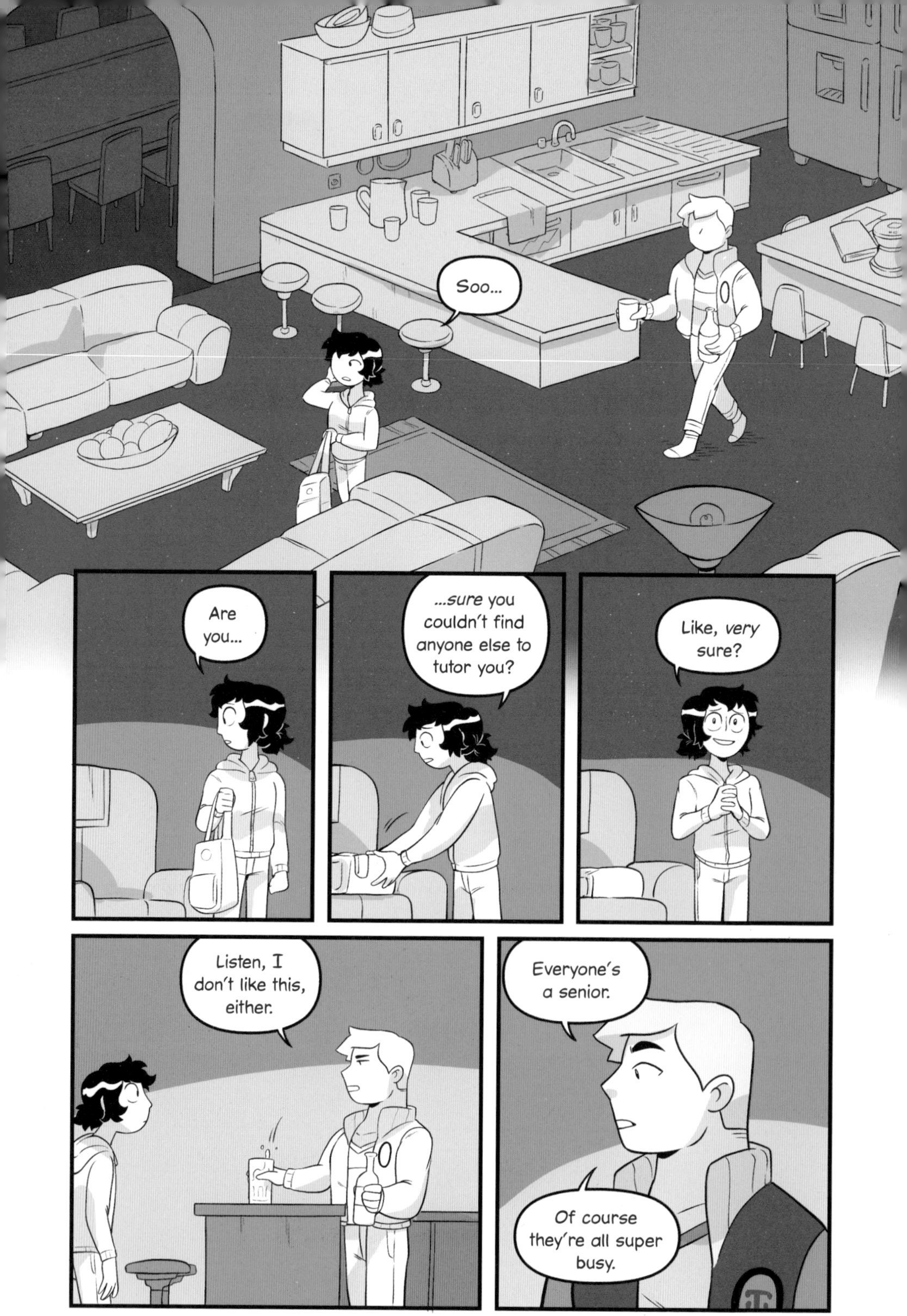
Soo...
Are you...
...*sure* you couldn't find anyone else to tutor you?
Like, *very* sure?
Listen, I don't like this, either.
Everyone's a senior.
Of course they're all super busy.

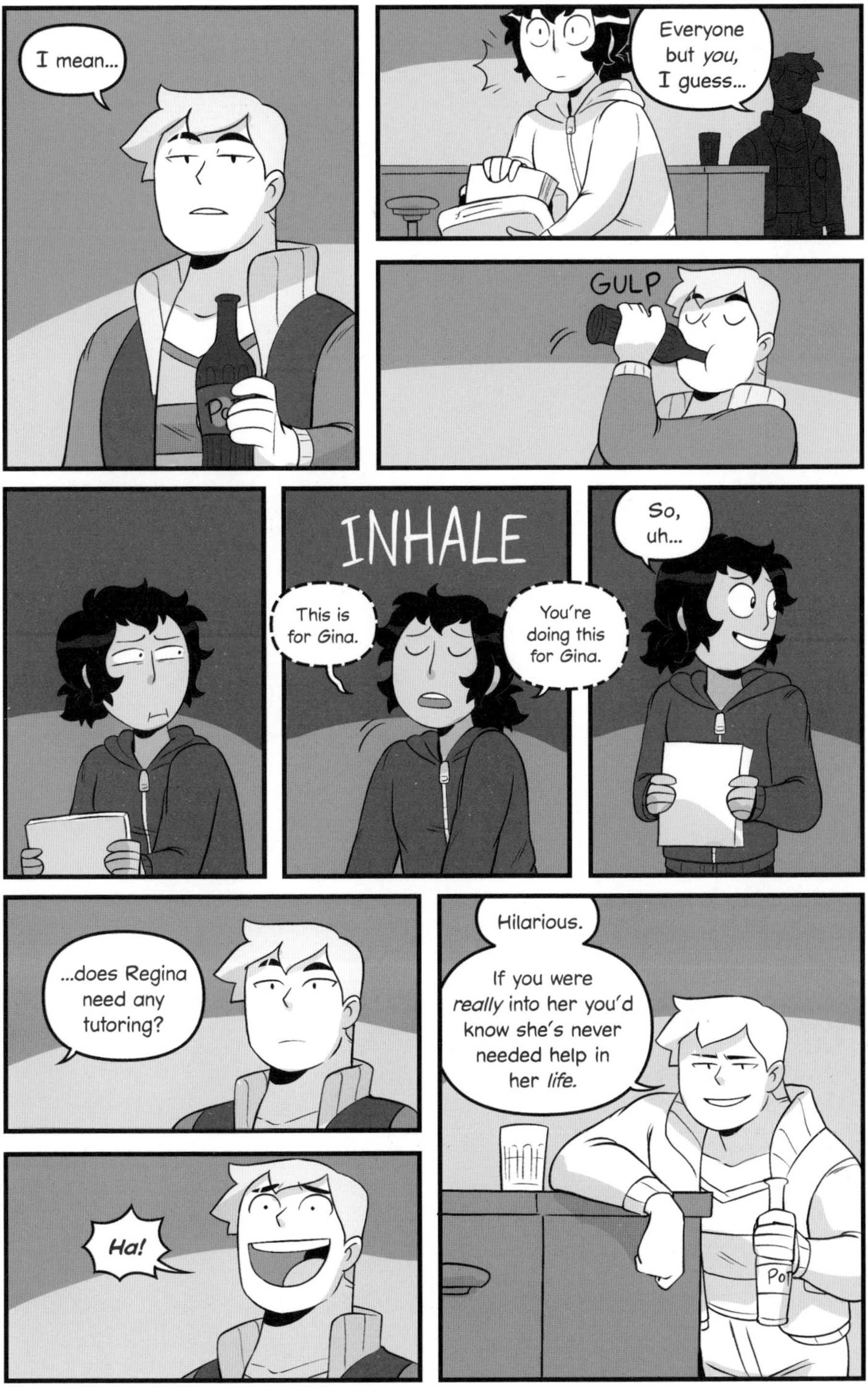
I mean...
Everyone but *you*, I guess...
GULP
INHALE
This is for Gina.
You're doing this for Gina.
So, uh...
...does Regina need any tutoring?
Ha!
Hilarious.
If you were *really* into her you'd know she's never needed help in her *life.*

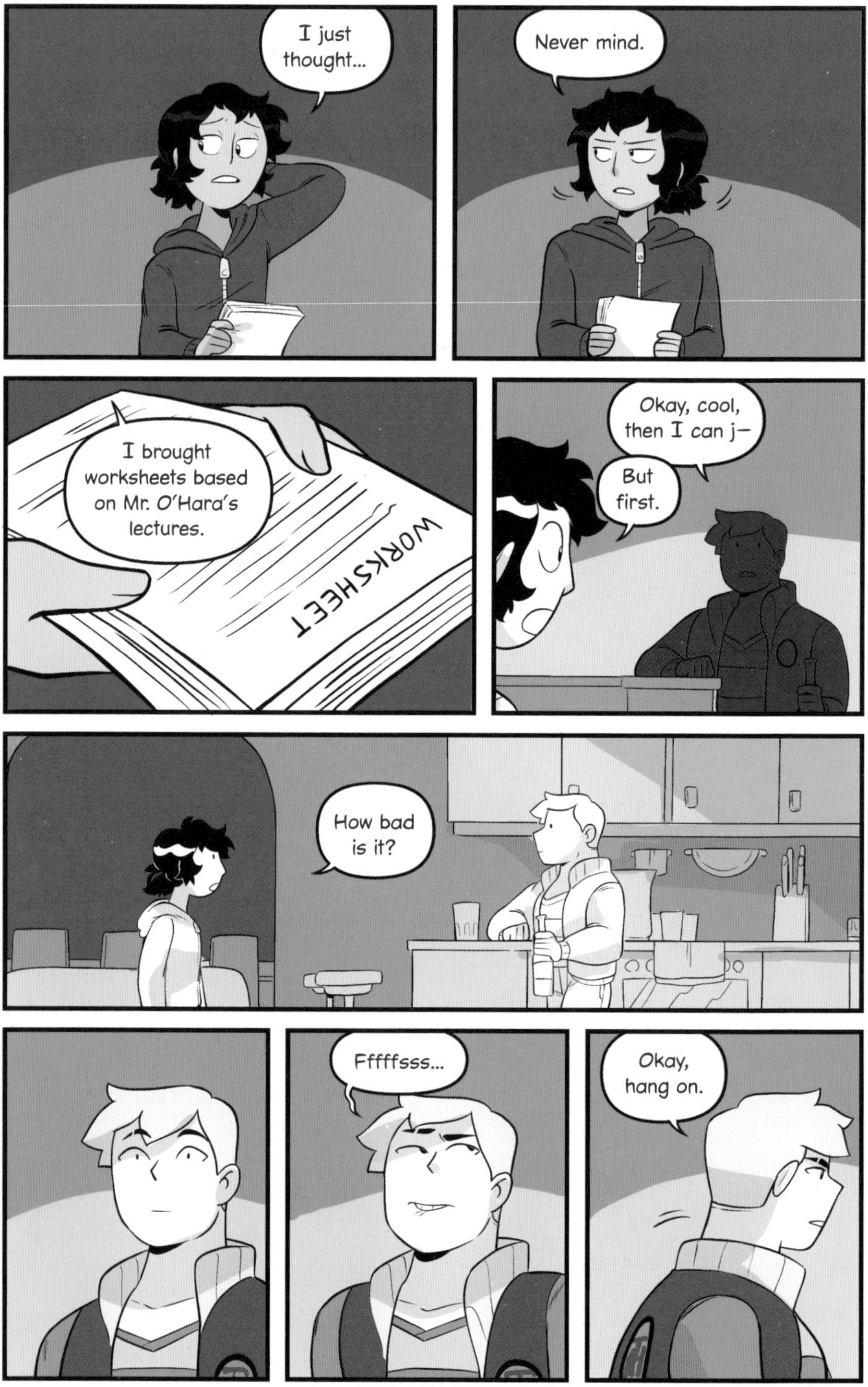
I just thought...
Never mind.
I brought worksheets based on Mr. O'Hara's lectures.
WORKSHEET
Okay, cool, then I can j—
But first.
How bad is it?
Fffffsss...
Okay, hang on.

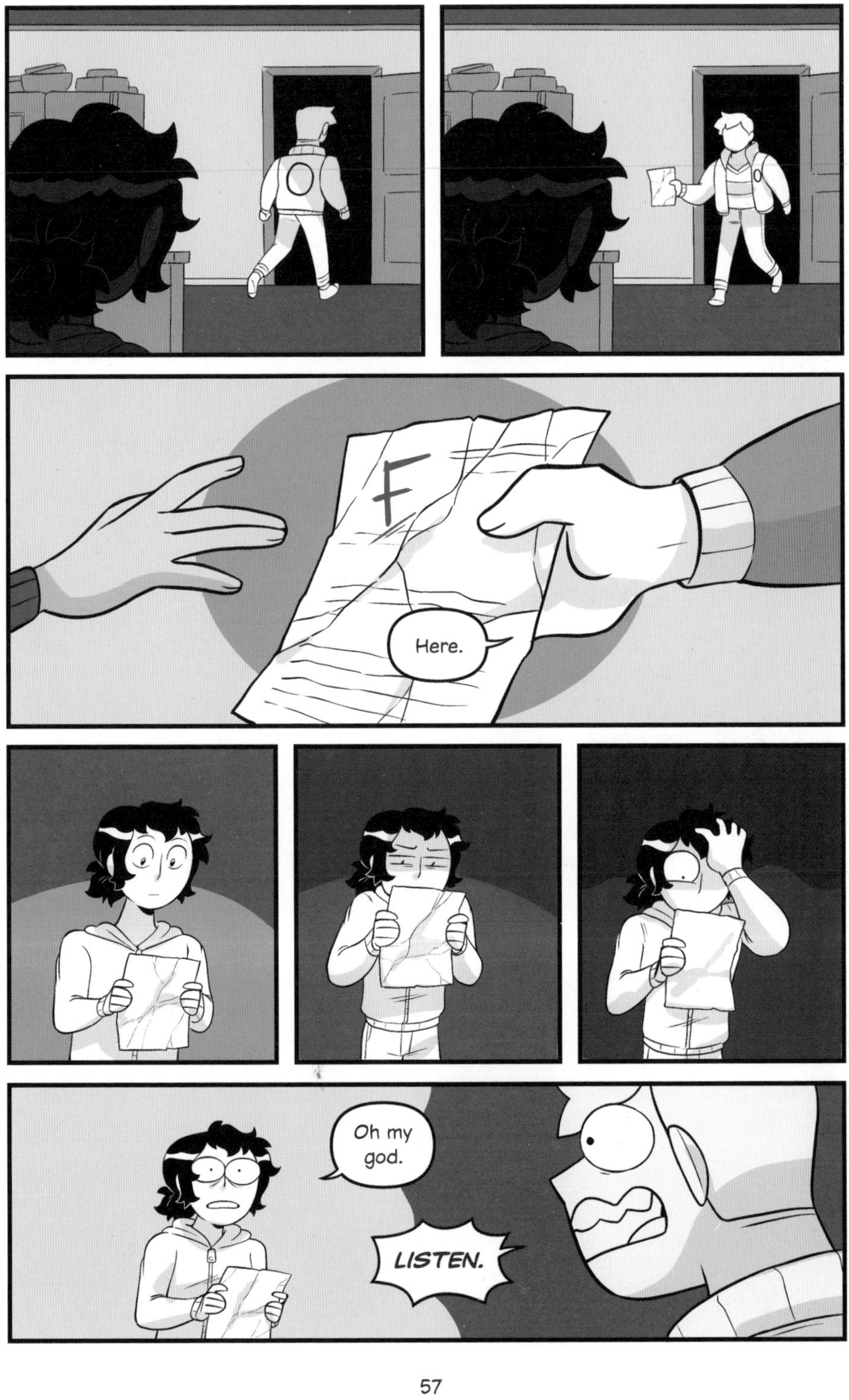
F
Here.
Oh my god.
LISTEN.

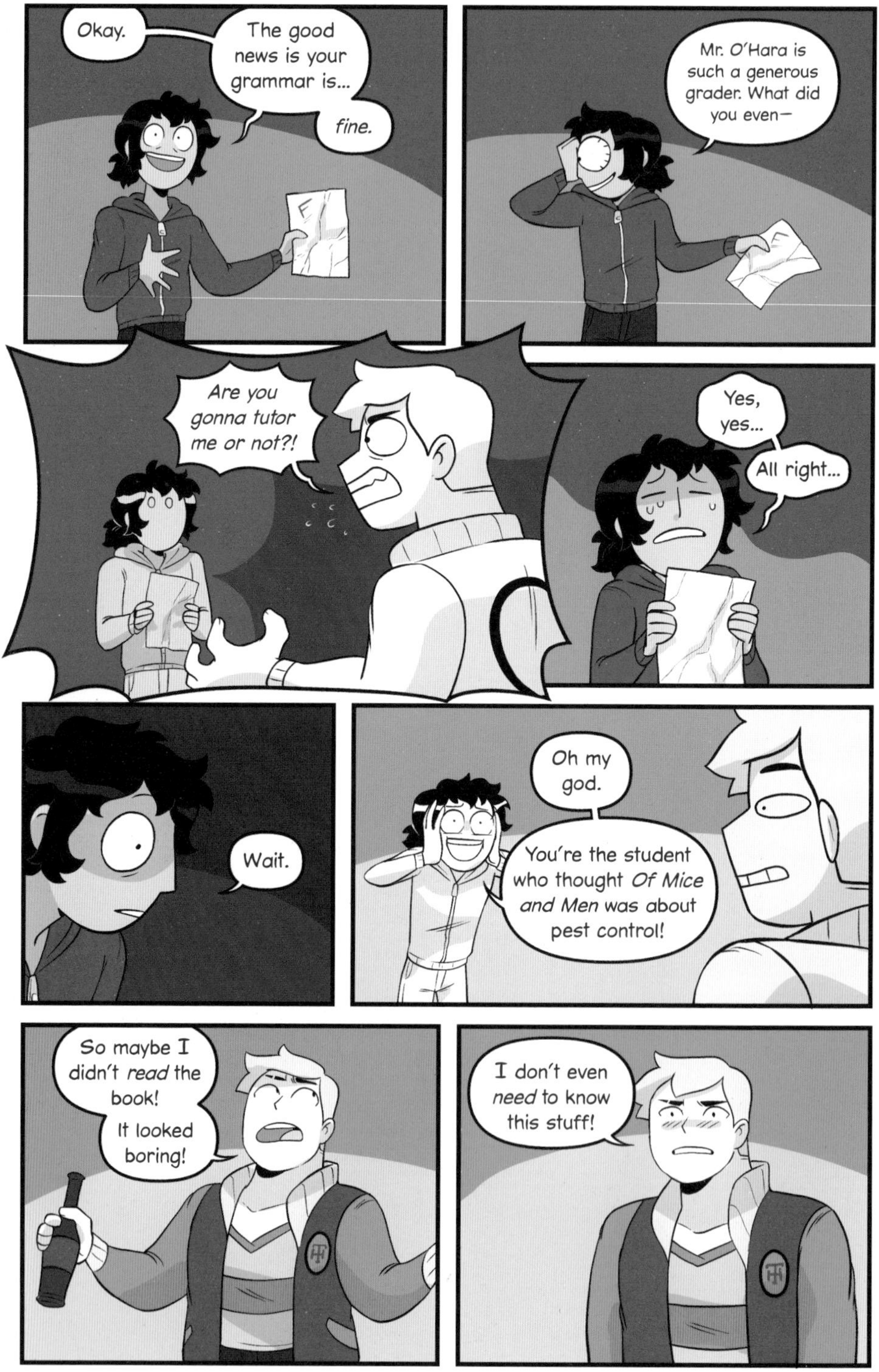
Okay.
The good news is your grammar is...
fine.
Mr. O'Hara is such a generous grader. What did you even—
Are you gonna tutor me or not?!
Yes, yes...
All right...
Wait.
Oh my god.
You're the student who thought *Of Mice and Men* was about pest control!
So maybe I didn't *read* the book!
It looked boring!
I don't even *need* to know this stuff!

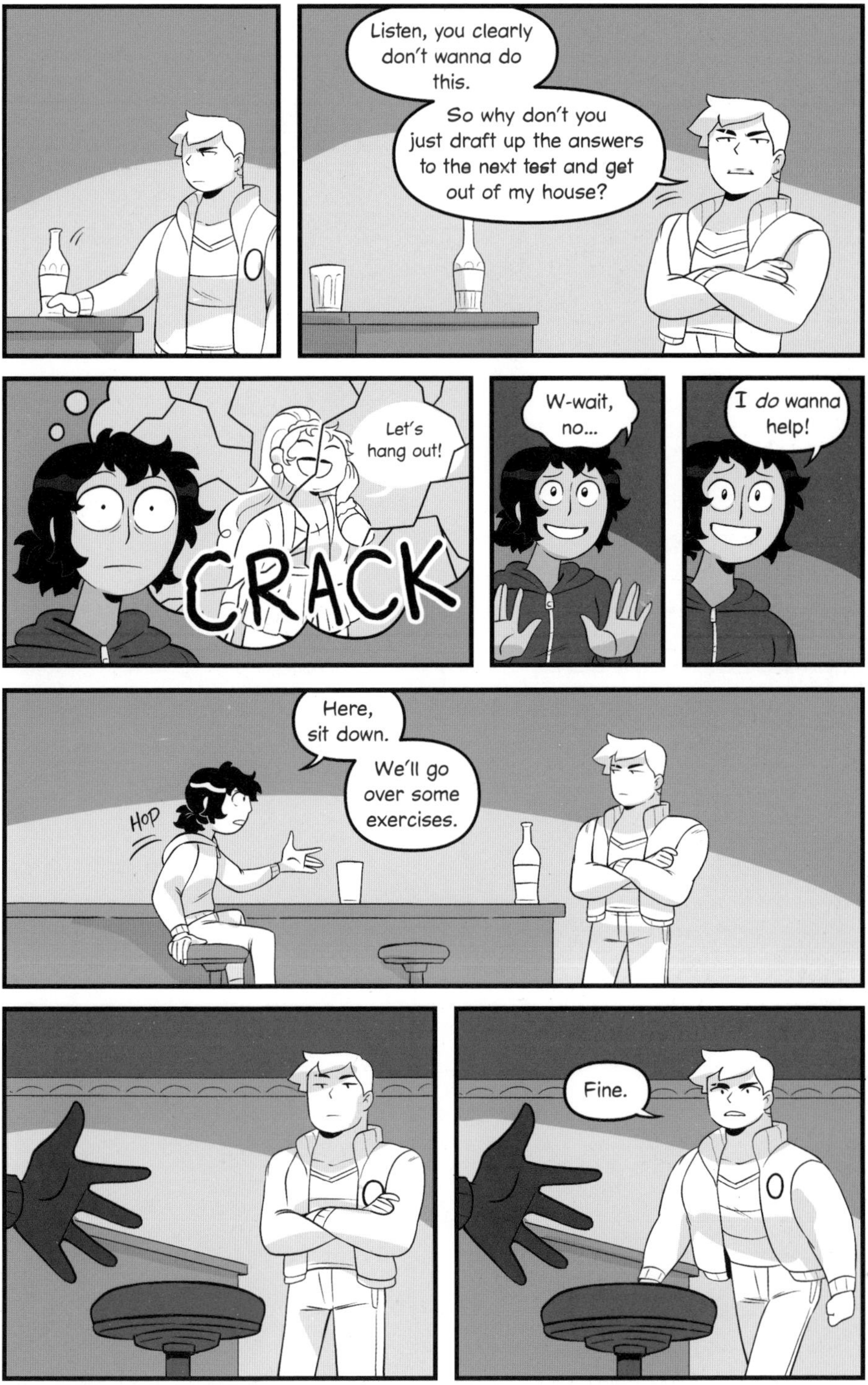
Listen, you clearly don't wanna do this.
So why don't you just draft up the answers to the next test and get out of my house?
Let's hang out!
CRACK
W-wait, no...
I *do* wanna help!
Here, sit down.
We'll go over some exercises.
HOP
Fine.

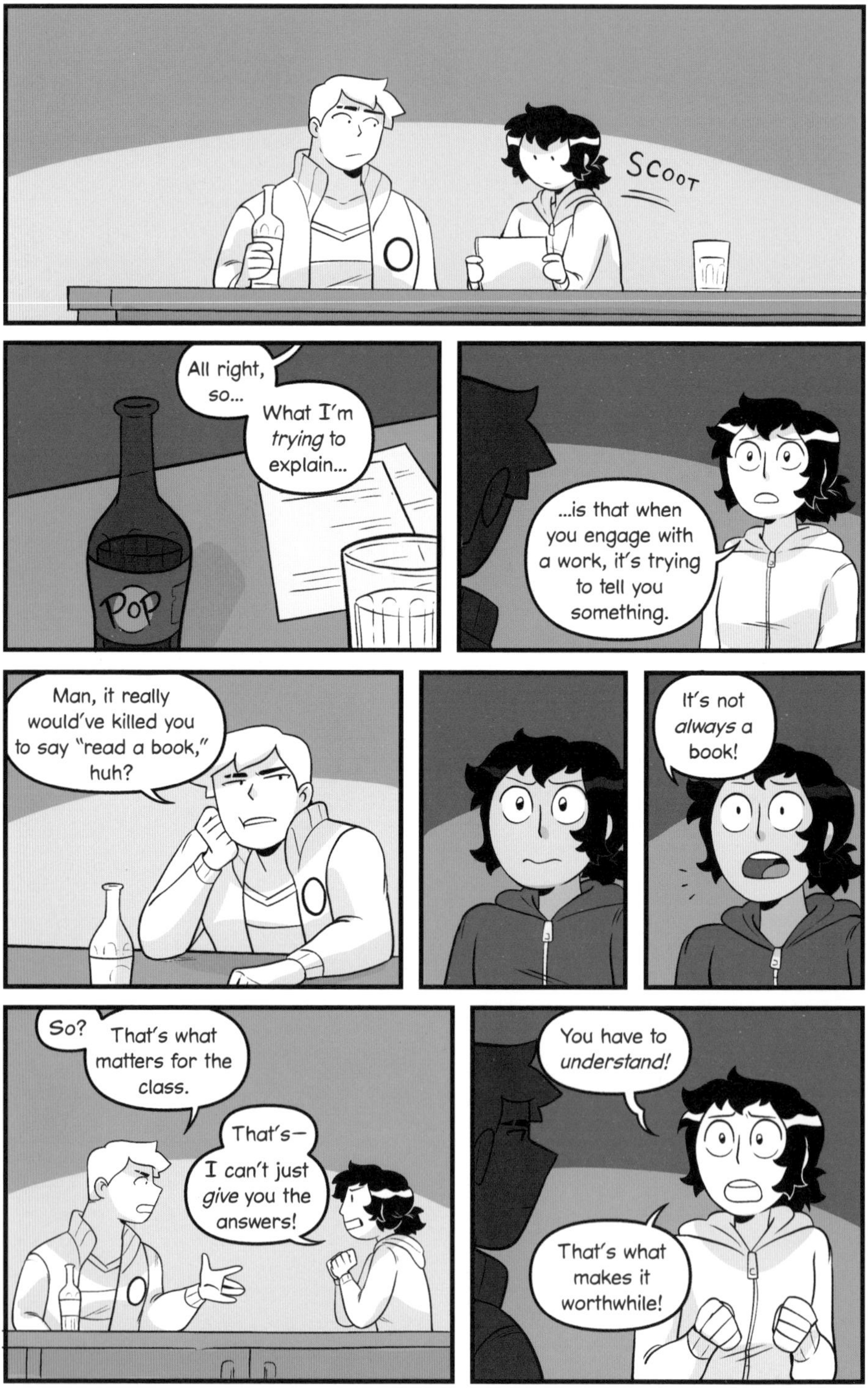
SCOOT
All right, so...
What I'm *trying* to explain...
...is that when you engage with a work, it's trying to tell you something.
Man, it really would've killed you to say "read a book," huh?
It's not *always* a book!
So?
That's what matters for the class.
That's—
I can't just *give* you the answers!
You have to *understand!*
That's what makes it worthwhile!

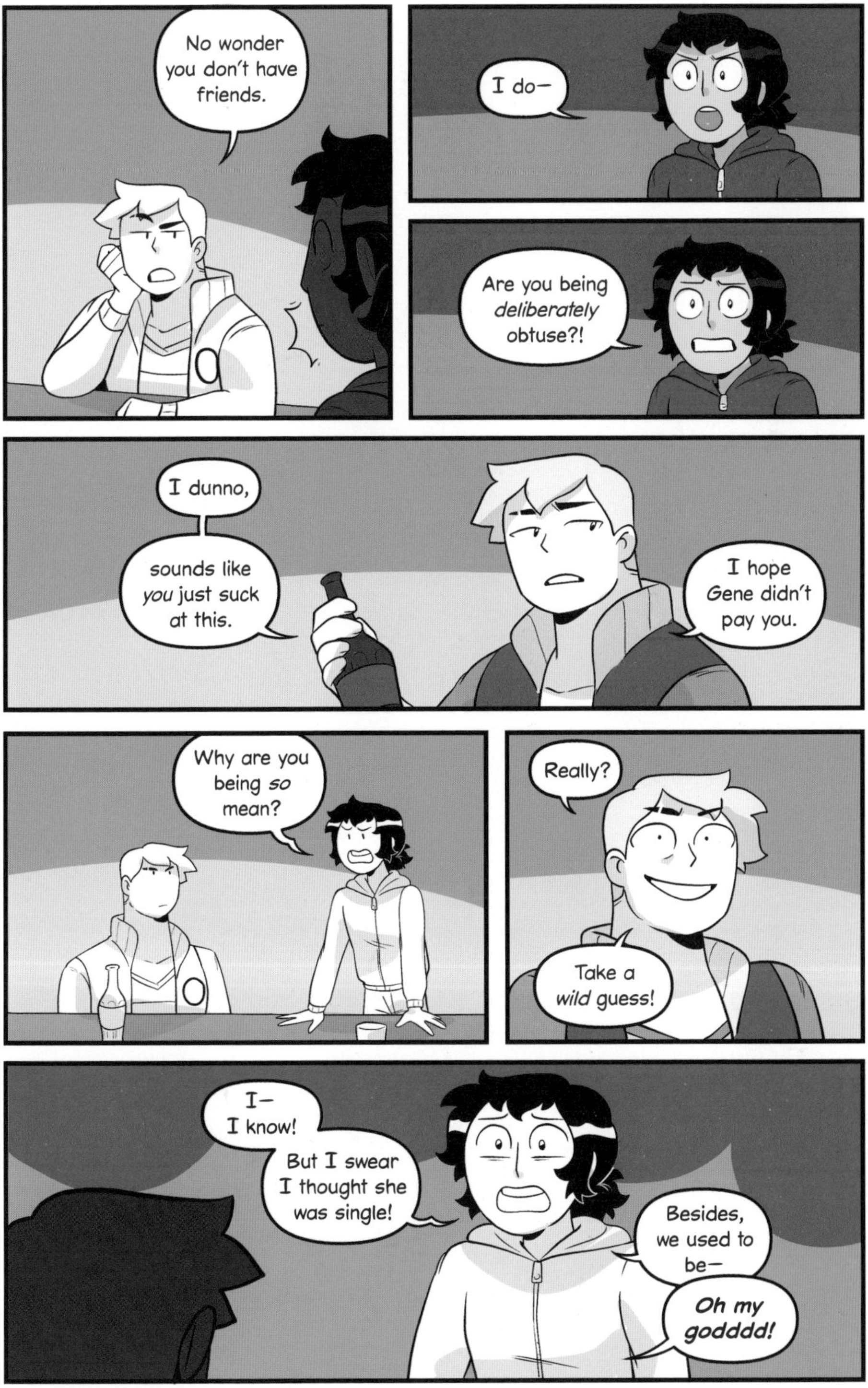
No wonder you don't have friends.
I do—
Are you being *deliberately* obtuse?!
I dunno,
sounds like *you* just suck at this.
I hope Gene didn't pay you.
Why are you being *so* mean?
Really?
Take a *wild* guess!
I— I know!
But I swear I thought she was single!
Besides, we used to be—
Oh my godddd!

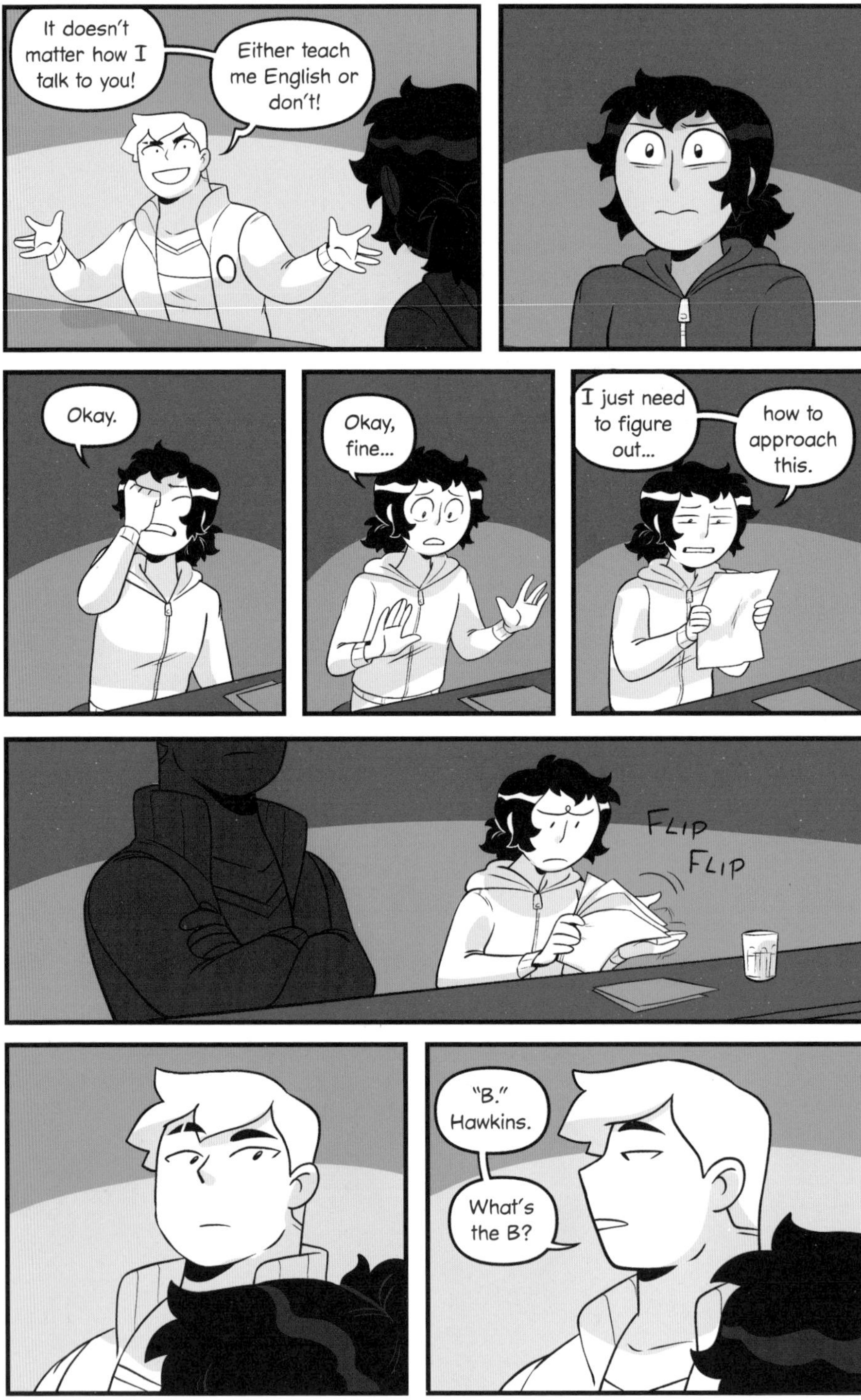
It doesn't matter how I talk to you!
Either teach me English or don't!
Okay.
Okay, fine...
I just need to figure out...
how to approach this.
FLIP
FLIP
"B." Hawkins.
What's the B?

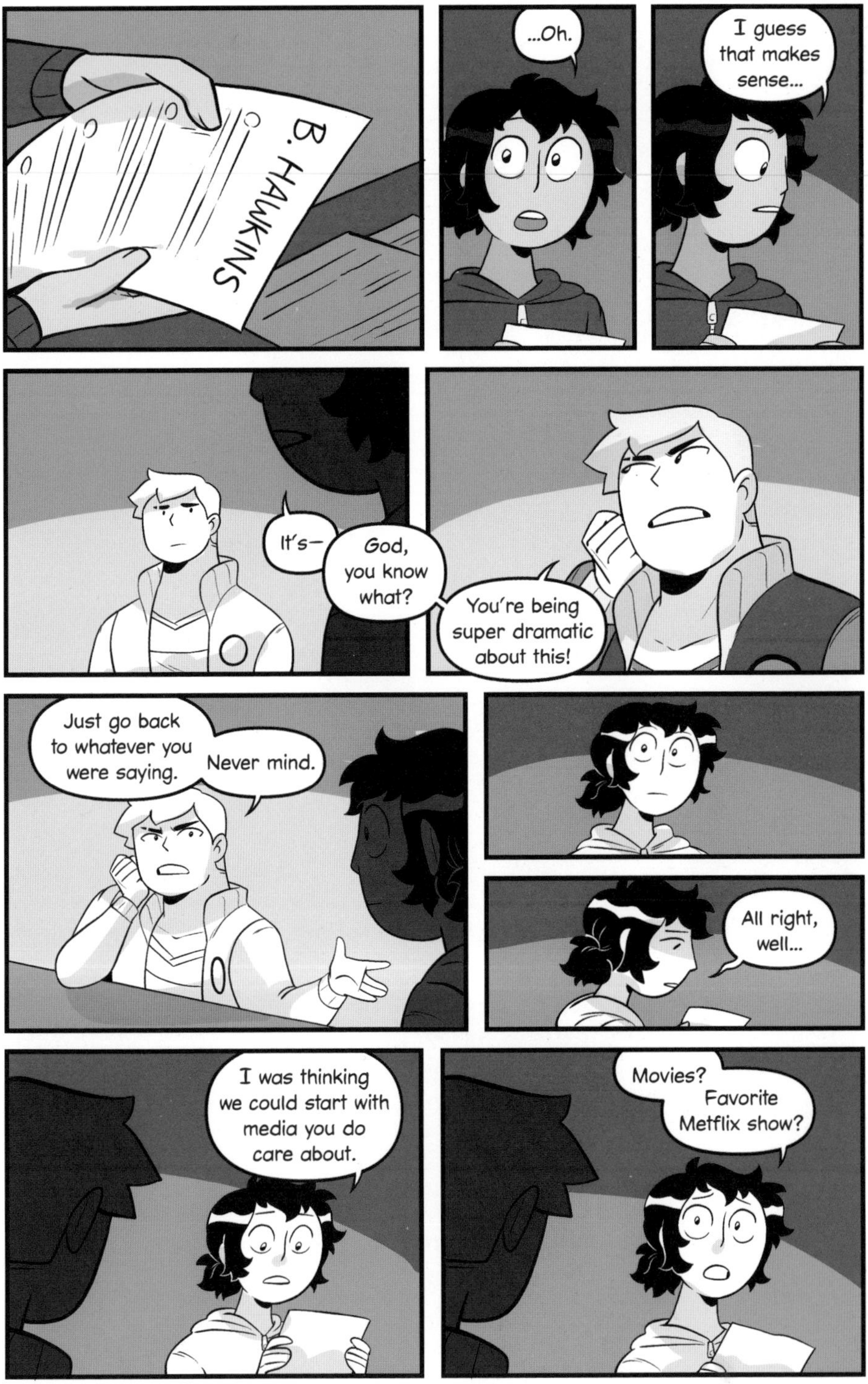
B. HAWKINS
...Oh.
I guess that makes sense...
It's—
God, you know what?
You're being super dramatic about this!
Just go back to whatever you were saying.
Never mind.
All right, well...
I was thinking we could start with media you do care about.
Movies?
Favorite Metflix show?

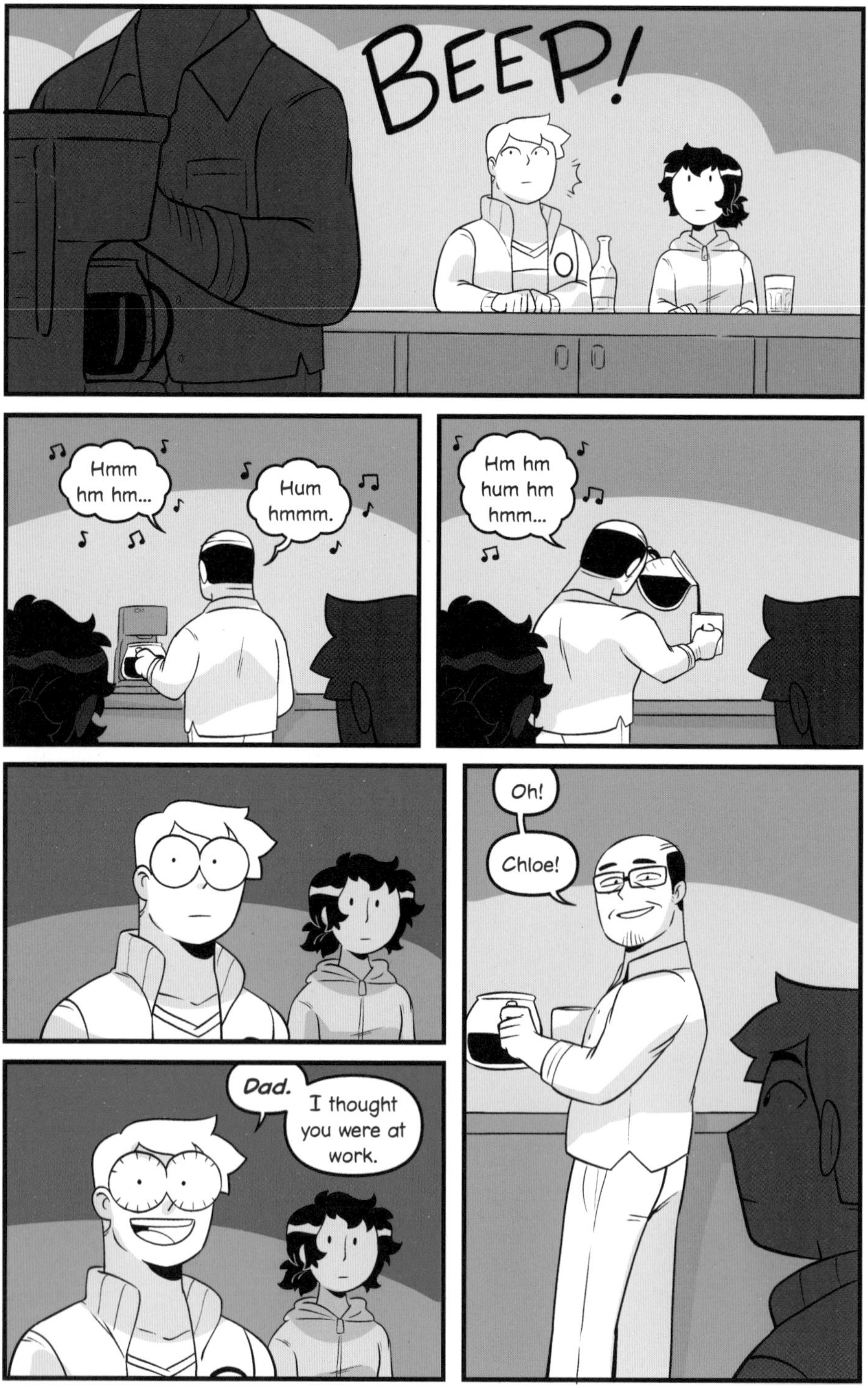
BEEP!
Hmm hm hm...
Hum hmmm.
Hm hm hum hm hmm...
Oh!
Chloe!
Dad. I thought you were at work.

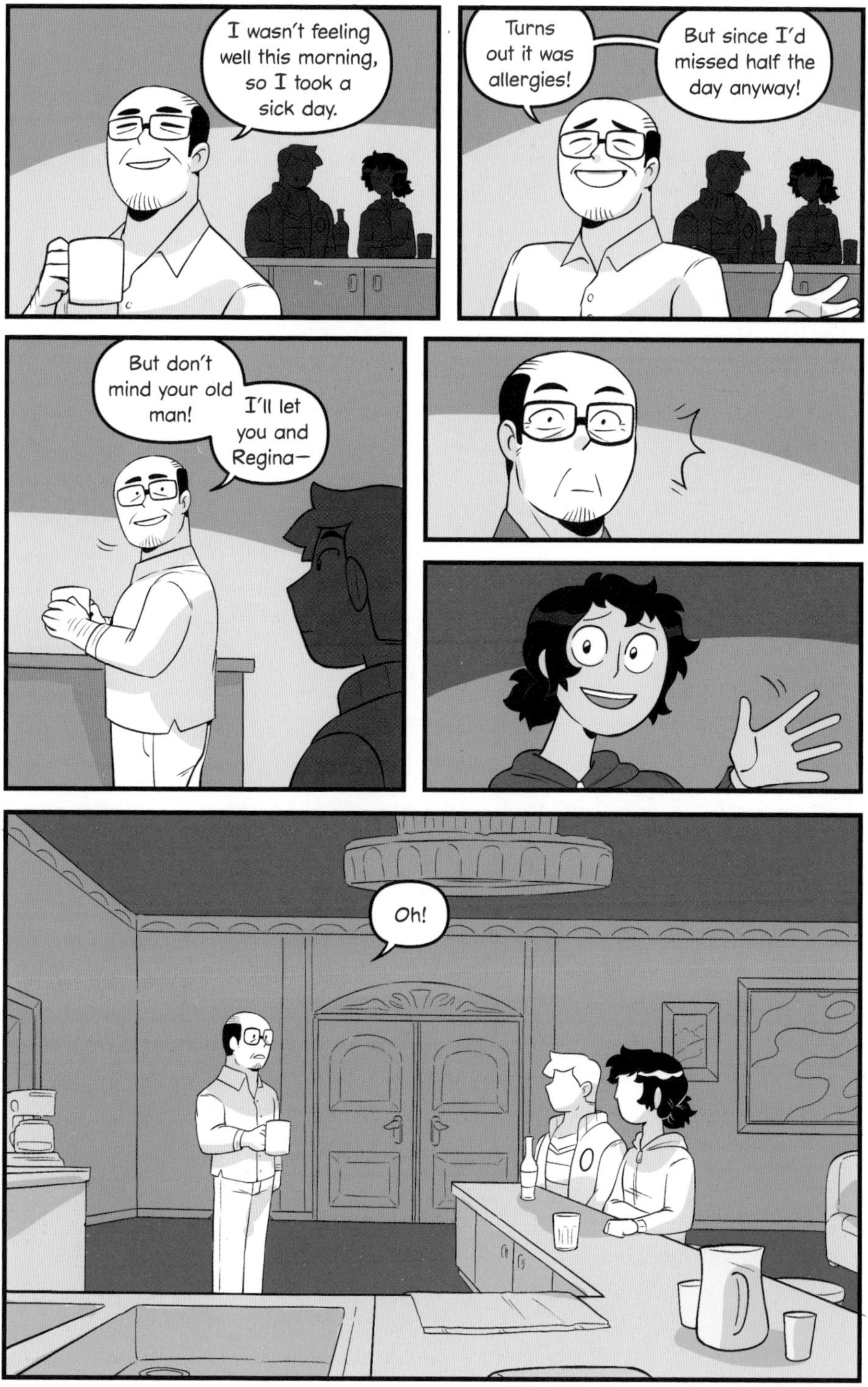
I wasn't feeling well this morning, so I took a sick day.
Turns out it was allergies!
But since I'd missed half the day anyway!
But don't mind your old man!
I'll let you and Regina—
Oh!

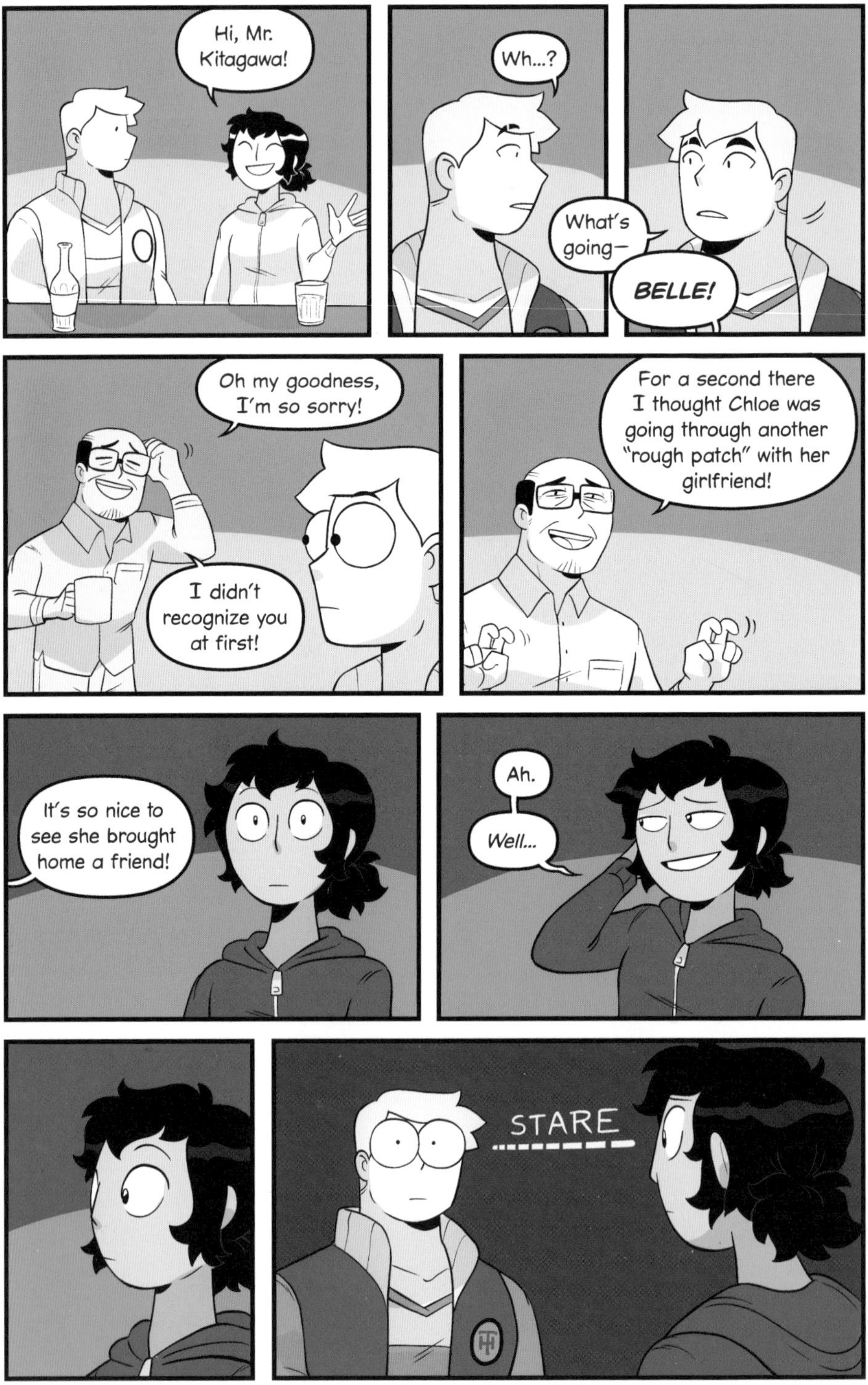
Hi, Mr. Kitagawa!
Wh...?
What's going—
BELLE!
Oh my goodness, I'm so sorry!
I didn't recognize you at first!
For a second there I thought Chloe was going through another "rough patch" with her girlfriend!
It's so nice to see she brought home a friend!
Ah.
Well...
STARE

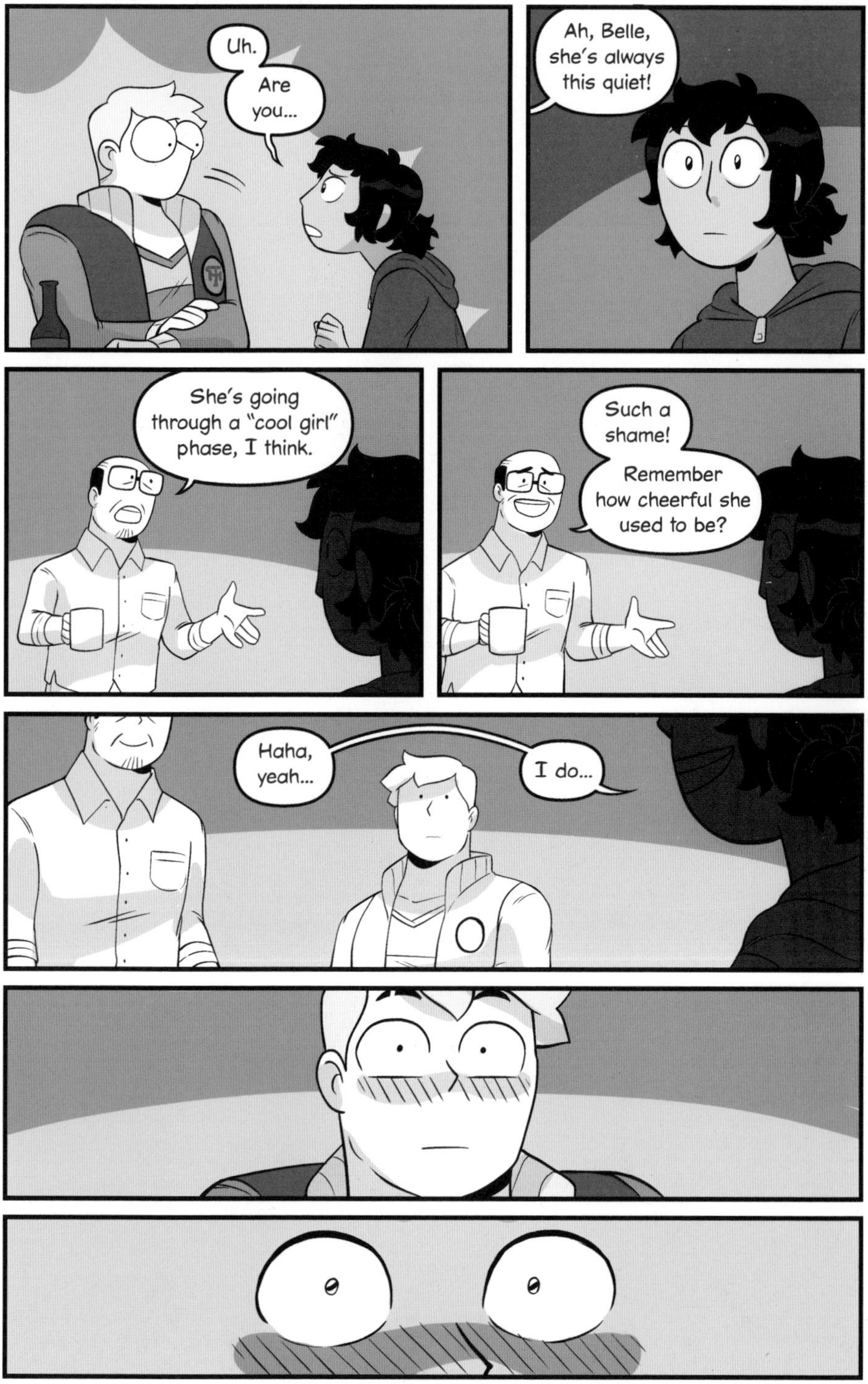
Uh.
Are you...
Ah, Belle, she's always this quiet!
She's going through a "cool girl" phase, I think.
Such a shame!
Remember how cheerful she used to be?
Haha, yeah...
I do...

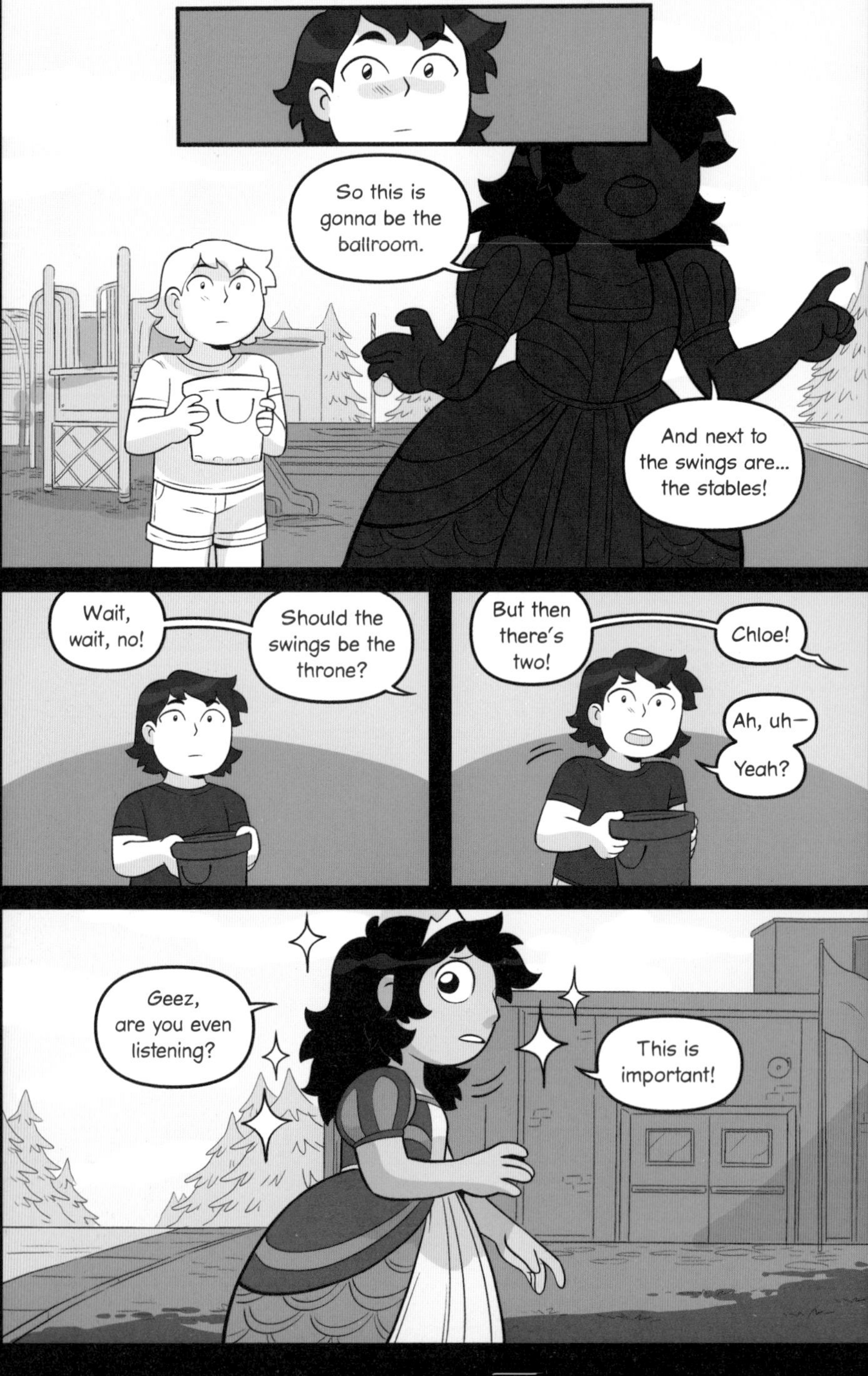

So this is gonna be the ballroom.
And next to the swings are... the stables!
Wait, wait, no!
Should the swings be the throne?
But then there's two!
Chloe!
Ah, uh—
Yeah?
Geez, are you even listening?
This is important!

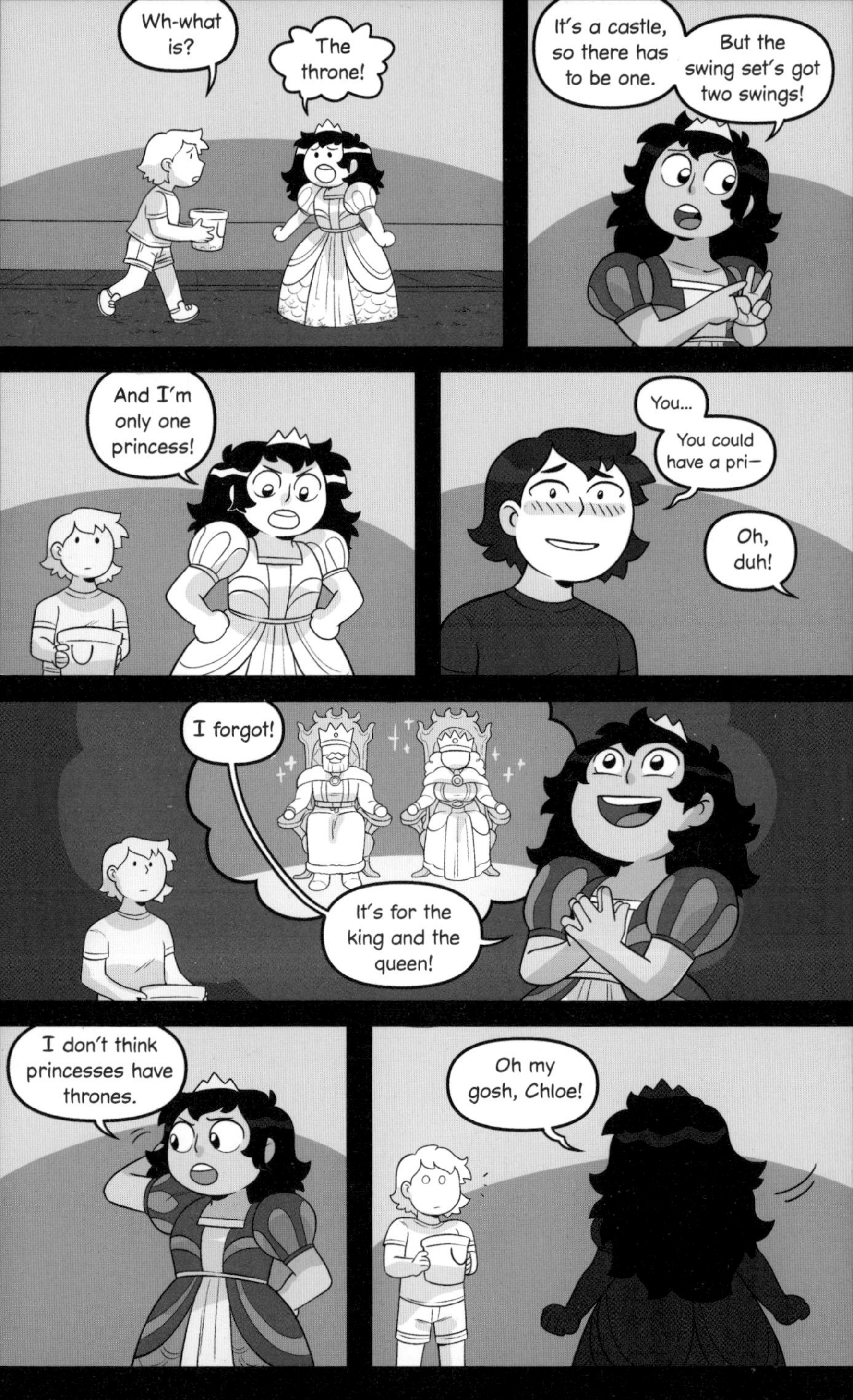

Wh-what is?
The throne!
It's a castle, so there has to be one.
But the swing set's got two swings!
And I'm only one princess!
You...
You could have a pri—
Oh, duh!
I forgot!
It's for the king and the queen!
I don't think princesses have thrones.
Oh my gosh, Chloe!

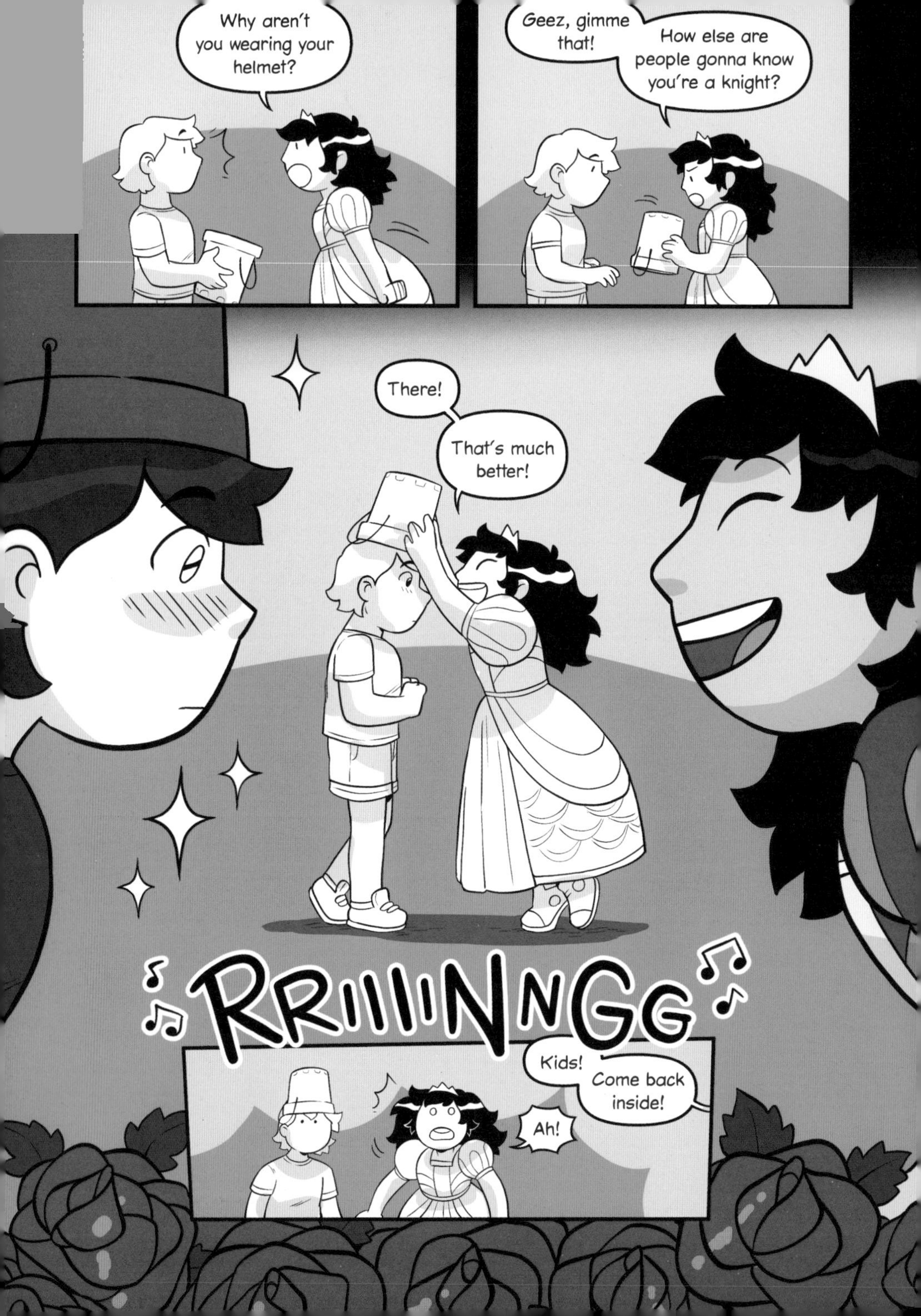
Why aren't you wearing your helmet?
Geez, gimme that!
How else are people gonna know you're a knight?
There!
That's much better!
RRIIIINNGG
Kids!
Come back inside!
Ah!

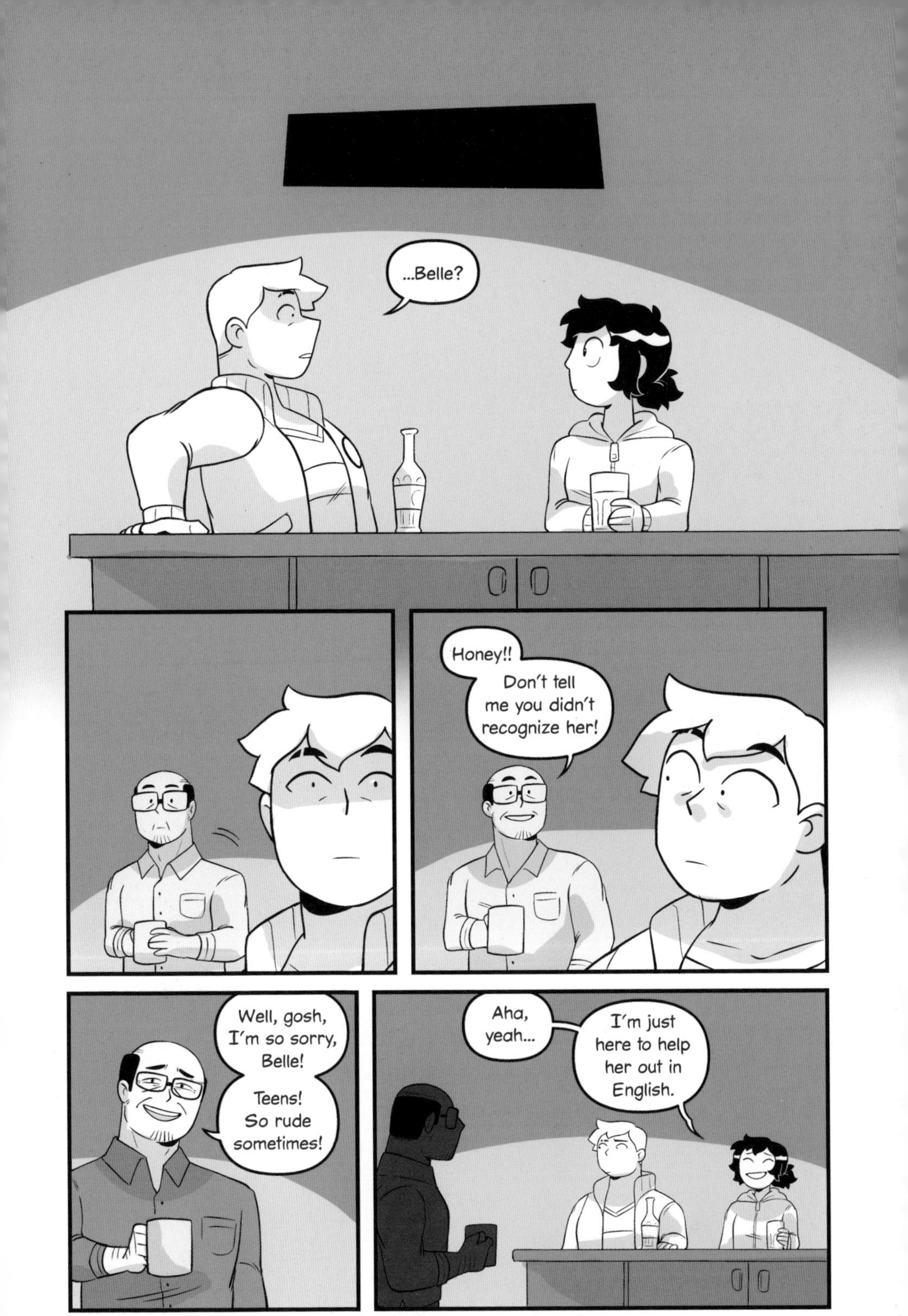
...Belle?
Honey!!
Don't tell me you didn't recognize her!
Well, gosh, I'm so sorry, Belle!
Teens! So rude sometimes!
Aha, yeah...
I'm just here to help her out in English.

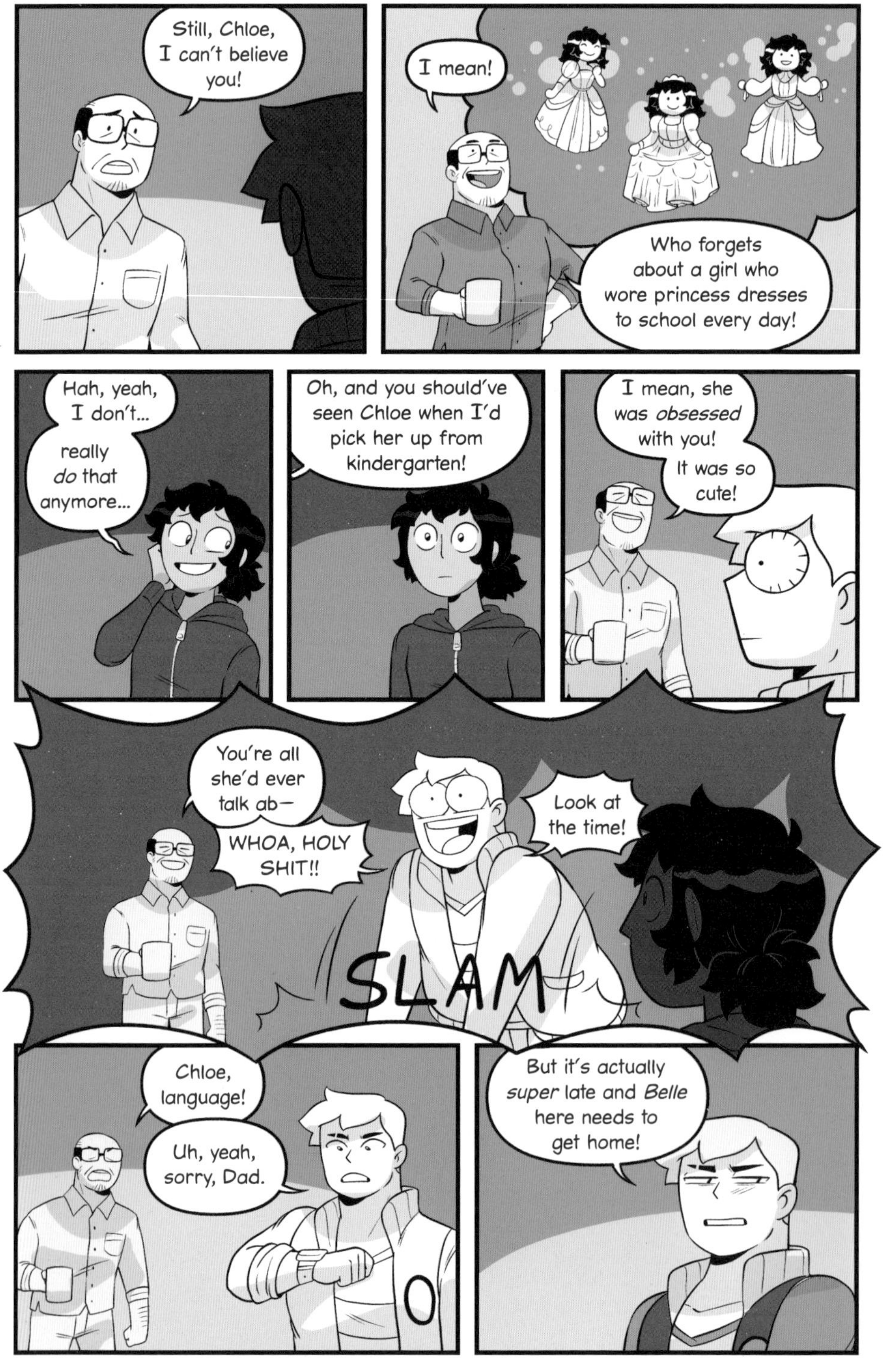
Still, Chloe, I can't believe you!
I mean!
Who forgets about a girl who wore princess dresses to school every day!
Hah, yeah, I don't...
really *do* that anymore...
Oh, and you should've seen Chloe when I'd pick her up from kindergarten!
I mean, she was *obsessed* with you!
It was so cute!
You're all she'd ever talk ab—
WHOA, HOLY SHIT!!
Look at the time!
SLAM
Chloe, language!
Uh, yeah, sorry, Dad.
But it's actually *super* late and *Belle* here needs to get home!

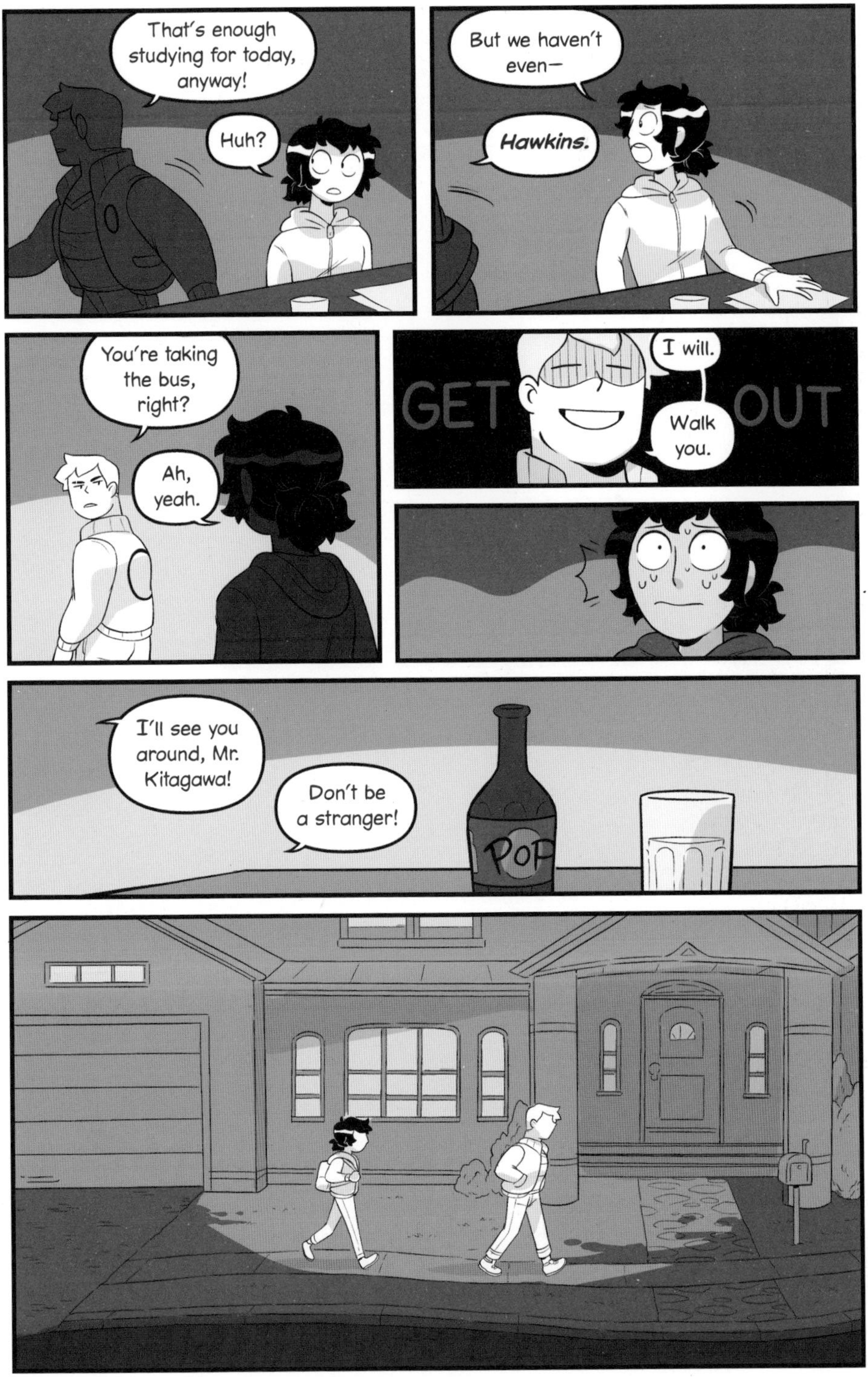
That's enough studying for today, anyway!
Huh?
But we haven't even—
Hawkins.
You're taking the bus, right?
Ah, yeah.
GET
OUT
I will.
Walk you.
I'll see you around, Mr. Kitagawa!
Don't be a stranger!
POP

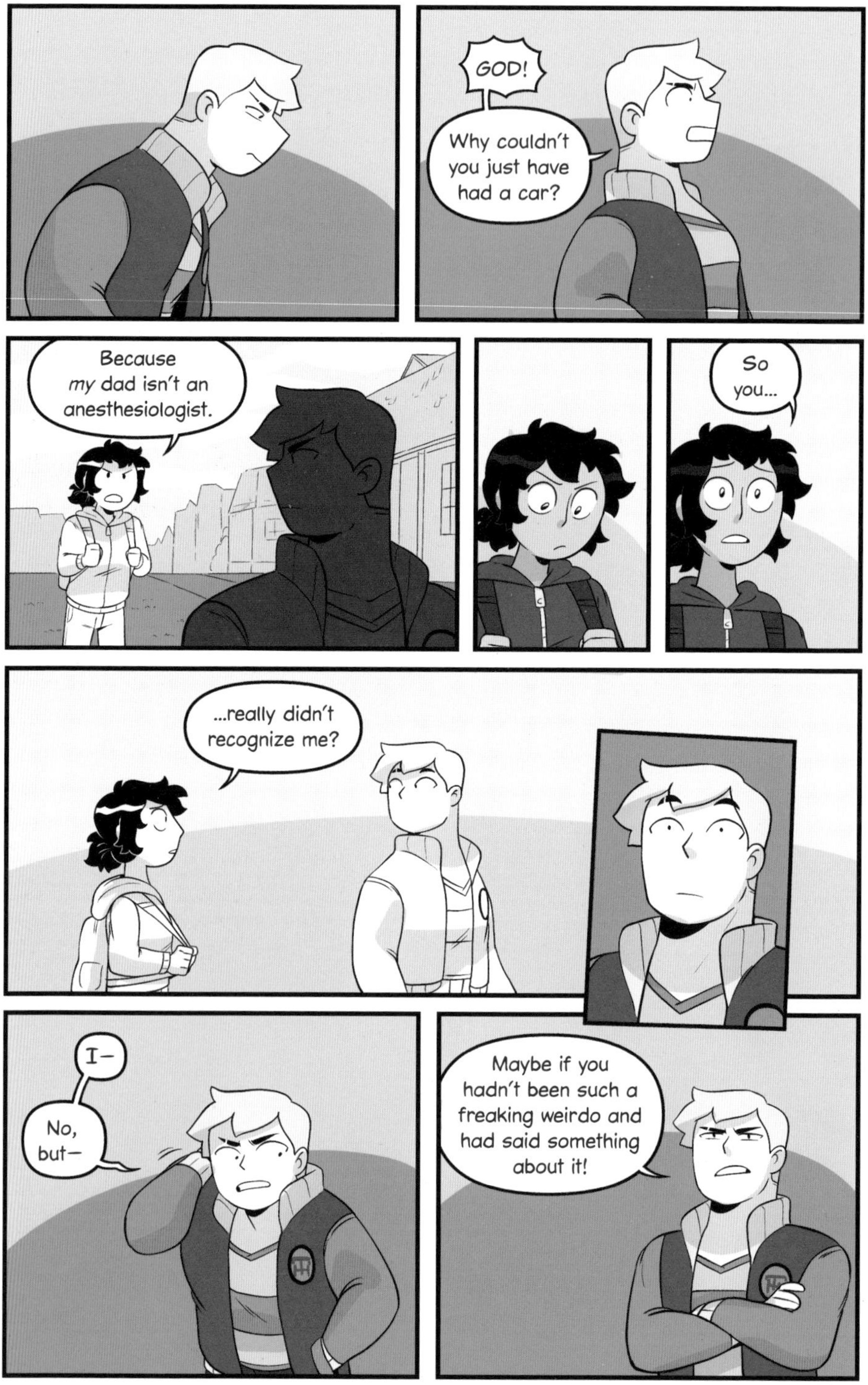
GOD!
Why couldn't you just have had a car?
Because *my* dad isn't an anesthesiologist.
So you...
...really didn't recognize me?
I–
No, but–
Maybe if you hadn't been such a freaking weirdo and had said something about it!

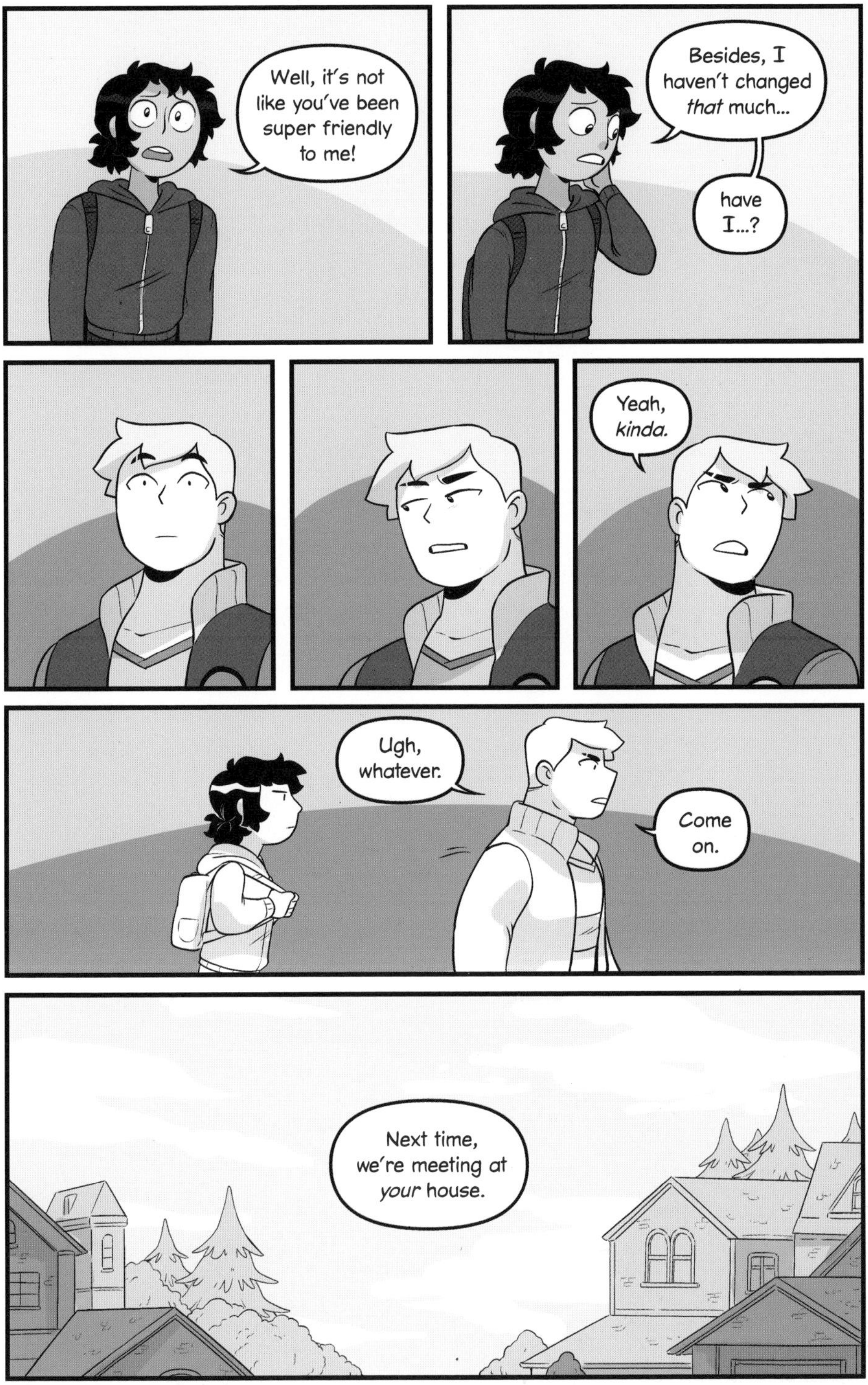

Well, it's not like you've been super friendly to me!
Besides, I haven't changed *that* much...
have I...?
Yeah, *kinda.*
Ugh, whatever.
Come on.
Next time, we're meeting at *your* house.

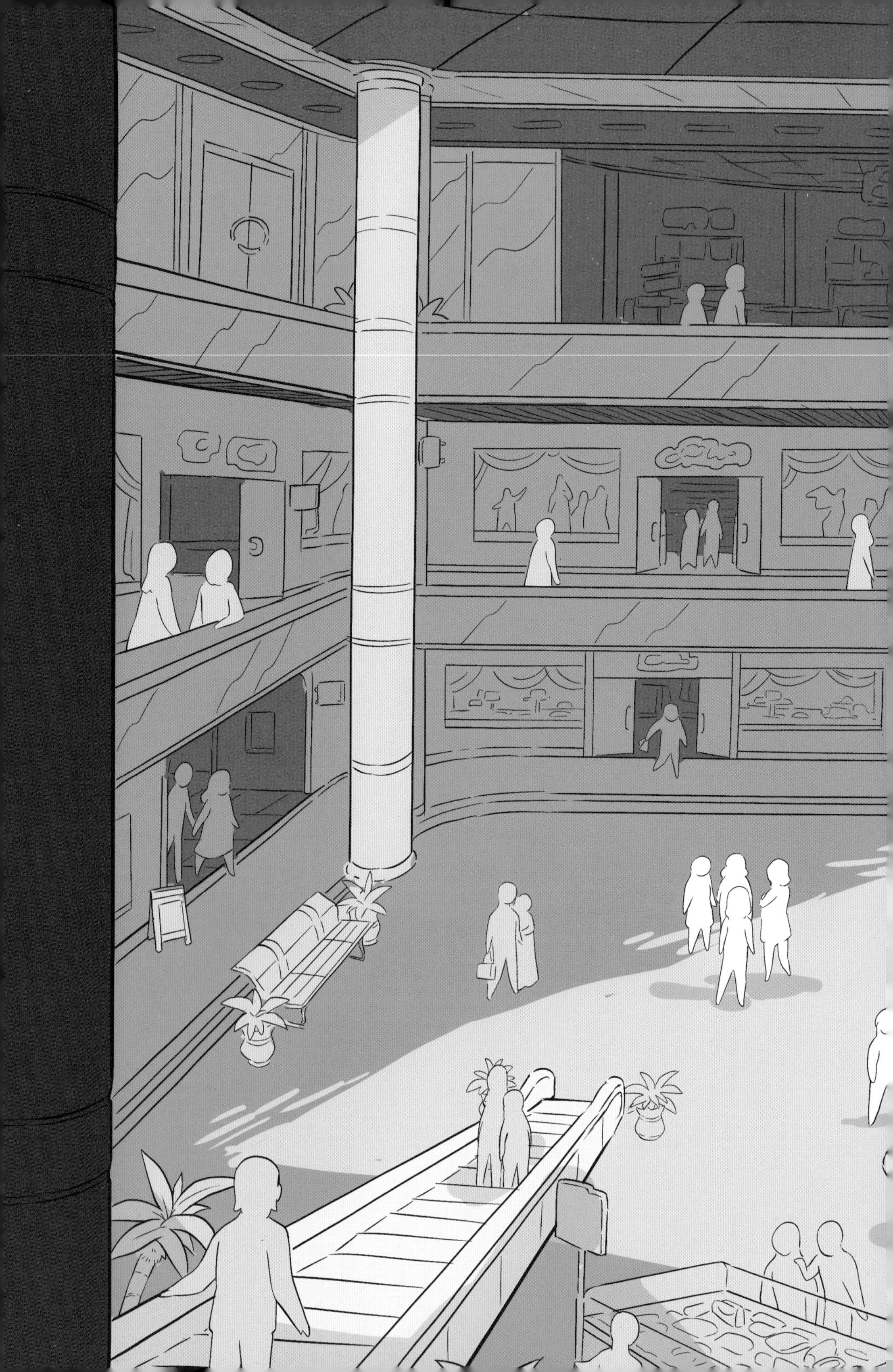

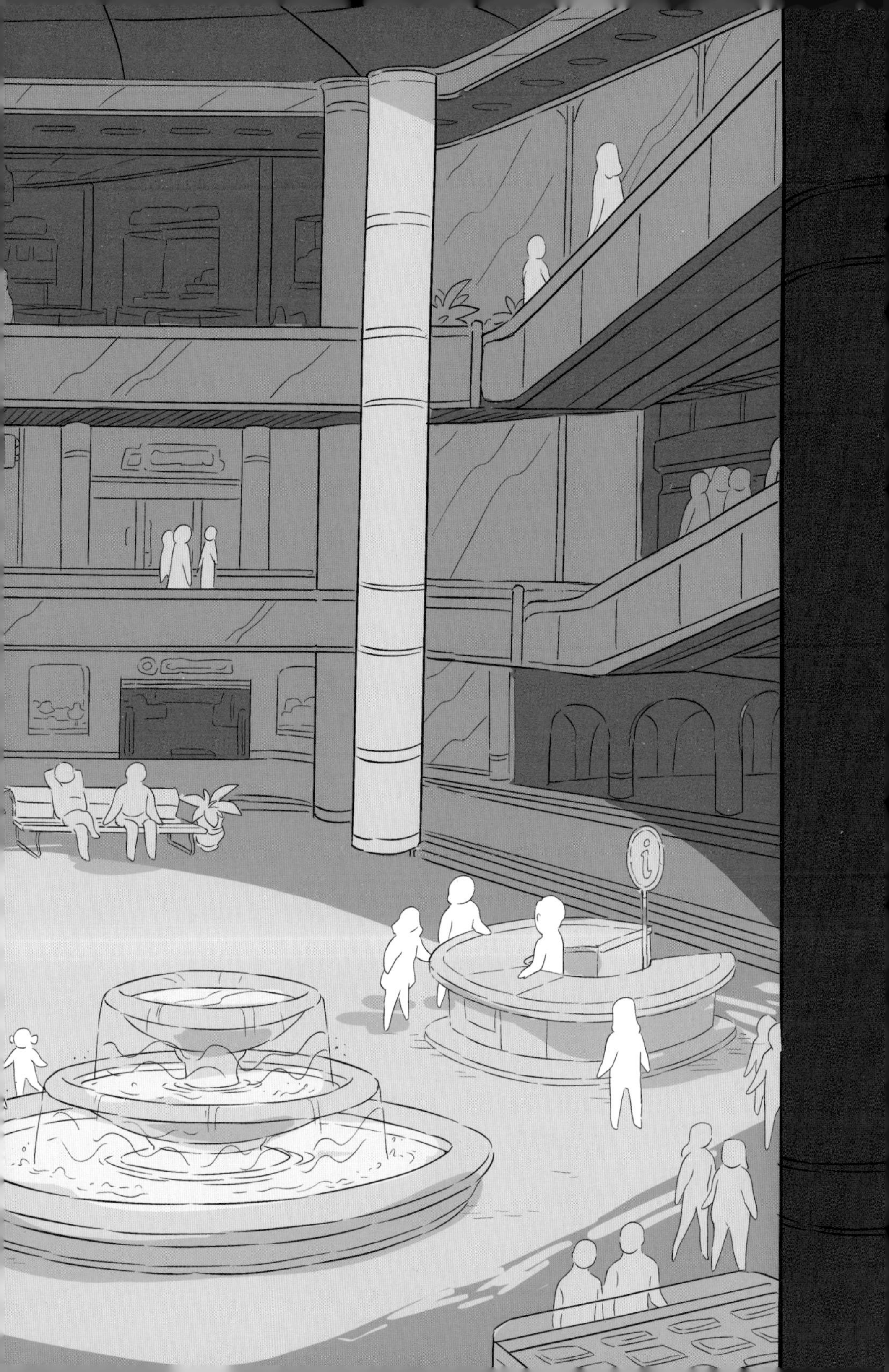

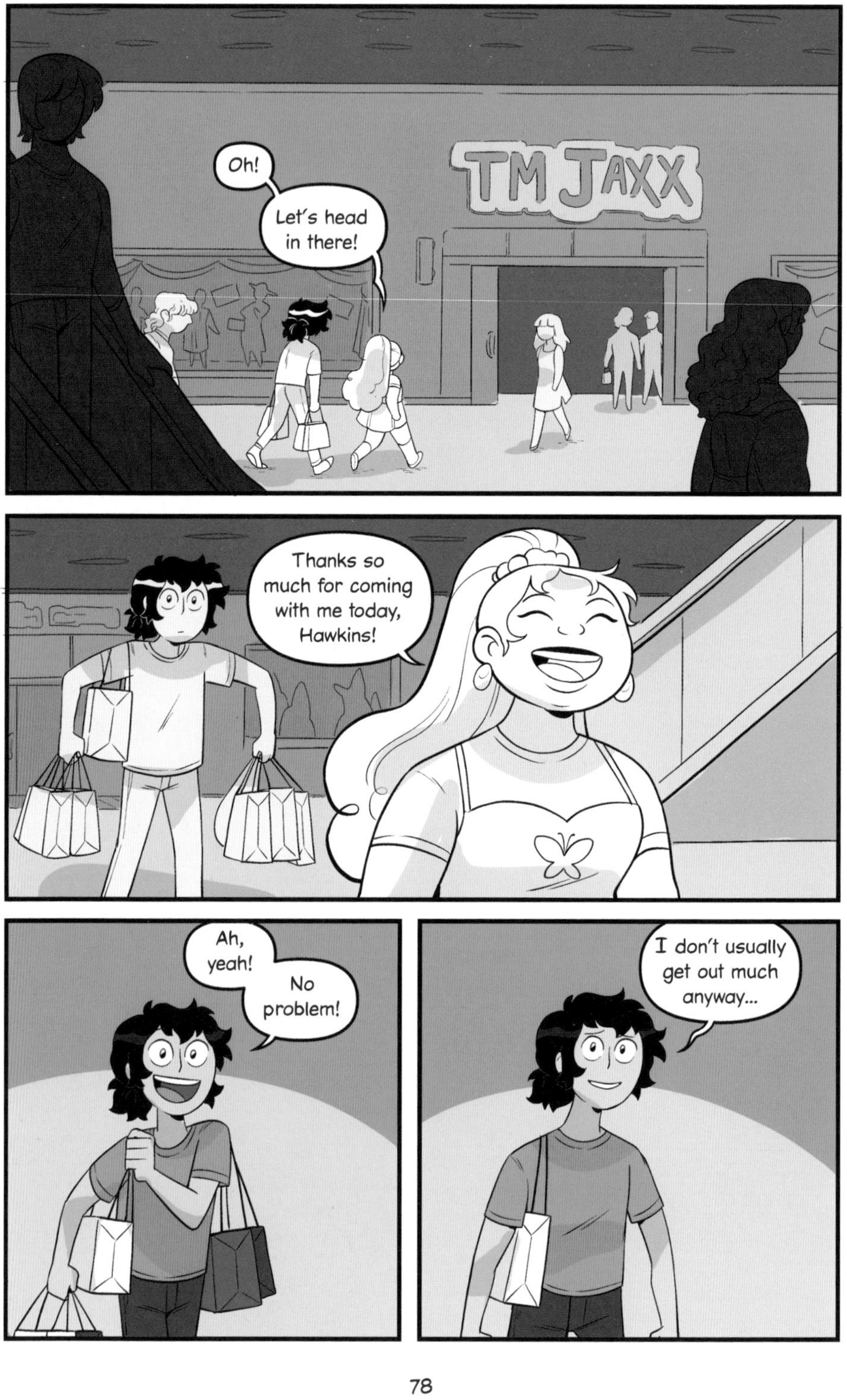
TM JAXX
Oh!
Let's head in there!
Thanks so much for coming with me today, Hawkins!
Ah, yeah!
No problem!
I don't usually get out much anyway...

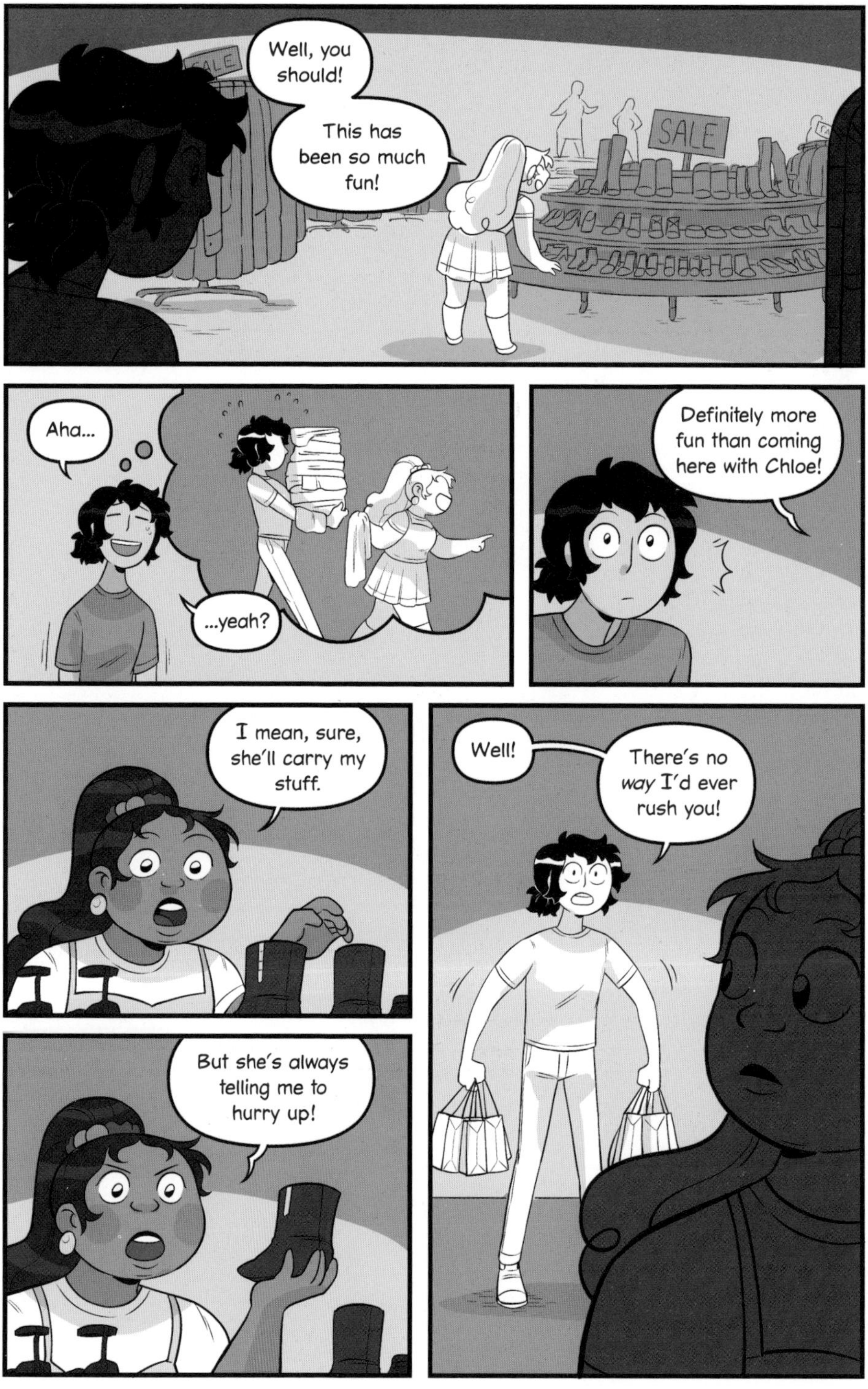

Well, you should!
This has been so much fun!
SALE
SALE
Aha...
...yeah?
Definitely more fun than coming here with Chloe!
I mean, sure, she'll carry my stuff.
But she's always telling me to hurry up!
Well!
There's no *way* I'd ever rush you!

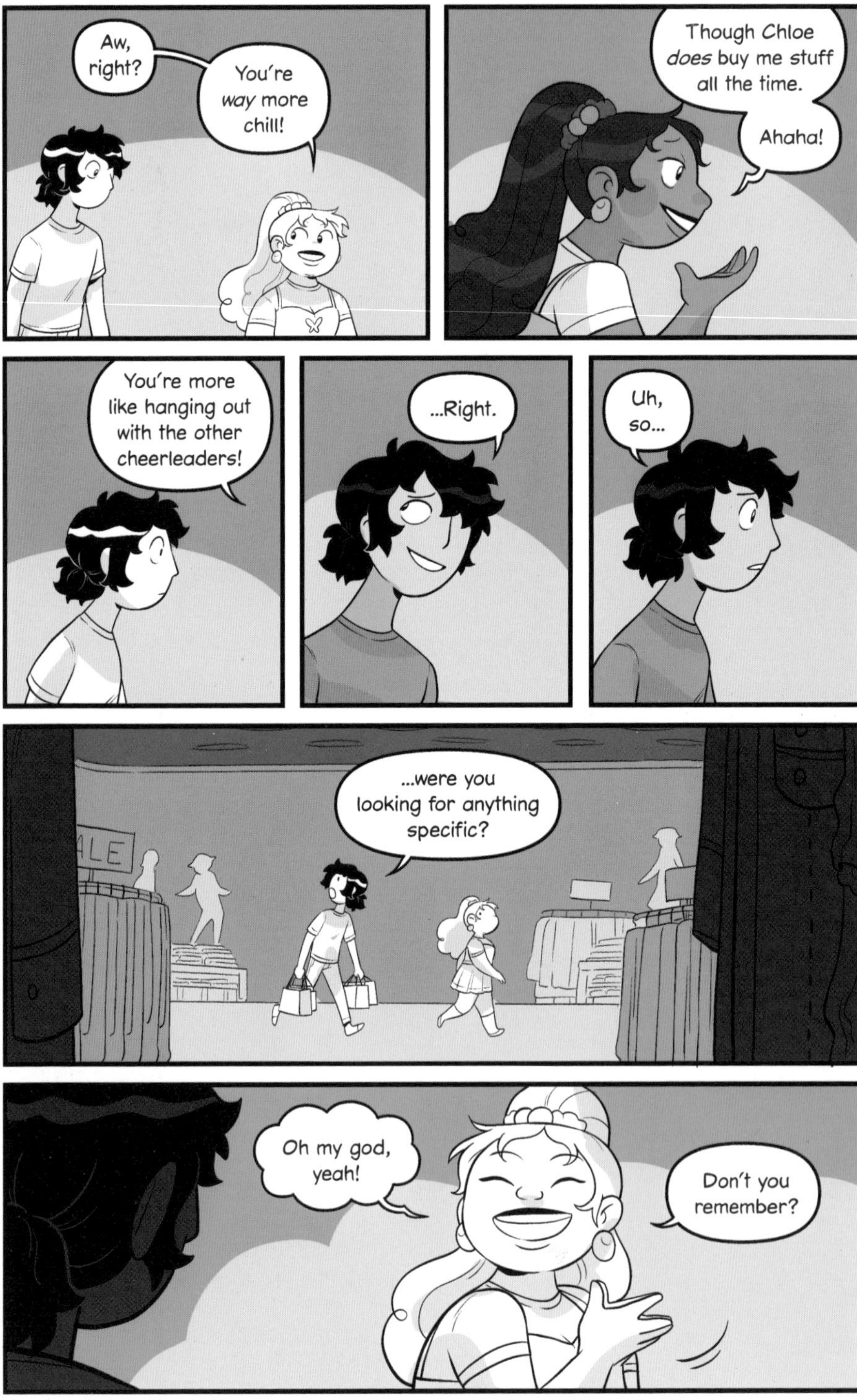
Aw, right?
You're *way* more chill!
Though Chloe *does* buy me stuff all the time.
Ahaha!
You're more like hanging out with the other cheerleaders!
...Right.
Uh, so...
...were you looking for anything specific?
ALE
Oh my god, yeah!
Don't you remember?

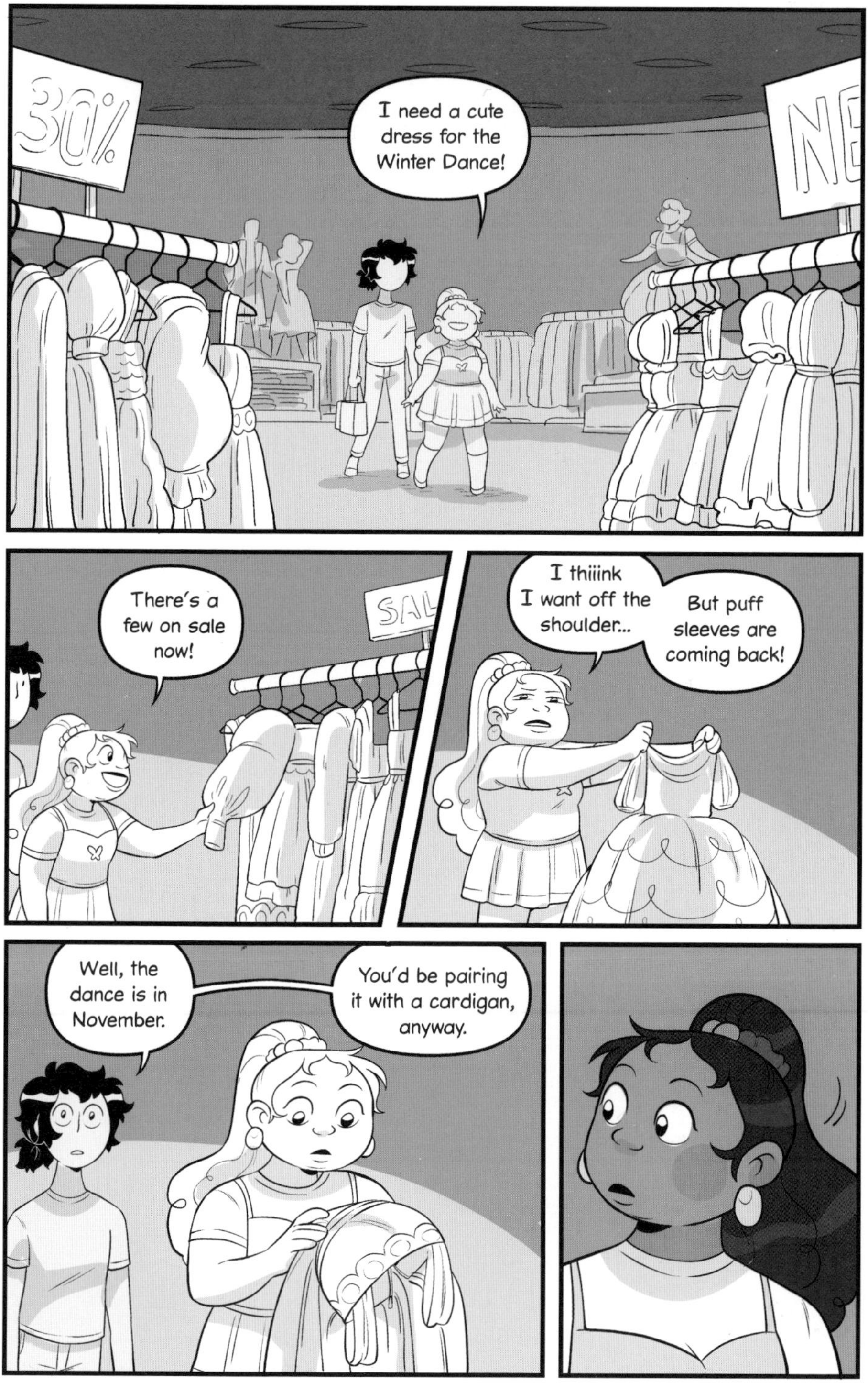
30%
I need a cute dress for the Winter Dance!
NE
There's a few on sale now!
SAL
I thiiink I want off the shoulder...
But puff sleeves are coming back!
Well, the dance is in November.
You'd be pairing it with a cardigan, anyway.

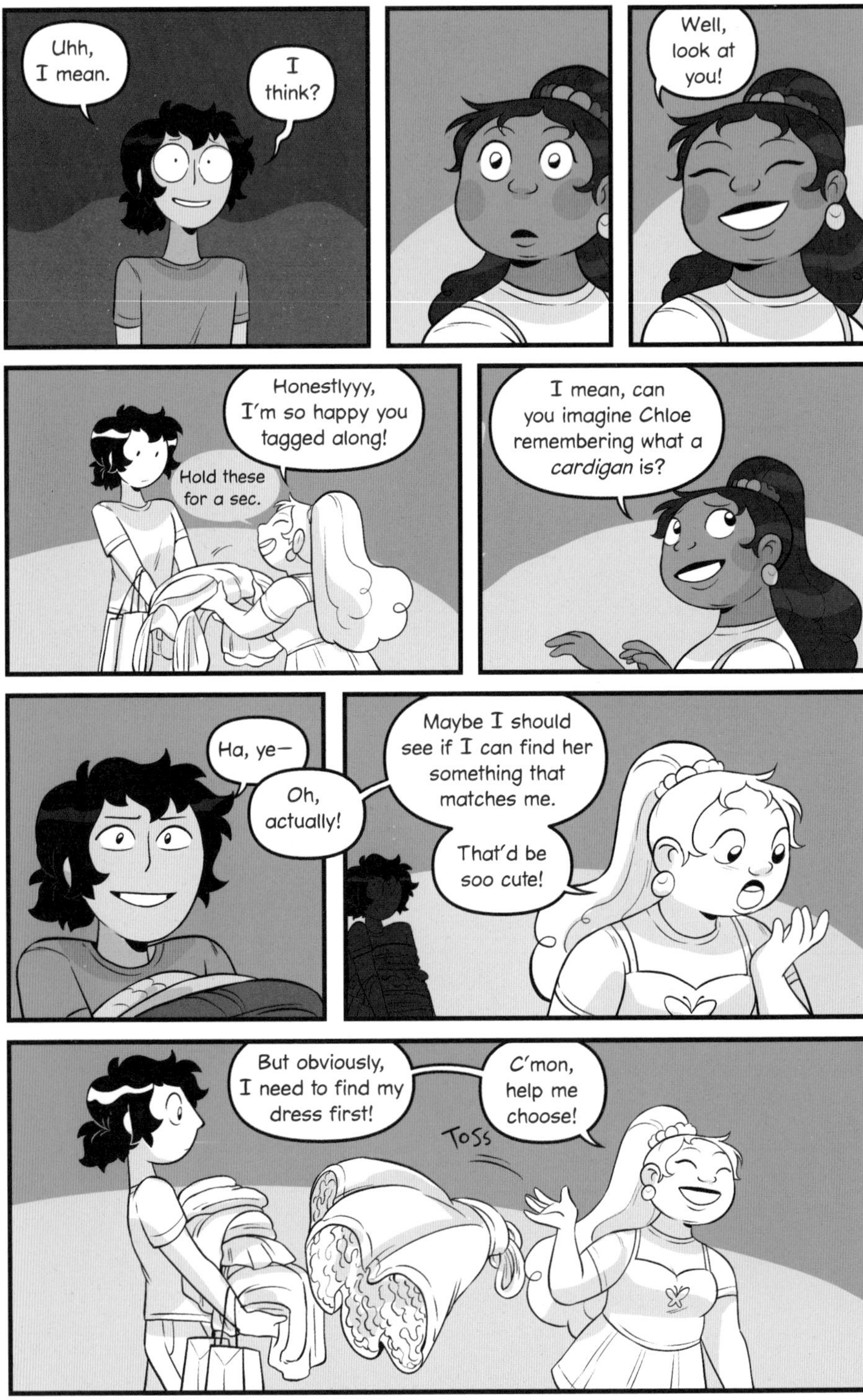
Uhh, I mean.
I think?
Well, look at you!
Honestlyyy, I'm so happy you tagged along!
Hold these for a sec.
I mean, can you imagine Chloe remembering what a *cardigan* is?
Ha, ye—
Oh, actually!
Maybe I should see if I can find her something that matches me.
That'd be soo cute!
But obviously, I need to find my dress first!
C'mon, help me choose!
TOSS

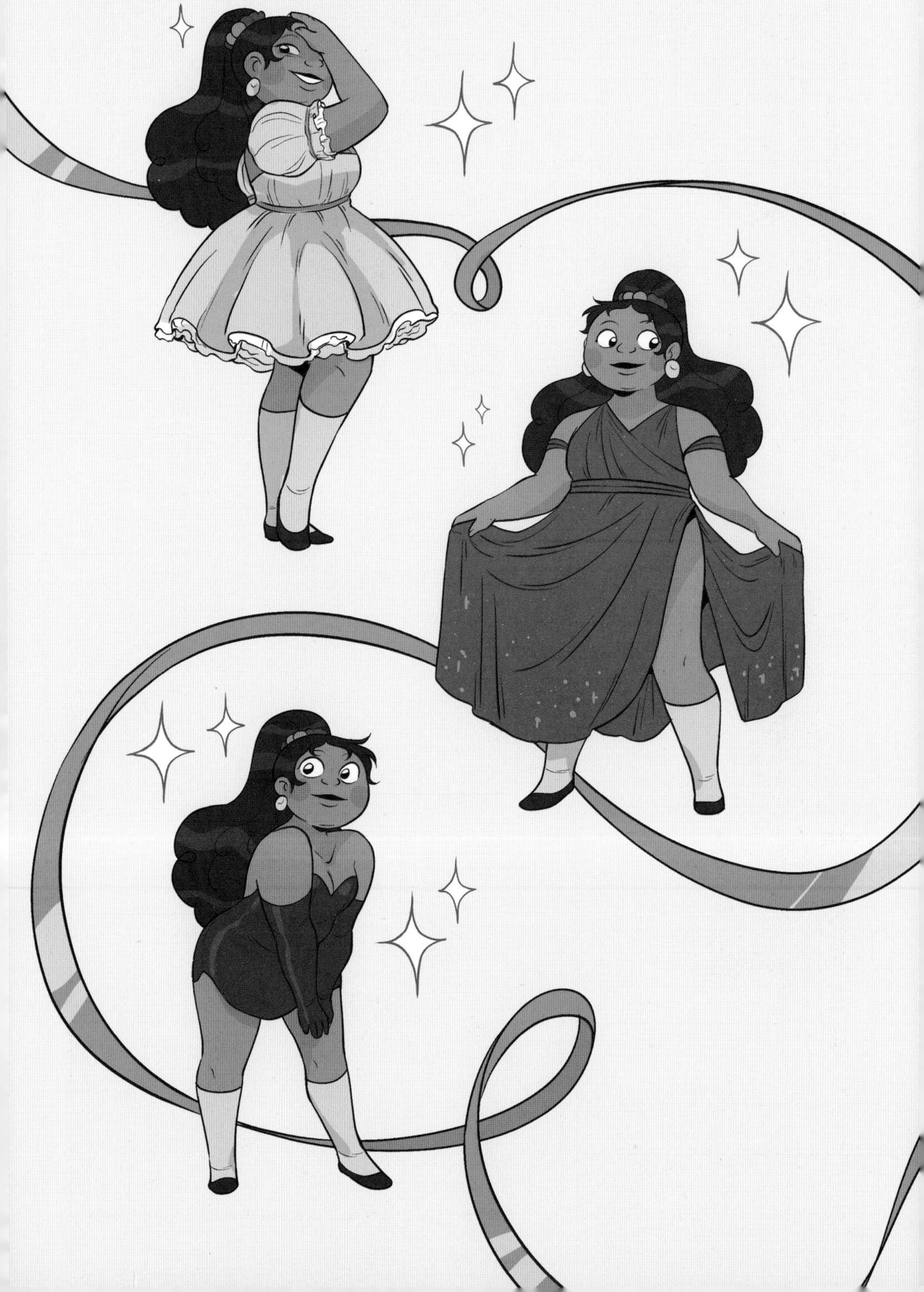

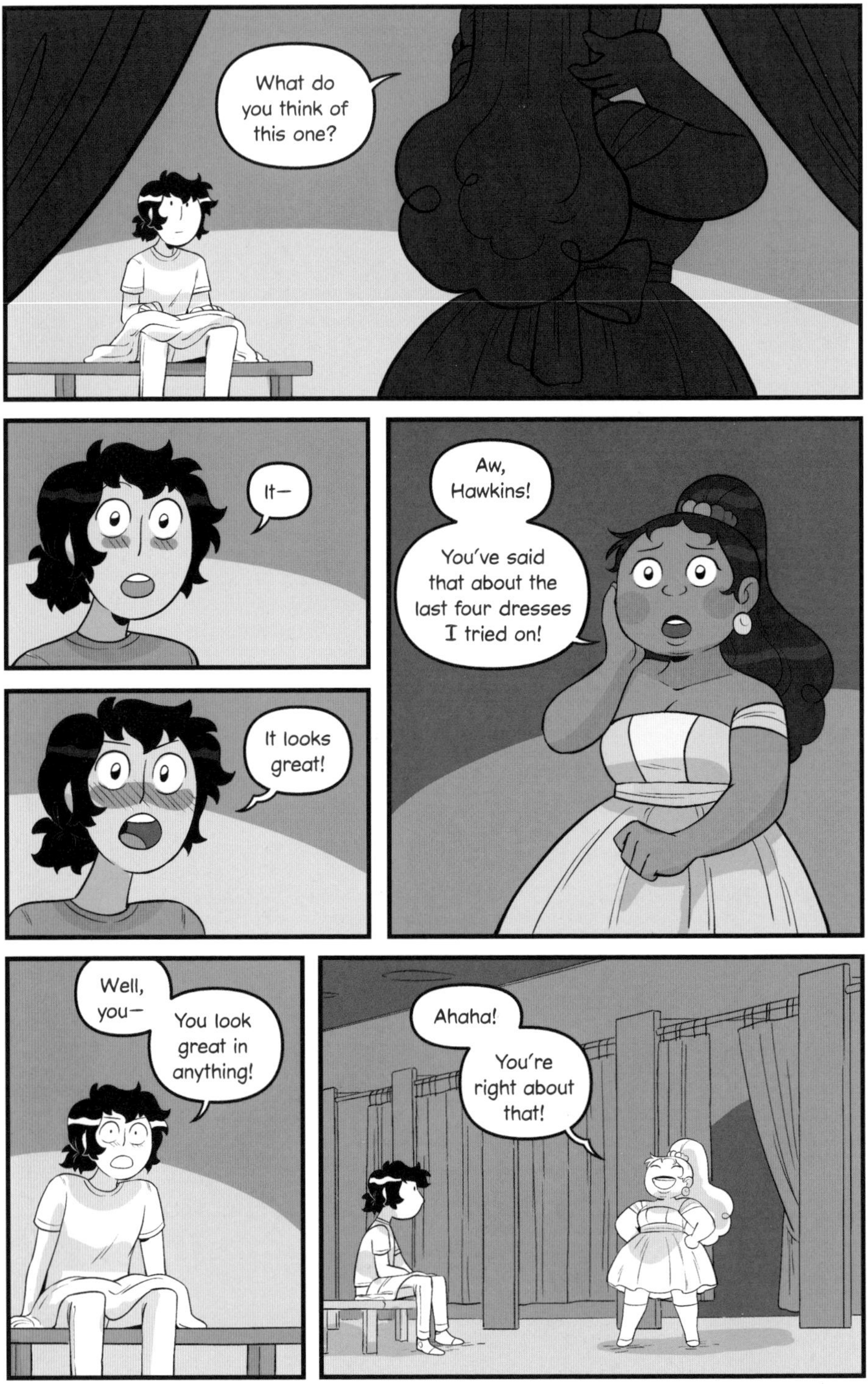

What do you think of this one?
It—
It looks great!
Aw, Hawkins!
You've said that about the last four dresses I tried on!
Well, you—
You look great in anything!
Ahaha!
You're right about that!

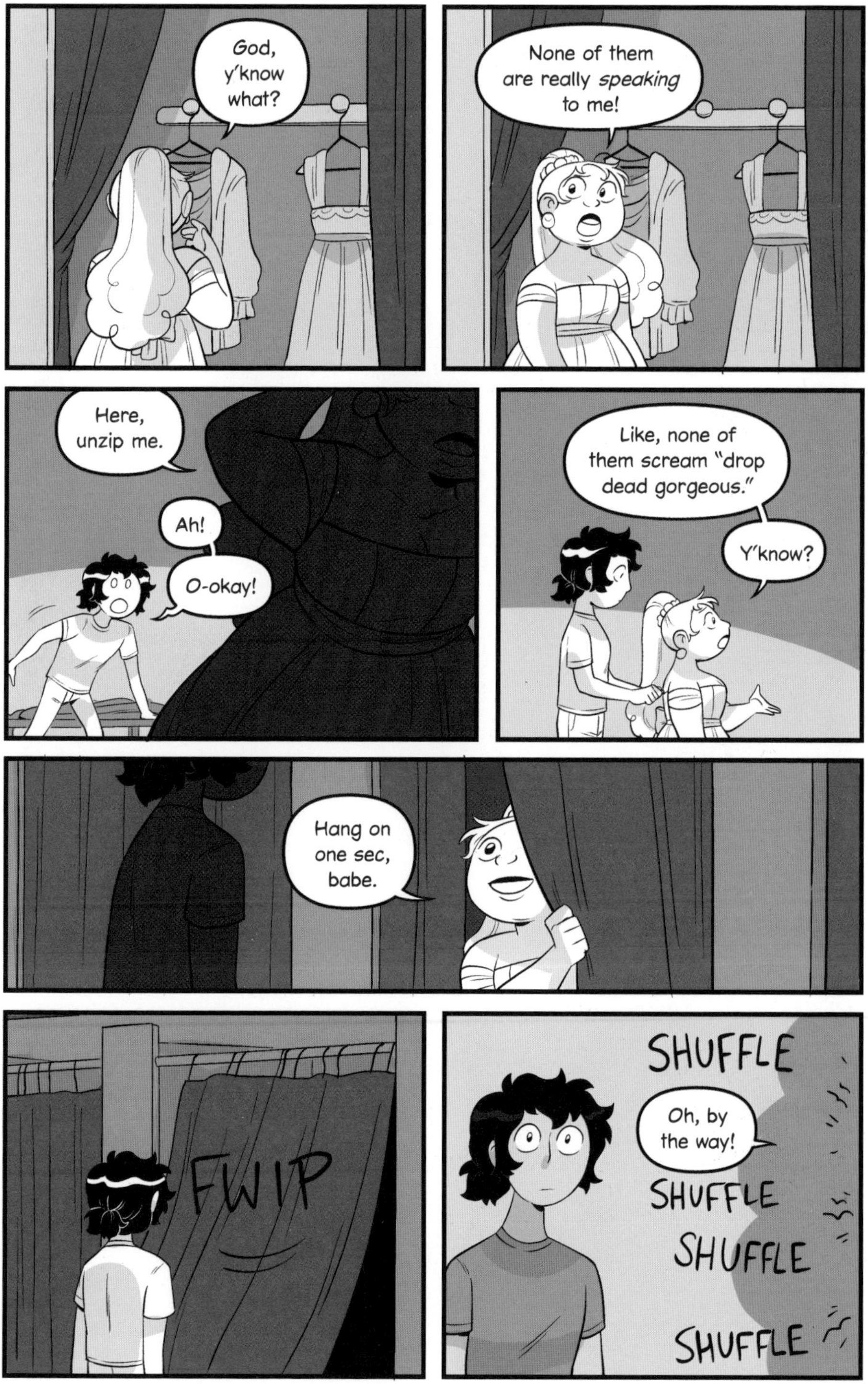
God, y'know what?
None of them are really *speaking* to me!
Here, unzip me.
Ah!
O-okay!
Like, none of them scream "drop dead gorgeous."
Y'know?
Hang on one sec, babe.
FWIP
SHUFFLE
Oh, by the way!
SHUFFLE
SHUFFLE
SHUFFLE

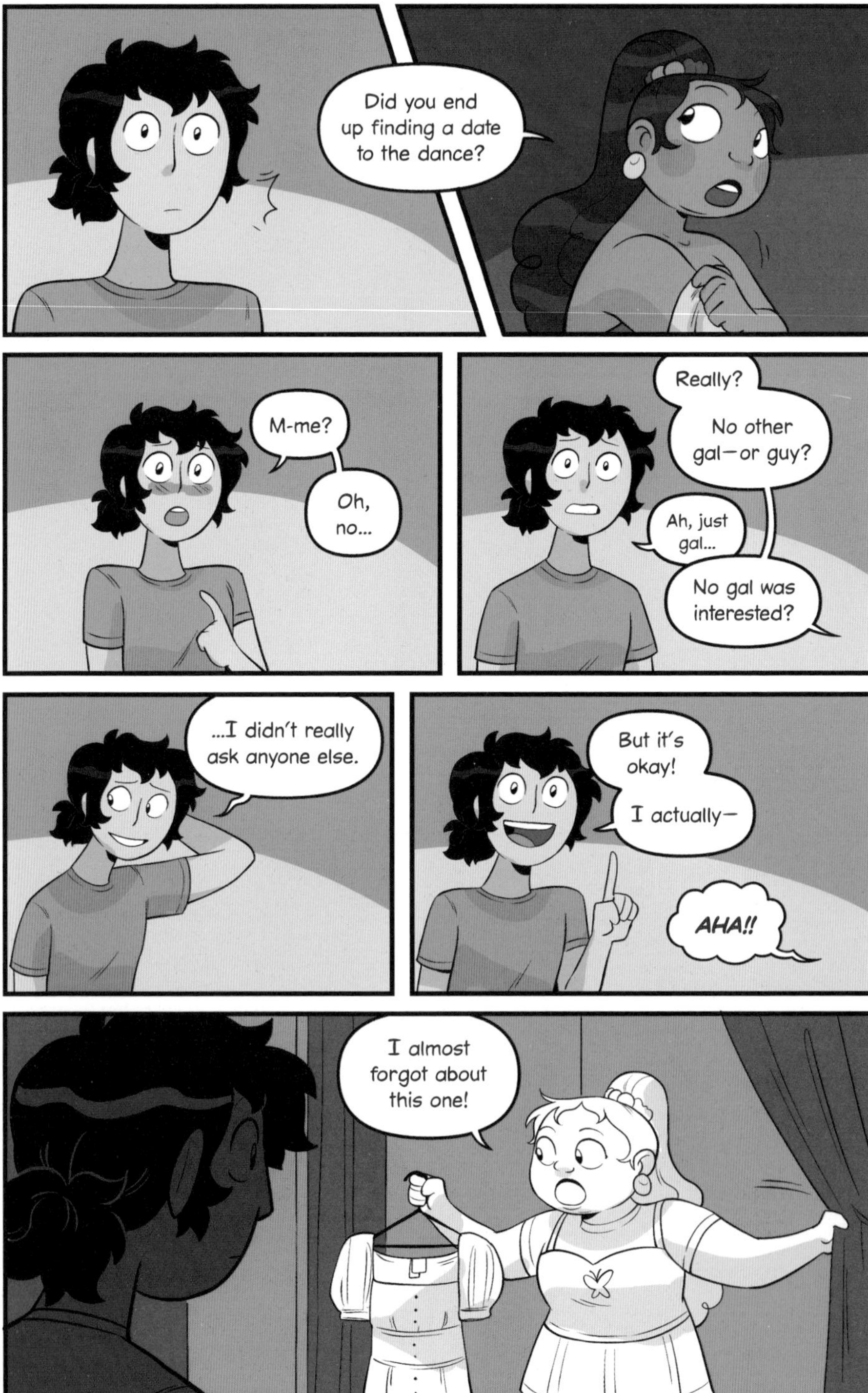
Did you end up finding a date to the dance?
M-me?
Oh, no...
Really?
No other gal—or guy?
Ah, just gal...
No gal was interested?
...I didn't really ask anyone else.
But it's okay!
I actually—
AHA!!
I almost forgot about this one!

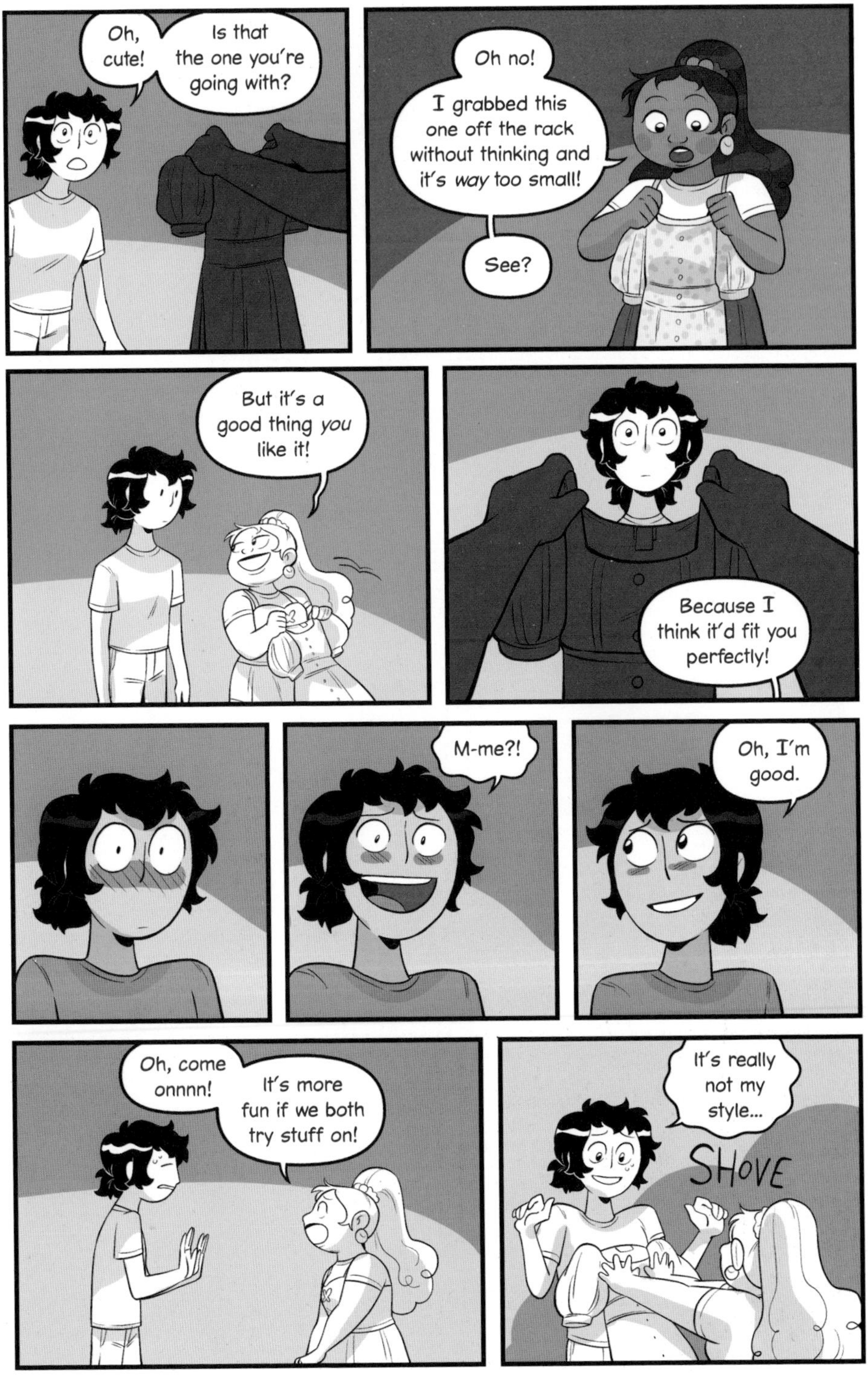
Oh, cute!
Is that the one you're going with?
Oh no!
I grabbed this one off the rack without thinking and it's *way* too small!
See?
But it's a good thing *you* like it!
Because I think it'd fit you perfectly!
M-me?!
Oh, I'm good.
Oh, come onnnn!
It's more fun if we both try stuff on!
It's really not my style...
SHOVE

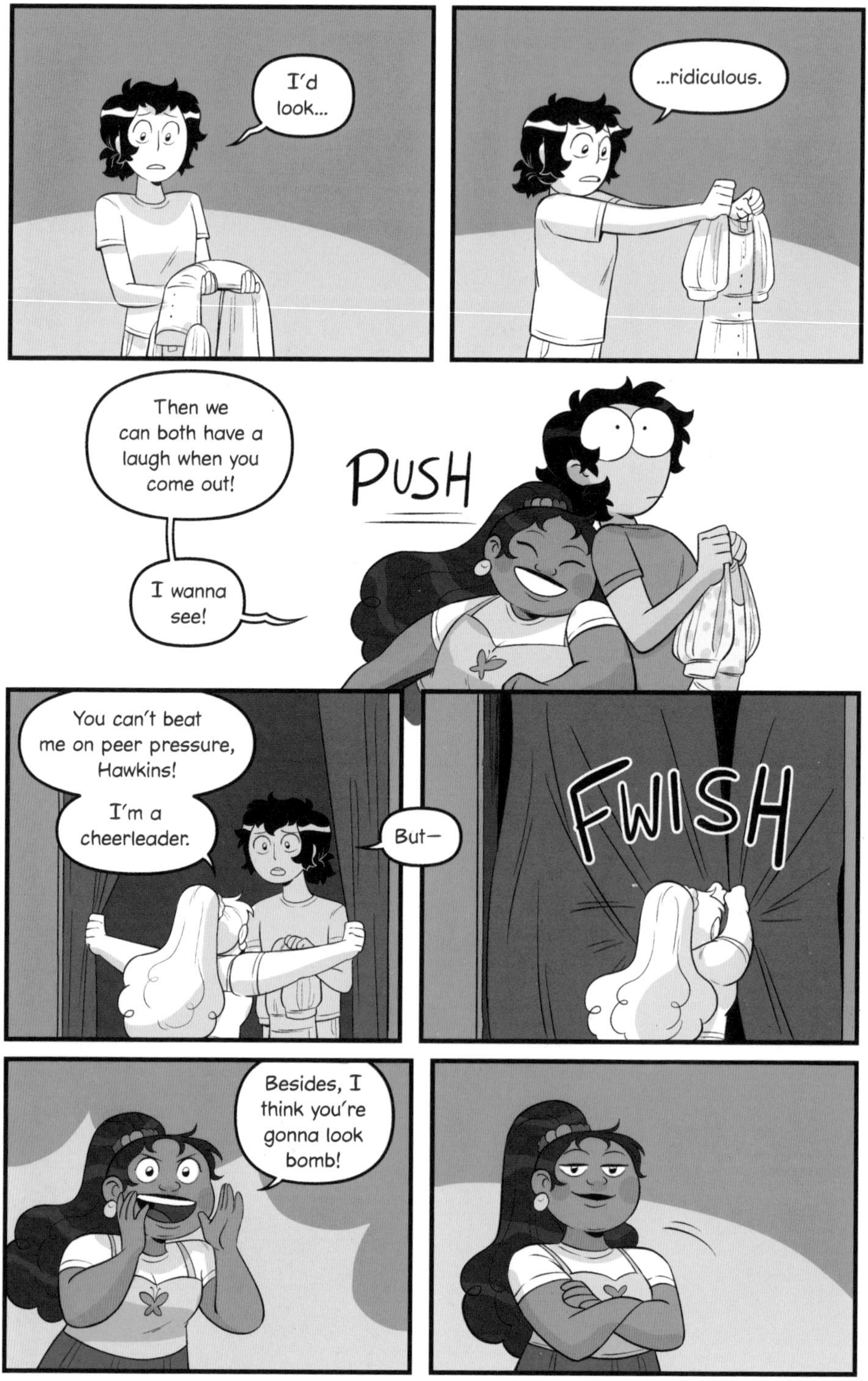
I'd look...
...ridiculous.
Then we can both have a laugh when you come out!
I wanna see!
PUSH
You can't beat me on peer pressure, Hawkins!
I'm a cheerleader.
But—
FWISH
Besides, I think you're gonna look bomb!

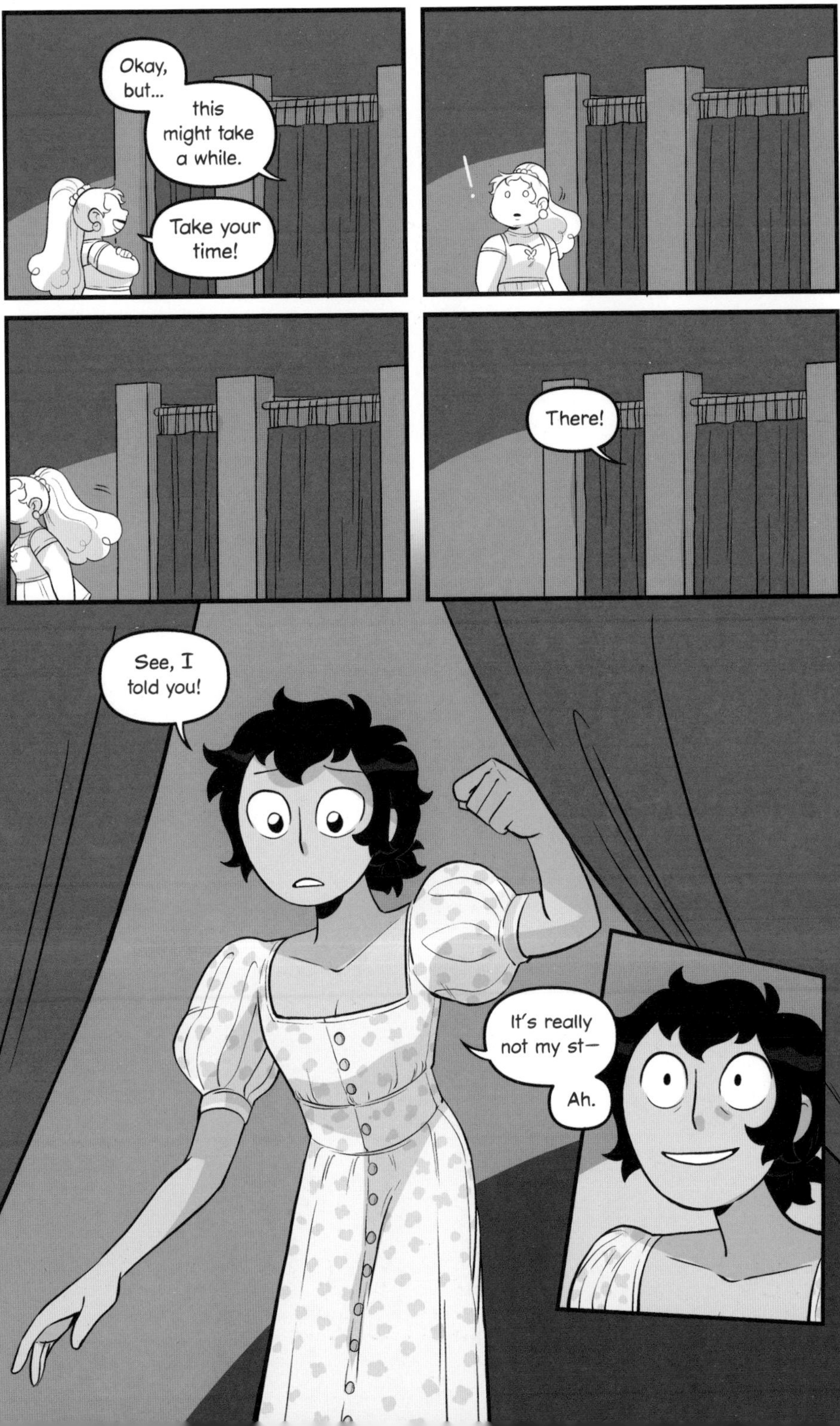

Okay, but...
this might take a while.
Take your time!
There!
See, I told you!
It's really not my st—
Ah.

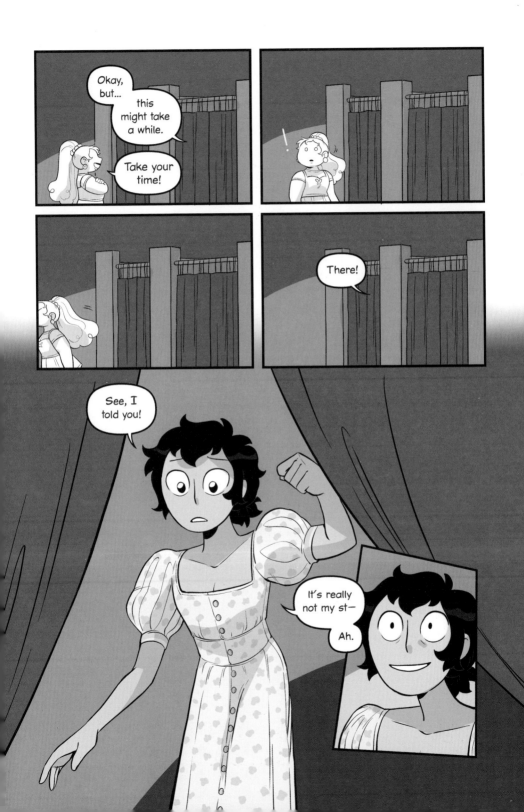

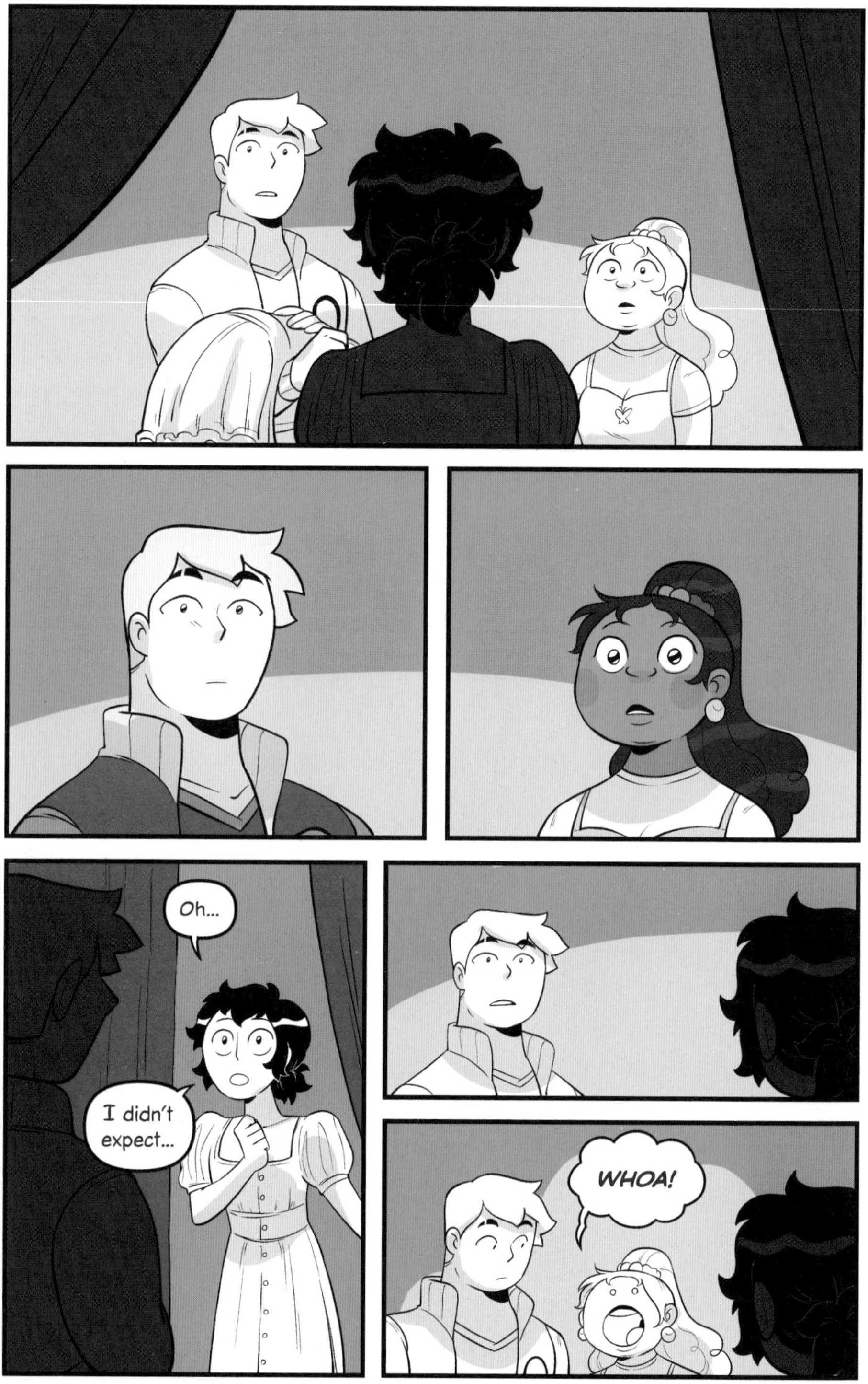
Oh...
I didn't expect...
WHOA!

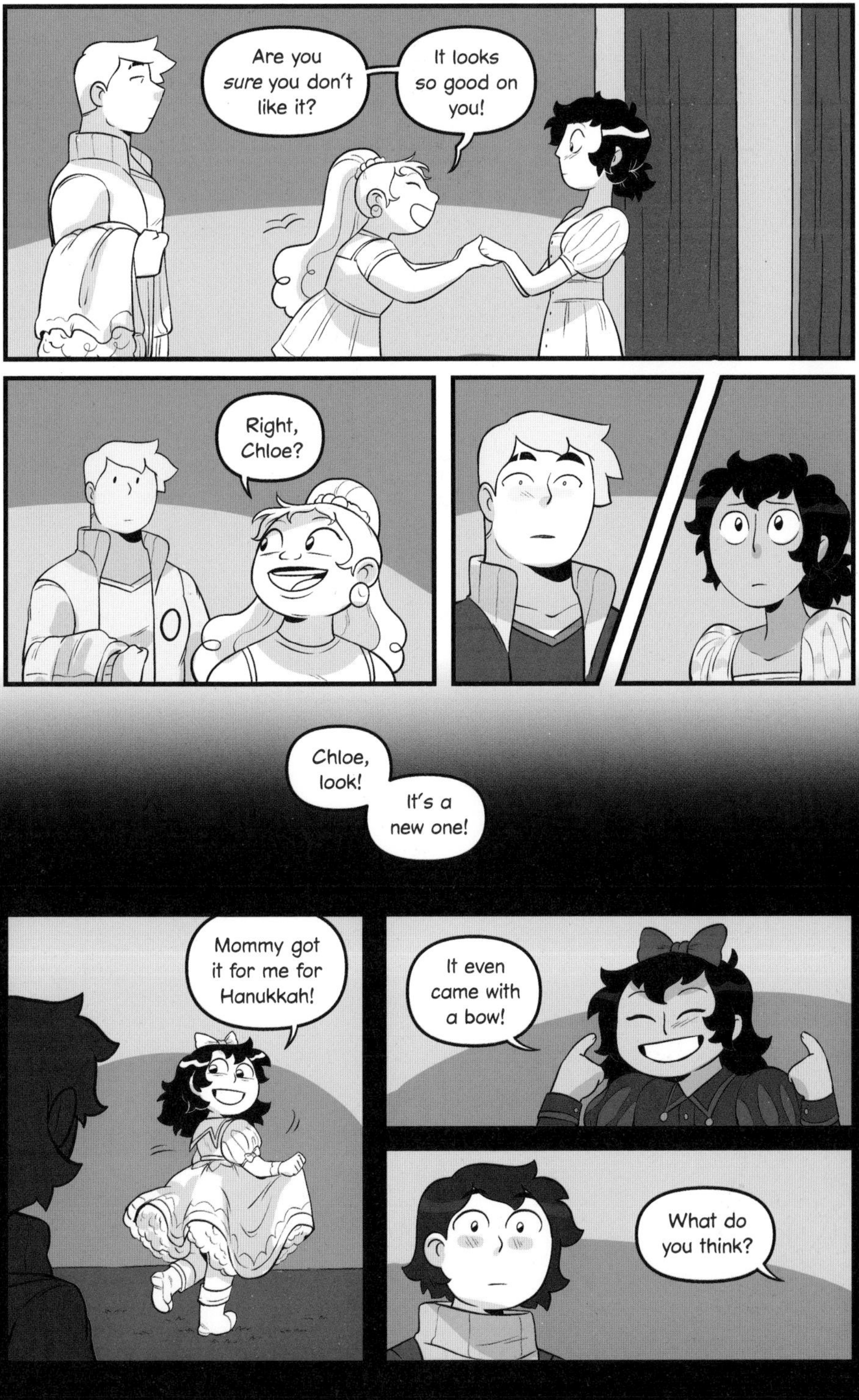
Are you *sure* you don't like it?
It looks so good on you!
Right, Chloe?
Chloe, look!
It's a new one!
Mommy got it for me for Hanukkah!
It even came with a bow!
What do you think?

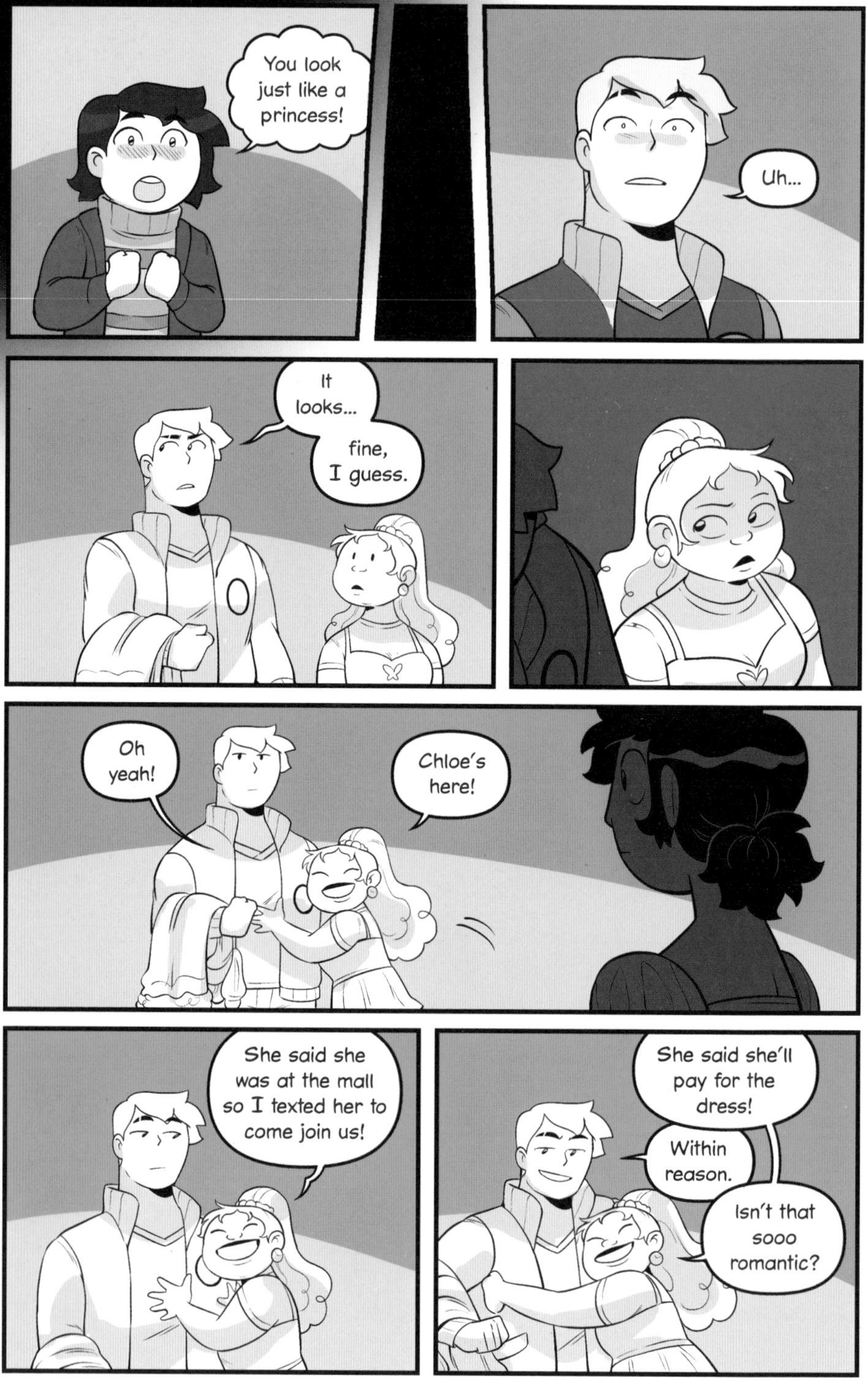
You look just like a princess!
Uh...
It looks...
fine, I guess.
Oh yeah!
Chloe's here!
She said she was at the mall so I texted her to come join us!
She said she'll pay for the dress!
Within reason.
Isn't that sooo romantic?

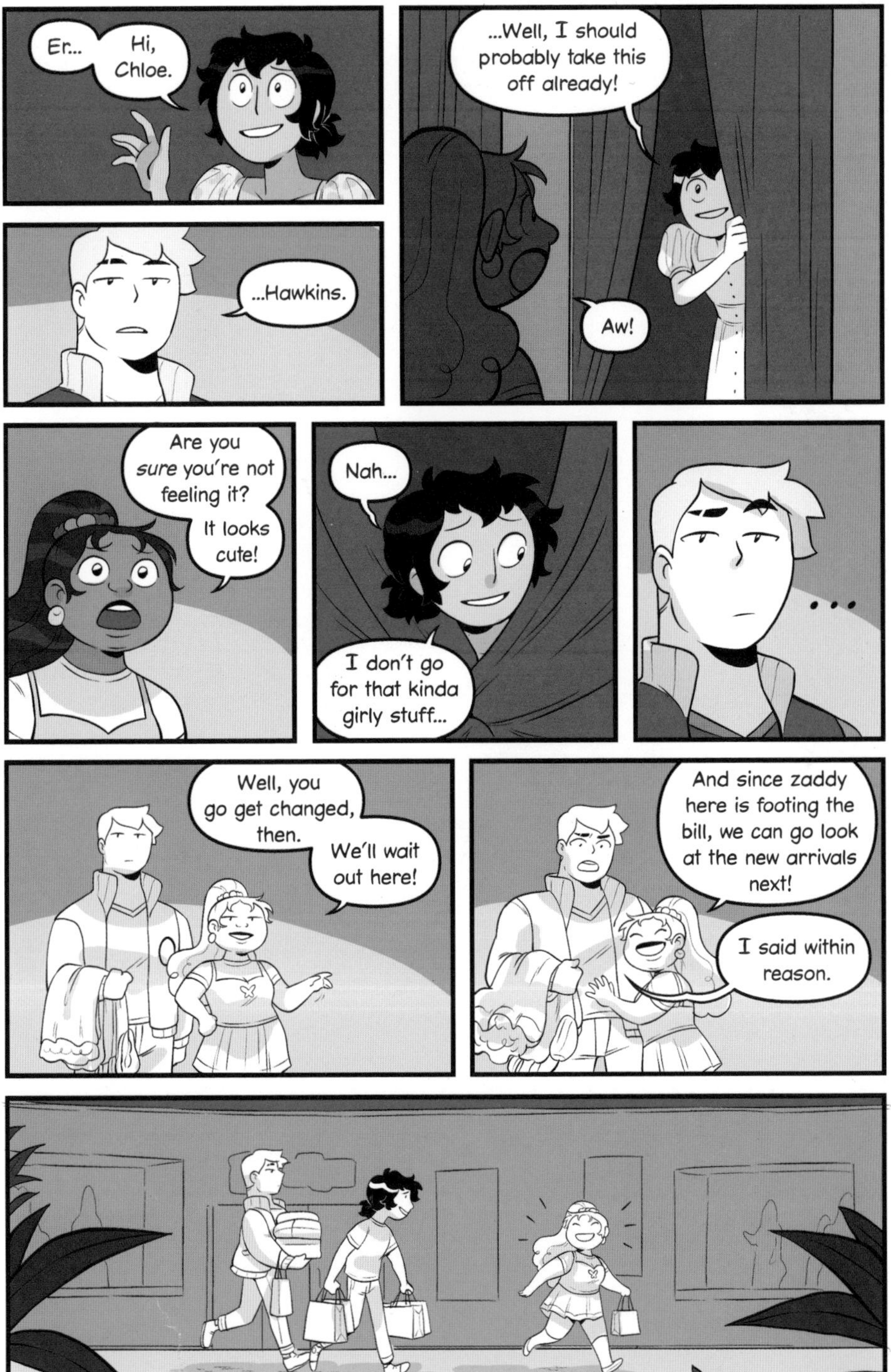
Er...
Hi, Chloe.
...Hawkins.
...Well, I should probably take this off already!
Aw!
Are you *sure* you're not feeling it?
It looks cute!
Nah...
I don't go for that kinda girly stuff...
...
Well, you go get changed, then.
We'll wait out here!
And since zaddy here is footing the bill, we can go look at the new arrivals next!
I said within reason.

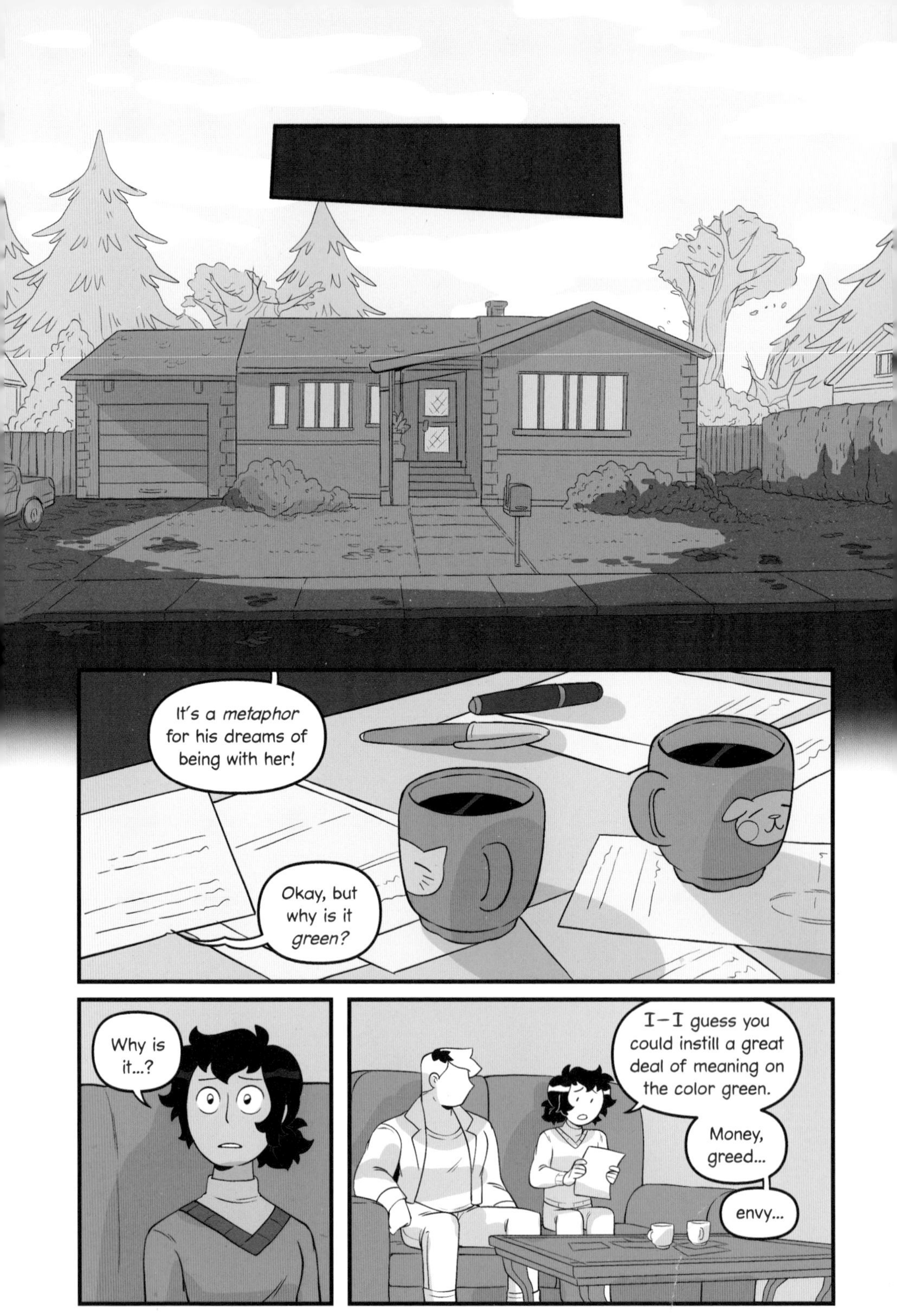
[redacted]
It's a *metaphor* for his dreams of being with her!
Okay, but why is it *green?*
Why is it...?
I—I guess you could instill a great deal of meaning on the color green.
Money, greed...
envy...

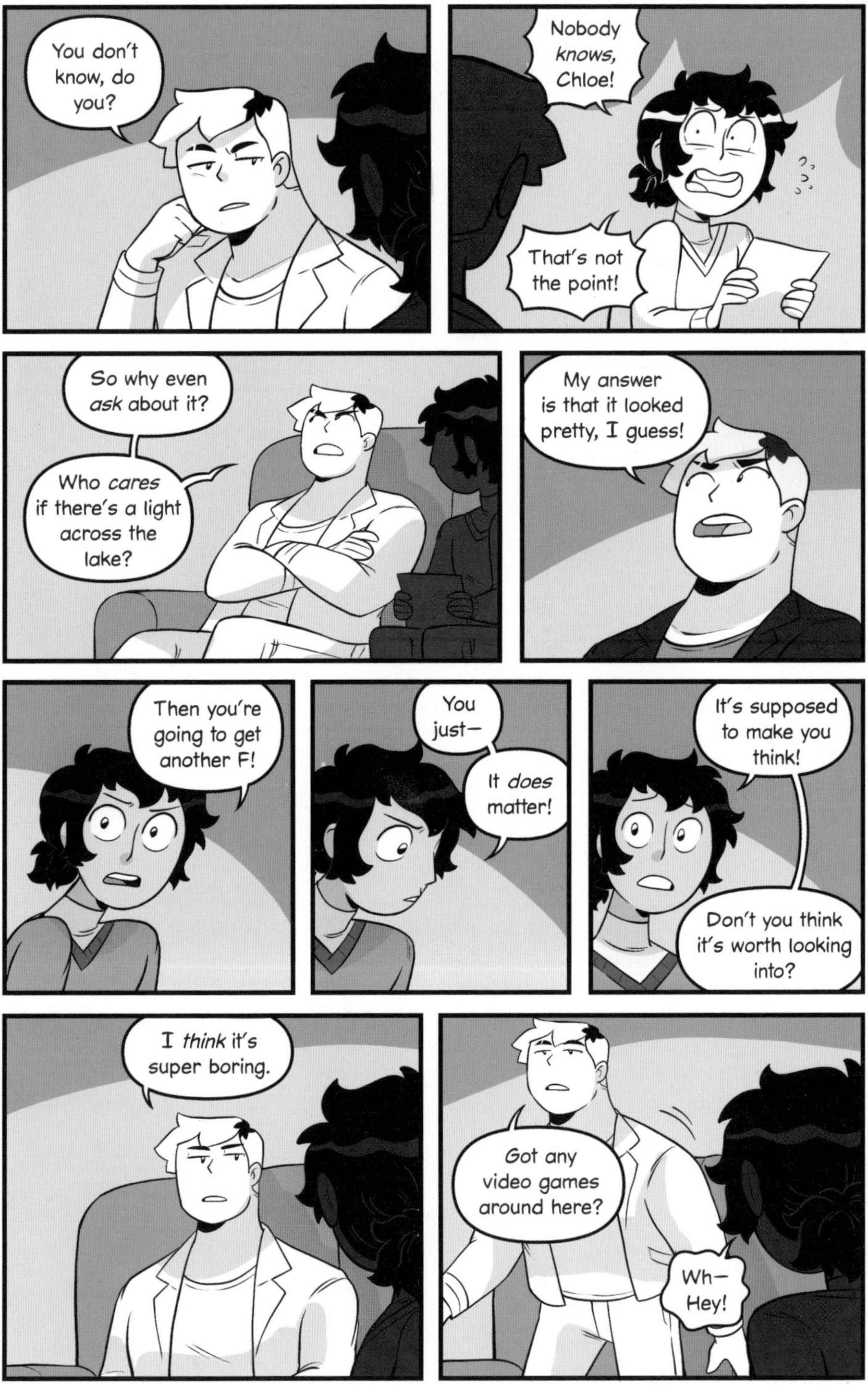
You don't know, do you?
Nobody *knows*, Chloe!
That's not the point!
So why even *ask* about it?
Who *cares* if there's a light across the lake?
My answer is that it looked pretty, I guess!
Then you're going to get another F!
You just—
It *does* matter!
It's supposed to make you think!
Don't you think it's worth looking into?
I *think* it's super boring.
Got any video games around here?
Wh—Hey!

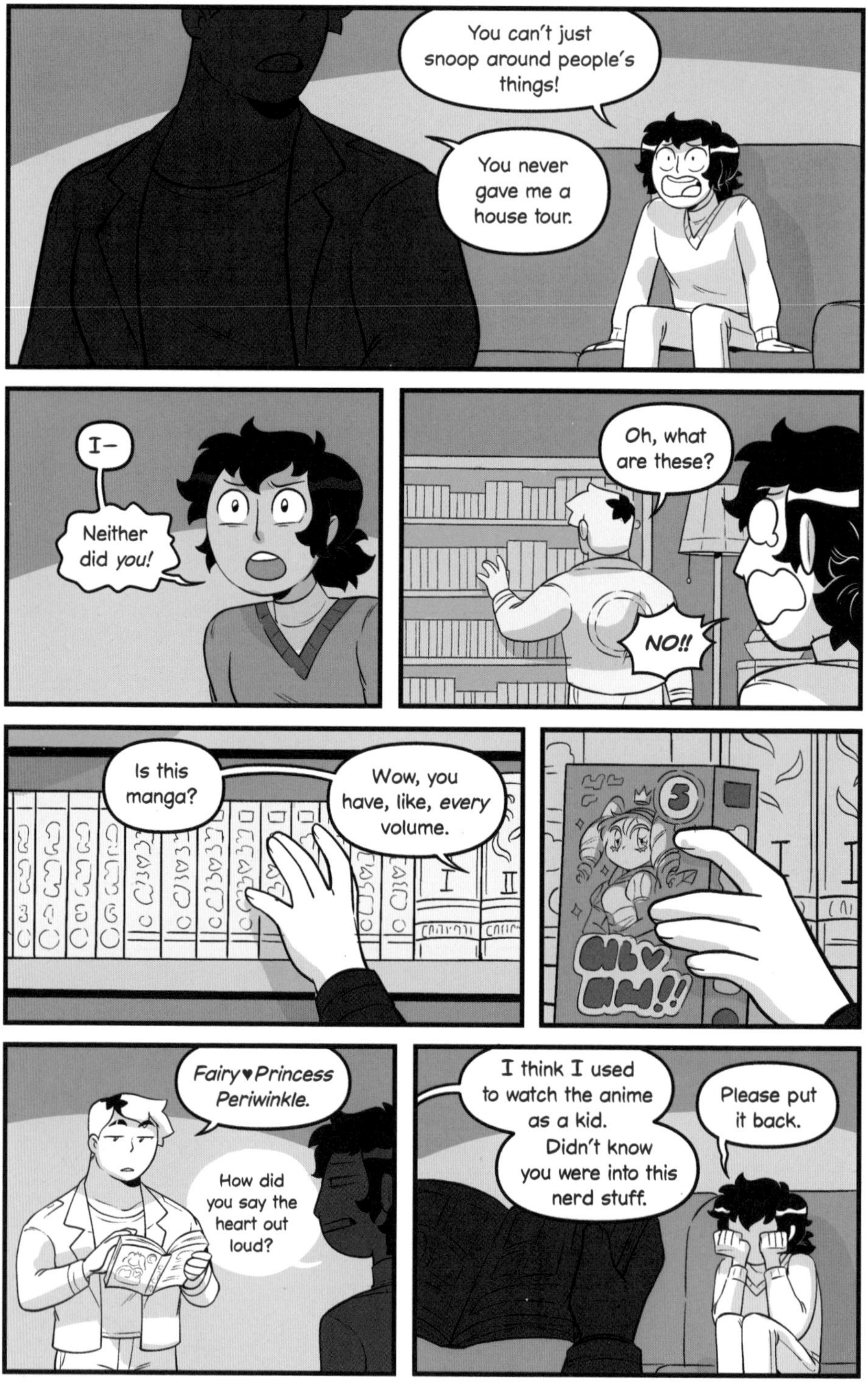
You can't just snoop around people's things!
You never gave me a house tour.
I–
Neither did *you!*
Oh, what are these?
NO!!
Is this manga?
Wow, you have, like, *every* volume.
Fairy♥Princess Periwinkle.
How did you say the heart out loud?
I think I used to watch the anime as a kid.
Didn't know you were into this nerd stuff.
Please put it back.

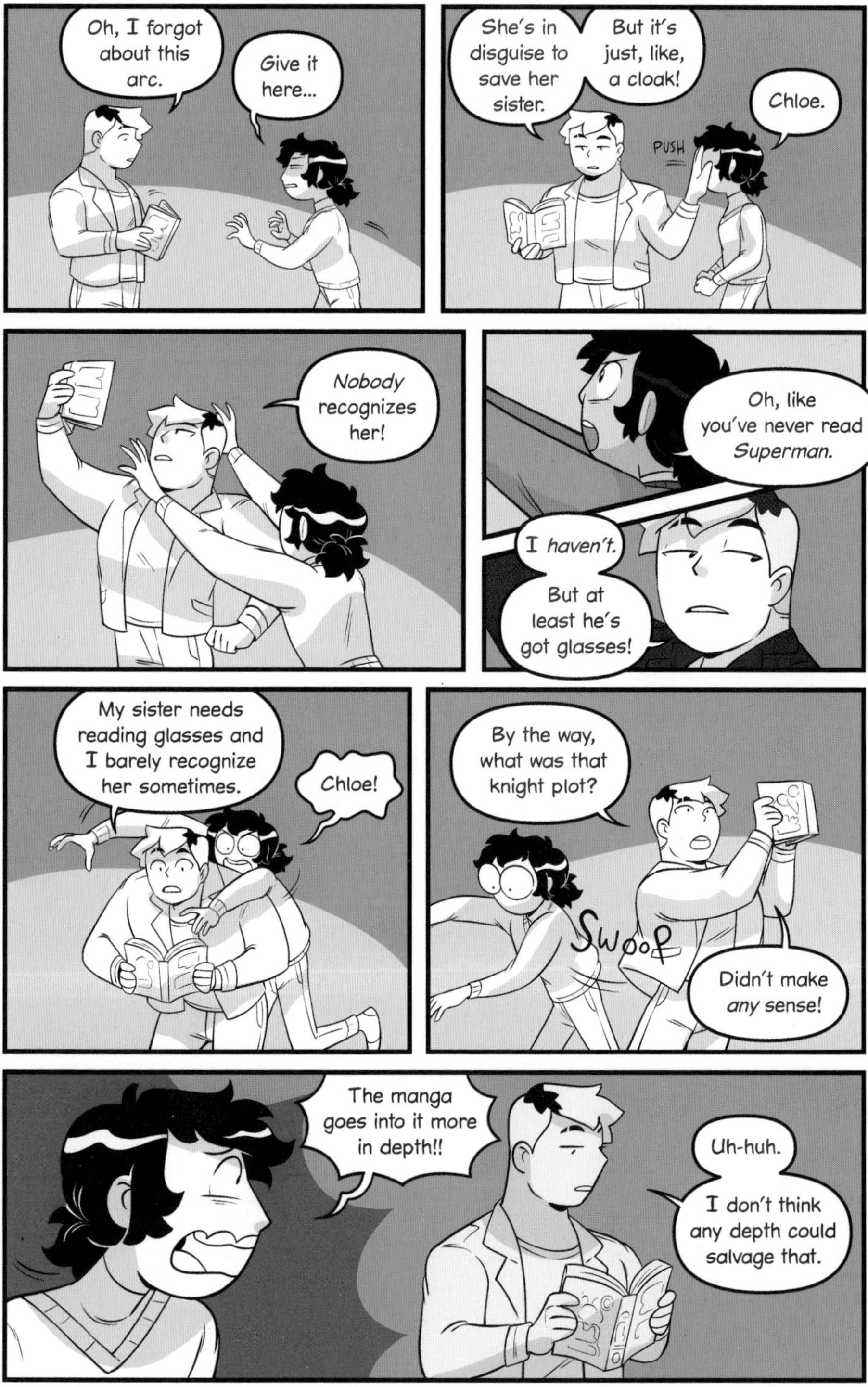
Oh, I forgot about this arc.
Give it here...
She's in disguise to save her sister.
But it's just, like, a cloak!
PUSH
Chloe.
Nobody recognizes her!
Oh, like you've never read *Superman.*
I *haven't.*
But at least he's got glasses!
My sister needs reading glasses and I barely recognize her sometimes.
Chloe!
By the way, what was that knight plot?
SWOOP
Didn't make *any* sense!
The manga goes into it more in depth!!
Uh-huh.
I don't think any depth could salvage that.

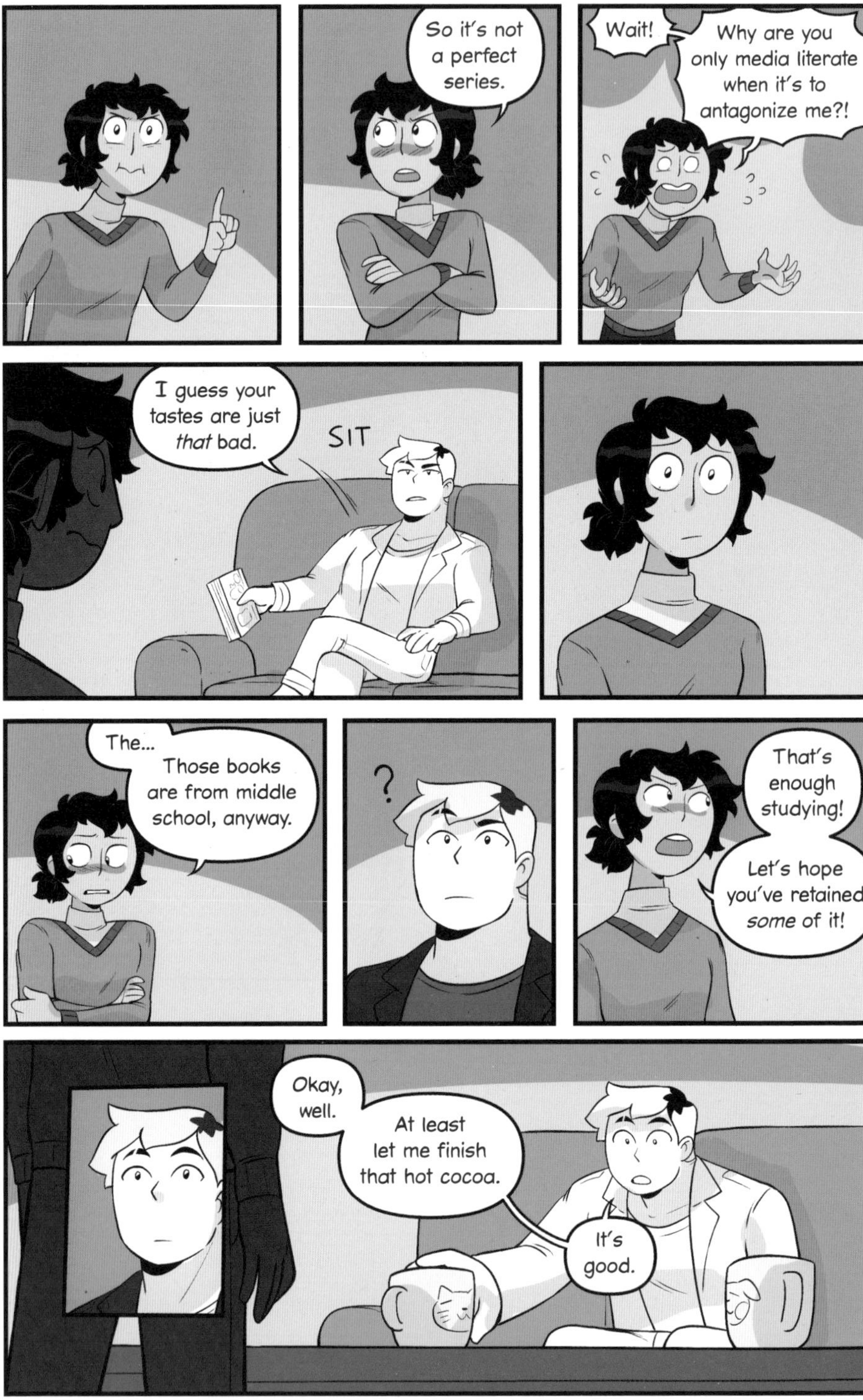

So it's not a perfect series.
Wait!
Why are you only media literate when it's to antagonize me?!
I guess your tastes are just *that* bad.
SIT
The...
Those books are from middle school, anyway.
?
That's enough studying!
Let's hope you've retained *some* of it!
Okay, well.
At least let me finish that hot cocoa.
It's good.

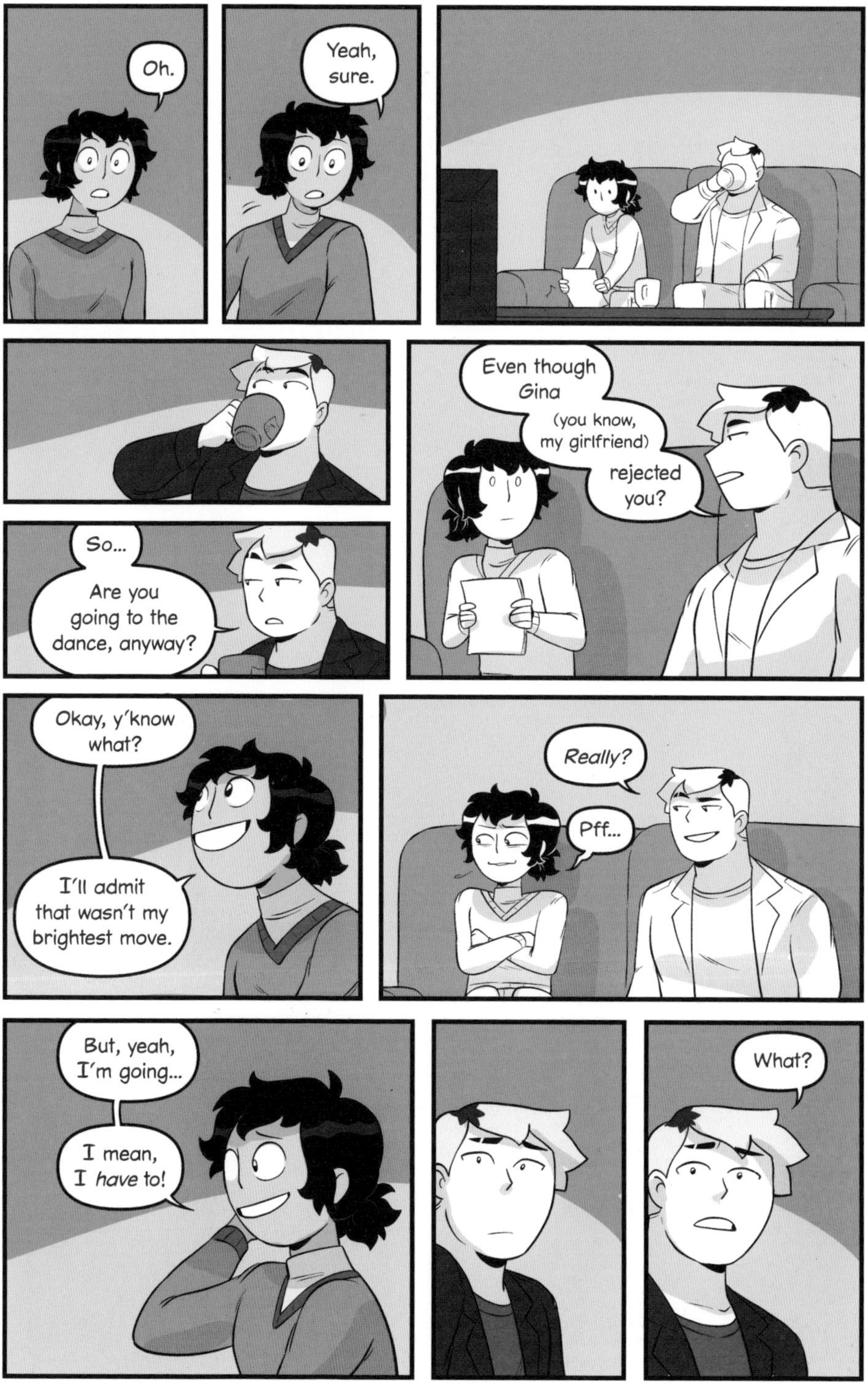
Oh.
Yeah, sure.
Even though Gina
(you know, my girlfriend)
rejected you?
So...
Are you going to the dance, anyway?
Okay, y'know what?
I'll admit that wasn't my brightest move.
Really?
Pff...
But, yeah, I'm going...
I mean, I *have* to!
What?

CHAPTER

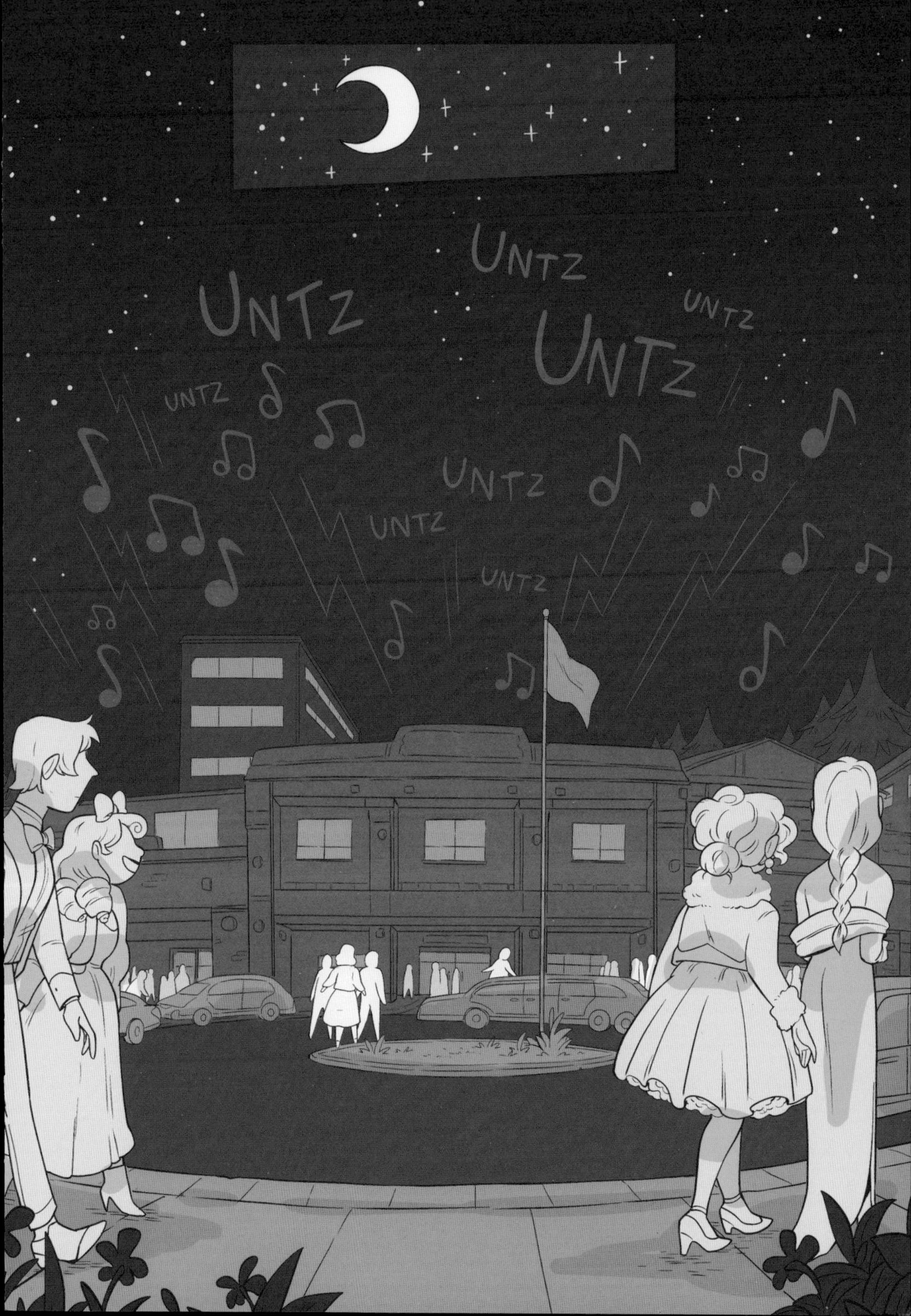

UNTZ
UNTZ
UNTZ
UNTZ
UNTZ
UNTZ
UNTZ
UNTZ

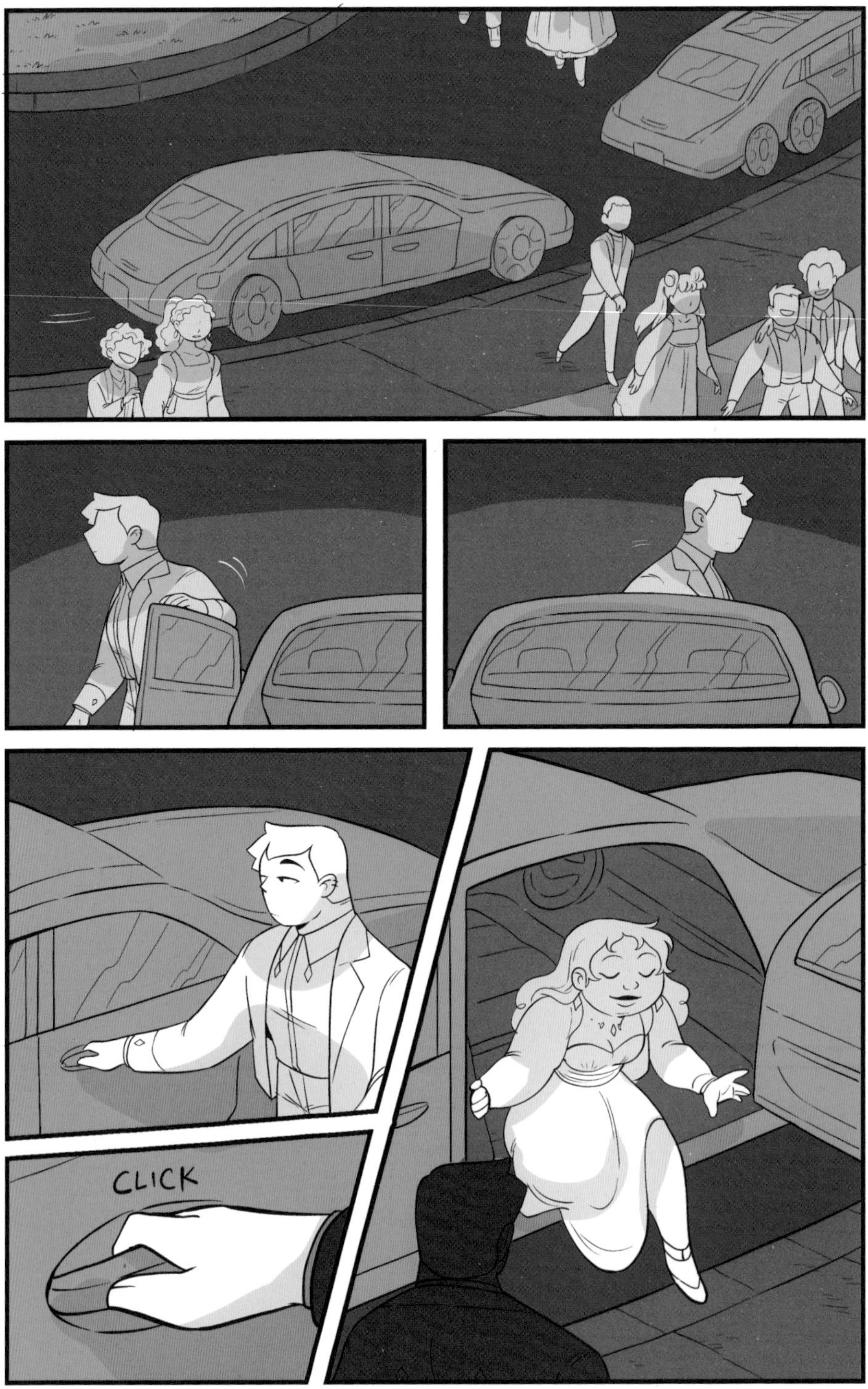
CLICK

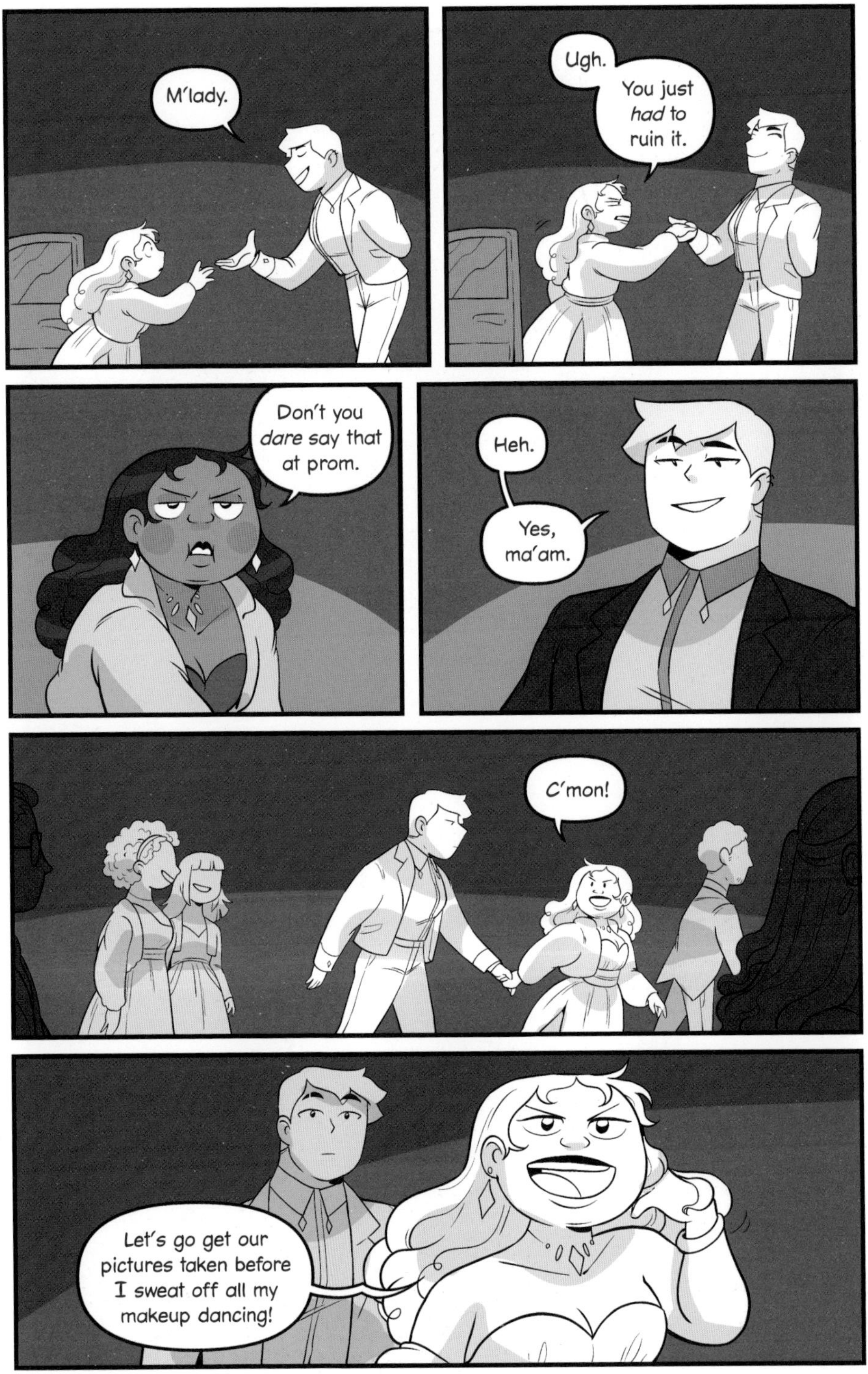
M'lady.
Ugh.
You just *had* to ruin it.
Don't you *dare* say that at prom.
Heh.
Yes, ma'am.
C'mon!
Let's go get our pictures taken before I sweat off all my makeup dancing!

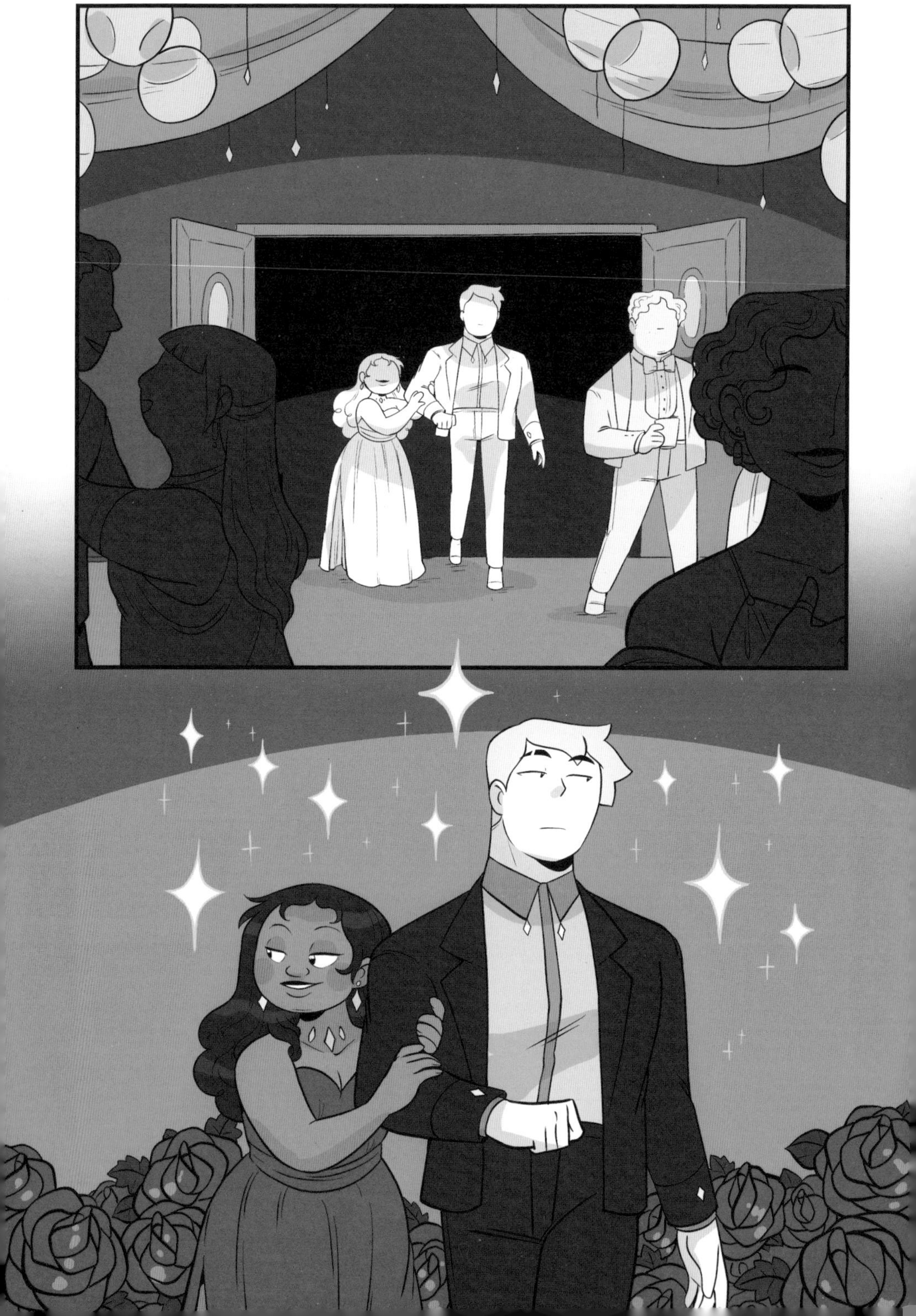

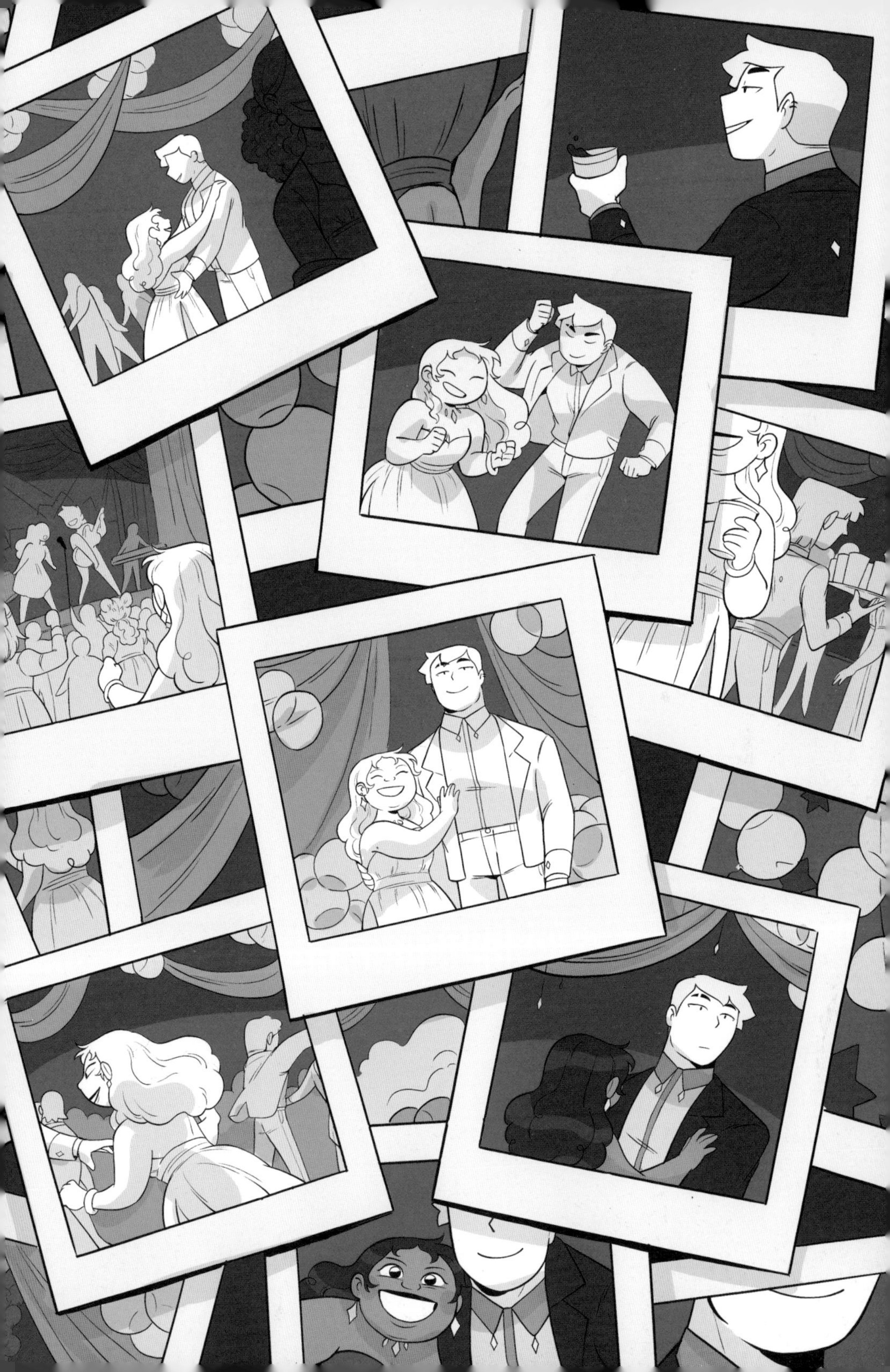

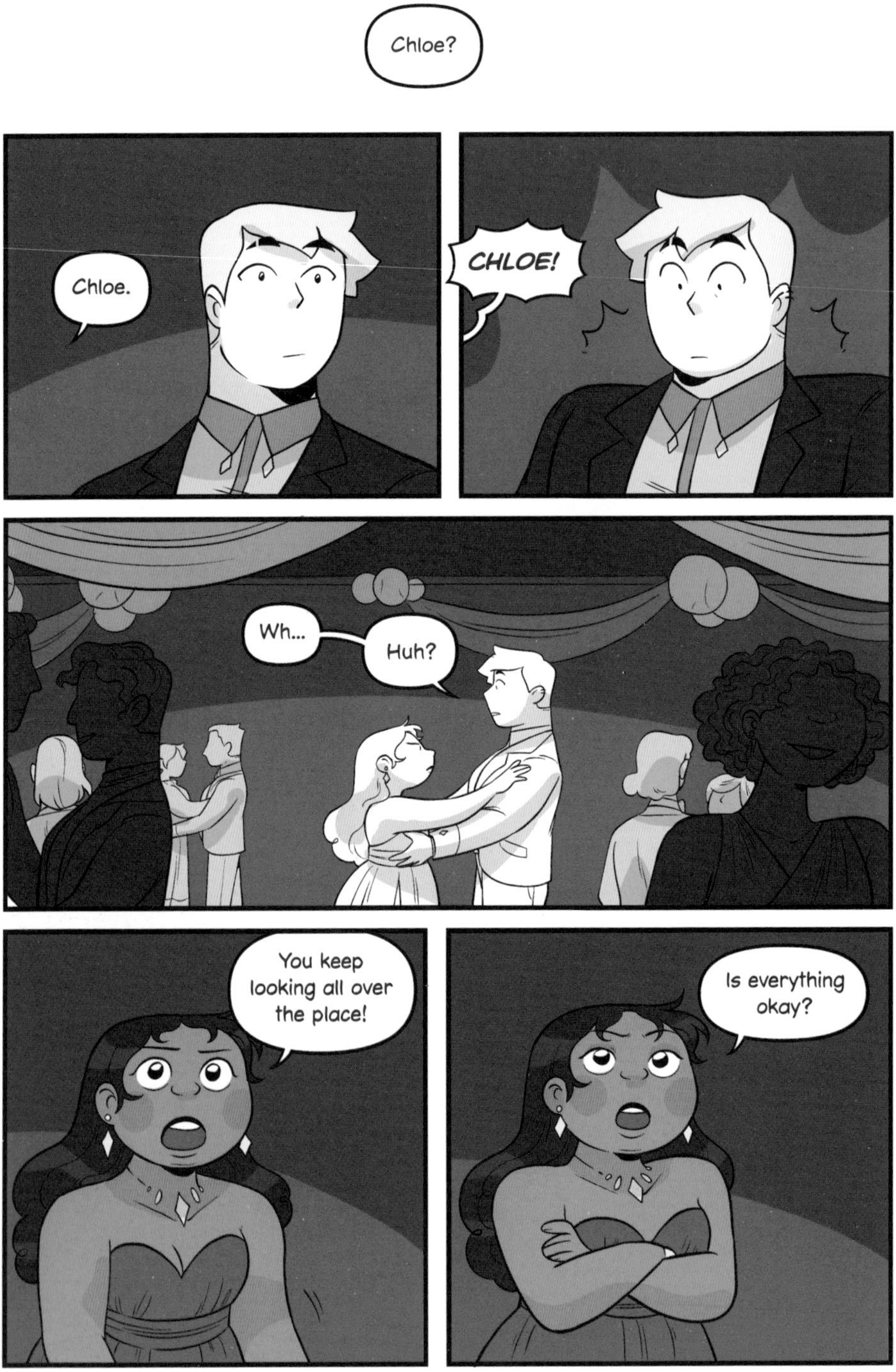
Chloe?
Chloe.
CHLOE!
Wh...
Huh?
You keep looking all over the place!
Is everything okay?

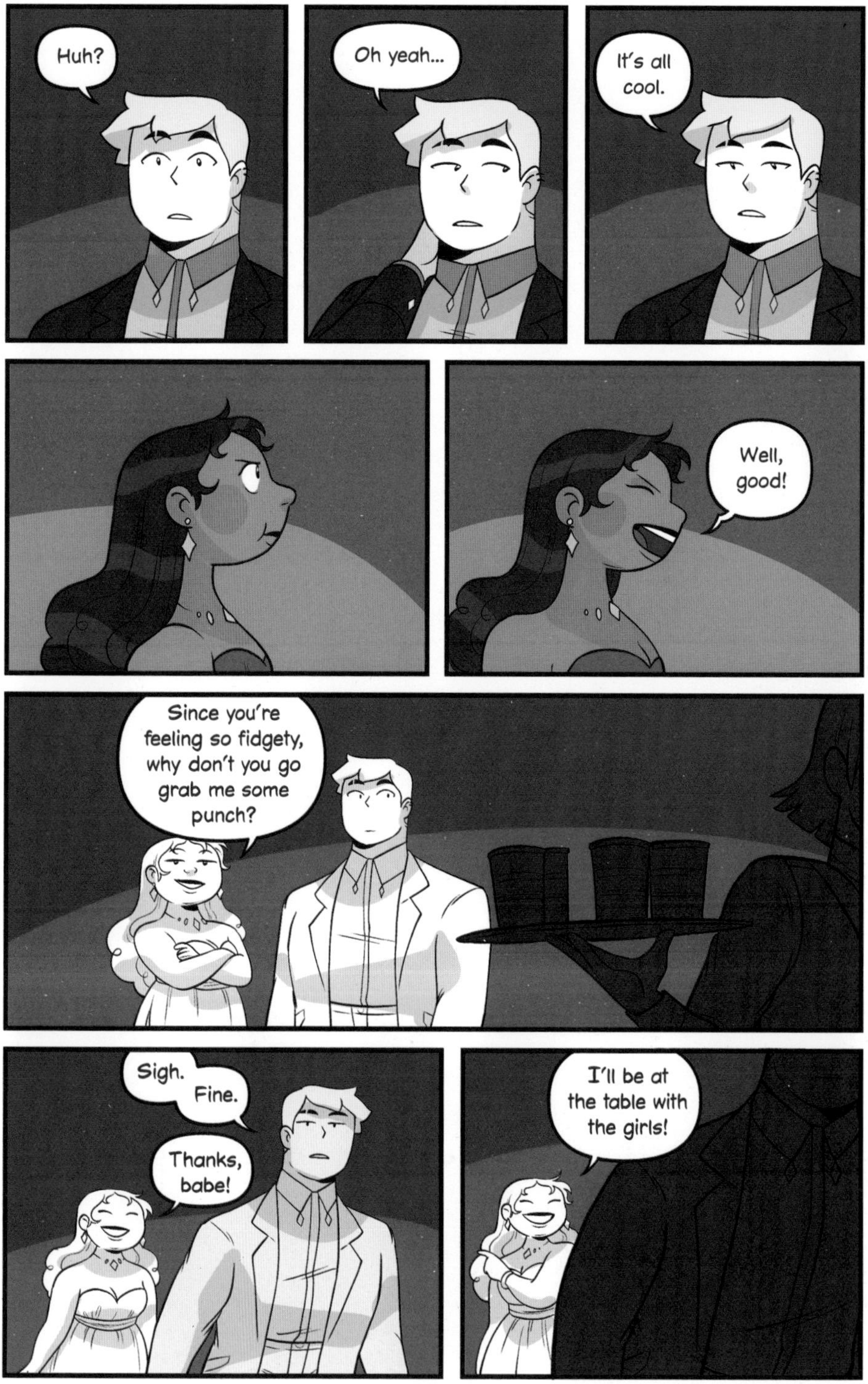
Huh?
Oh yeah...
It's all cool.
Well, good!
Since you're feeling so fidgety, why don't you go grab me some punch?
Sigh.
Fine.
Thanks, babe!
I'll be at the table with the girls!

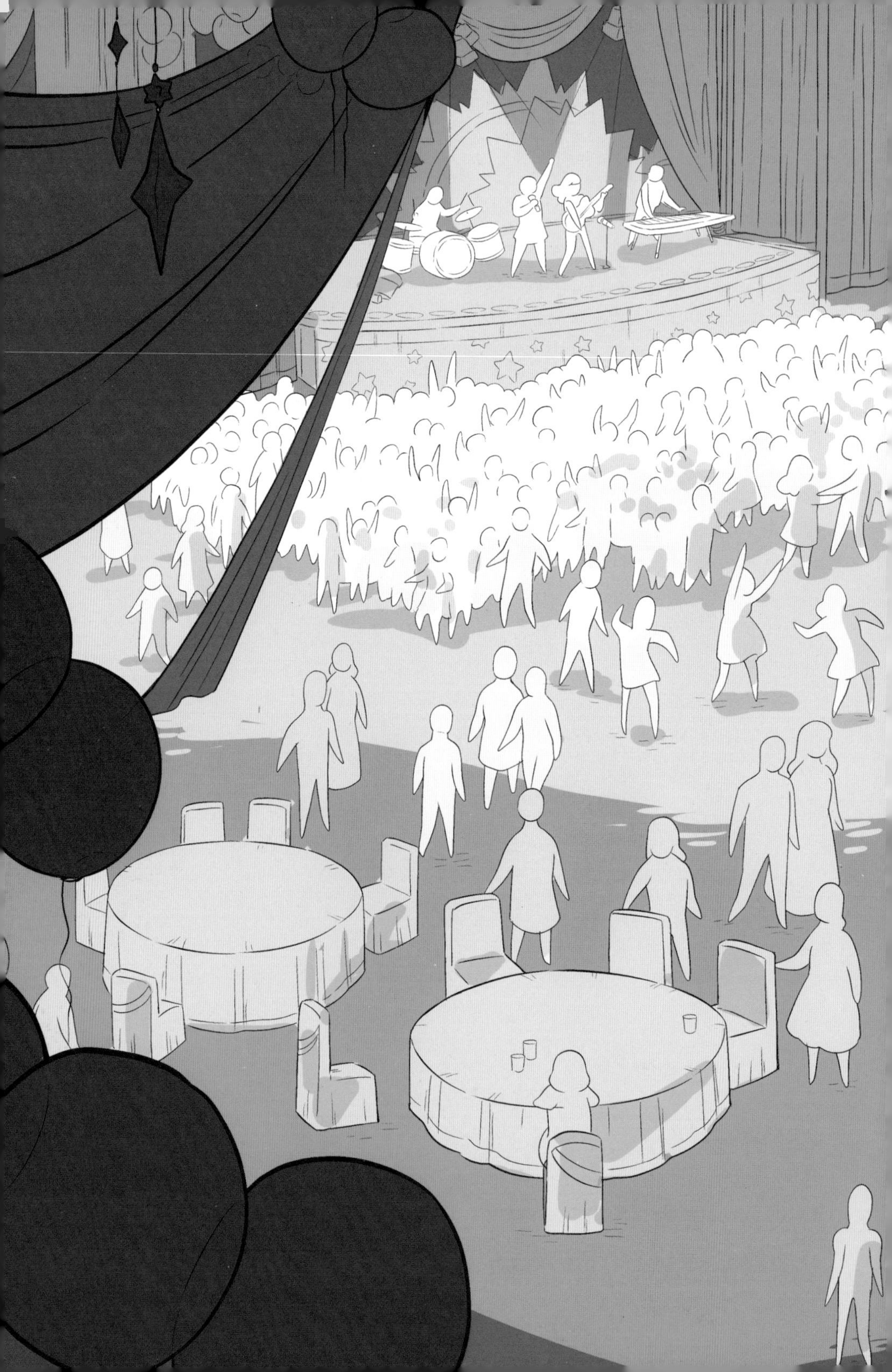

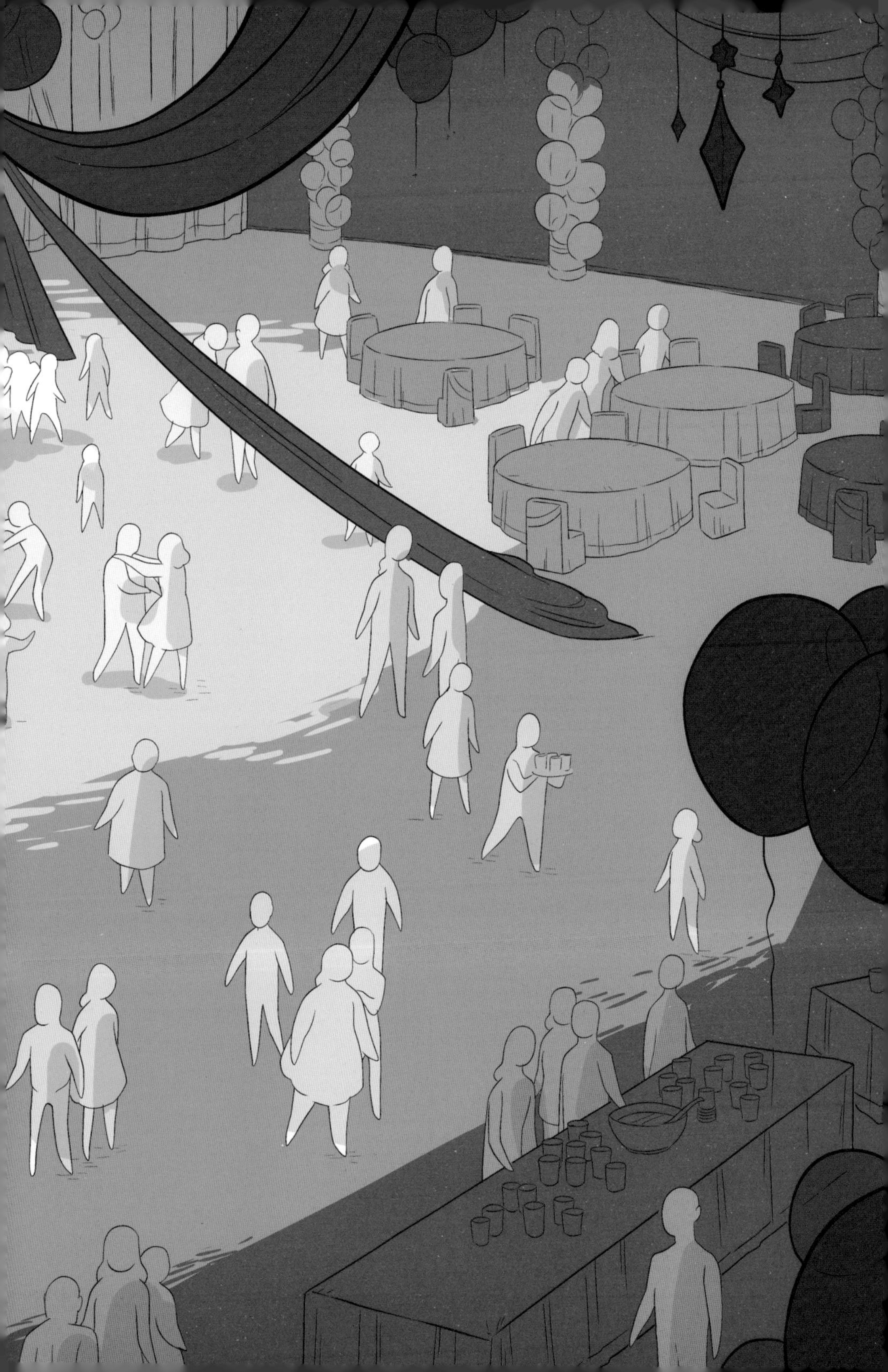

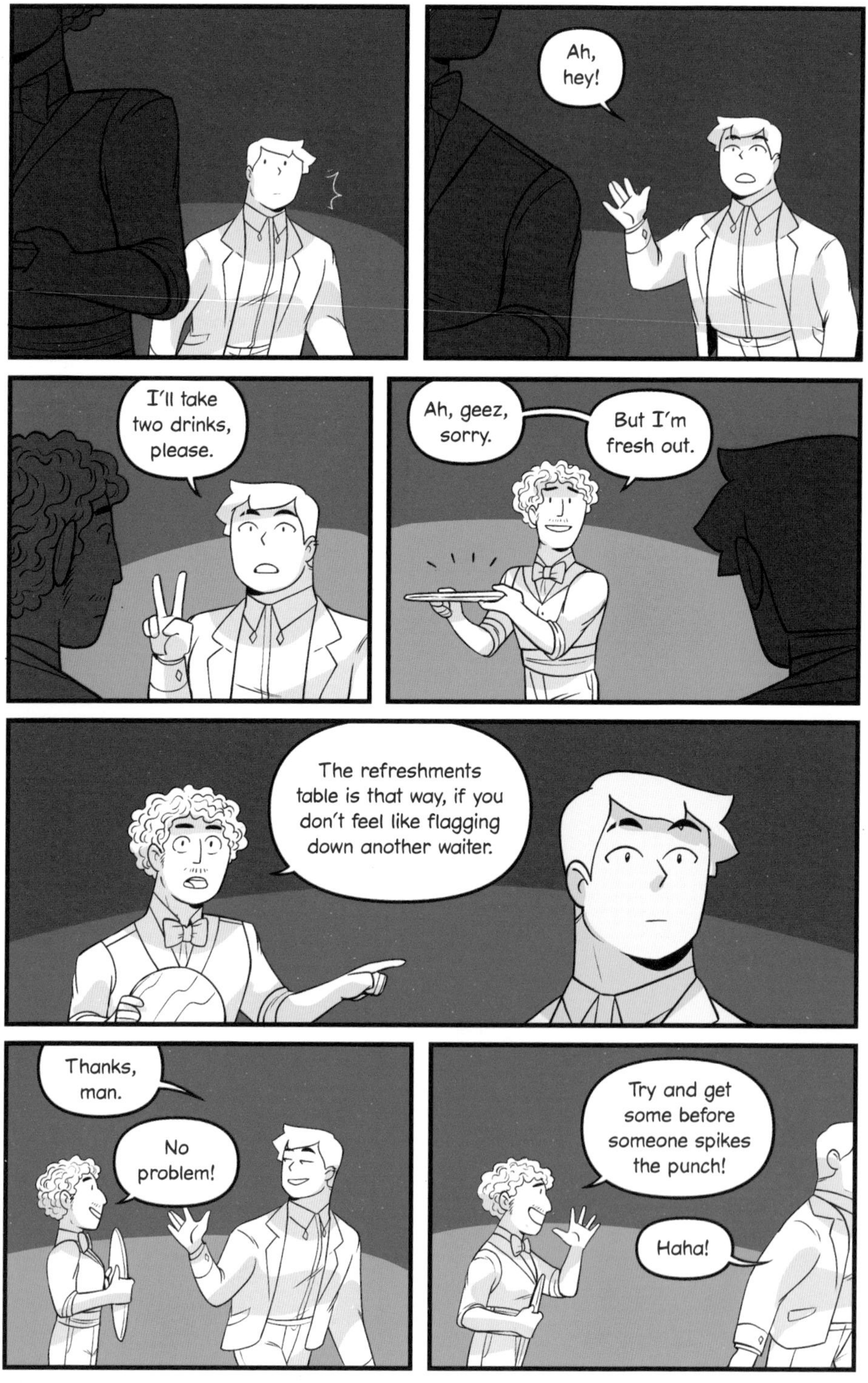
Ah, hey!
I'll take two drinks, please.
Ah, geez, sorry.
But I'm fresh out.
The refreshments table is that way, if you don't feel like flagging down another waiter.
Thanks, man.
No problem!
Try and get some before someone spikes the punch!
Haha!

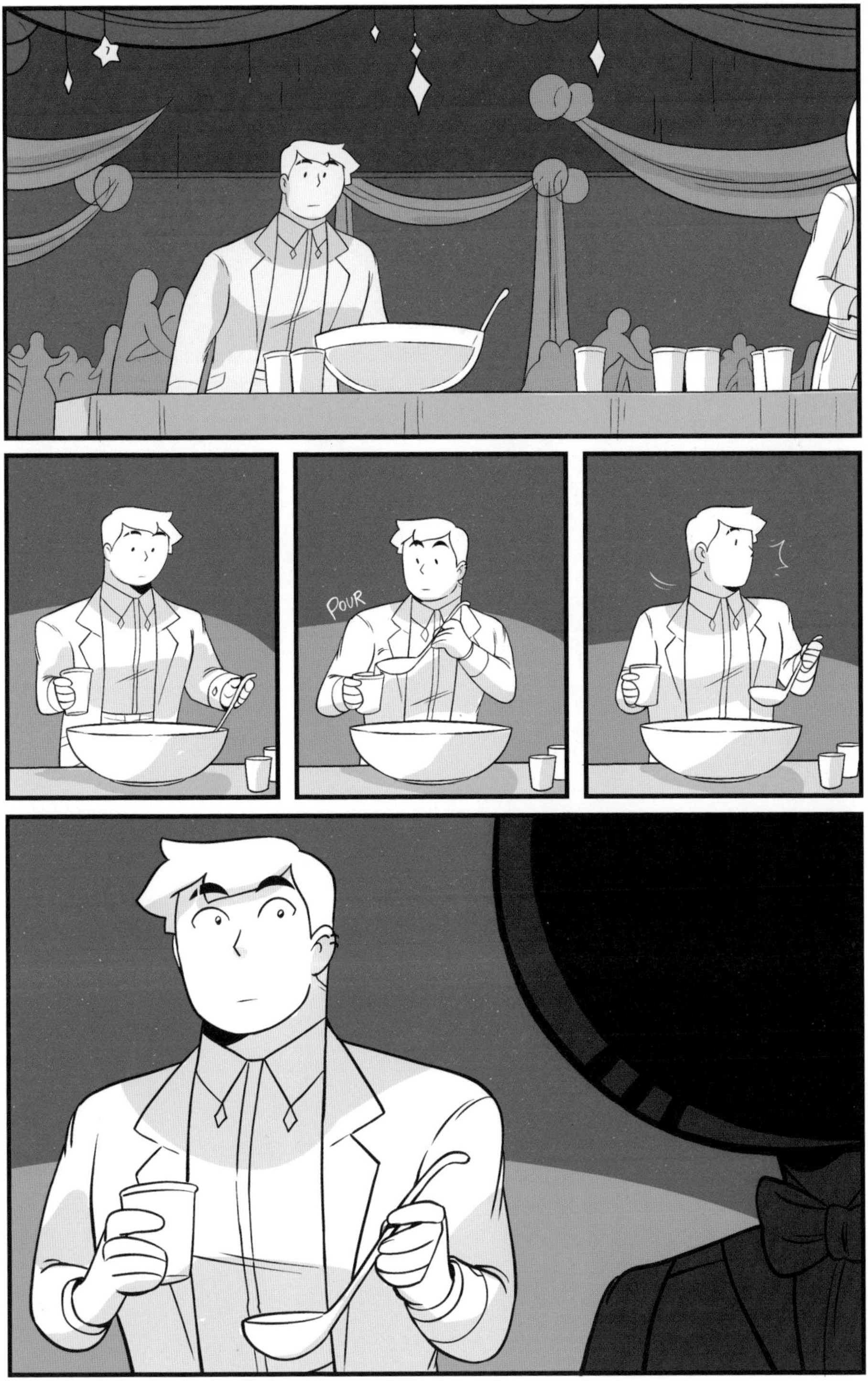
POUR

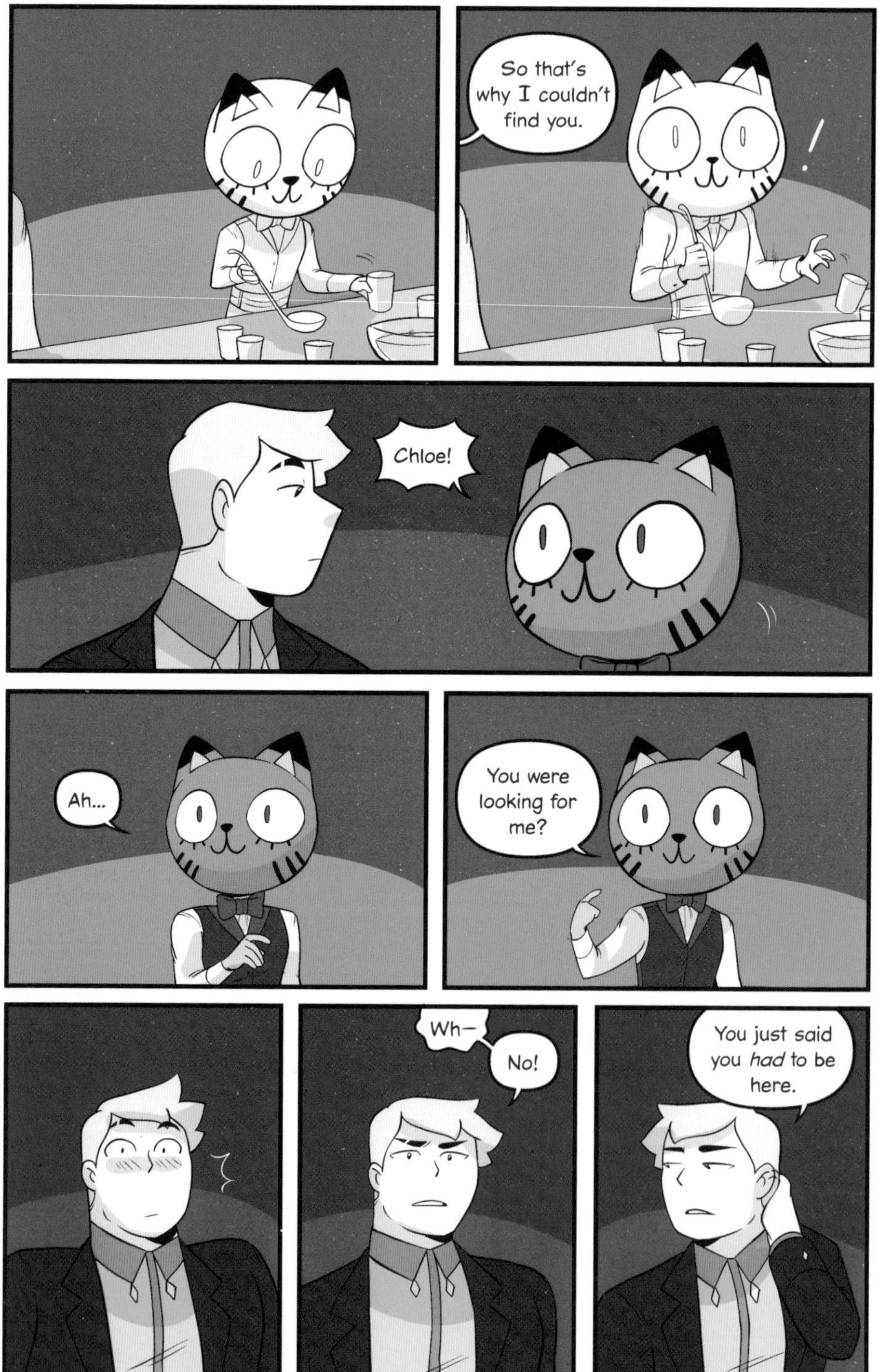

So that's why I couldn't find you.
!
Chloe!
Ah...
You were looking for me?
Wh—
No!
You just said you *had* to be here.

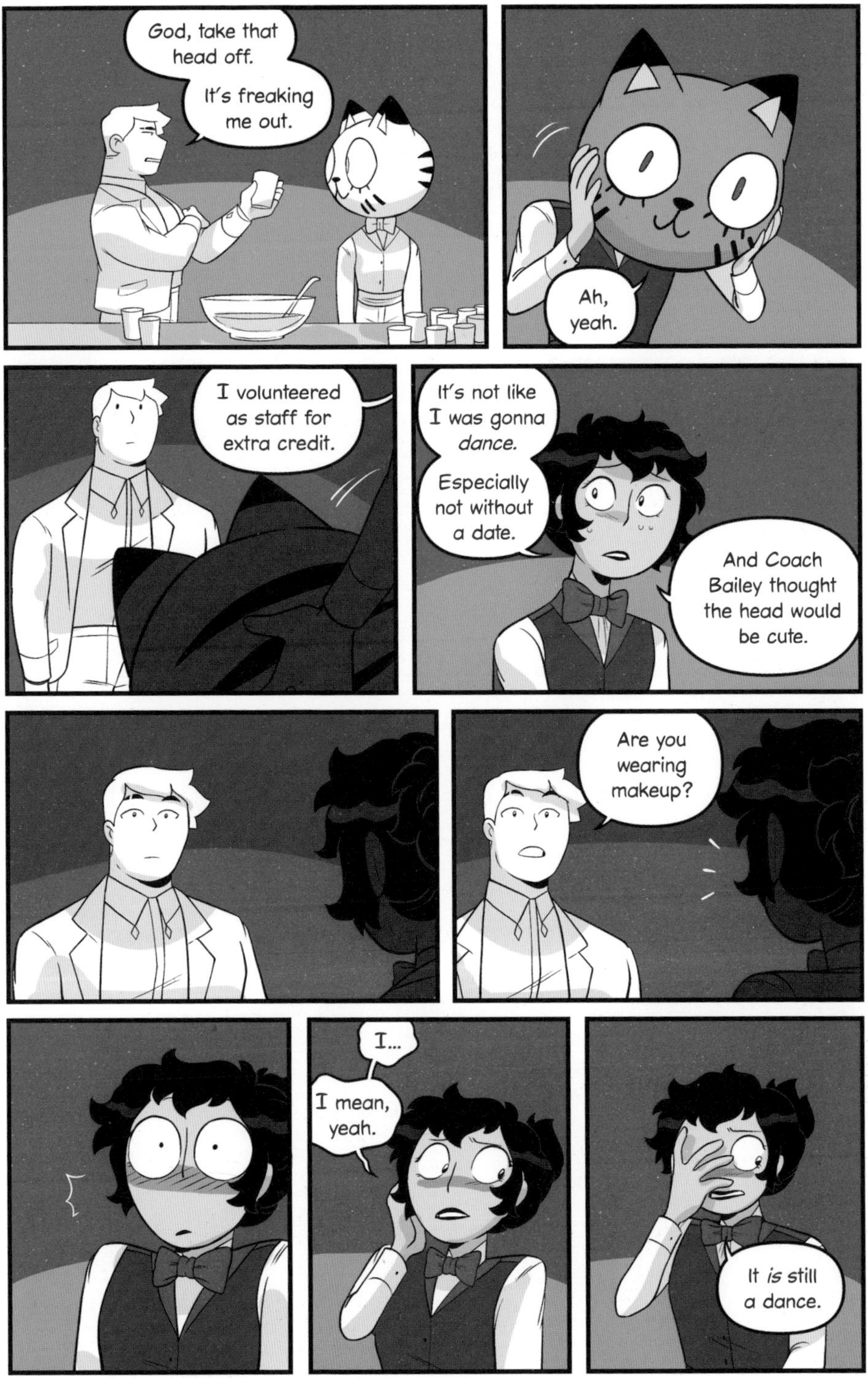
God, take that head off.
It's freaking me out.
Ah, yeah.
I volunteered as staff for extra credit.
It's not like I was gonna *dance.*
Especially not without a date.
And Coach Bailey thought the head would be cute.
Are you wearing makeup?
I...
I mean, yeah.
It *is* still a dance.

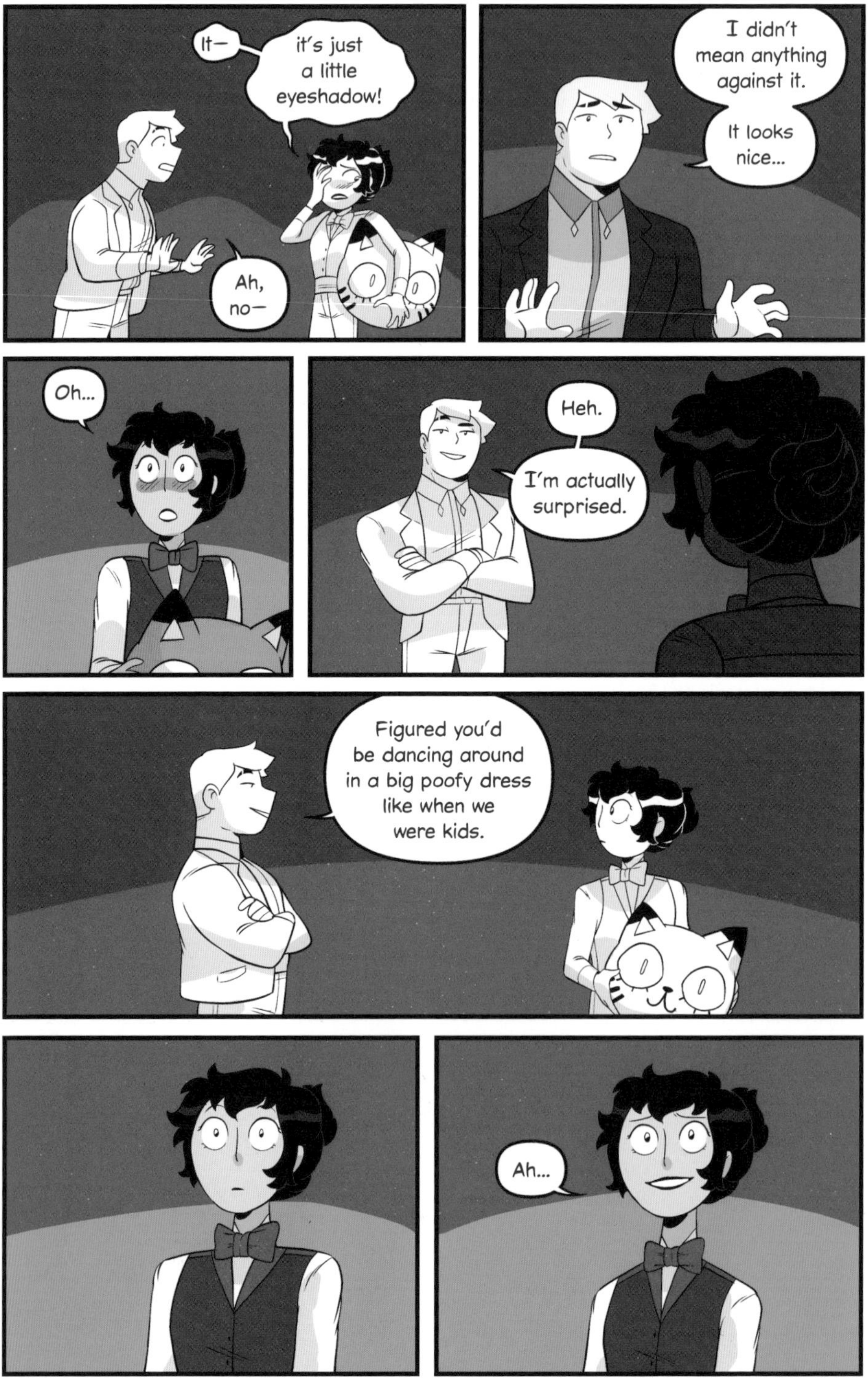
It—
it's just a little eyeshadow!
Ah, no—
I didn't mean anything against it.
It looks nice...
Oh...
Heh.
I'm actually surprised.
Figured you'd be dancing around in a big poofy dress like when we were kids.
Ah...

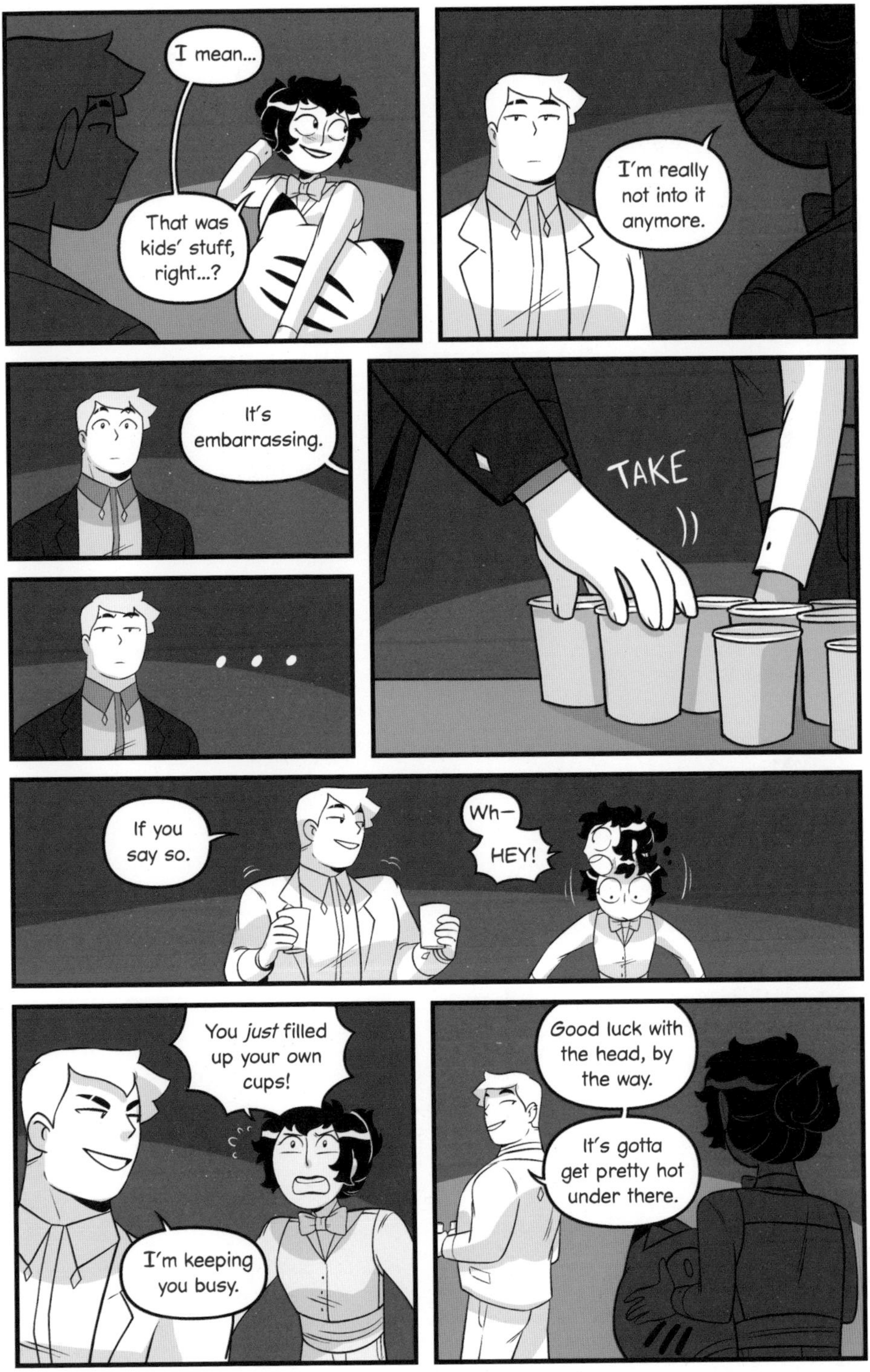
I mean...
That was kids' stuff, right...?
I'm really not into it anymore.
It's embarrassing.
. . .
TAKE
If you say so.
Wh–
HEY!
You *just* filled up your own cups!
I'm keeping you busy.
Good luck with the head, by the way.
It's gotta get pretty hot under there.

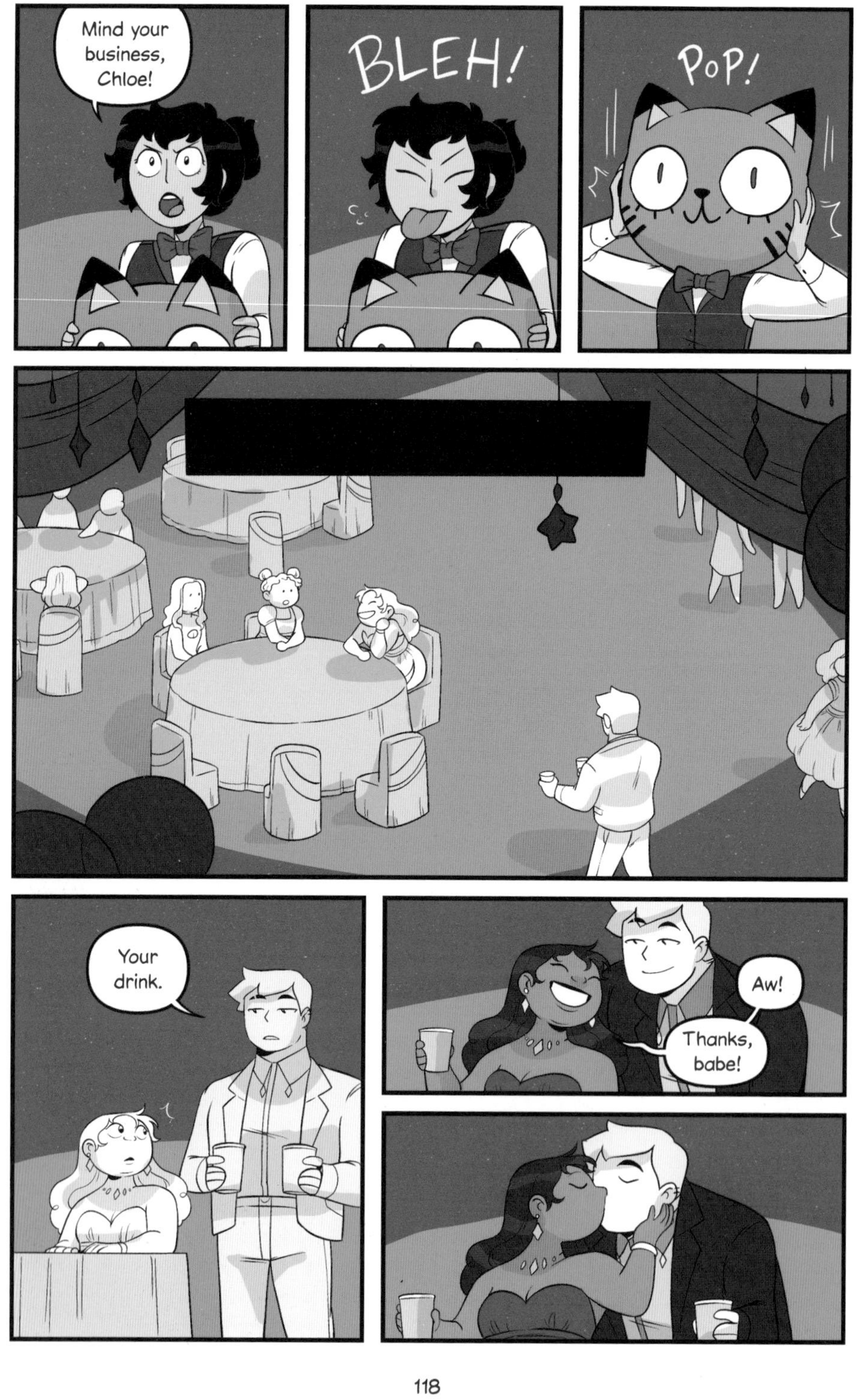
Mind your business, Chloe!
BLEH!
POP!
[redacted]
Your drink.
Aw!
Thanks, babe!

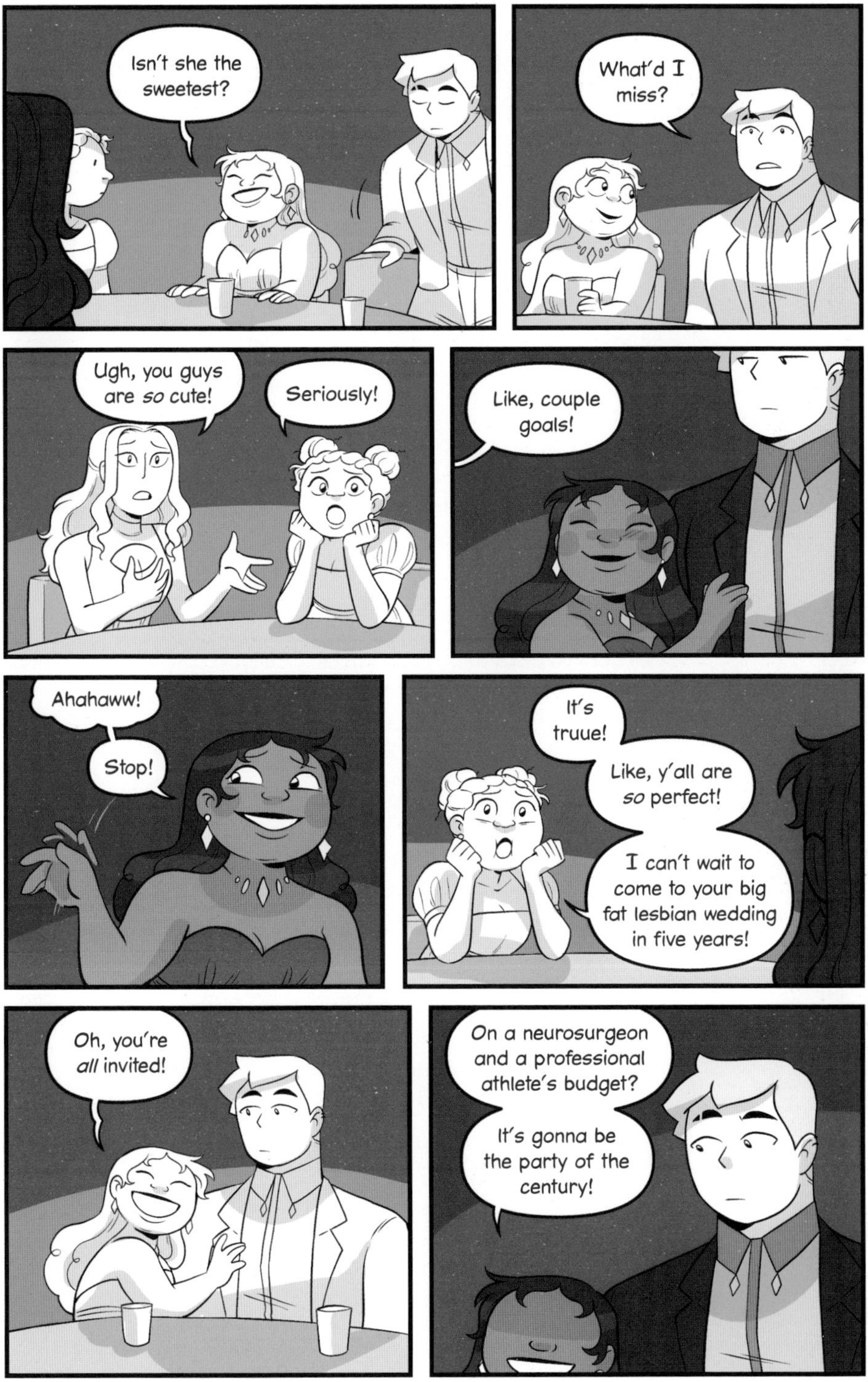
Isn't she the sweetest?
What'd I miss?
Ugh, you guys are *so* cute!
Seriously!
Like, couple goals!
Ahahaww!
Stop!
It's truue!
Like, y'all are *so* perfect!
I can't wait to come to your big fat lesbian wedding in five years!
Oh, you're *all* invited!
On a neurosurgeon and a professional athlete's budget?
It's gonna be the party of the century!

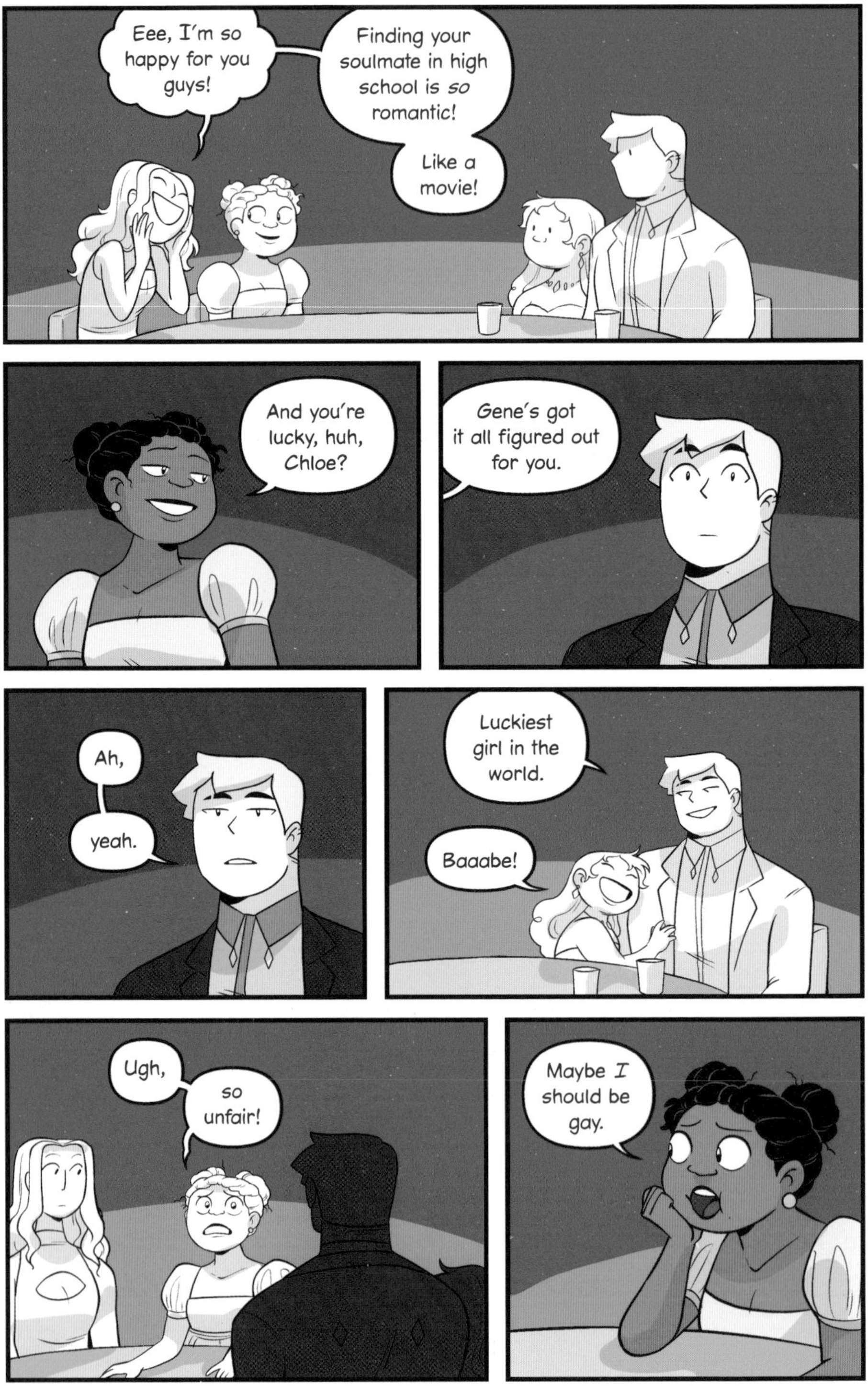
Eee, I'm so happy for you guys!
Finding your soulmate in high school is *so* romantic!
Like a movie!
And you're lucky, huh, Chloe?
Gene's got it all figured out for you.
Ah,
yeah.
Luckiest girl in the world.
Baaabe!
Ugh,
so unfair!
Maybe *I* should be gay.

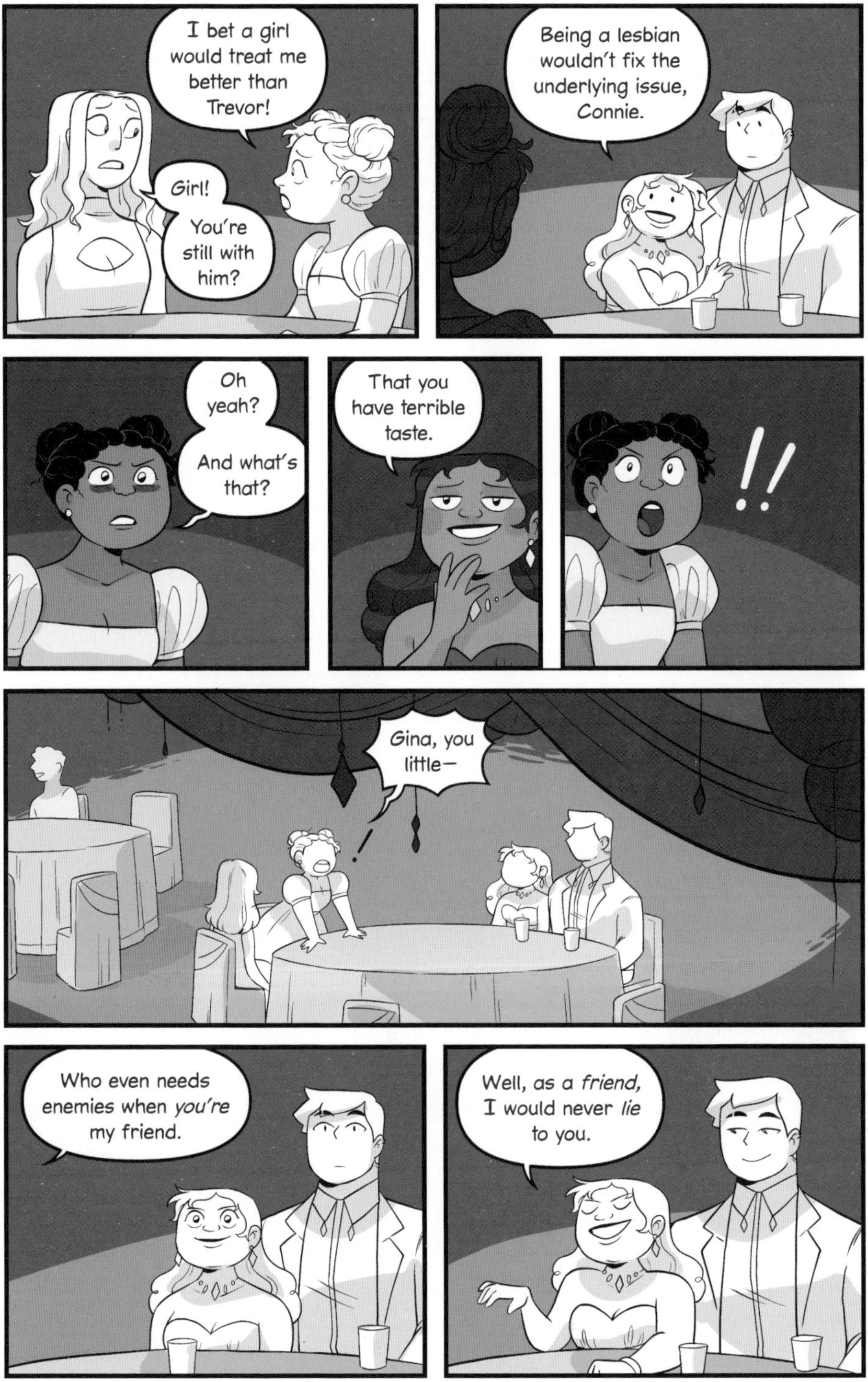
I bet a girl would treat me better than Trevor!
Girl!
You're still with him?
Being a lesbian wouldn't fix the underlying issue, Connie.
Oh yeah?
And what's that?
That you have terrible taste.
!!
Gina, you little—
!
Who even needs enemies when *you're* my friend.
Well, as a *friend,* I would never *lie* to you.

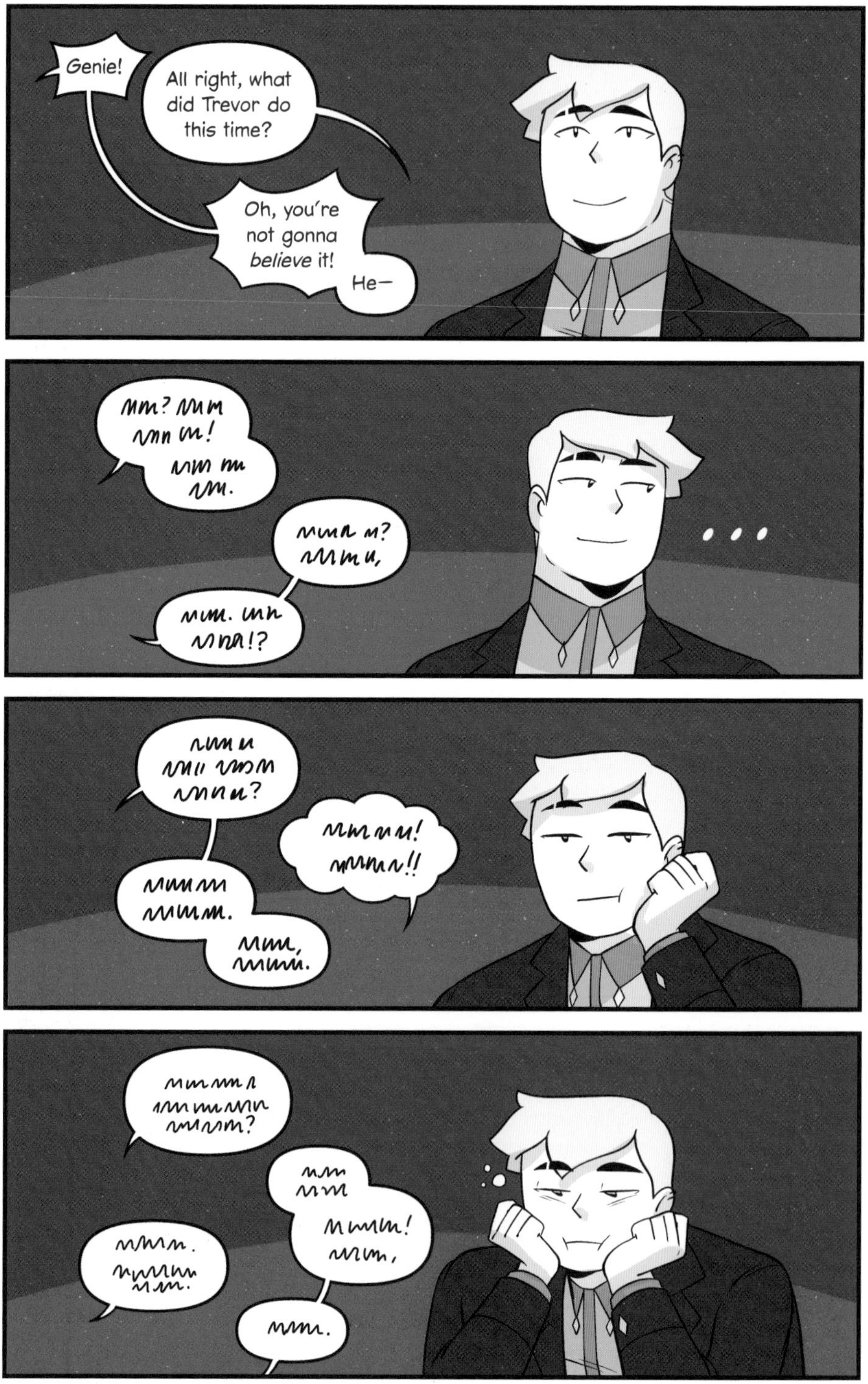
Genie!
All right, what did Trevor do this time?
Oh, you're not gonna *believe* it!
He—

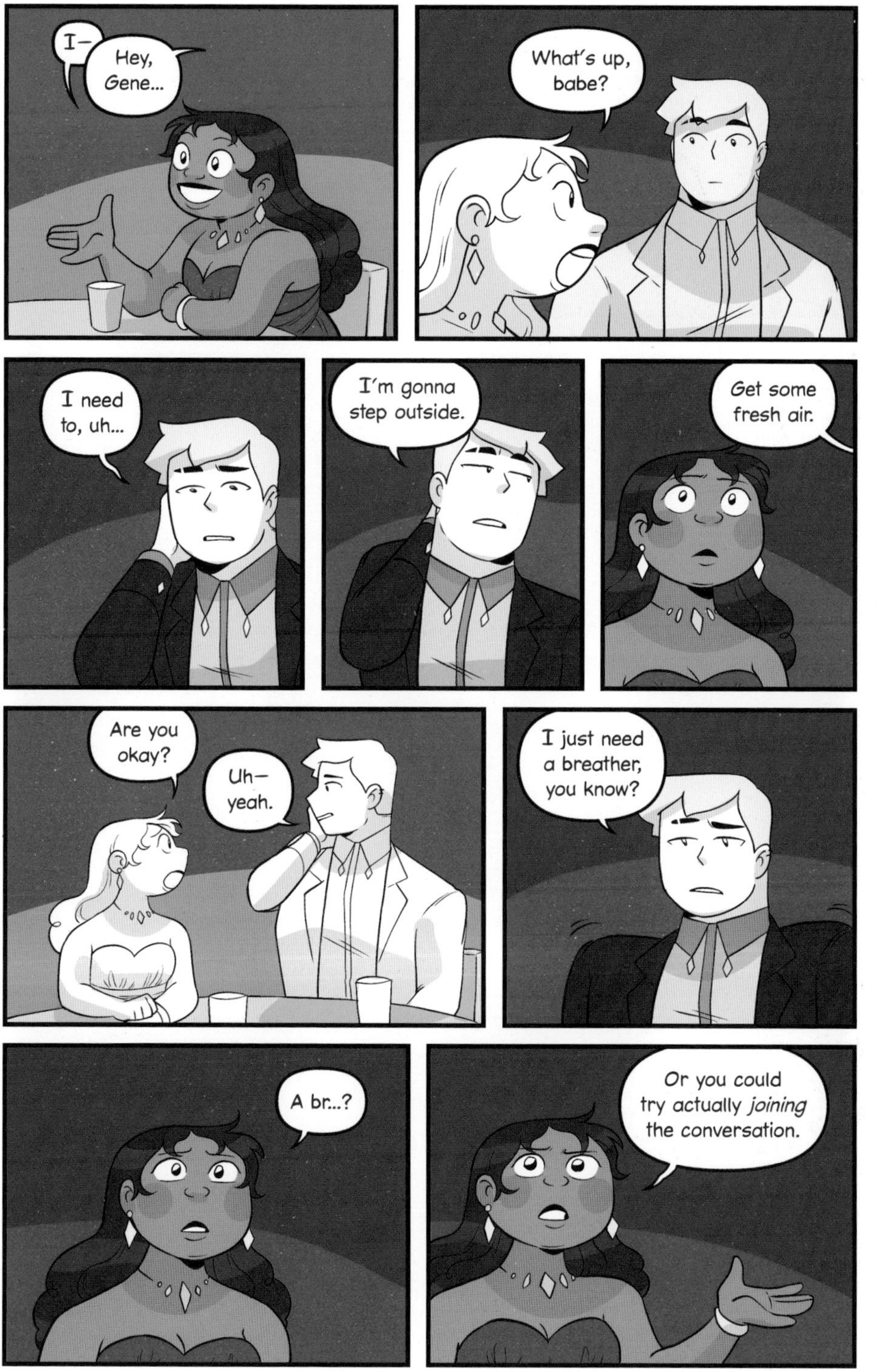
I—
Hey, Gene...
What's up, babe?
I need to, uh...
I'm gonna step outside.
Get some fresh air.
Are you okay?
Uh— yeah.
I just need a breather, you know?
A br...?
Or you could try actually *joining* the conversation.

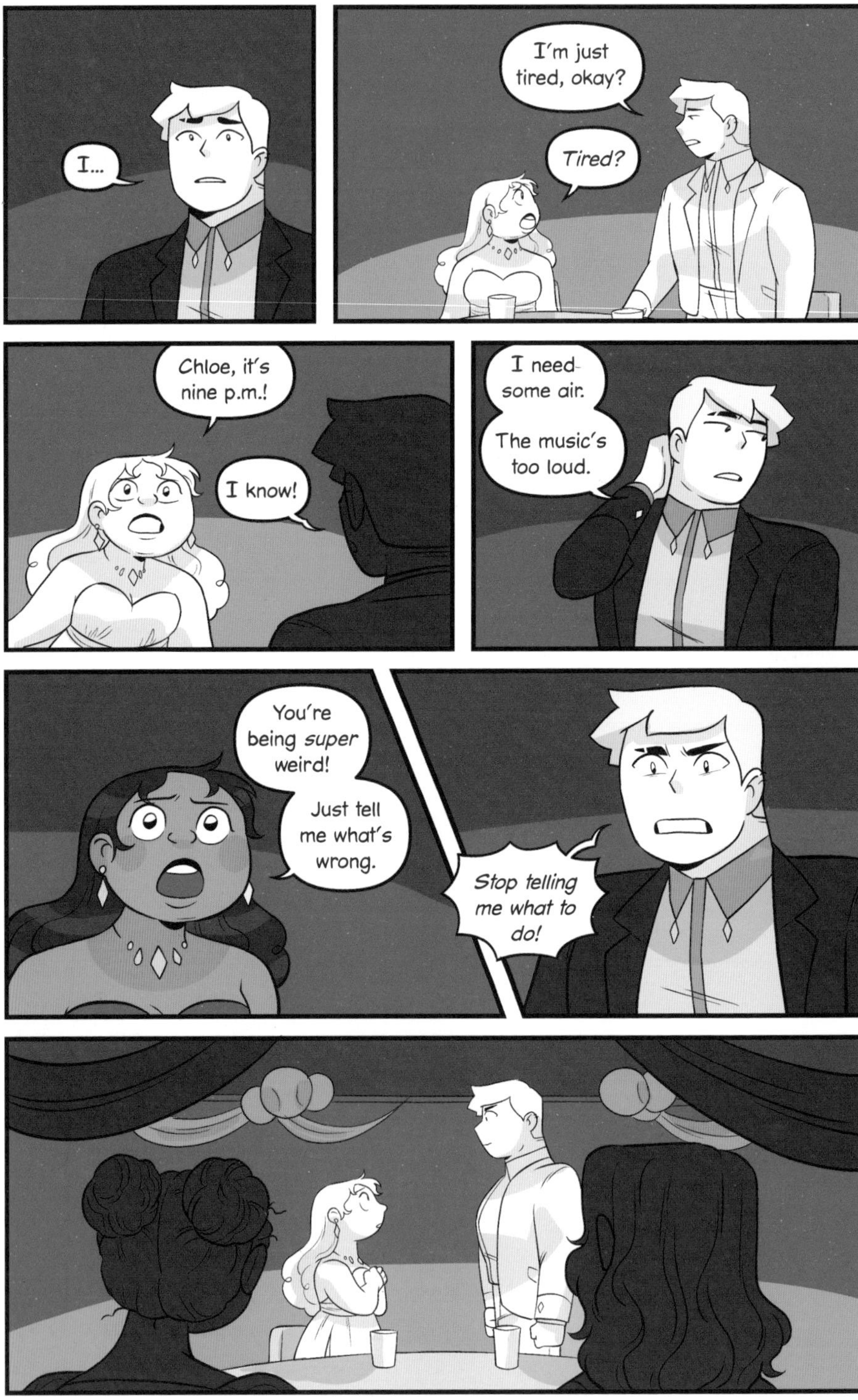
I...
I'm just tired, okay?
Tired?
Chloe, it's nine p.m.!
I know!
I need some air.
The music's too loud.
You're being *super* weird!
Just tell me what's wrong.
Stop telling me what to do!

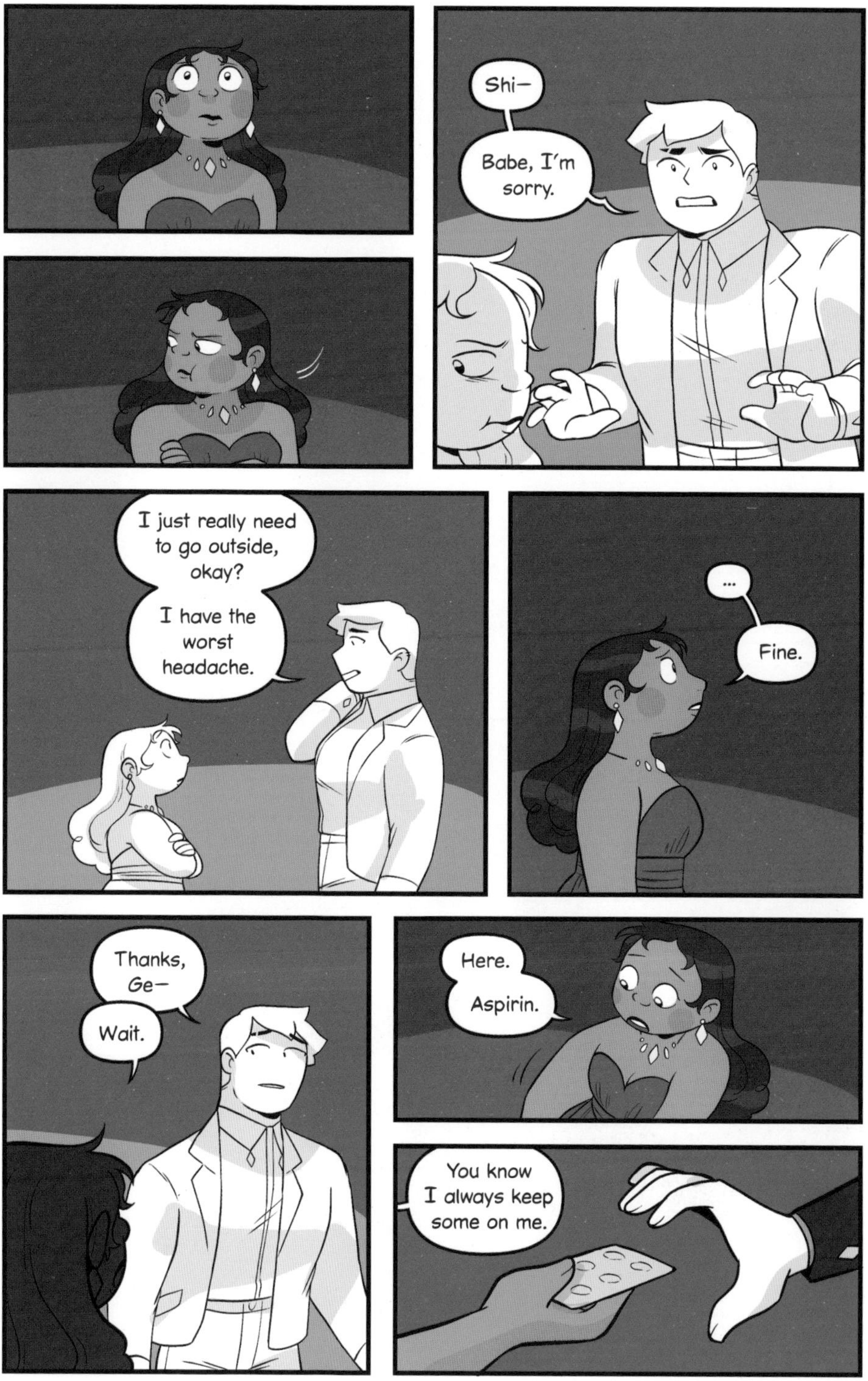
Shi—
Babe, I'm sorry.
I just really need to go outside, okay?
I have the worst headache.
...
Fine.
Thanks, Ge—
Wait.
Here.
Aspirin.
You know I always keep some on me.

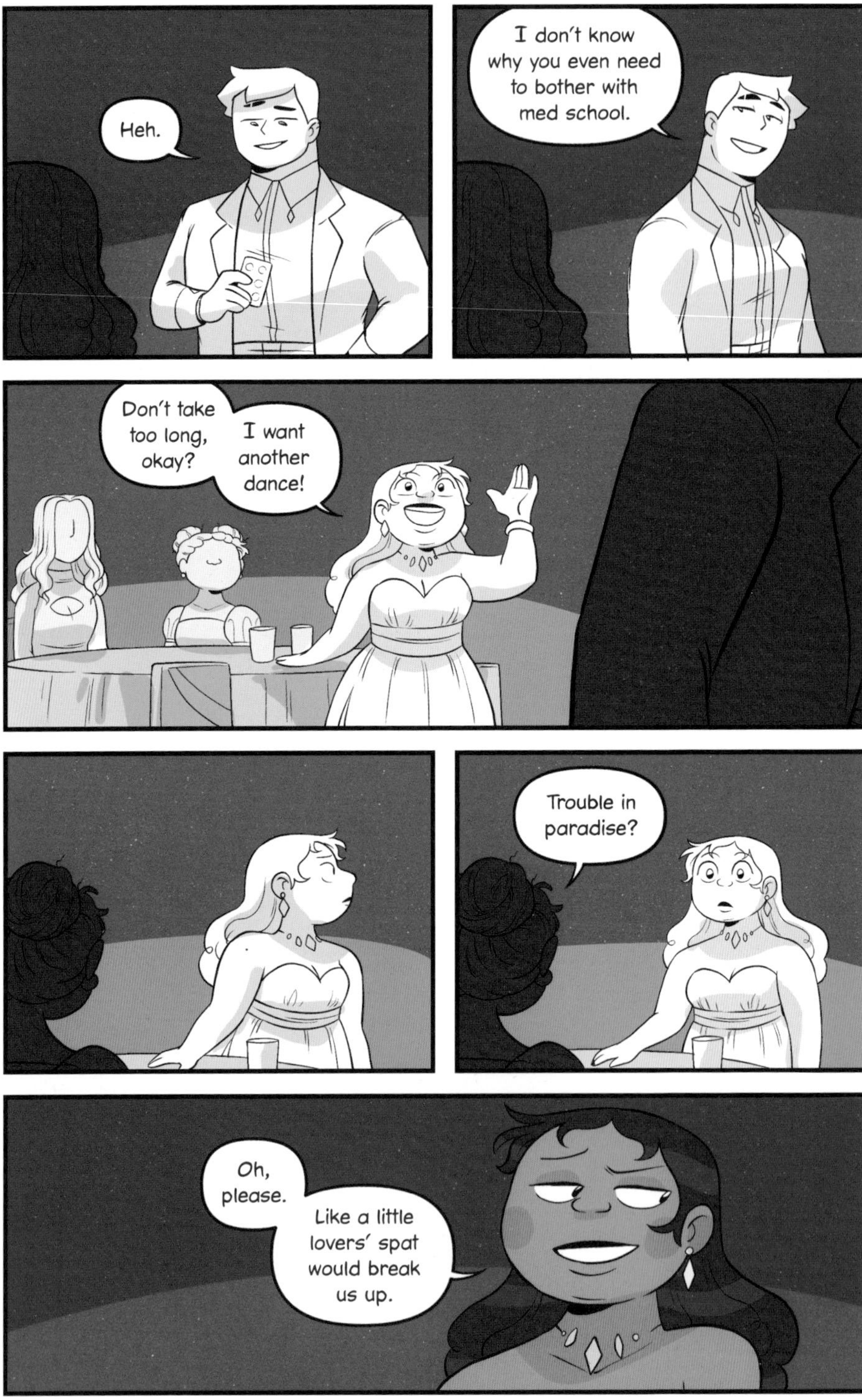
Heh.
I don't know why you even need to bother with med school.
Don't take too long, okay?
I want another dance!
Trouble in paradise?
Oh, please.
Like a little lovers' spat would break us up.

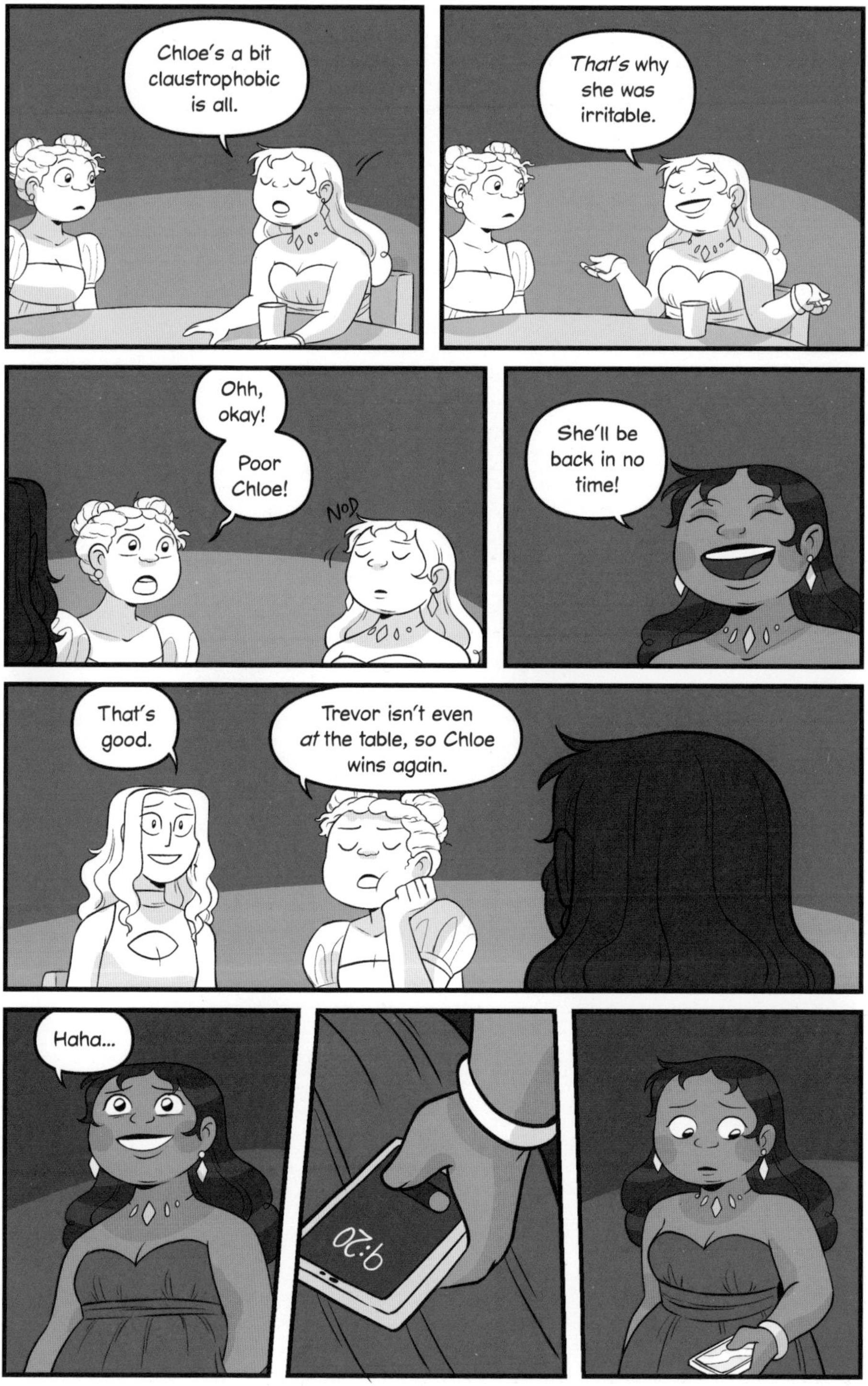
Chloe's a bit claustrophobic is all.
That's why she was irritable.
Ohh, okay!
Poor Chloe!
NOD
She'll be back in no time!
That's good.
Trevor isn't even *at* the table, so Chloe wins again.
Haha...
9:20

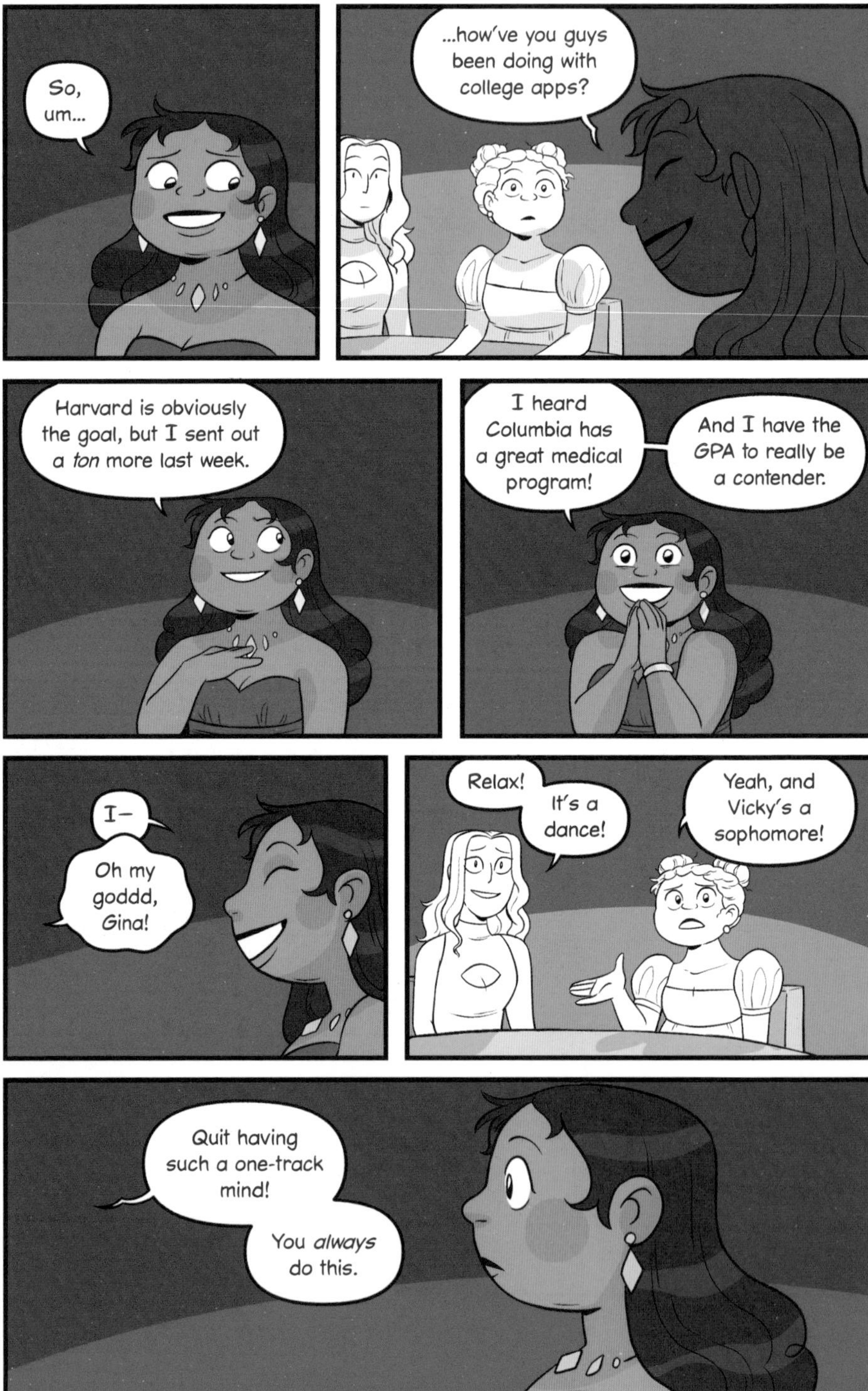
So, um...
...how've you guys been doing with college apps?
Harvard is obviously the goal, but I sent out a *ton* more last week.
I heard Columbia has a great medical program!
And I have the GPA to really be a contender.
I—
Oh my goddd, Gina!
Relax!
It's a dance!
Yeah, and Vicky's a sophomore!
Quit having such a one-track mind!
You *always* do this.

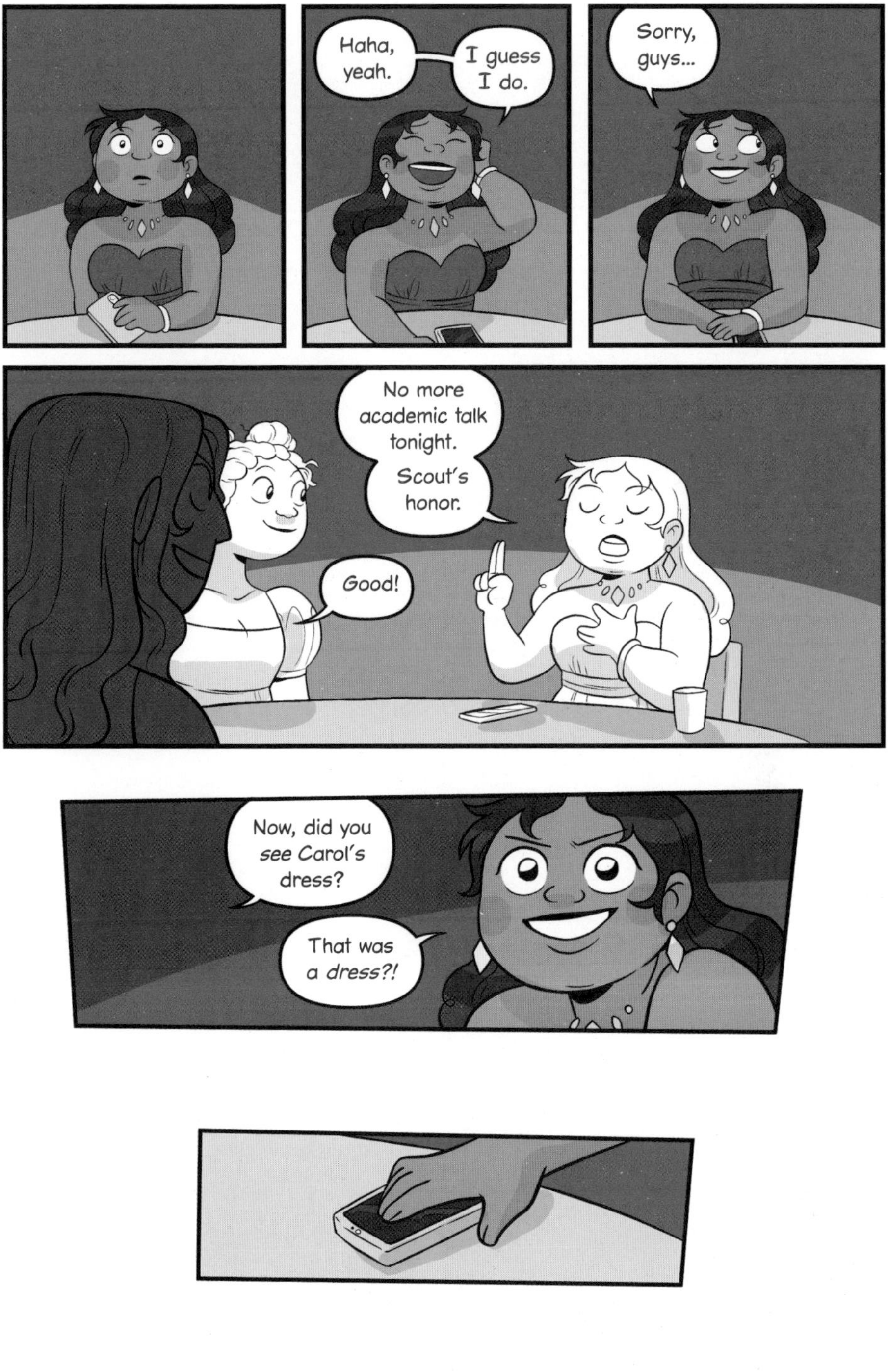
Haha, yeah.
I guess I do.
Sorry, guys...
No more academic talk tonight.
Scout's honor.
Good!
Now, did you *see* Carol's dress?
That was a *dress?!*

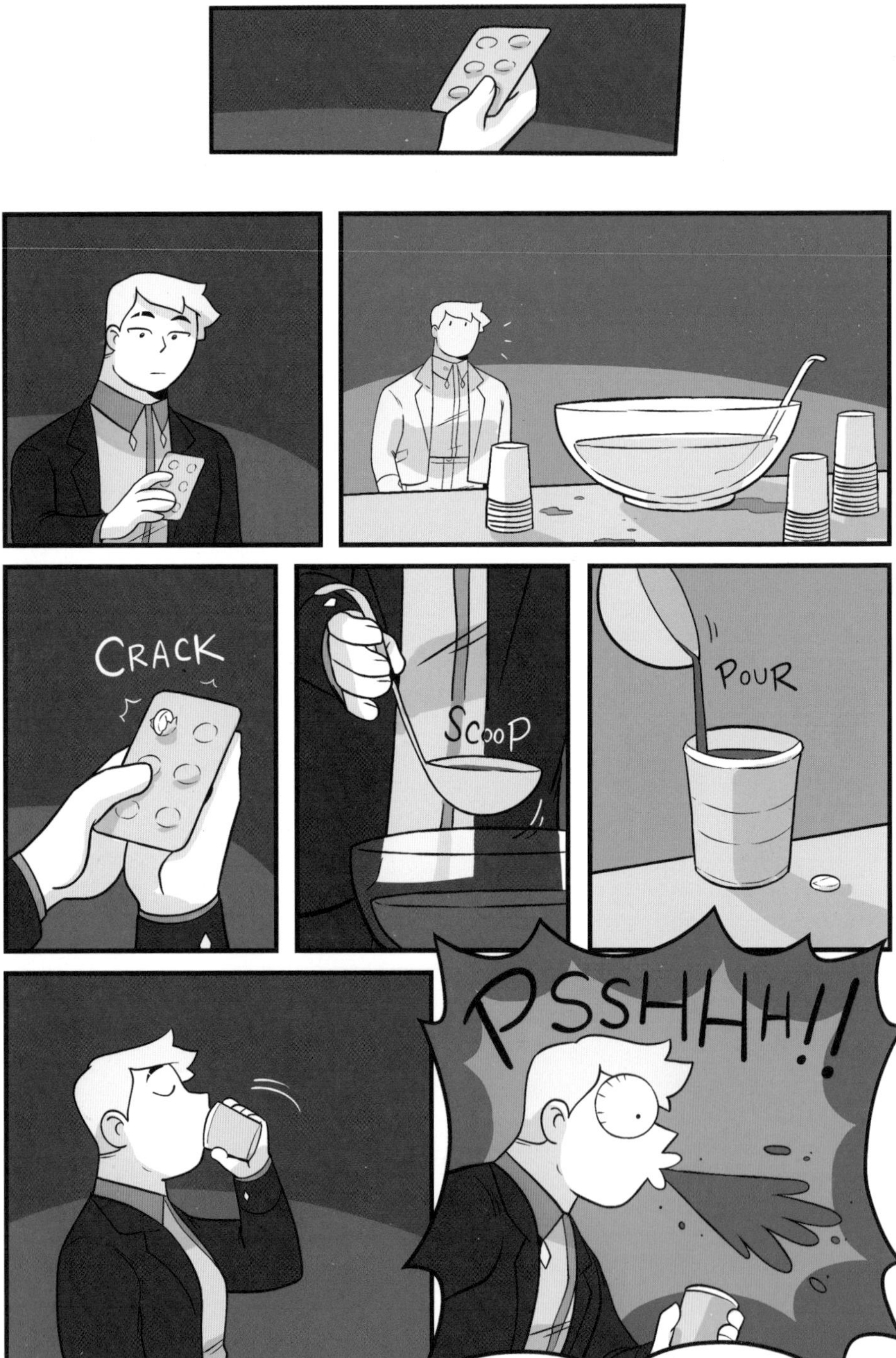
CRACK
SCOOP
POUR
PSSHHH!!

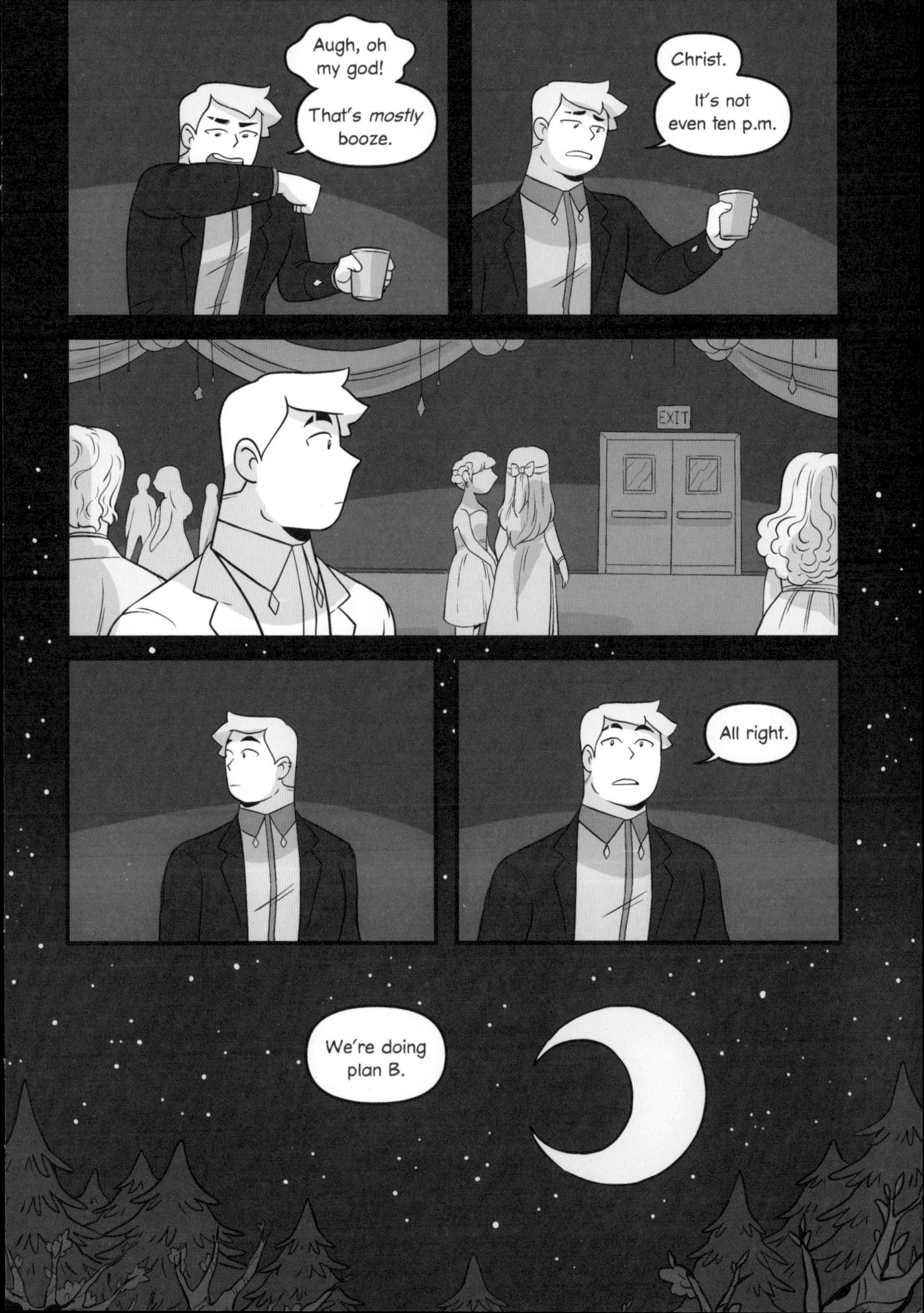
Augh, oh my god!
That's *mostly* booze.
Christ.
It's not even ten p.m.
EXIT
All right.
We're doing plan B.

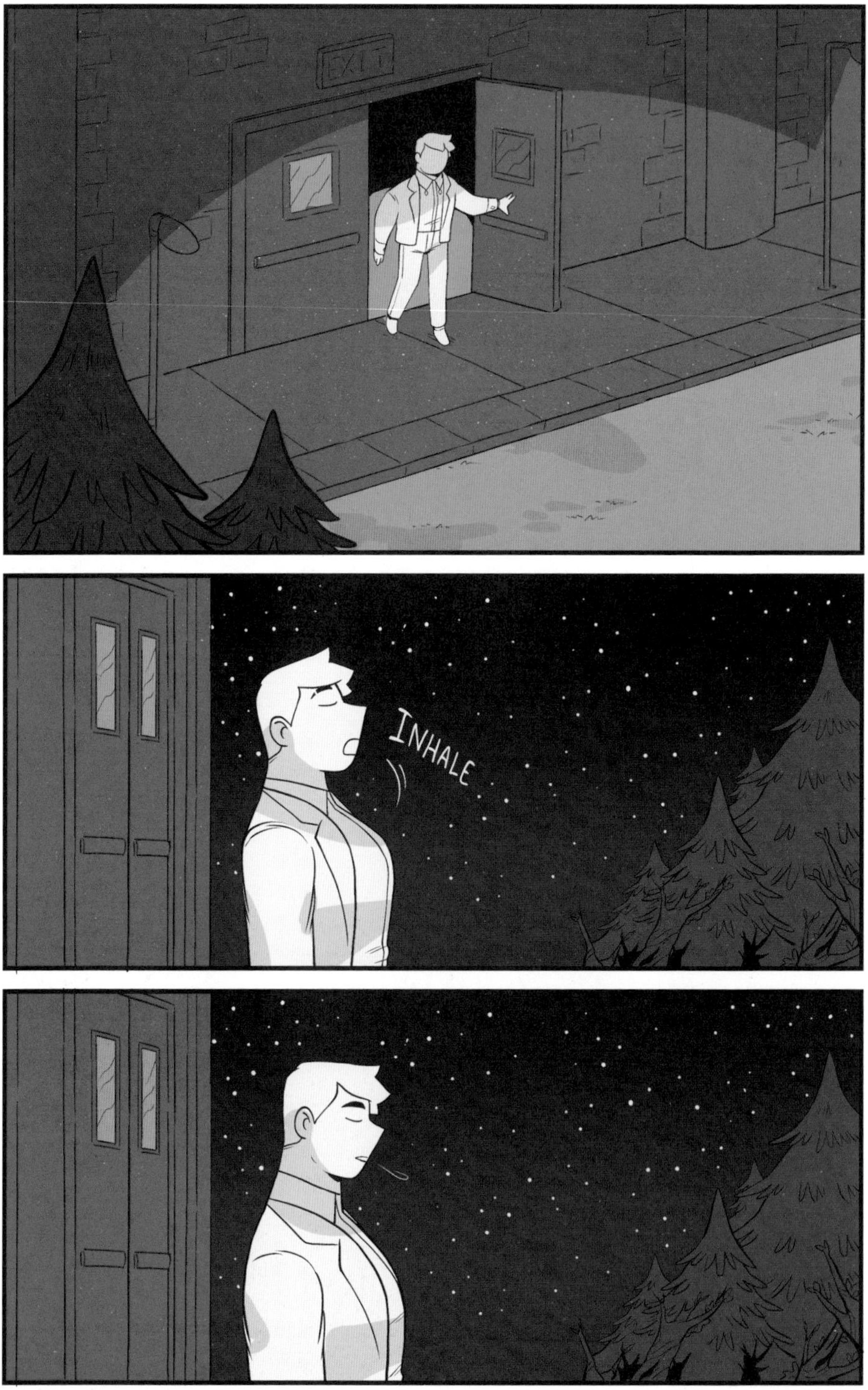
EXIT
INHALE

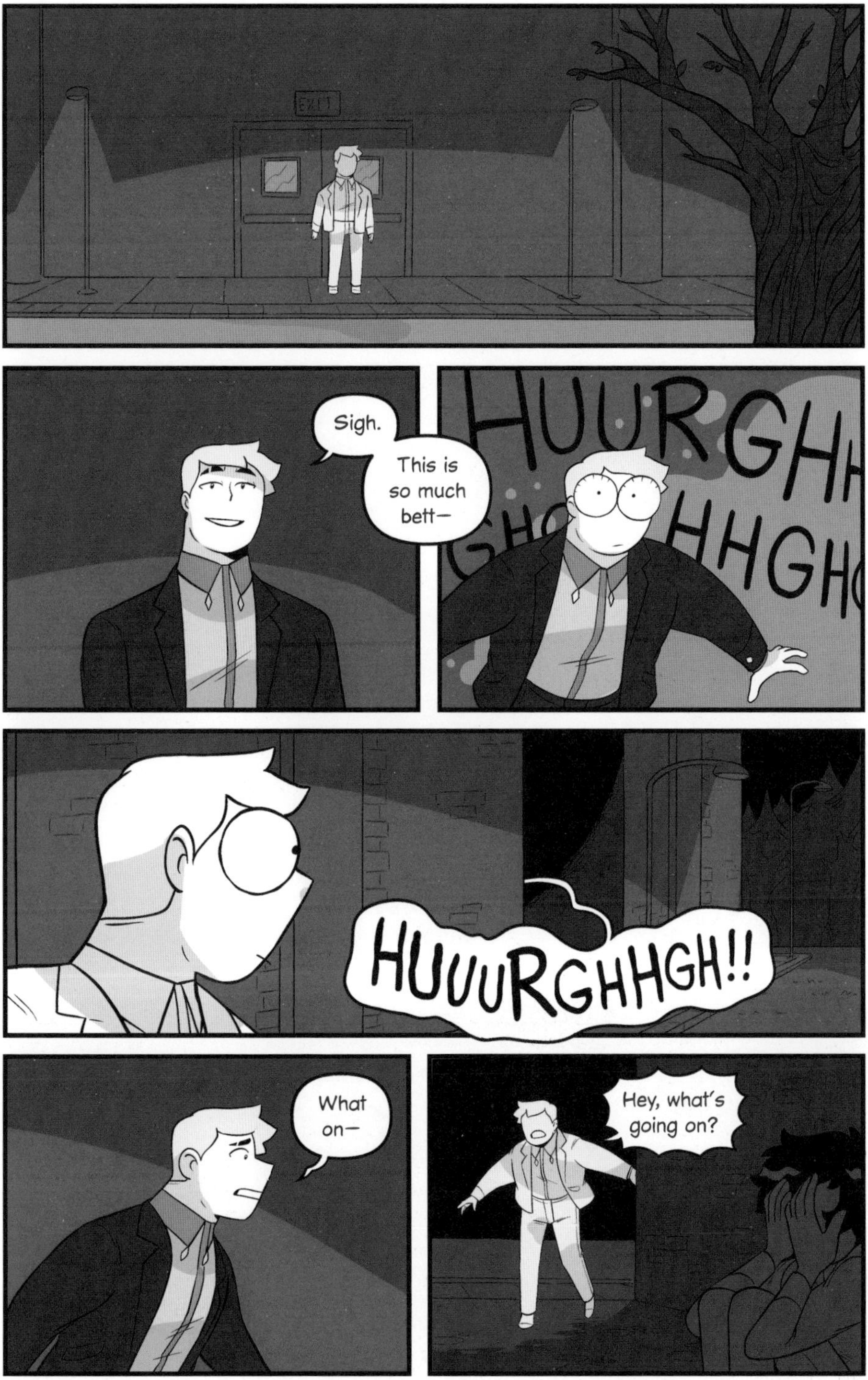
Sigh.
This is so much bett—
HUURGHHGHOHHGHO
HUUURGHHGH!!
What on—
Hey, what's going on?

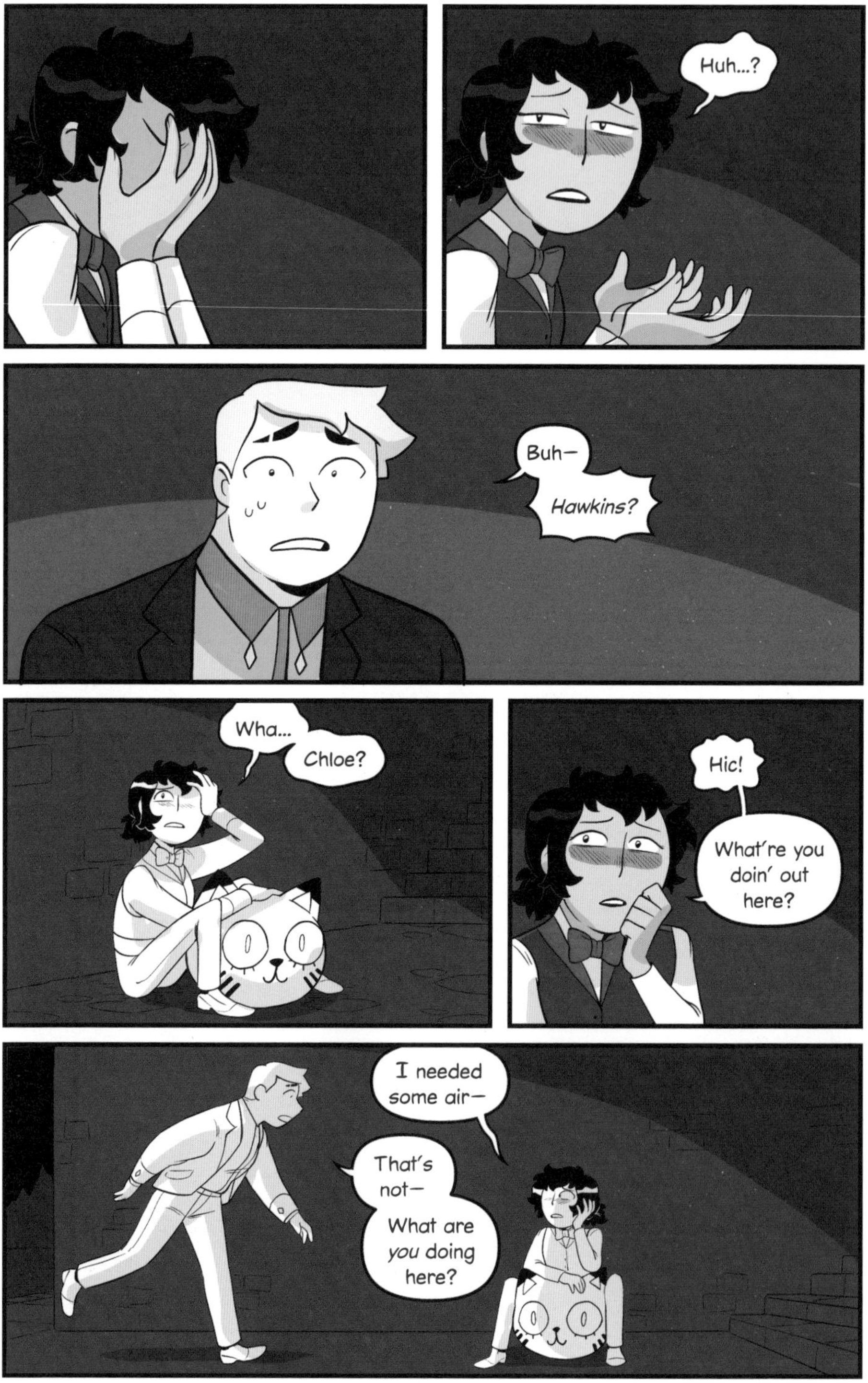
Huh...?
Buh—
Hawkins?
Wha...
Chloe?
Hic!
What're you doin' out here?
I needed some air—
That's not—
What are *you* doing here?

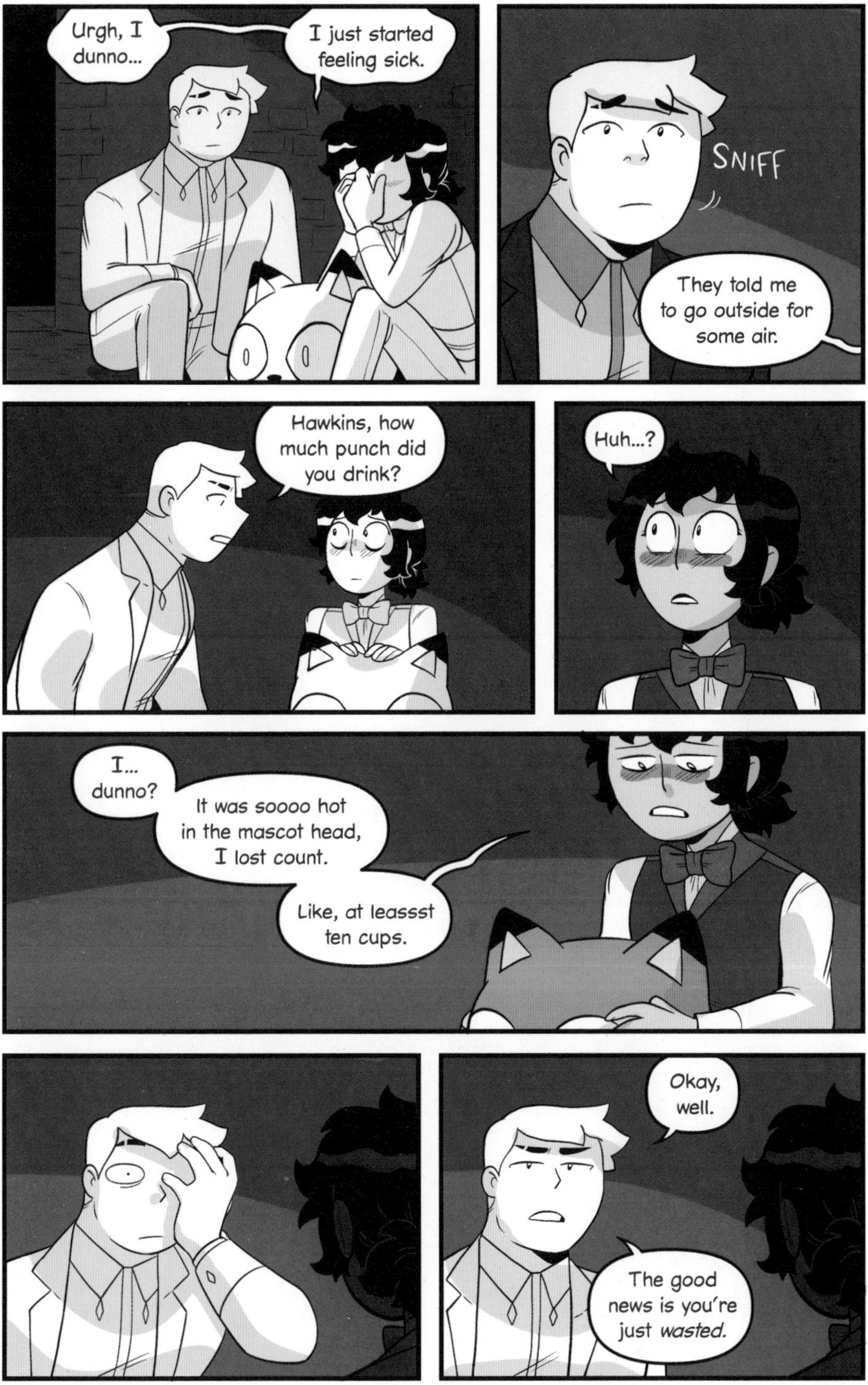
Urgh, I dunno...
I just started feeling sick.
SNIFF
They told me to go outside for some air.
Hawkins, how much punch did you drink?
Huh...?
I... dunno?
It was soooo hot in the mascot head, I lost count.
Like, at leassst ten cups.
Okay, well.
The good news is you're just *wasted*.

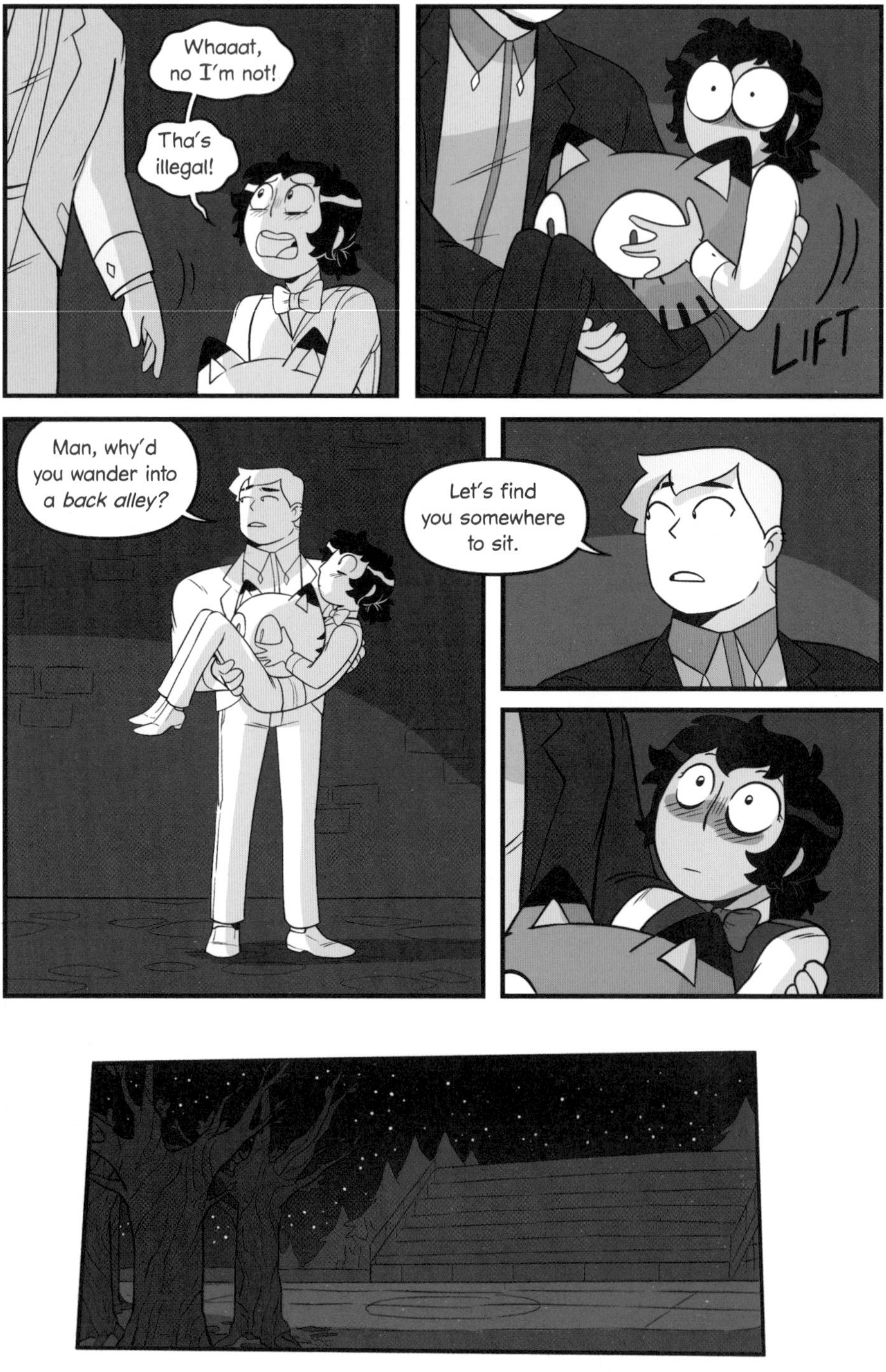
Whaaat, no I'm not!
Tha's illegal!
LIFT
Man, why'd you wander into a *back alley?*
Let's find you somewhere to sit.

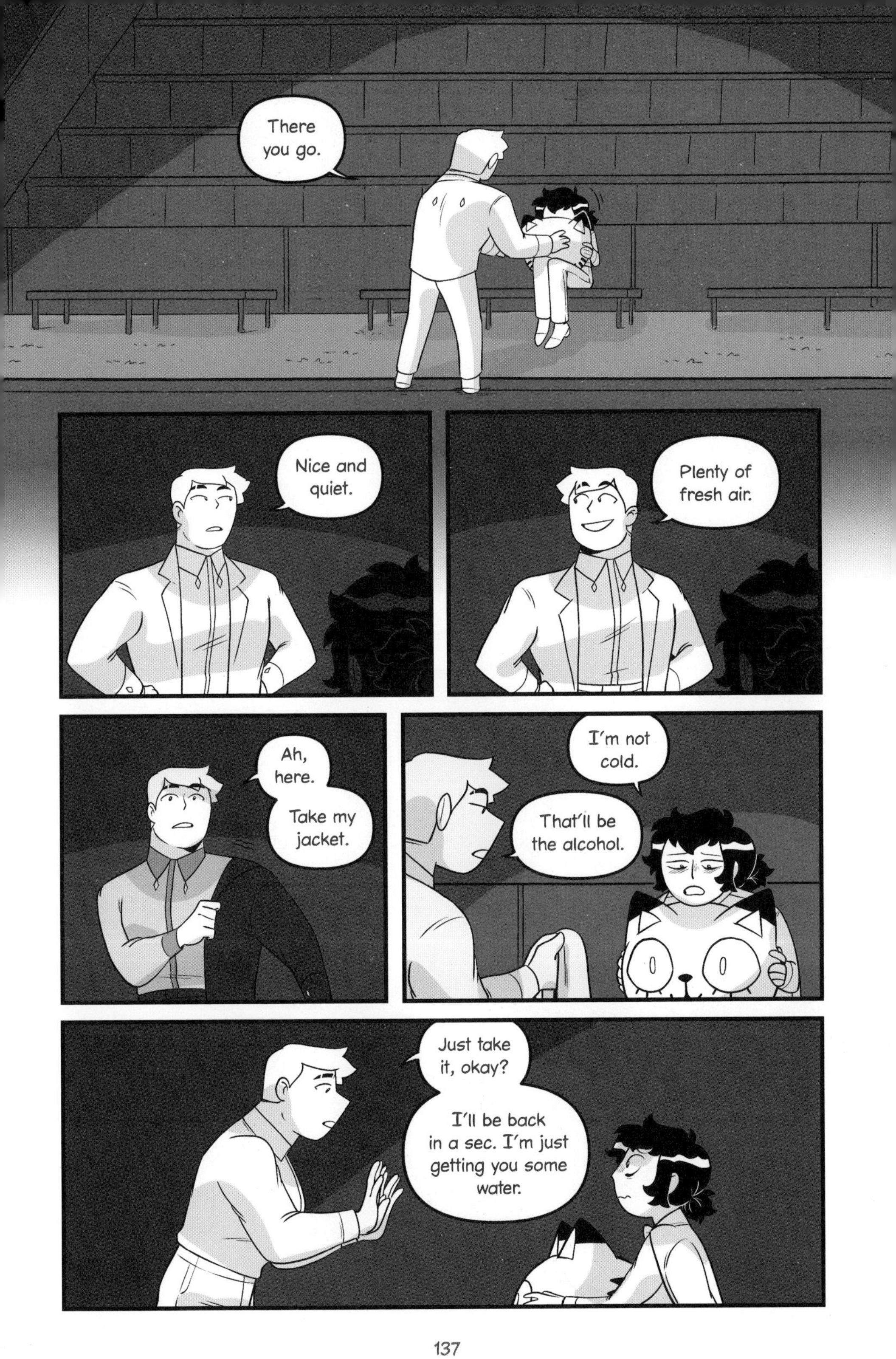
There you go.
Nice and quiet.
Plenty of fresh air.
Ah, here.
Take my jacket.
I'm not cold.
That'll be the alcohol.
Just take it, okay?
I'll be back in a sec. I'm just getting you some water.

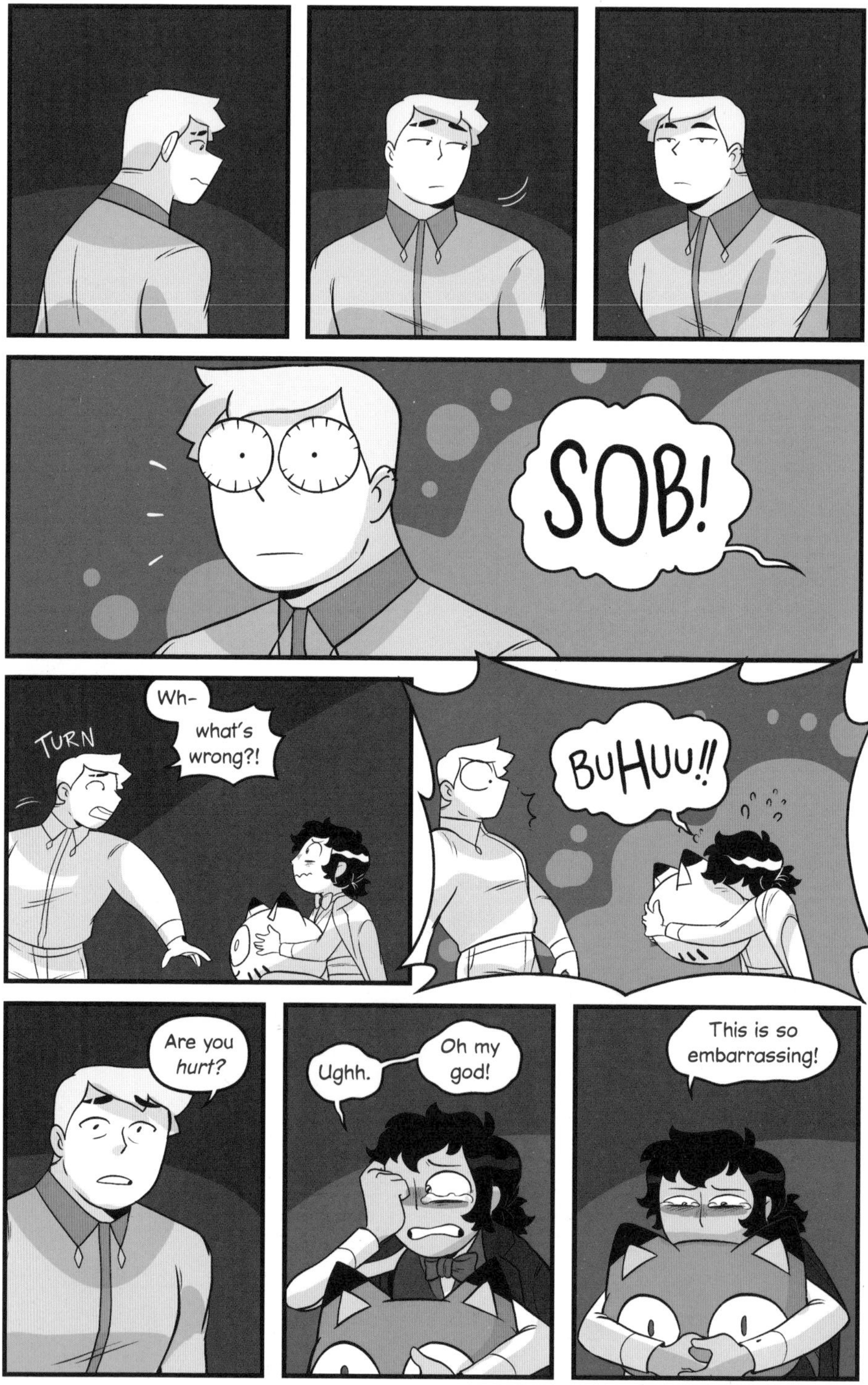
SOB!
TURN
Wh-
what's wrong?!
BuHuu!!
Are you *hurt?*
Ugh.
Oh my god!
This is so embarrassing!

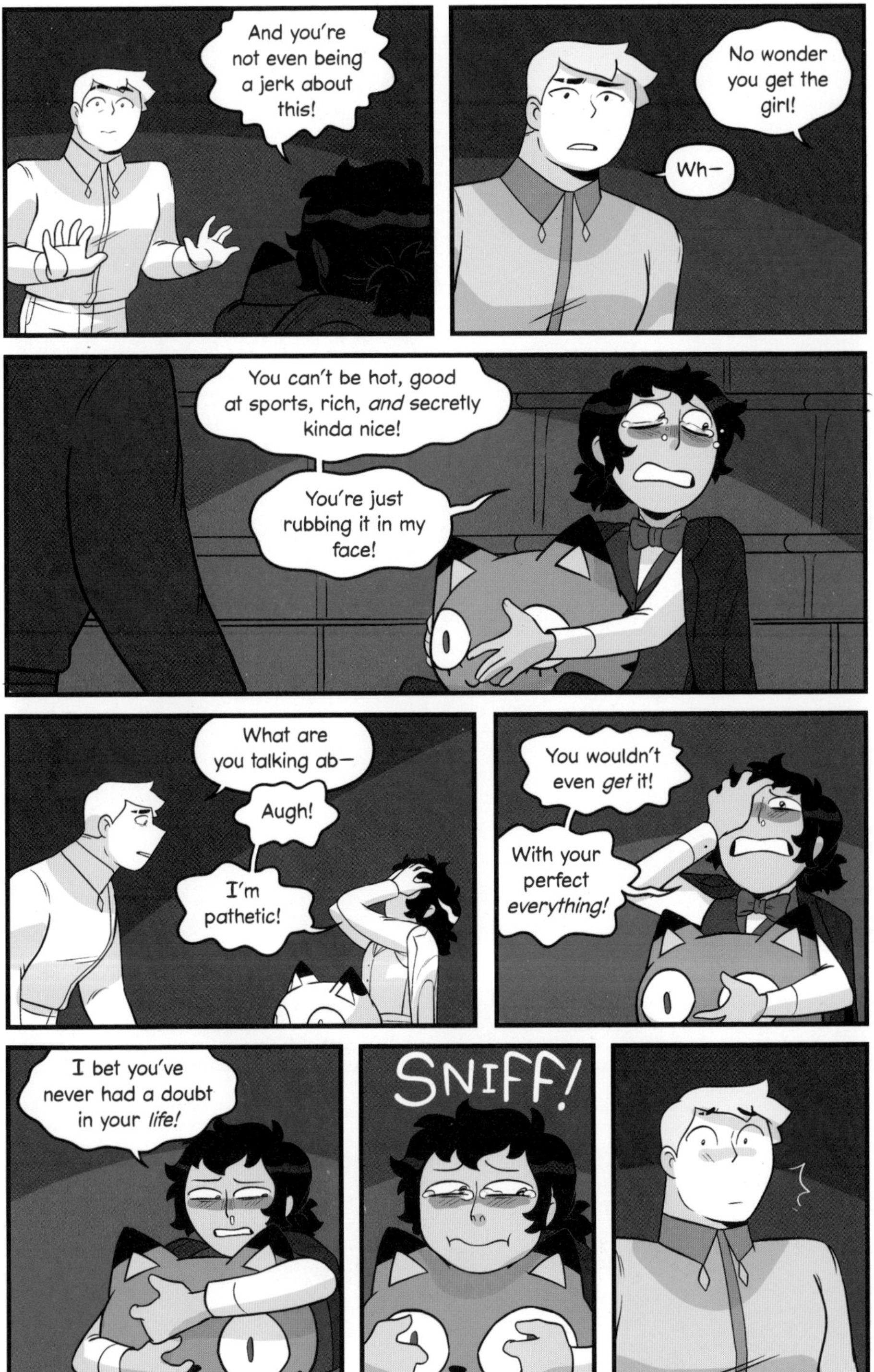

And you're not even being a jerk about this!
No wonder you get the girl!
Wh—
You can't be hot, good at sports, rich, *and* secretly kinda nice!
You're just rubbing it in my face!
What are you talking ab—
Augh!
I'm pathetic!
You wouldn't even *get* it!
With your perfect *everything!*
I bet you've never had a doubt in your *life!*
SNIFF!

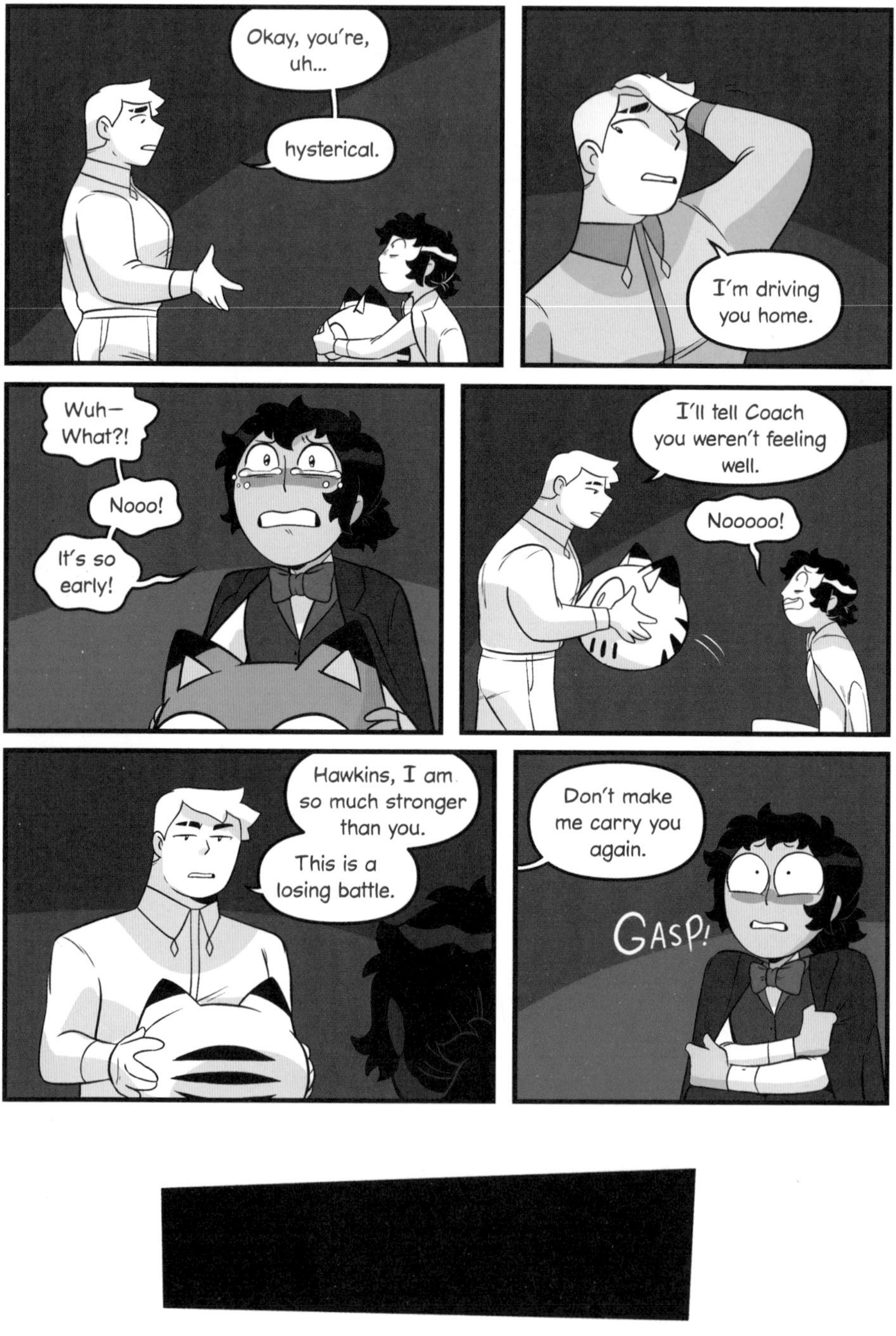
Okay, you're, uh...
hysterical.
I'm driving you home.
Wuh— What?!
Nooo!
It's so early!
I'll tell Coach you weren't feeling well.
Nooooo!
Hawkins, I am so much stronger than you.
This is a losing battle.
Don't make me carry you again.
GASP!

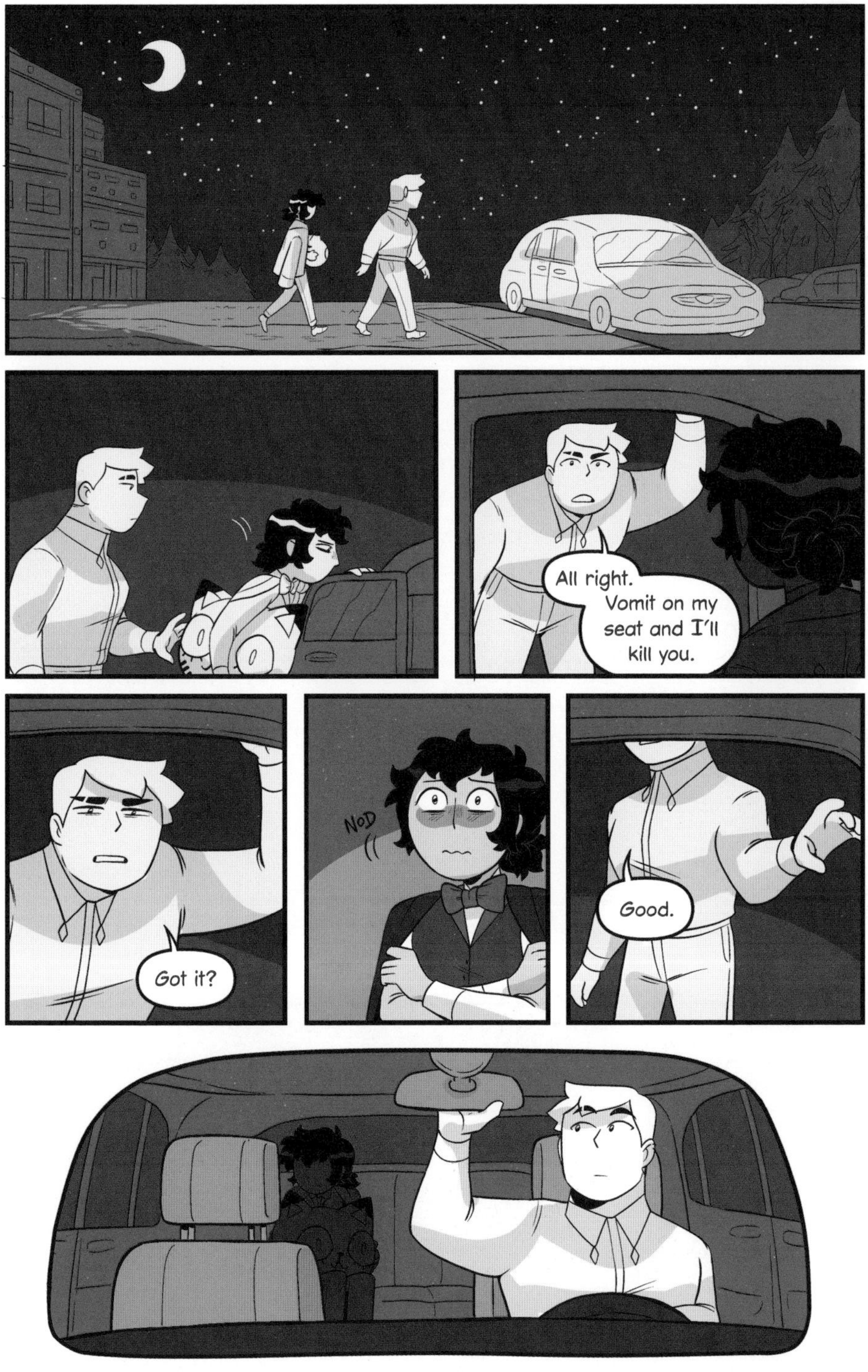
All right. Vomit on my seat and I'll kill you.
Got it?
NOD
Good.

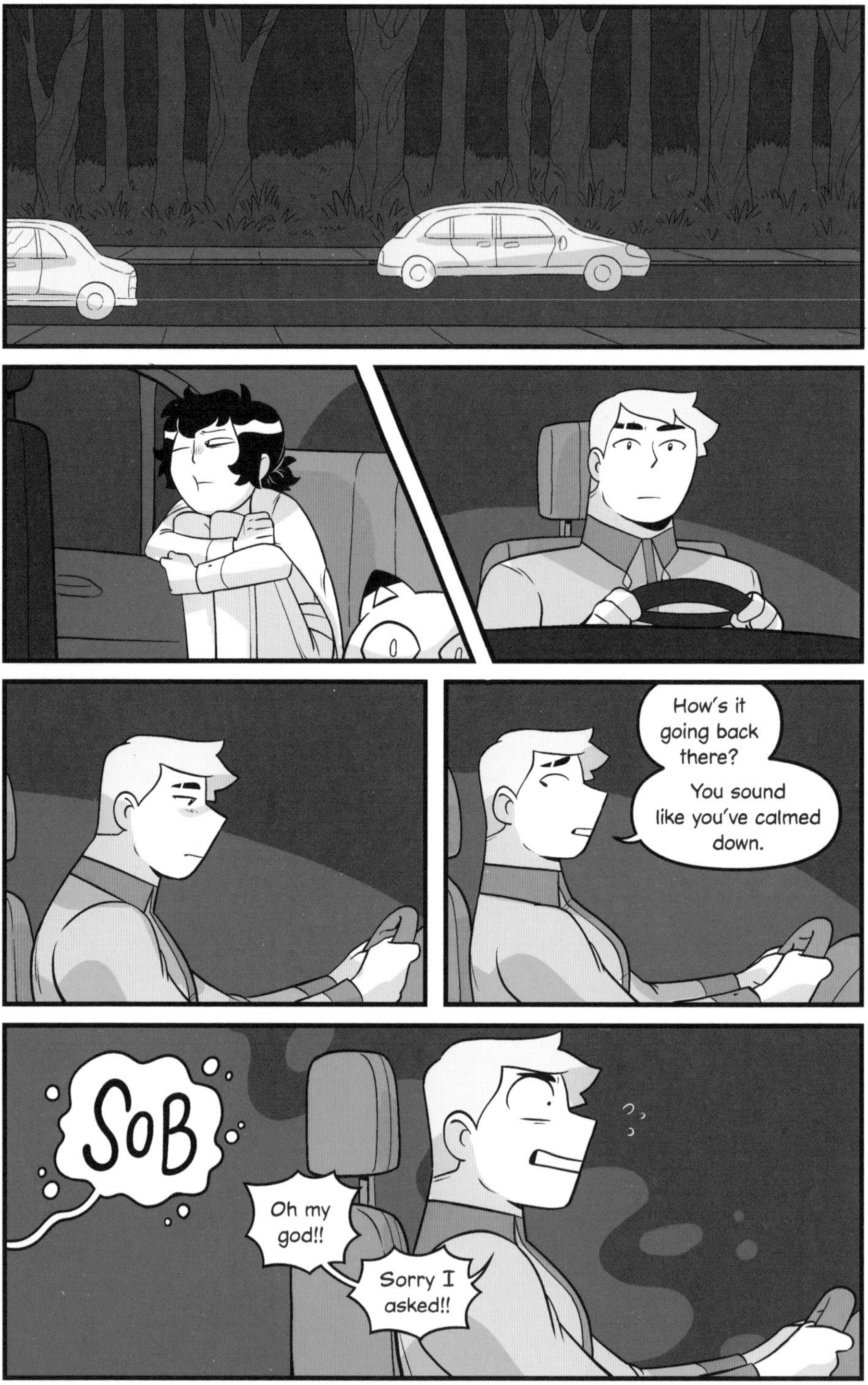
How's it going back there?
You sound like you've calmed down.
SOB
Oh my god!!
Sorry I asked!!

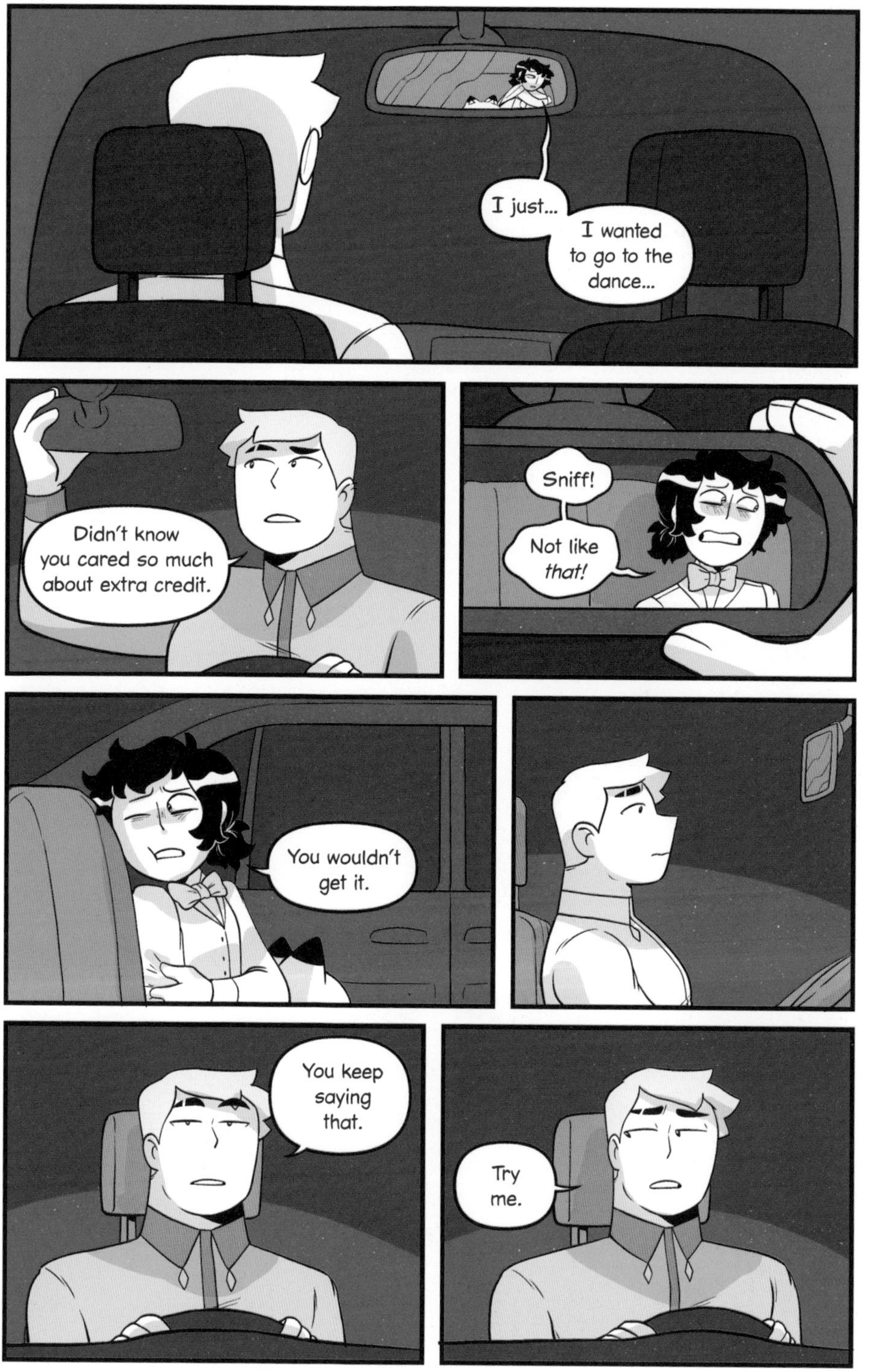
I just...
I wanted to go to the dance...
Didn't know you cared so much about extra credit.
Sniff!
Not like *that!*
You wouldn't get it.
You keep saying that.
Try me.

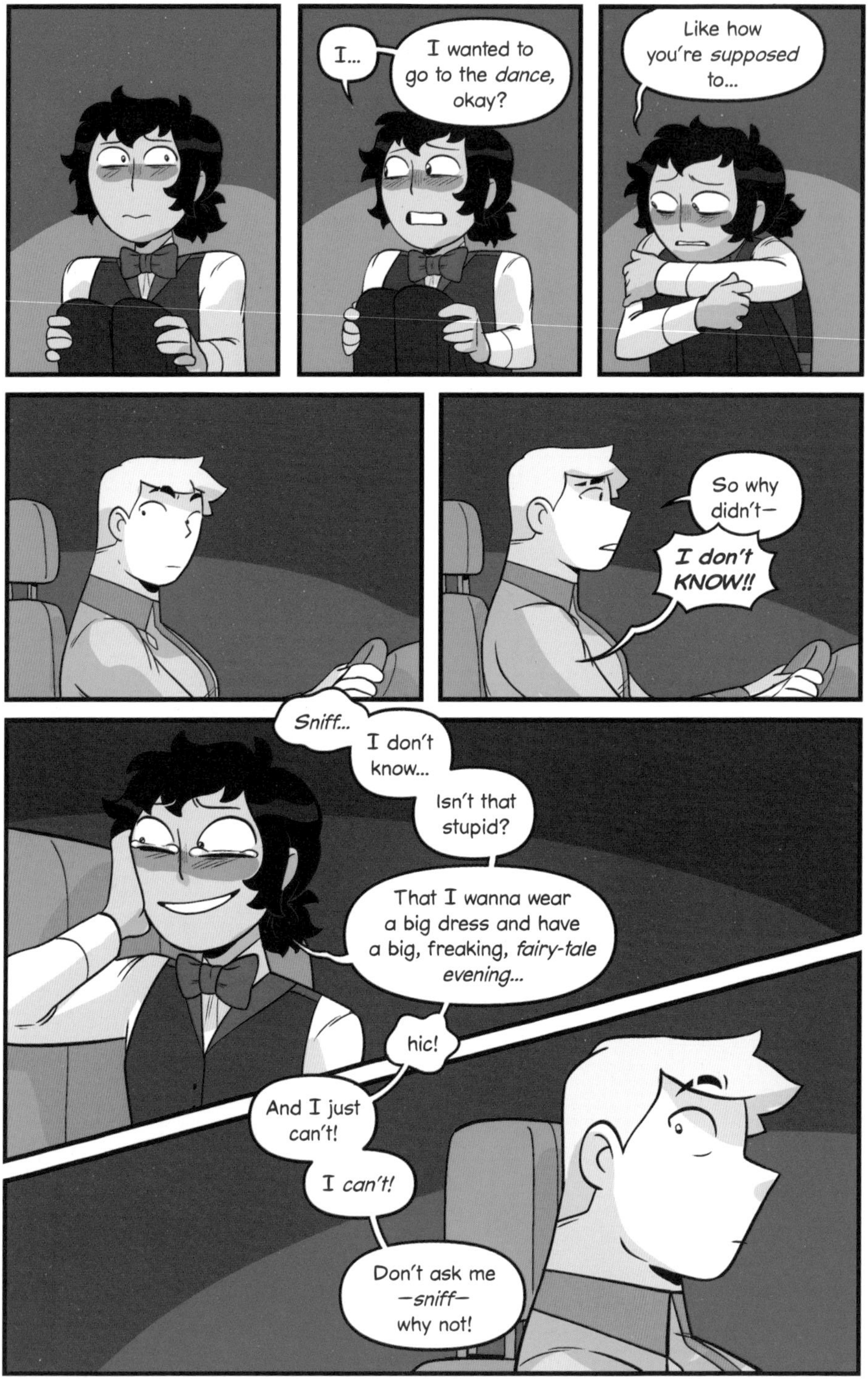
I...
I wanted to go to the *dance,* okay?
Like how you're *supposed* to...
So why didn't—
I don't KNOW!!
Sniff...
I don't know...
Isn't that stupid?
That I wanna wear a big dress and have a big, freaking, *fairy-tale evening...*
hic!
And I just can't!
I *can't!*
Don't ask me —*sniff*— why not!

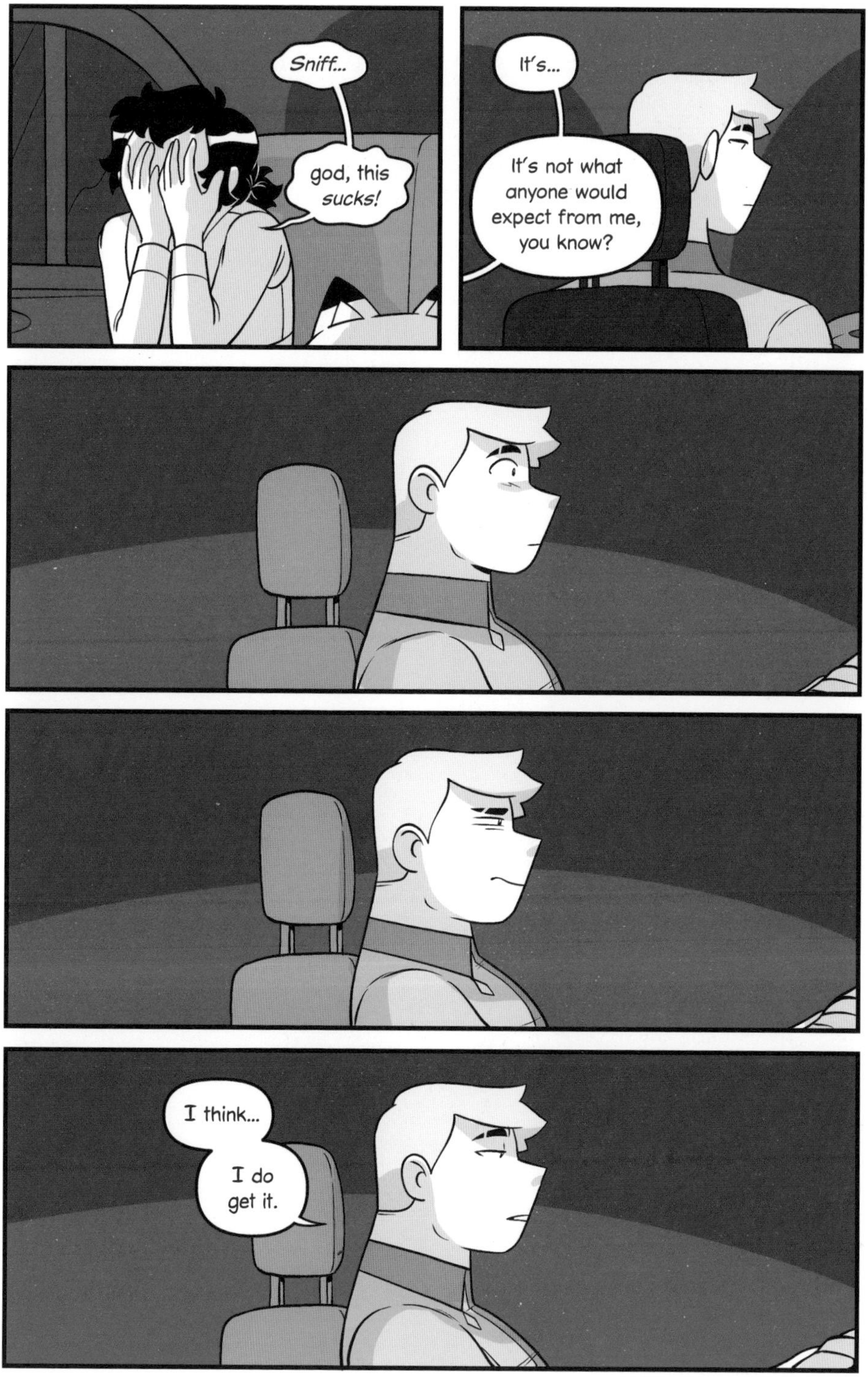
Sniff...
god, this sucks!
It's...
It's not what anyone would expect from me, you know?
I think...
I do get it.

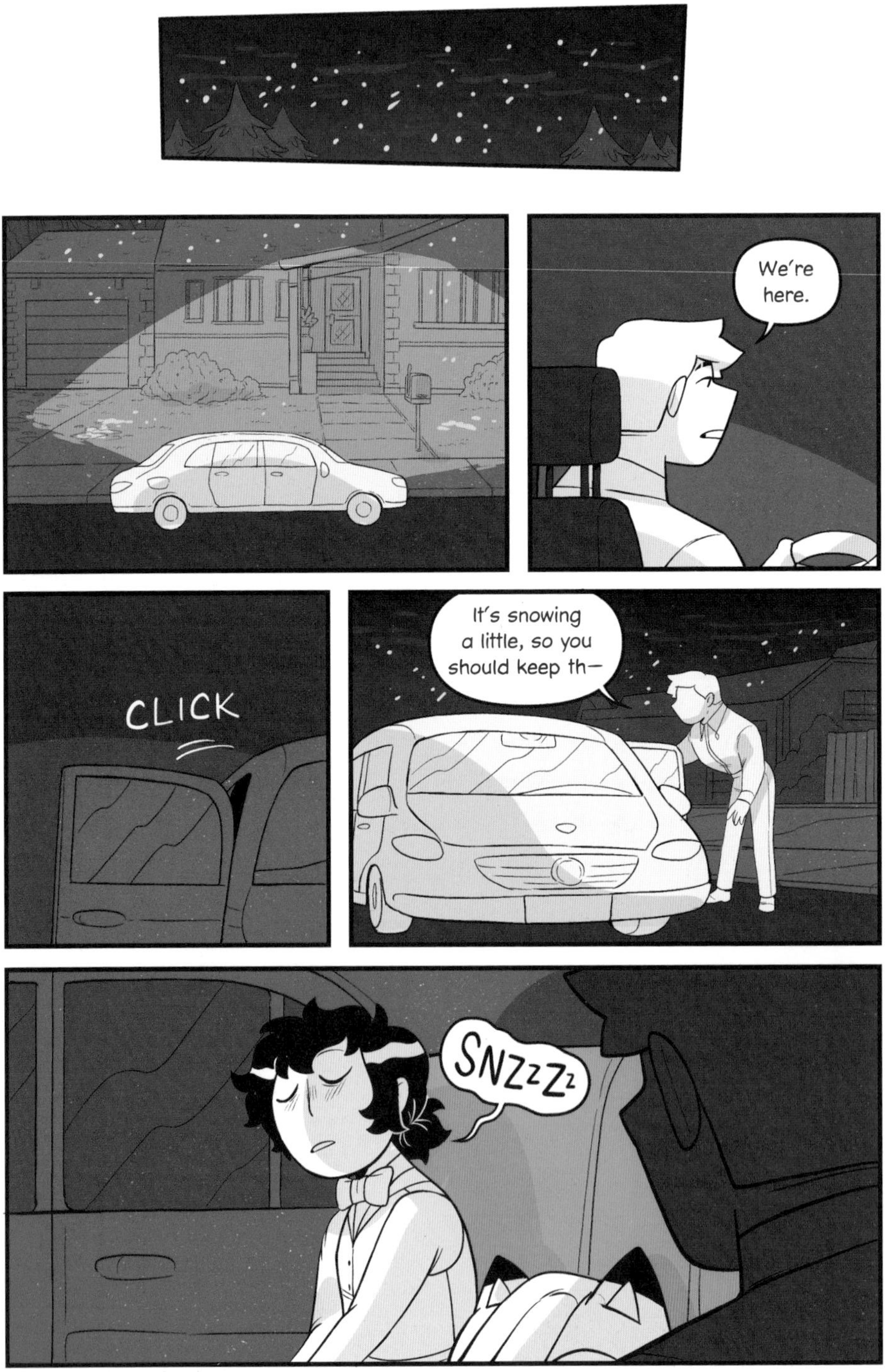
We're here.
CLICK
It's snowing a little, so you should keep th—
SNZzZz

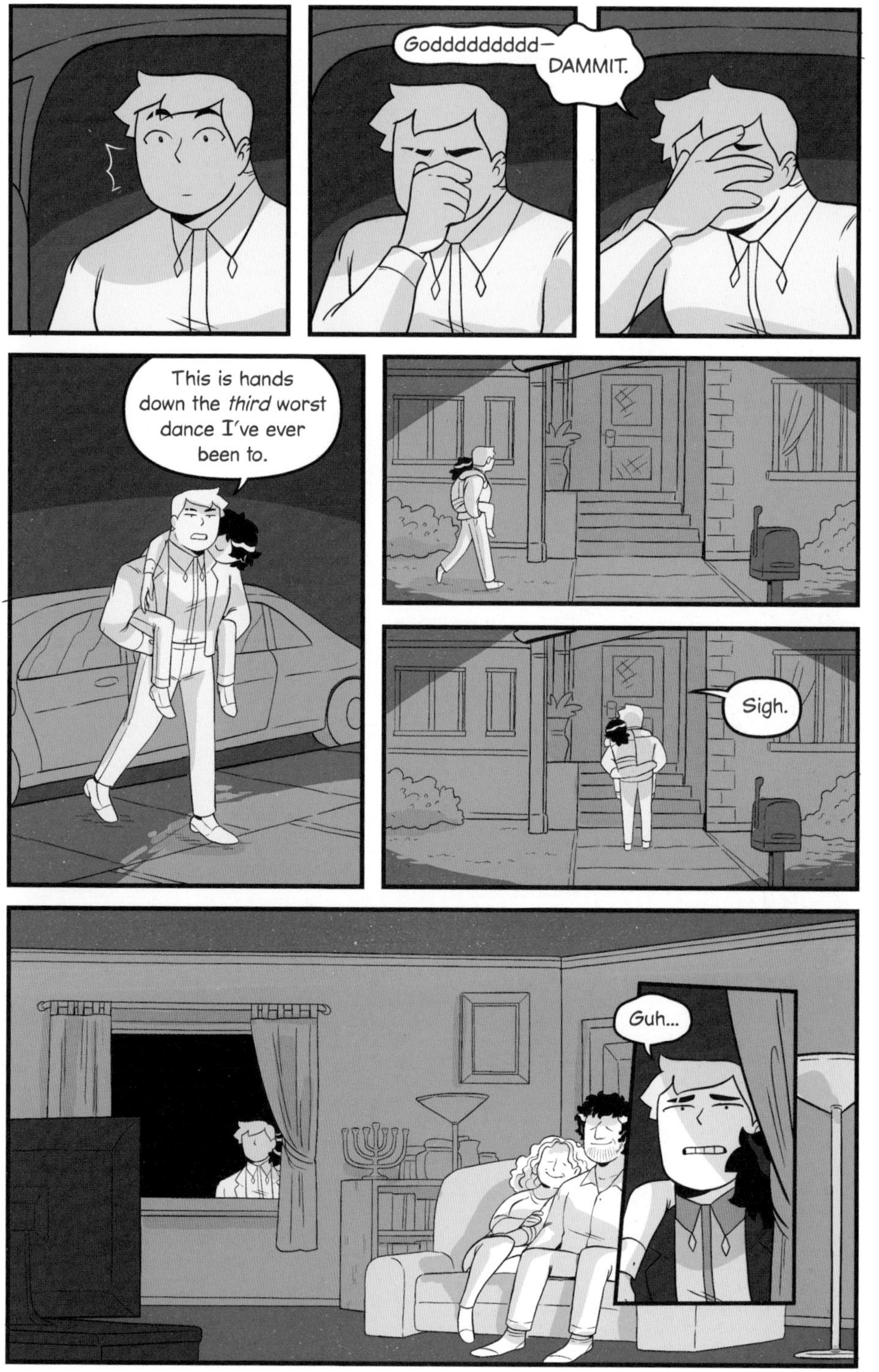
Goddddddddd—
DAMMIT.
This is hands down the *third* worst dance I've ever been to.
Sigh.
Guh...

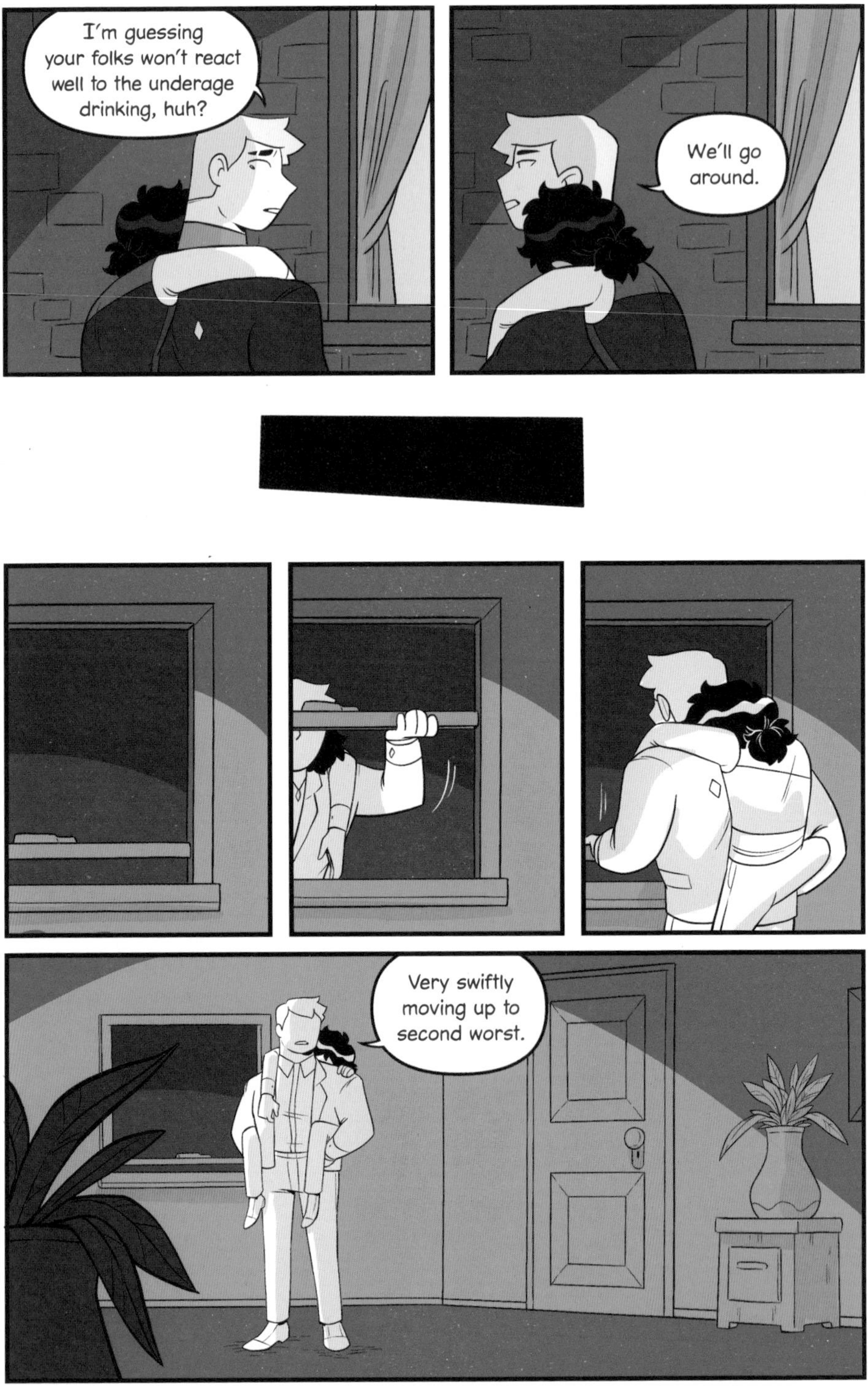
I'm guessing your folks won't react well to the underage drinking, huh?
We'll go around.
Very swiftly moving up to second worst.

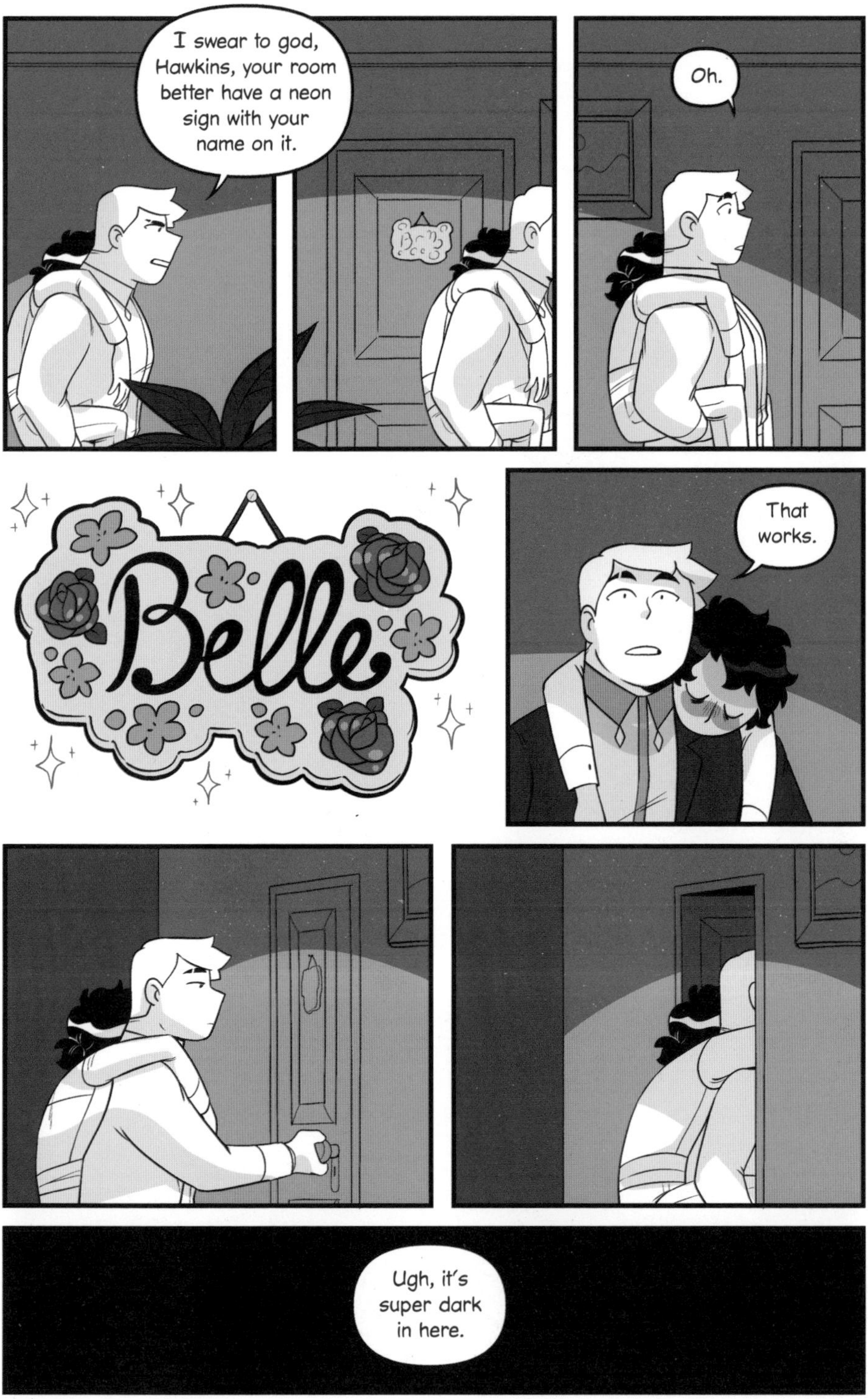
I swear to god, Hawkins, your room better have a neon sign with your name on it.
Oh.
Belle
That works.
Ugh, it's super dark in here.

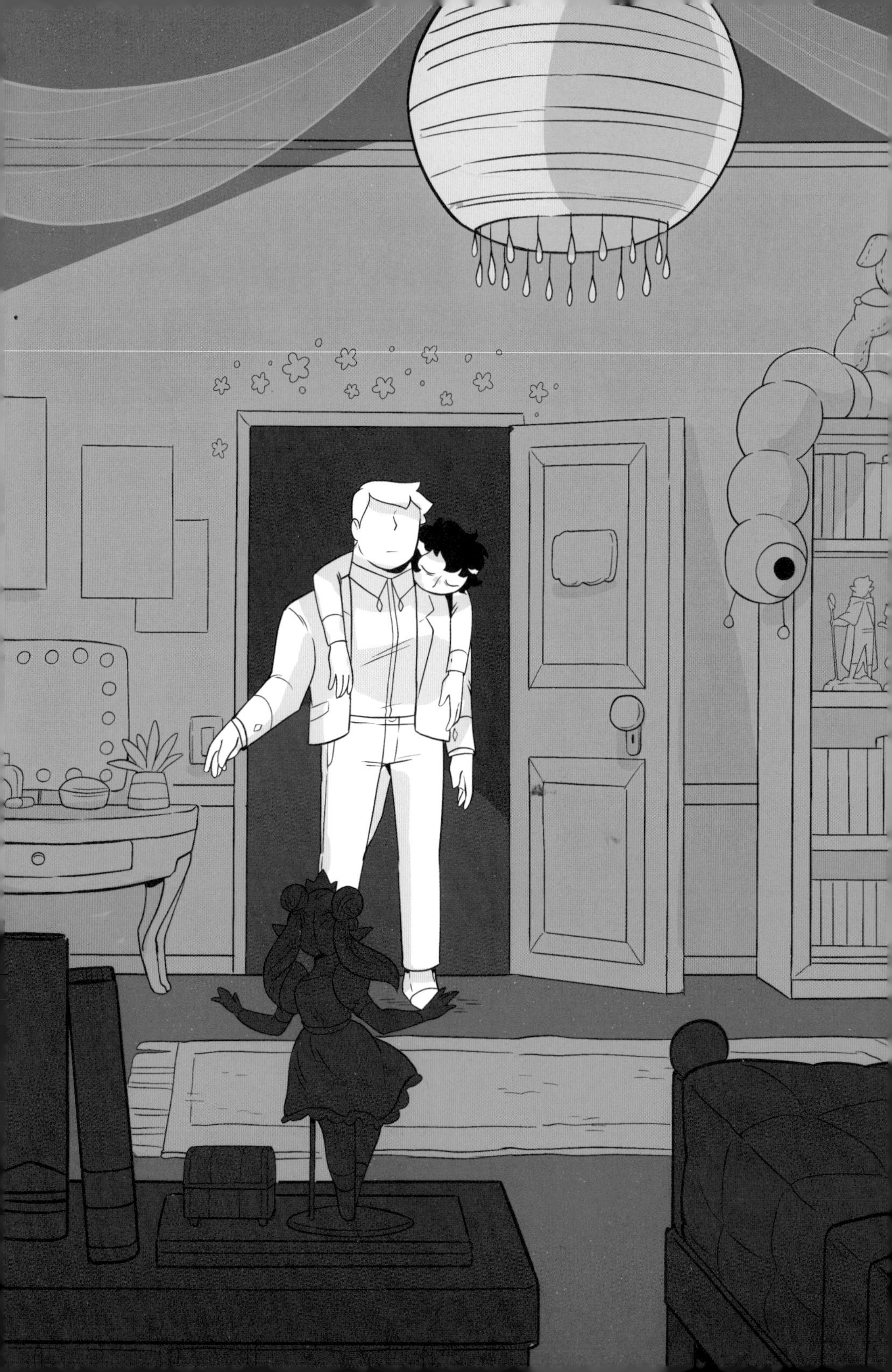

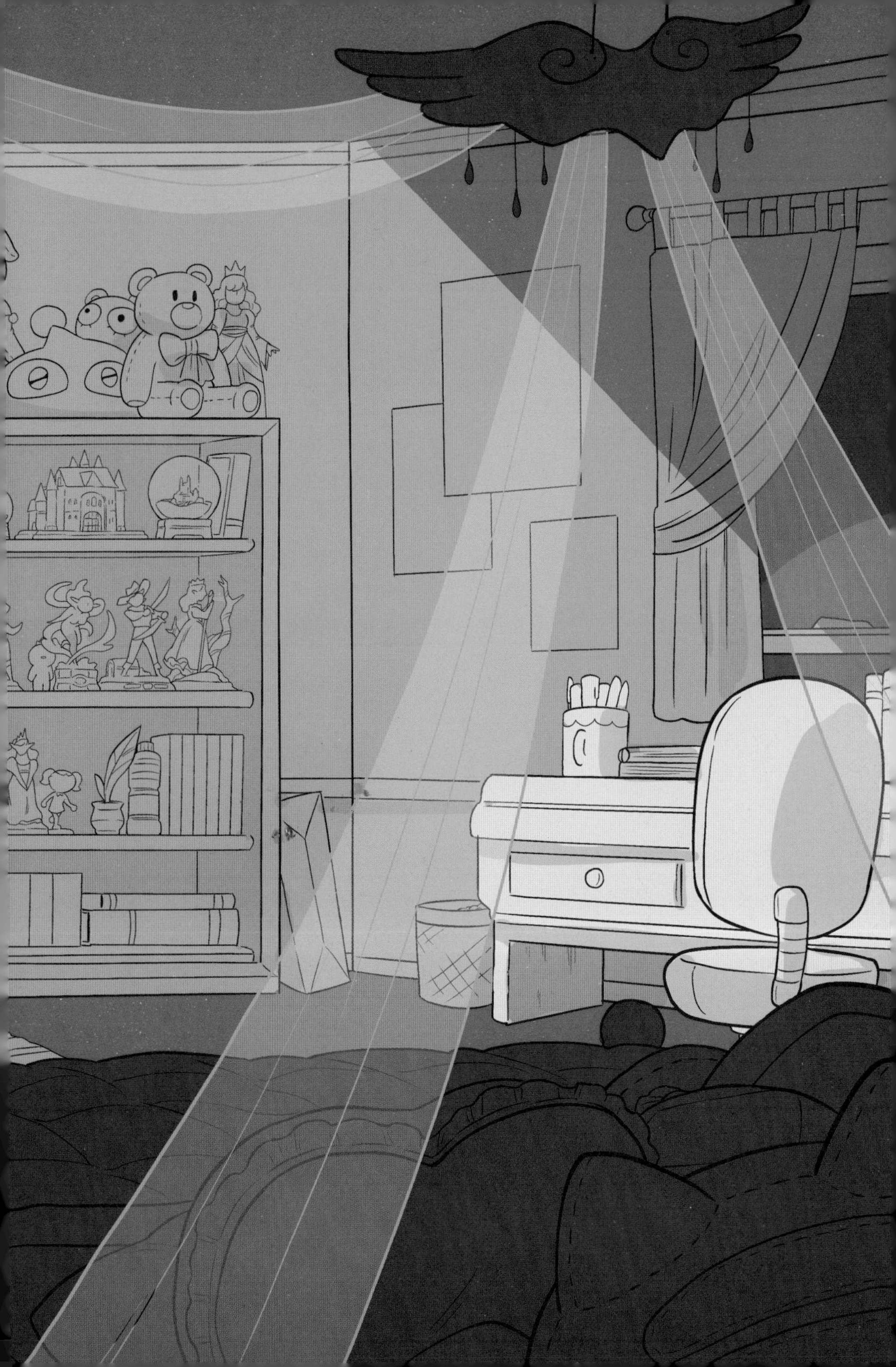

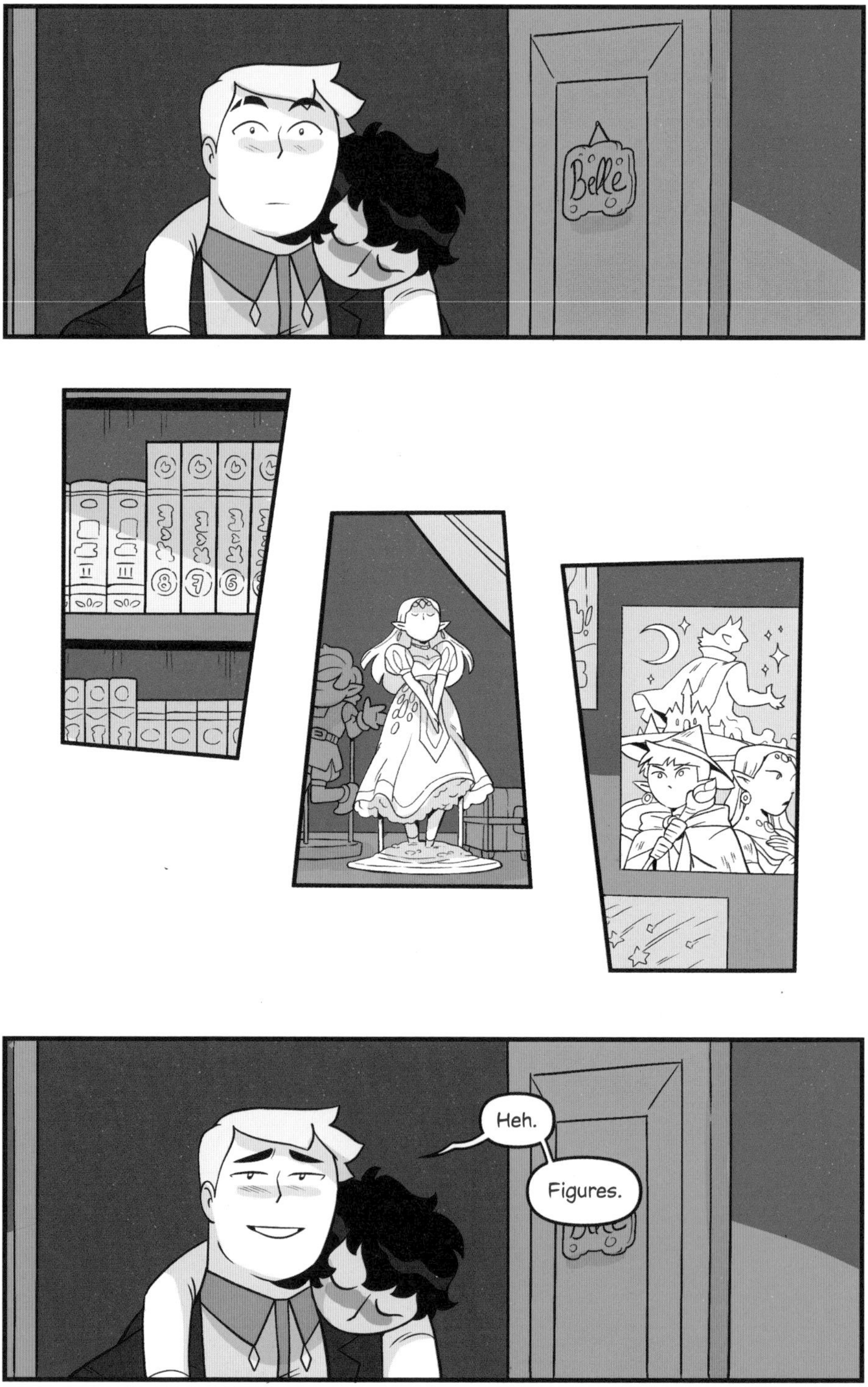
Belle
Heh.
Figures.

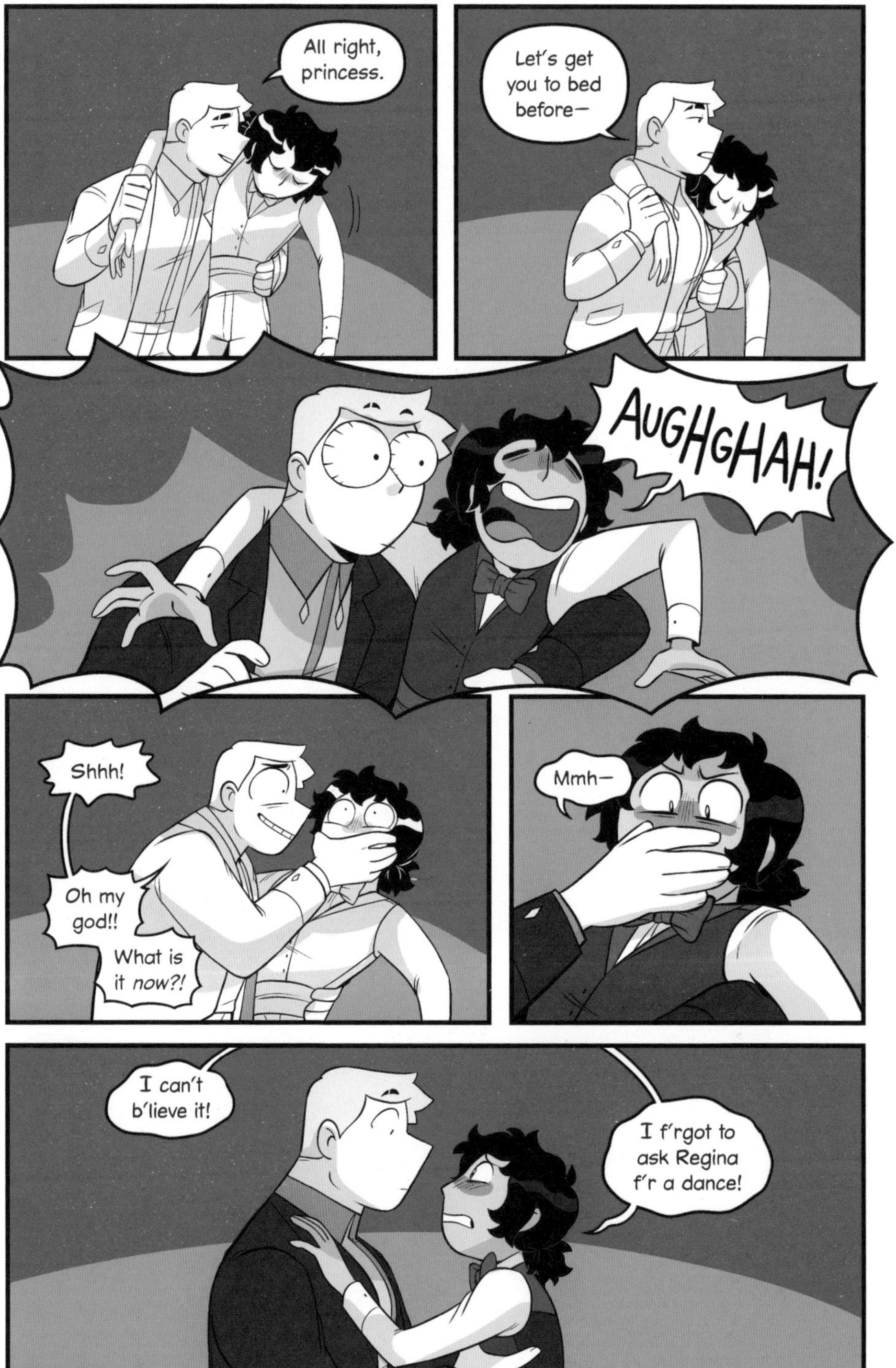
All right, princess.
Let's get you to bed before—
AUGHGHAH!
Shhh!
Oh my god!!
What is it *now?!*
Mmh—
I can't b'lieve it!
I f'rgot to ask Regina f'r a dance!

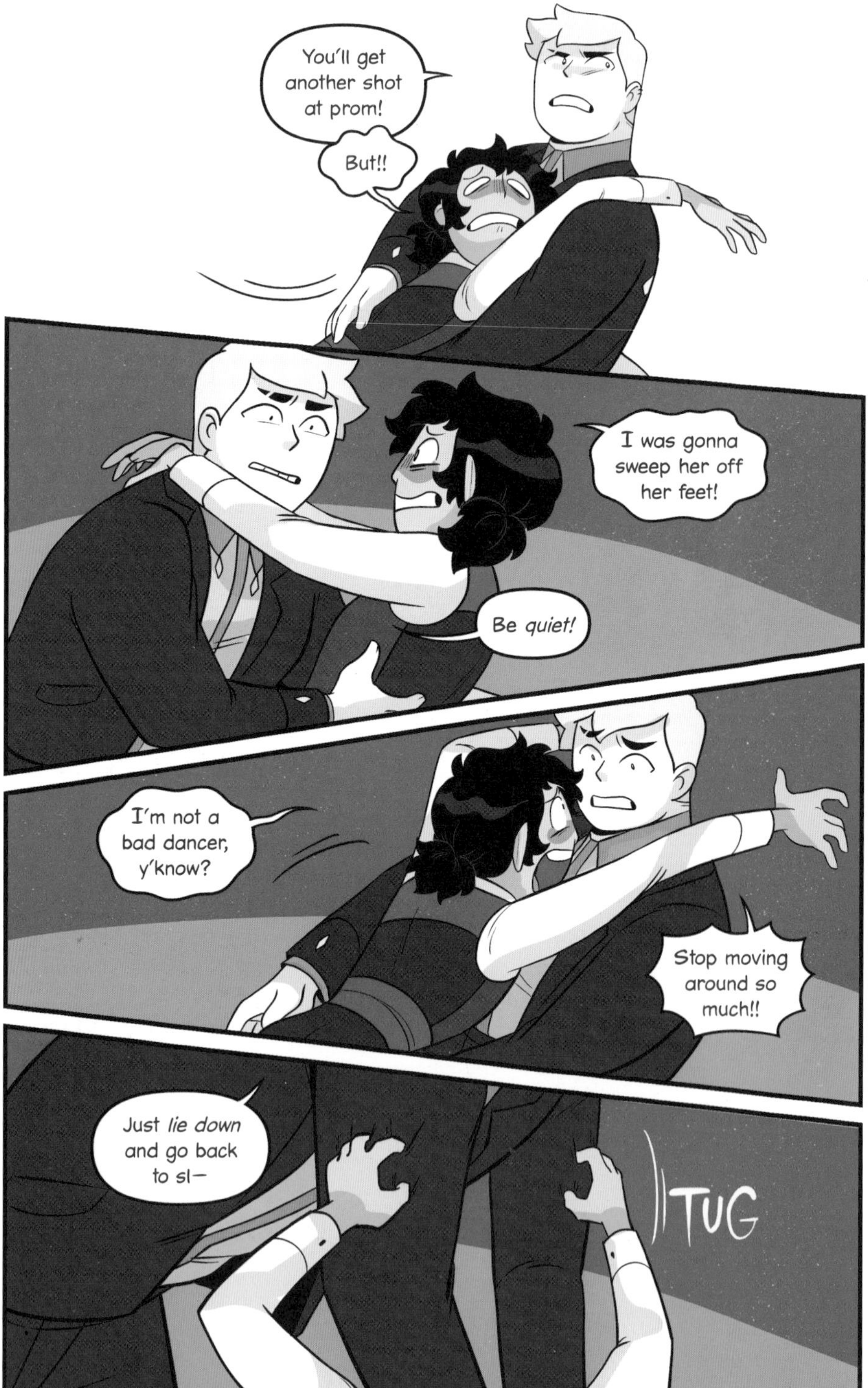
You'll get another shot at prom!
But!!
I was gonna sweep her off her feet!
Be *quiet!*
I'm not a bad dancer, y'know?
Stop moving around so much!!
Just *lie down* and go back to sl—
TUG

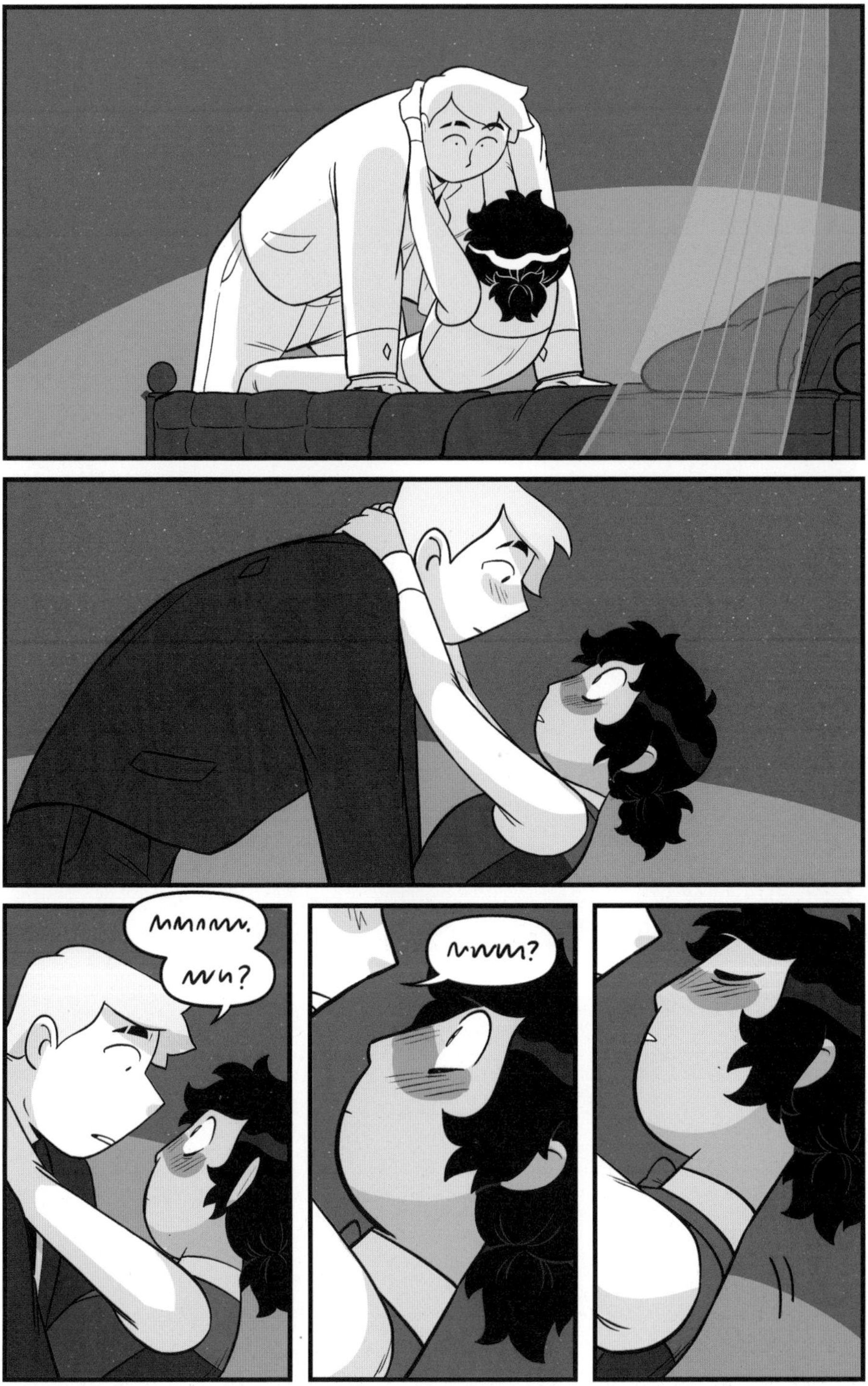
MMMMM.
MMM?
MMM?

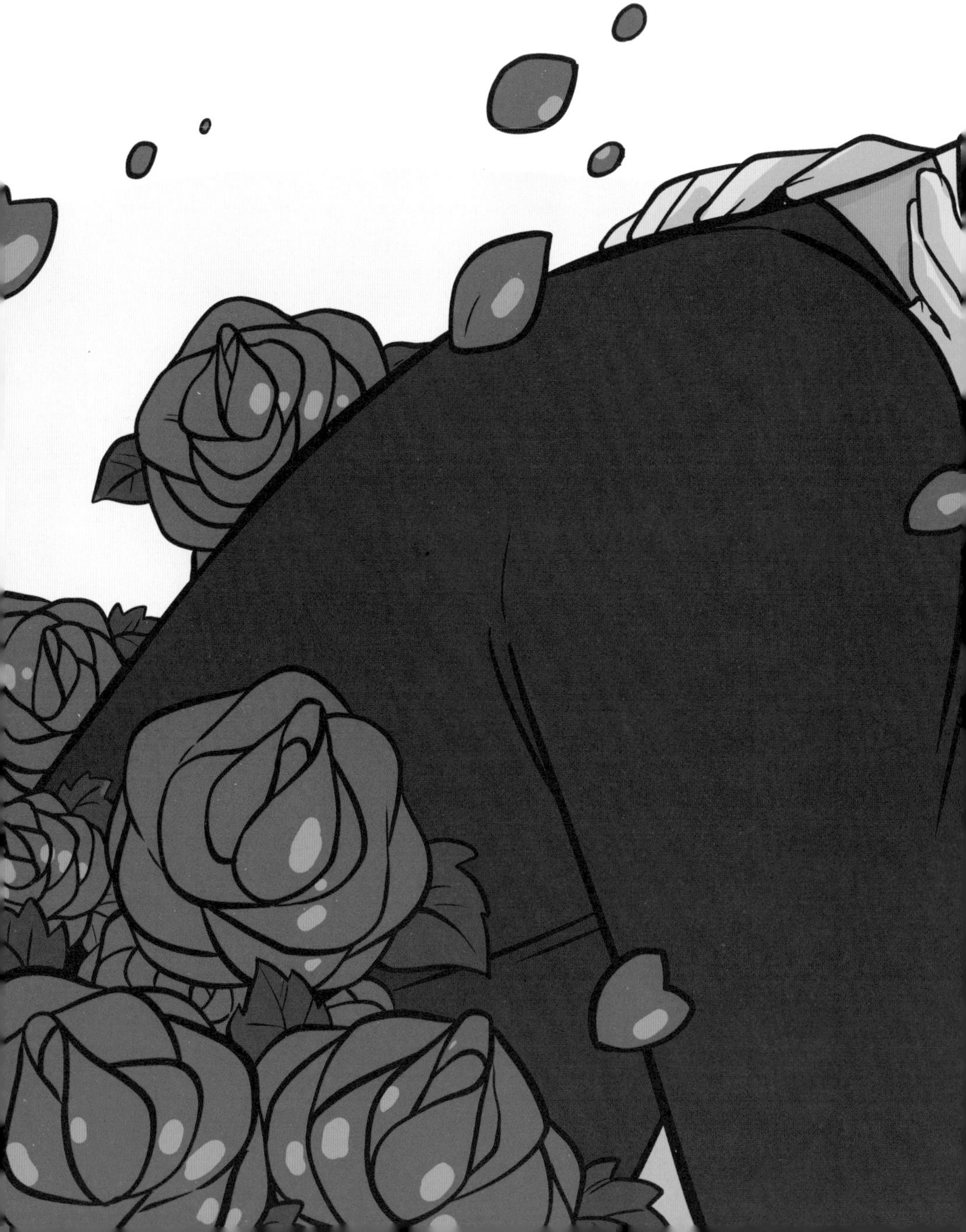

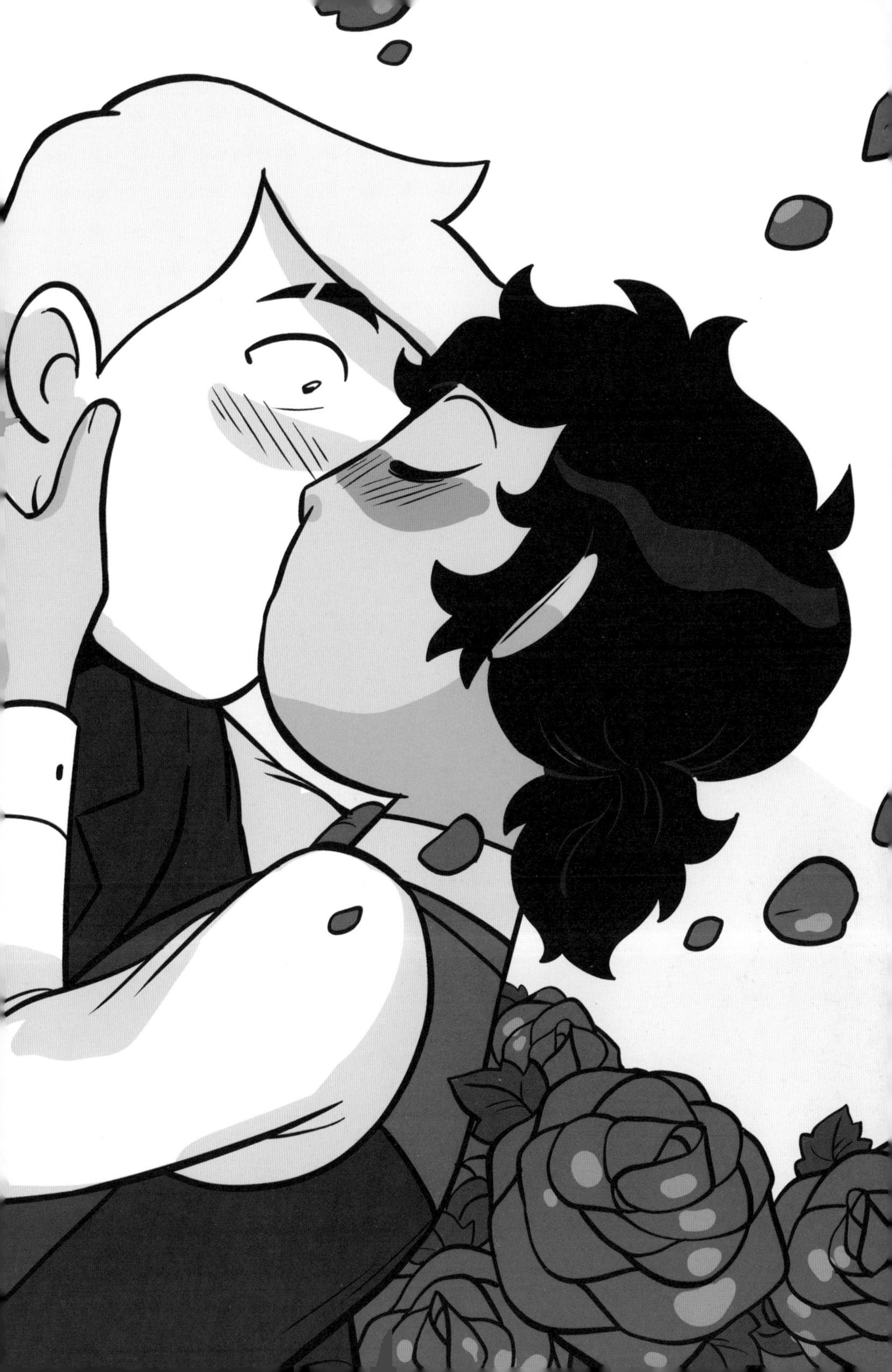

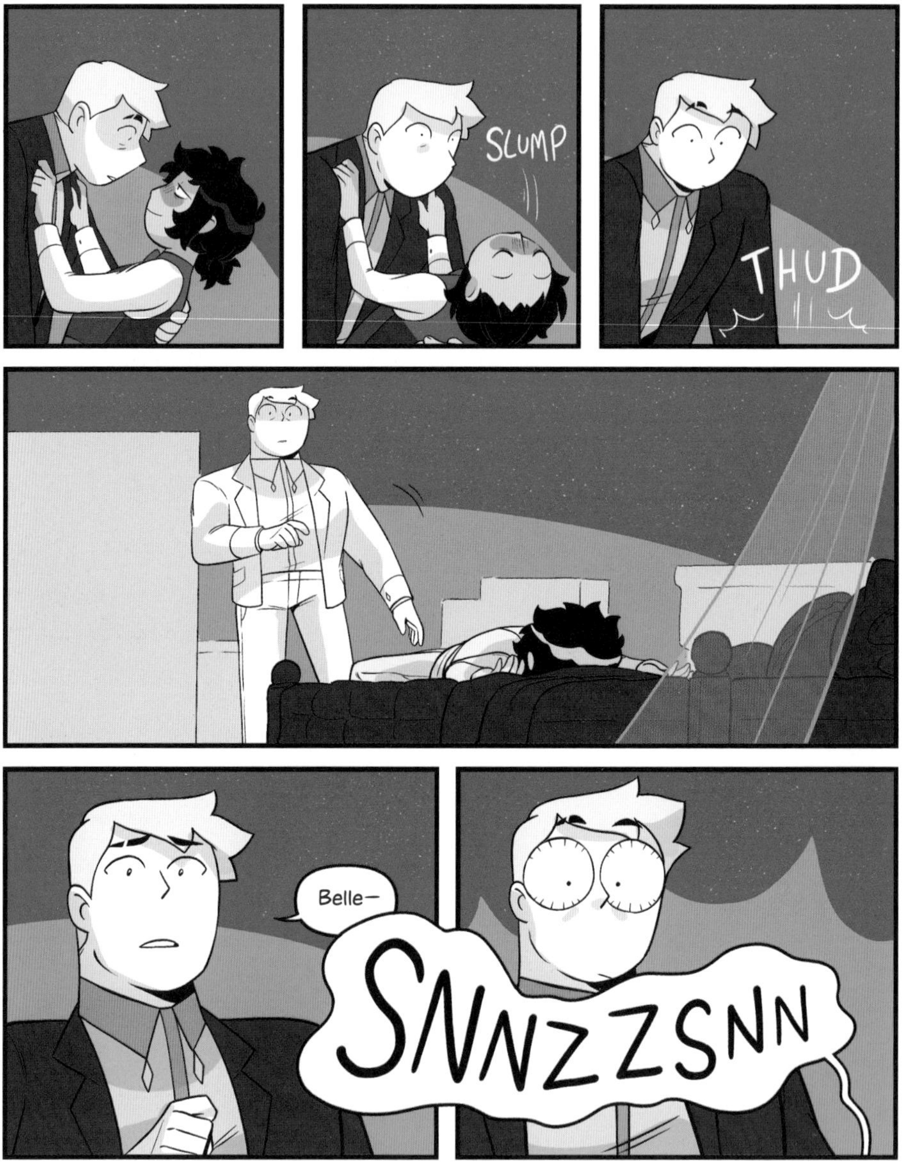
SLUMP
THUD
Belle—
SNZZSNN

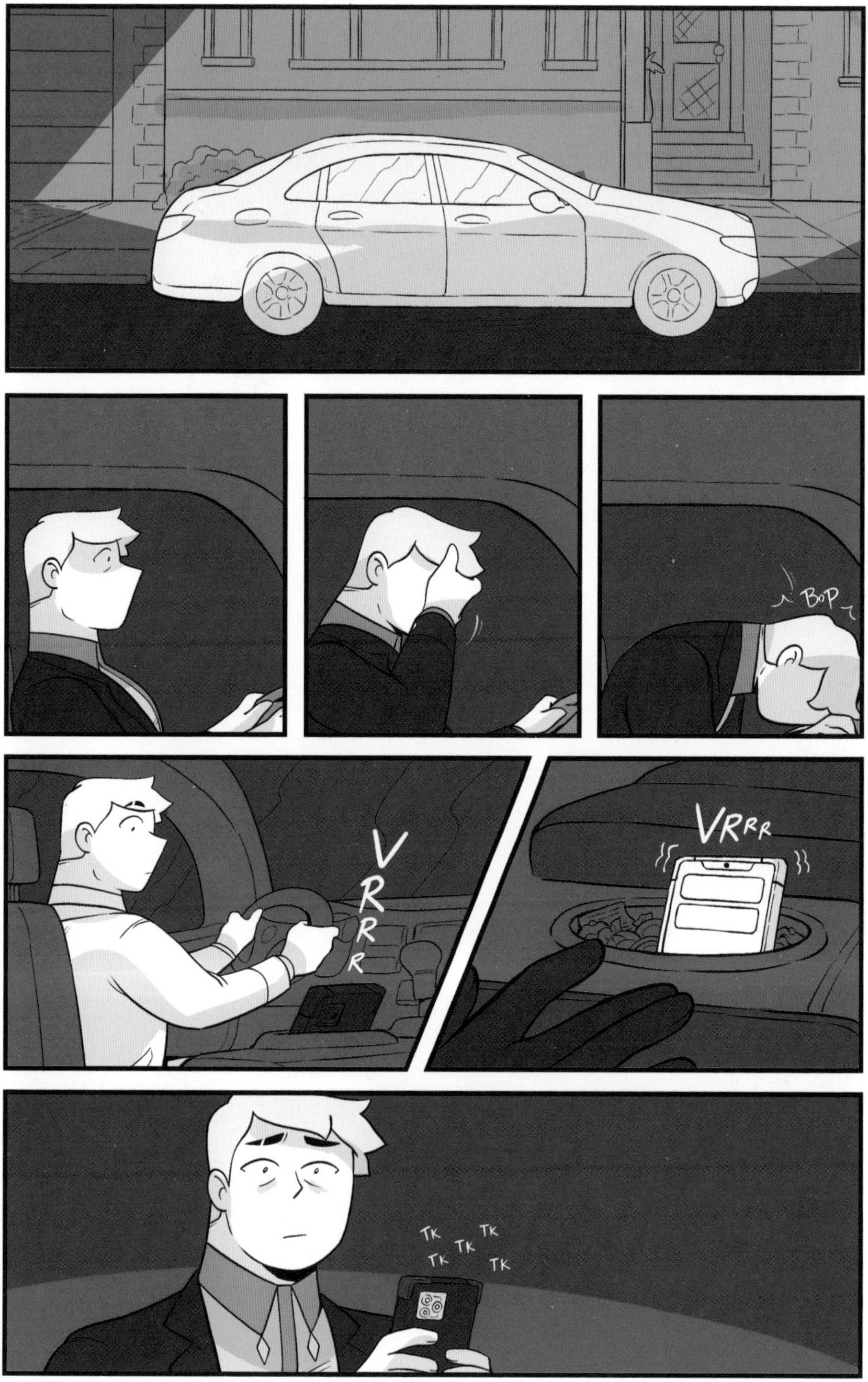
BOP
VRRR
VRRR
TK TK TK
TK TK

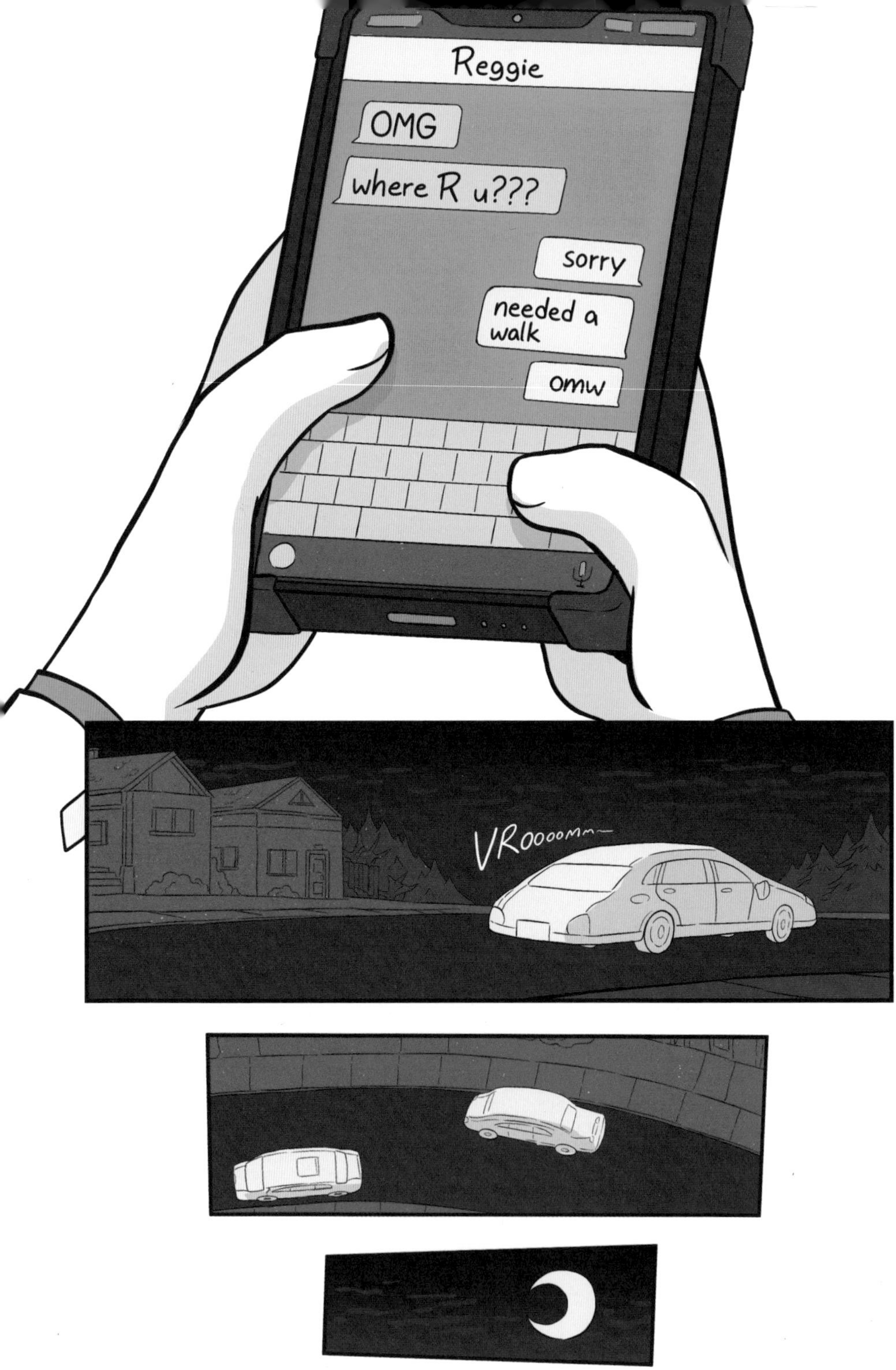
Reggie
OMG
where R u???
sorry
needed a walk
omw
VROoooMM~

CHAPTER

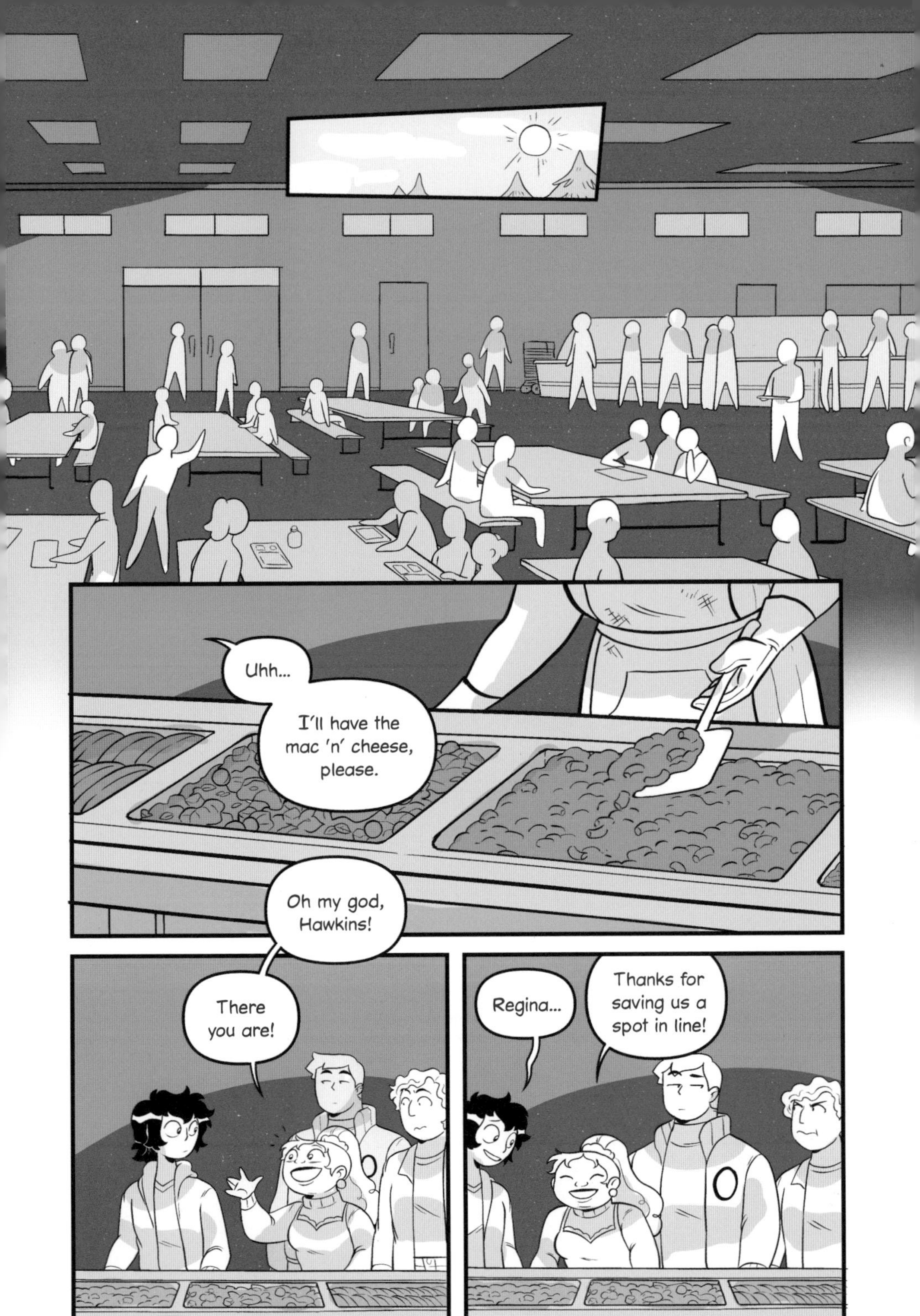
Uhh...
I'll have the mac 'n' cheese, please.
Oh my god, Hawkins!
There you are!
Regina...
Thanks for saving us a spot in line!

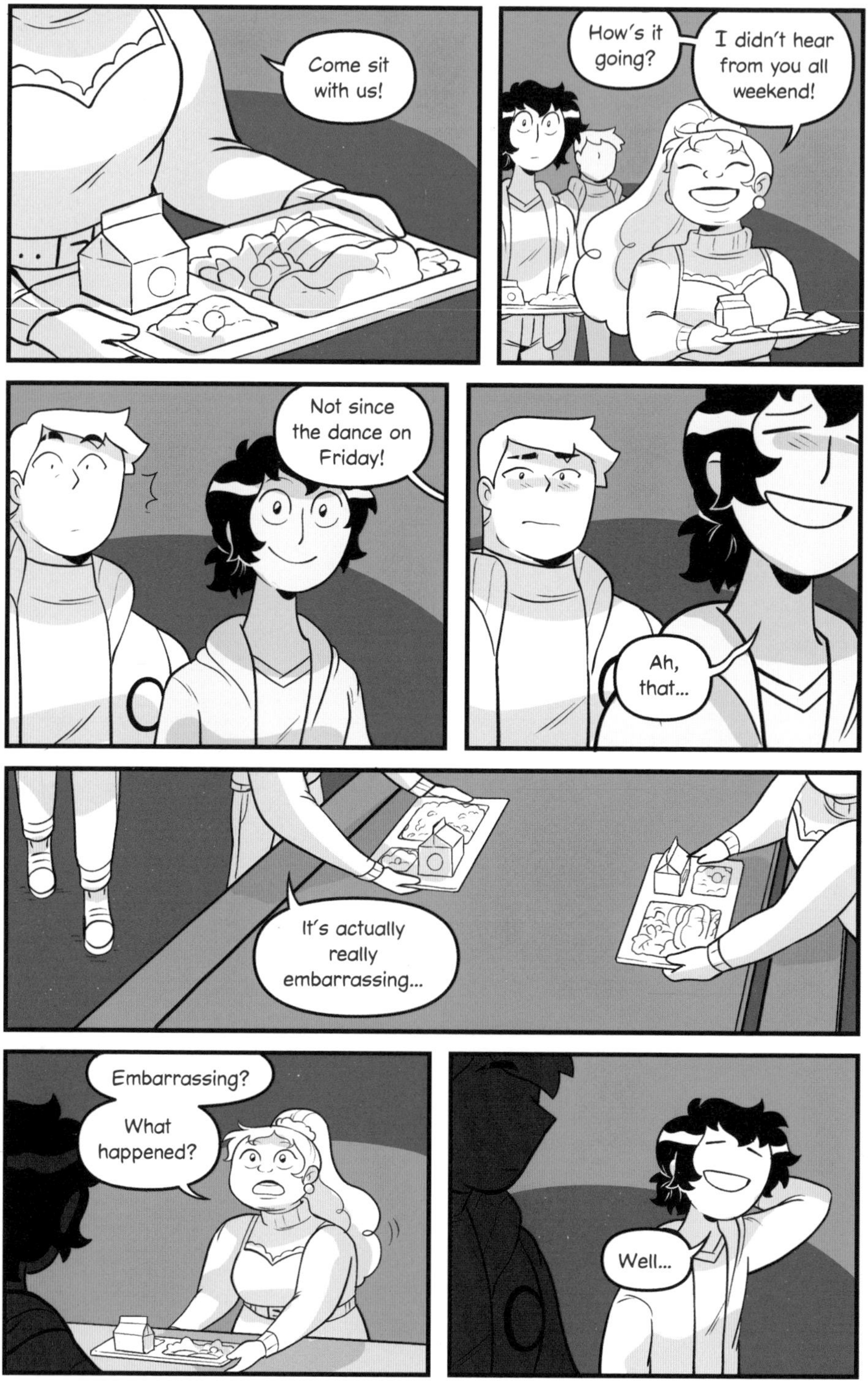
Come sit with us!
How's it going?
I didn't hear from you all weekend!
Not since the dance on Friday!
Ah, that...
It's actually really embarrassing...
Embarrassing?
What happened?
Well...

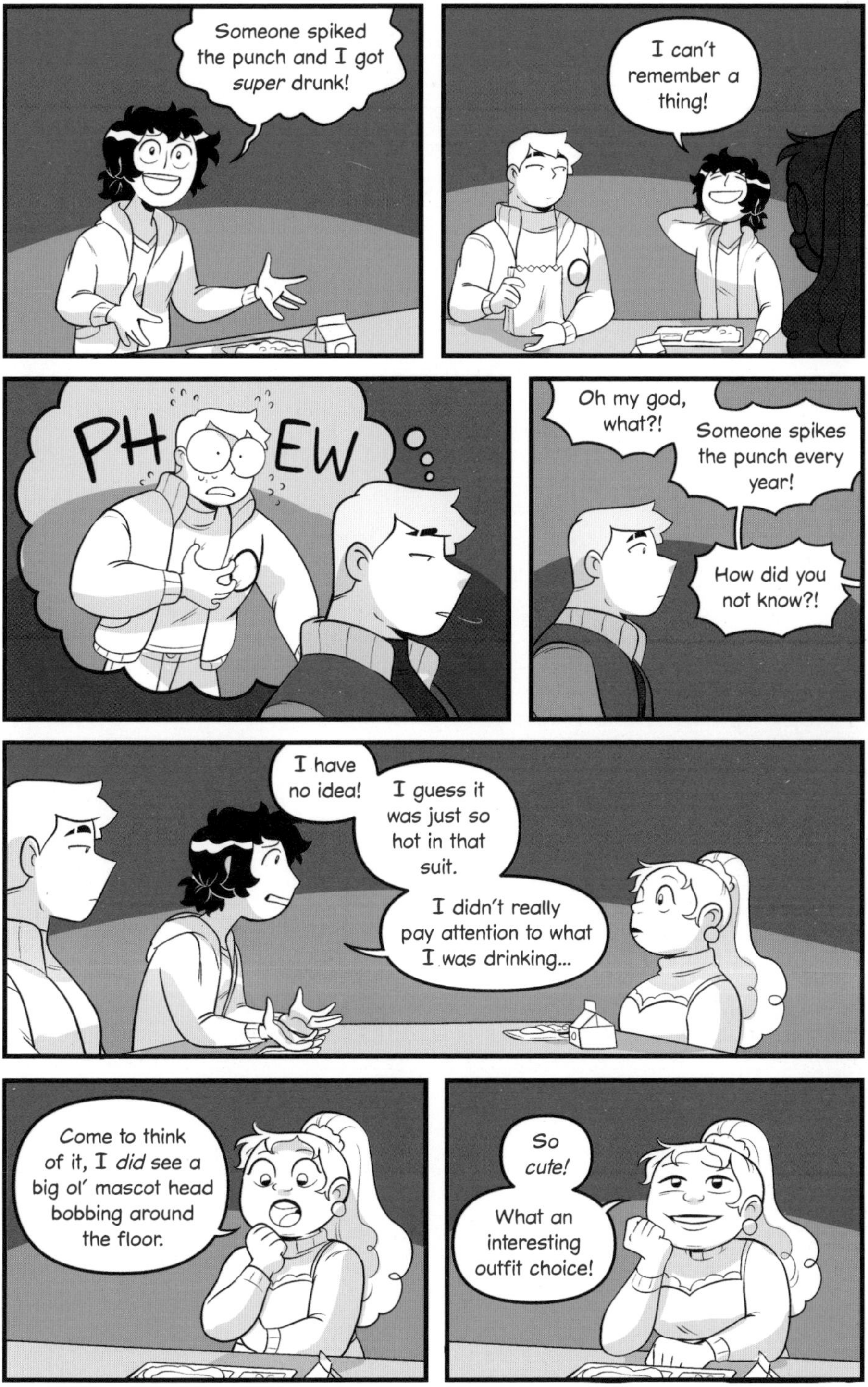
Someone spiked the punch and I got *super* drunk!
I can't remember a thing!
PHEW
Oh my god, what?!
Someone spikes the punch every year!
How did you not know?!
I have no idea!
I guess it was just so hot in that suit.
I didn't really pay attention to what I was drinking...
Come to think of it, I *did* see a big ol' mascot head bobbing around the floor.
So *cute!*
What an interesting outfit choice!

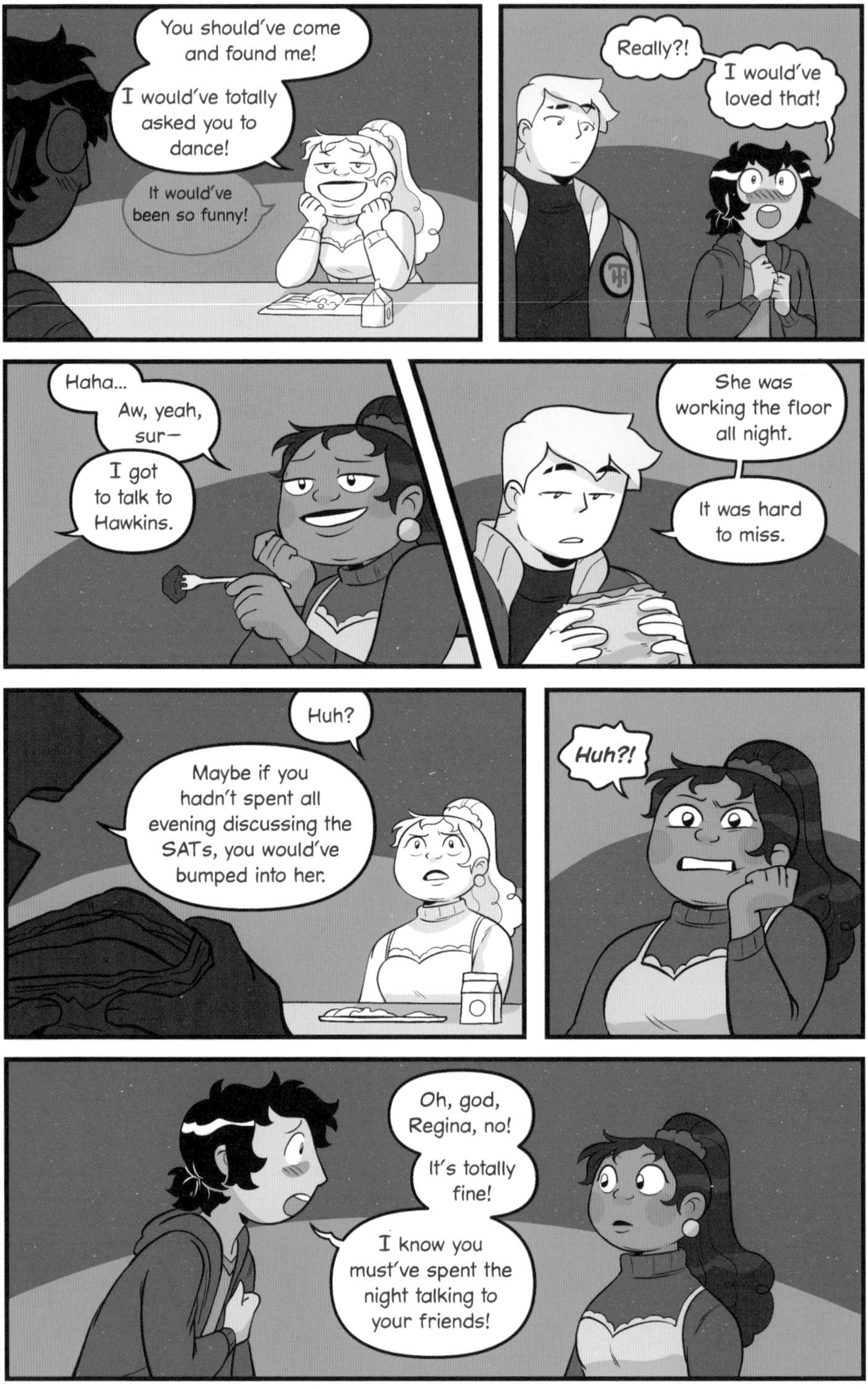
You should've come and found me!
I would've totally asked you to dance!
It would've been so funny!
Really?!
I would've loved that!
Haha...
Aw, yeah, sur—
I got to talk to Hawkins.
She was working the floor all night.
It was hard to miss.
Huh?
Maybe if you hadn't spent all evening discussing the SATs, you would've bumped into her.
Huh?!
Oh, god, Regina, no!
It's totally fine!
I know you must've spent the night talking to your friends!

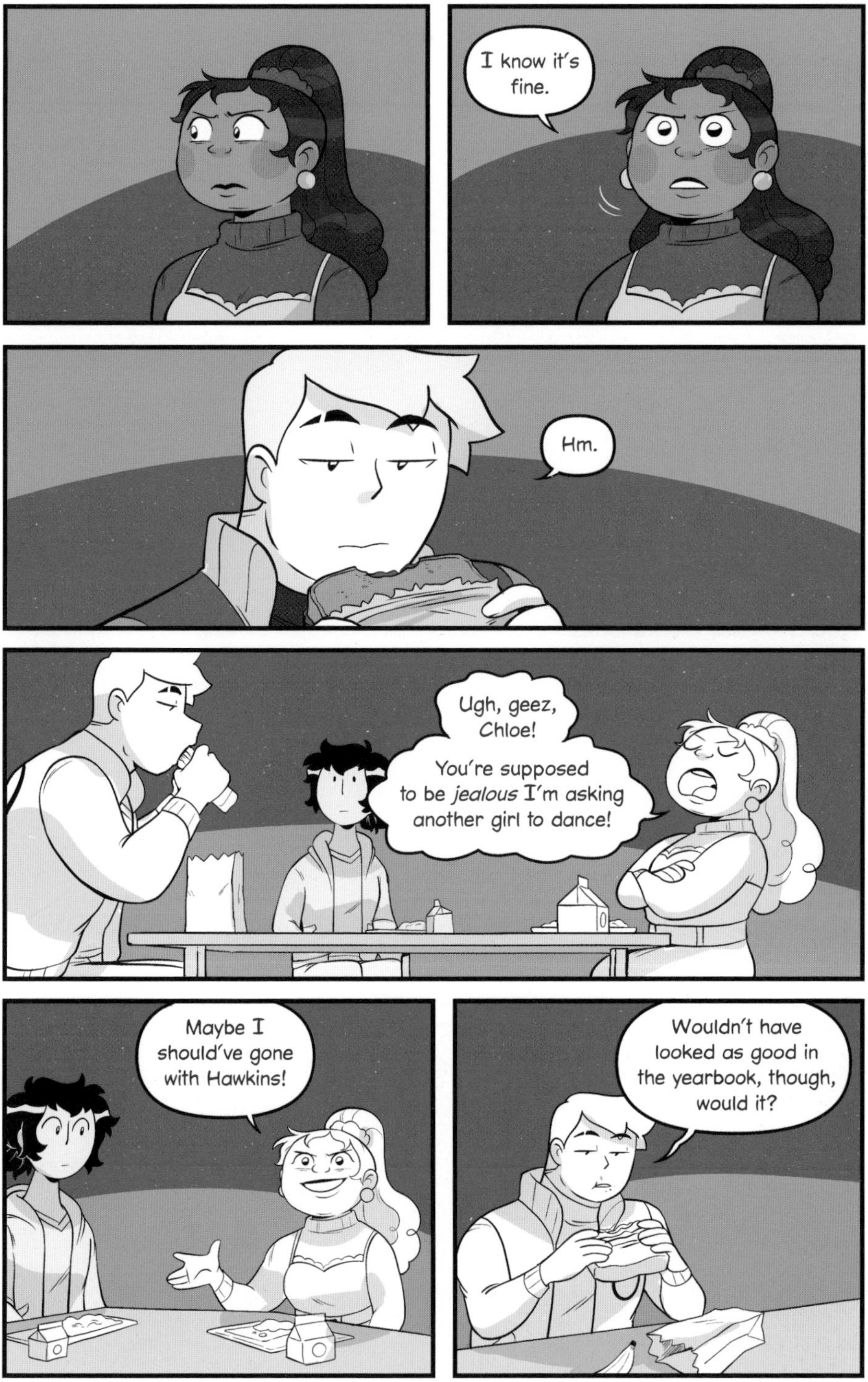
I know it's fine.
Hm.
Ugh, geez, Chloe!
You're supposed to be *jealous* I'm asking another girl to dance!
Maybe I should've gone with Hawkins!
Wouldn't have looked as good in the yearbook, though, would it?

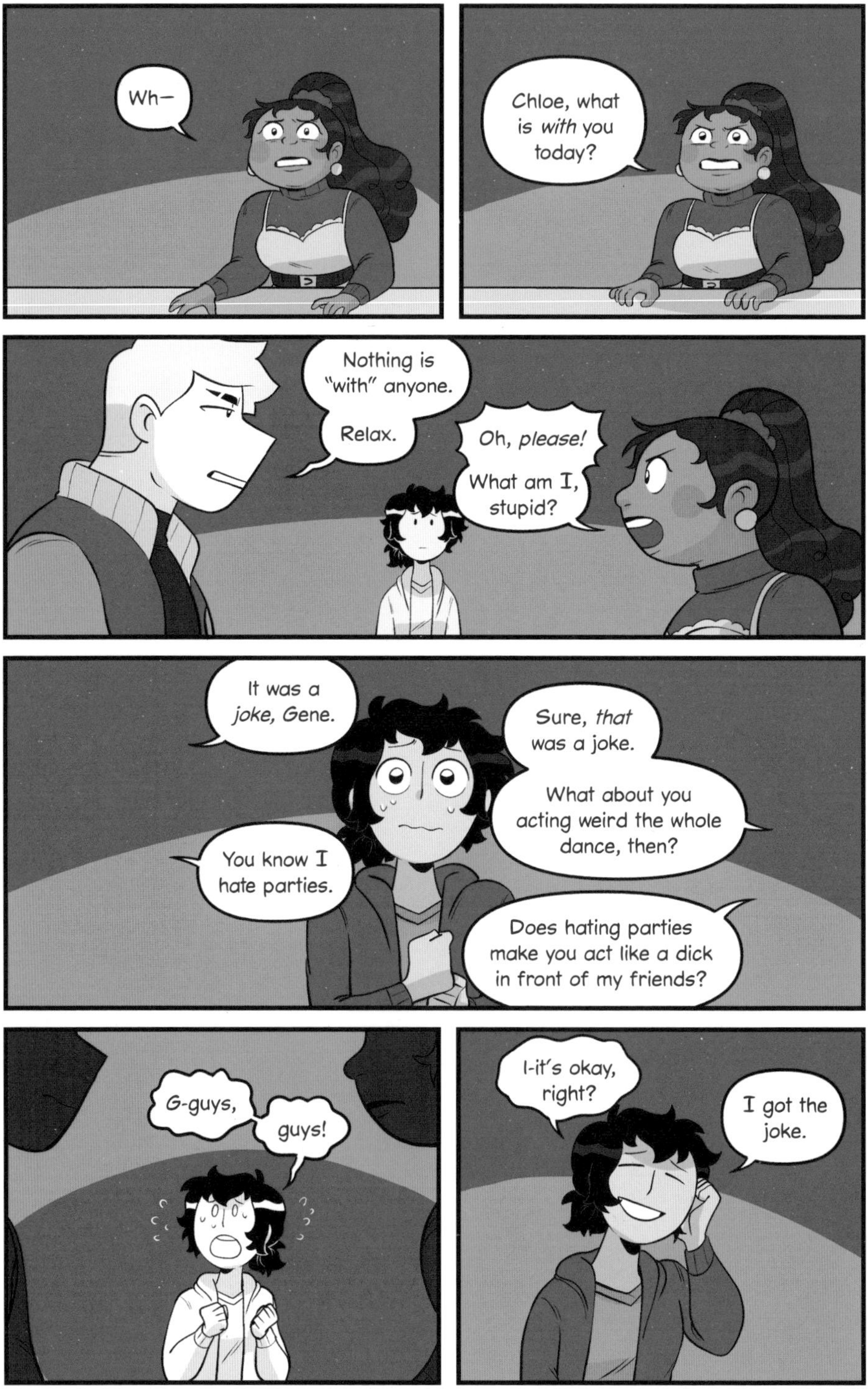

Wh—
Chloe, what is *with* you today?
Nothing is "with" anyone.
Relax.
Oh, please!
What am I, stupid?
It was a *joke,* Gene.
Sure, *that* was a joke.
What about you acting weird the whole dance, then?
You know I hate parties.
Does hating parties make you act like a dick in front of my friends?
G-guys,
guys!
I-it's okay, right?
I got the joke.

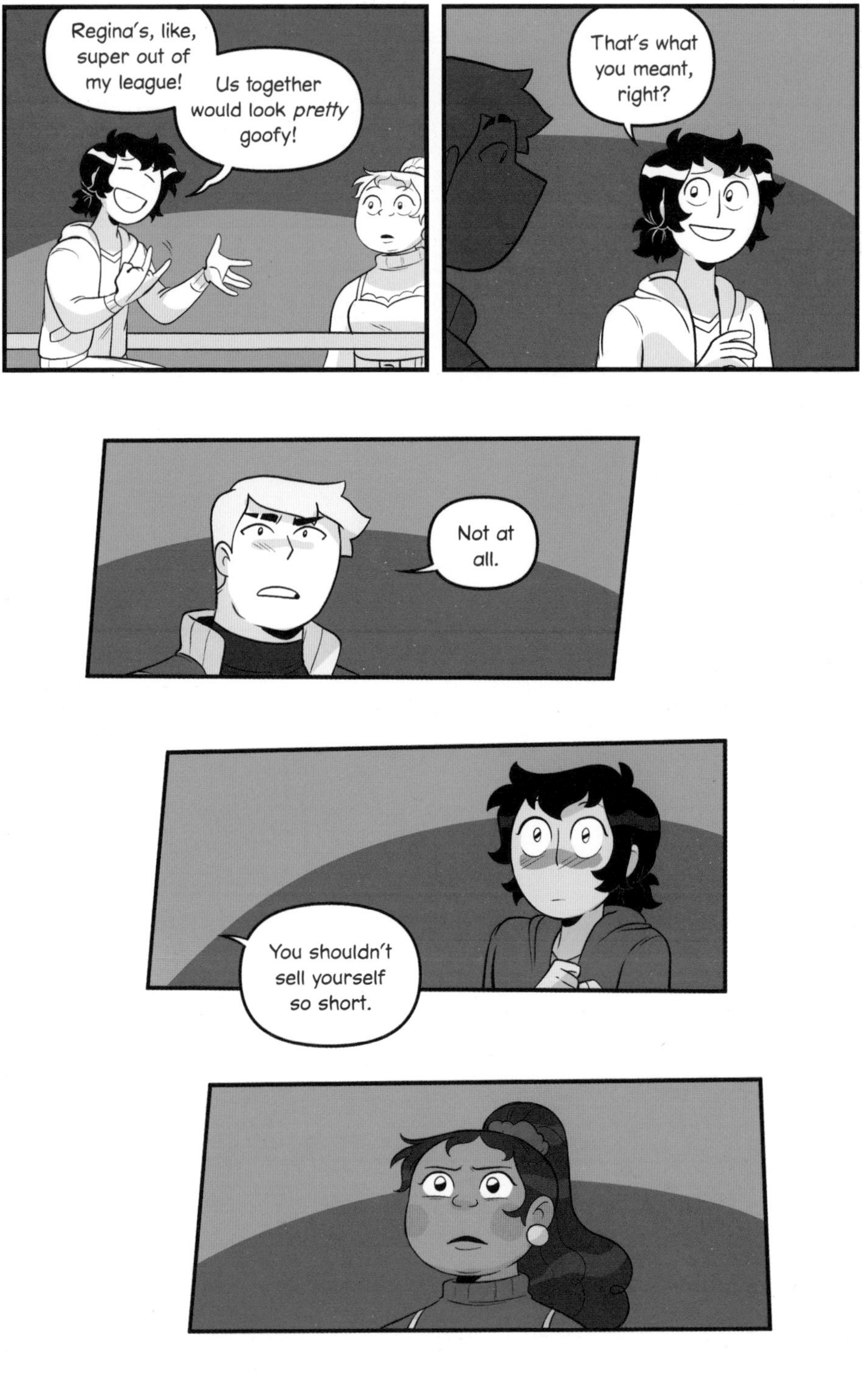
Regina's, like, super out of my league!
Us together would look *pretty* goofy!
That's what you meant, right?
Not at all.
You shouldn't sell yourself so short.

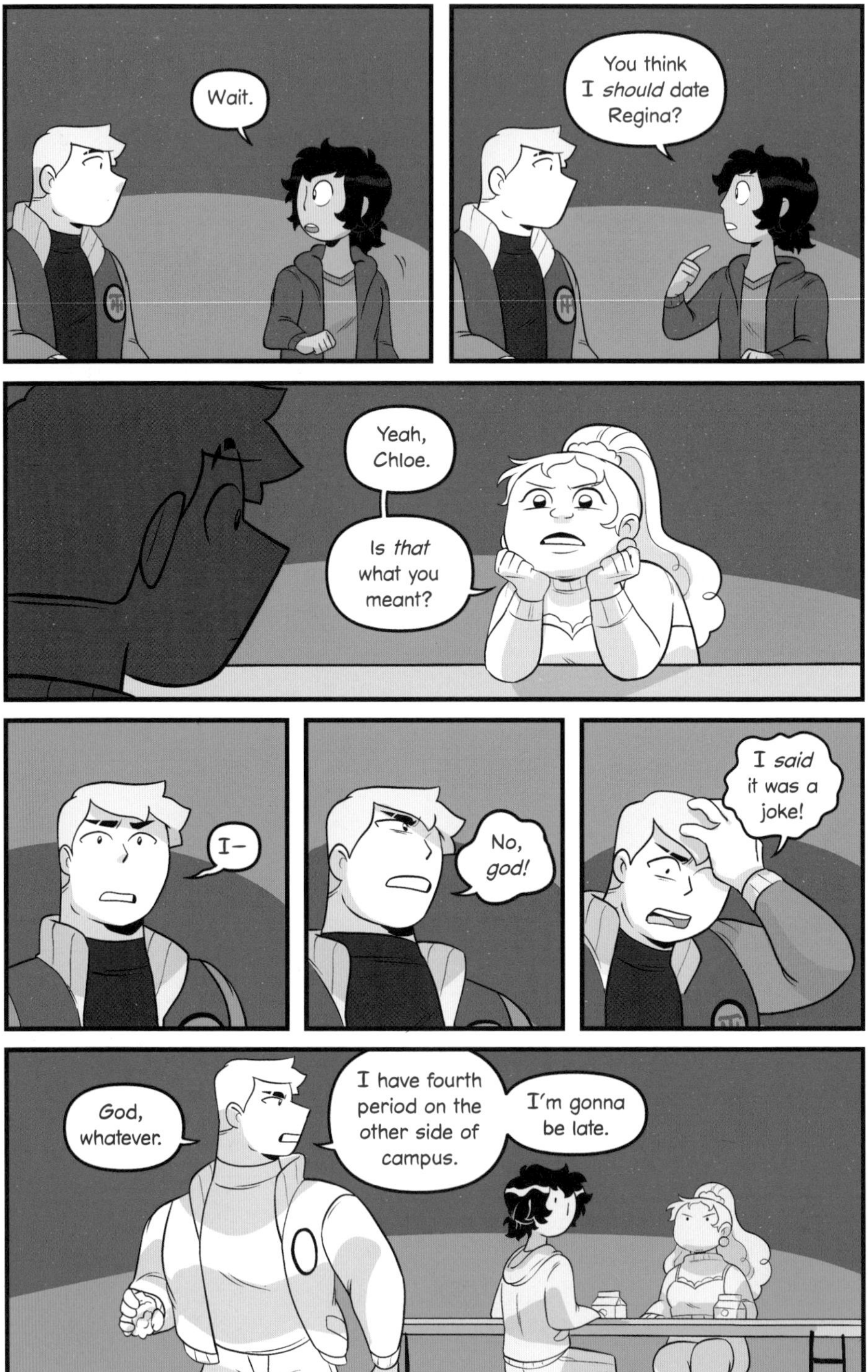
Wait.
You think I *should* date Regina?
Yeah, Chloe.
Is *that* what you meant?
I—
No, *god!*
I *said* it was a joke!
God, whatever.
I have fourth period on the other side of campus.
I'm gonna be late.

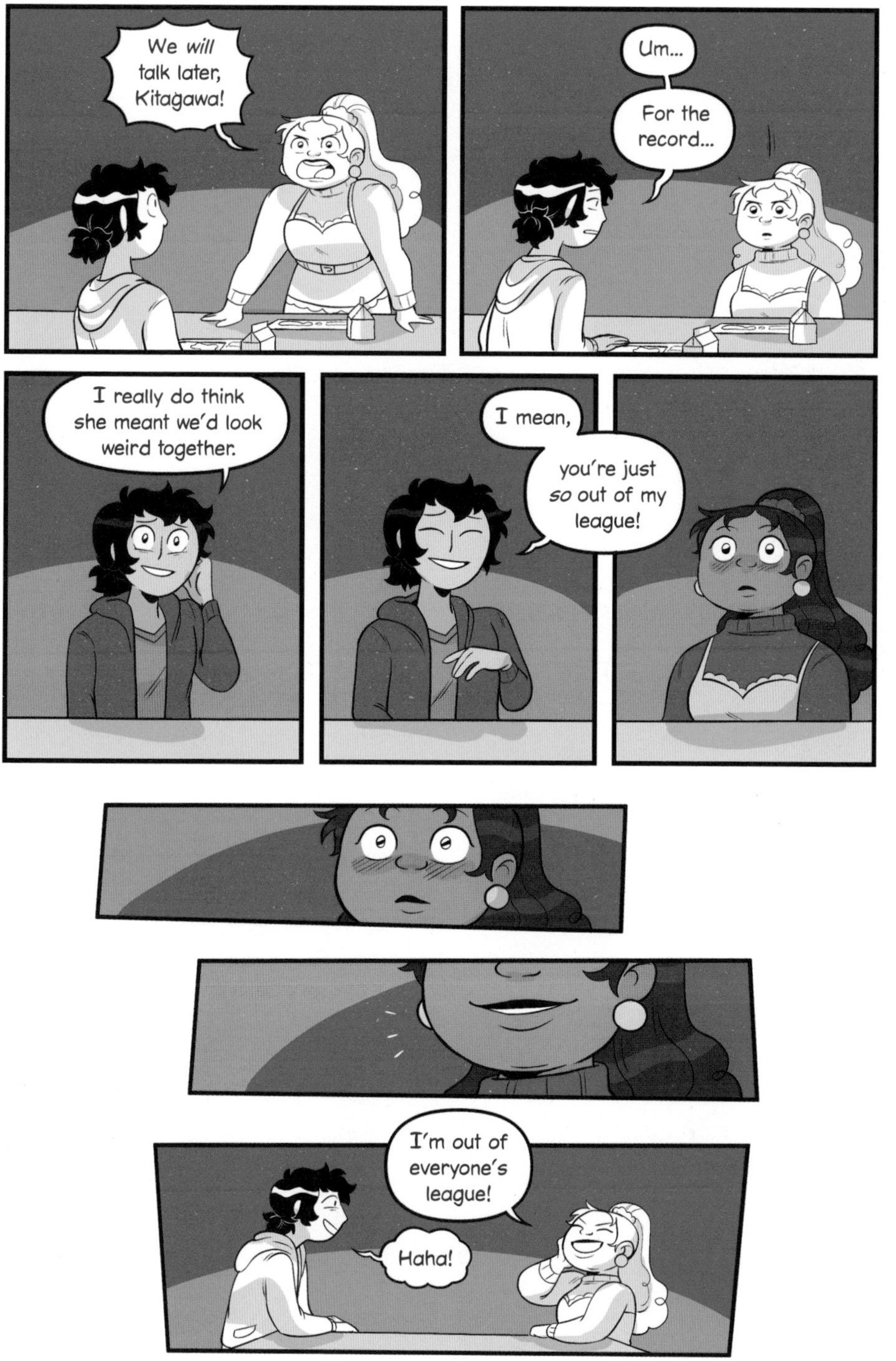
We *will* talk later, Kitagawa!
Um...
For the record...
I really do think she meant we'd look weird together.
I mean,
you're just *so* out of my league!
I'm out of everyone's league!
Haha!

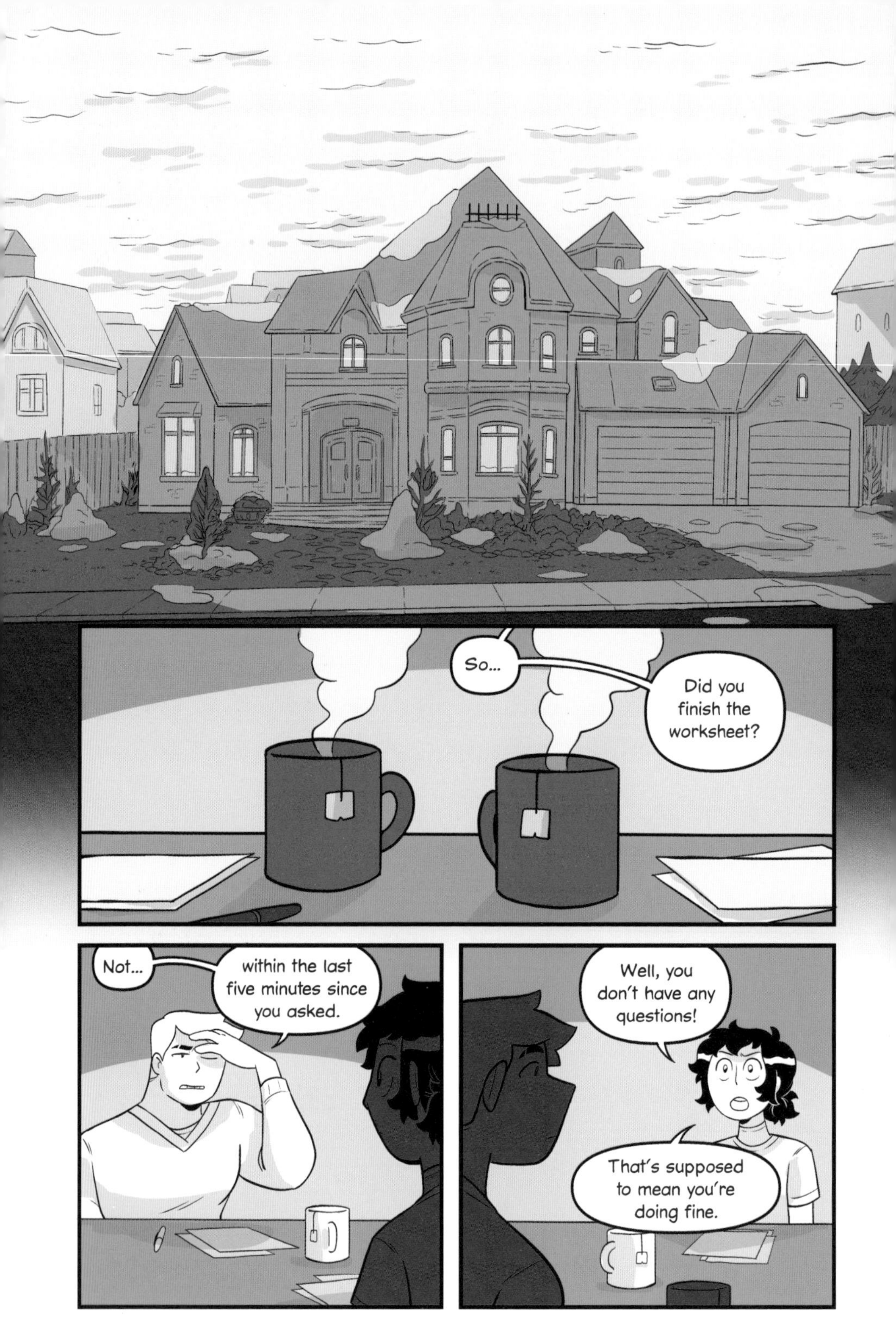
So...
Did you finish the worksheet?
Not...
within the last five minutes since you asked.
Well, you don't have any questions!
That's supposed to mean you're doing fine.

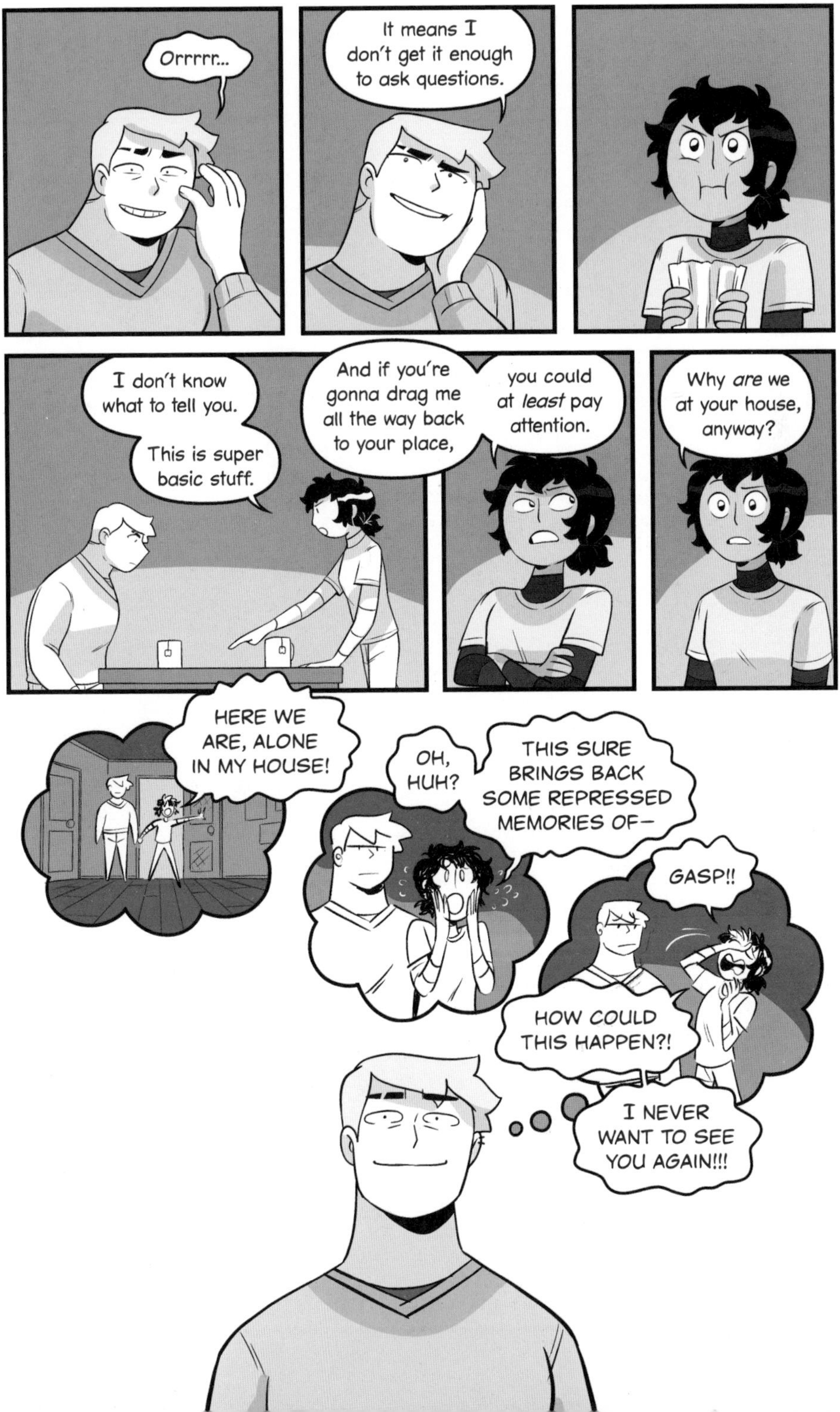
Orrrrr...
It means I don't get it enough to ask questions.
I don't know what to tell you.
This is super basic stuff.
And if you're gonna drag me all the way back to your place,
you could at *least* pay attention.
Why *are* we at your house, anyway?
HERE WE ARE, ALONE IN MY HOUSE!
OH, HUH?
THIS SURE BRINGS BACK SOME REPRESSED MEMORIES OF—
GASP!!
HOW COULD THIS HAPPEN?!
I NEVER WANT TO SEE YOU AGAIN!!!

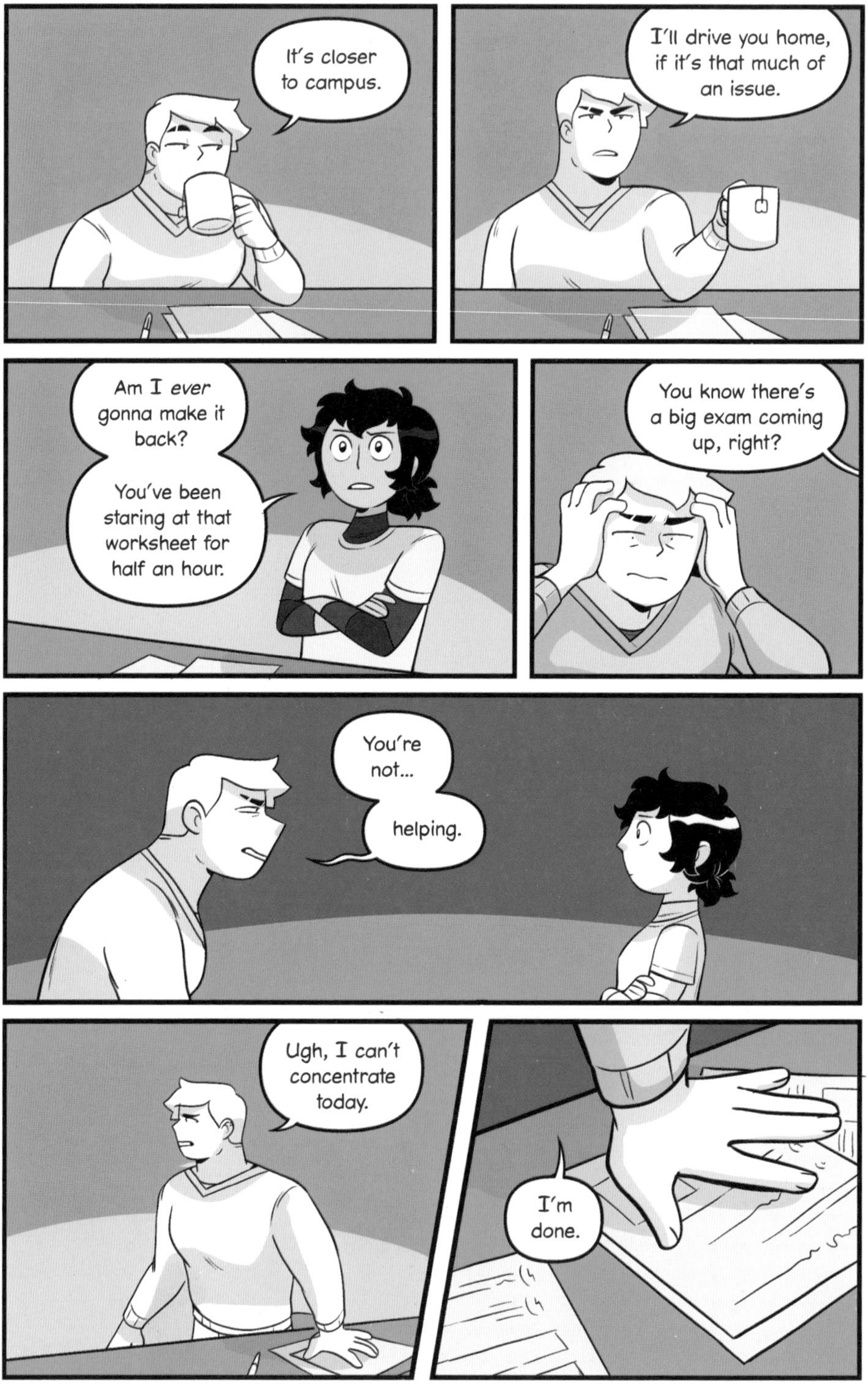
It's closer to campus.
I'll drive you home, if it's that much of an issue.
Am I *ever* gonna make it back?
You've been staring at that worksheet for half an hour.
You know there's a big exam coming up, right?
You're not...
helping.
Ugh, I can't concentrate today.
I'm done.

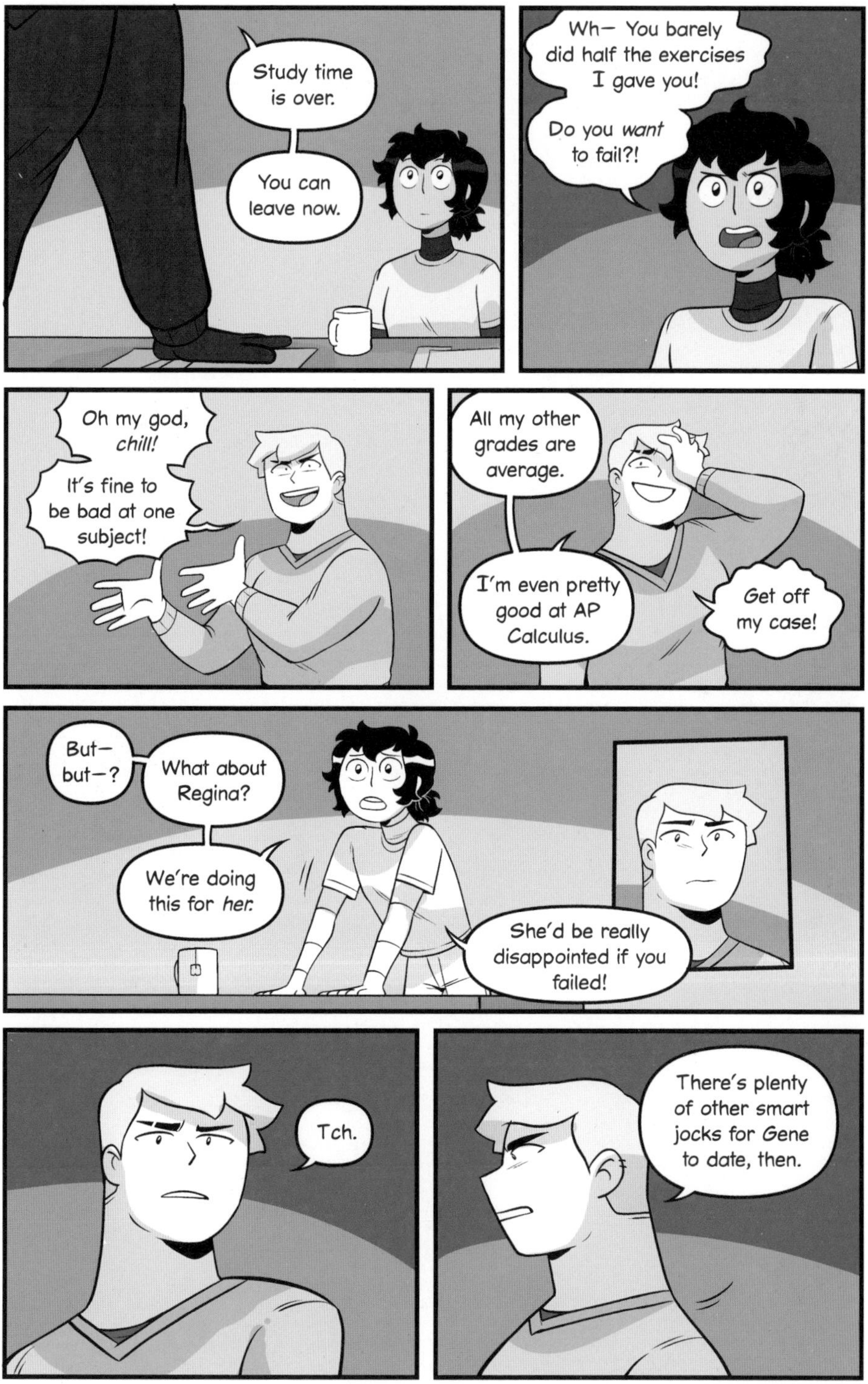

Study time is over.
You can leave now.
Wh— You barely did half the exercises I gave you!
Do you *want* to fail?!
Oh my god, *chill!*
It's fine to be bad at one subject!
All my other grades are average.
I'm even pretty good at AP Calculus.
Get off my case!
But— but—?
What about Regina?
We're doing this for *her.*
She'd be really disappointed if you failed!
Tch.
There's plenty of other smart jocks for Gene to date, then.

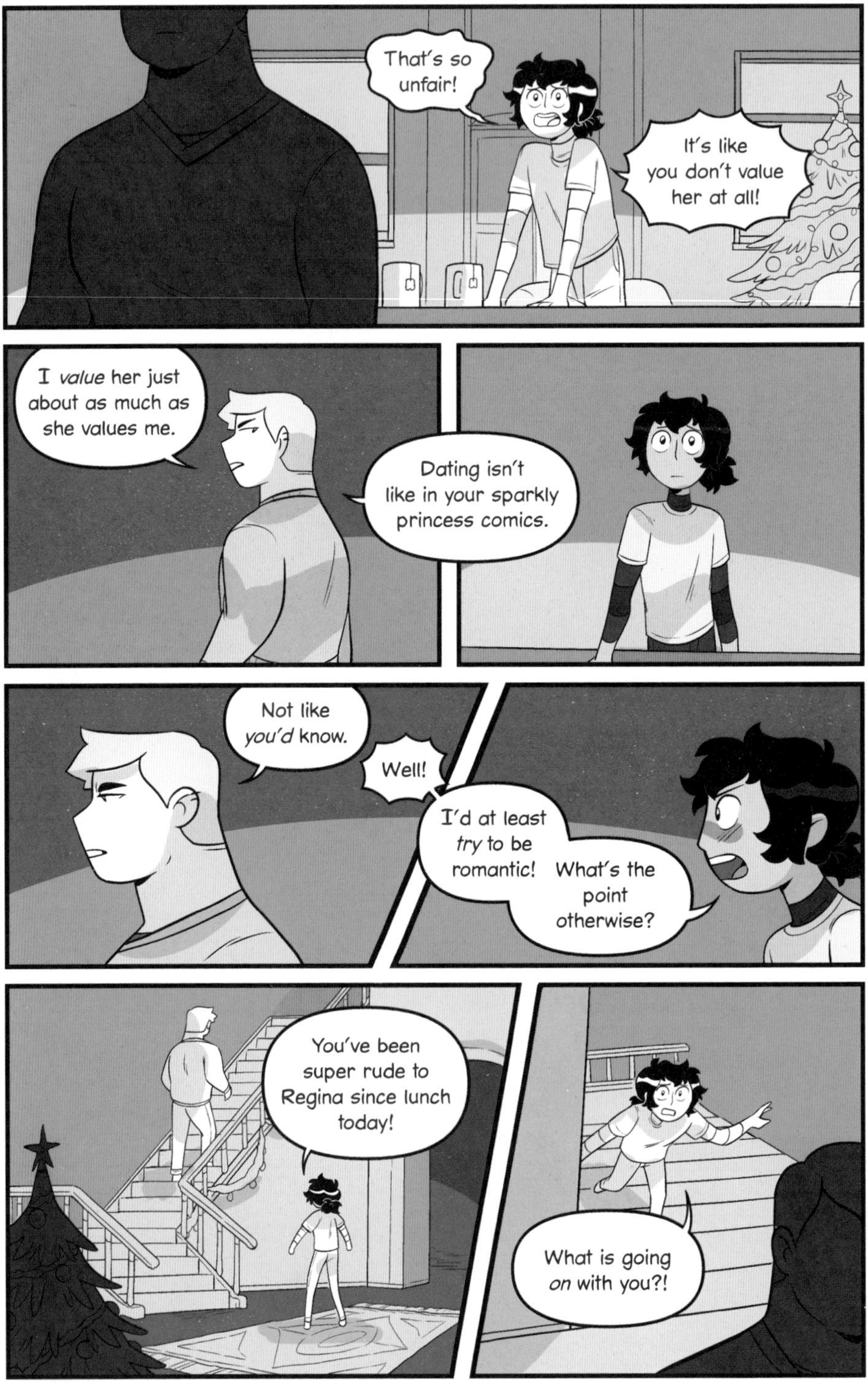
That's so unfair!
It's like you don't value her at all!
I *value* her just about as much as she values me.
Dating isn't like in your sparkly princess comics.
Not like *you'd* know.
Well!
I'd at least *try* to be romantic!
What's the point otherwise?
You've been super rude to Regina since lunch today!
What is going *on* with you?!

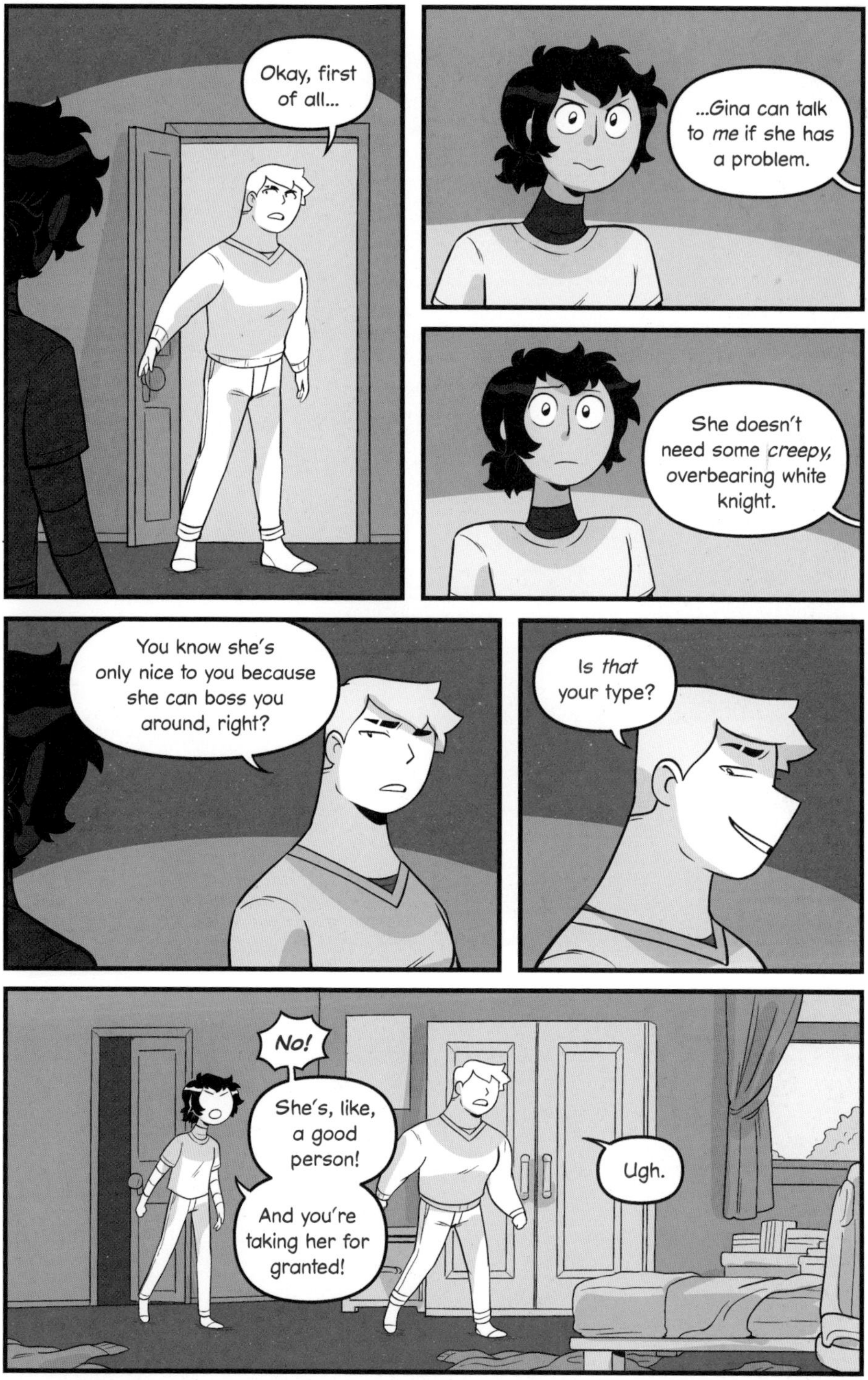
Okay, first of all...
...Gina can talk to *me* if she has a problem.
She doesn't need some *creepy,* overbearing white knight.
You know she's only nice to you because she can boss you around, right?
Is *that* your type?
No!
She's, like, a good person!
And you're taking her for granted!
Ugh.

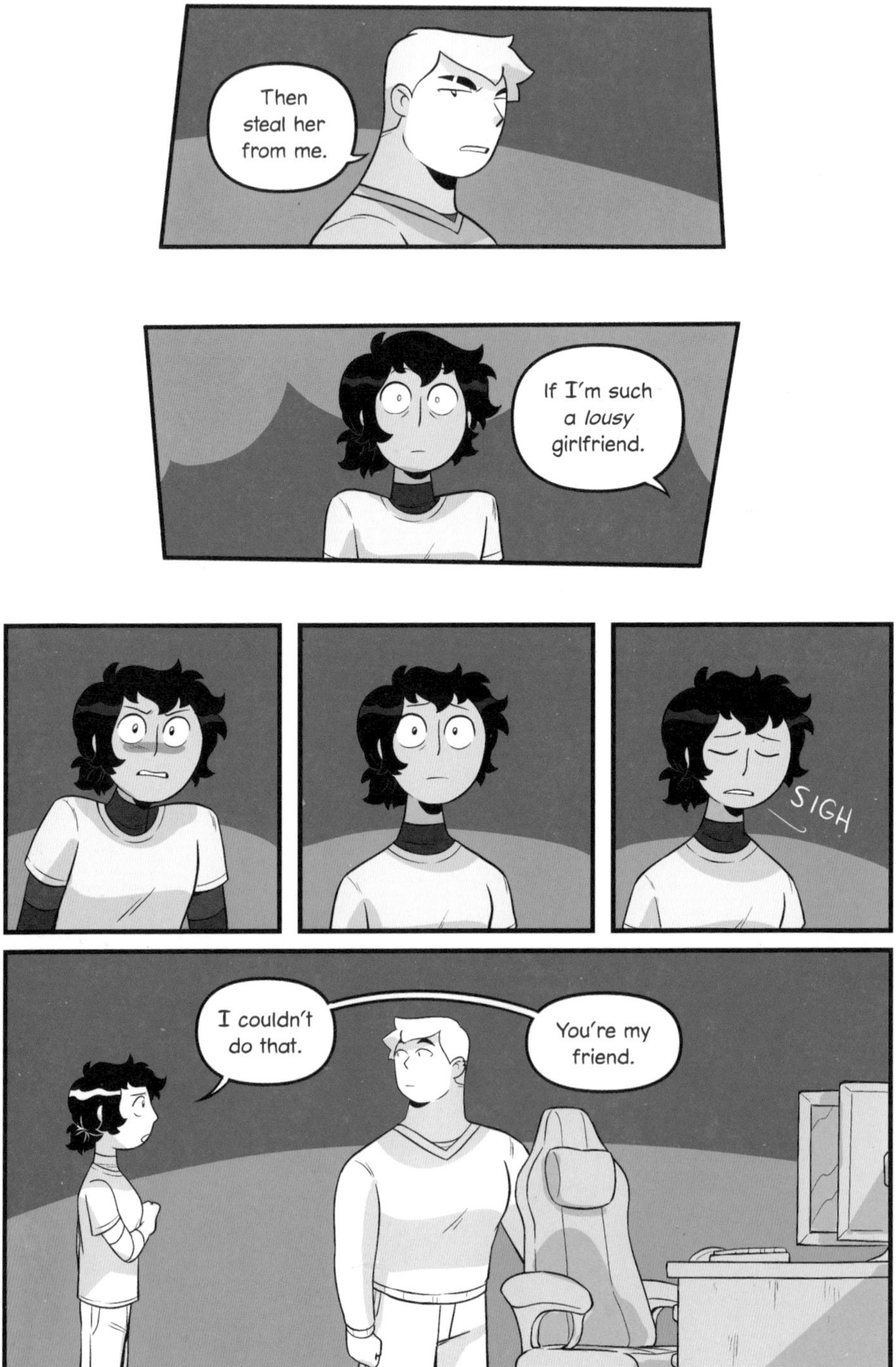
Then steal her from me.
If I'm such a *lousy* girlfriend.
SIGH
I couldn't do that.
You're my friend.

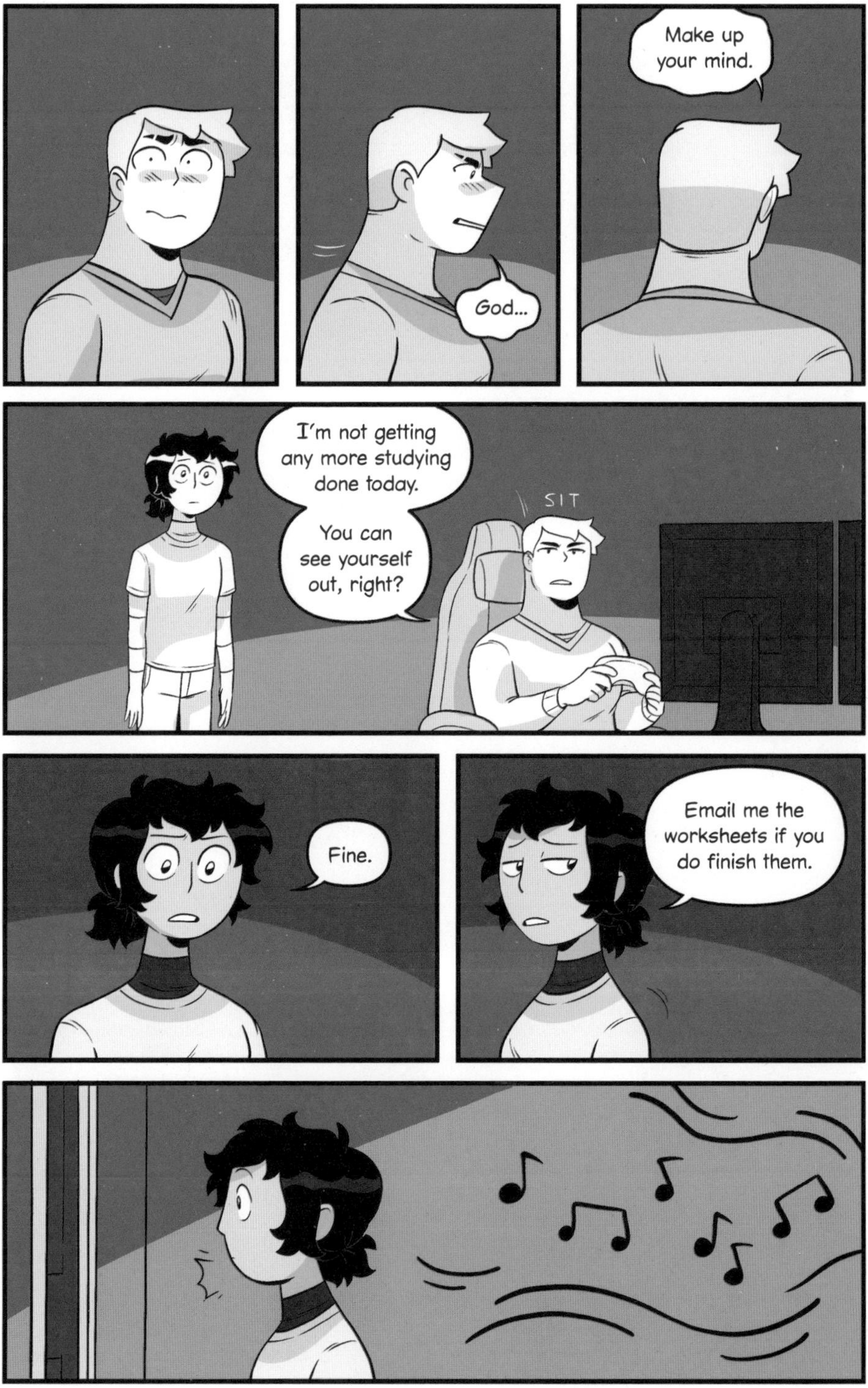
God...
Make up your mind.
I'm not getting any more studying done today.
You can see yourself out, right?
SIT
Fine.
Email me the worksheets if you do finish them.

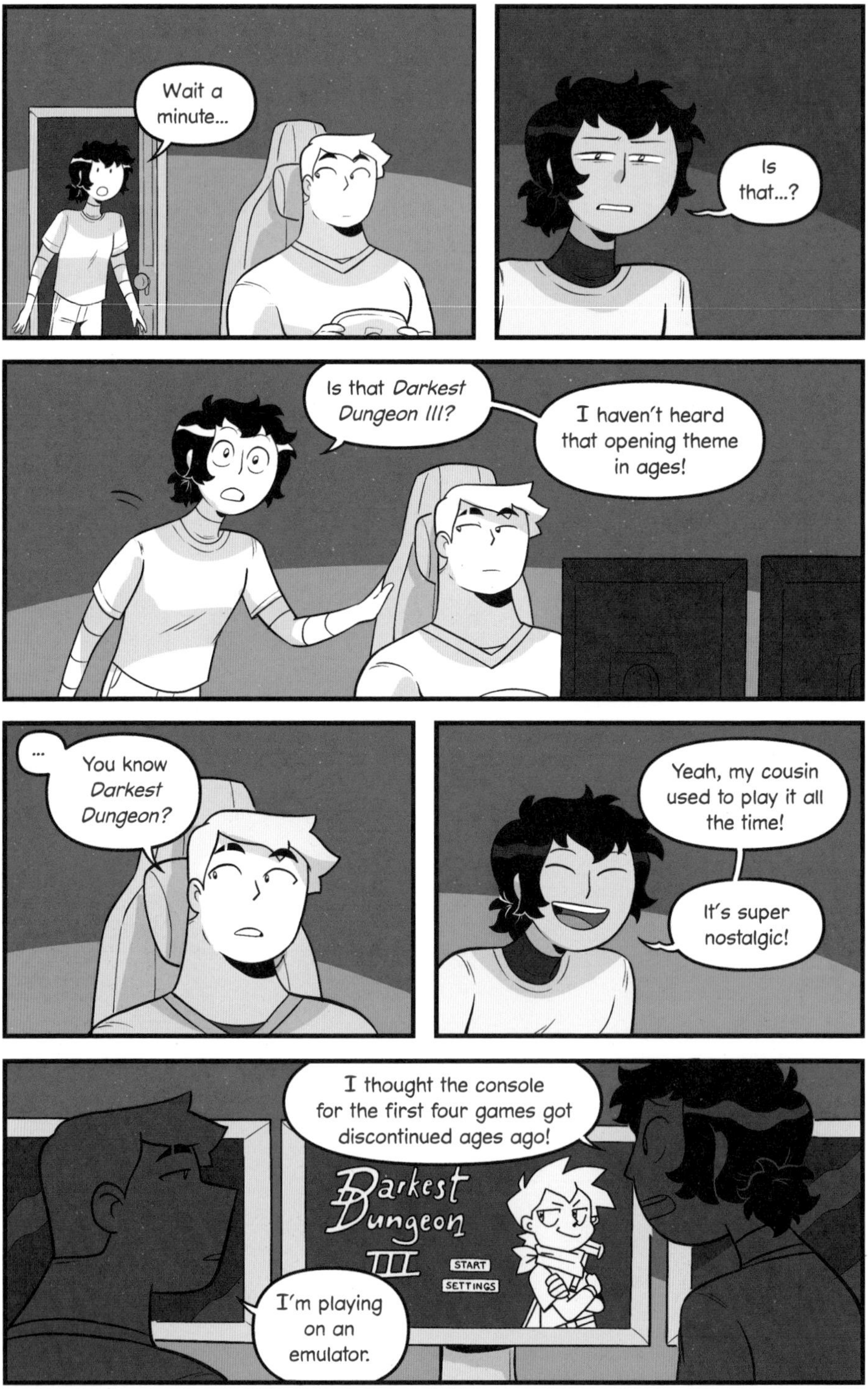
Wait a minute...
Is that...?
Is that *Darkest Dungeon III*?
I haven't heard that opening theme in ages!
...
You know *Darkest Dungeon*?
Yeah, my cousin used to play it all the time!
It's super nostalgic!
I thought the console for the first four games got discontinued ages ago!
Darkest Dungeon III
START
SETTINGS
I'm playing on an emulator.

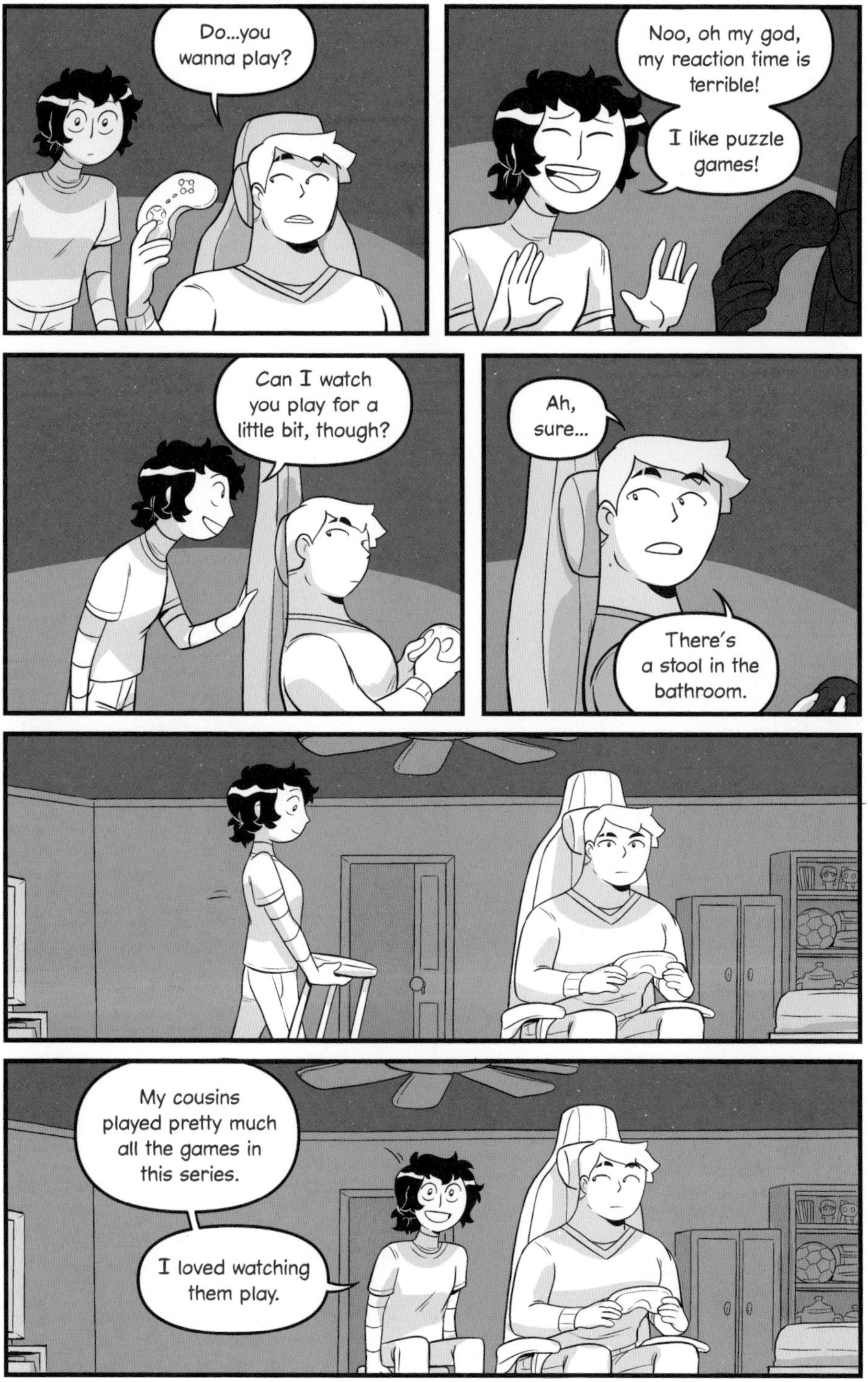
Do...you wanna play?
Noo, oh my god, my reaction time is terrible!
I like puzzle games!
Can I watch you play for a little bit, though?
Ah, sure...
There's a stool in the bathroom.
My cousins played pretty much all the games in this series.
I loved watching them play.

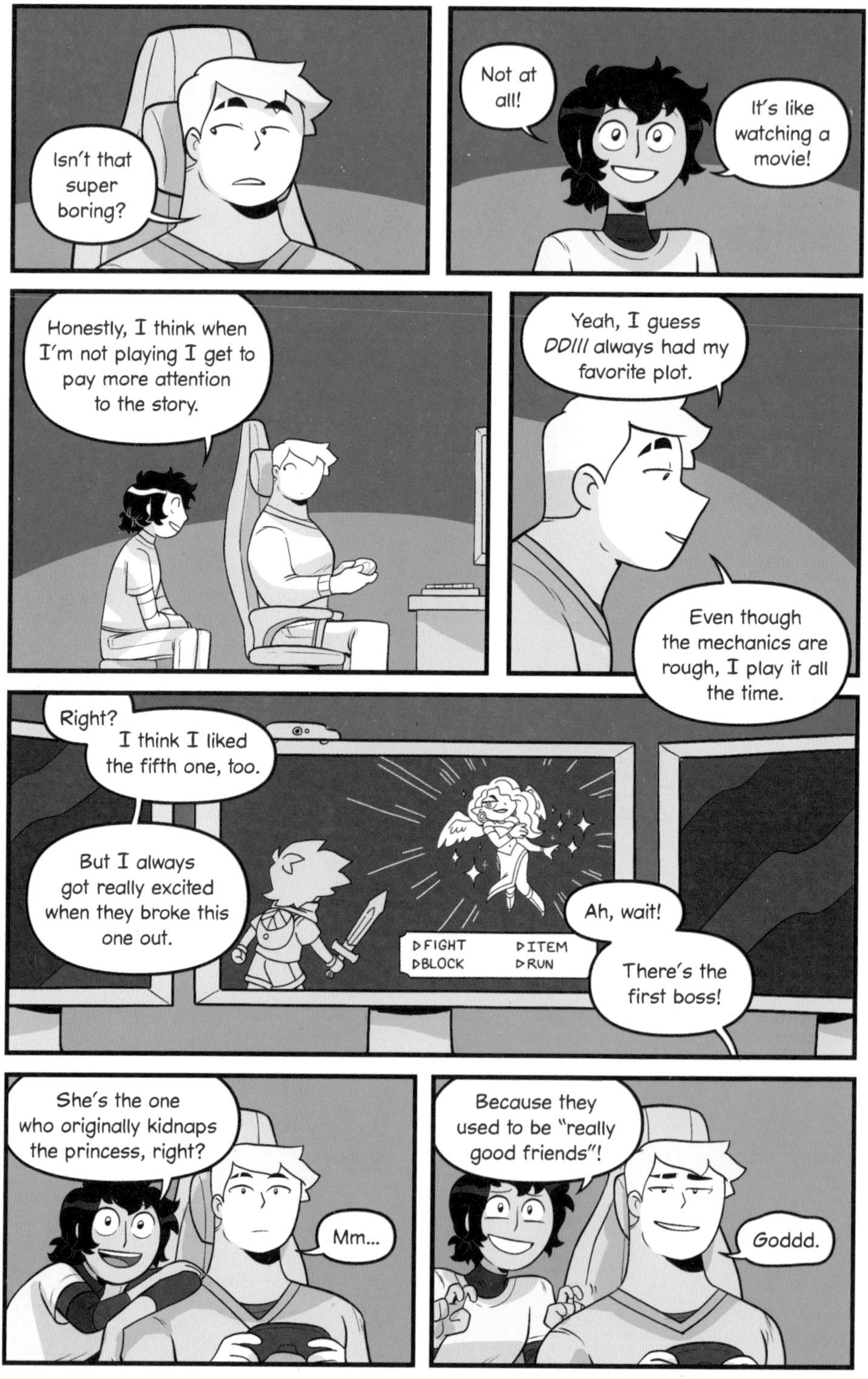
Isn't that super boring?
Not at all!
It's like watching a movie!
Honestly, I think when I'm not playing I get to pay more attention to the story.
Yeah, I guess *DDIII* always had my favorite plot.
Even though the mechanics are rough, I play it all the time.
Right? I think I liked the fifth one, too.
But I always got really excited when they broke this one out.
▷FIGHT ▷ITEM
▷BLOCK ▷RUN
Ah, wait!
There's the first boss!
She's the one who originally kidnaps the princess, right?
Mm...
Because they used to be "really good friends"!
Goddd.

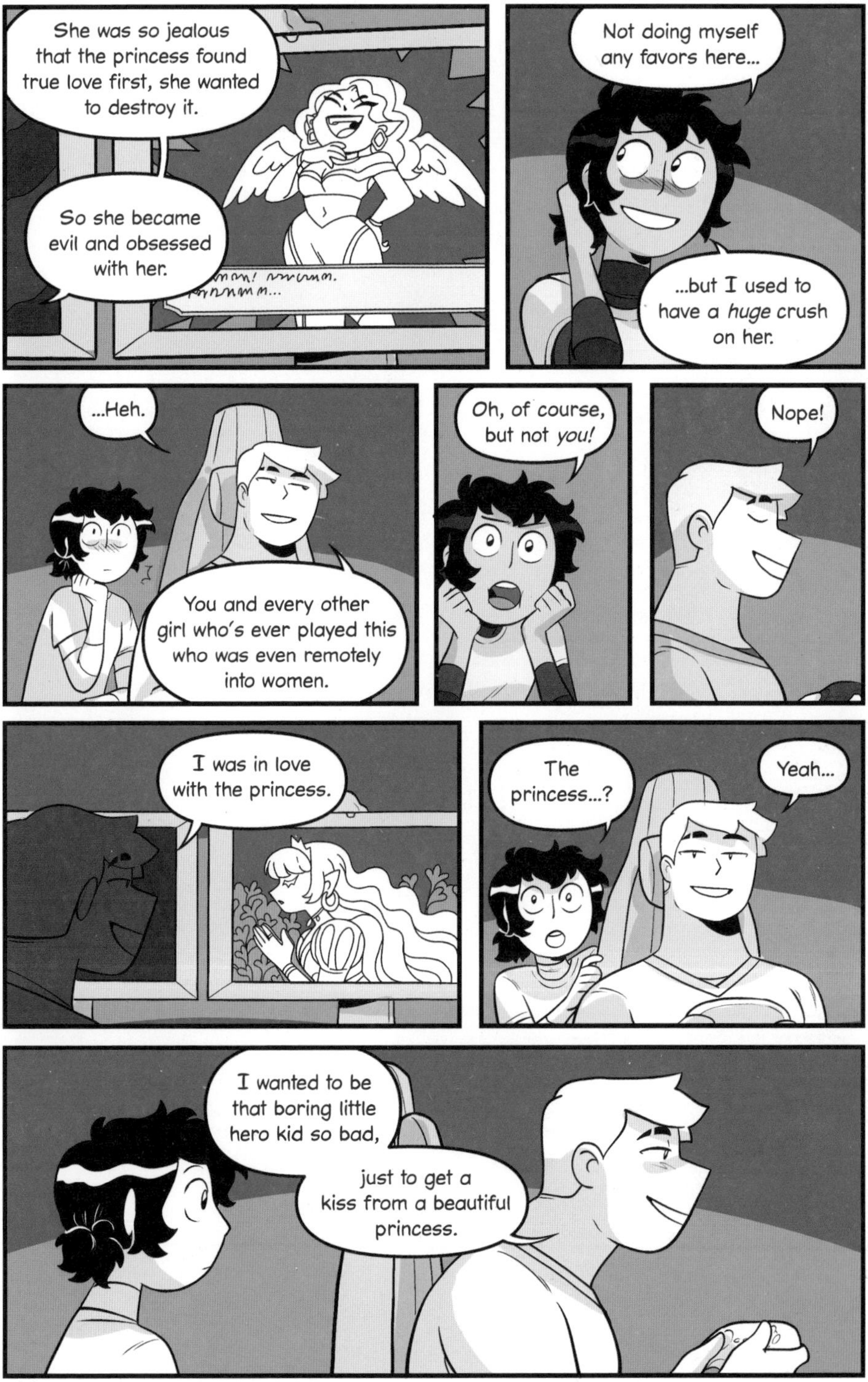

She was so jealous that the princess found true love first, she wanted to destroy it.
So she became evil and obsessed with her.
Not doing myself any favors here...
...but I used to have a *huge* crush on her.
...Heh.
You and every other girl who's ever played this who was even remotely into women.
Oh, of course, but not *you!*
Nope!
I was in love with the princess.
The princess...?
Yeah...
I wanted to be that boring little hero kid so bad,
just to get a kiss from a beautiful princess.

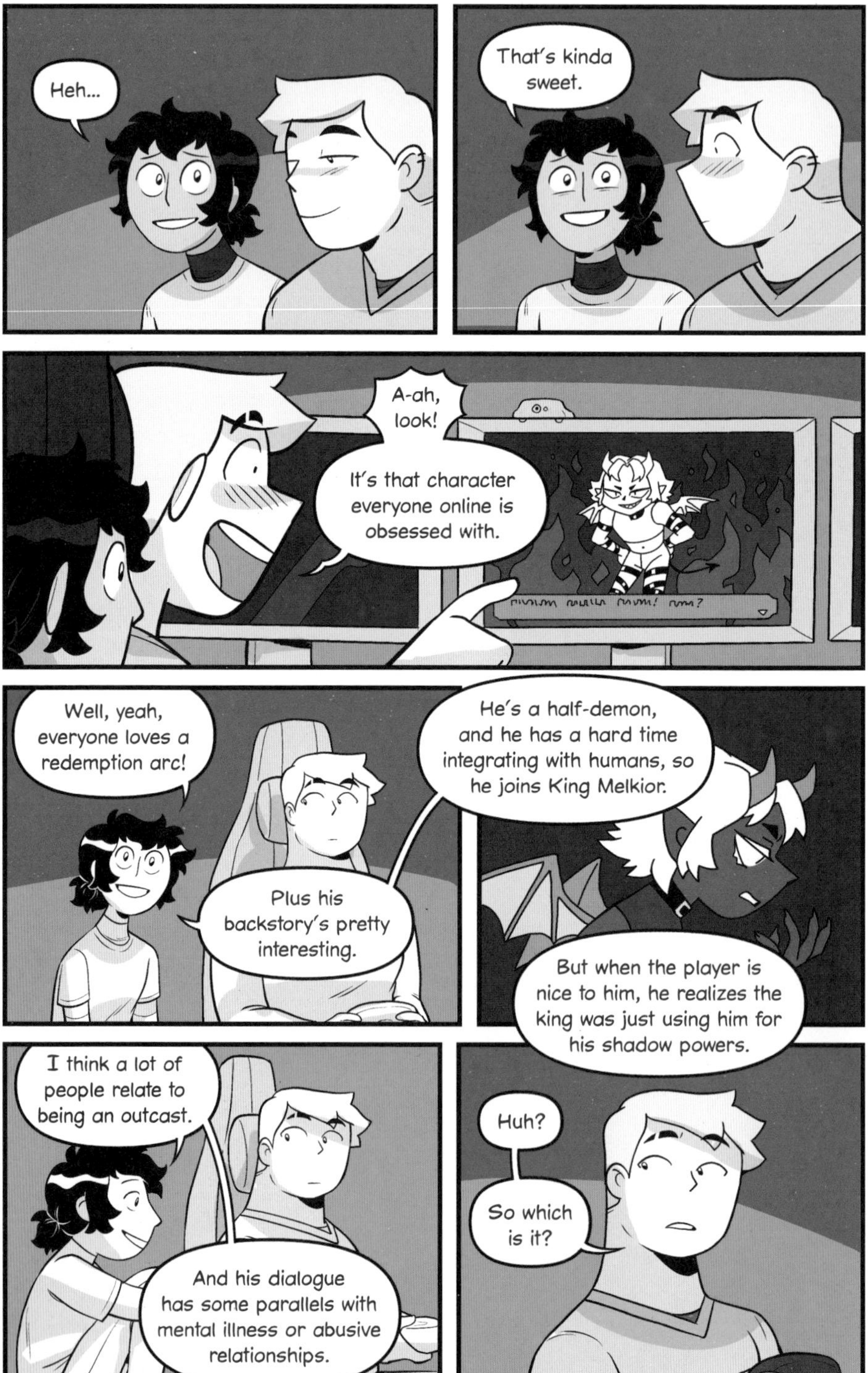

Heh...
That's kinda sweet.
A-ah, look!
It's that character everyone online is obsessed with.
Well, yeah, everyone loves a redemption arc!
Plus his backstory's pretty interesting.
He's a half-demon, and he has a hard time integrating with humans, so he joins King Melkior.
But when the player is nice to him, he realizes the king was just using him for his shadow powers.
I think a lot of people relate to being an outcast.
And his dialogue has some parallels with mental illness or abusive relationships.
Huh?
So which is it?

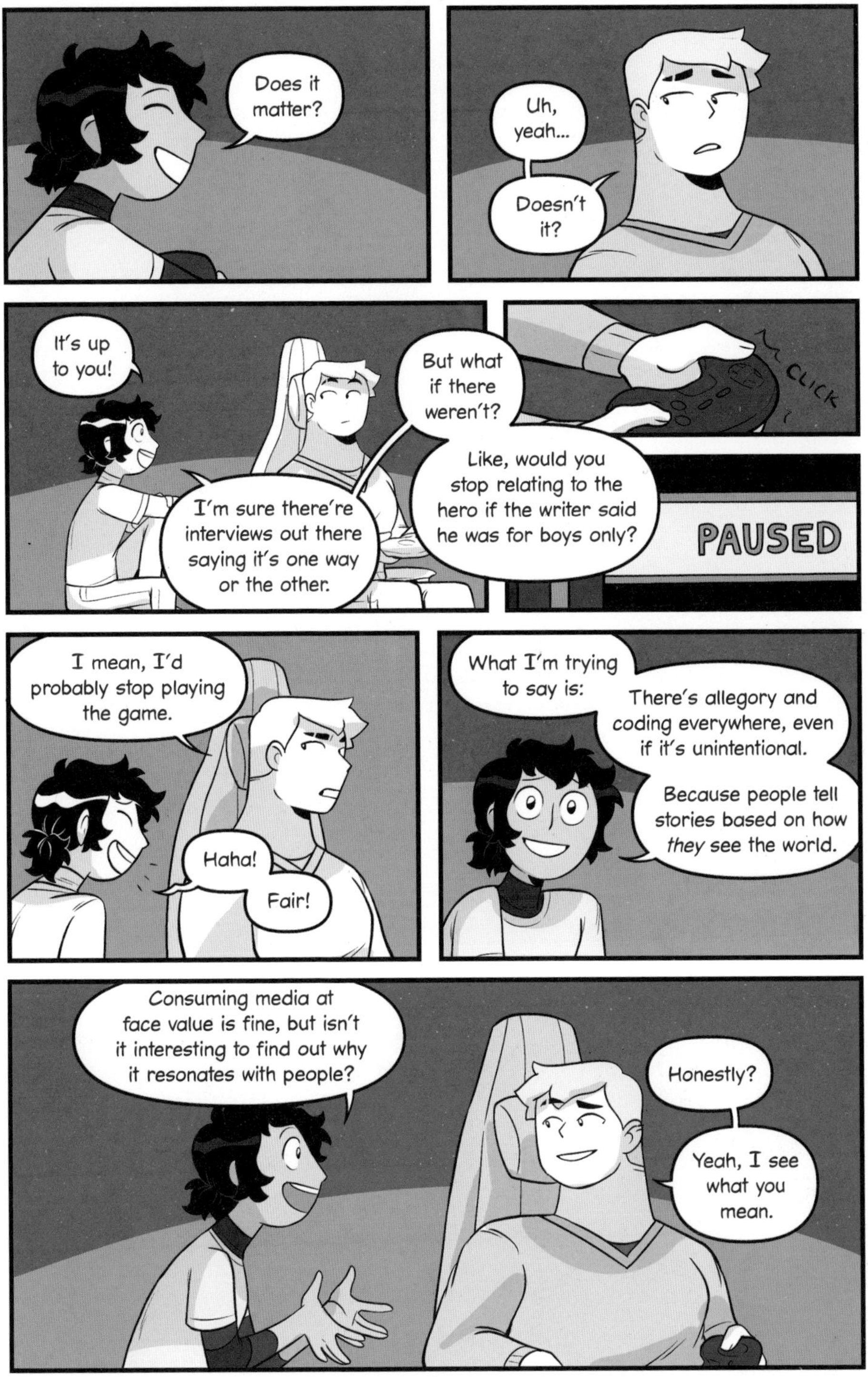
Does it matter?
Uh, yeah...
Doesn't it?
It's up to you!
I'm sure there're interviews out there saying it's one way or the other.
But what if there weren't?
Like, would you stop relating to the hero if the writer said he was for boys only?
CLICK
PAUSED
I mean, I'd probably stop playing the game.
Haha!
Fair!
What I'm trying to say is:
There's allegory and coding everywhere, even if it's unintentional.
Because people tell stories based on how *they* see the world.
Consuming media at face value is fine, but isn't it interesting to find out why it resonates with people?
Honestly?
Yeah, I see what you mean.

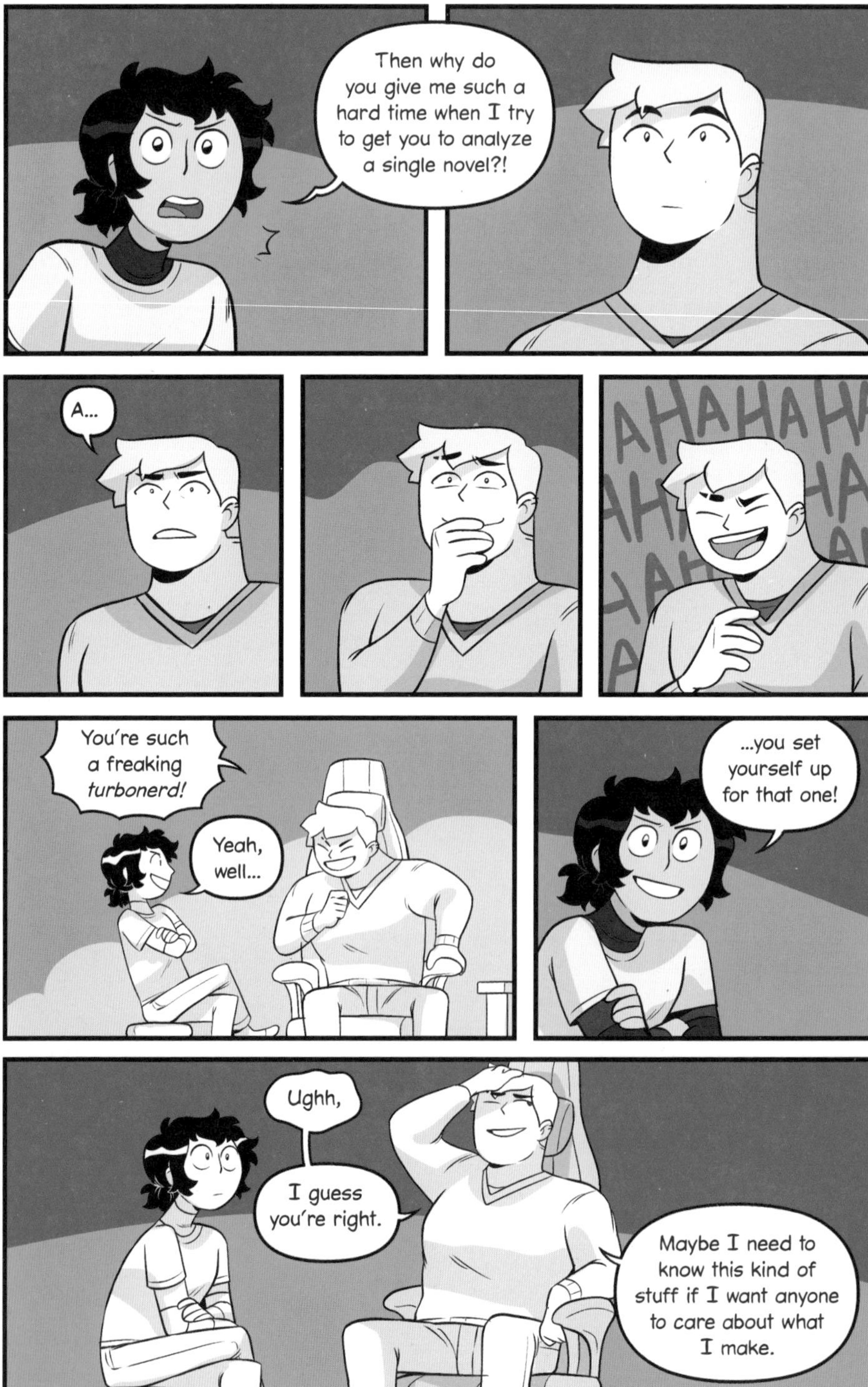
Then why do you give me such a hard time when I try to get you to analyze a single novel?!
A...
HAHAHAHA
You're such a freaking *turbonerd!*
Yeah, well...
...you set yourself up for that one!
Ughh,
I guess you're right.
Maybe I need to know this kind of stuff if I want anyone to care about what I make.

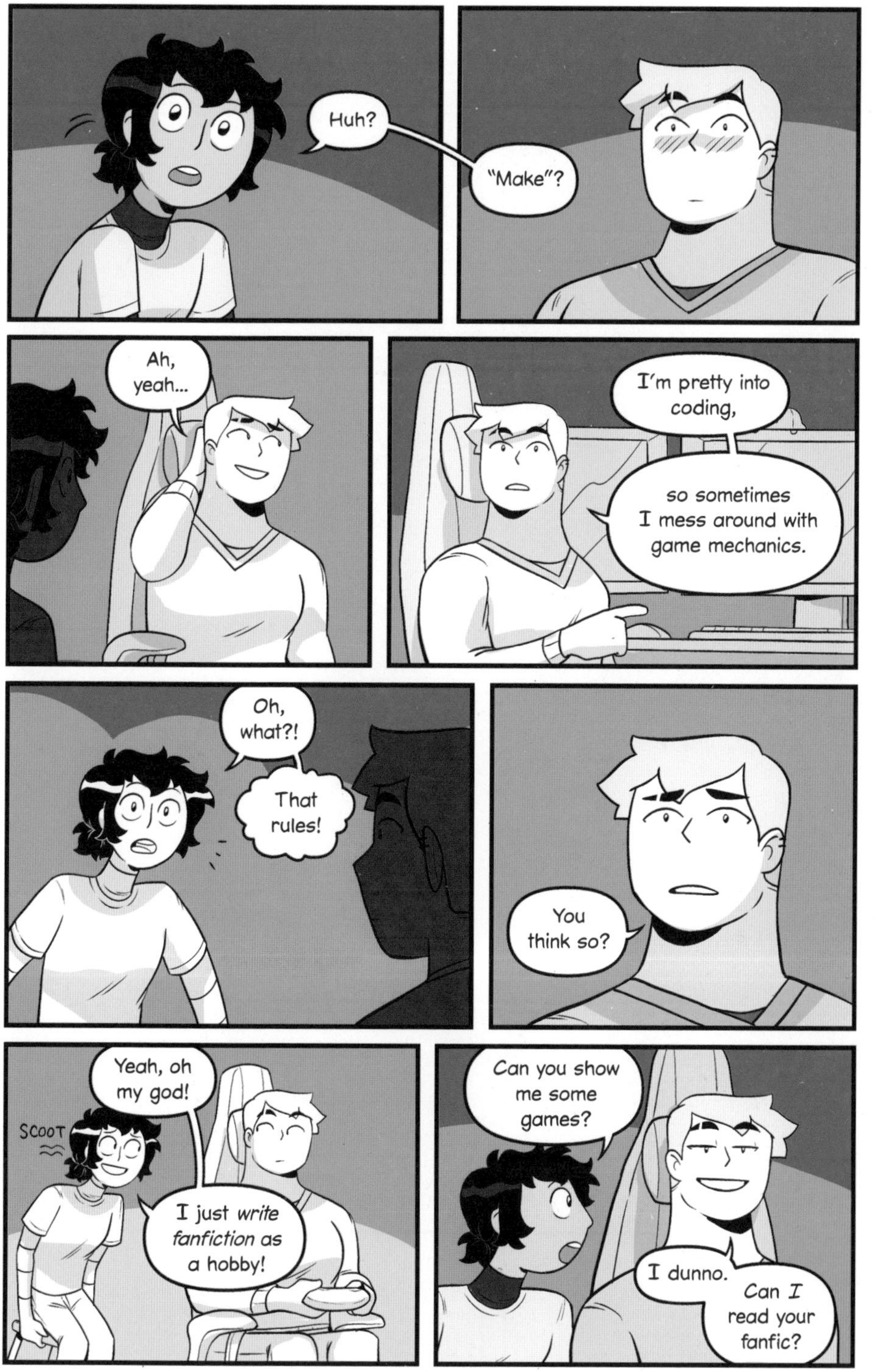
Huh?
"Make"?
Ah, yeah...
I'm pretty into coding,
so sometimes I mess around with game mechanics.
Oh, what?!
That rules!
You think so?
Yeah, oh my god!
SCOOT
I just *write fanfiction* as a hobby!
Can you show me some games?
I dunno.
Can *I* read your fanfic?

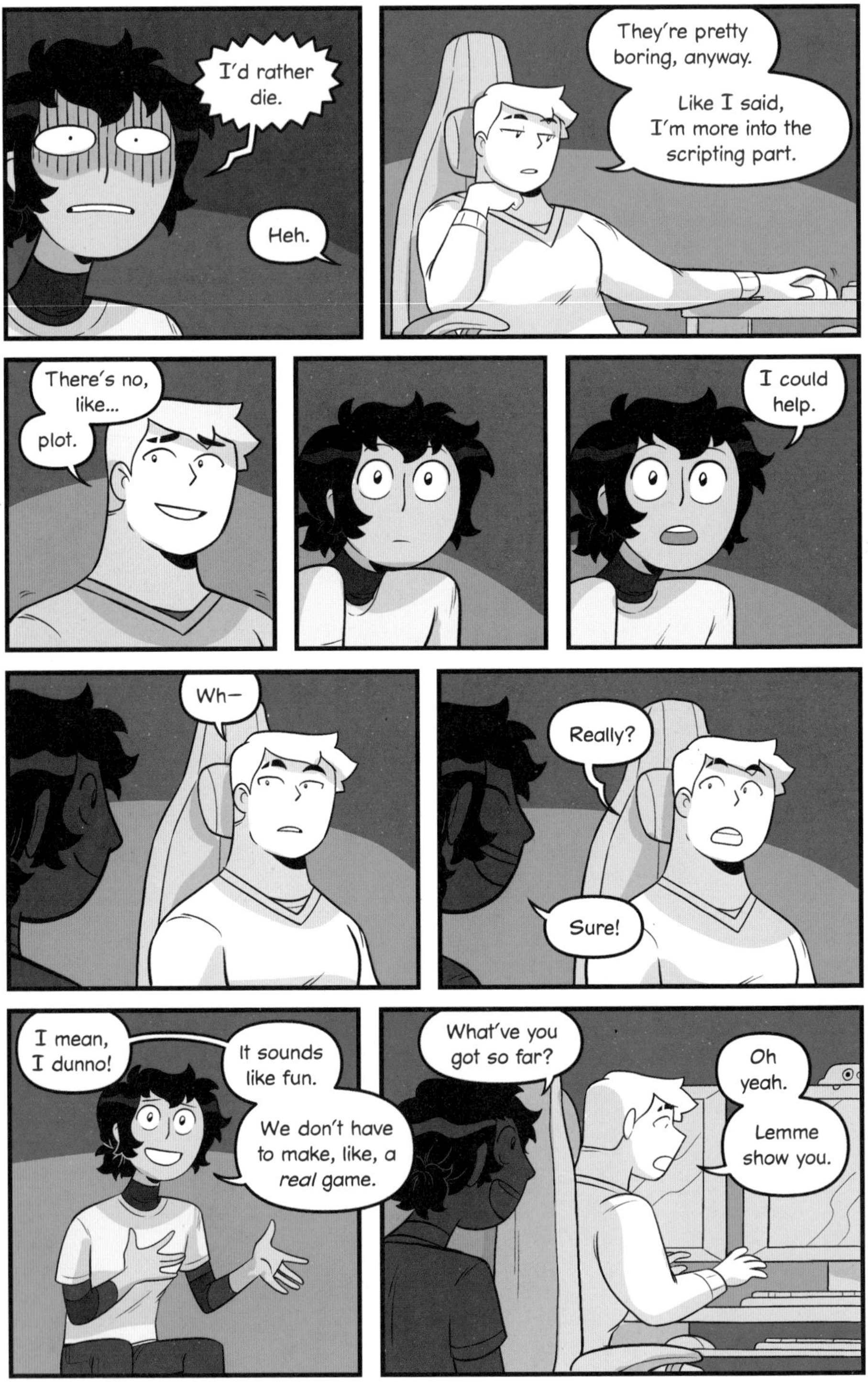

I'd rather die.
Heh.
They're pretty boring, anyway.
Like I said, I'm more into the scripting part.
There's no, like...
plot.
I could help.
Wh–
Really?
Sure!
I mean, I dunno!
It sounds like fun.
We don't have to make, like, a *real* game.
What've you got so far?
Oh yeah.
Lemme show you.

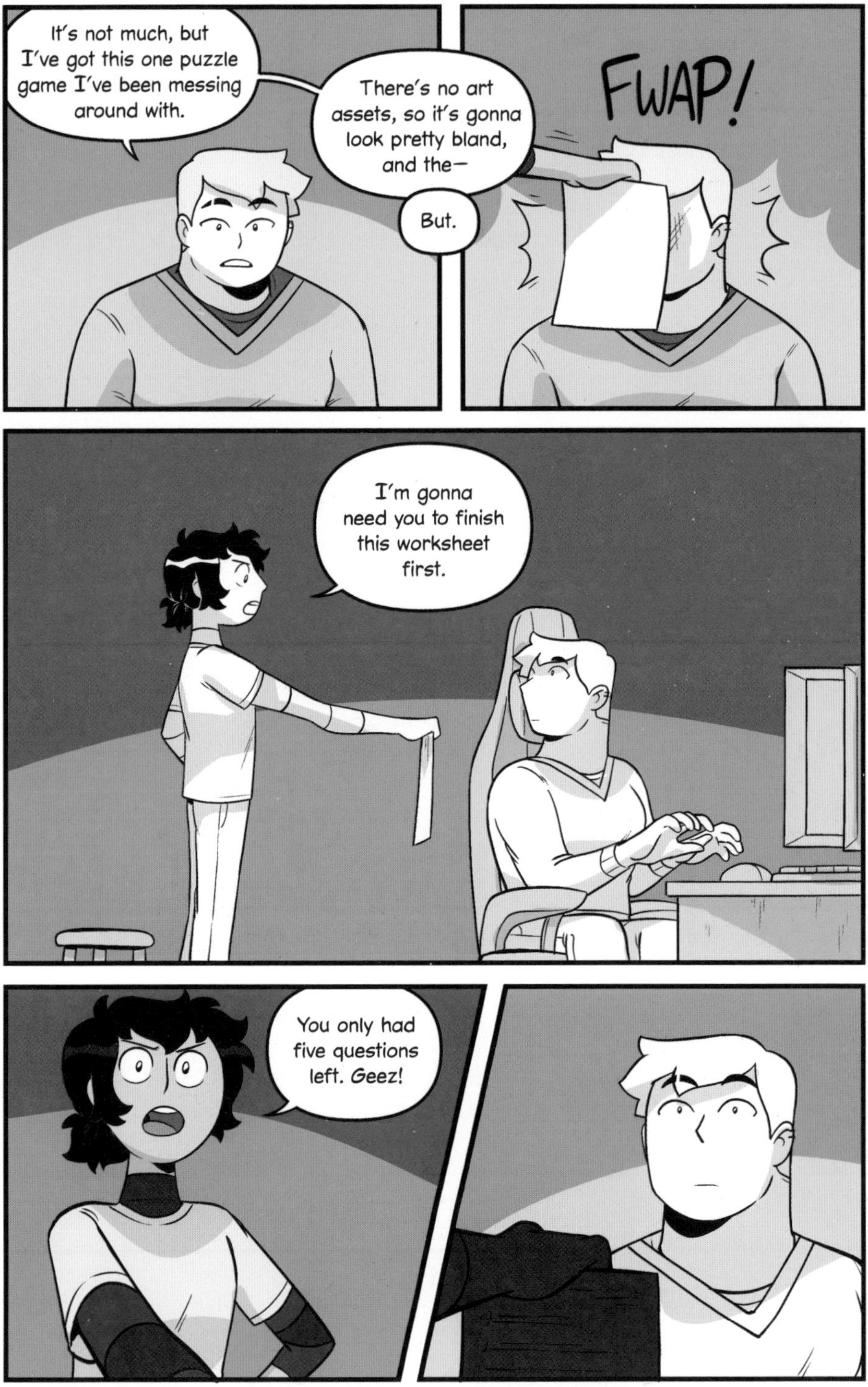
It's not much, but I've got this one puzzle game I've been messing around with.
There's no art assets, so it's gonna look pretty bland, and the—
But.
FWAP!
I'm gonna need you to finish this worksheet first.
You only had five questions left. Geez!

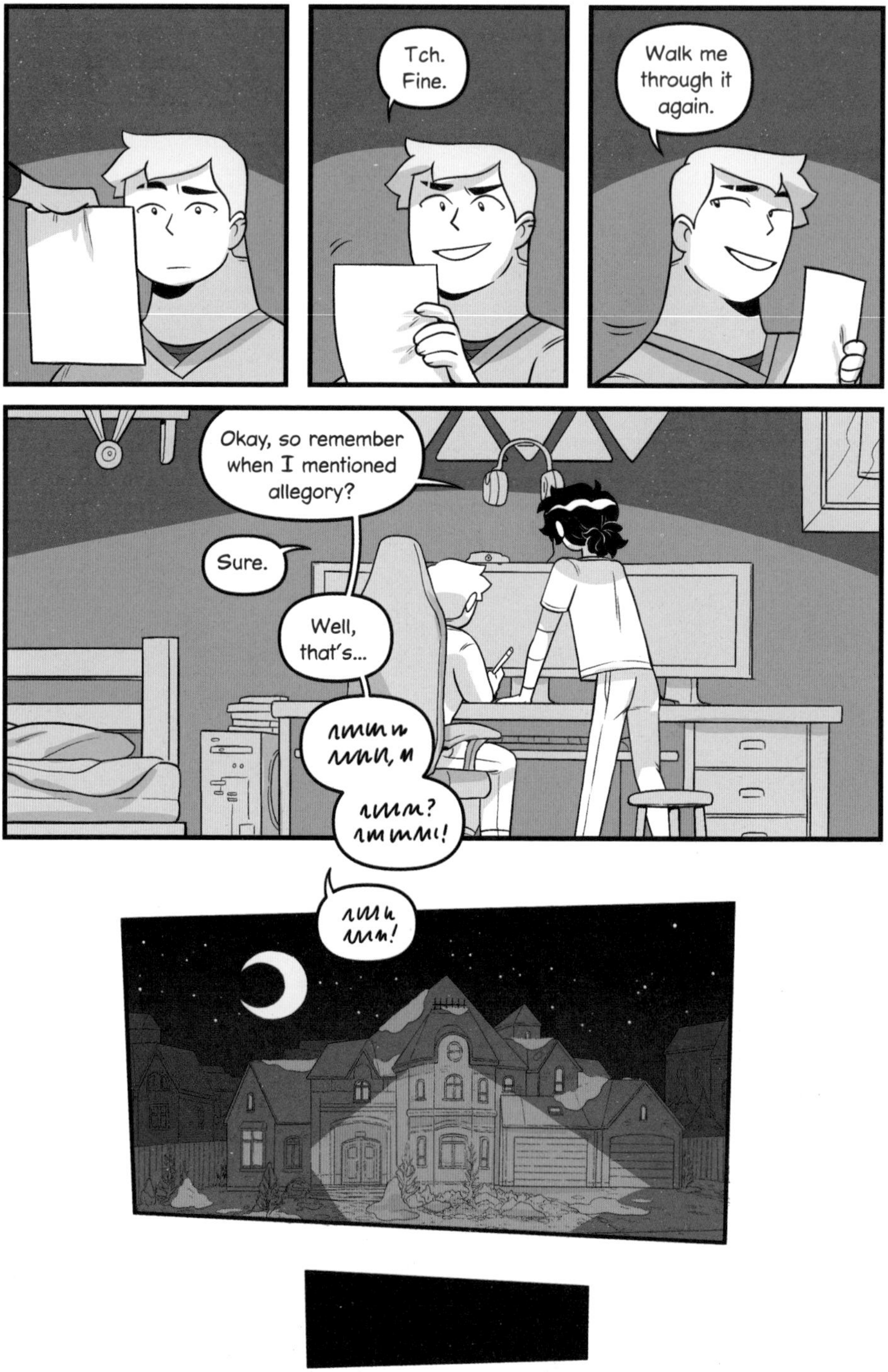
Tch. Fine.
Walk me through it again.
Okay, so remember when I mentioned allegory?
Sure.
Well, that's...

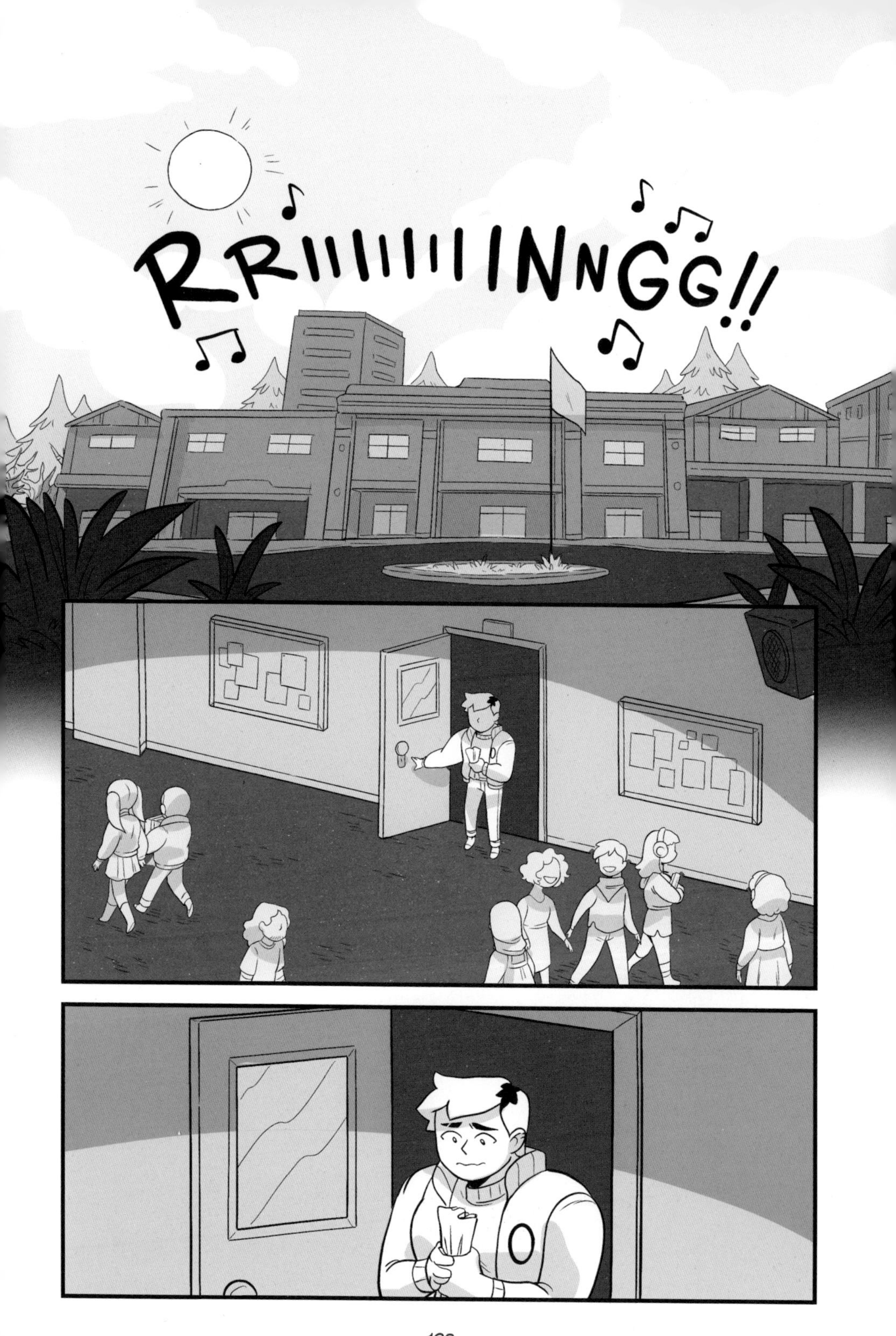
RRIIIIIIIINNGG!!

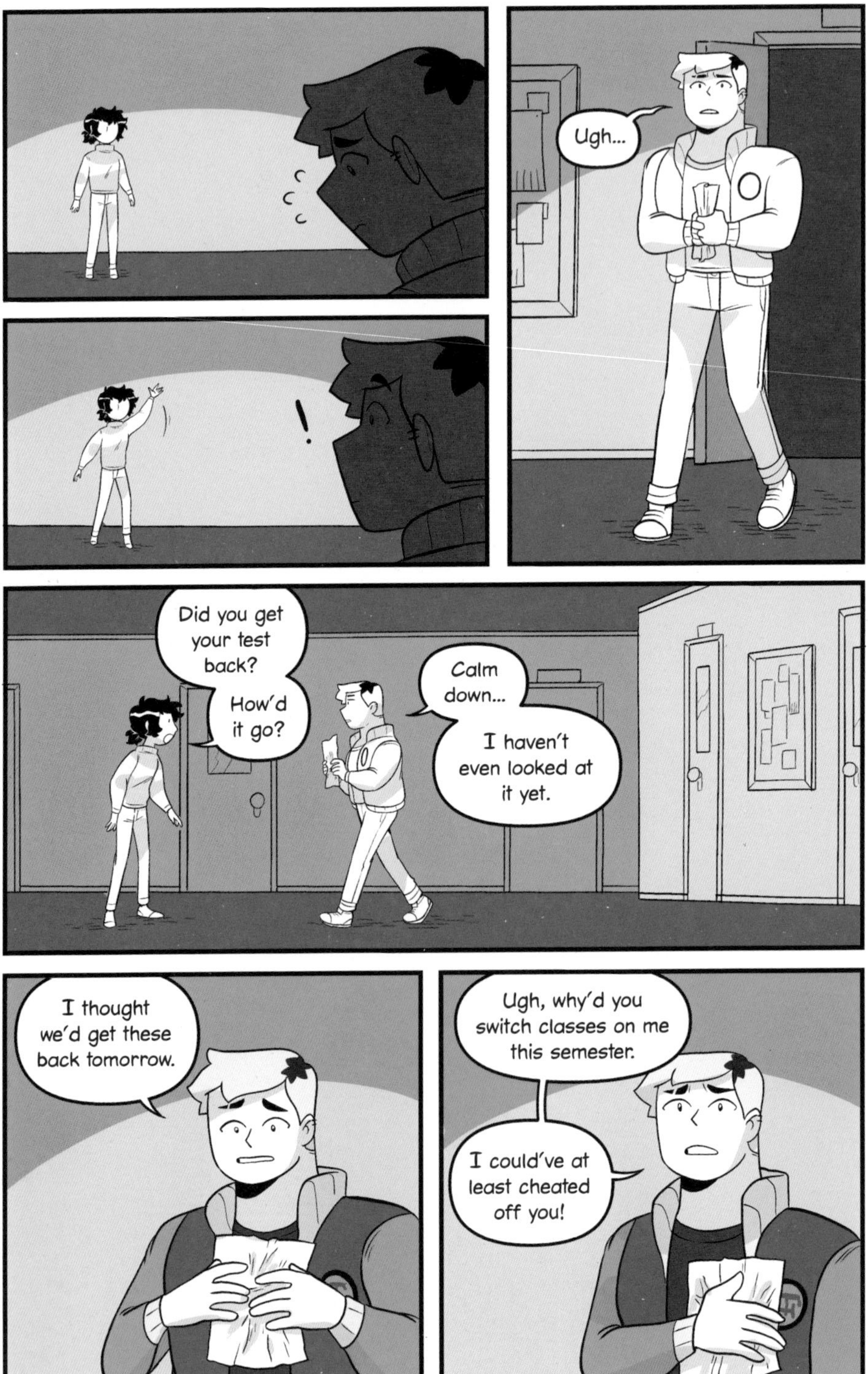
Ugh...
Did you get your test back?
How'd it go?
Calm down...
I haven't even looked at it yet.
I thought we'd get these back tomorrow.
Ugh, why'd you switch classes on me this semester.
I could've at least cheated off you!

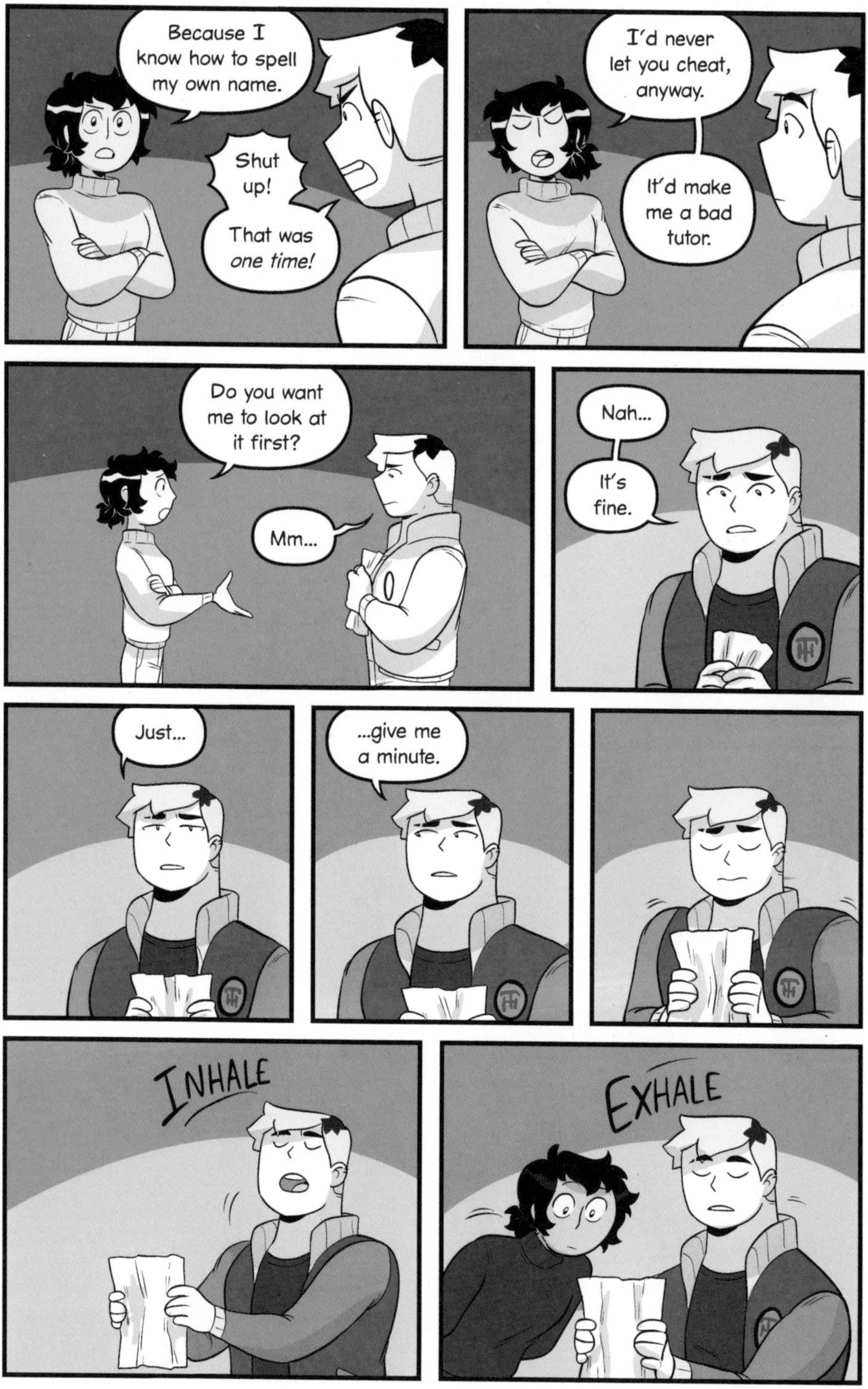
Because I know how to spell my own name.
Shut up!
That was *one time!*
I'd never let you cheat, anyway.
It'd make me a bad tutor.
Do you want me to look at it first?
Mm...
Nah...
It's fine.
Just...
...give me a minute.
INHALE
EXHALE

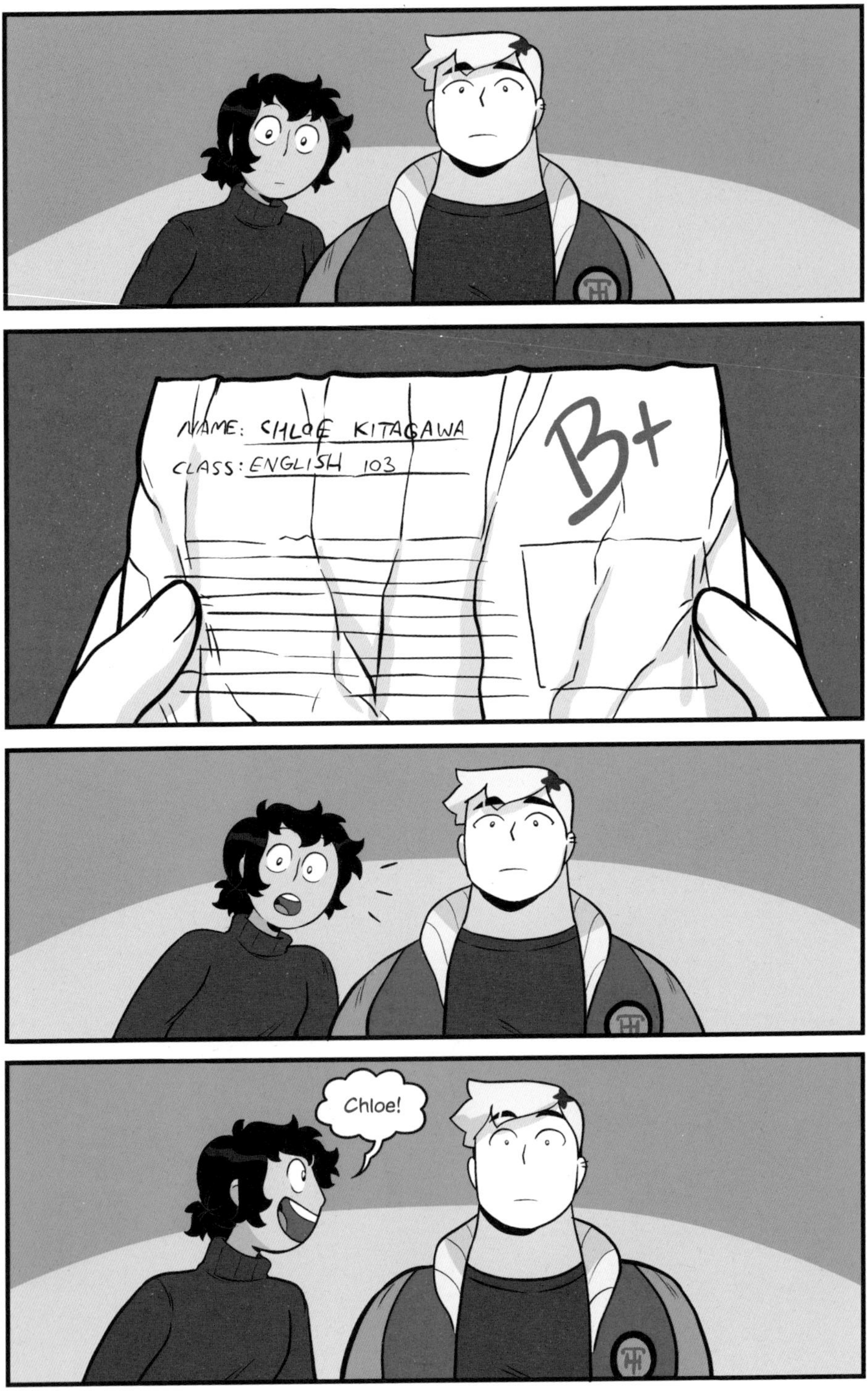
NAME: CHLOE KITAGAWA
CLASS: ENGLISH 103
B+
Chloe!

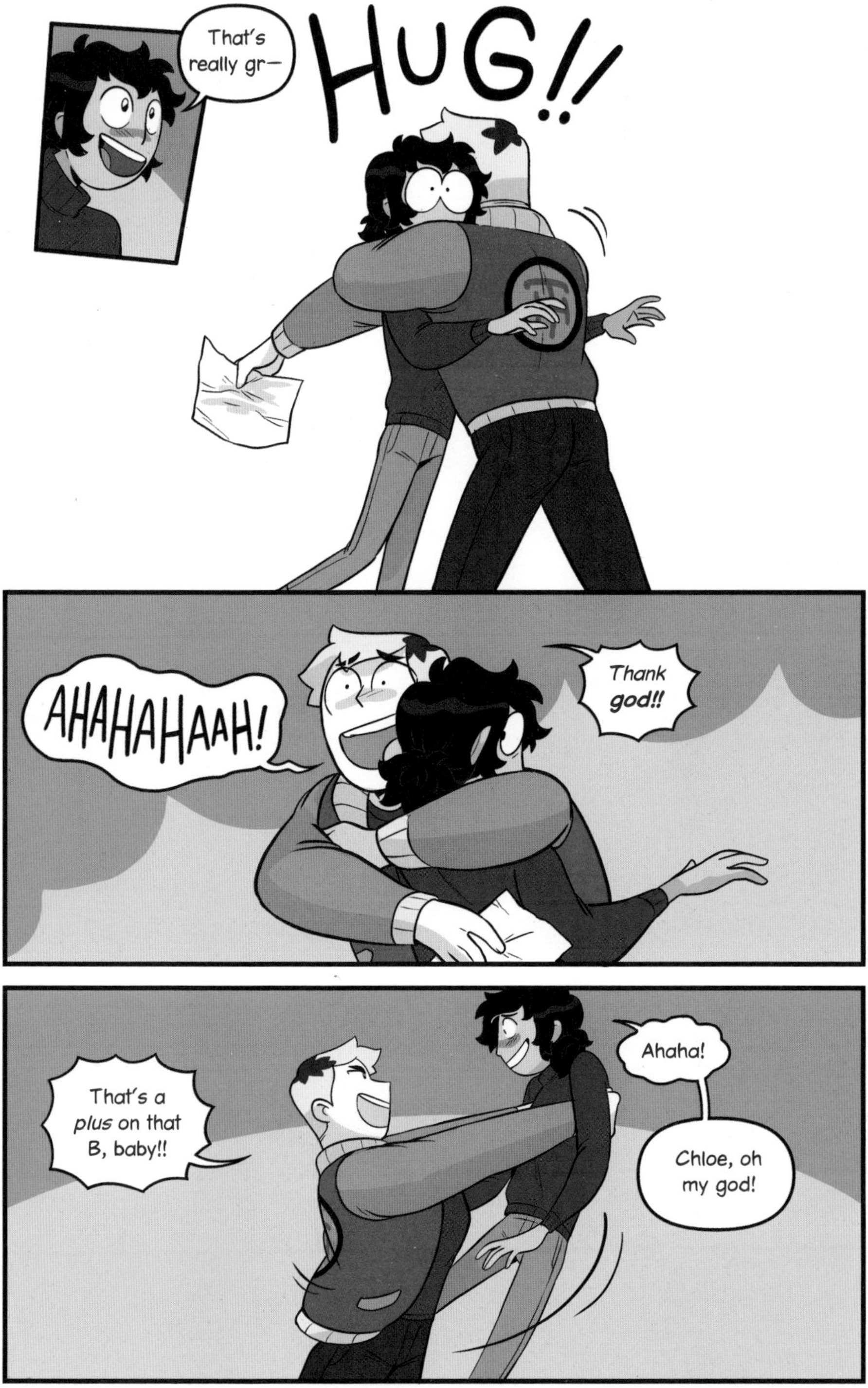
That's really gr—
HUG!!
AHAHAHAAH!
Thank *god!!*
That's a *plus* on that B, baby!!
Ahaha!
Chloe, oh my god!

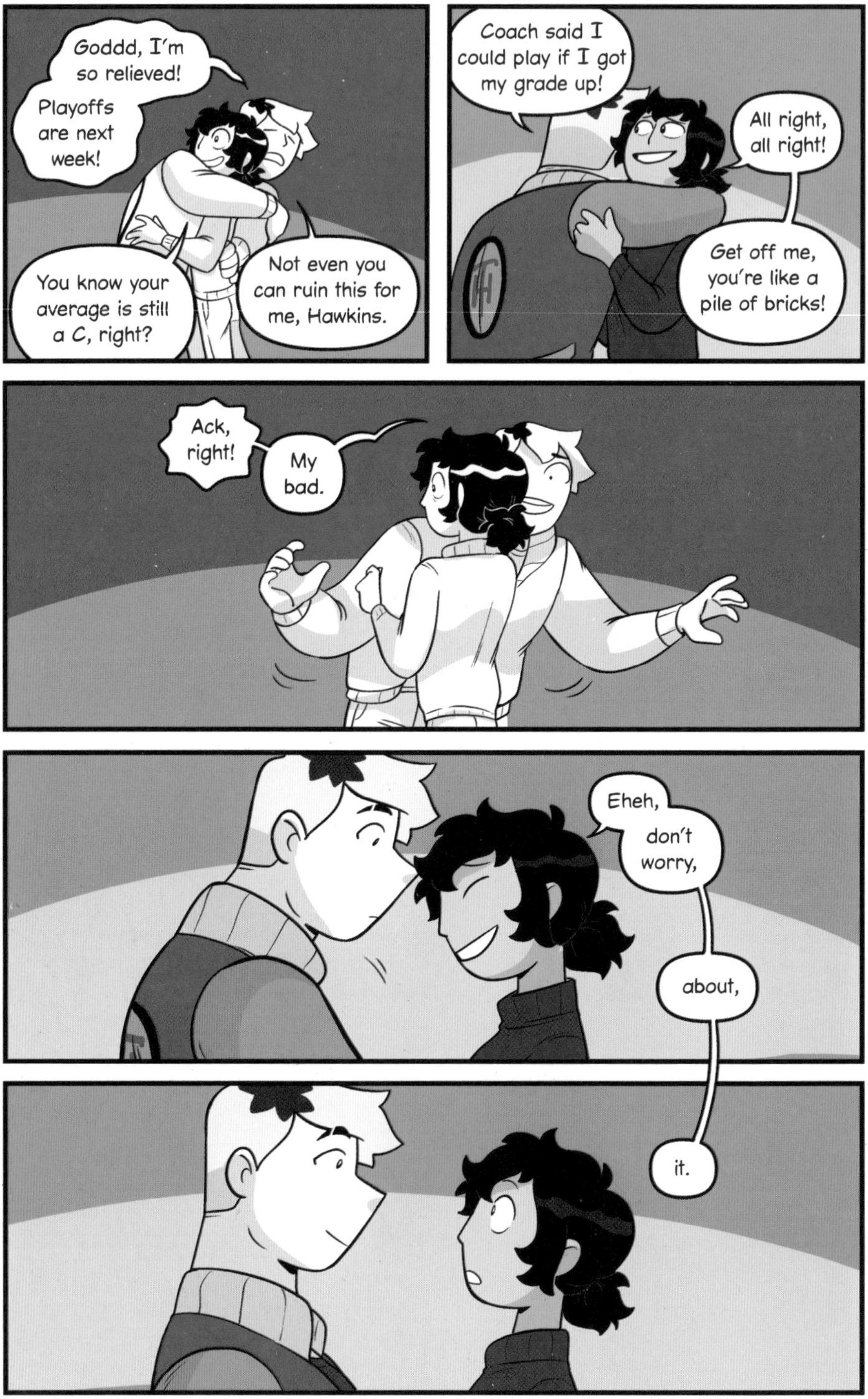

Goddd, I'm so relieved!
Playoffs are next week!
You know your average is still a C, right?
Not even you can ruin this for me, Hawkins.
Coach said I could play if I got my grade up!
All right, all right!
Get off me, you're like a pile of bricks!
Ack, right!
My bad.
Eheh,
don't worry,
about,
it.

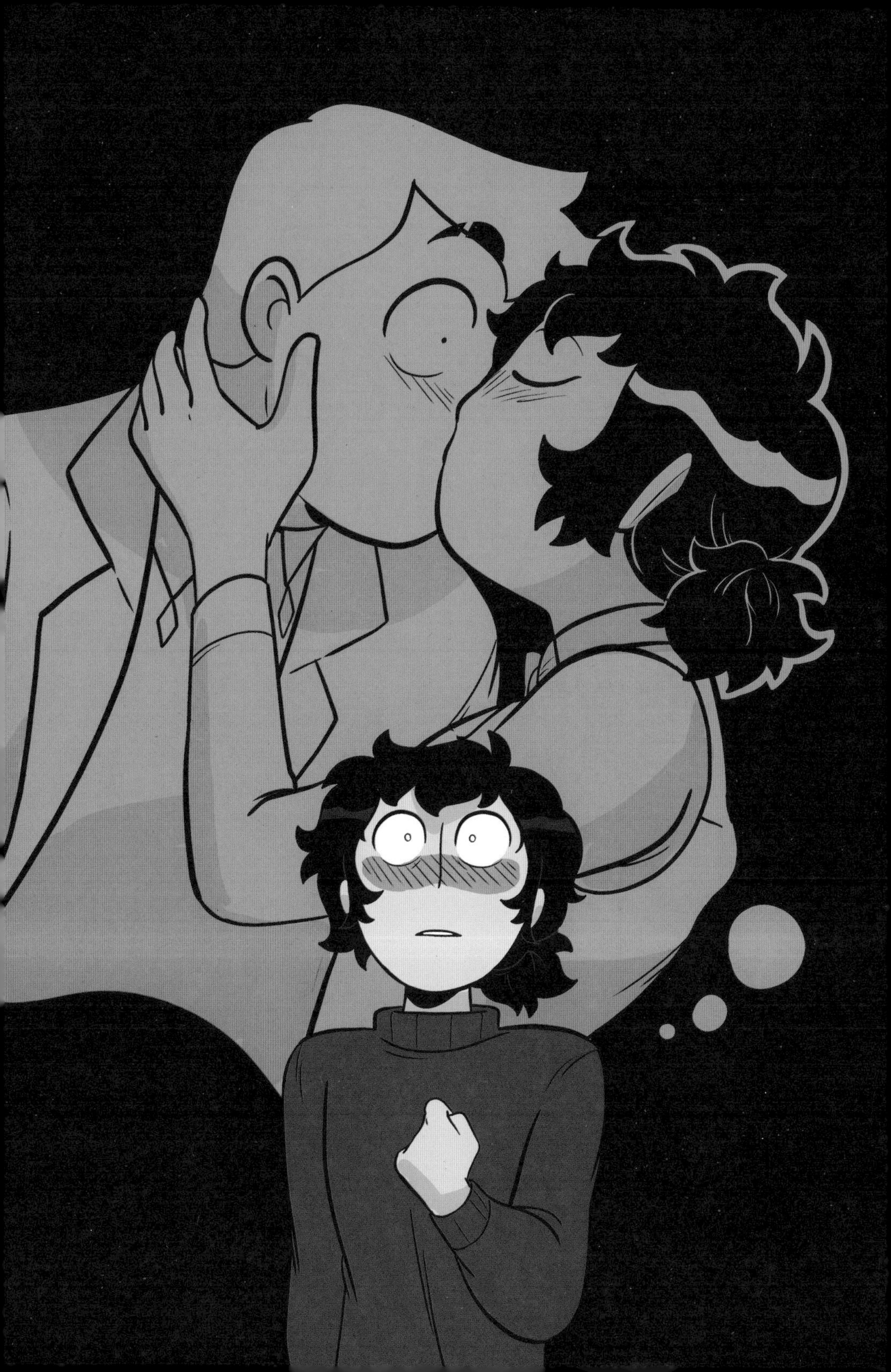

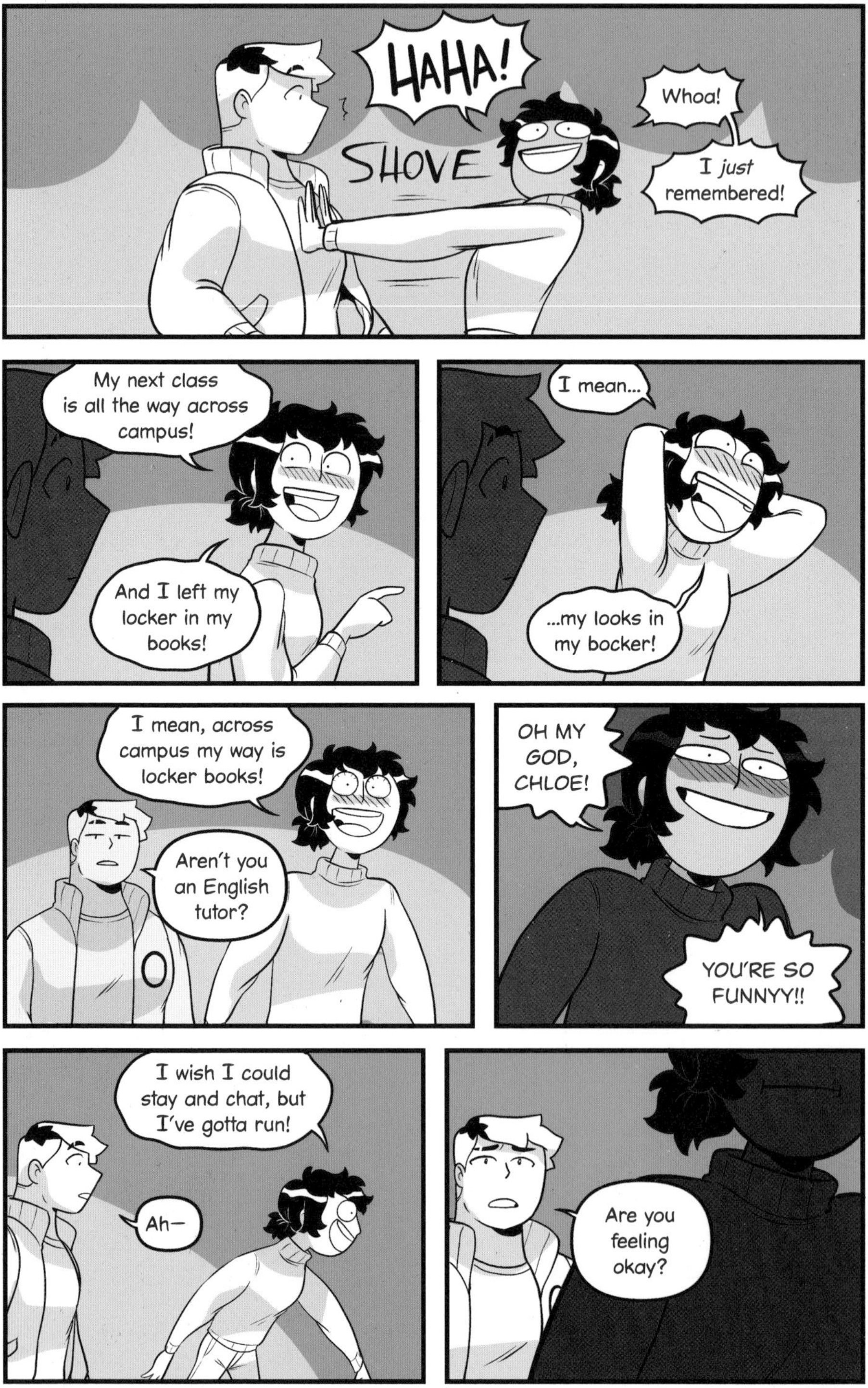
HAHA!
SHOVE
Whoa!
I *just* remembered!
My next class is all the way across campus!
And I left my locker in my books!
I mean...
...my looks in my bocker!
I mean, across campus my way is locker books!
Aren't you an English tutor?
OH MY GOD, CHLOE!
YOU'RE SO FUNNYY!!
I wish I could stay and chat, but I've gotta run!
Ah—
Are you feeling okay?

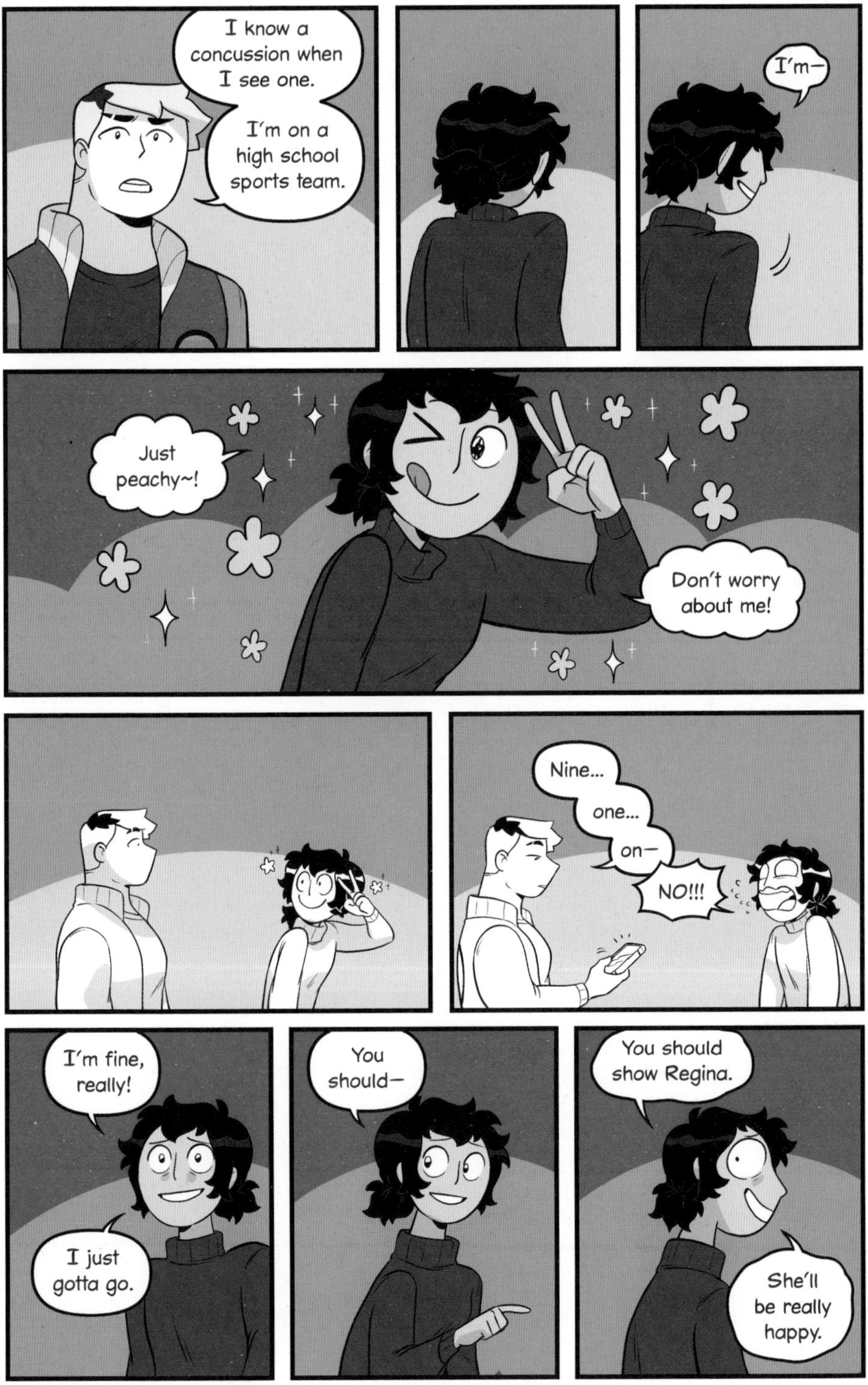

I know a concussion when I see one.
I'm on a high school sports team.
I'm—
Just peachy~!
Don't worry about me!
Nine...
one...
on—
NO!!!
I'm fine, really!
I just gotta go.
You should—
You should show Regina.
She'll be really happy.

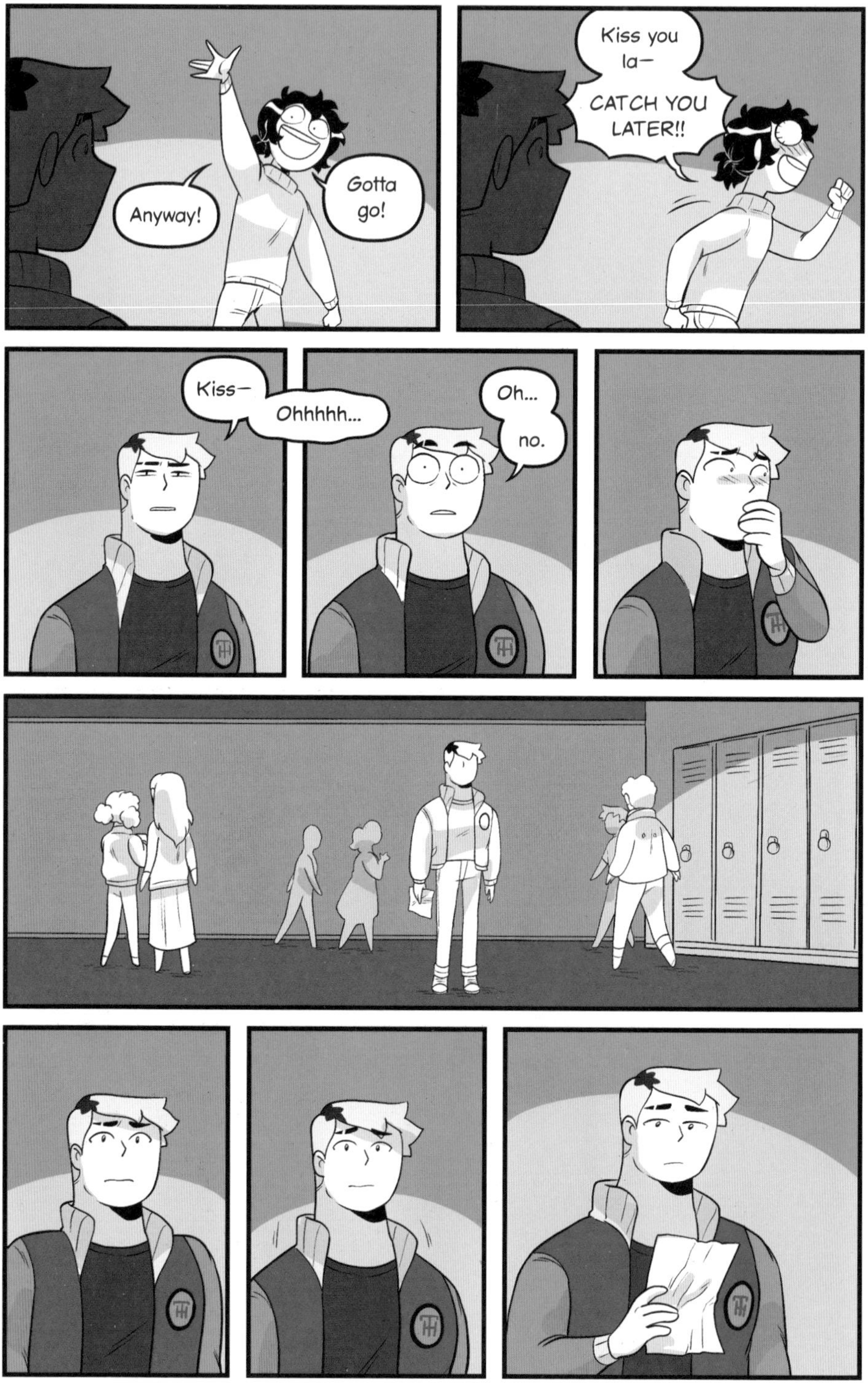
Anyway!
Gotta go!
Kiss you la—
CATCH YOU LATER!!
Kiss—
Ohhhhh...
Oh...
no.

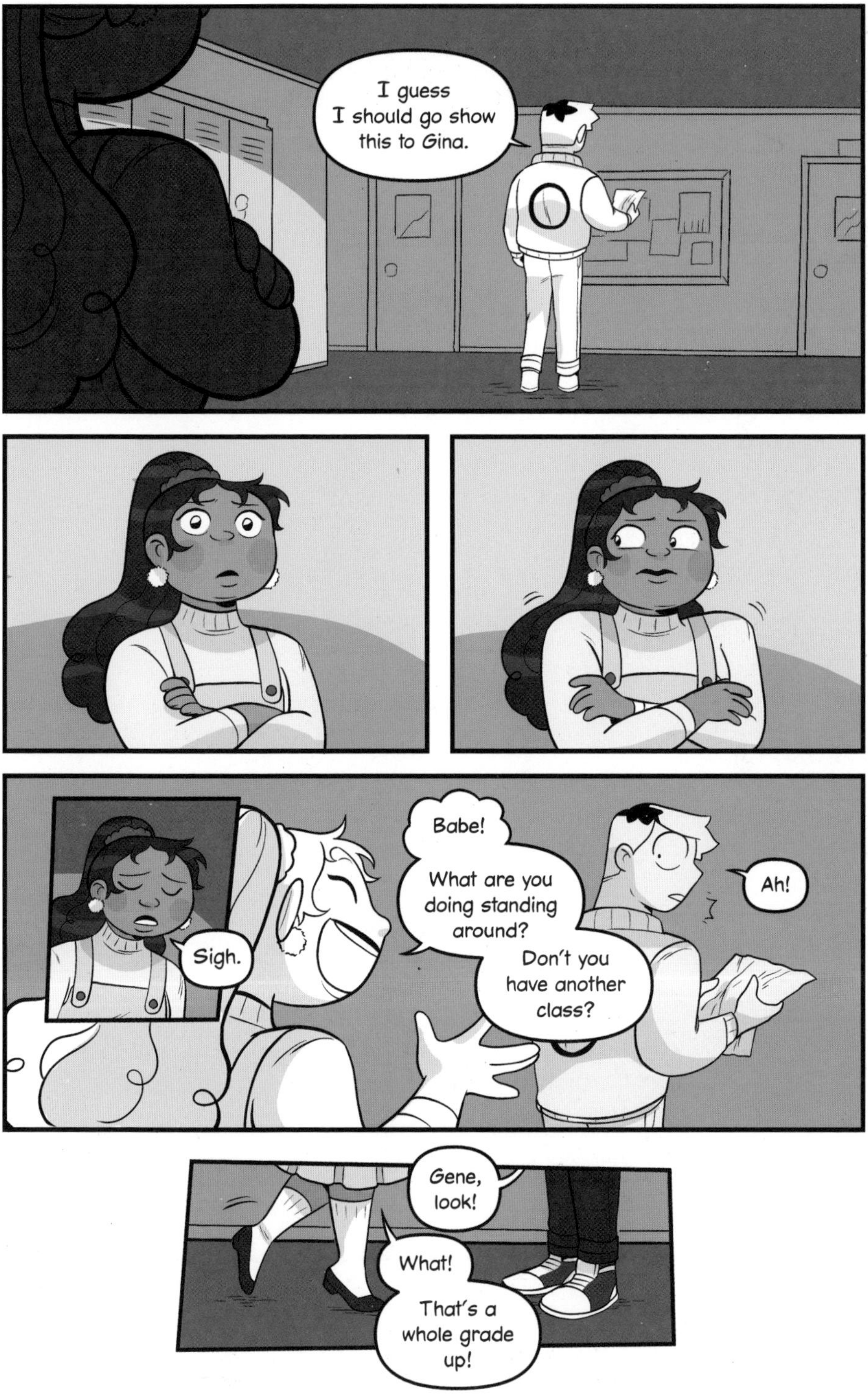
I guess I should go show this to Gina.
Sigh.
Babe!
What are you doing standing around?
Don't you have another class?
Ah!
Gene, look!
What!
That's a whole grade up!

[redacted]

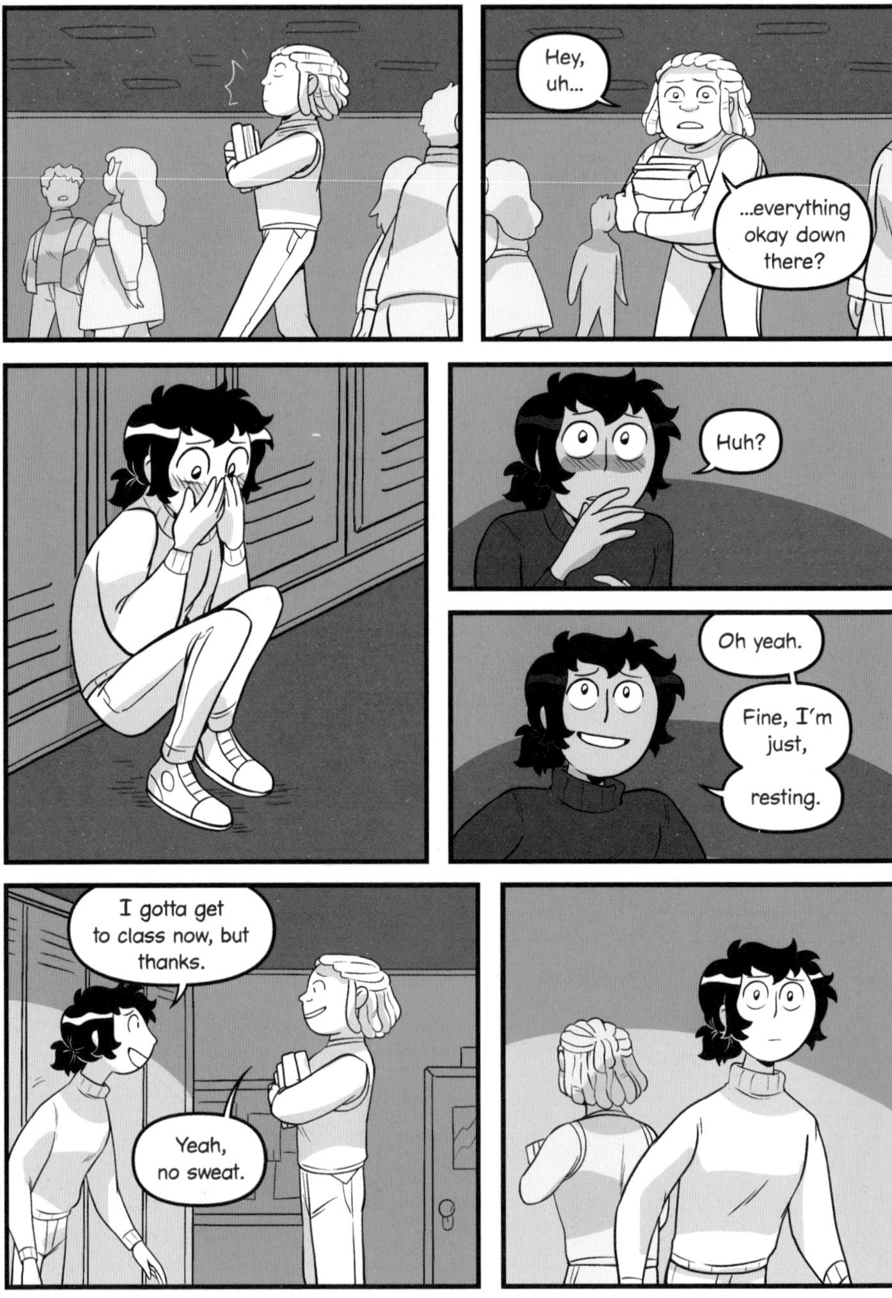
Hey, uh...
...everything okay down there?
Huh?
Oh yeah.
Fine, I'm just,
resting.
I gotta get to class now, but thanks.
Yeah, no sweat.

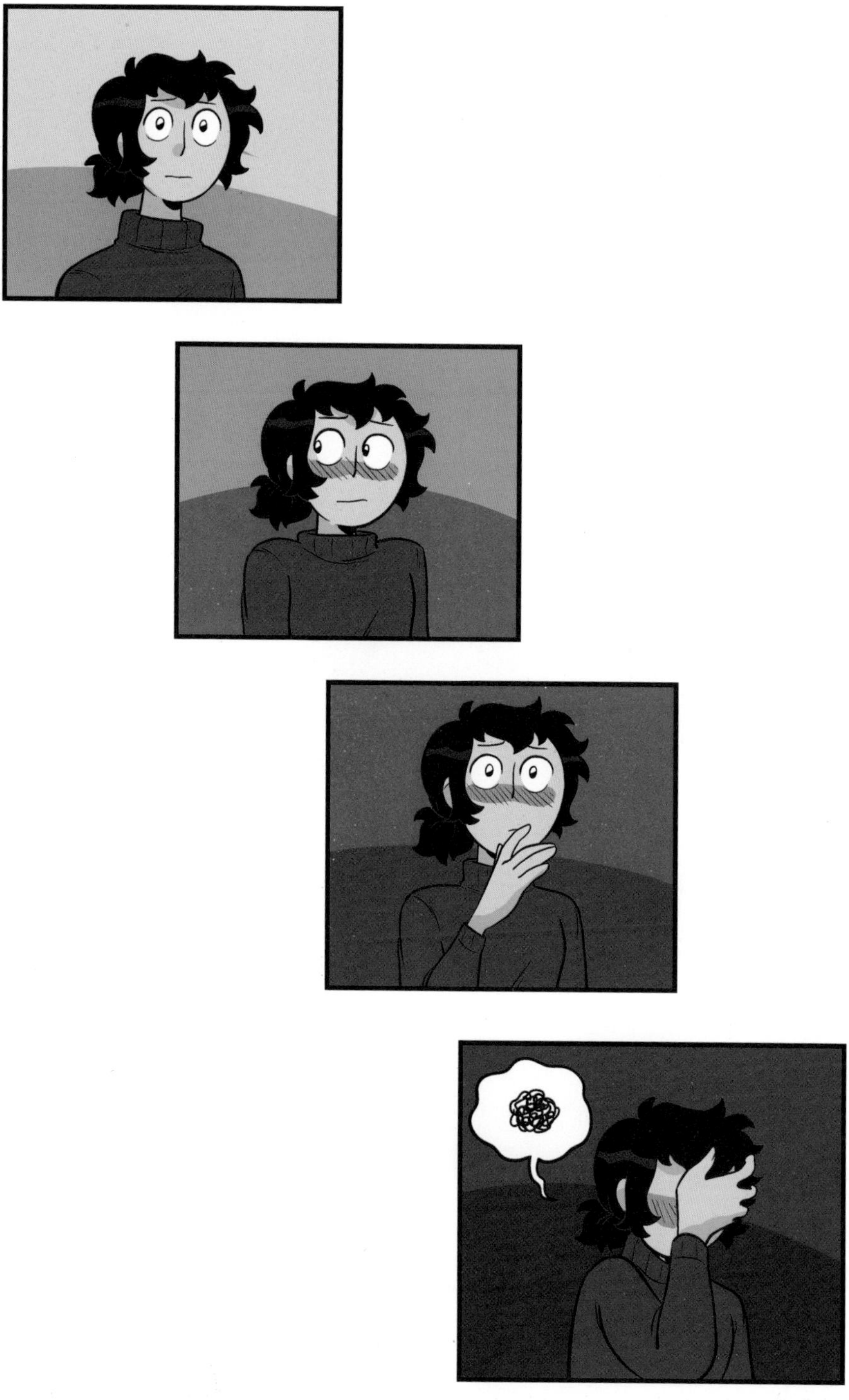

CHAPTER

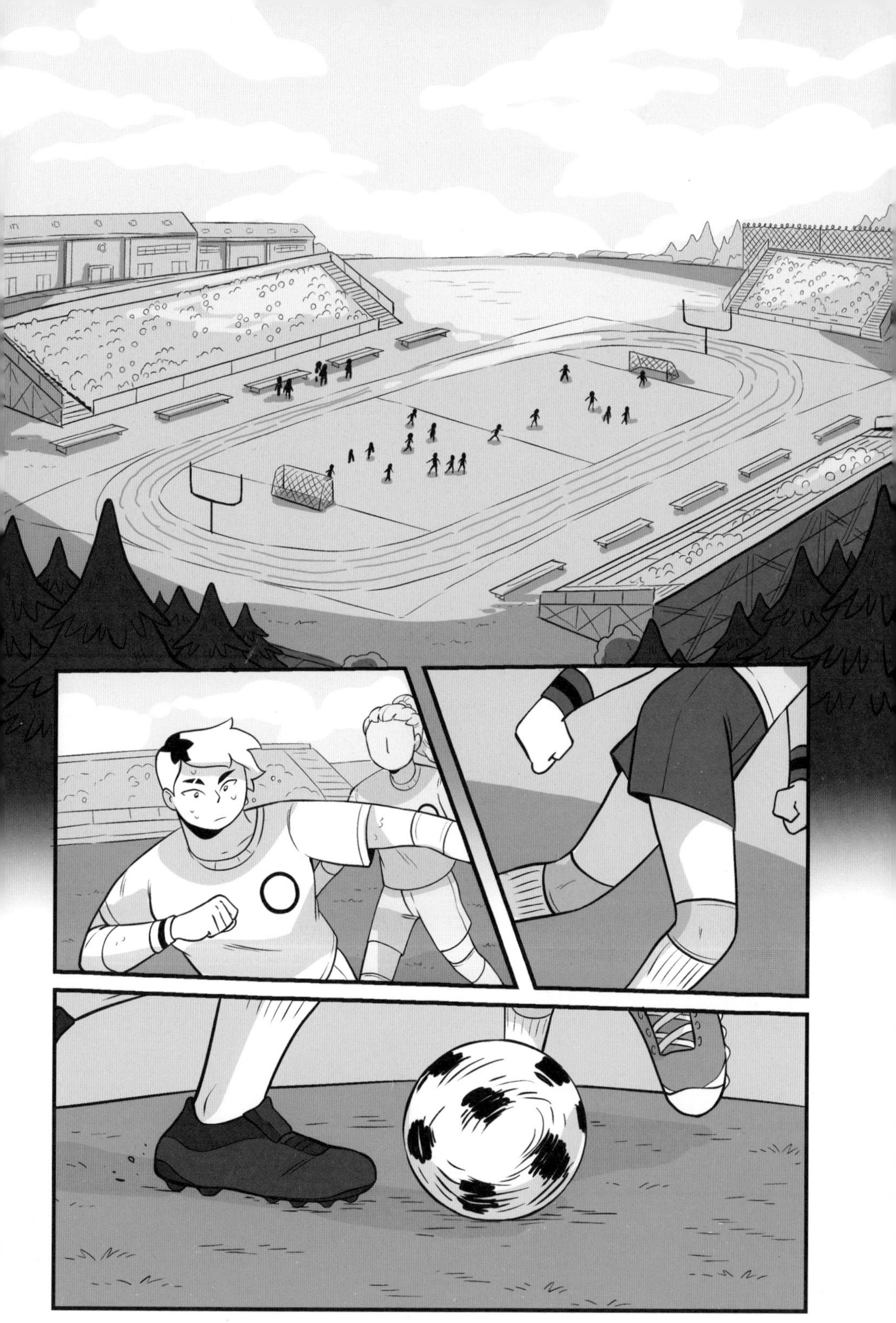

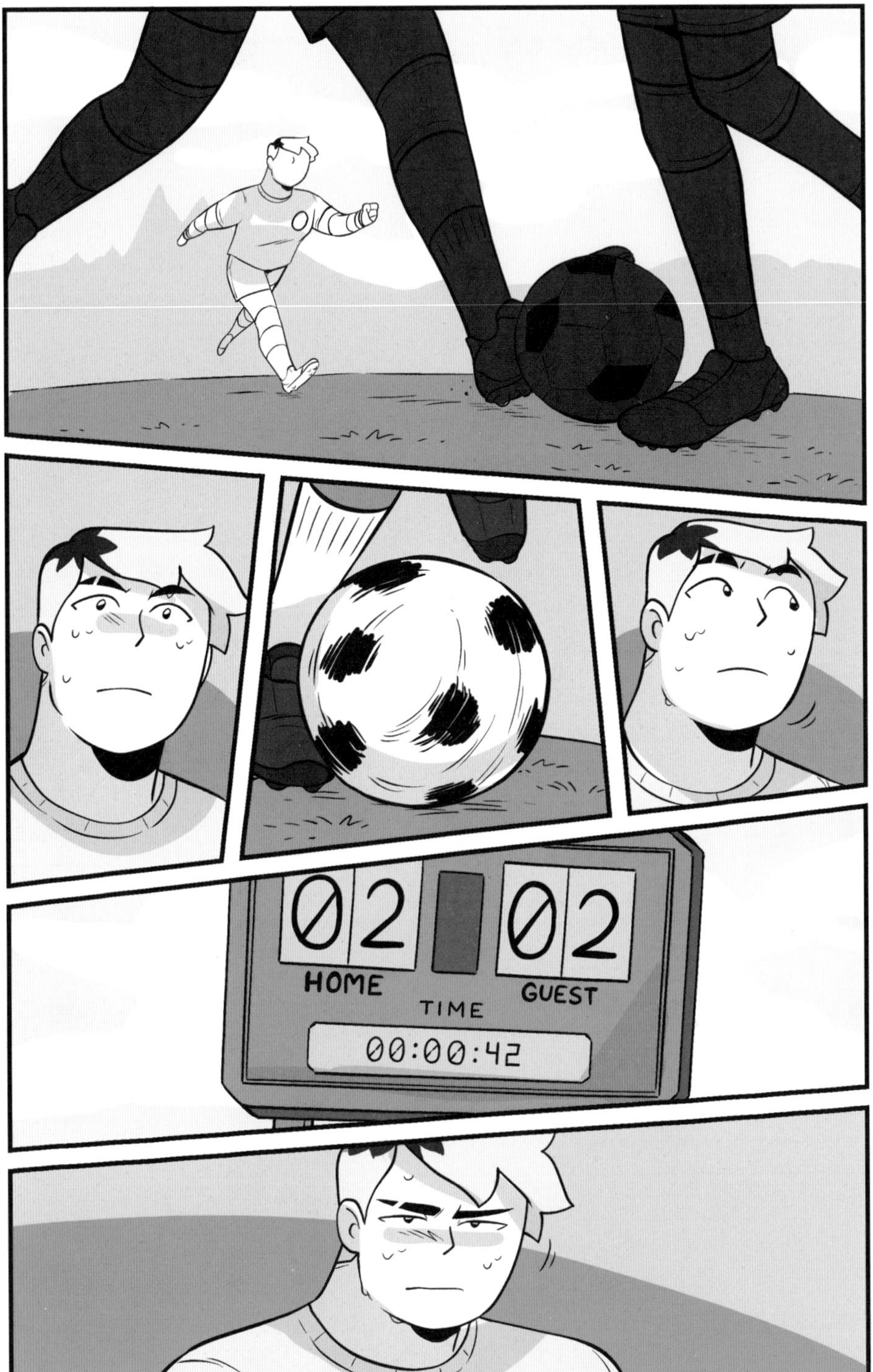
02 02
HOME
TIME
GUEST
00:00:42

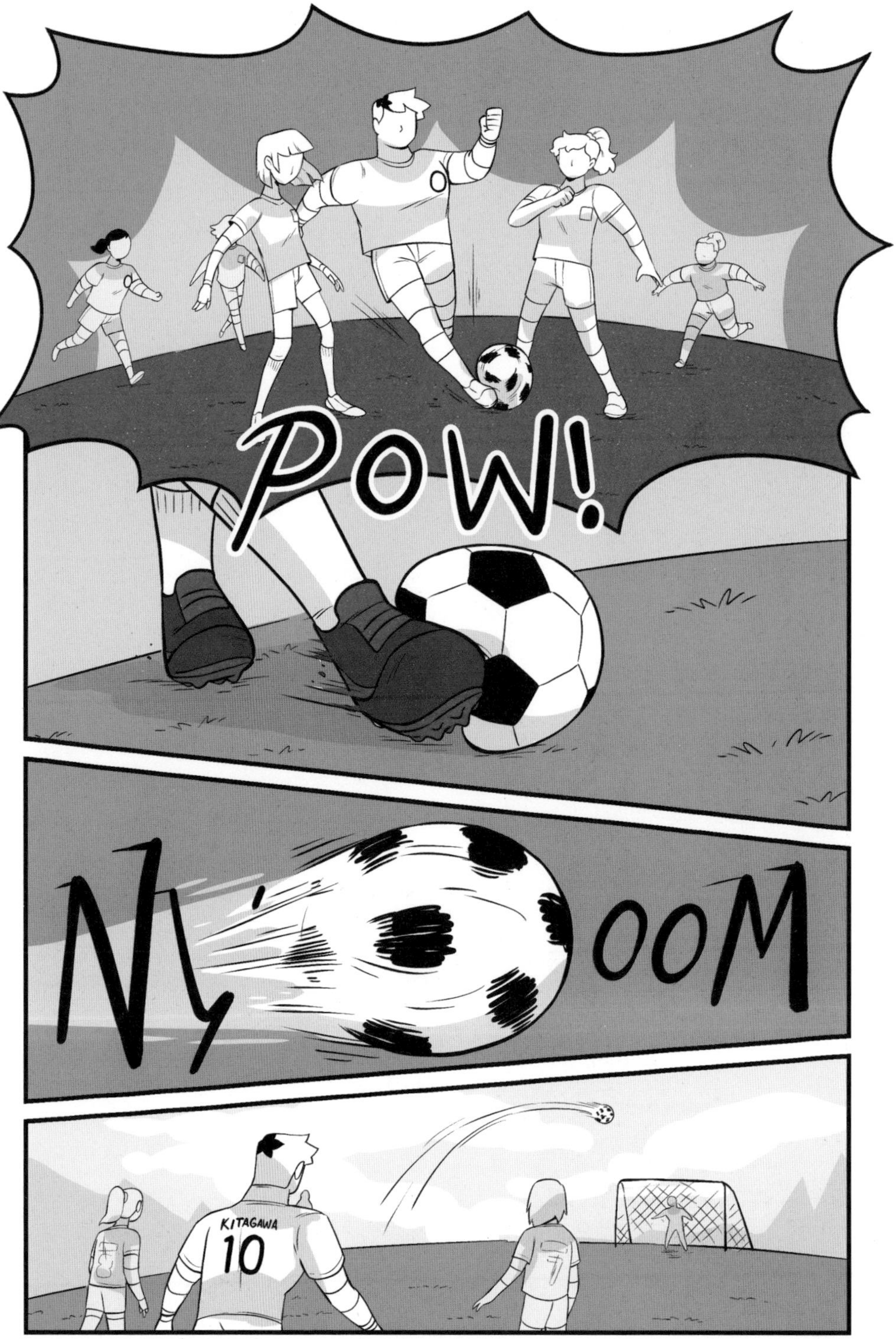
POW!
NYOOOM
KITAGAWA
10

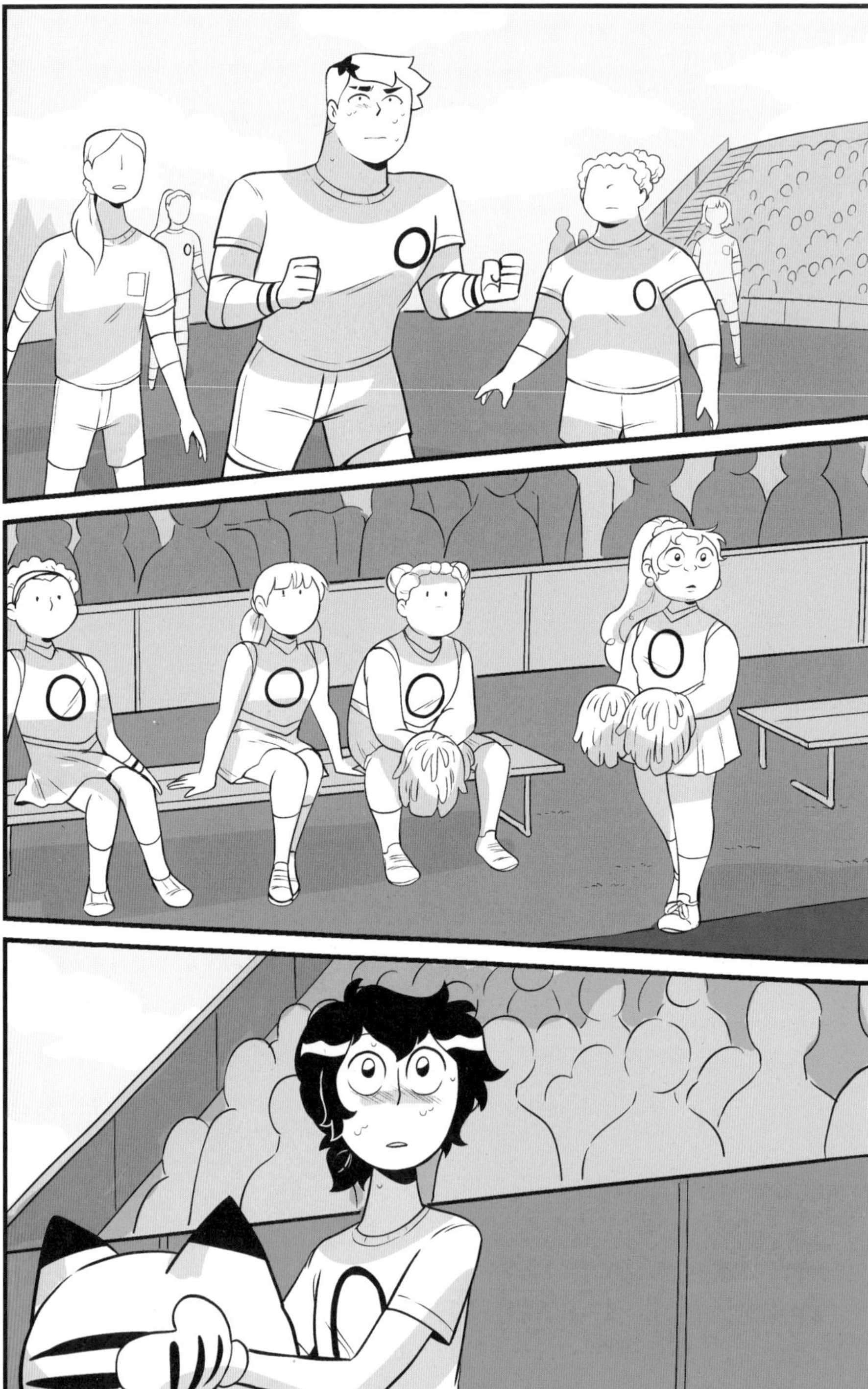

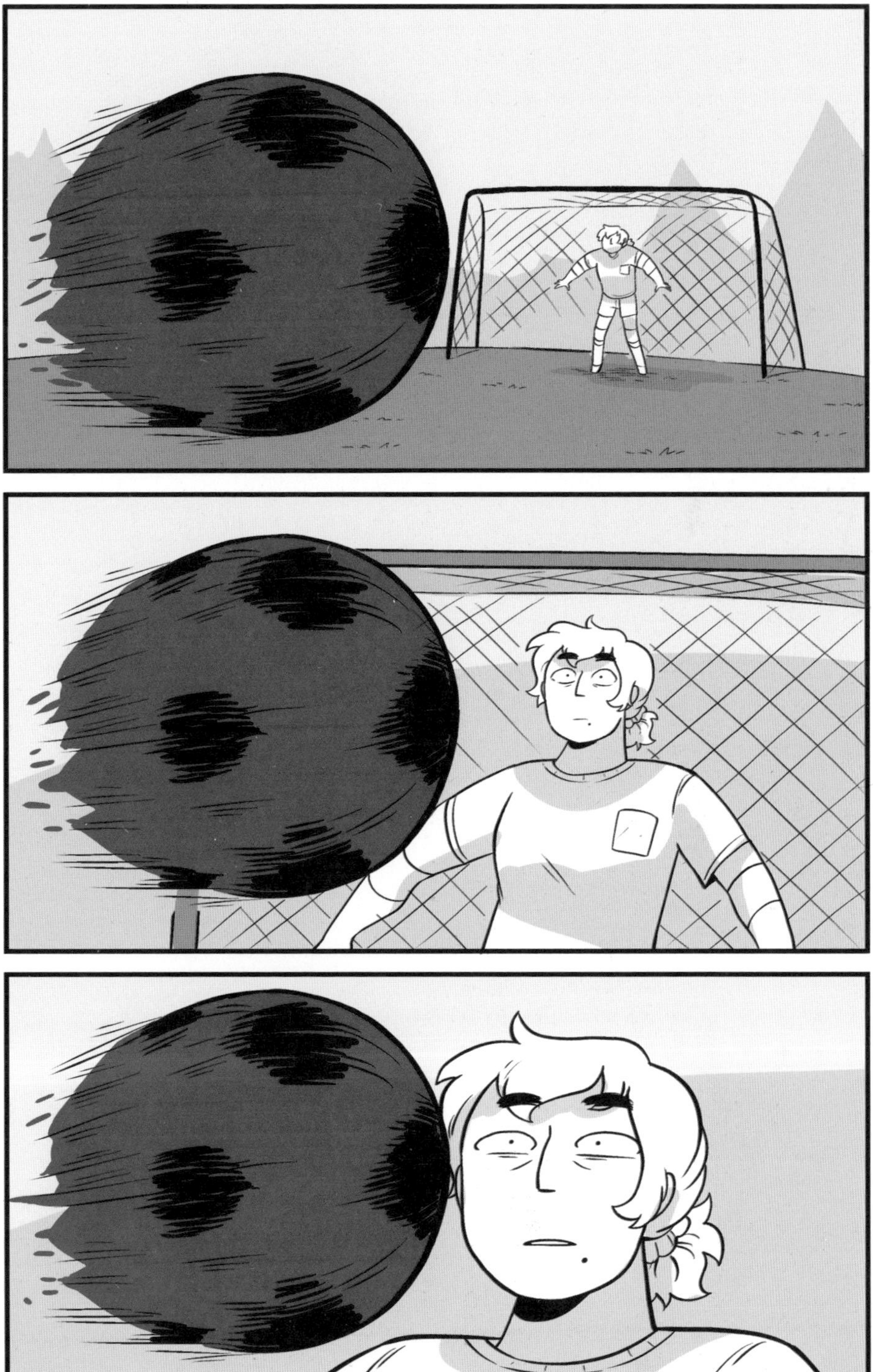

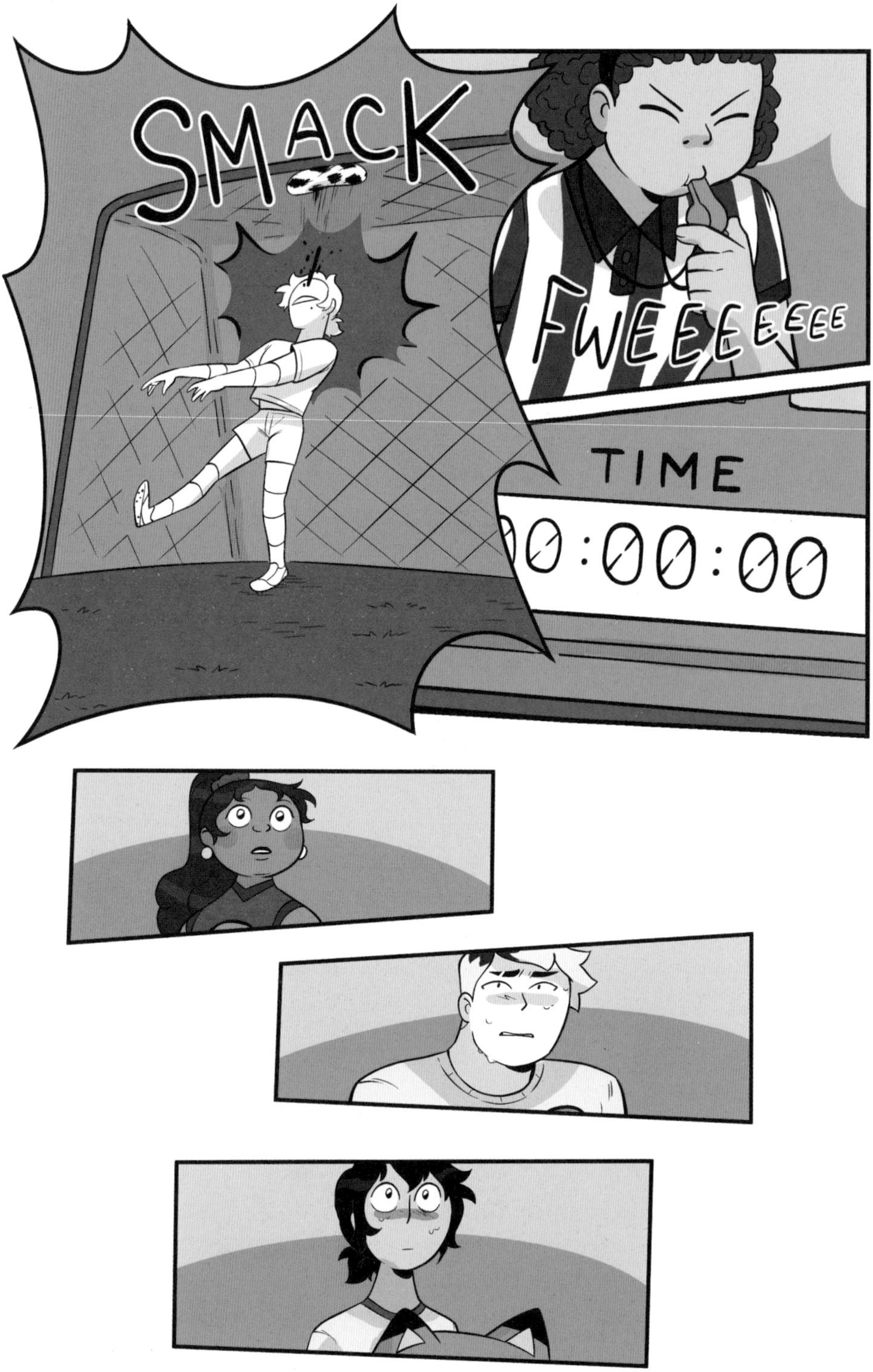
SMACK
FWEEEEEEE
TIME
00:00:00

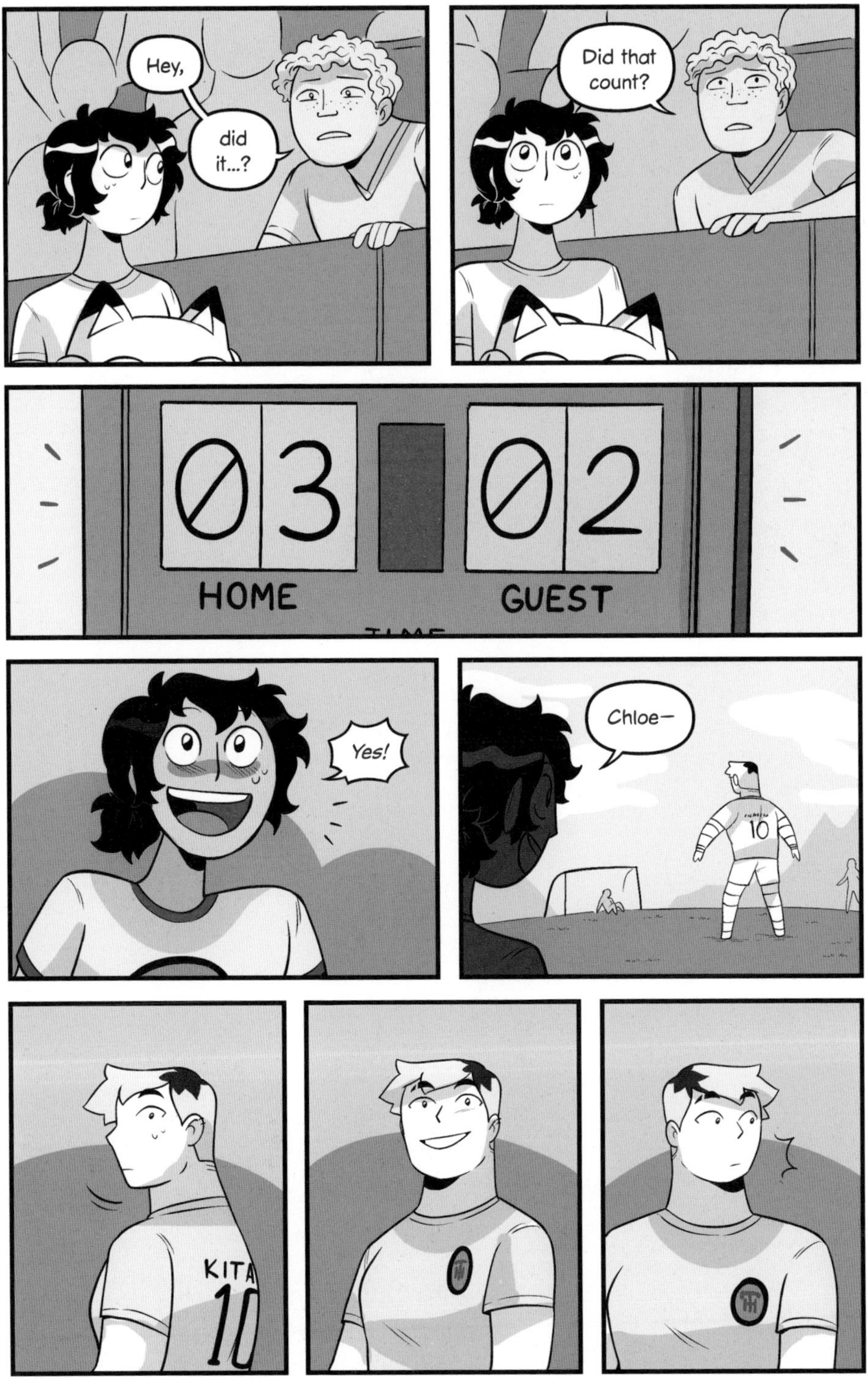
Hey,
did it...?
Did that count?
03
02
HOME
GUEST
Yes!
Chloe–
KITA
10

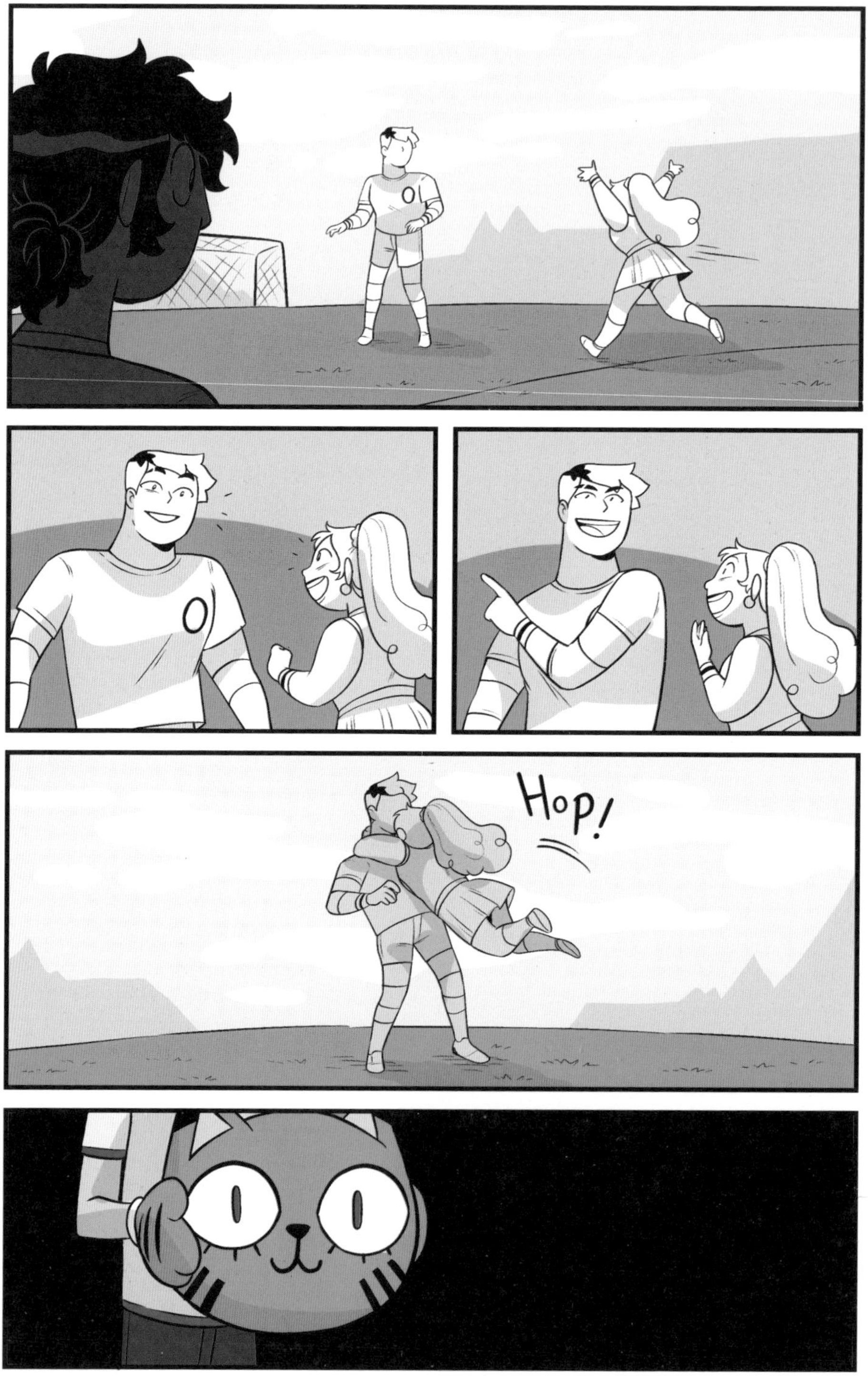
Hop!

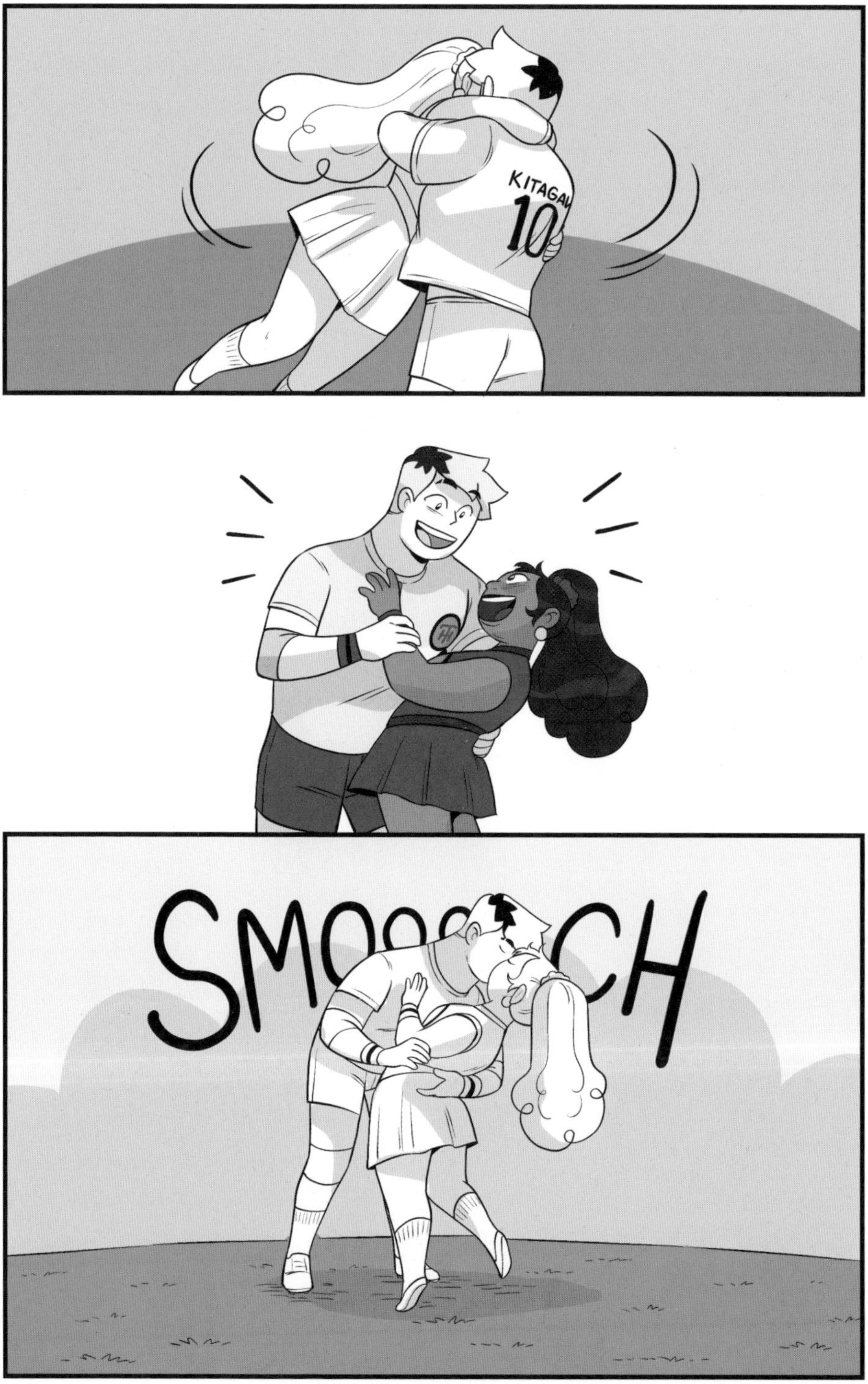
KITAGAW
10
SMOO
CH

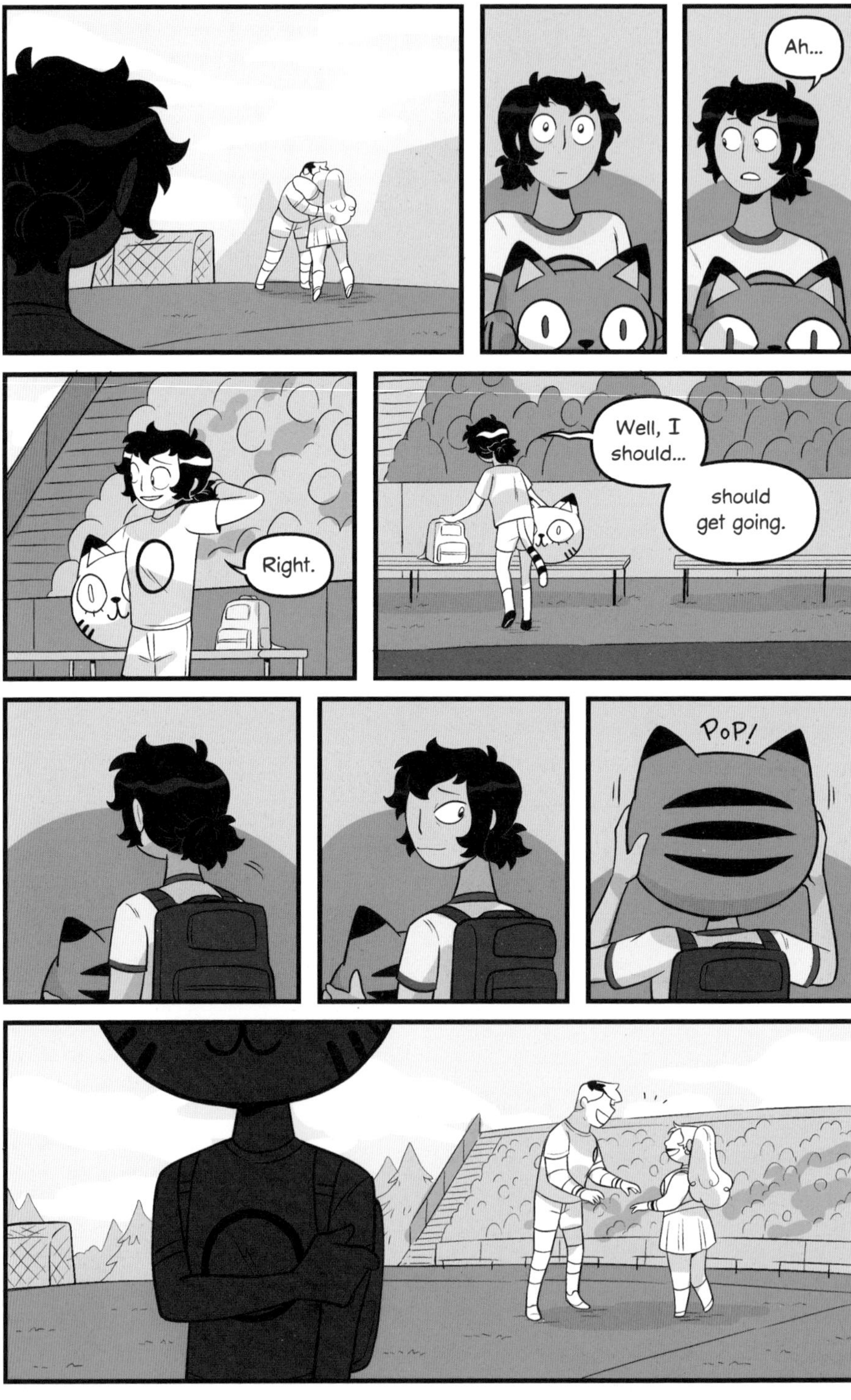
Ah...
Right.
Well, I should...
should get going.
PoP!

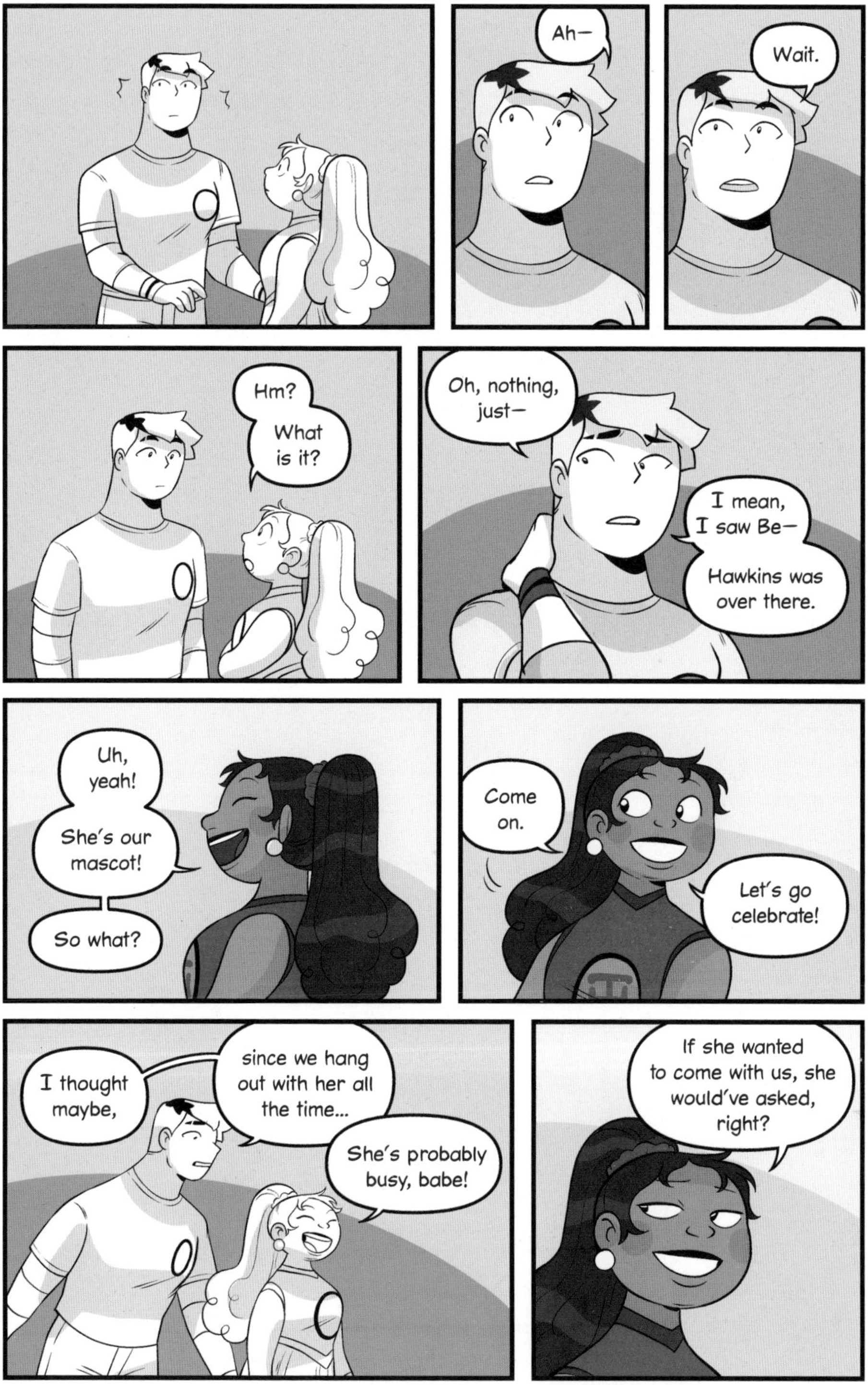

Ah—
Wait.
Hm?
What is it?
Oh, nothing, just—
I mean, I saw Be—
Hawkins was over there.
Uh, yeah!
She's our mascot!
So what?
Come on.
Let's go celebrate!
I thought maybe,
since we hang out with her all the time...
She's probably busy, babe!
If she wanted to come with us, she would've asked, right?

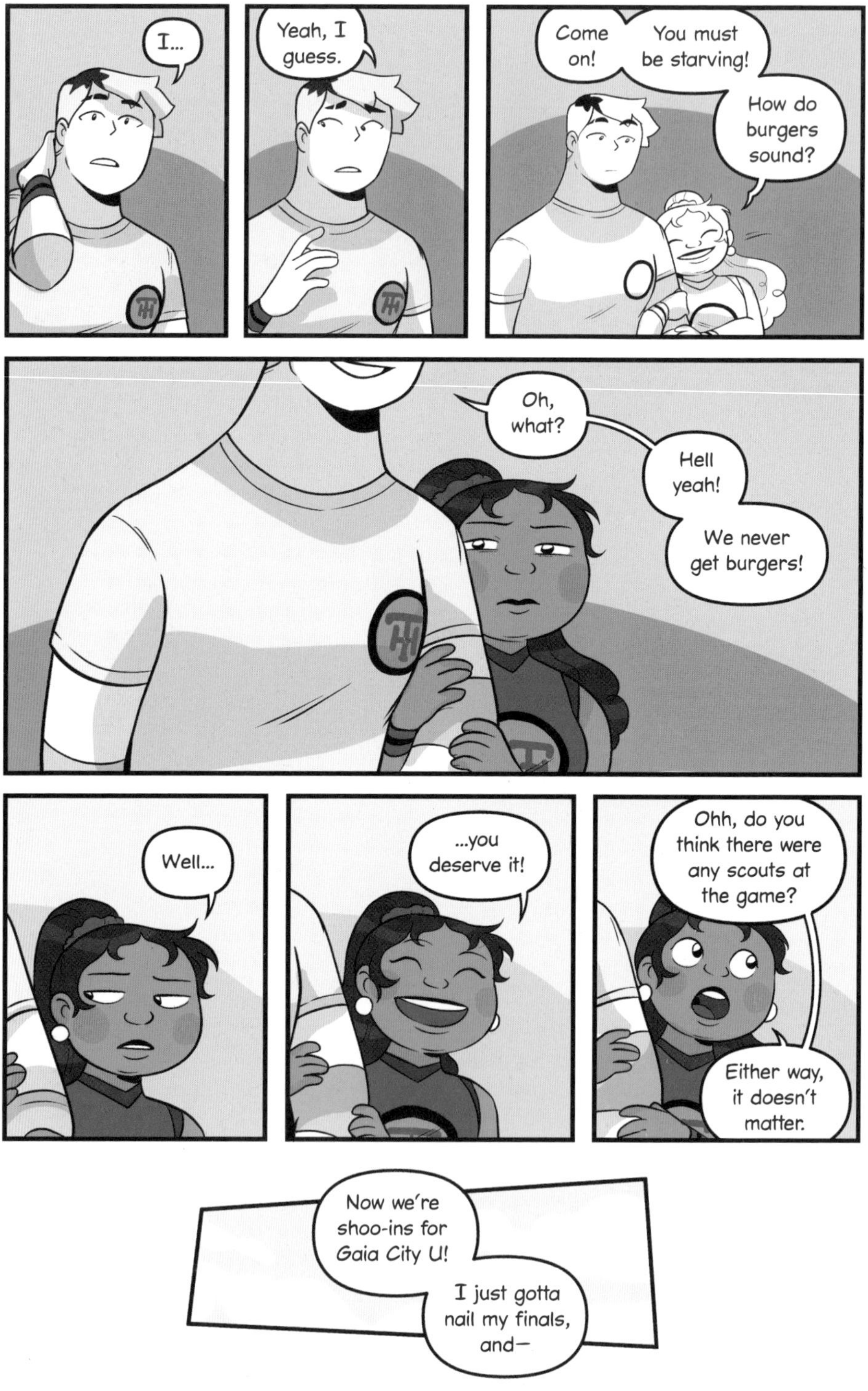
I...
Yeah, I guess.
Come on!
You must be starving!
How do burgers sound?
Oh, what?
Hell yeah!
We never get burgers!
Well...
...you deserve it!
Ohh, do you think there were any scouts at the game?
Either way, it doesn't matter.
Now we're shoo-ins for Gaia City U!
I just gotta nail my finals, and—

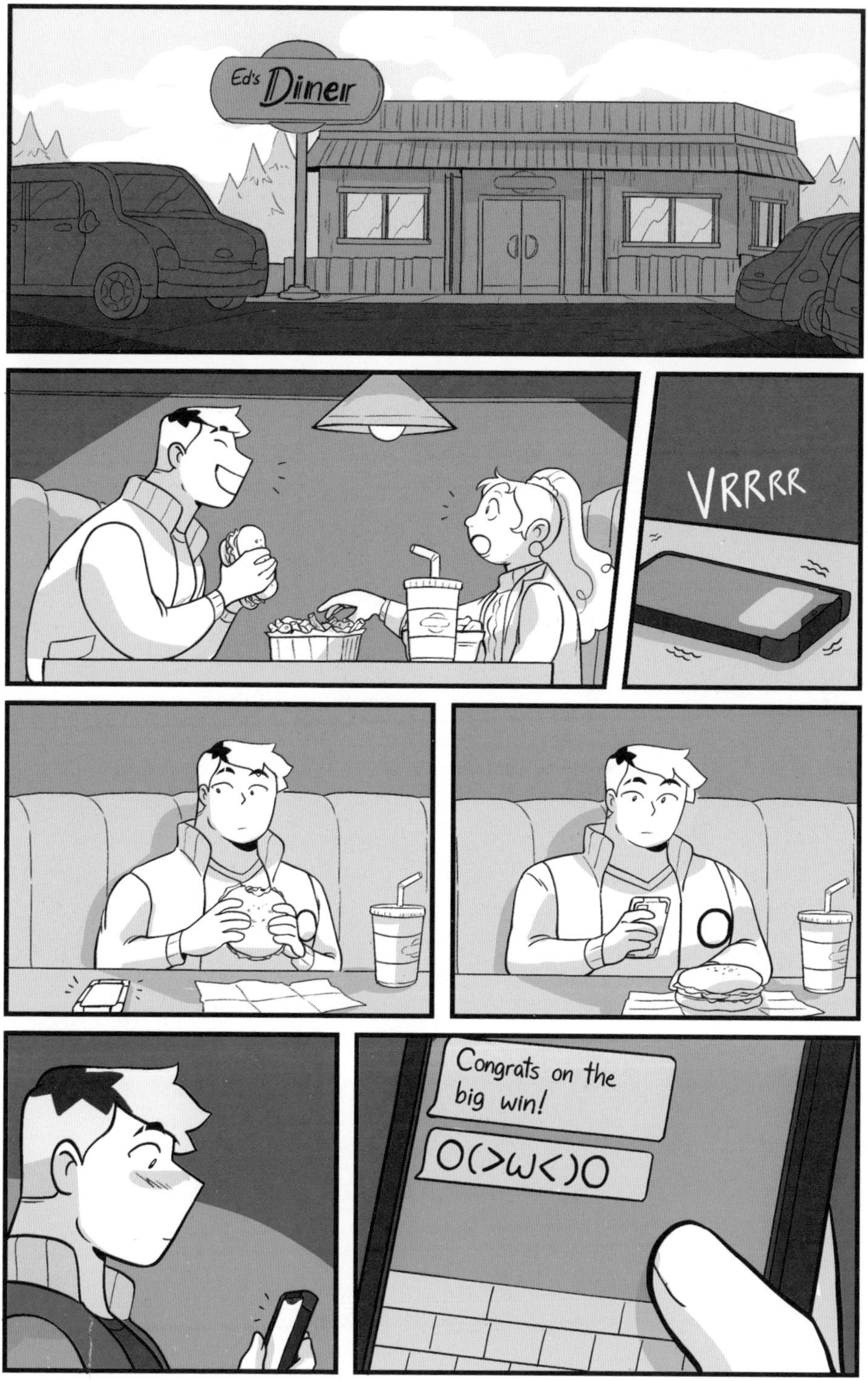
Ed's Diner
VRRRR
Congrats on the big win!
O(>ω<)O

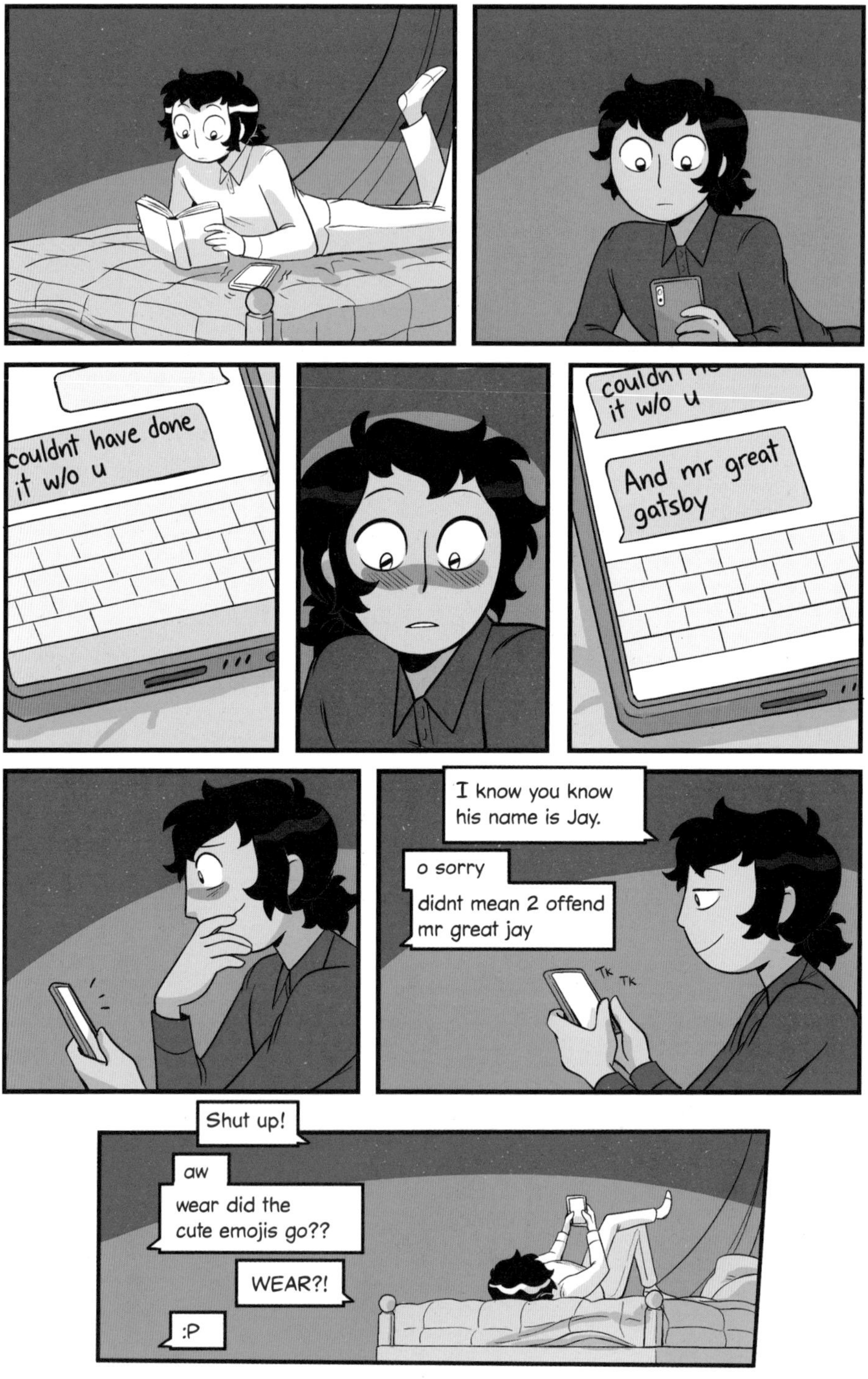
couldnt have done it w/o u
And mr great gatsby
I know you know his name is Jay.
o sorry
didnt mean 2 offend mr great jay
TK TK
Shut up!
aw
wear did the cute emojis go??
WEAR?!
:P

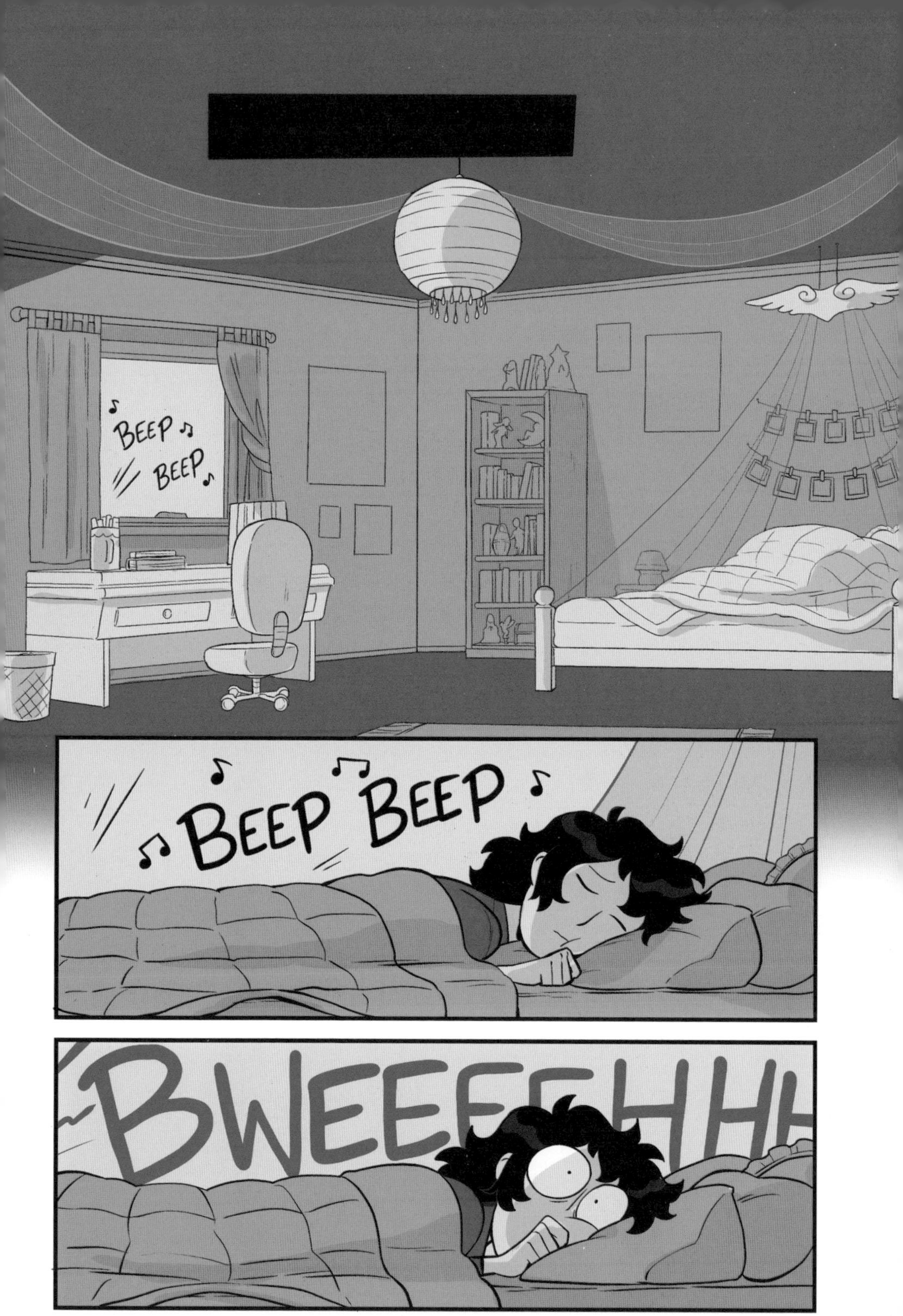
[redacted]
BEEP BEEP
BEEP BEEP
BWEEEHH

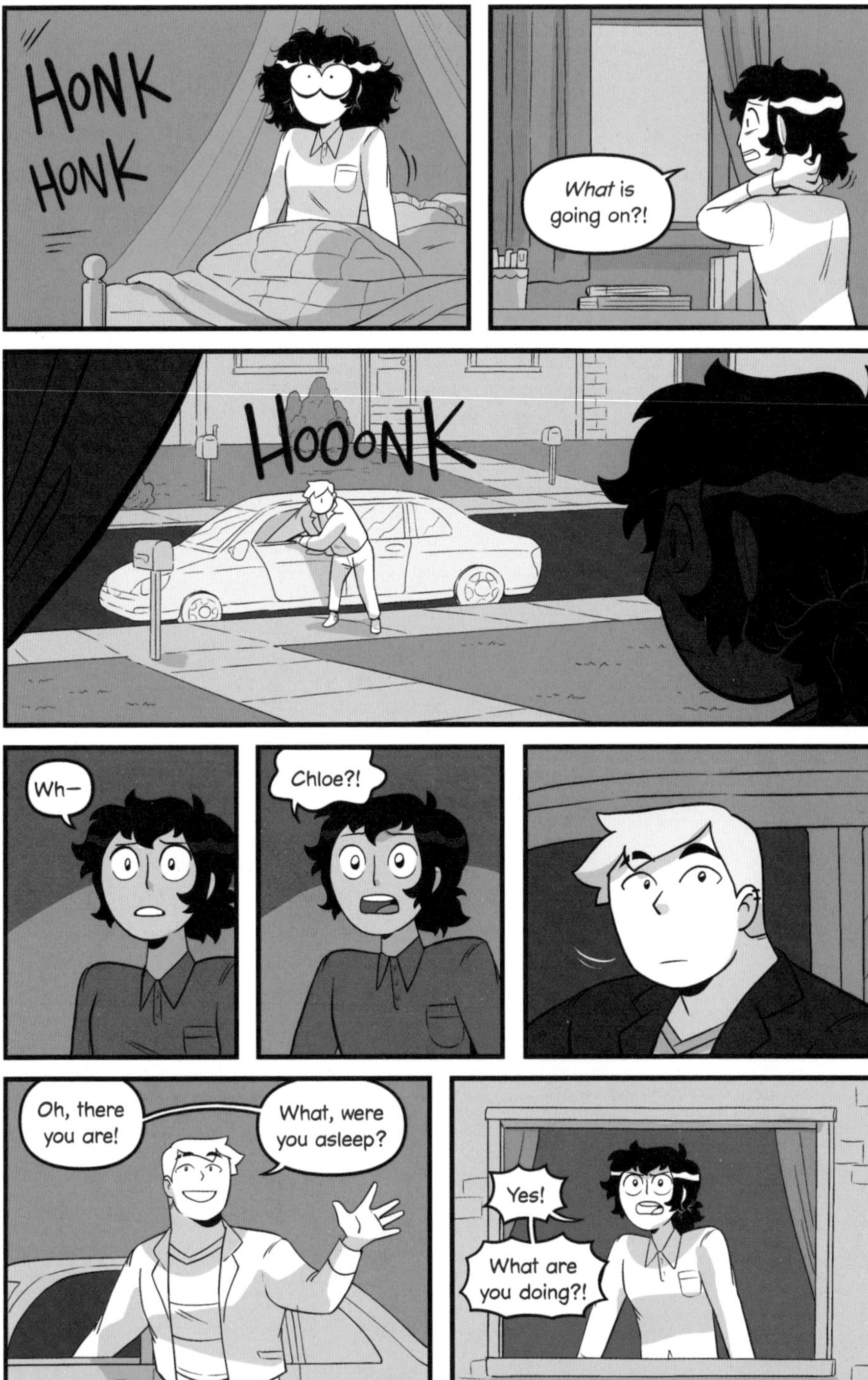
HONK
HONK
What is going on?!
HOOONK
Wh—
Chloe?!
Oh, there you are!
What, were you asleep?
Yes!
What are you doing?!

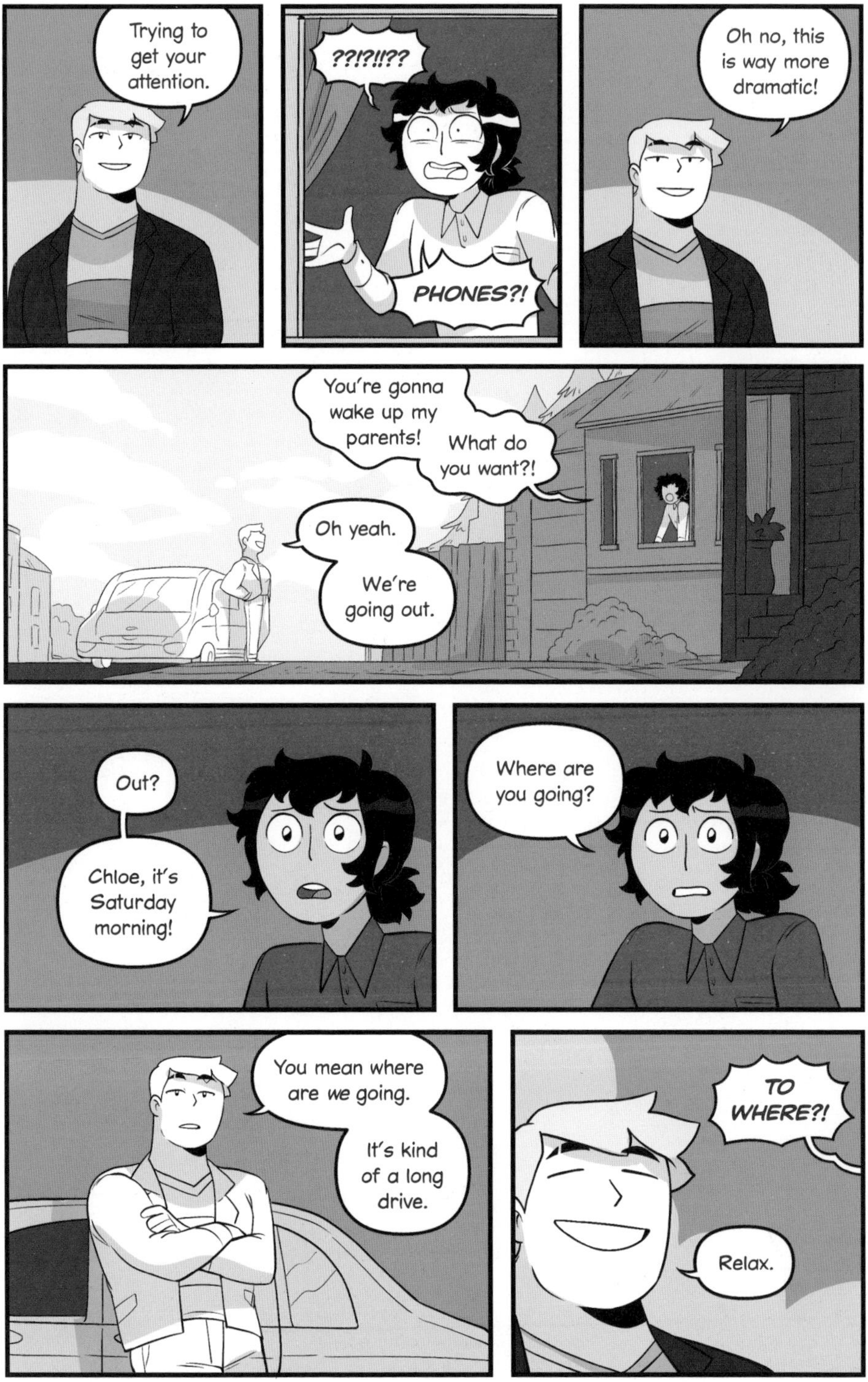
Trying to get your attention.
??!?!!??
PHONES?!
Oh no, this is way more dramatic!
You're gonna wake up my parents!
What do you want?!
Oh yeah.
We're going out.
Out?
Chloe, it's Saturday morning!
Where are you going?
You mean where are we going.
It's kind of a long drive.
TO WHERE?!
Relax.

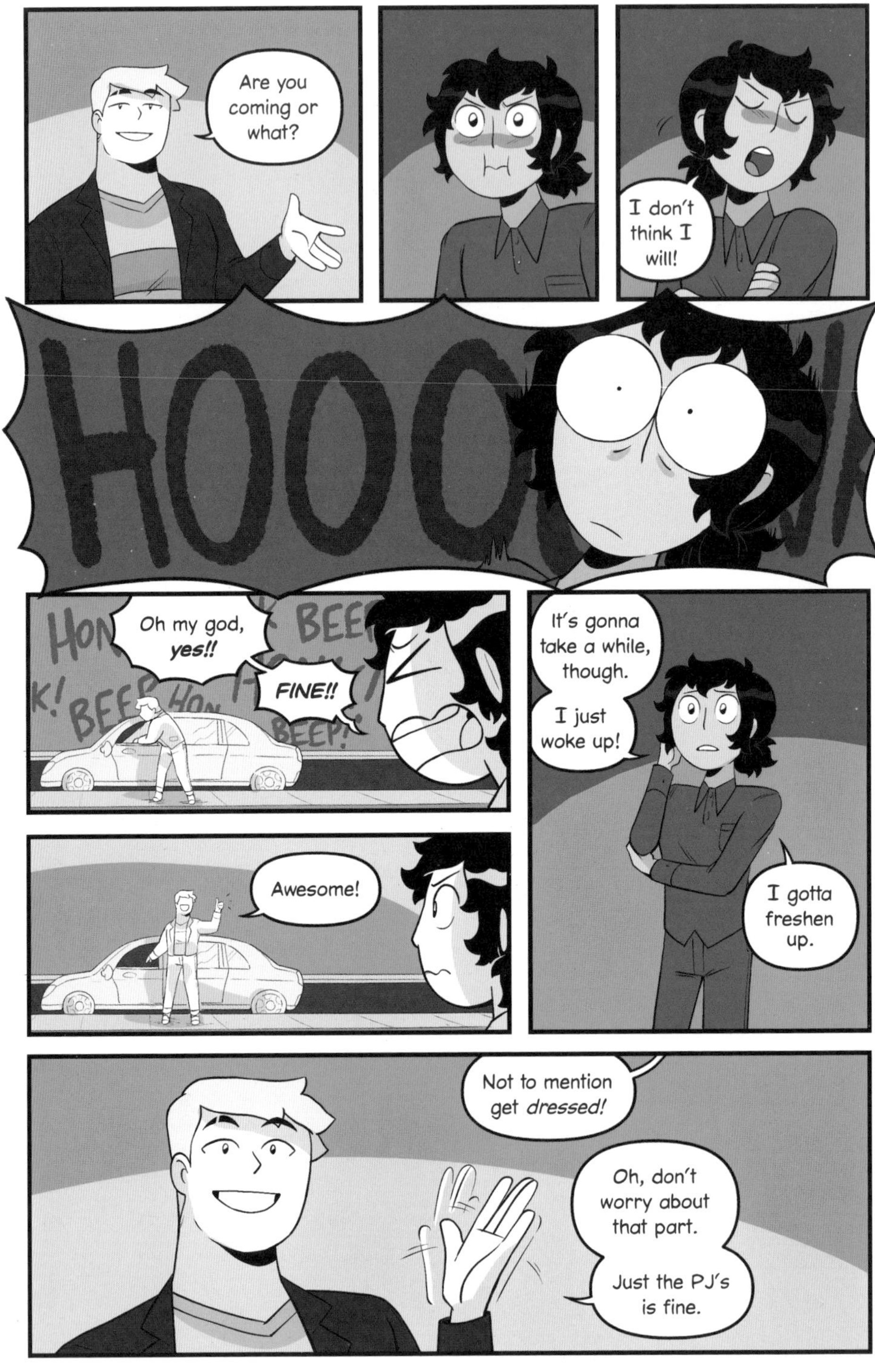
Are you coming or what?
I don't think I will!
Oh my god, *yes!!*
FINE!!
It's gonna take a while, though.
I just woke up!
Awesome!
I gotta freshen up.
Not to mention get *dressed!*
Oh, don't worry about that part.
Just the PJ's is fine.

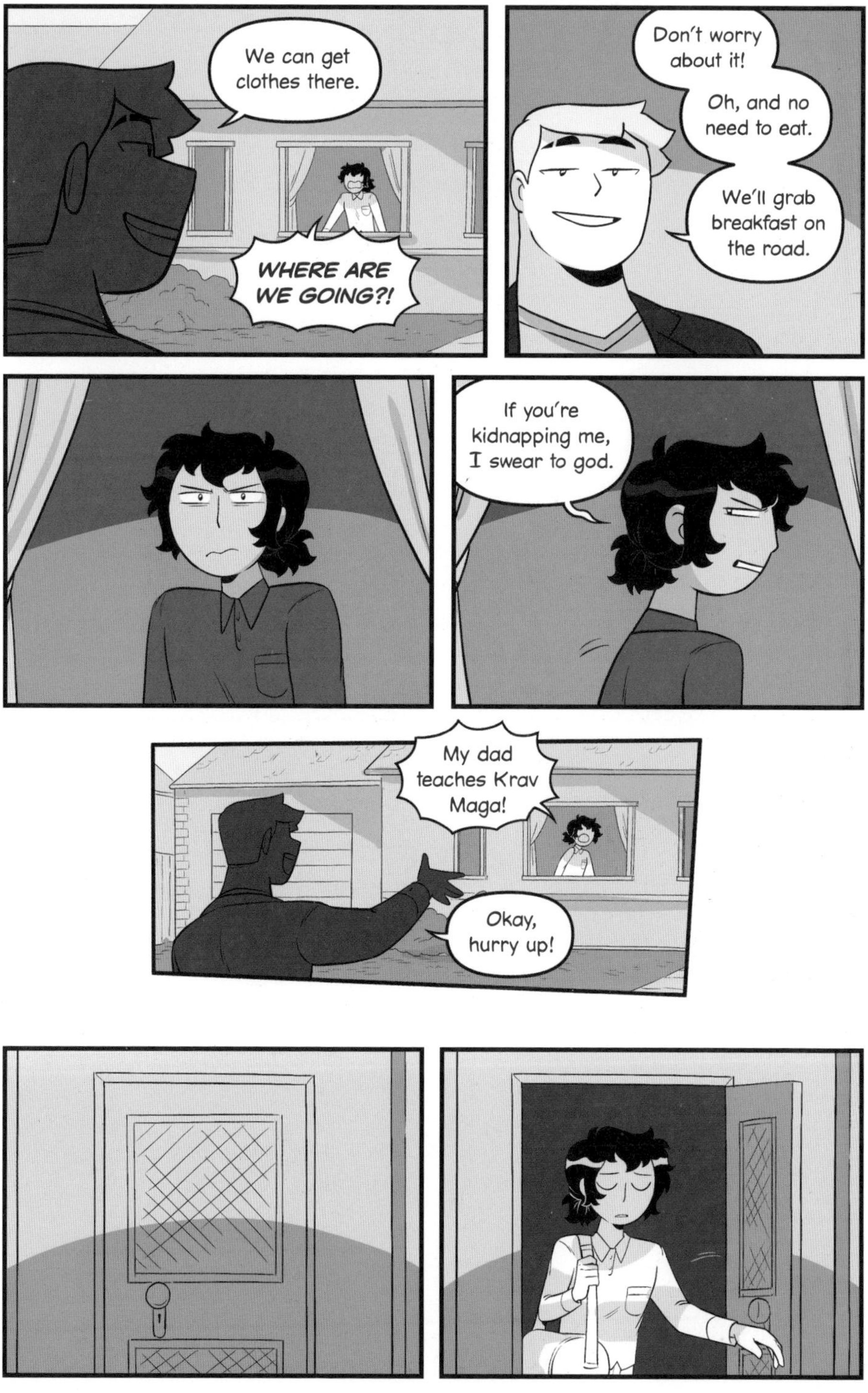
We can get clothes there.
WHERE ARE WE GOING?!
Don't worry about it!
Oh, and no need to eat.
We'll grab breakfast on the road.
If you're kidnapping me, I swear to god.
My dad teaches Krav Maga!
Okay, hurry up!

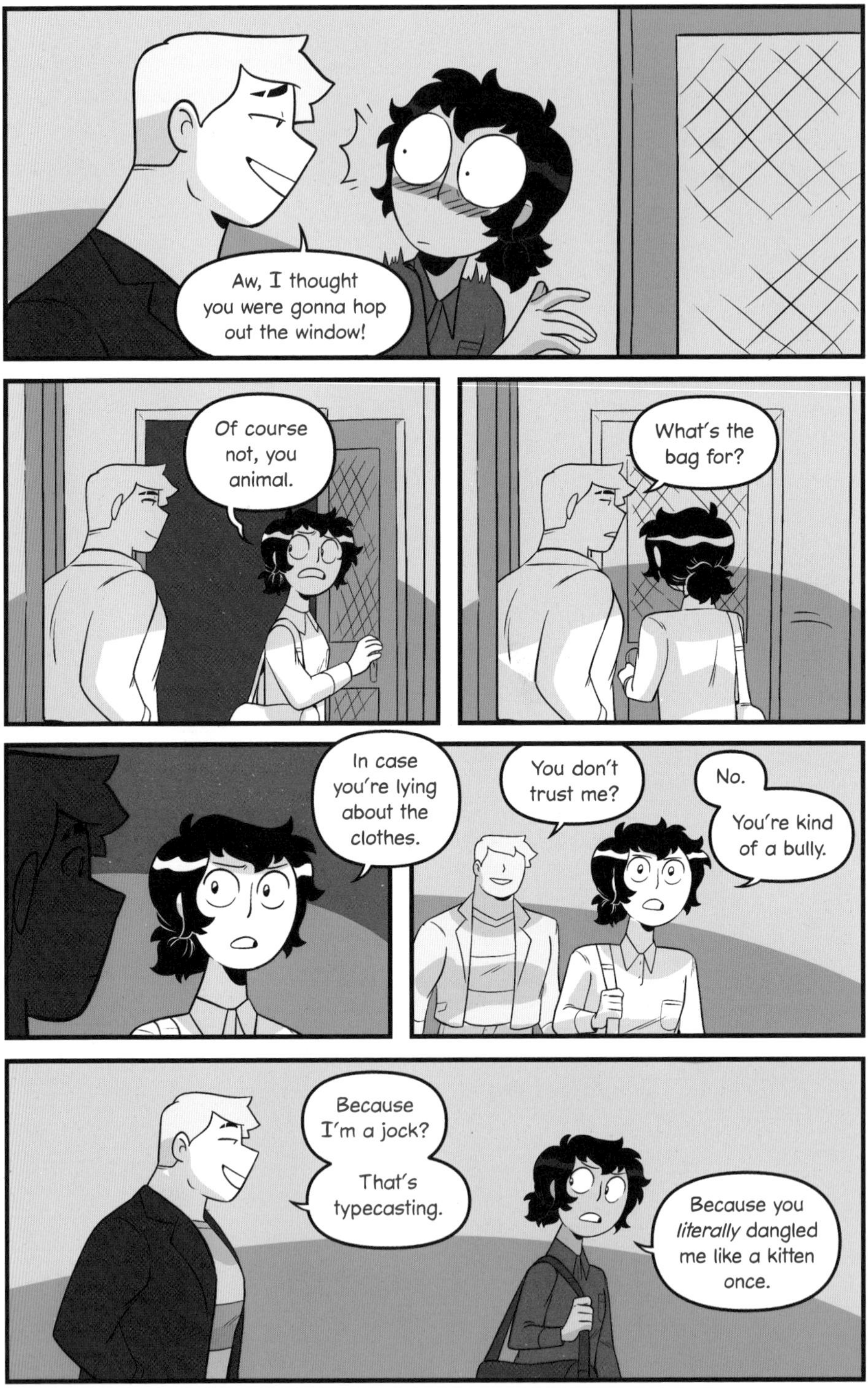
Aw, I thought you were gonna hop out the window!
Of course not, you animal.
What's the bag for?
In case you're lying about the clothes.
You don't trust me?
No.
You're kind of a bully.
Because I'm a jock?
That's typecasting.
Because you *literally* dangled me like a kitten once.

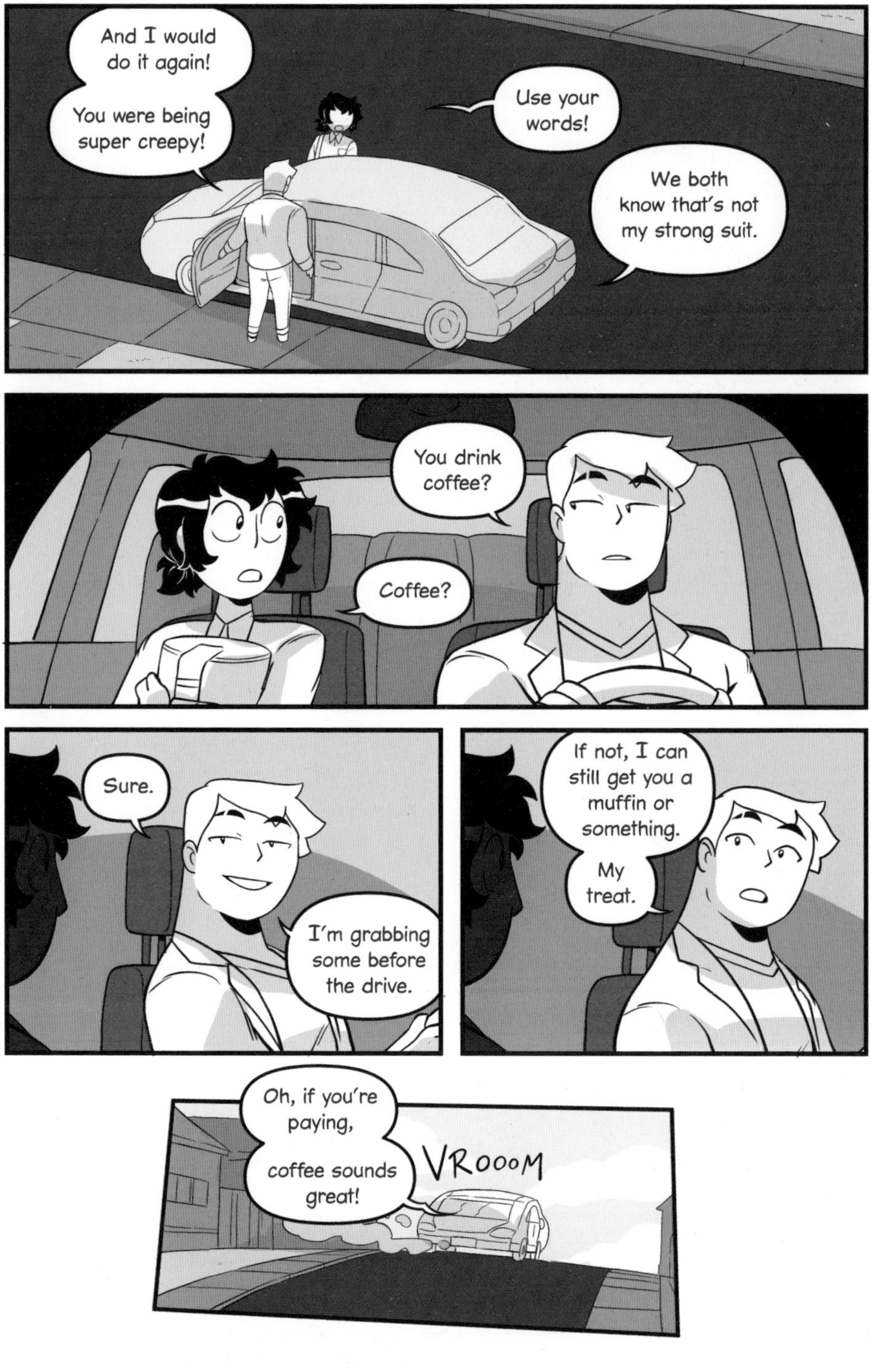
And I would do it again!
You were being super creepy!
Use your words!
We both know that's not my strong suit.
You drink coffee?
Coffee?
Sure.
I'm grabbing some before the drive.
If not, I can still get you a muffin or something.
My treat.
Oh, if you're paying,
coffee sounds great!
VROOOM

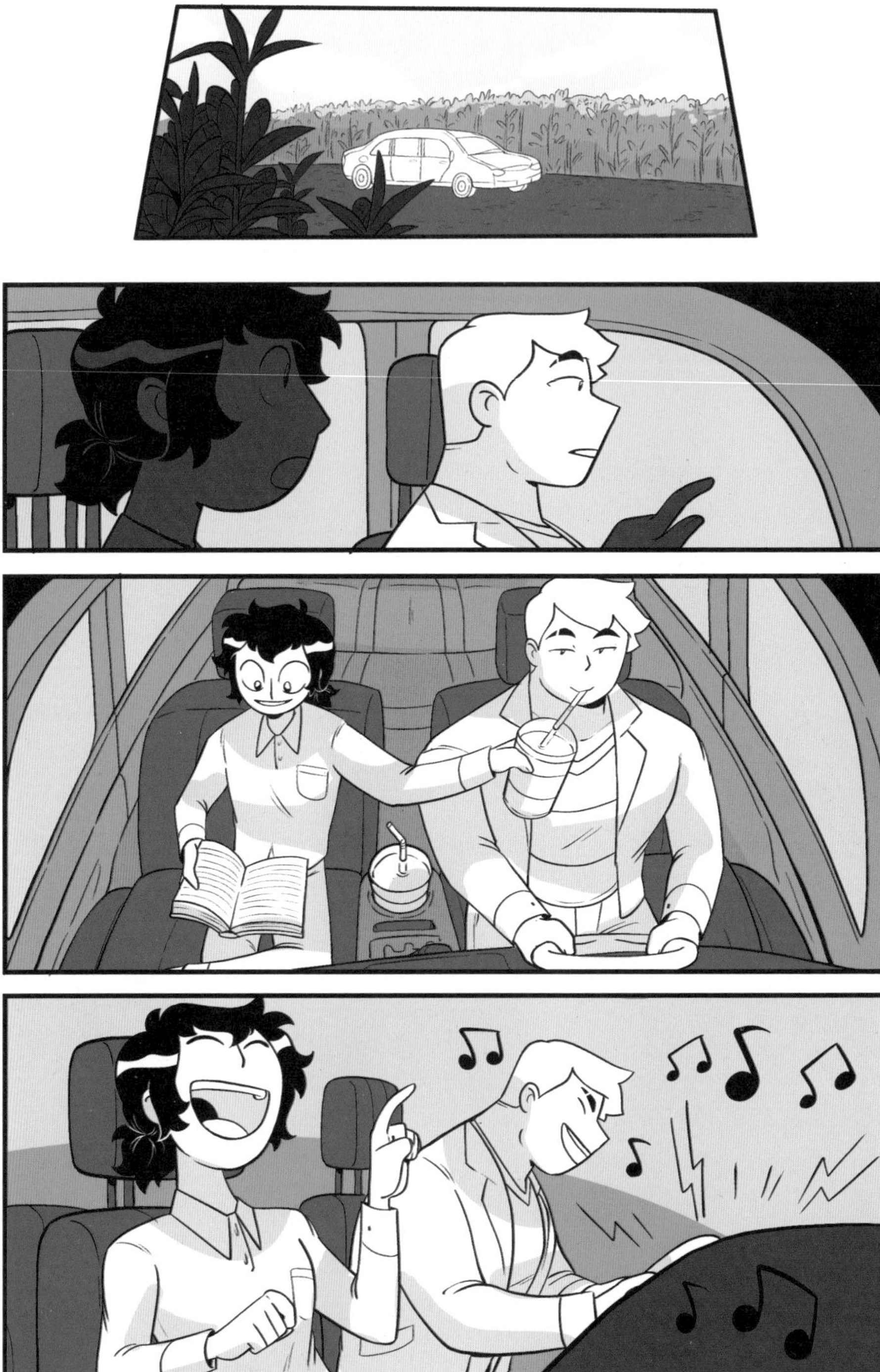

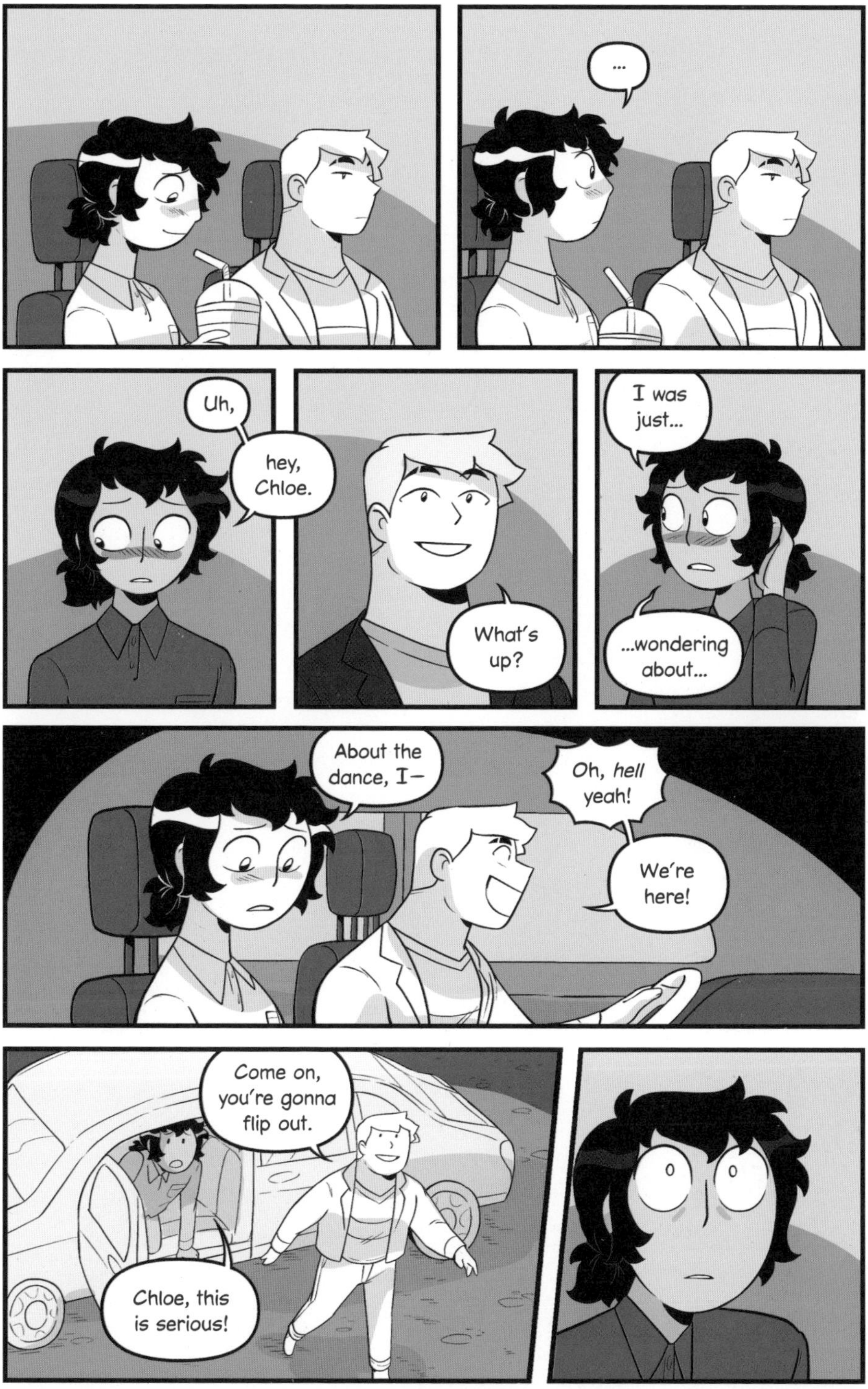
...
Uh,
hey, Chloe.
What's up?
I was just...
...wondering about...
About the dance, I—
Oh, *hell* yeah!
We're here!
Come on, you're gonna flip out.
Chloe, this is serious!

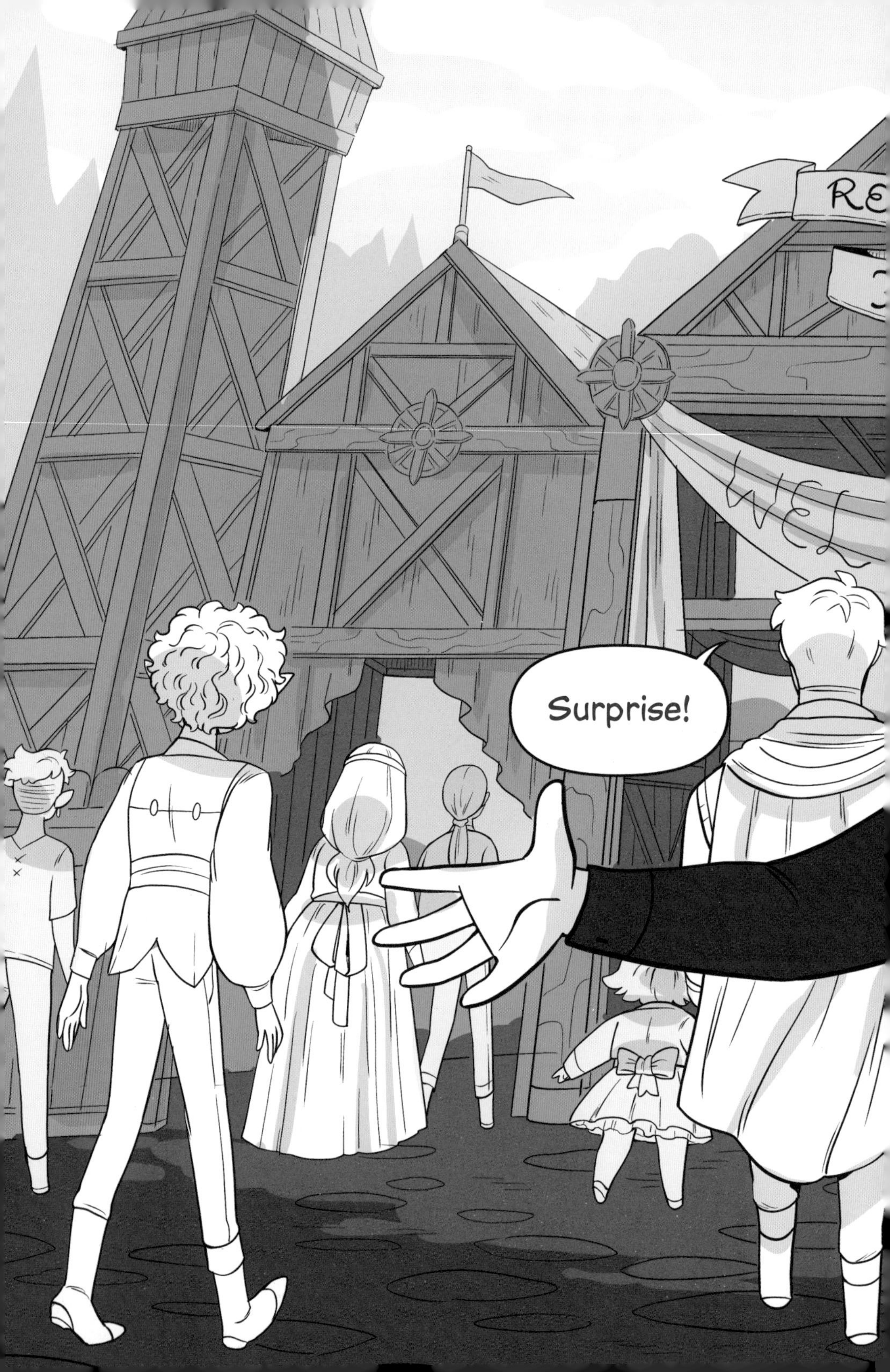
Surprise!

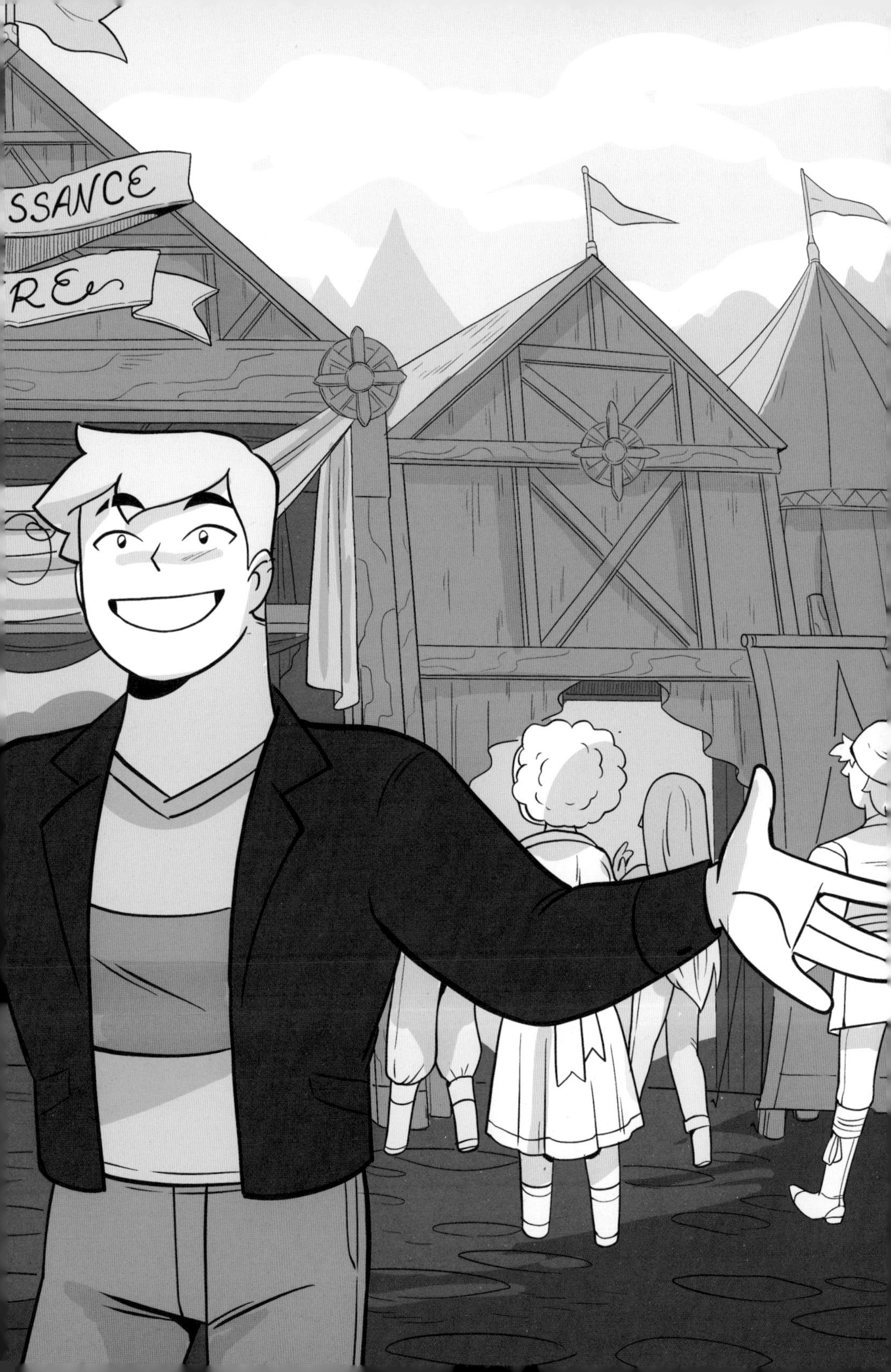
SSANCE
RE

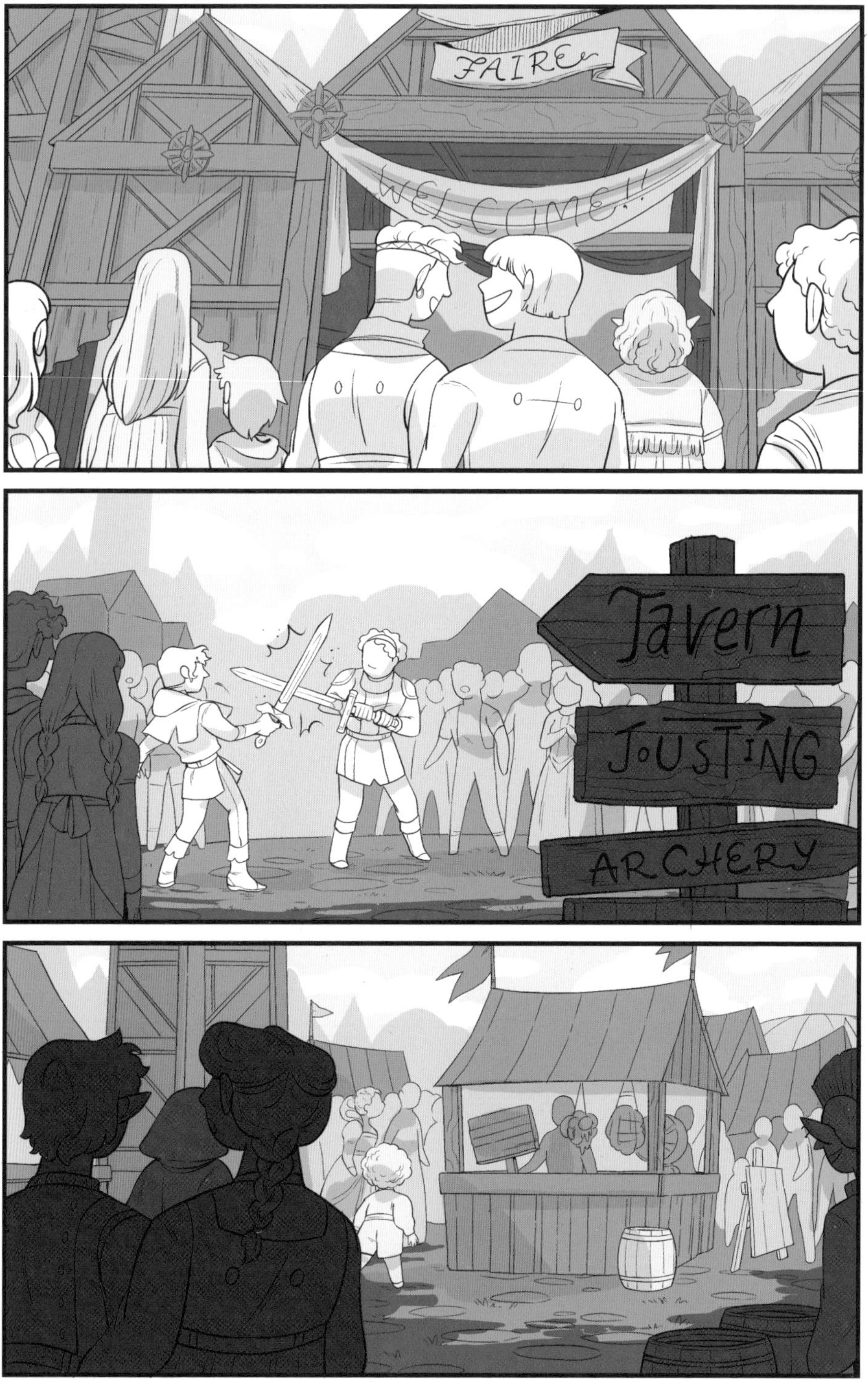
FAIRE
WELCOME!!
Tavern
JOUSTING
ARCHERY

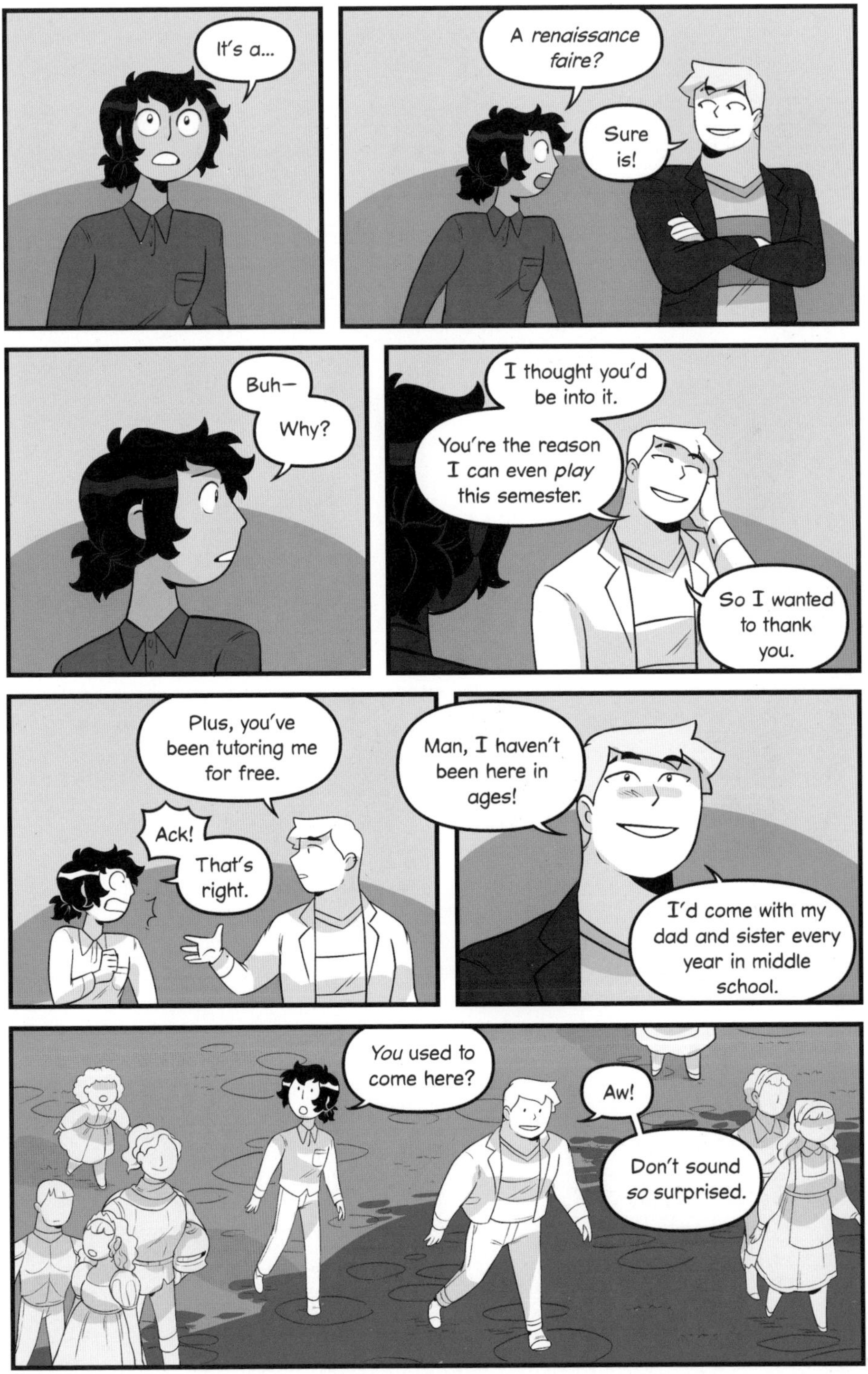
It's a...
A *renaissance faire?*
Sure is!
Buh—
Why?
I thought you'd be into it.
You're the reason I can even *play* this semester.
So I wanted to thank you.
Plus, you've been tutoring me for free.
Ack!
That's right.
Man, I haven't been here in ages!
I'd come with my dad and sister every year in middle school.
You used to come here?
Aw!
Don't sound *so* surprised.

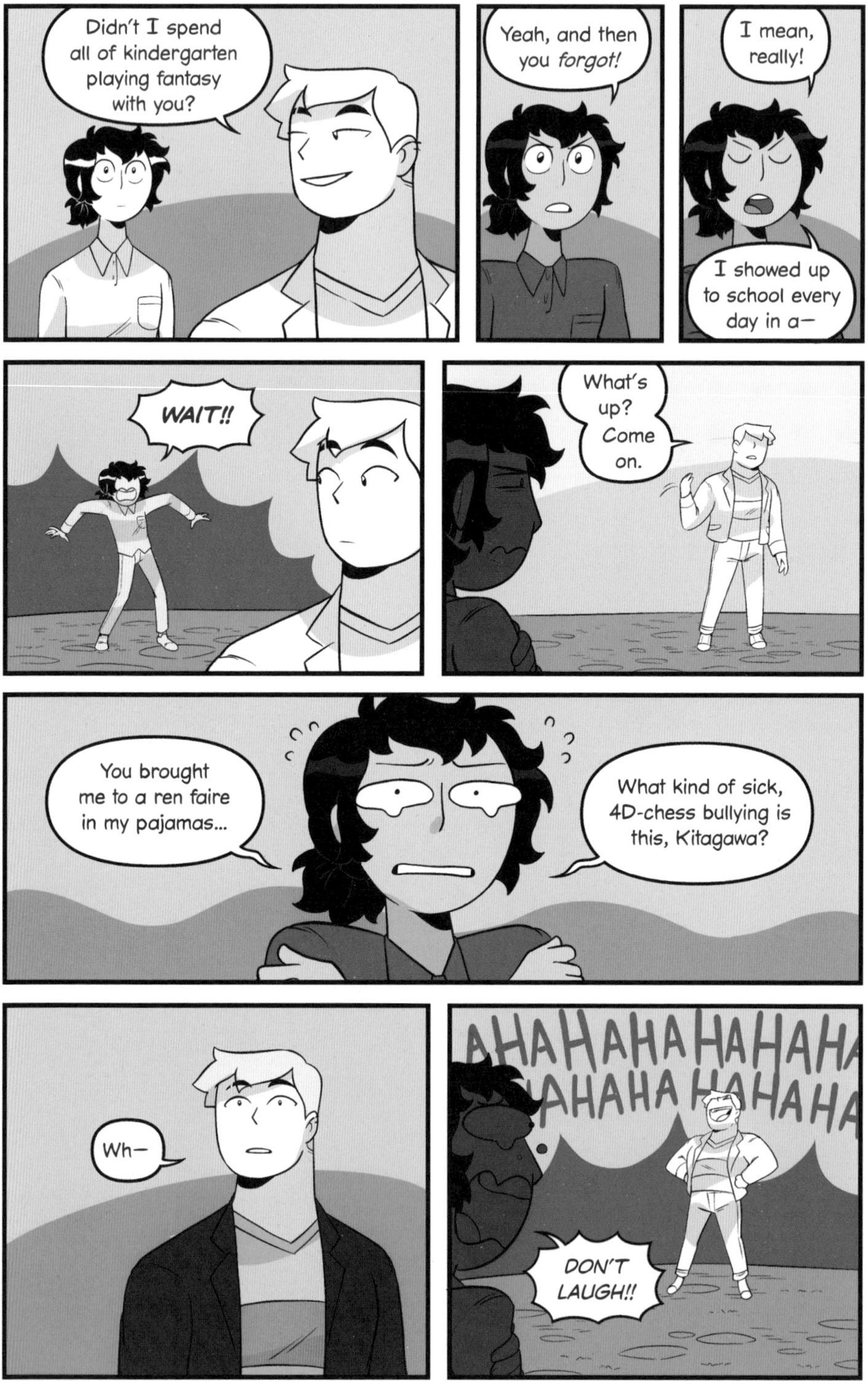
Didn't I spend all of kindergarten playing fantasy with you?
Yeah, and then you *forgot!*
I mean, really!
I showed up to school every day in a—
WAIT!!
What's up? Come on.
You brought me to a ren faire in my pajamas...
What kind of sick, 4D-chess bullying is this, Kitagawa?
Wh—
AHAHAHAHAHAHAHA
HAHAHAHAHAHAHA
DON'T LAUGH!!

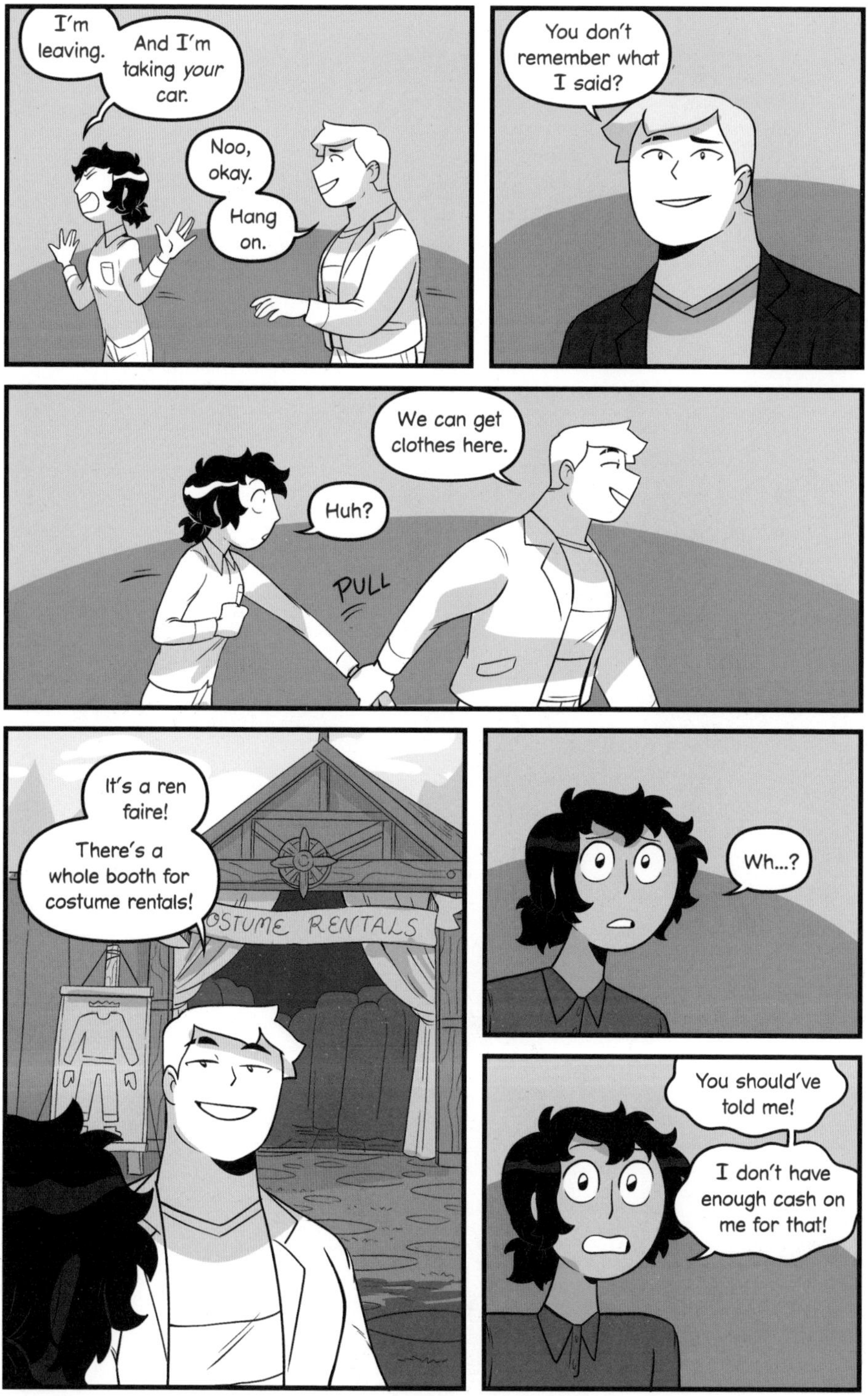
I'm leaving.
And I'm taking *your* car.
Noo, okay.
Hang on.
You don't remember what I said?
We can get clothes here.
Huh?
PULL
It's a ren faire!
There's a whole booth for costume rentals!
OSTUME RENTALS
Wh...?
You should've told me!
I don't have enough cash on me for that!

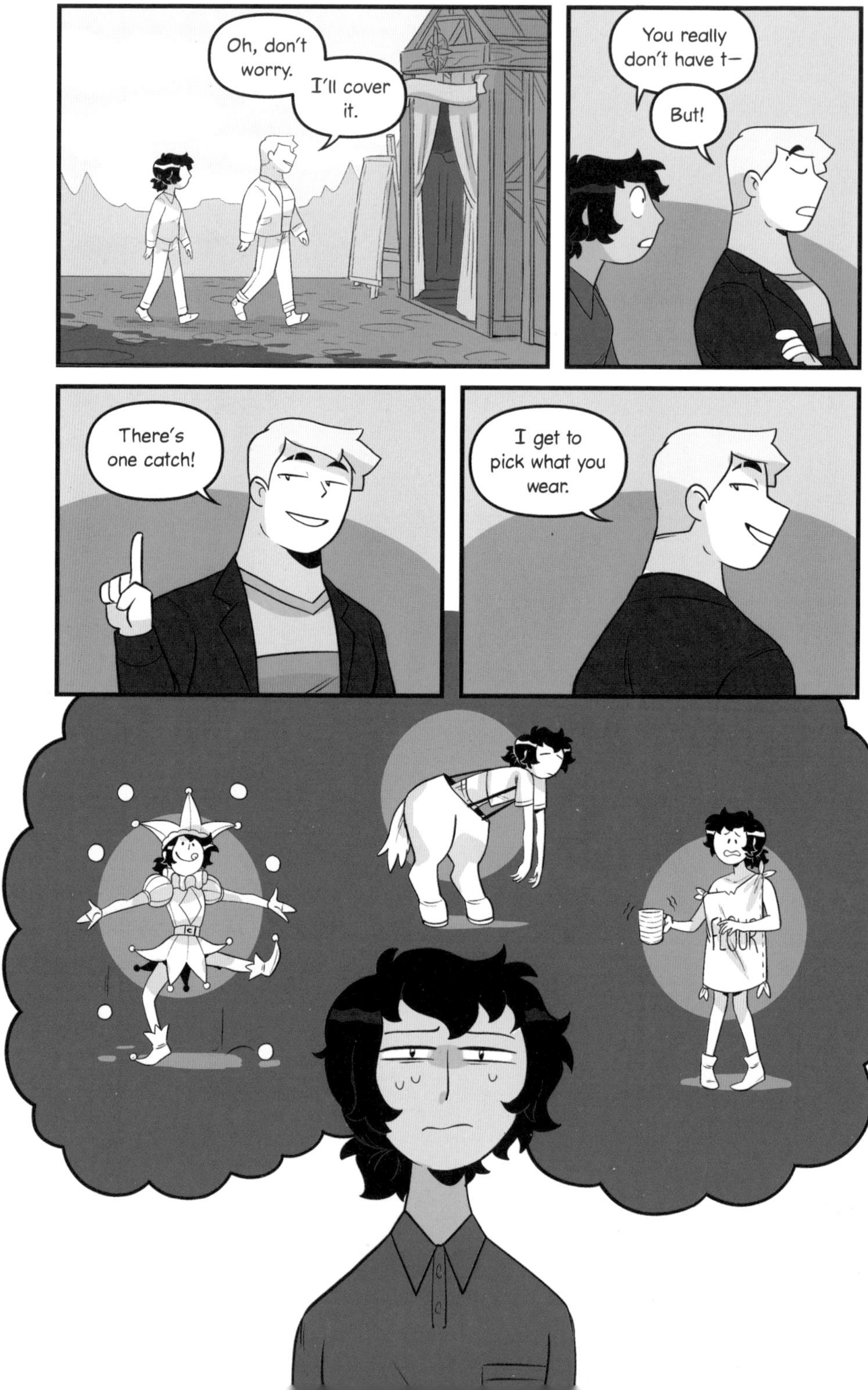
Oh, don't worry.
I'll cover it.
You really don't have t—
But!
There's one catch!
I get to pick what you wear.
FLOUR

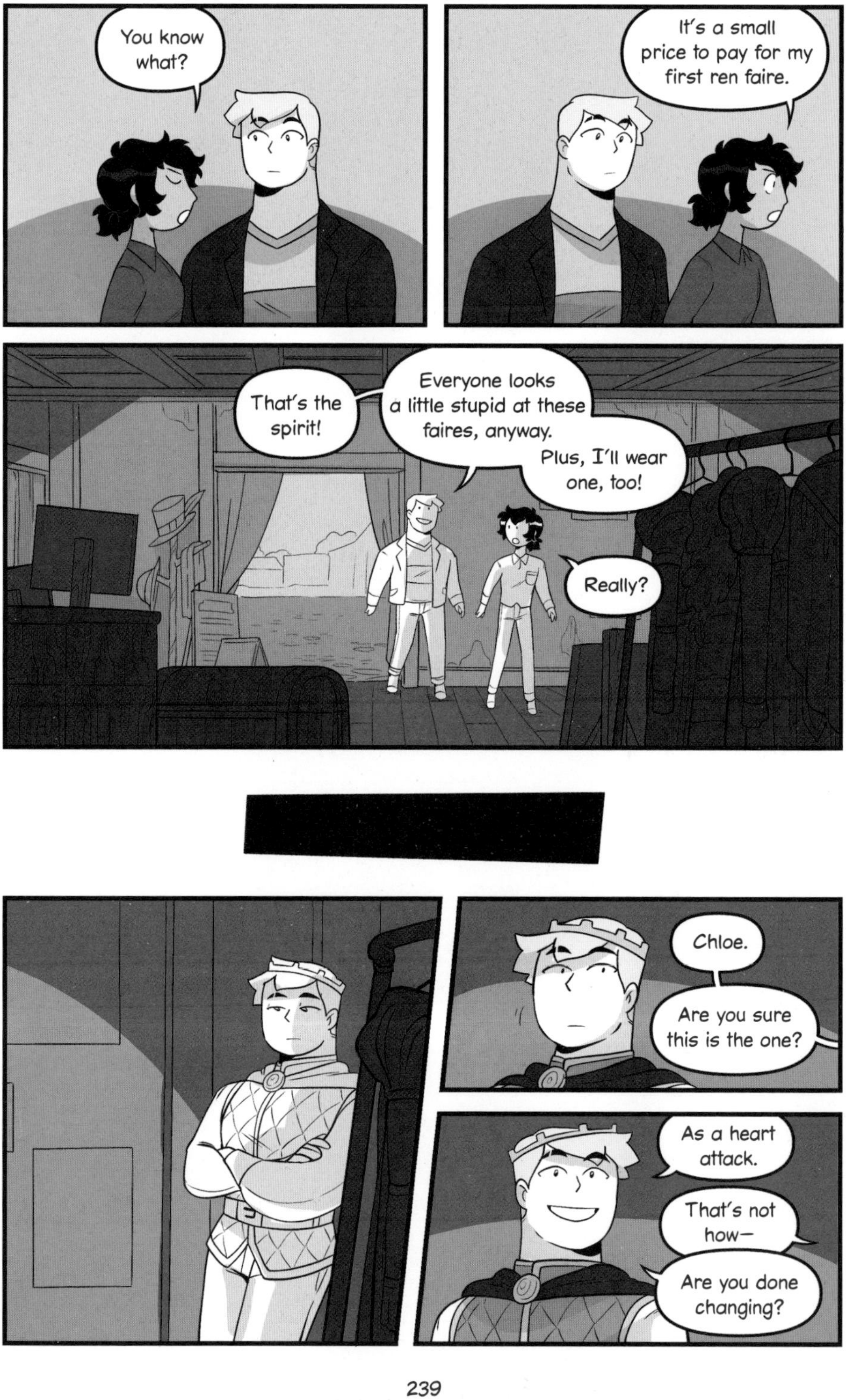
You know what?
It's a small price to pay for my first ren faire.
That's the spirit!
Everyone looks a little stupid at these faires, anyway.
Plus, I'll wear one, too!
Really?
Chloe.
Are you sure this is the one?
As a heart attack.
That's not how—
Are you done changing?

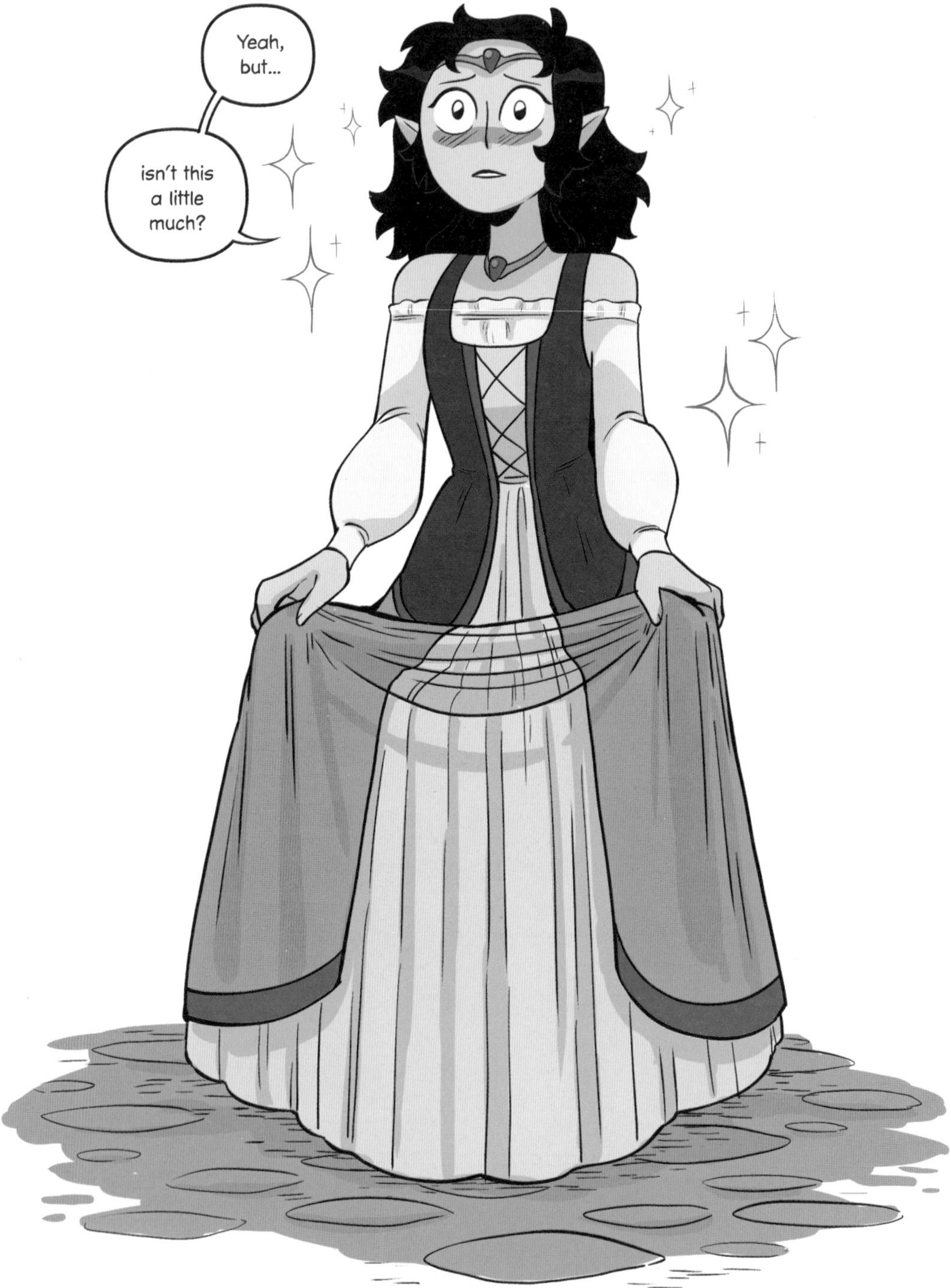
Yeah, but...
isn't this a little much?

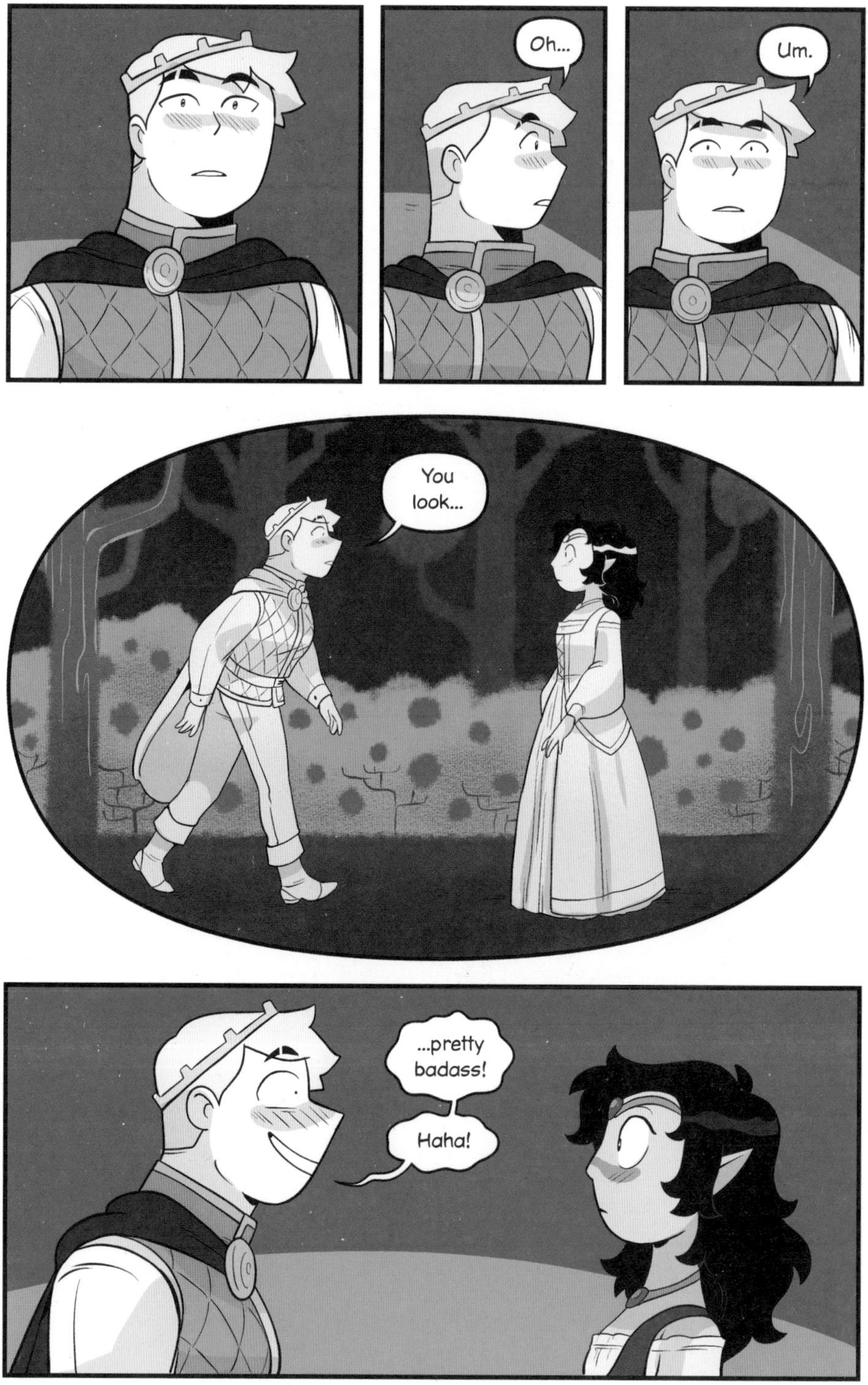
Oh...
Um.
You look...
...pretty badass!
Haha!

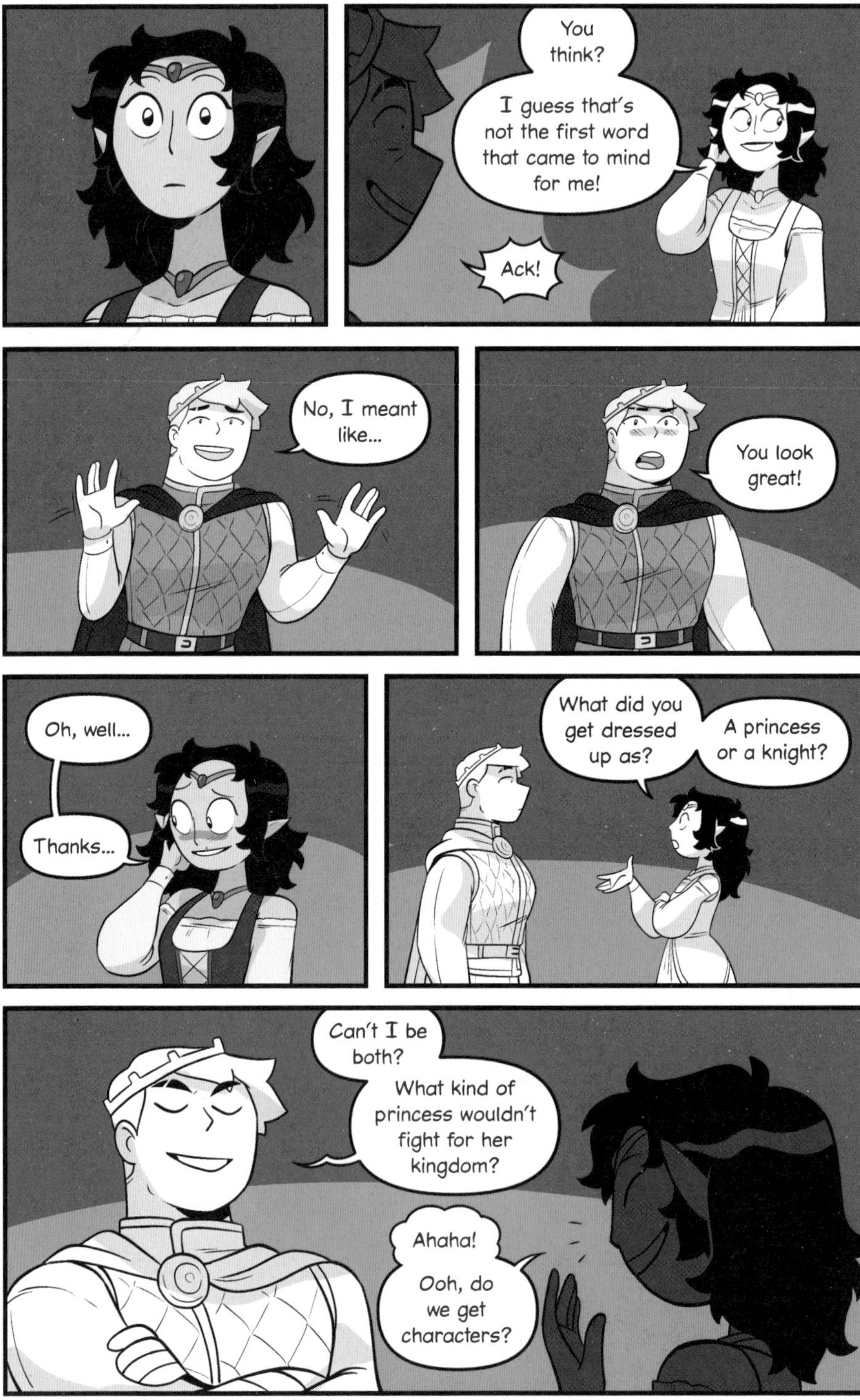
You think?
I guess that's not the first word that came to mind for me!
Ack!
No, I meant like...
You look great!
Oh, well...
Thanks...
What did you get dressed up as?
A princess or a knight?
Can't I be both?
What kind of princess wouldn't fight for her kingdom?
Ahaha!
Ooh, do we get characters?

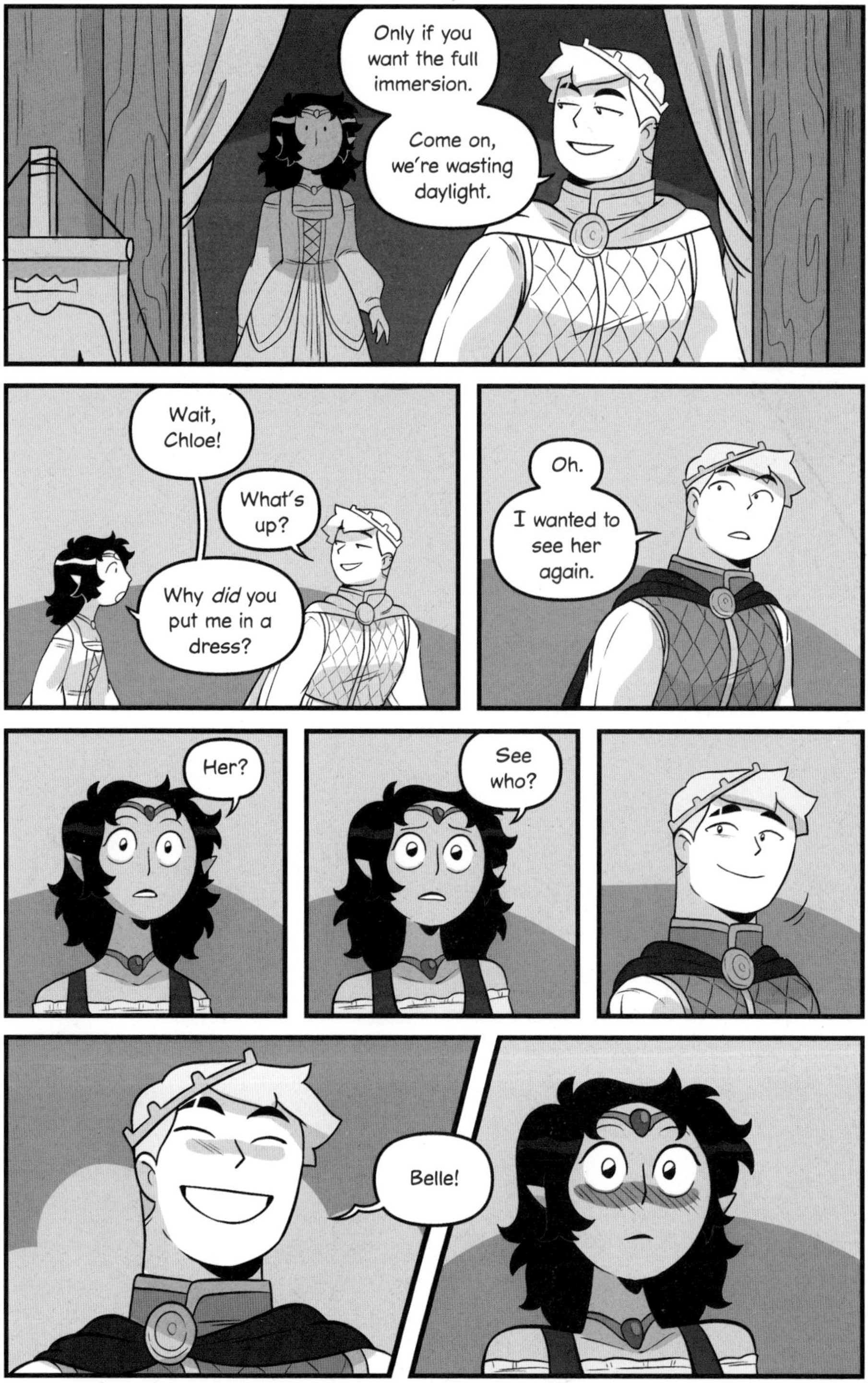
Only if you want the full immersion.
Come on, we're wasting daylight.
Wait, Chloe!
What's up?
Why *did* you put me in a dress?
Oh.
I wanted to see her again.
Her?
See who?
Belle!

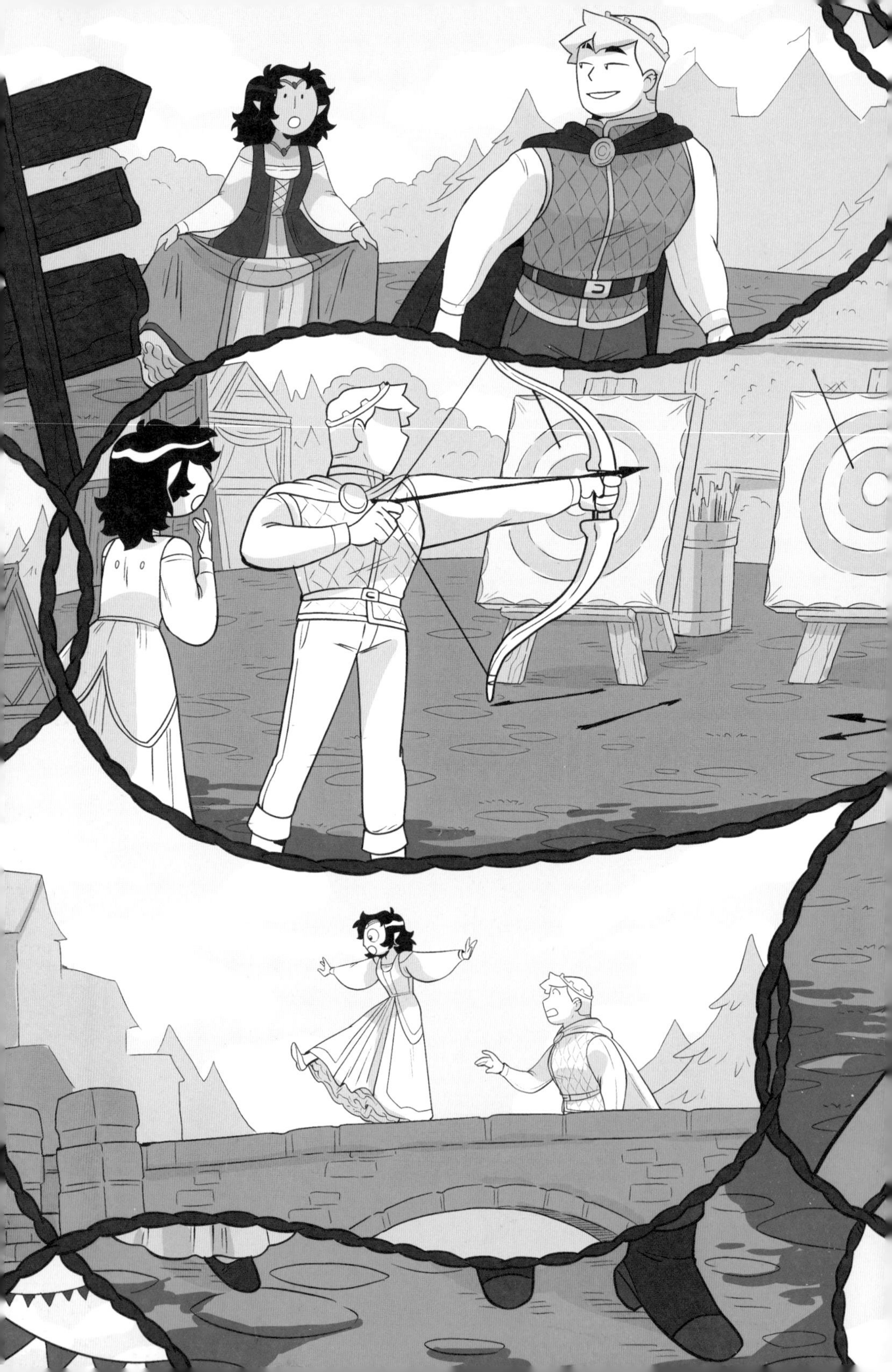

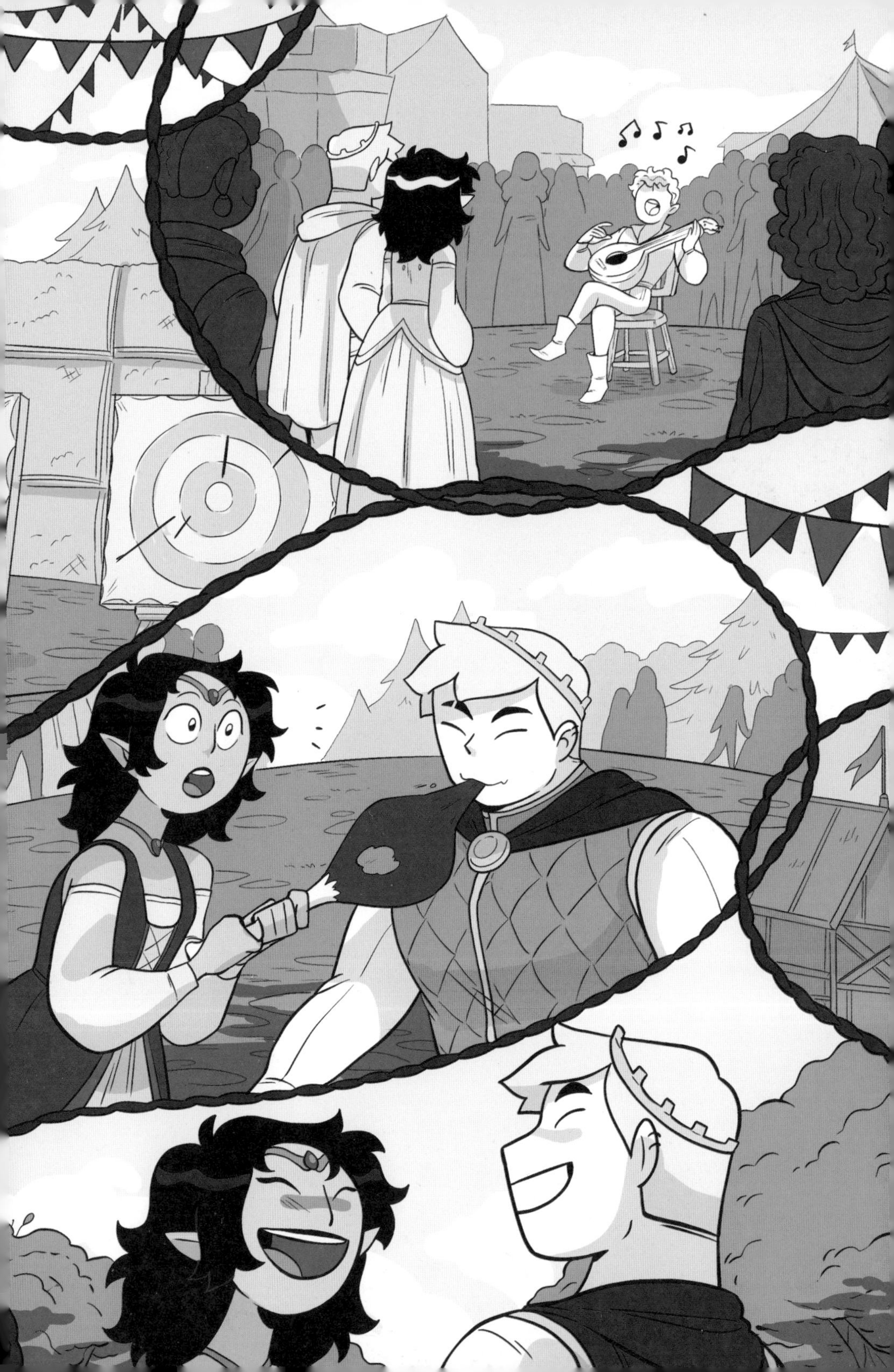

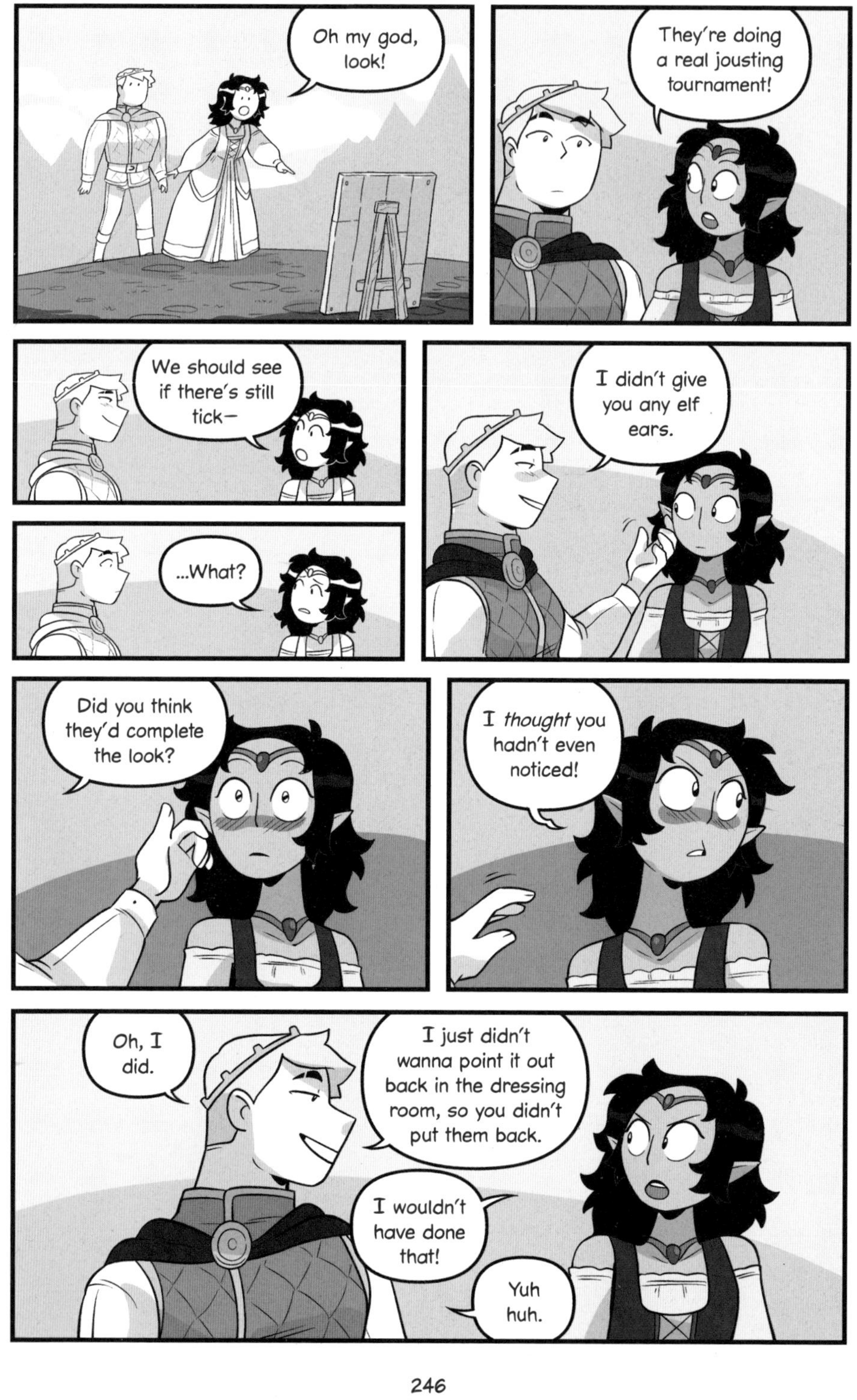
Oh my god, look!
They're doing a real jousting tournament!
We should see if there's still tick—
...What?
I didn't give you any elf ears.
Did you think they'd complete the look?
I *thought* you hadn't even noticed!
Oh, I did.
I just didn't wanna point it out back in the dressing room, so you didn't put them back.
I wouldn't have done that!
Yuh huh.

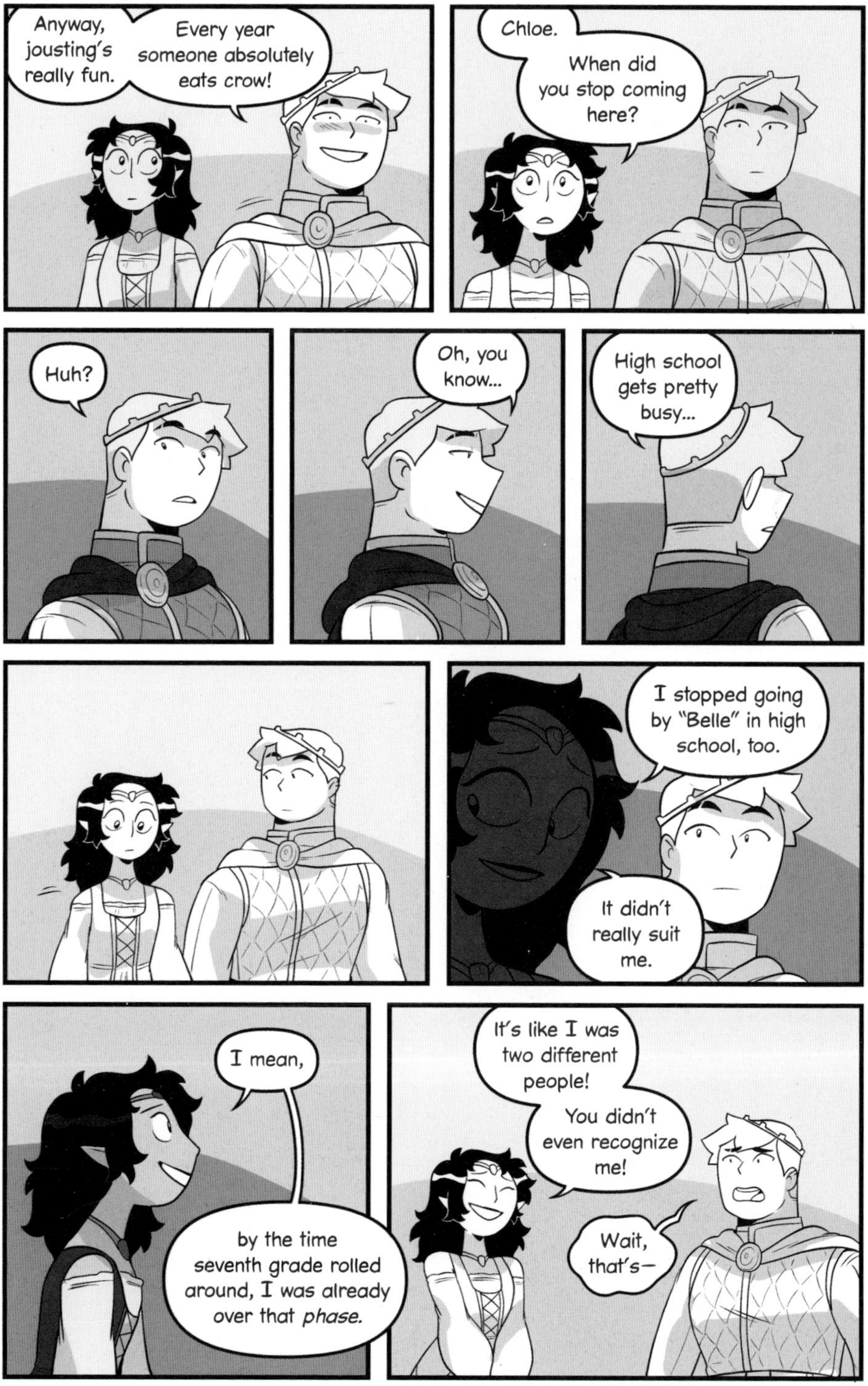

Anyway, jousting's really fun.
Every year someone absolutely eats crow!
Chloe.
When did you stop coming here?
Huh?
Oh, you know...
High school gets pretty busy...
I stopped going by "Belle" in high school, too.
It didn't really suit me.
I mean,
by the time seventh grade rolled around, I was already over that *phase.*
It's like I was two different people!
You didn't even recognize me!
Wait, that's—

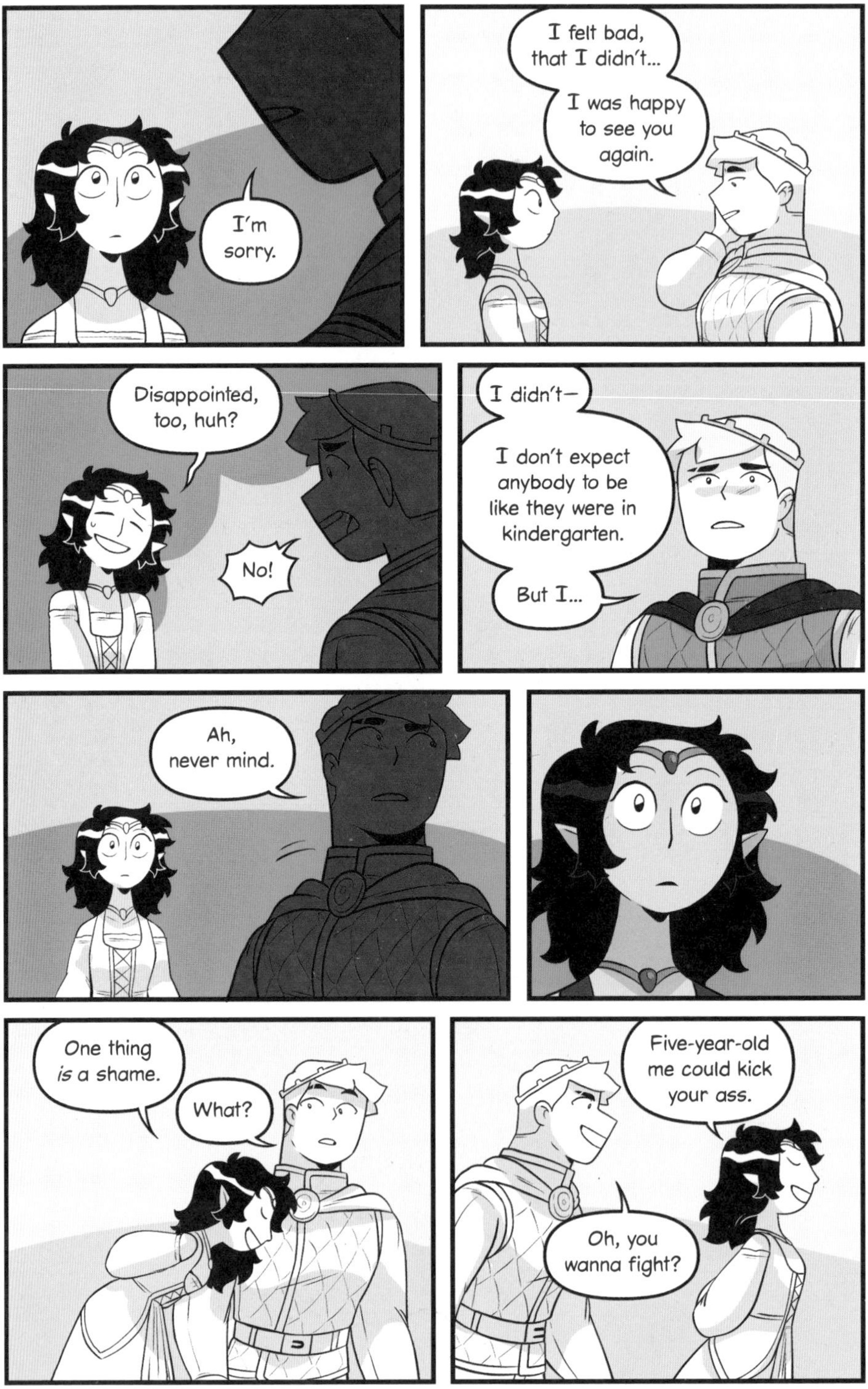
I'm sorry.
I felt bad, that I didn't...
I was happy to see you again.
Disappointed, too, huh?
No!
I didn't—
I don't expect anybody to be like they were in kindergarten.
But I...
Ah, never mind.
One thing *is* a shame.
What?
Five-year-old me could kick your ass.
Oh, you wanna fight?

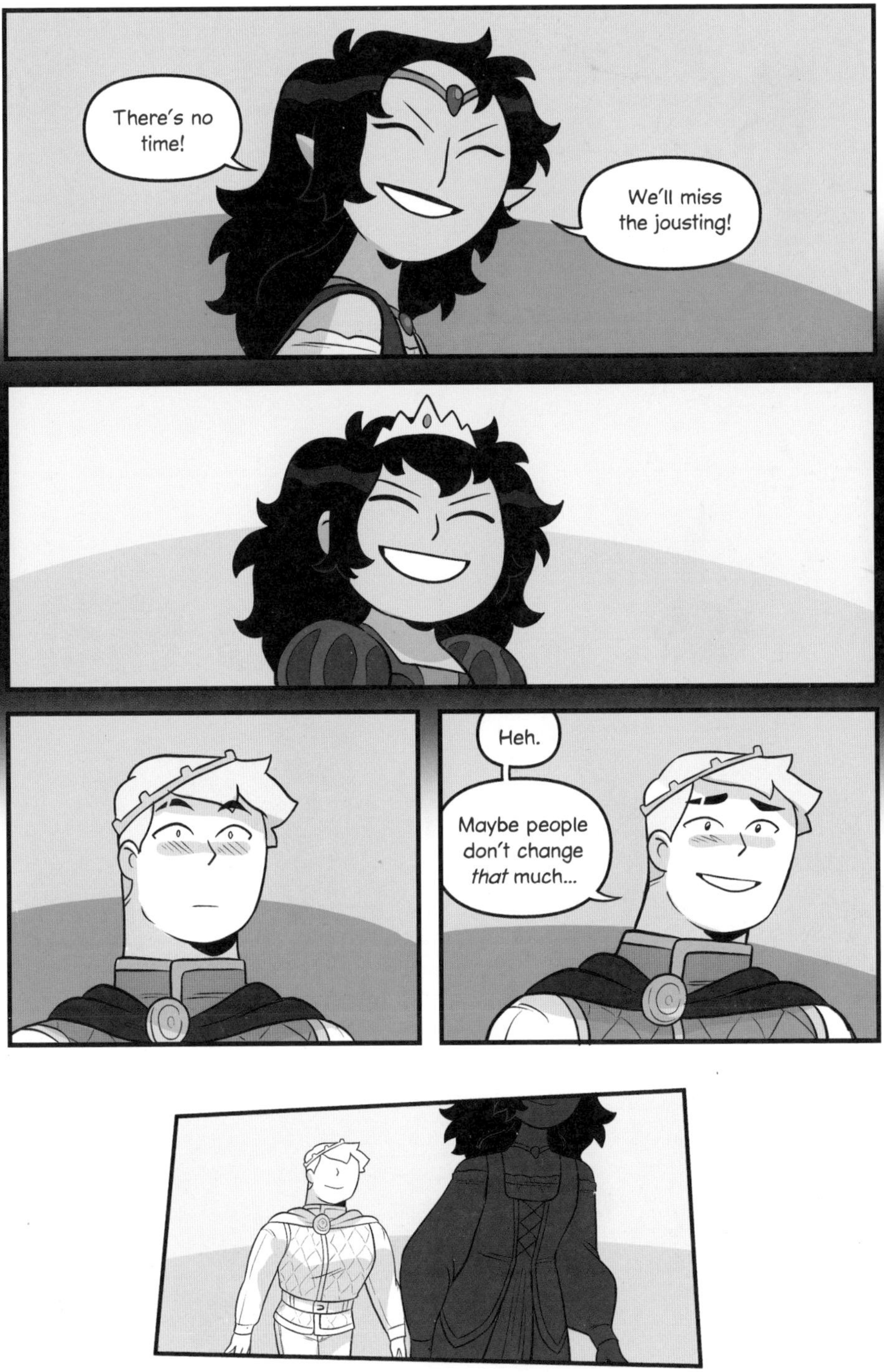
There's no time!
We'll miss the jousting!
Heh.
Maybe people don't change *that* much...

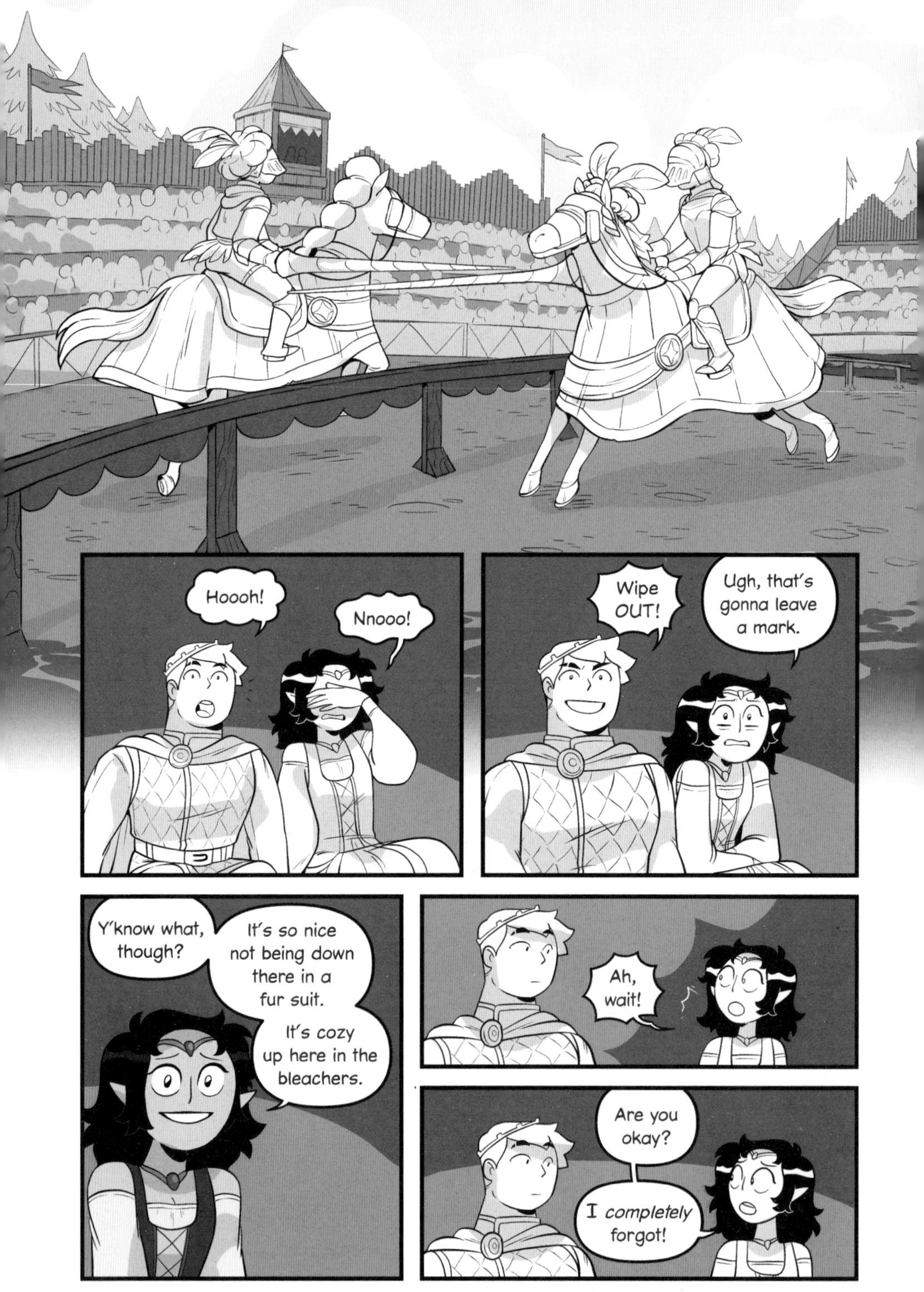
Hoooh!
Nnooo!
Wipe OUT!
Ugh, that's gonna leave a mark.
Y'know what, though?
It's so nice not being down there in a fur suit.
It's cozy up here in the bleachers.
Ah, wait!
Are you okay?
I *completely* forgot!

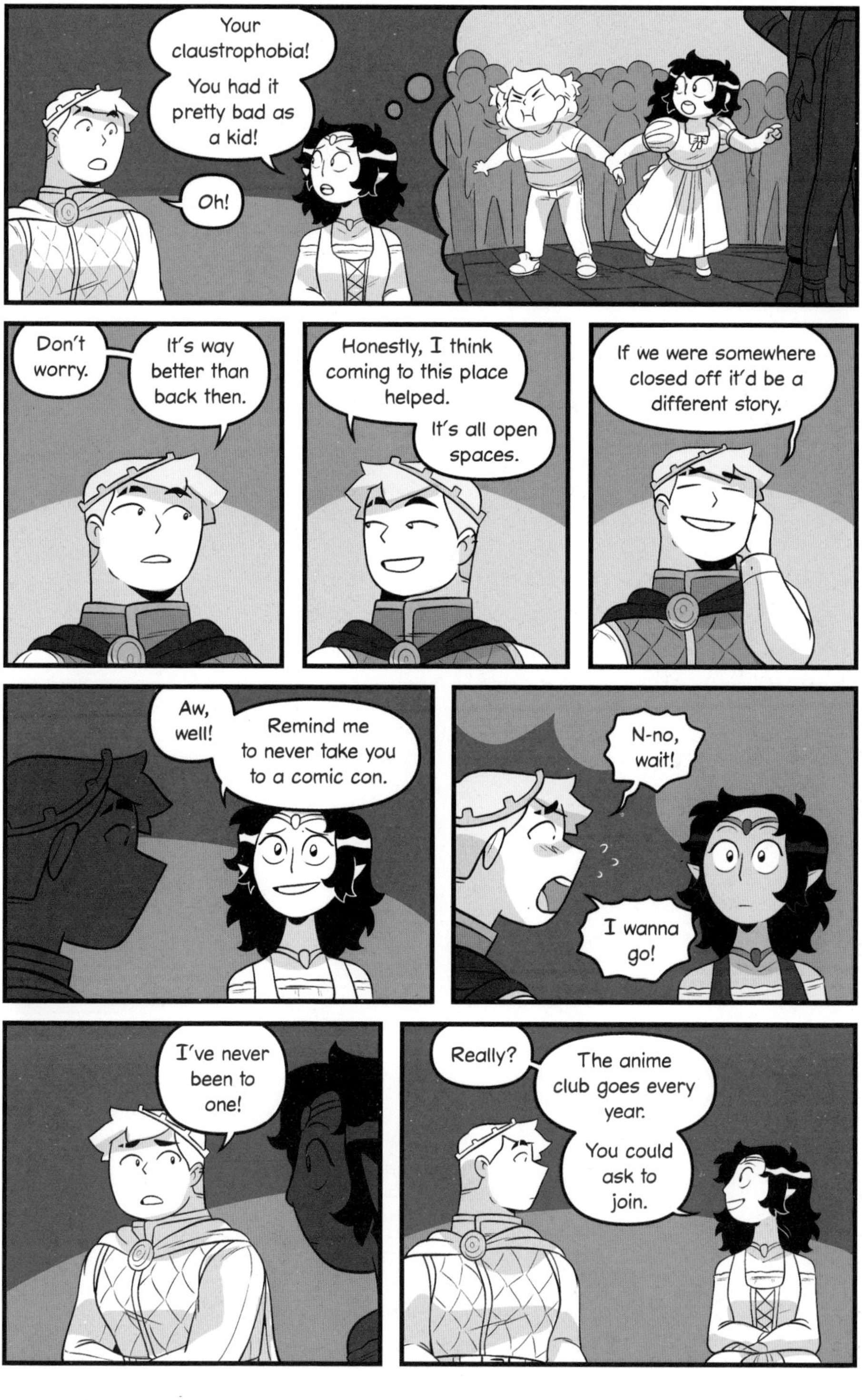
Your claustrophobia!
You had it pretty bad as a kid!
Oh!
Don't worry.
It's way better than back then.
Honestly, I think coming to this place helped.
It's all open spaces.
If we were somewhere closed off it'd be a different story.
Aw, well!
Remind me to never take you to a comic con.
N-no, wait!
I wanna go!
I've never been to one!
Really?
The anime club goes every year.
You could ask to join.

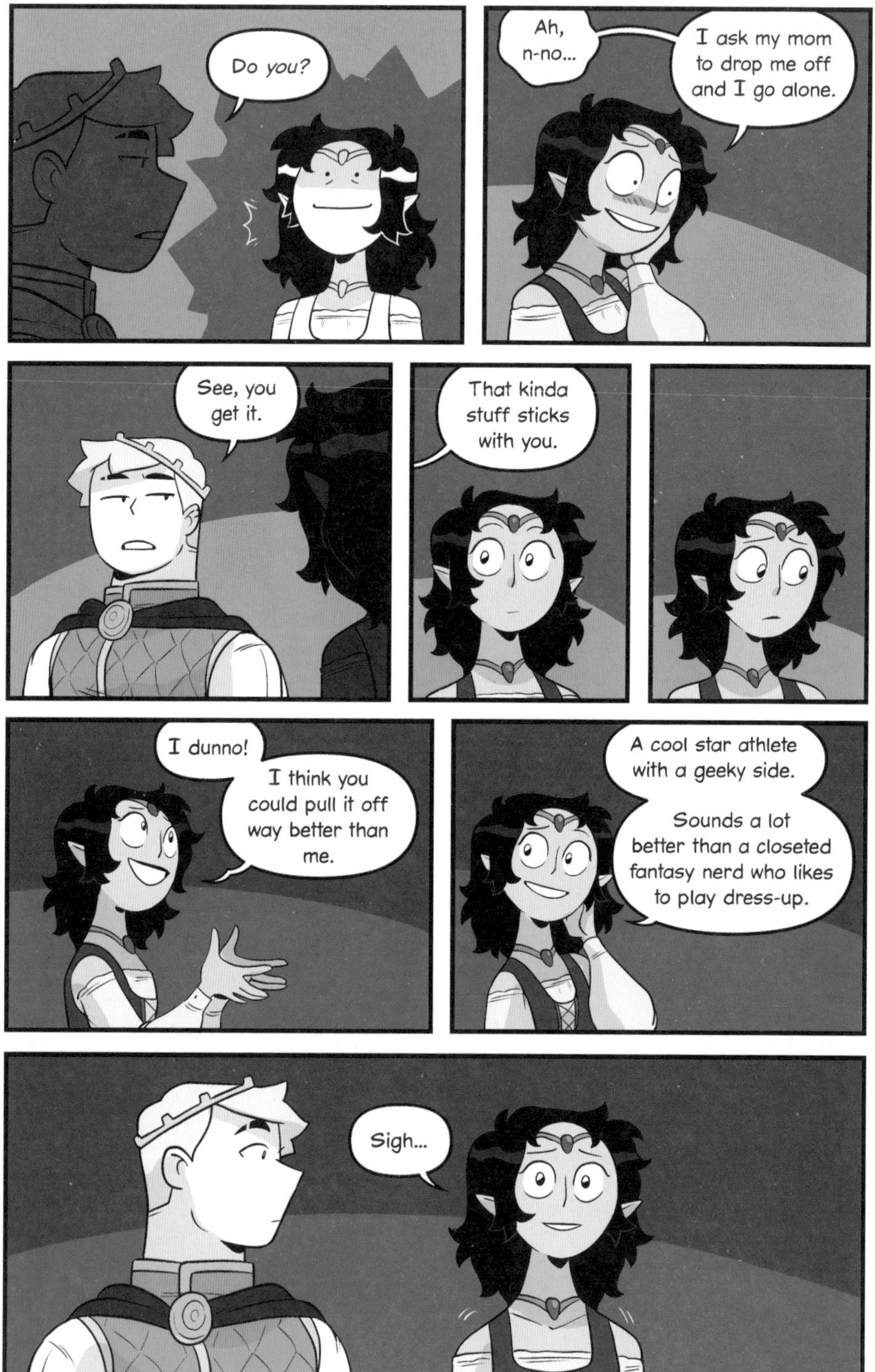

Do you?
Ah, n-no...
I ask my mom to drop me off and I go alone.
See, you get it.
That kinda stuff sticks with you.
I dunno!
I think you could pull it off way better than me.
A cool star athlete with a geeky side.
Sounds a lot better than a closeted fantasy nerd who likes to play dress-up.
Sigh...

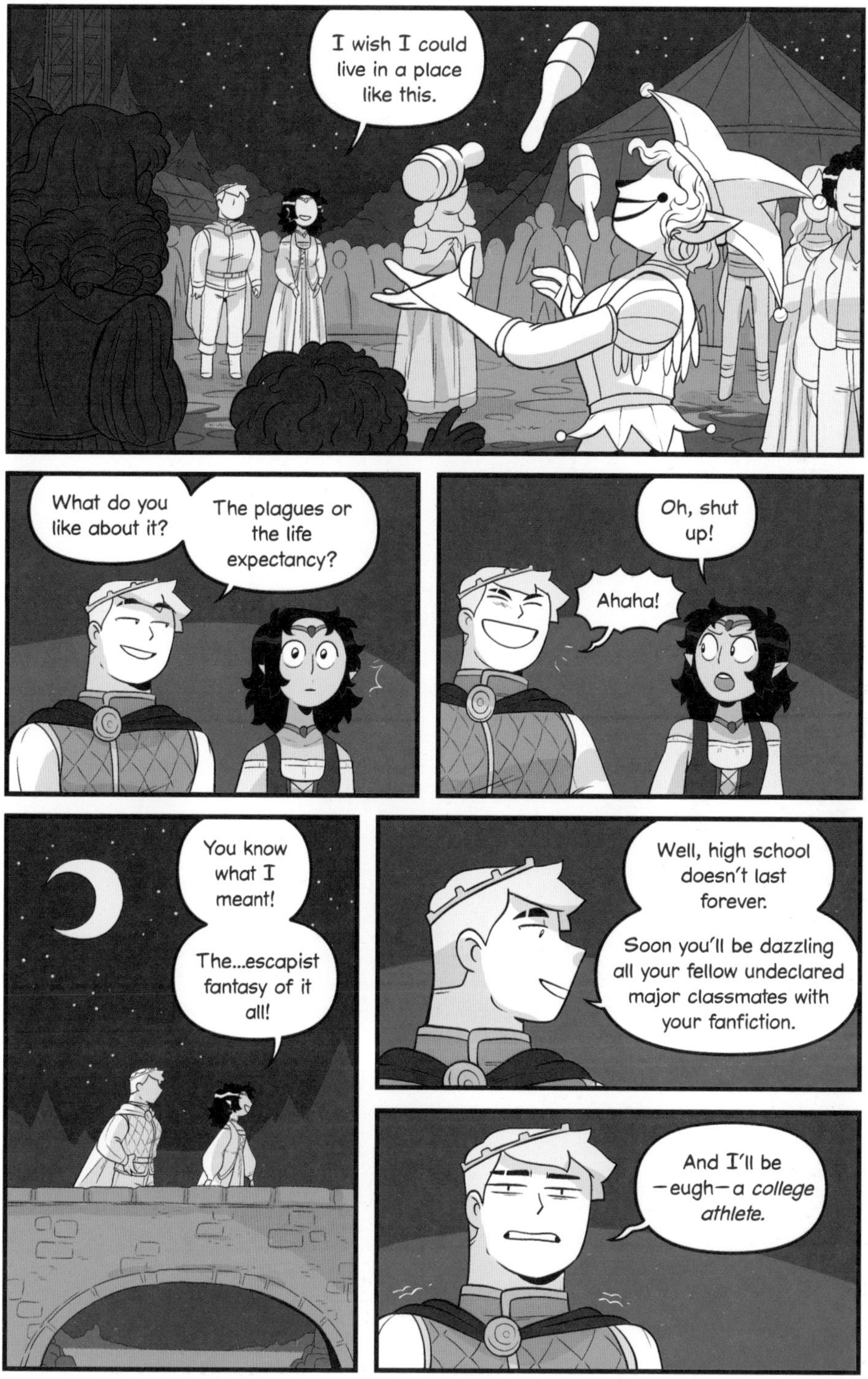

I wish I could live in a place like this.
What do you like about it?
The plagues or the life expectancy?
Oh, shut up!
Ahaha!
You know what I meant!
The...escapist fantasy of it all!
Well, high school doesn't last forever.
Soon you'll be dazzling all your fellow undeclared major classmates with your fanfiction.
And I'll be —eugh—a *college athlete.*

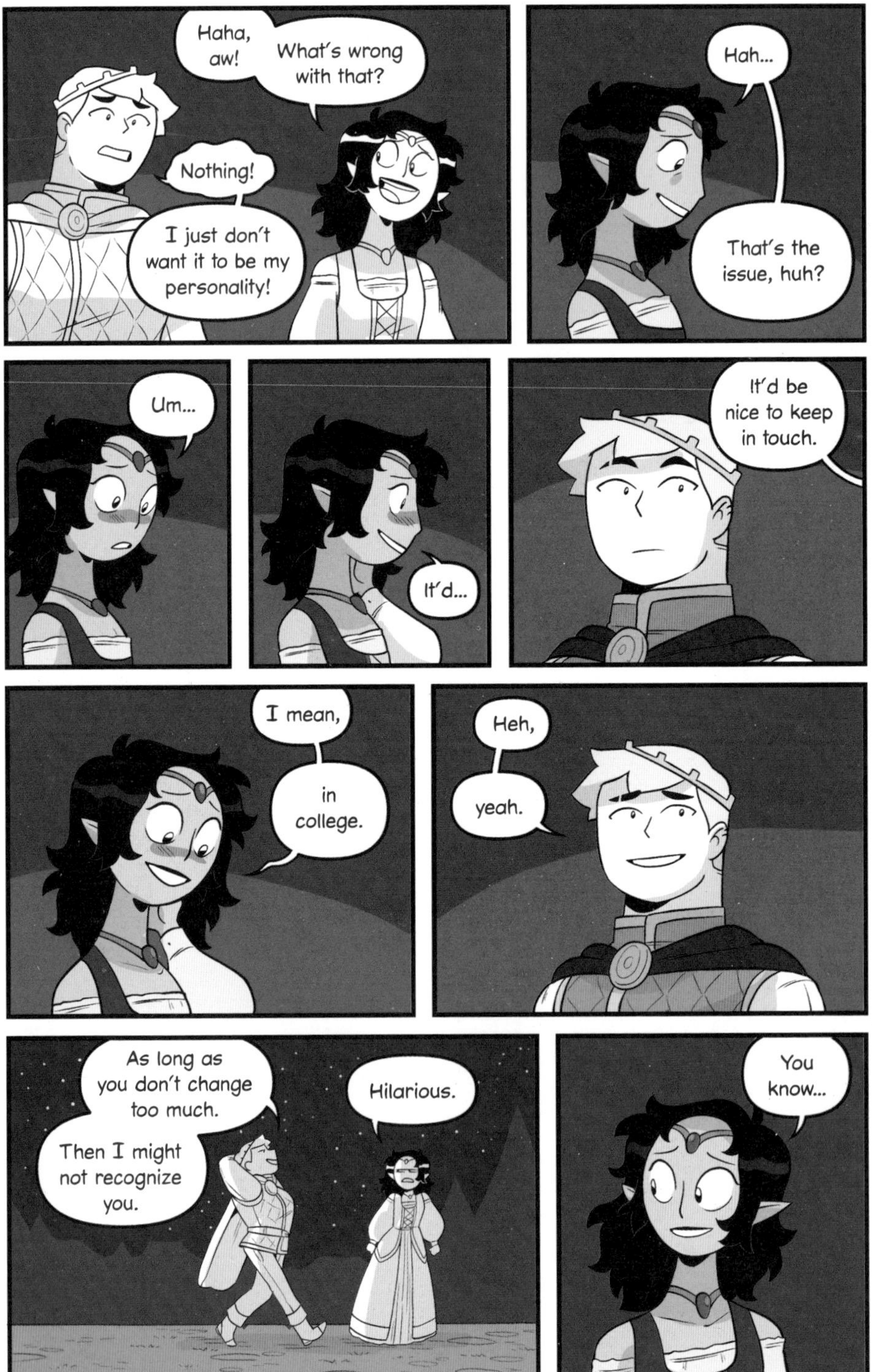

Haha, aw!
What's wrong with that?
Nothing!
I just don't want it to be my personality!
Hah...
That's the issue, huh?
Um...
It'd...
It'd be nice to keep in touch.
I mean,
in college.
Heh,
yeah.
As long as you don't change too much.
Then I might not recognize you.
Hilarious.
You know...

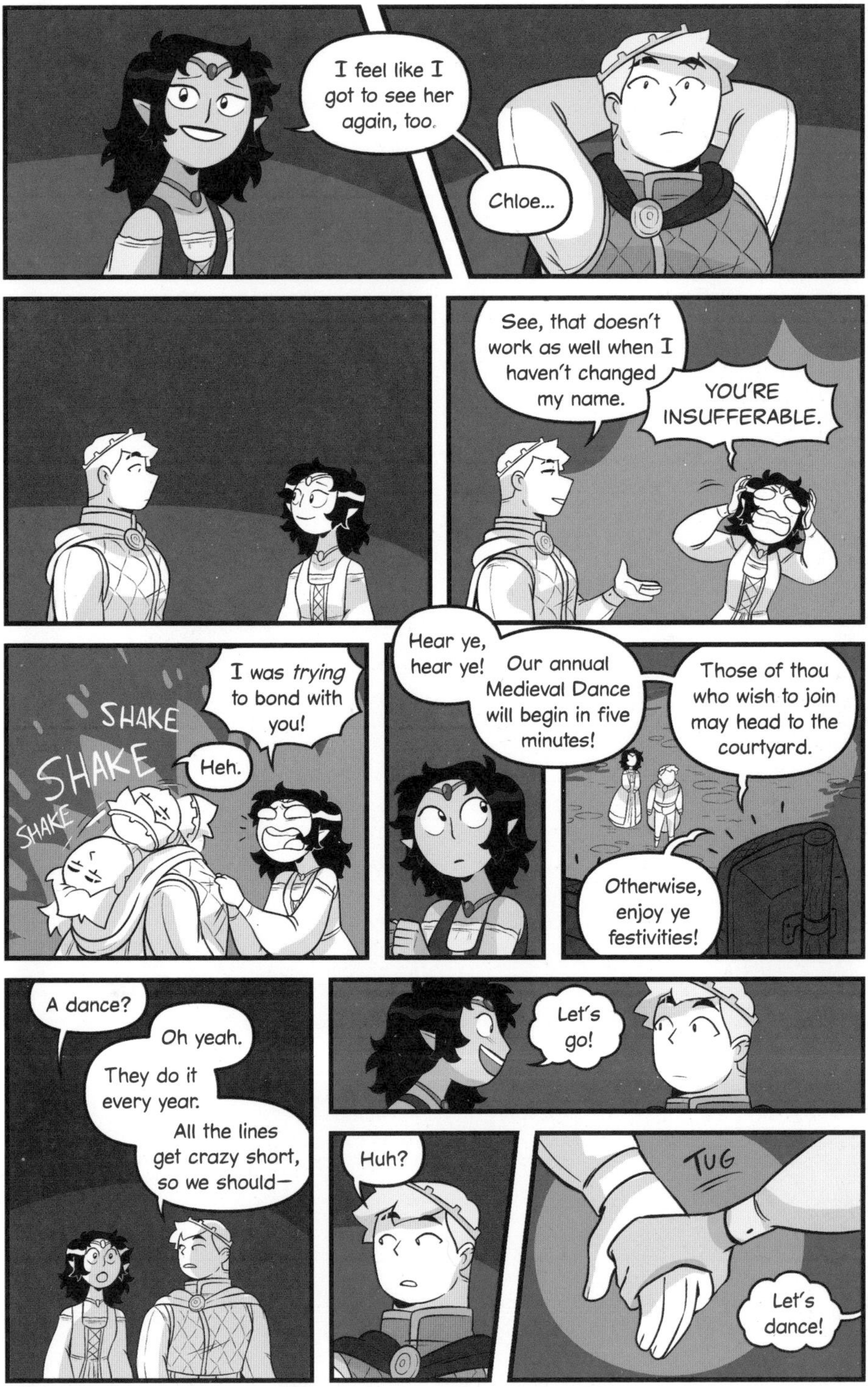
I feel like I got to see her again, too.
Chloe...
See, that doesn't work as well when I haven't changed my name.
YOU'RE INSUFFERABLE.
I was *trying* to bond with you!
SHAKE
SHAKE
SHAKE
Heh.
Hear ye, hear ye!
Our annual Medieval Dance will begin in five minutes!
Those of thou who wish to join may head to the courtyard.
Otherwise, enjoy ye festivities!
A dance?
Oh yeah.
They do it every year.
All the lines get crazy short, so we should—
Let's go!
Huh?
TUG
Let's dance!

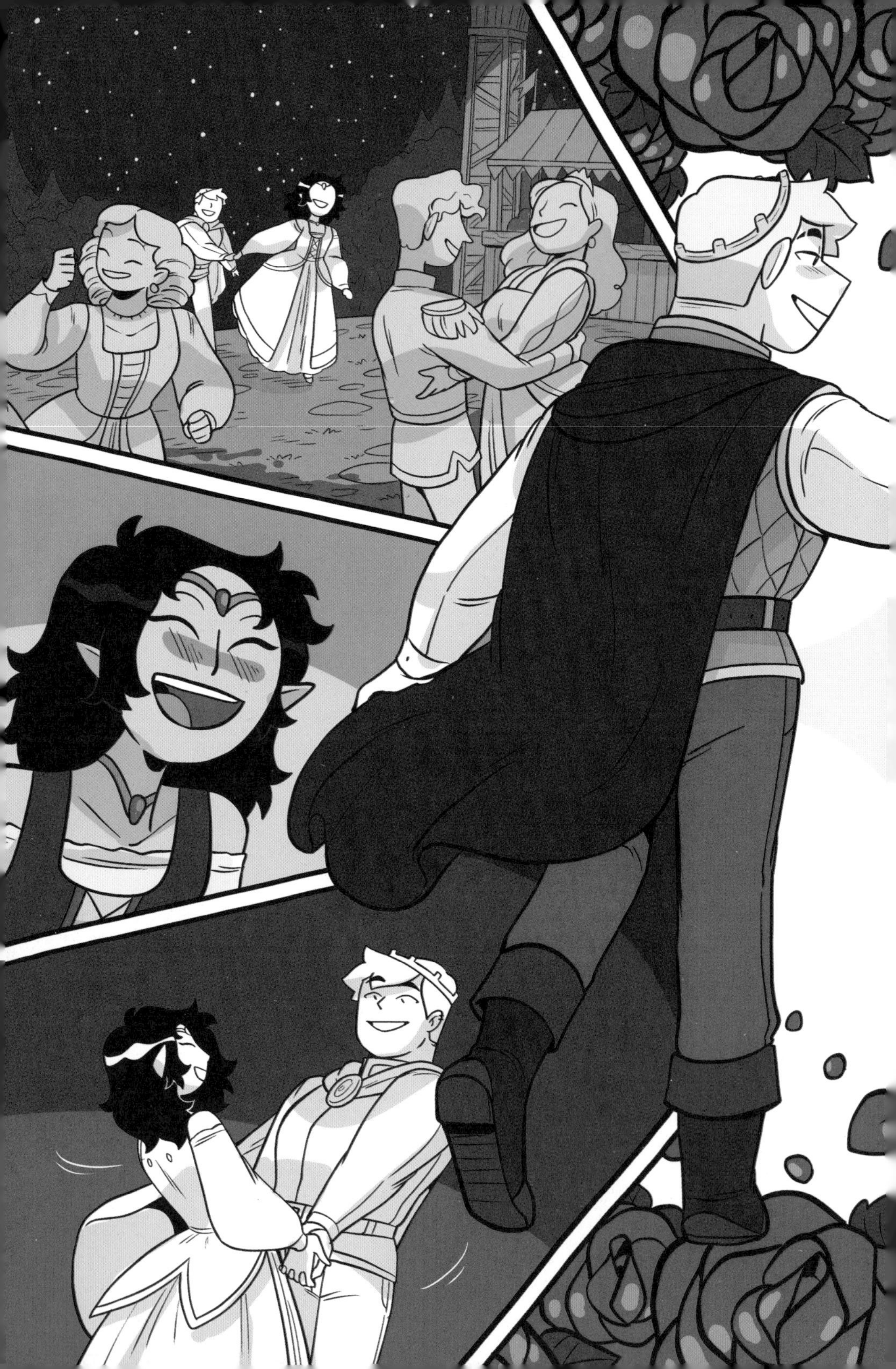

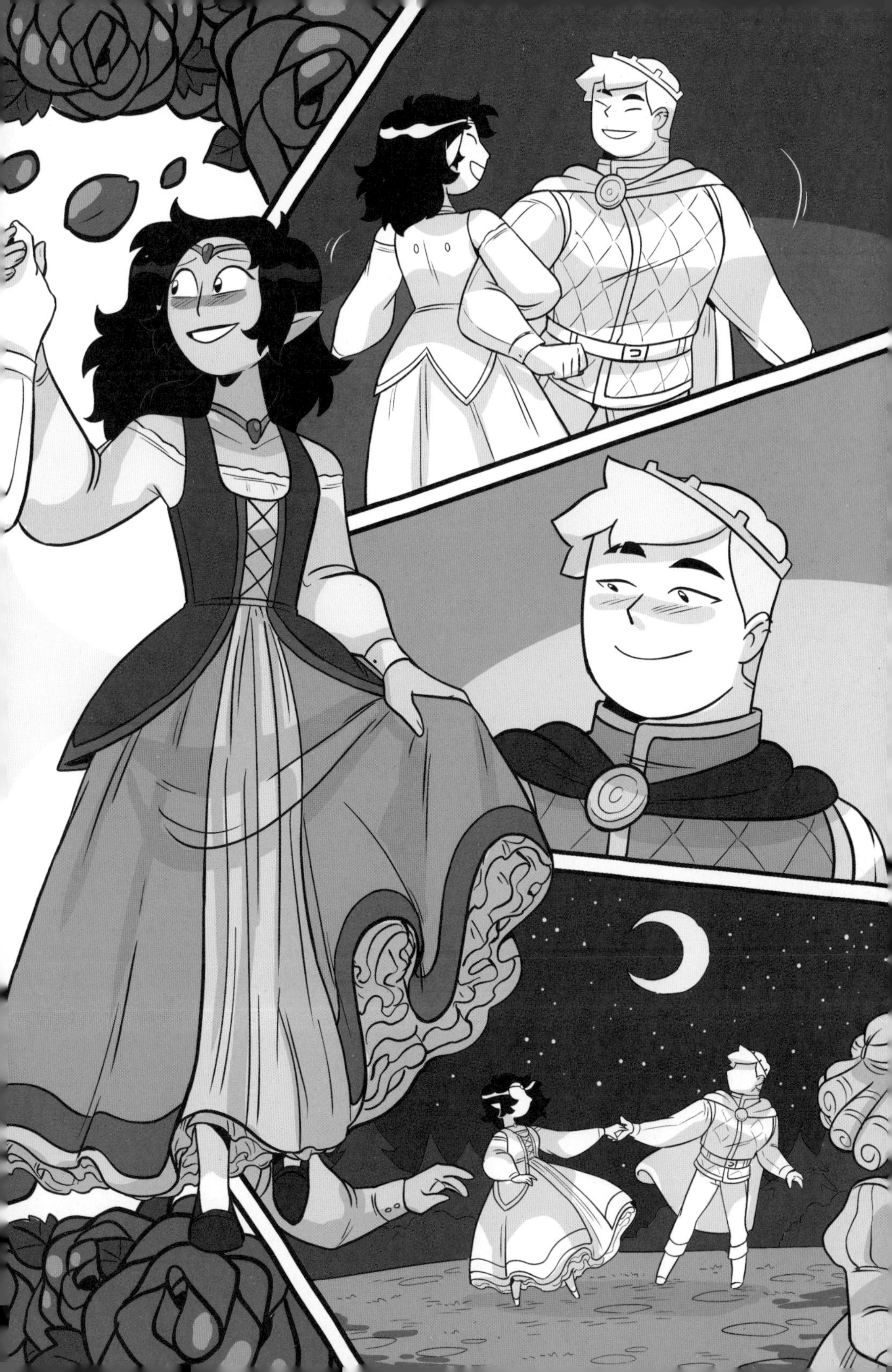

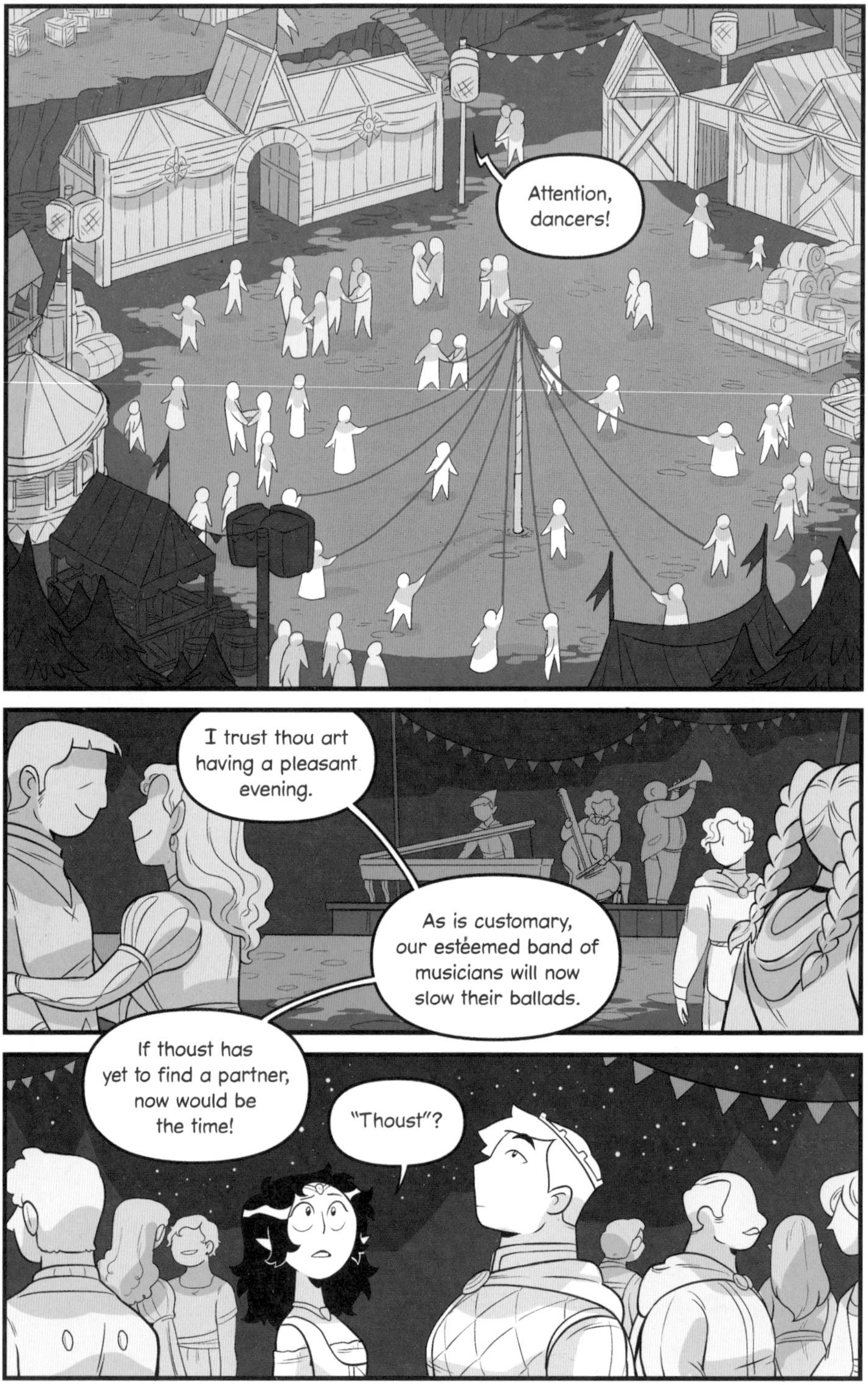
Attention, dancers!
I trust thou art having a pleasant evening.
As is customary, our estéemed band of musicians will now slow their ballads.
If thoust has yet to find a partner, now would be the time!
"Thoust"?

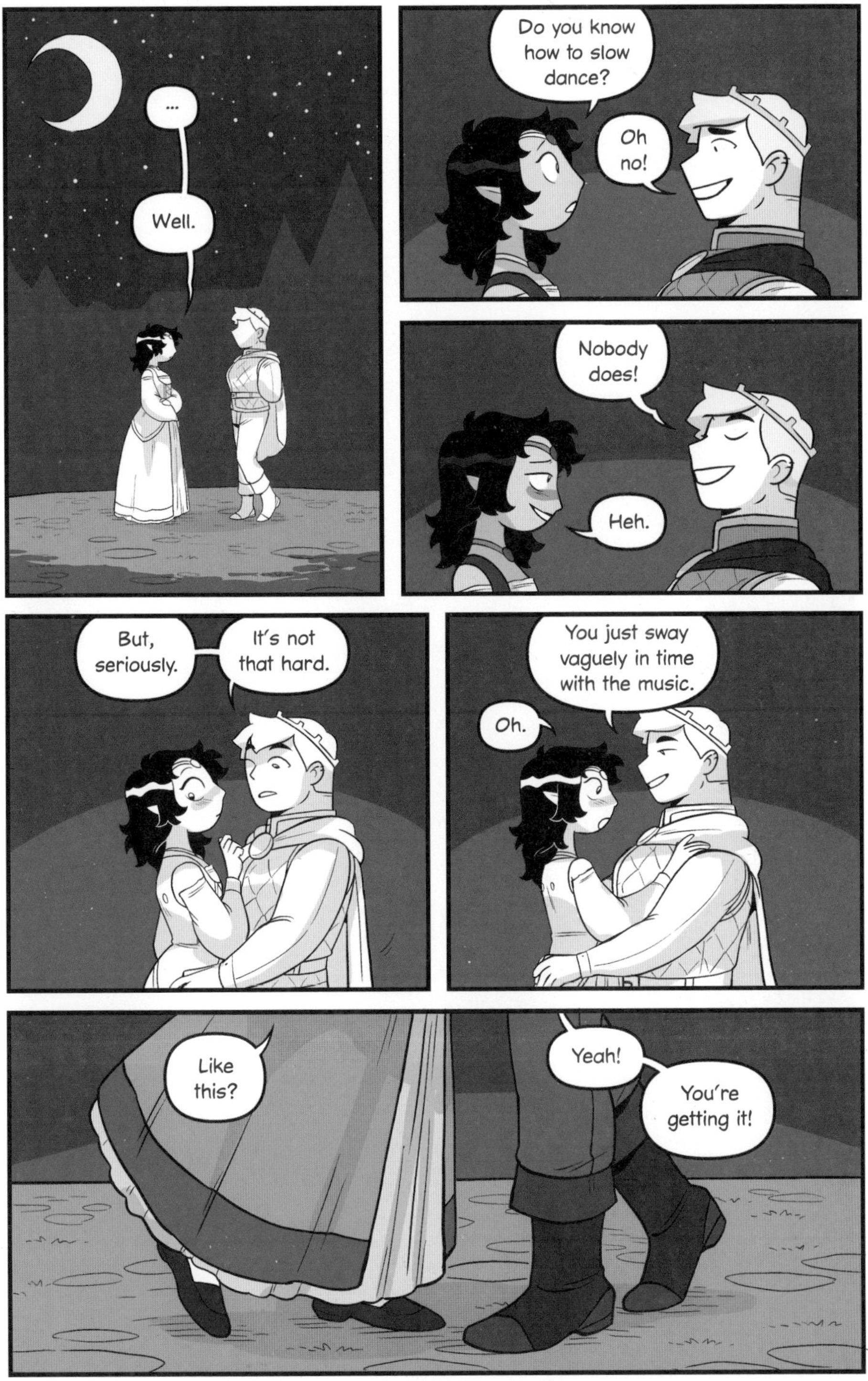
...
Well.
Do you know how to slow dance?
Oh no!
Nobody does!
Heh.
But, seriously.
It's not that hard.
You just sway vaguely in time with the music.
Oh.
Like this?
Yeah!
You're getting it!

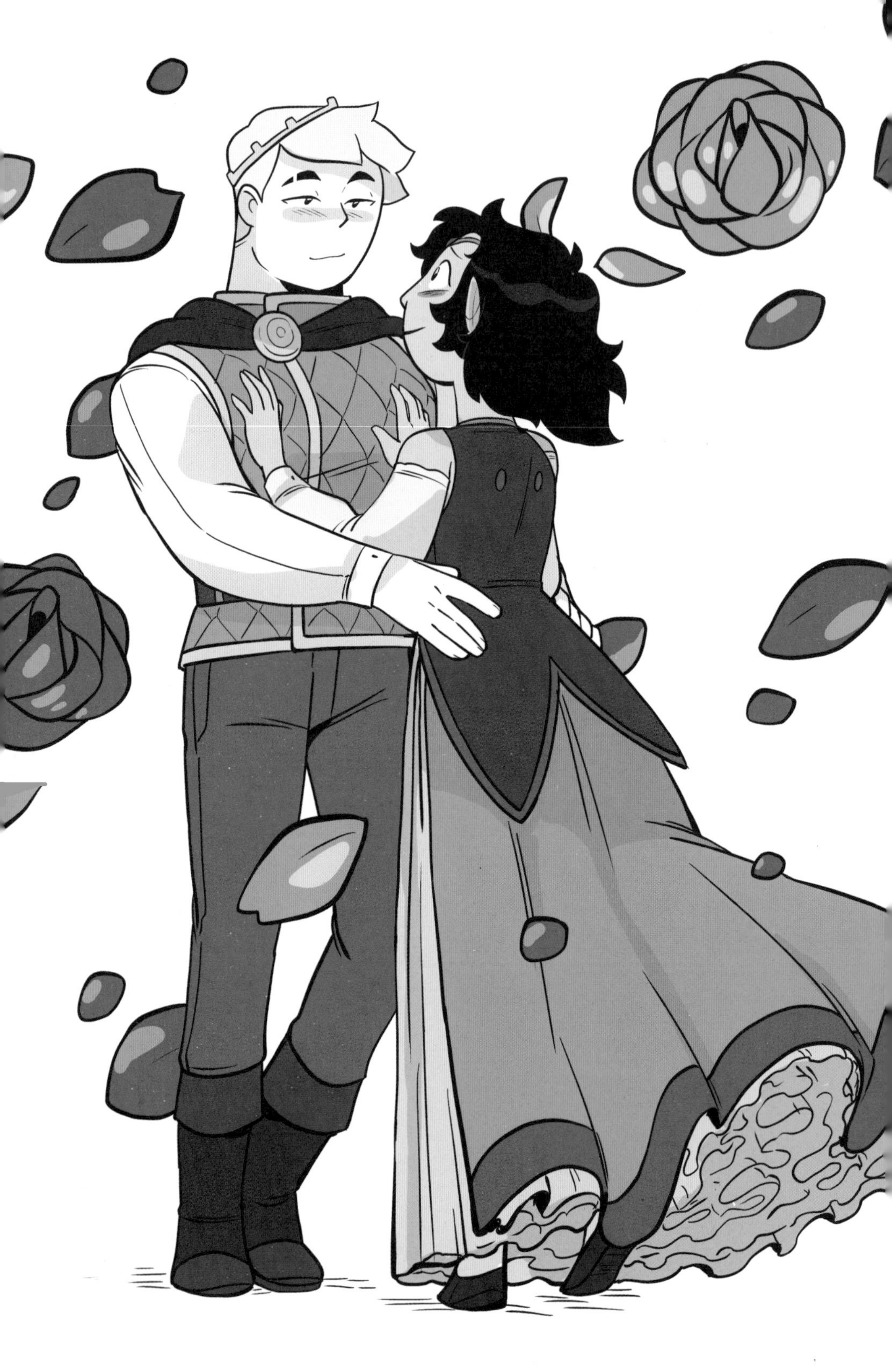

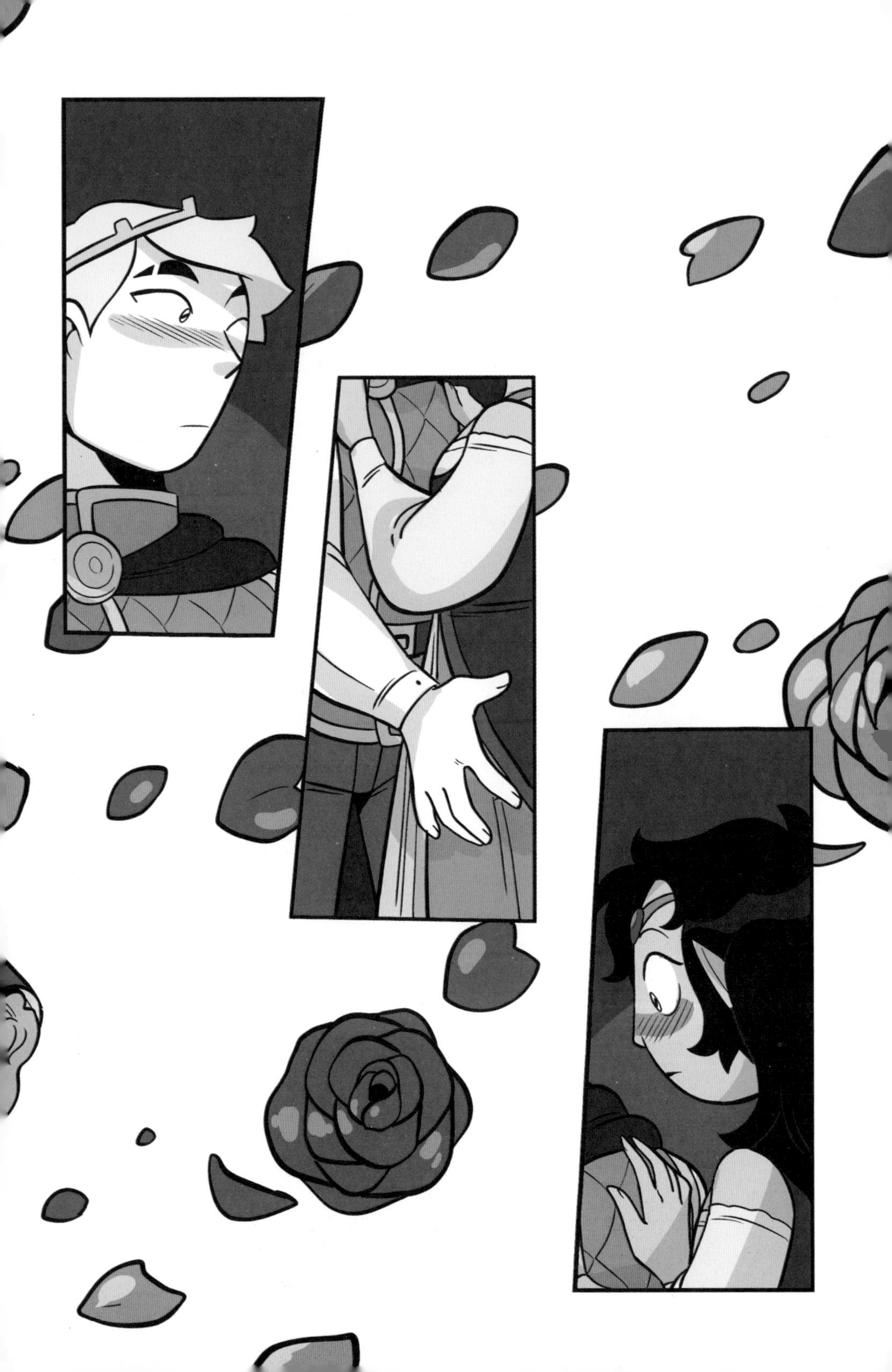

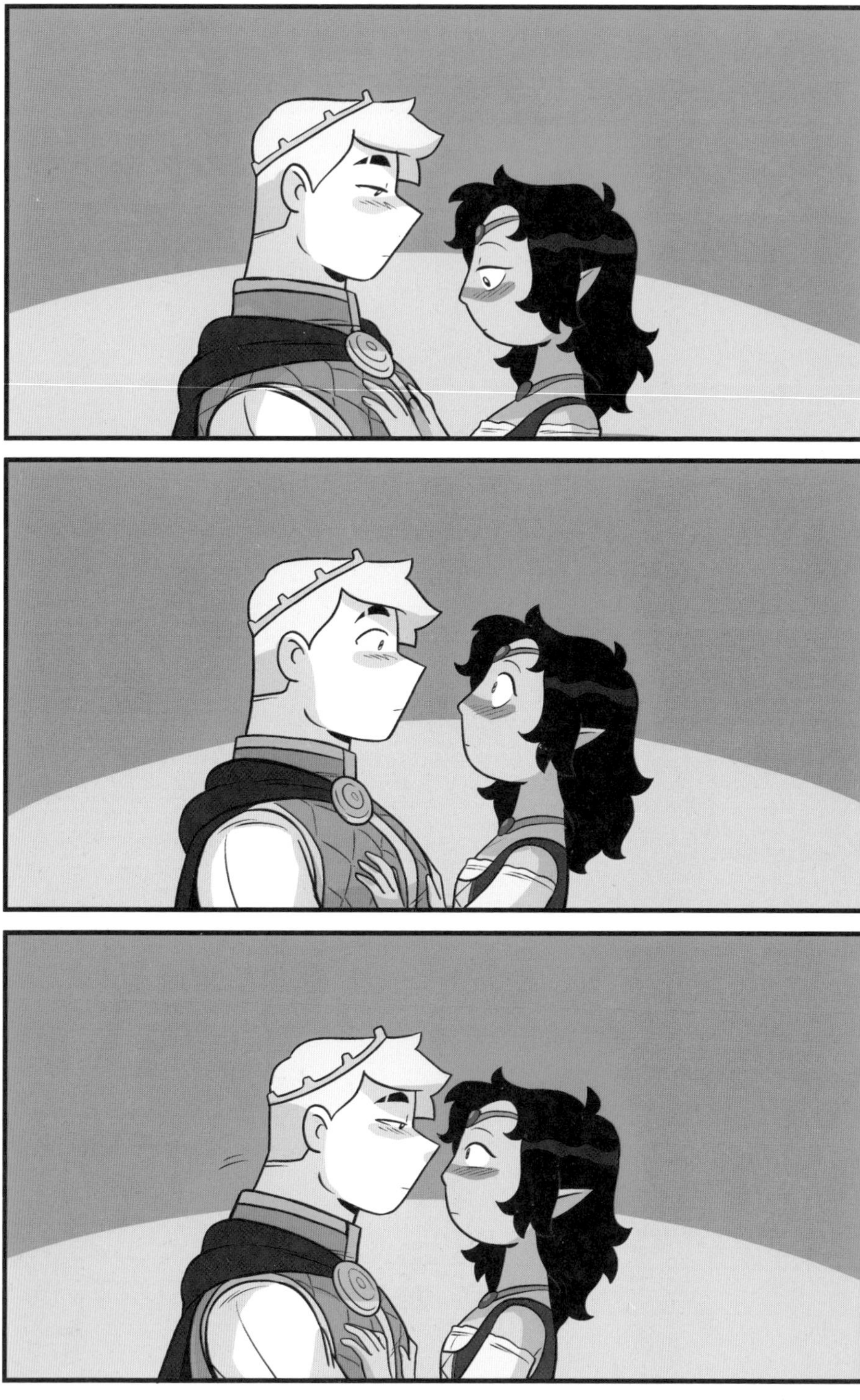

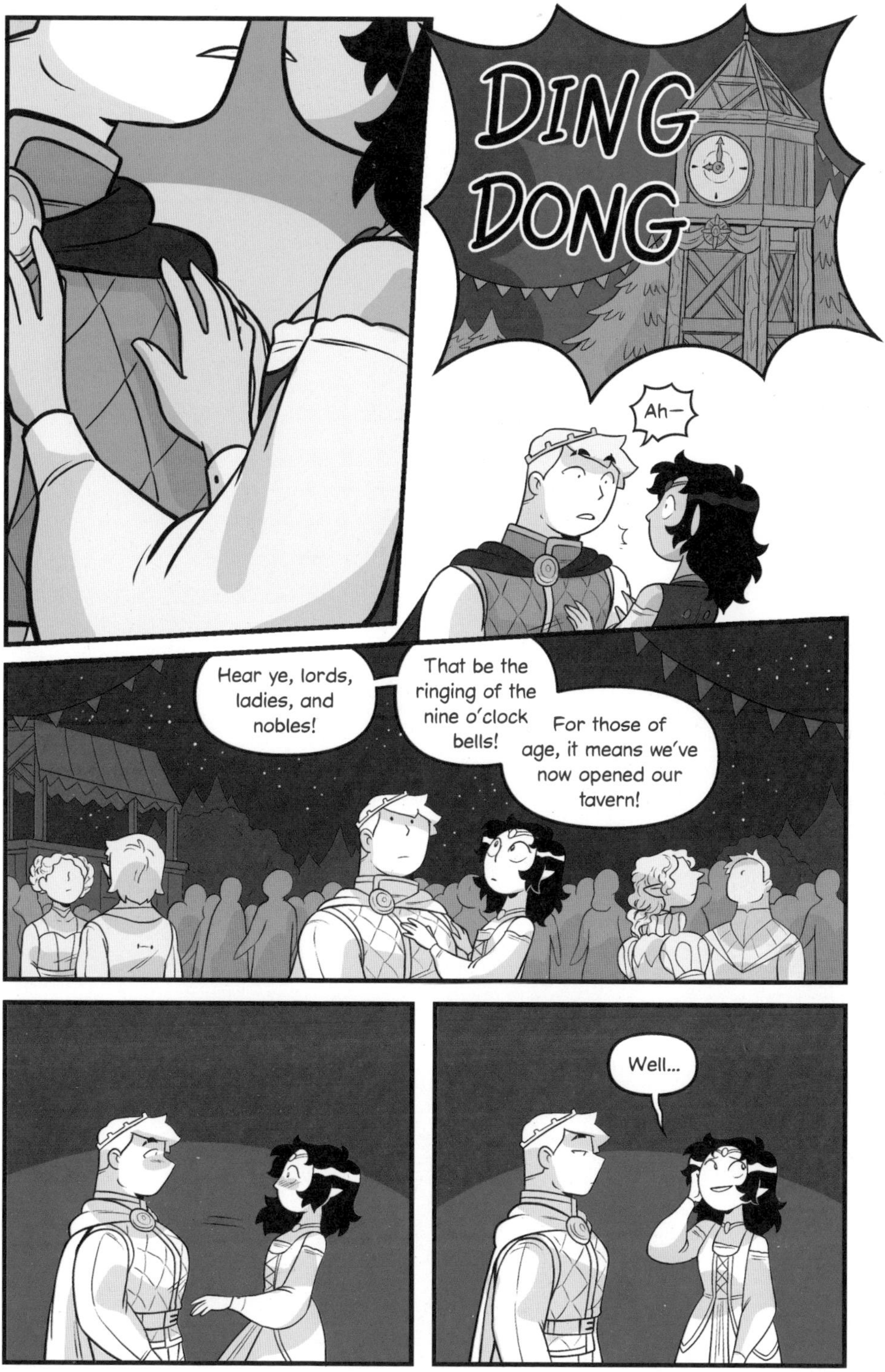
DING DONG
Ah—
Hear ye, lords, ladies, and nobles!
That be the ringing of the nine o'clock bells!
For those of age, it means we've now opened our tavern!
Well...

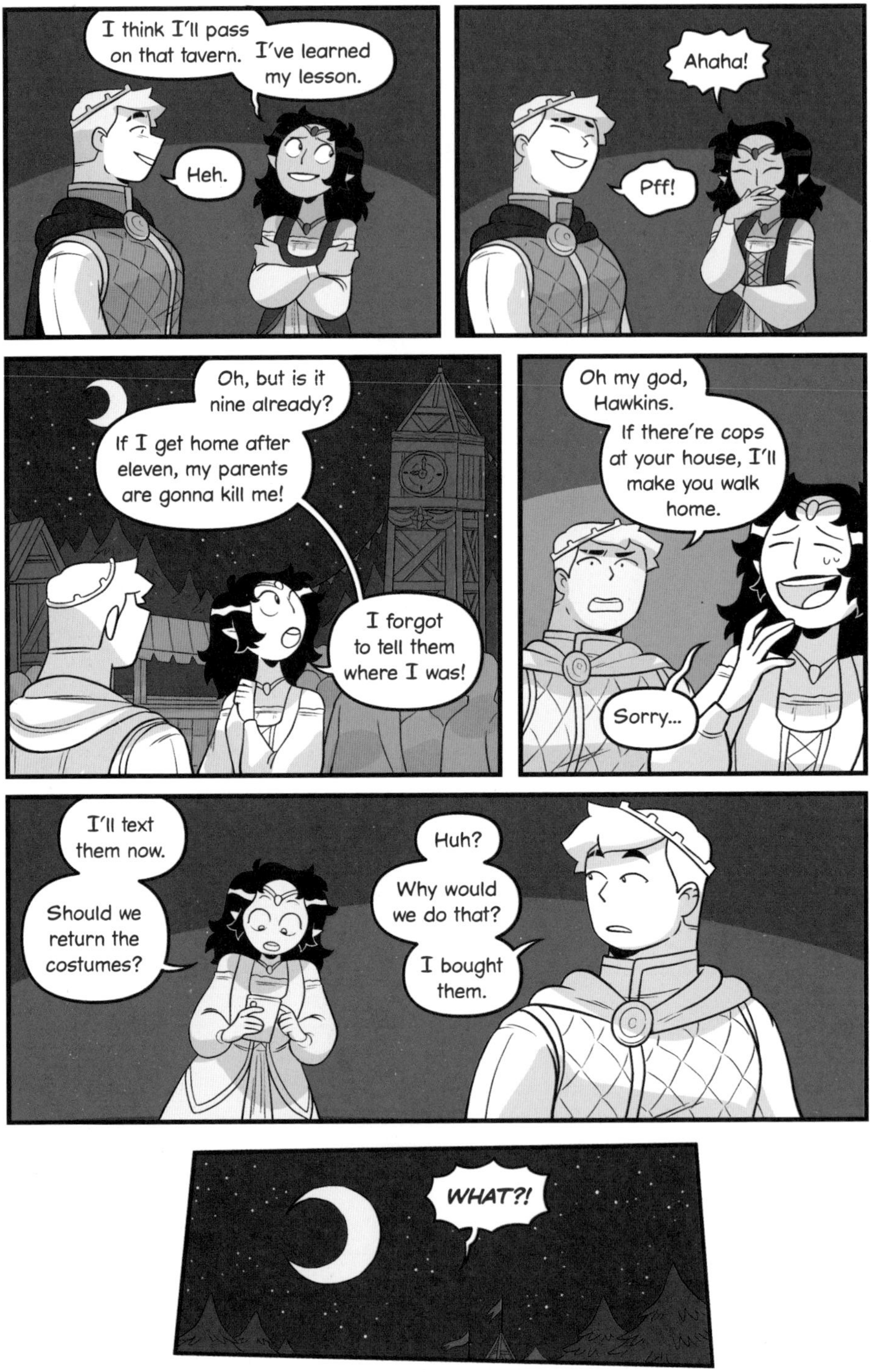
I think I'll pass on that tavern.
I've learned my lesson.
Heh.
Ahaha!
Pff!
Oh, but is it nine already?
If I get home after eleven, my parents are gonna kill me!
I forgot to tell them where I was!
Oh my god, Hawkins.
If there're cops at your house, I'll make you walk home.
Sorry...
I'll text them now.
Should we return the costumes?
Huh?
Why would we do that?
I bought them.
WHAT?!

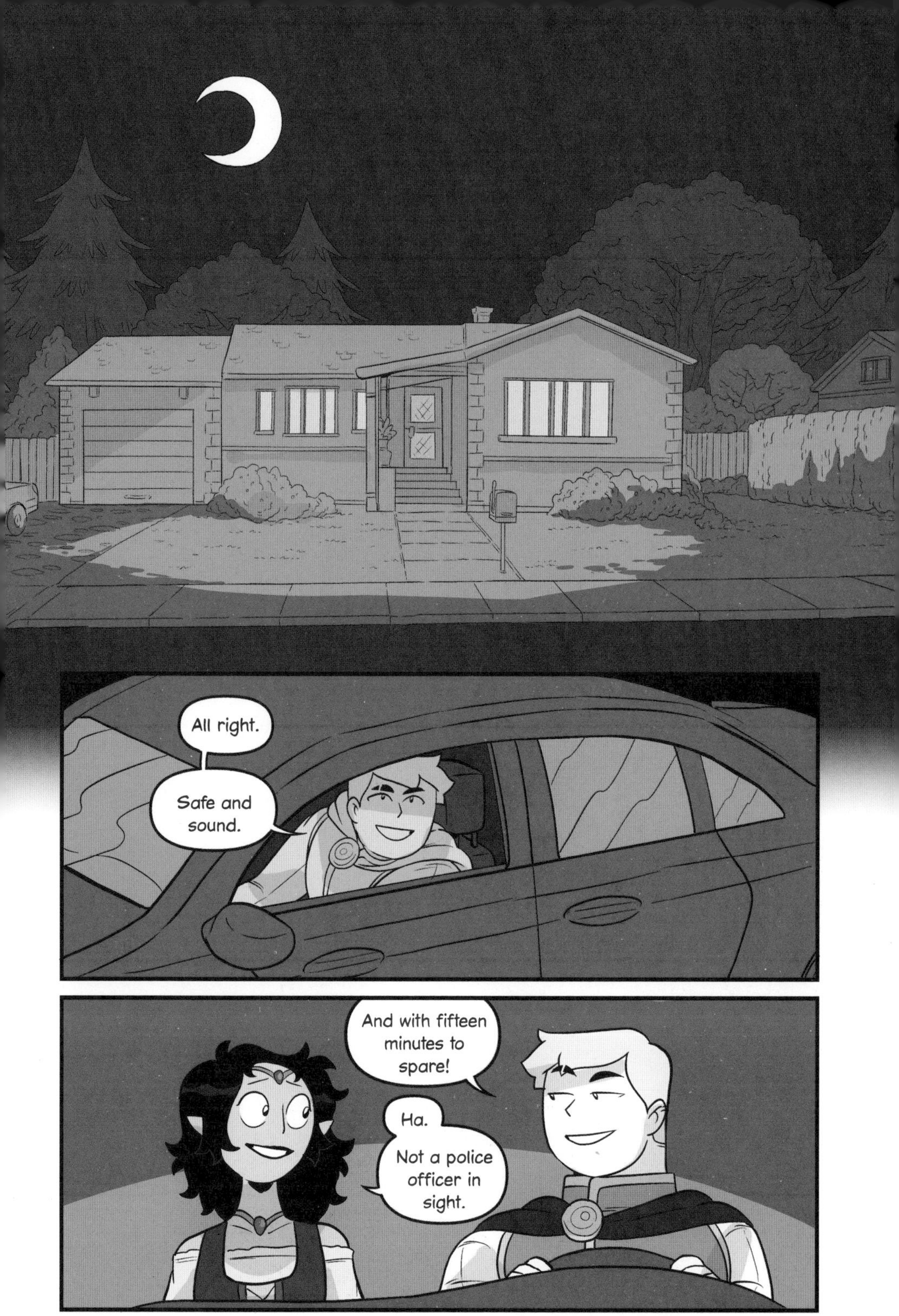
All right.
Safe and sound.
And with fifteen minutes to spare!
Ha.
Not a police officer in sight.

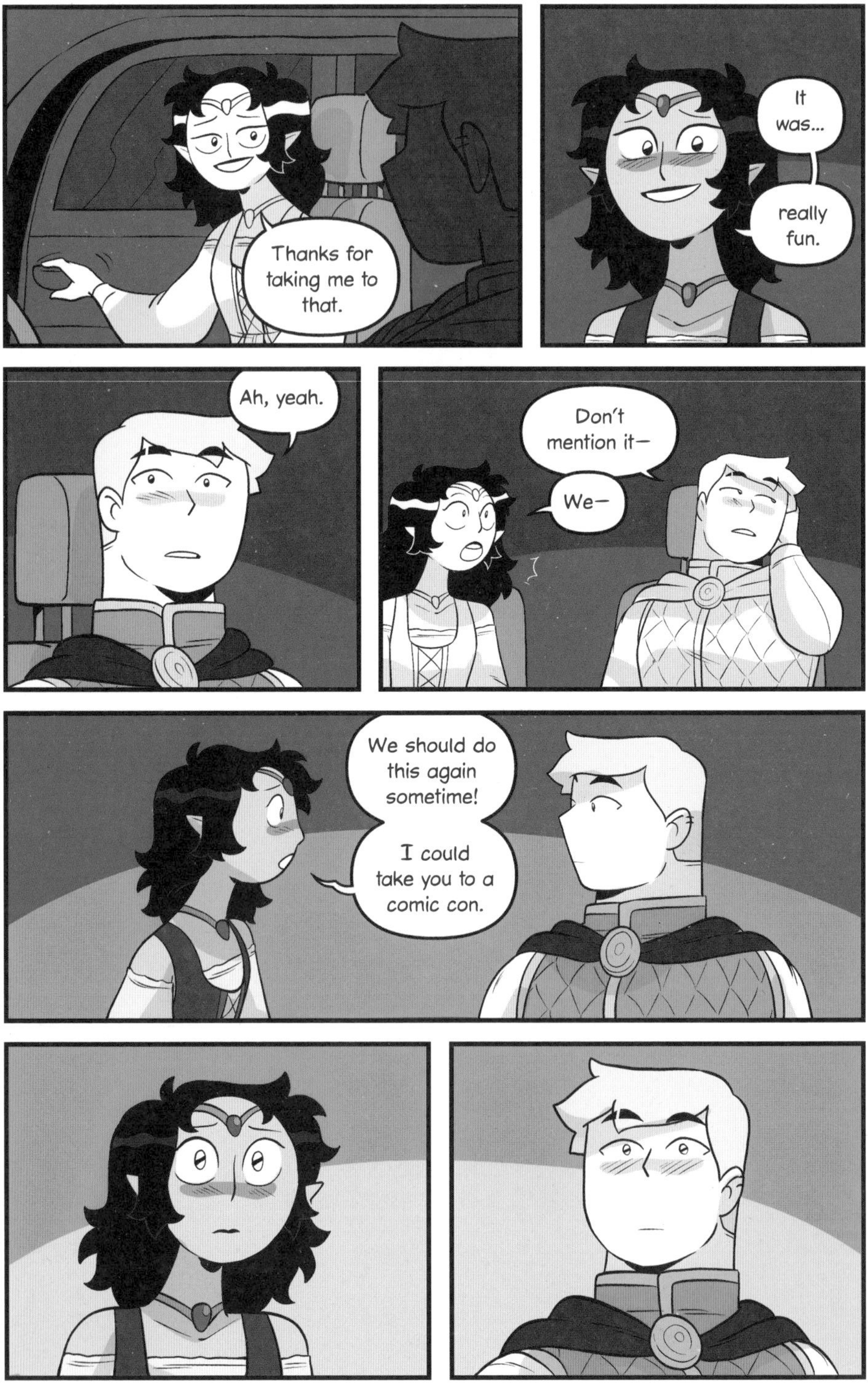
Thanks for taking me to that.
It was...
really fun.
Ah, yeah.
Don't mention it—
We—
We should do this again sometime!
I could take you to a comic con.

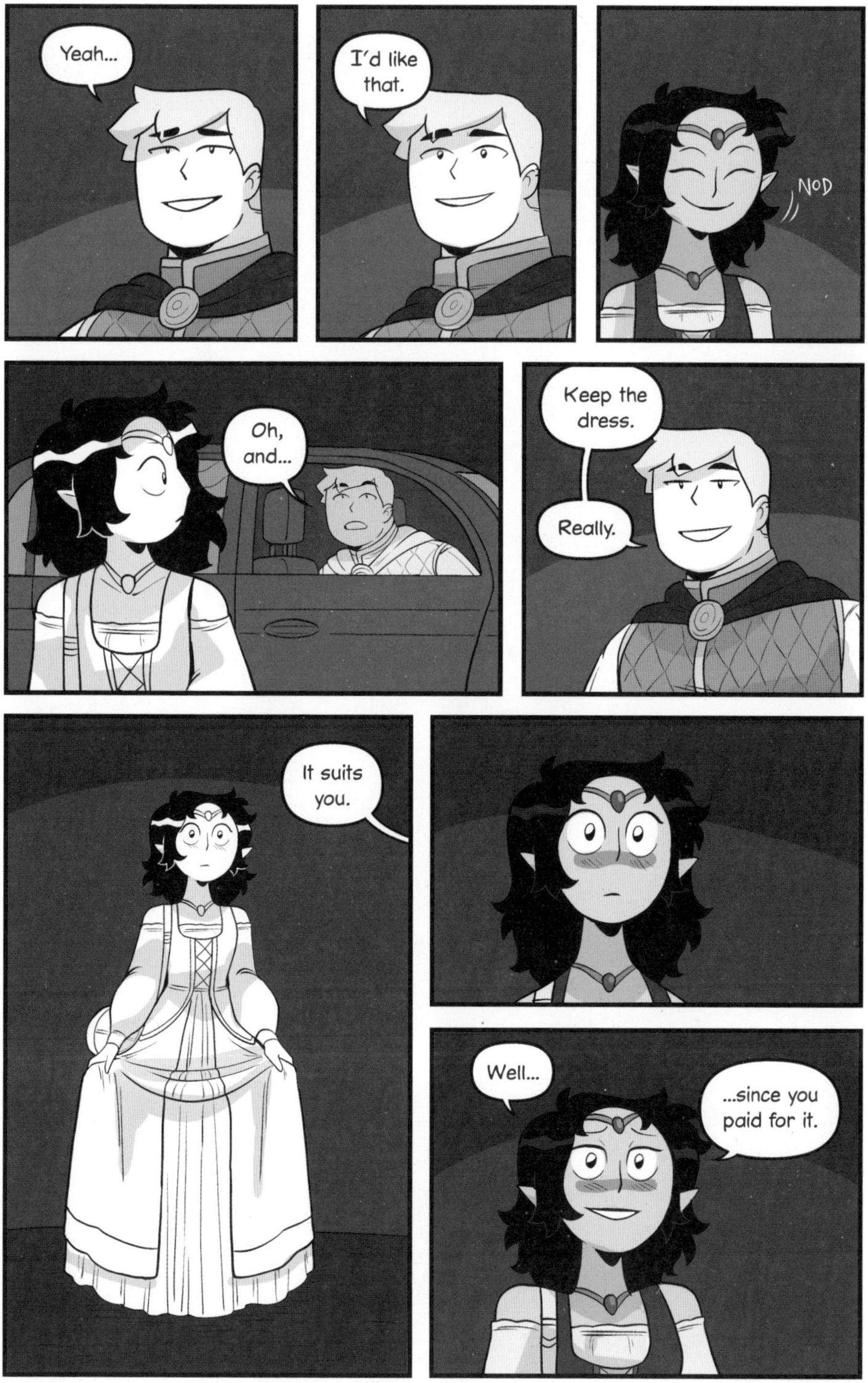

Yeah...
I'd like that.
NOD
Oh, and...
Keep the dress.
Really.
It suits you.
Well...
...since you paid for it.

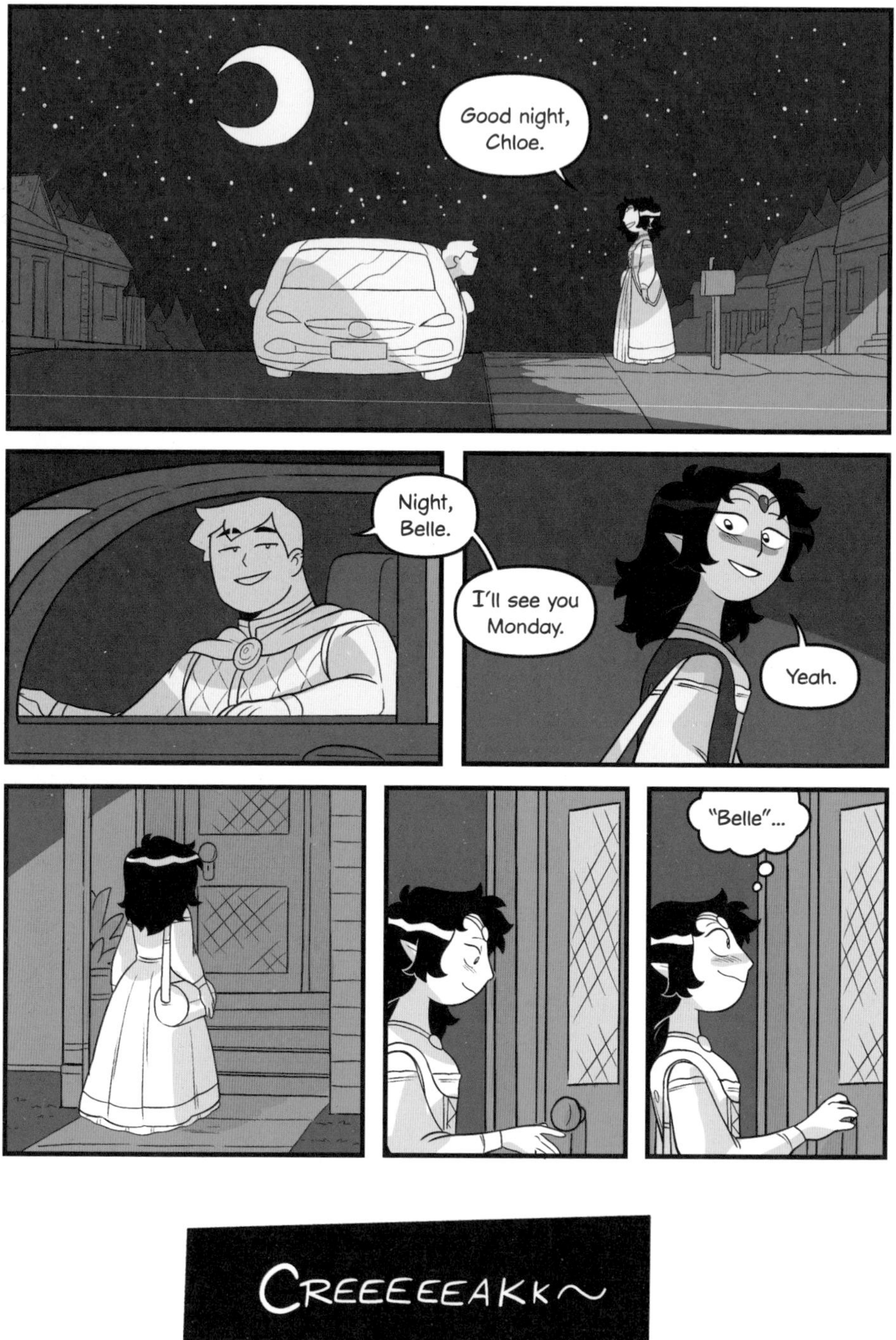
Good night, Chloe.
Night, Belle.
I'll see you Monday.
Yeah.
"Belle"...
CREEEEEEAKK~

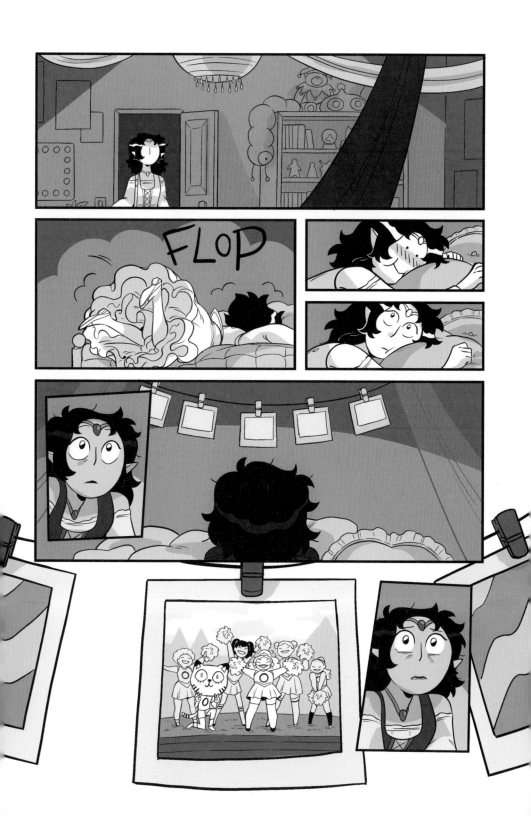

FLOP

CHAPTER

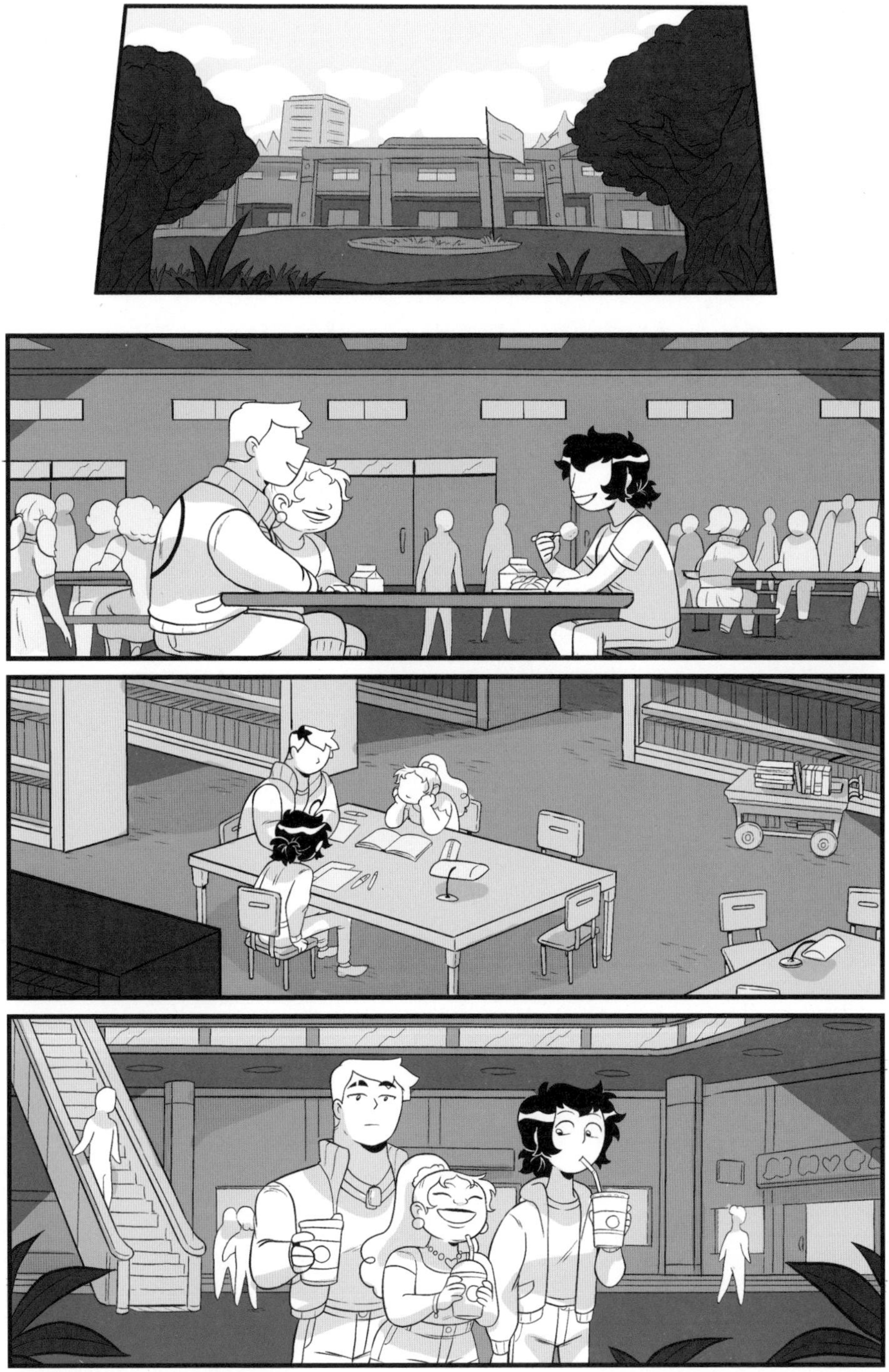

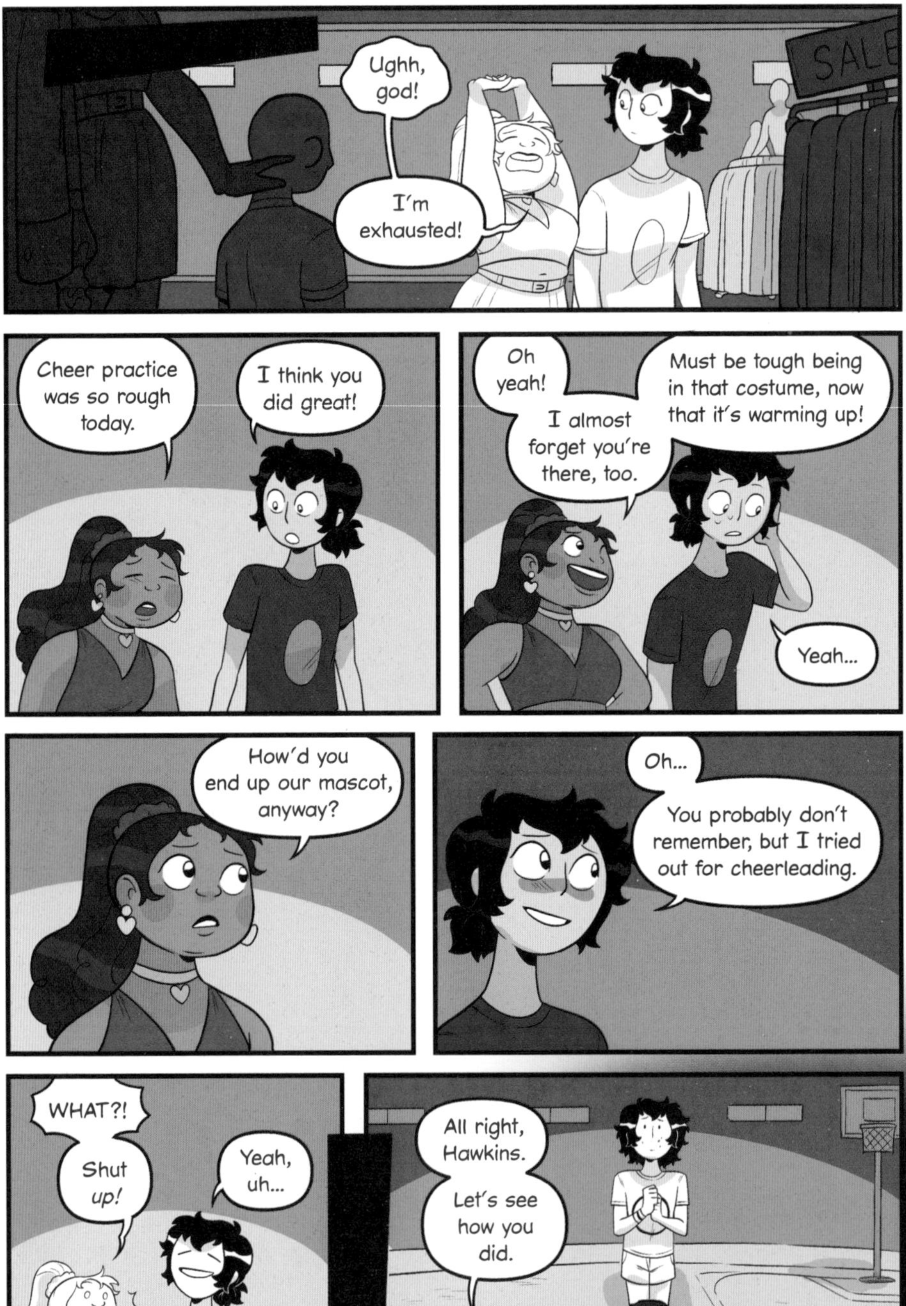

[redacted]
Ughh, god!
I'm exhausted!
Cheer practice was so rough today.
I think you did great!
Oh yeah!
I almost forget you're there, too.
Must be tough being in that costume, now that it's warming up!
Yeah...
How'd you end up our mascot, anyway?
Oh...
You probably don't remember, but I tried out for cheerleading.
WHAT?!
Shut up!
Yeah, uh...
[redacted]
All right, Hawkins.
Let's see how you did.

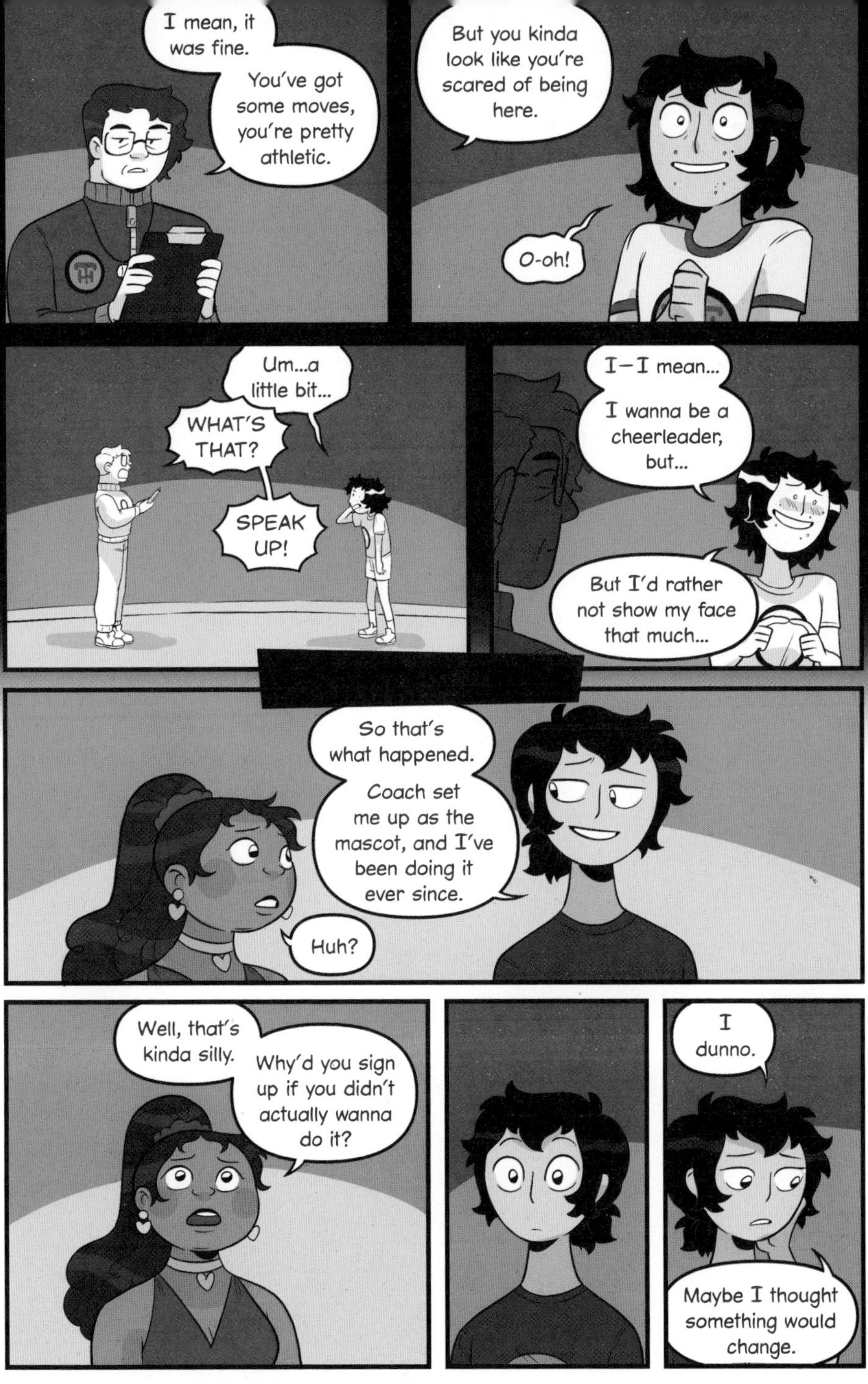
I mean, it was fine.
You've got some moves, you're pretty athletic.
But you kinda look like you're scared of being here.
O-oh!
Um...a little bit...
WHAT'S THAT?
SPEAK UP!
I—I mean...
I wanna be a cheerleader, but...
But I'd rather not show my face that much...
So that's what happened.
Coach set me up as the mascot, and I've been doing it ever since.
Huh?
Well, that's kinda silly.
Why'd you sign up if you didn't actually wanna do it?
I dunno.
Maybe I thought something would change.

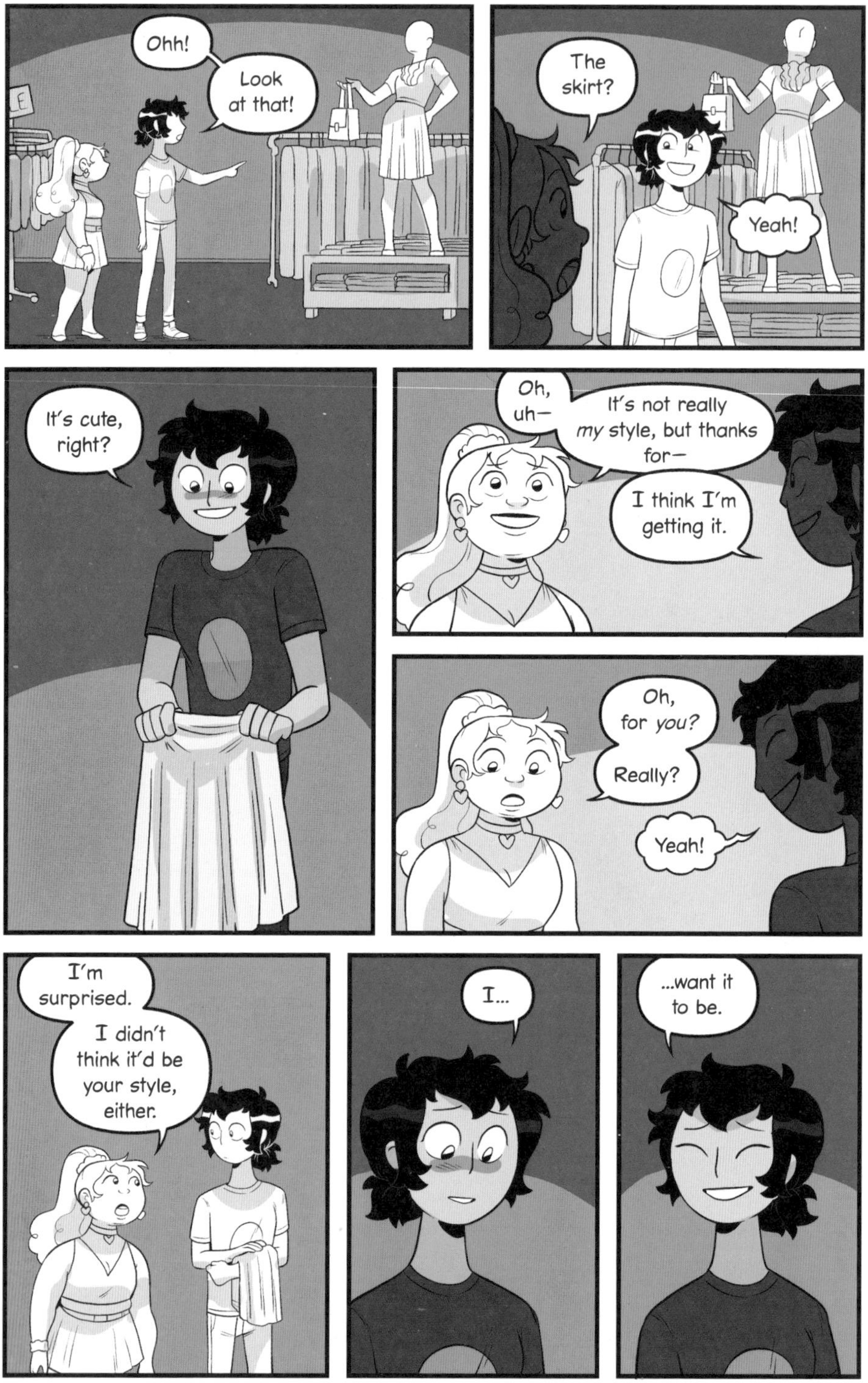
Ohh!
Look at that!
The skirt?
Yeah!
It's cute, right?
Oh, uh—
It's not really *my* style, but thanks for—
I think I'm getting it.
Oh, for *you?*
Really?
Yeah!
I'm surprised.
I didn't think it'd be your style, either.
I...
...want it to be.

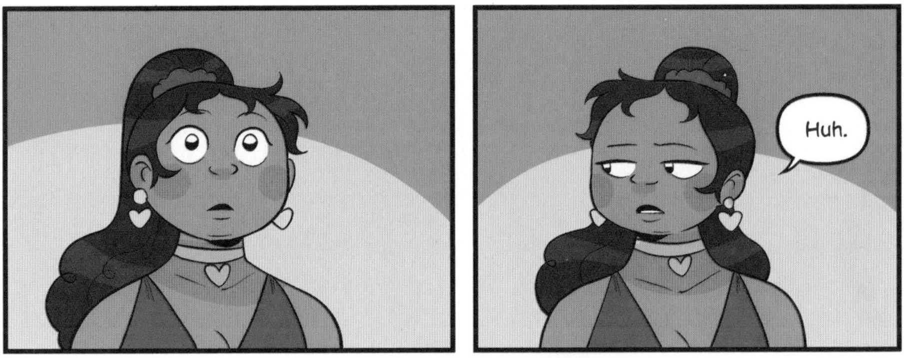
Huh.

[redacted]

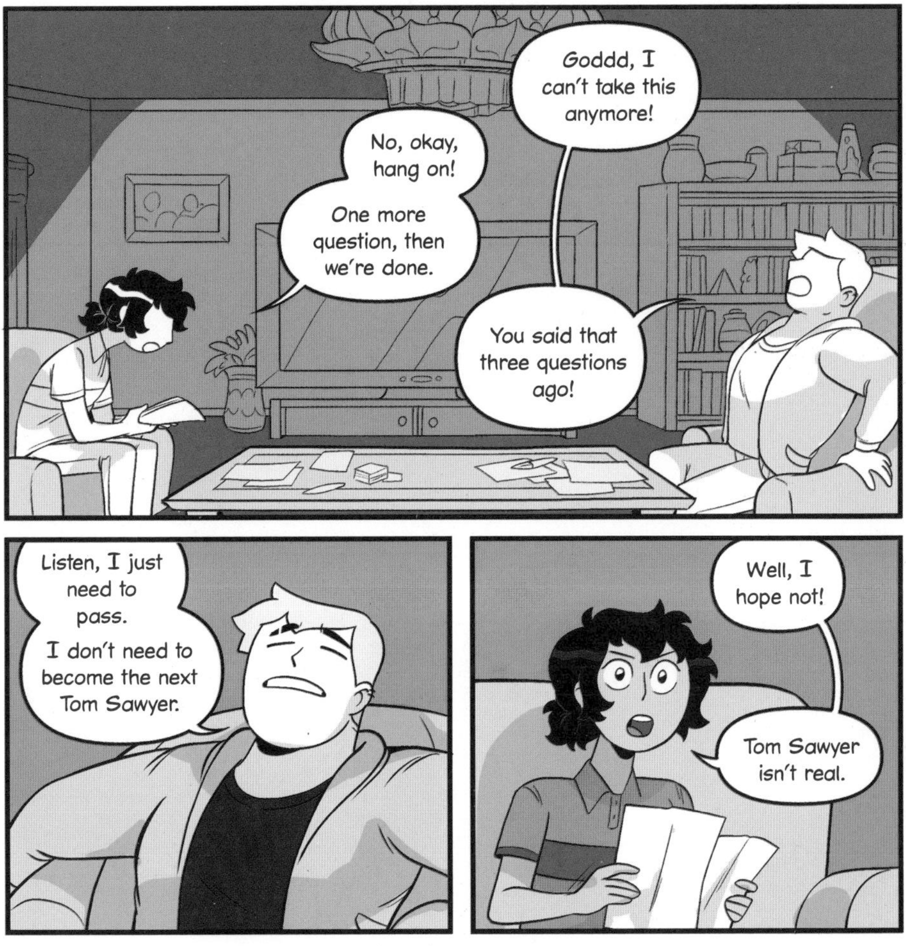
No, okay, hang on!
One more question, then we're done.
Goddd, I can't take this anymore!
You said that three questions ago!
Listen, I just need to pass.
I don't need to become the next Tom Sawyer.
Well, I hope not!
Tom Sawyer isn't real.

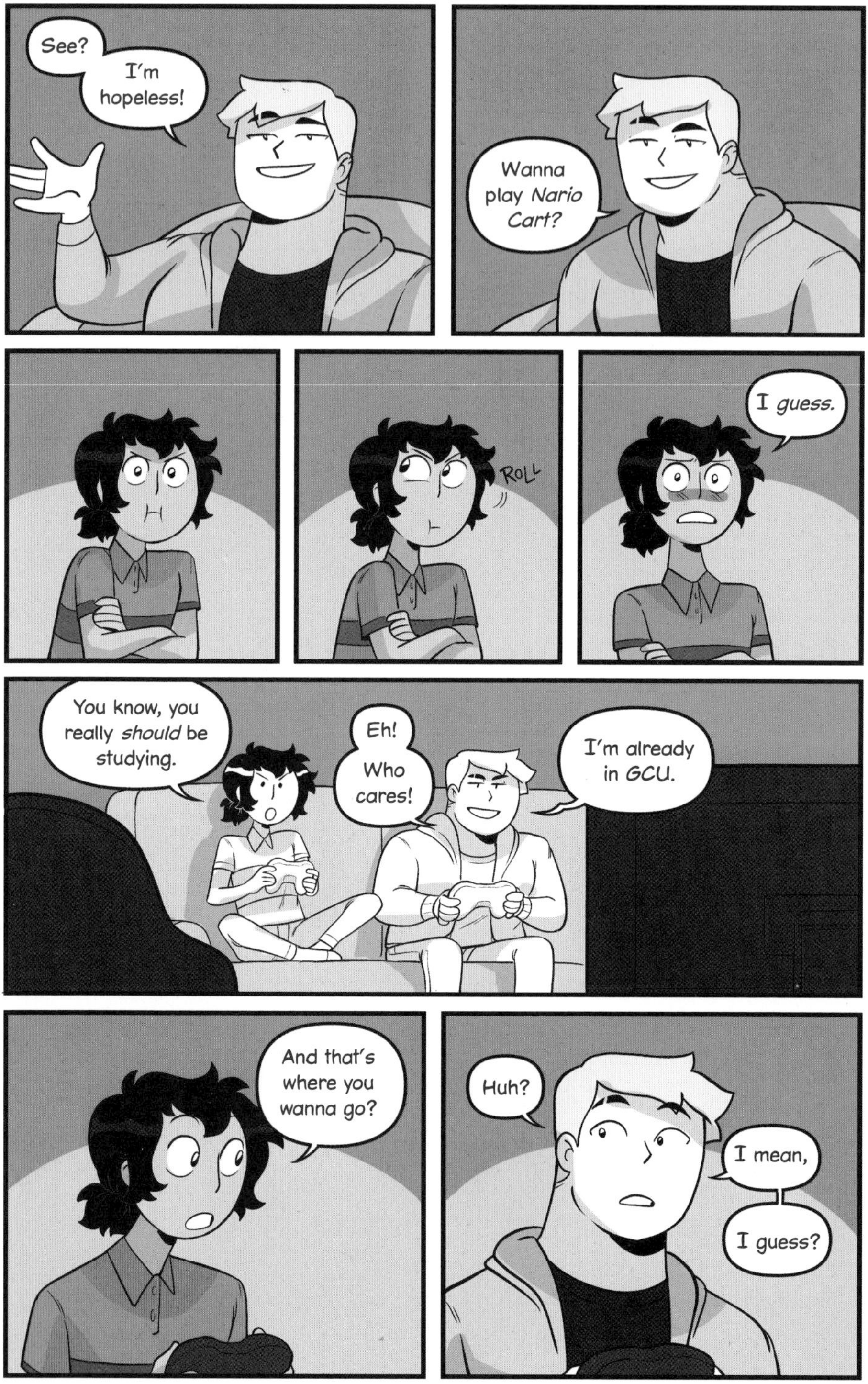
See?
I'm hopeless!
Wanna play *Nario Cart?*
ROLL
I *guess.*
You know, you really *should* be studying.
Eh!
Who cares!
I'm already in GCU.
And that's where you wanna go?
Huh?
I mean,
I guess?

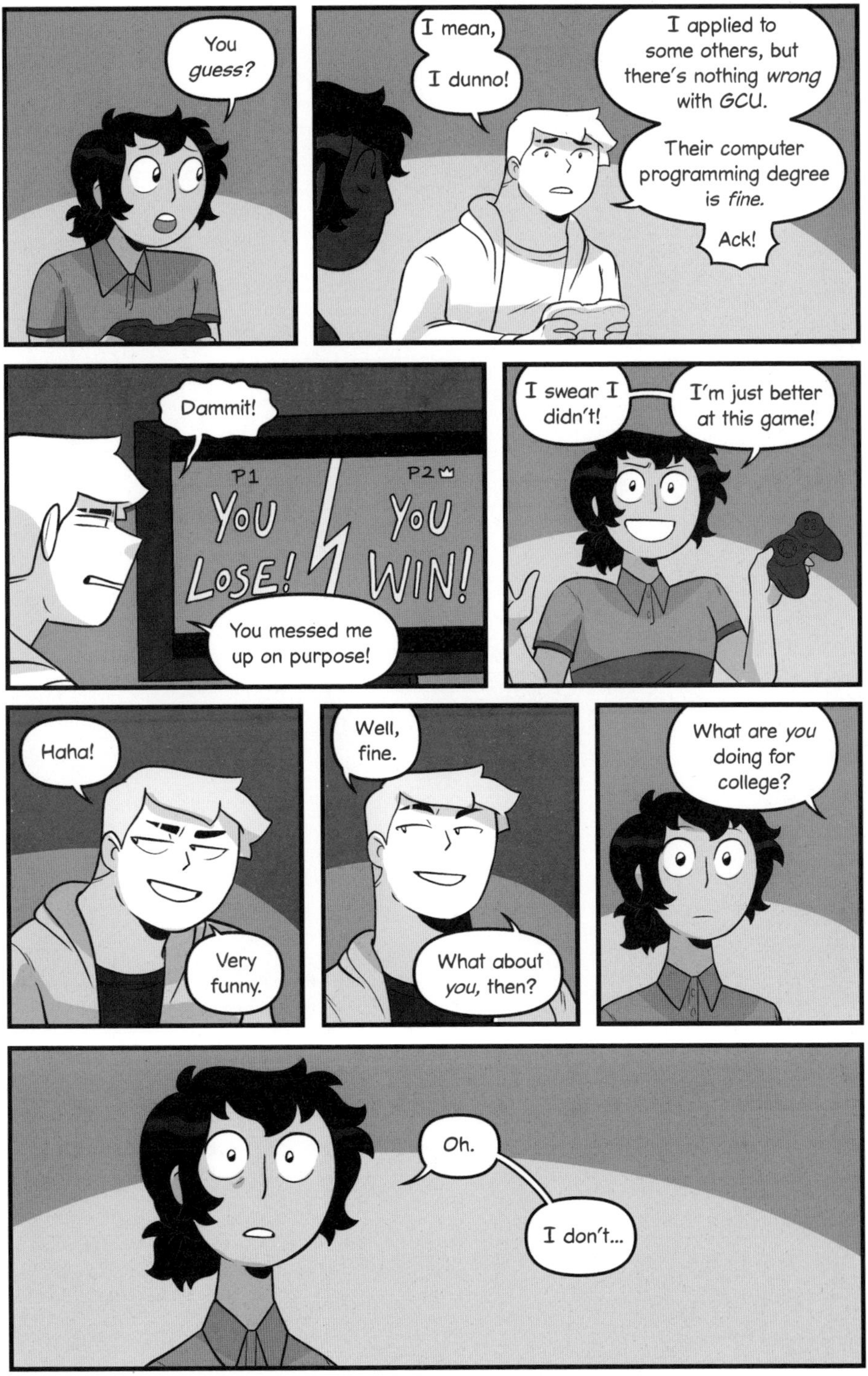
You *guess?*
I mean,
I dunno!
I applied to some others, but there's nothing *wrong* with GCU.
Their computer programming degree is *fine.*
Ack!
Dammit!
P1
YOU LOSE!
P2
YOU WIN!
You messed me up on purpose!
I swear I didn't!
I'm just better at this game!
Haha!
Very funny.
Well, fine.
What about *you,* then?
What are *you* doing for college?
Oh.
I don't...

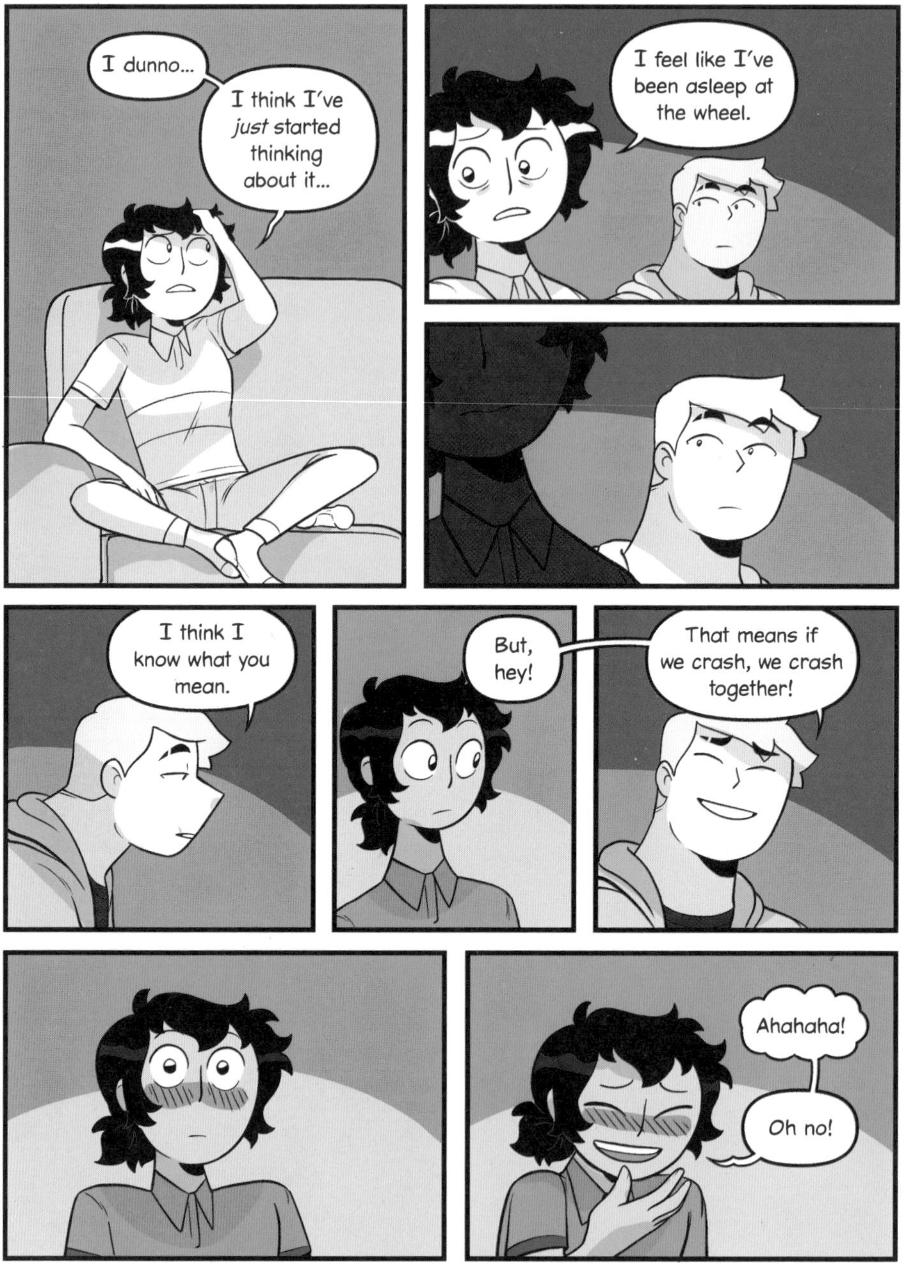
I dunno...
I think I've *just* started thinking about it...
I feel like I've been asleep at the wheel.
I think I know what you mean.
But, hey!
That means if we crash, we crash together!
Ahahaha!
Oh no!

[redacted]

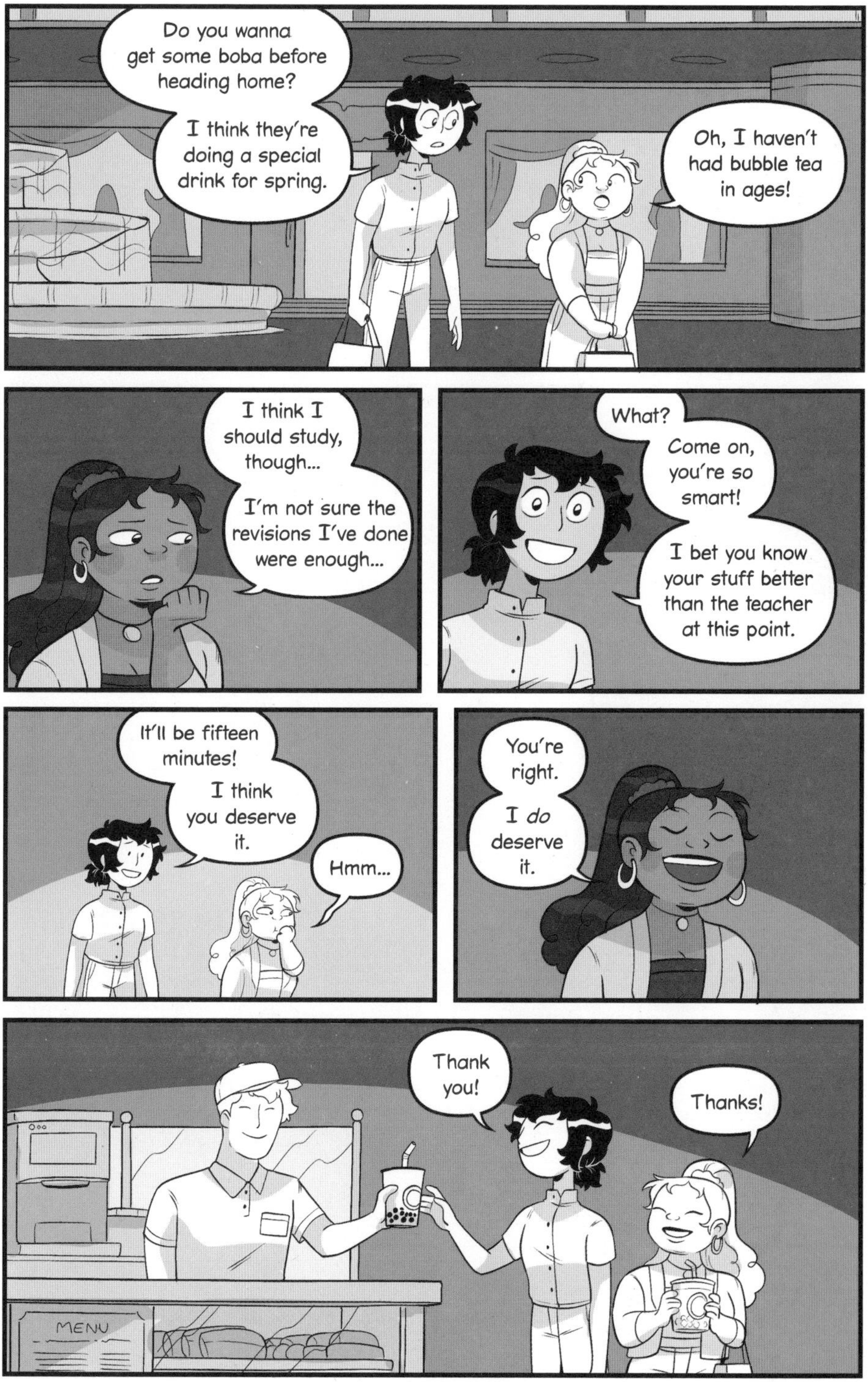
Do you wanna get some boba before heading home?
I think they're doing a special drink for spring.
Oh, I haven't had bubble tea in ages!
I think I should study, though...
I'm not sure the revisions I've done were enough...
What?
Come on, you're so smart!
I bet you know your stuff better than the teacher at this point.
It'll be fifteen minutes!
I think you deserve it.
Hmm...
You're right.
I *do* deserve it.
Thank you!
Thanks!
MENU

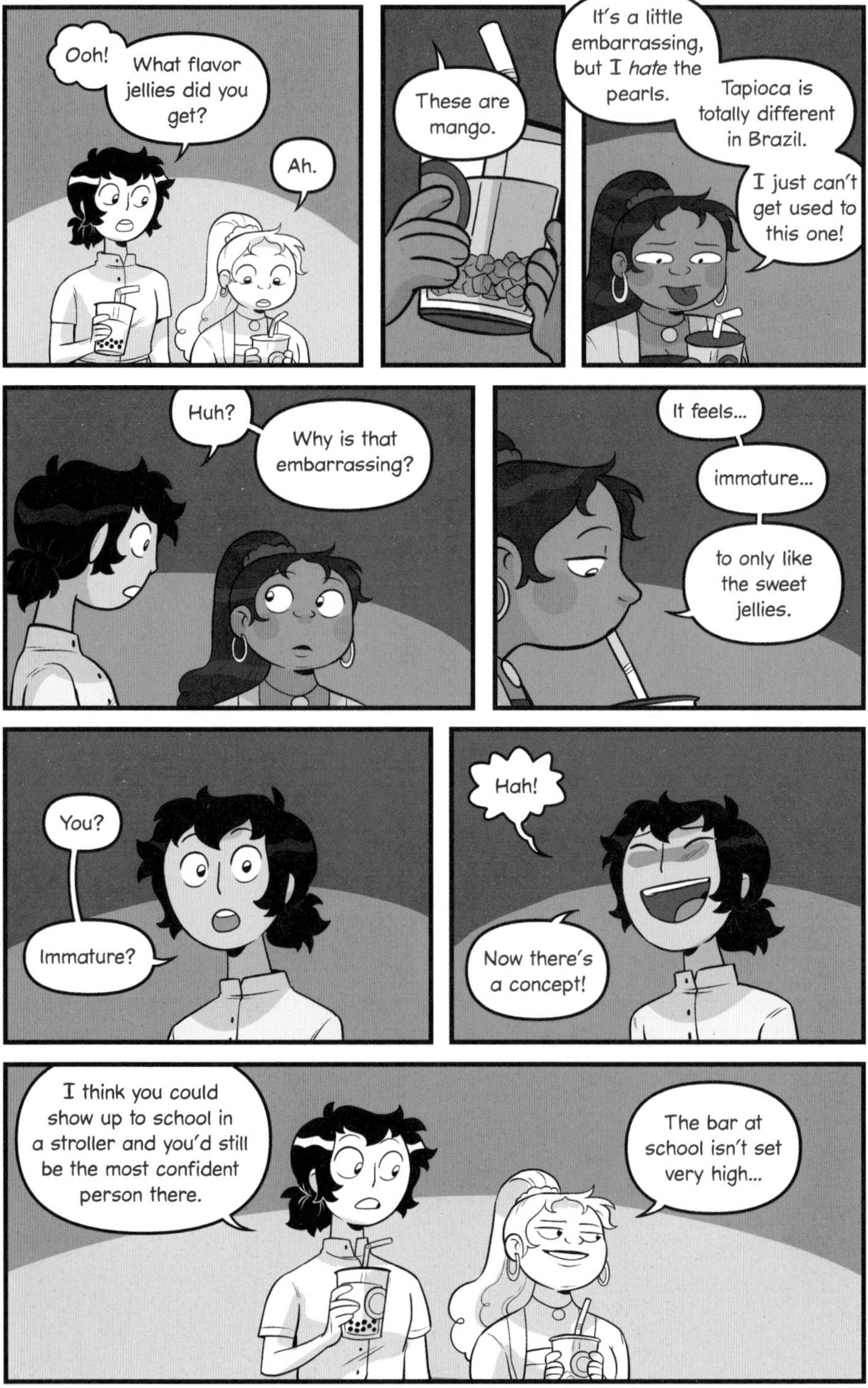
Ooh!
What flavor jellies did you get?
Ah.
These are mango.
It's a little embarrassing, but I *hate* the pearls.
Tapioca is totally different in Brazil.
I just can't get used to this one!
Huh?
Why is that embarrassing?
It feels...
immature...
to only like the sweet jellies.
You?
Immature?
Hah!
Now there's a concept!
I think you could show up to school in a stroller and you'd still be the most confident person there.
The bar at school isn't set very high...

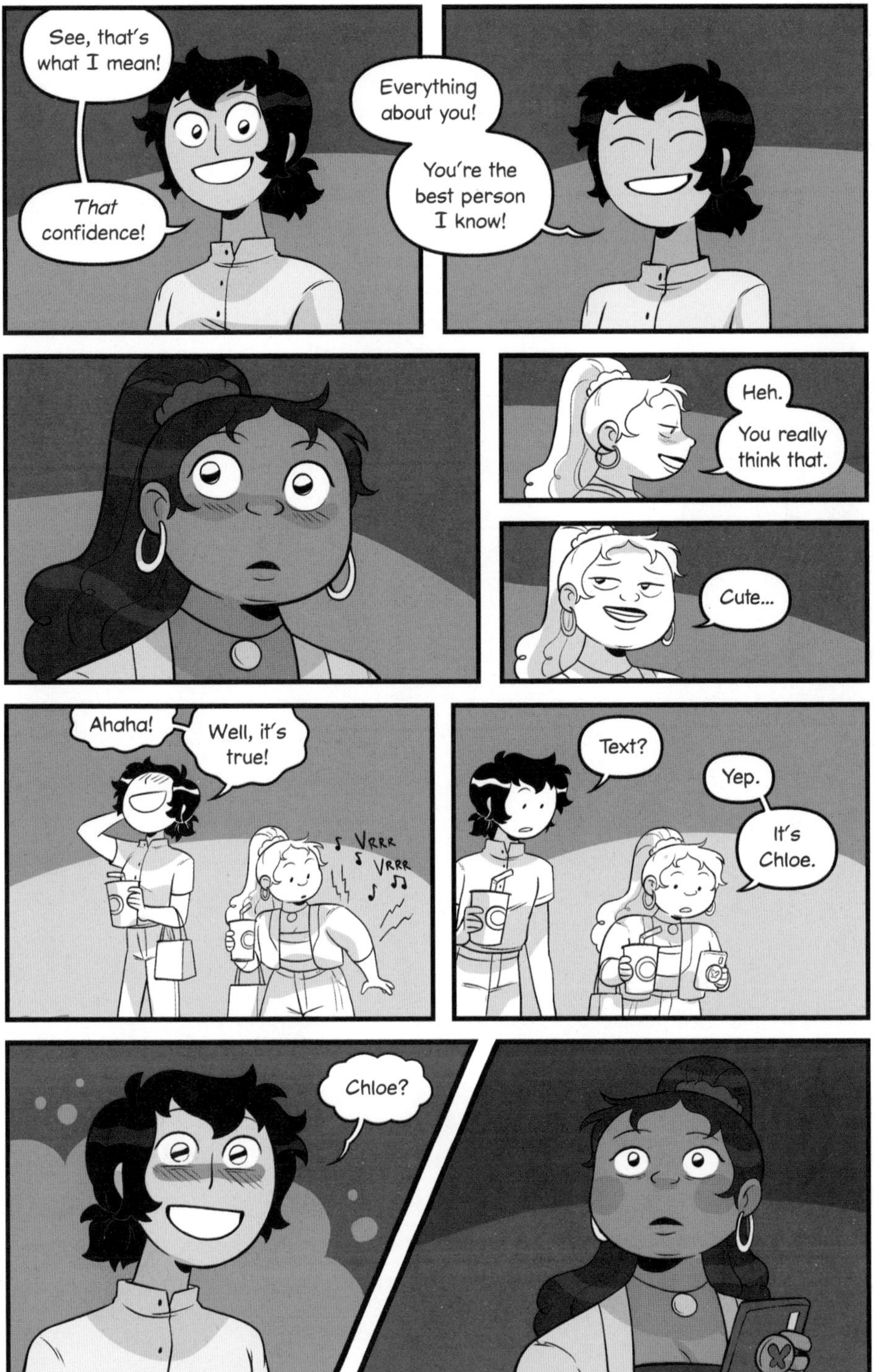
See, that's what I mean!
That confidence!
Everything about you!
You're the best person I know!
Heh.
You really think that.
Cute...
Ahaha!
Well, it's true!
VRRR
VRRR
Text?
Yep.
It's Chloe.
Chloe?

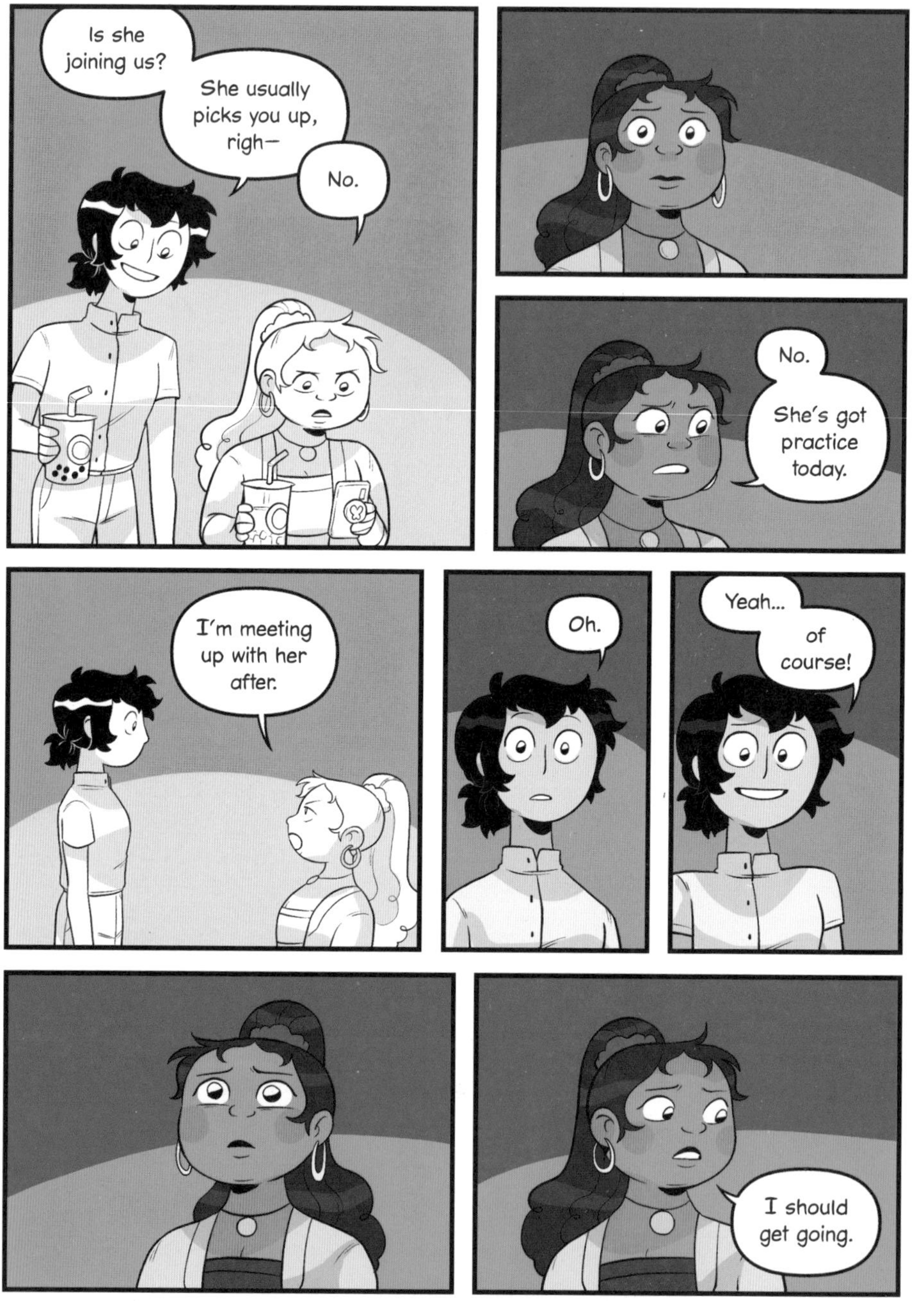
Is she joining us?
She usually picks you up, righ—
No.
No.
She's got practice today.
I'm meeting up with her after.
Oh.
Yeah...
of course!
I should get going.

[redacted]

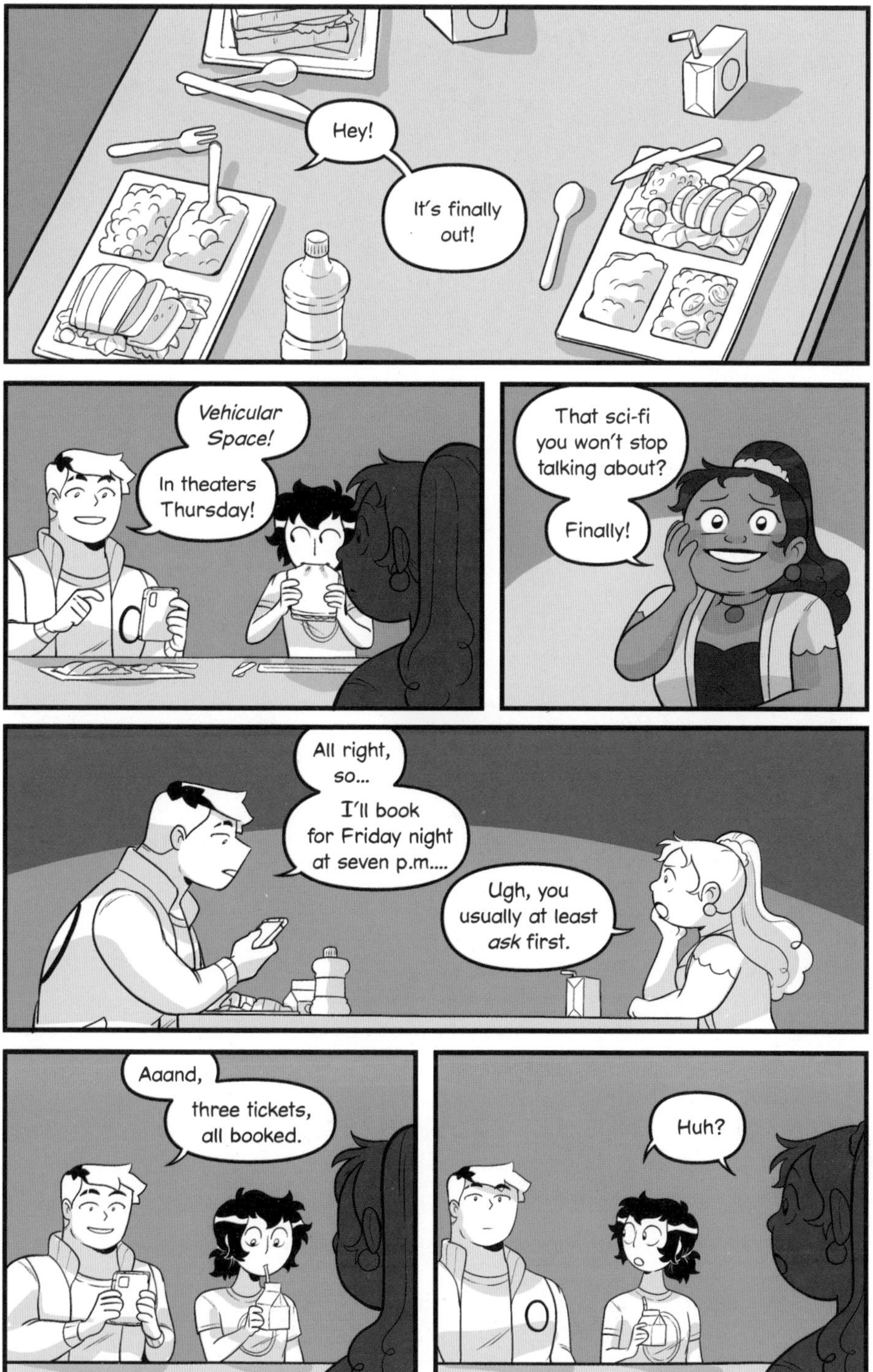

Hey!
It's finally out!
Vehicular Space!
In theaters Thursday!
That sci-fi you won't stop talking about?
Finally!
All right, so...
I'll book for Friday night at seven p.m....
Ugh, you usually at least *ask* first.
Aaand,
three tickets, all booked.
Huh?

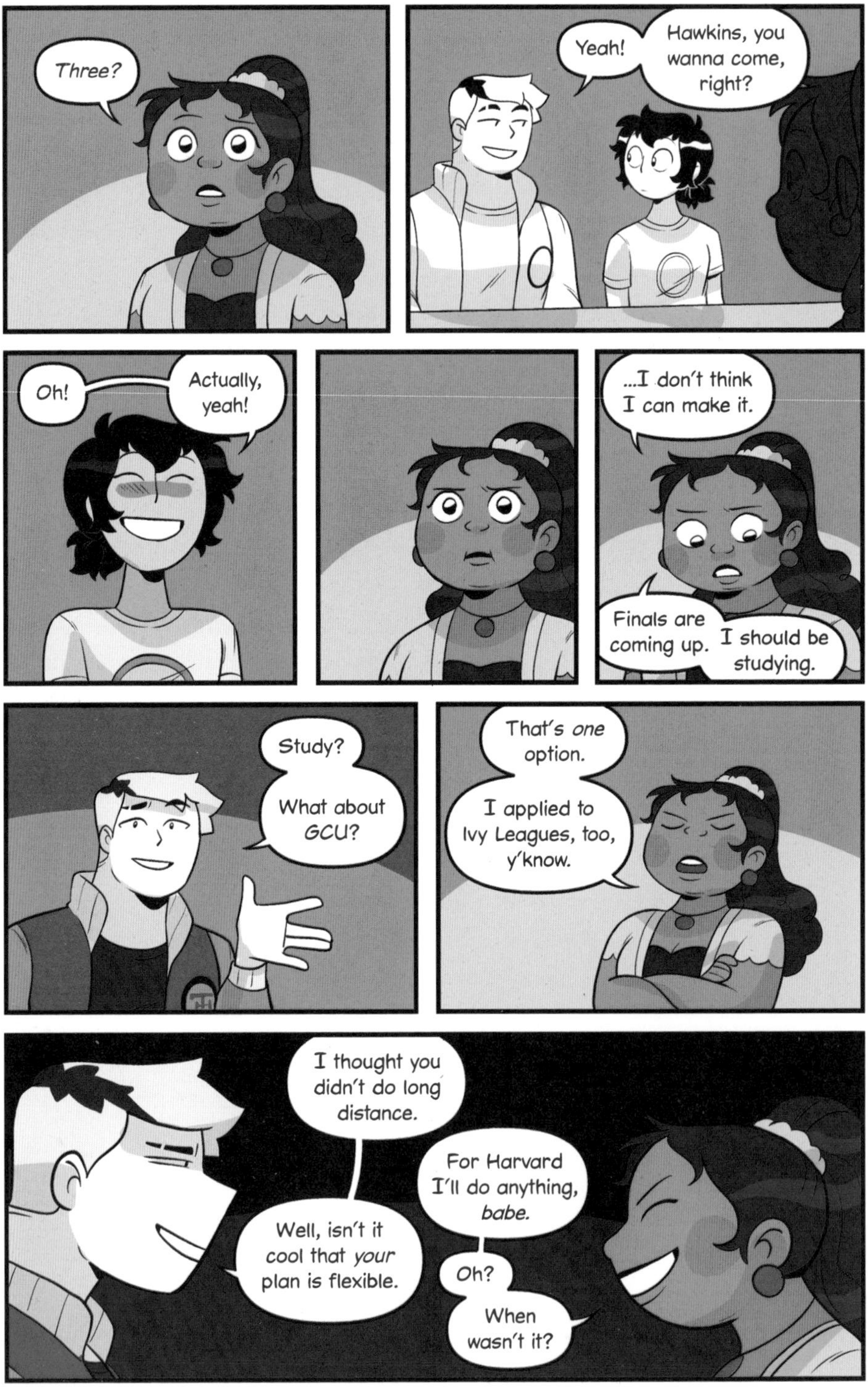
Three?
Yeah!
Hawkins, you wanna come, right?
Oh!
Actually, yeah!
...I don't think I can make it.
Finals are coming up.
I should be studying.
Study?
What about GCU?
That's *one* option.
I applied to Ivy Leagues, too, y'know.
I thought you didn't do long distance.
For Harvard I'll do anything, *babe.*
Well, isn't it cool that *your* plan is flexible.
Oh?
When wasn't it?

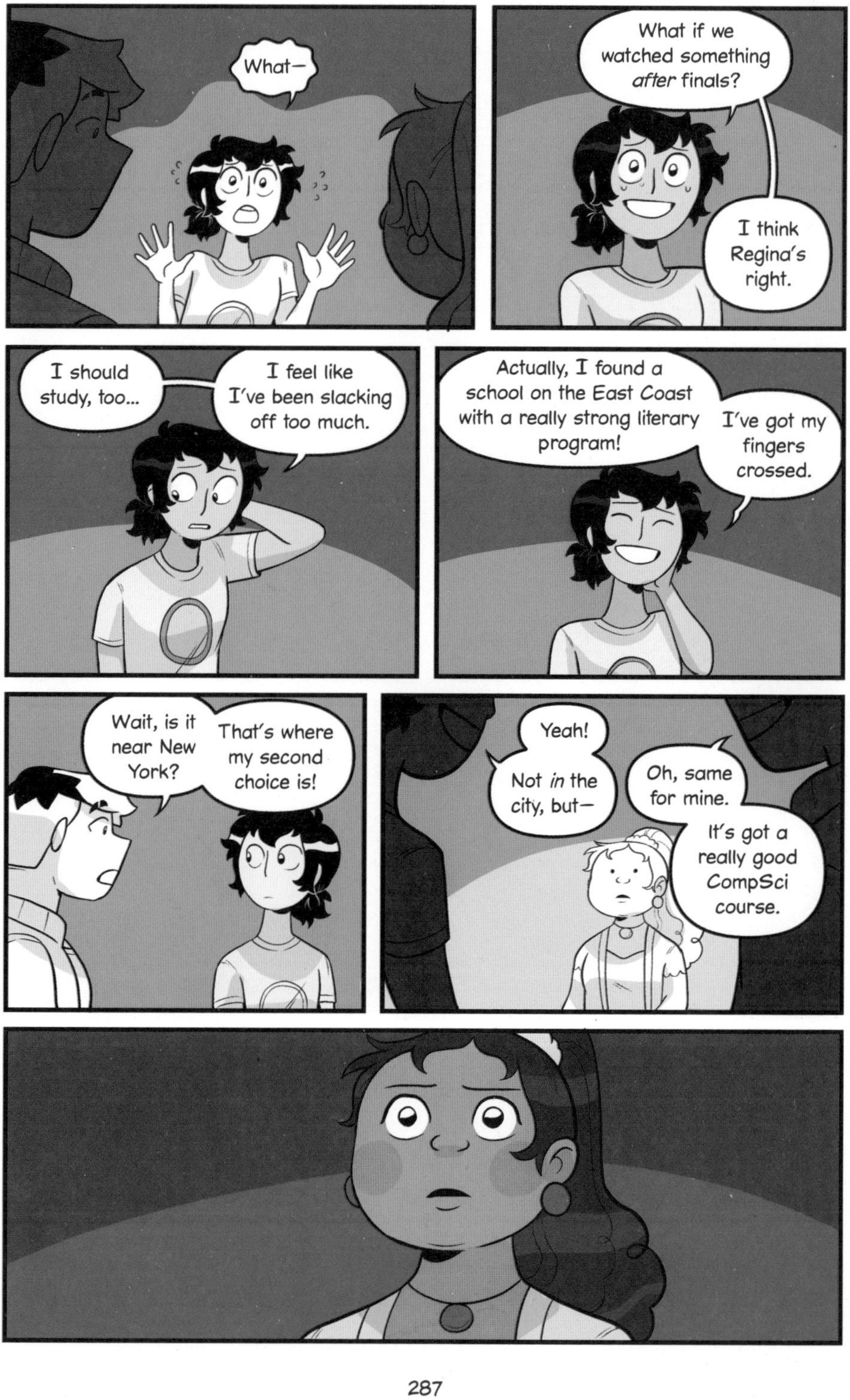
What—
What if we watched something *after* finals?
I think Regina's right.
I should study, too...
I feel like I've been slacking off too much.
Actually, I found a school on the East Coast with a really strong literary program!
I've got my fingers crossed.
Wait, is it near New York?
That's where my second choice is!
Yeah!
Not *in* the city, but—
Oh, same for mine.
It's got a really good CompSci course.

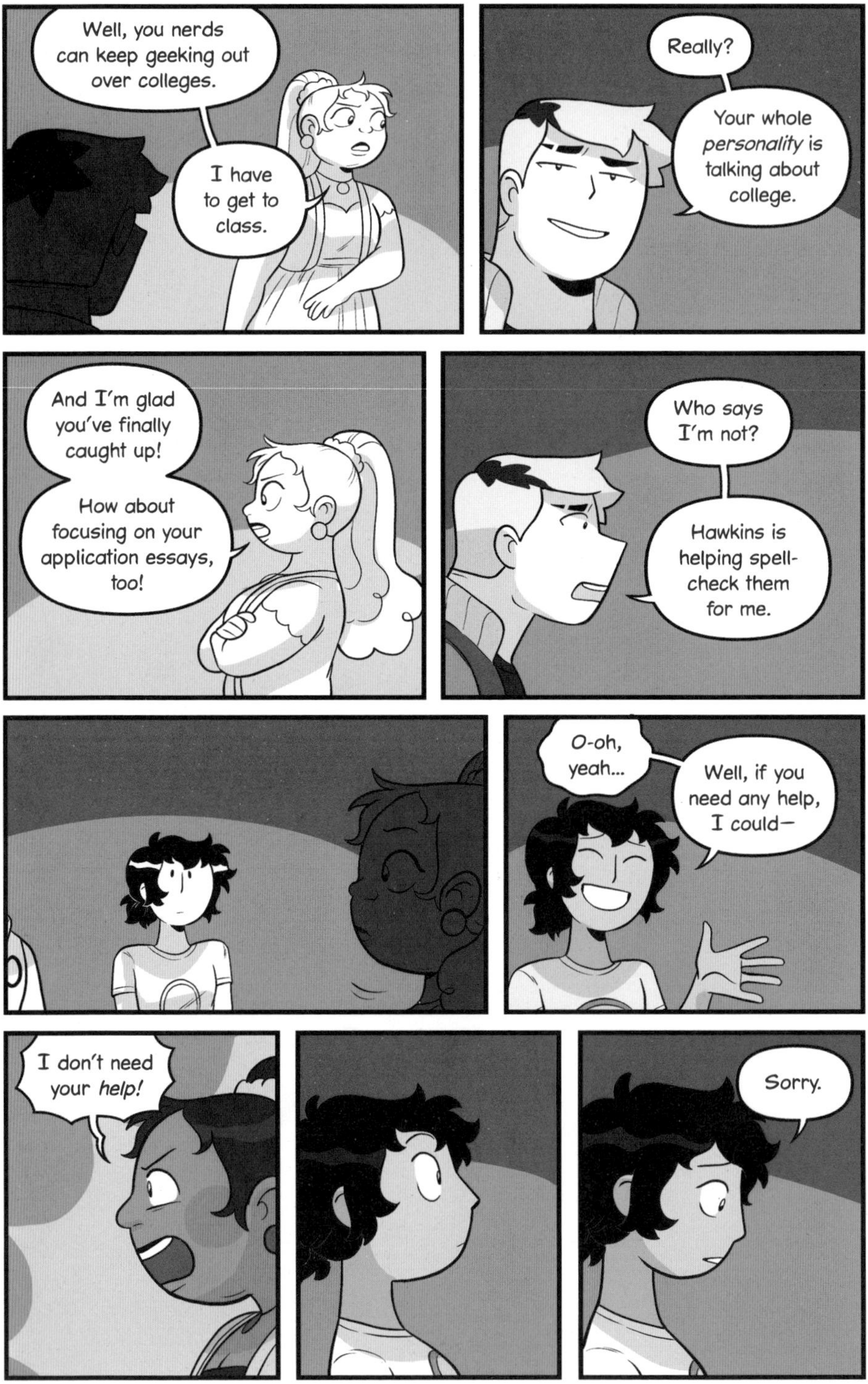
Well, you nerds can keep geeking out over colleges.
I have to get to class.
Really?
Your whole *personality* is talking about college.
And I'm glad you've finally caught up!
How about focusing on your application essays, too!
Who says I'm not?
Hawkins is helping spell-check them for me.
O-oh, yeah...
Well, if you need any help, I could—
I don't need your *help!*
Sorry.

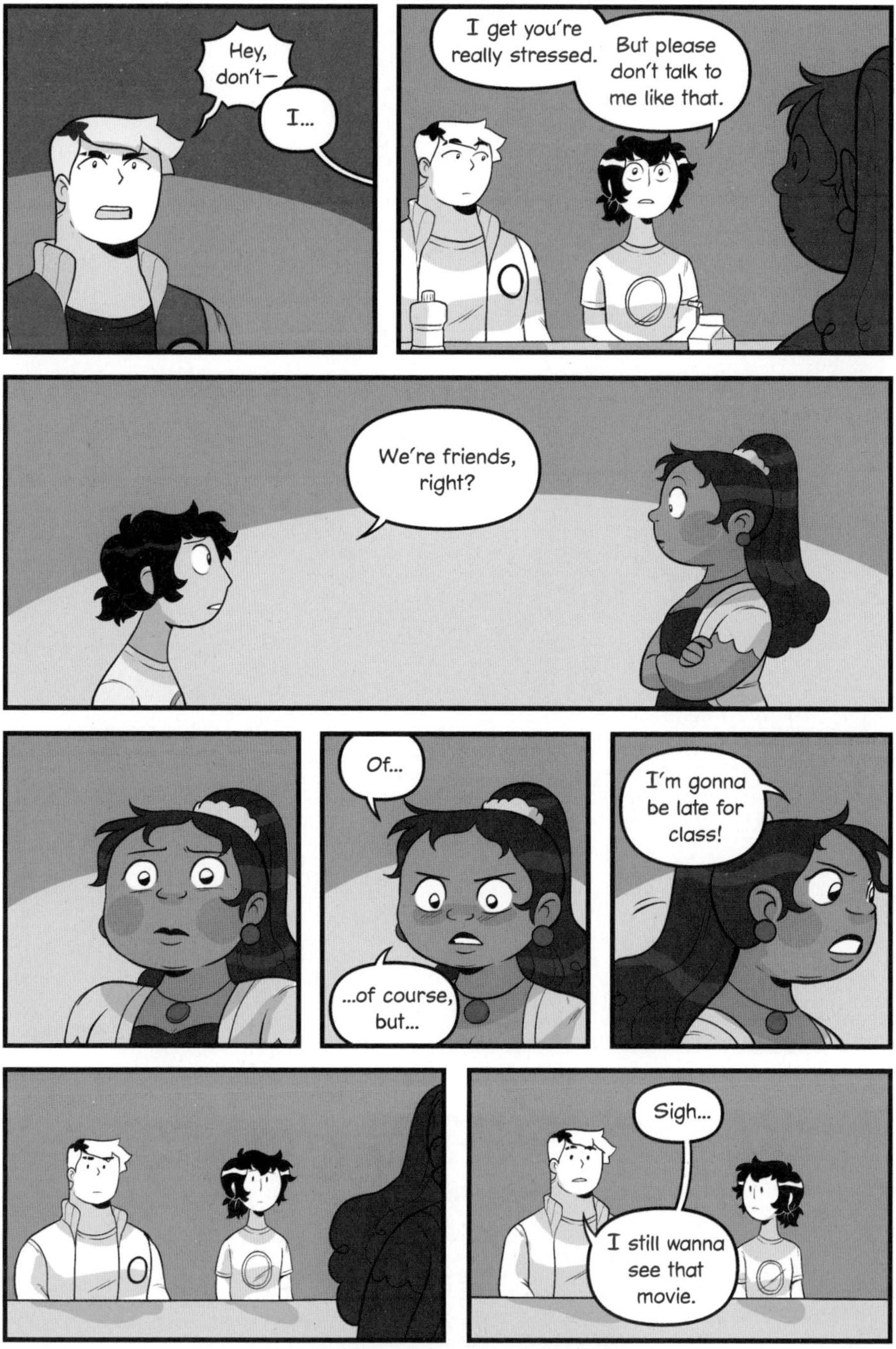
Hey, don't—
I...
I get you're really stressed.
But please don't talk to me like that.
We're friends, right?
Of...
...of course, but...
I'm gonna be late for class!
Sigh...
I still wanna see that movie.

[redacted]

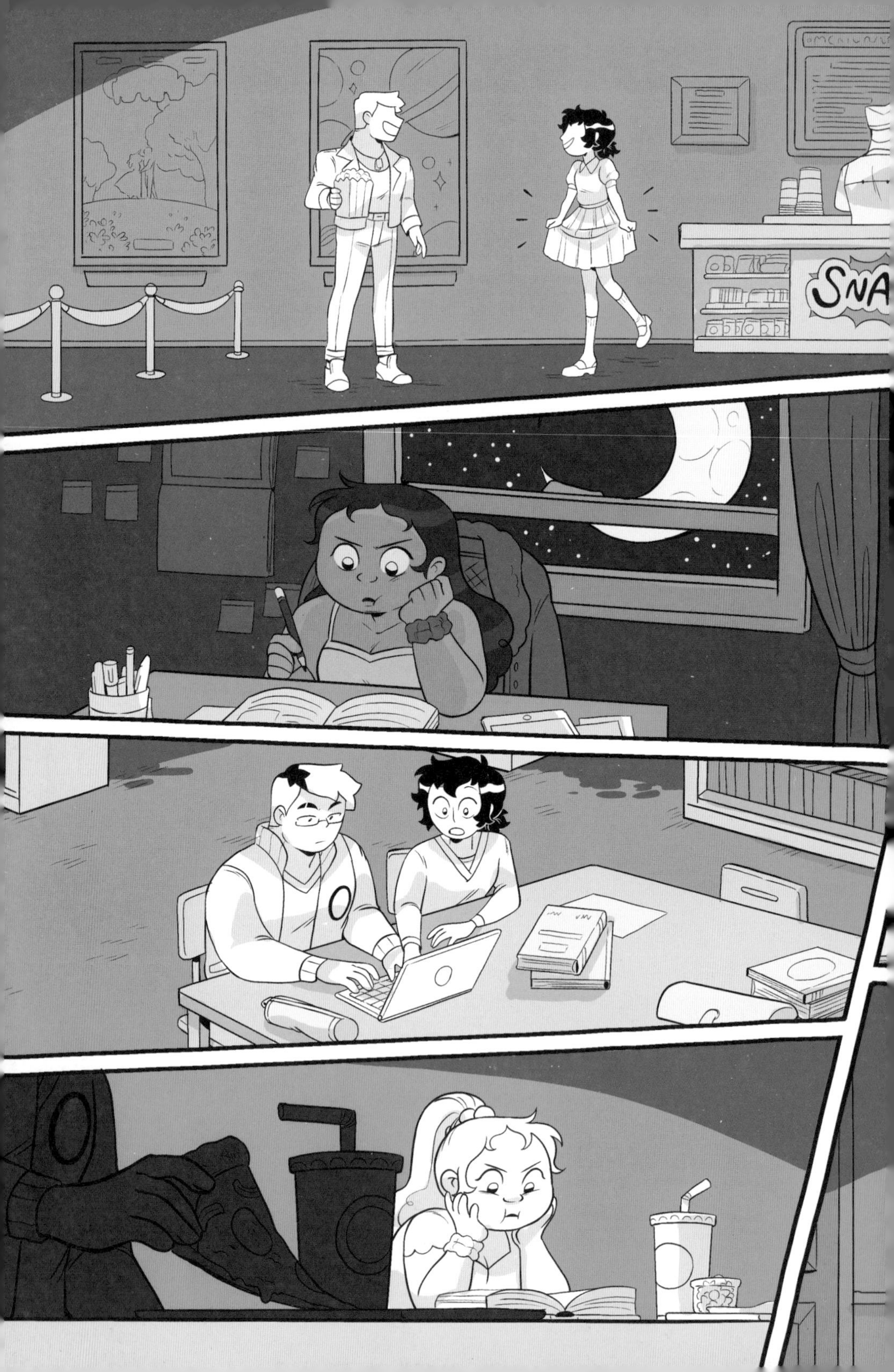
SNA

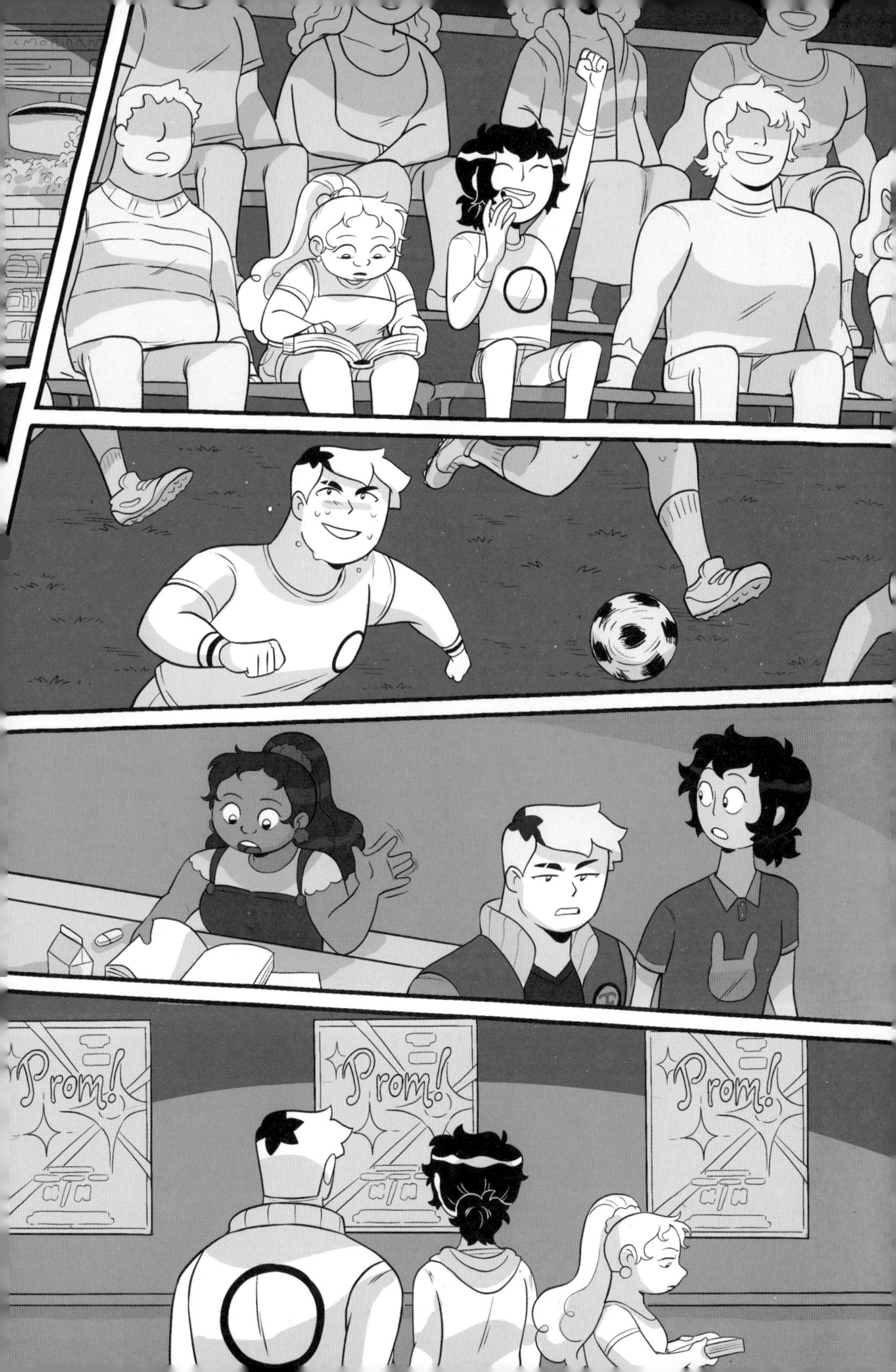
Prom!
Prom!
Prom!

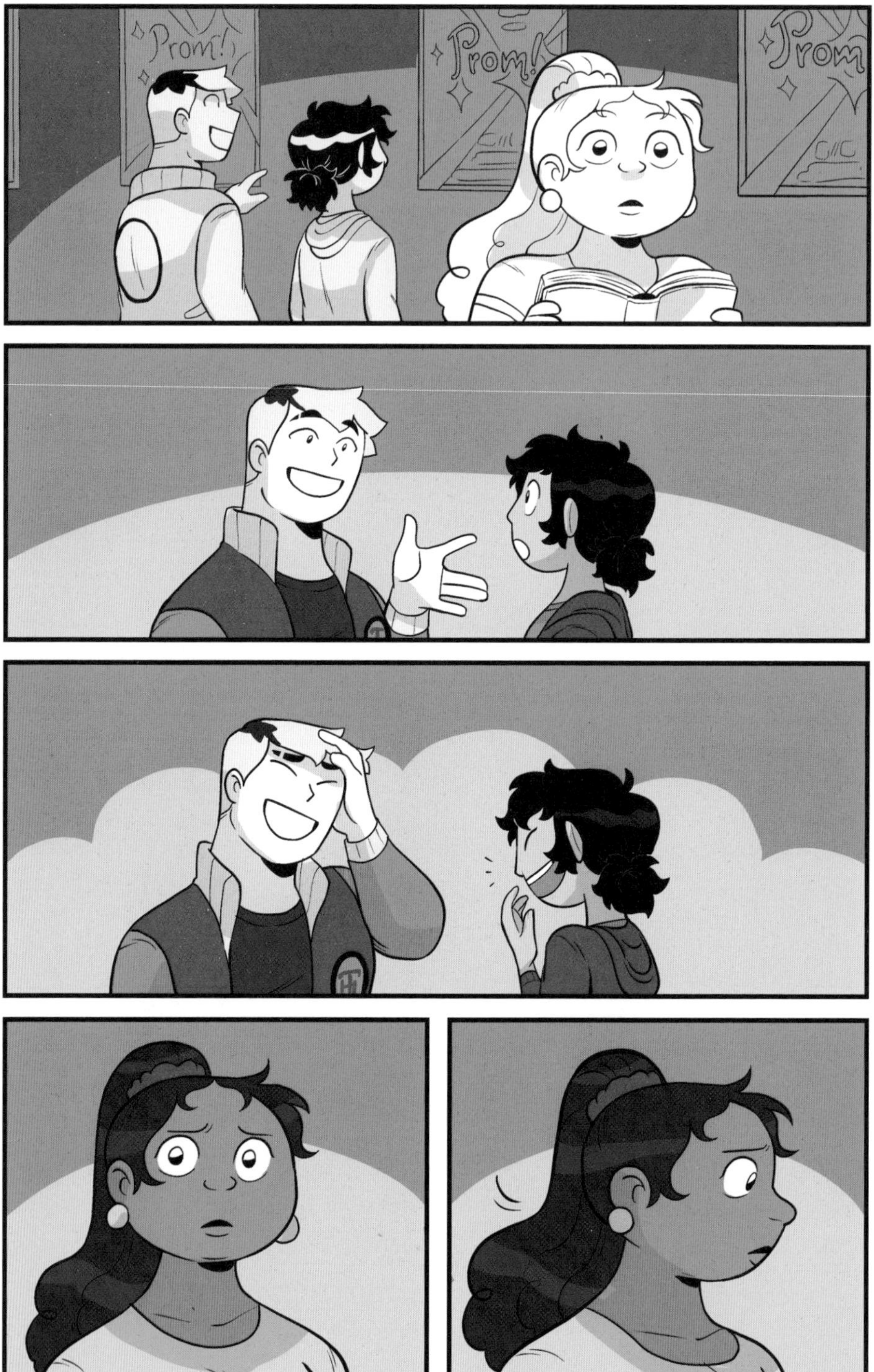
Prom!
Prom!
Prom

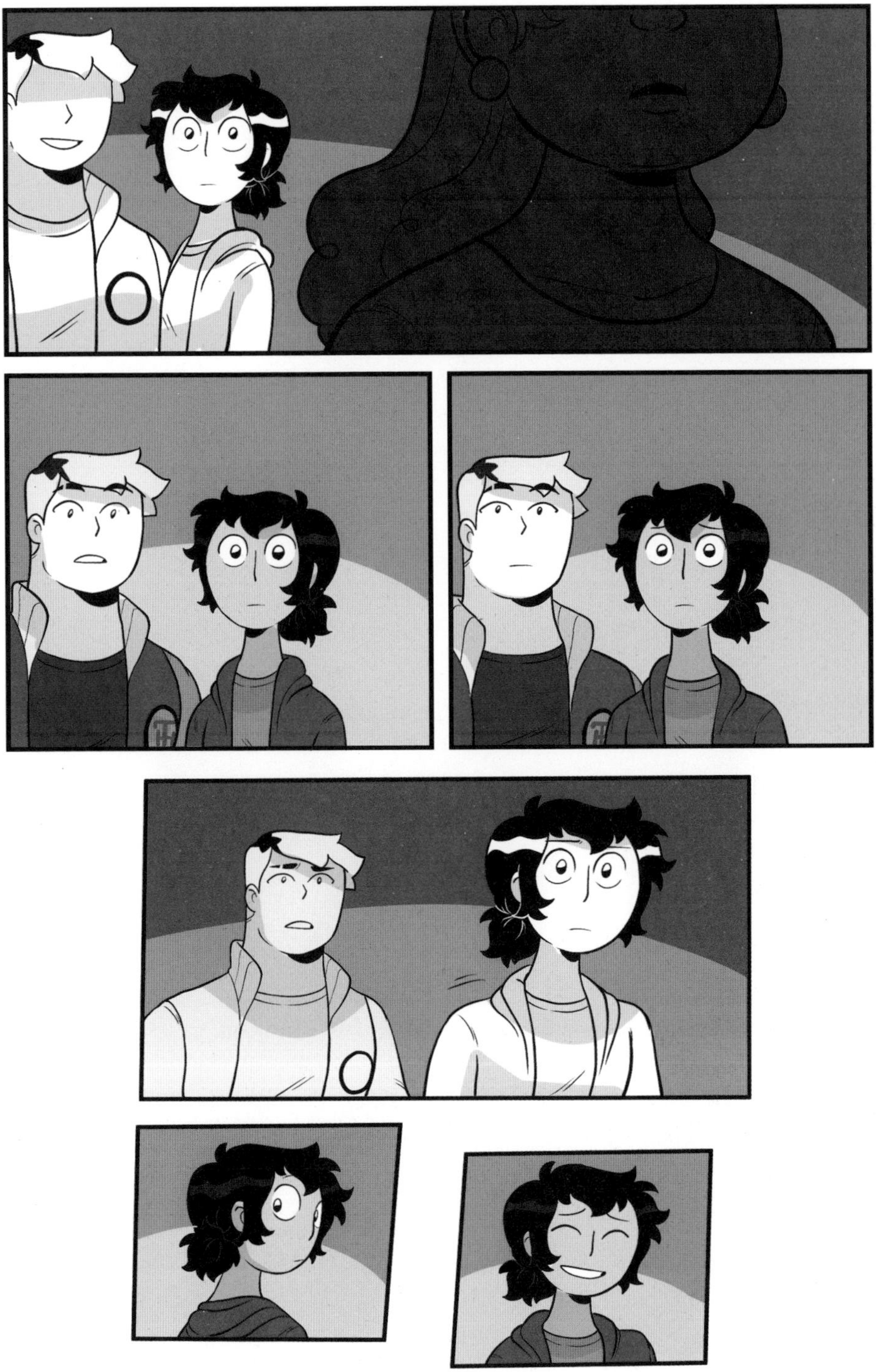

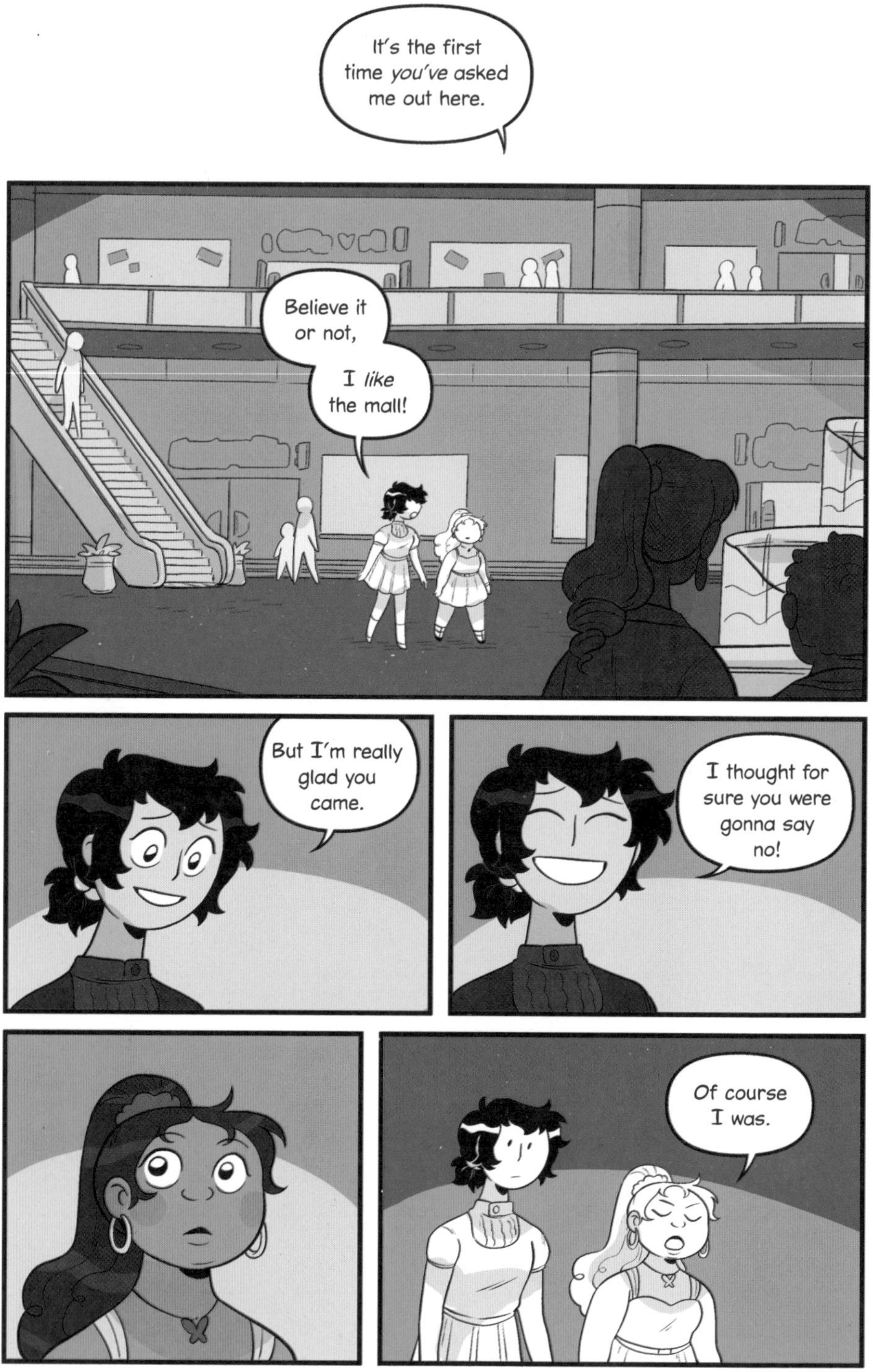
It's the first time *you've* asked me out here.
Believe it or not,
I *like* the mall!
But I'm really glad you came.
I thought for sure you were gonna say no!
Of course I was.

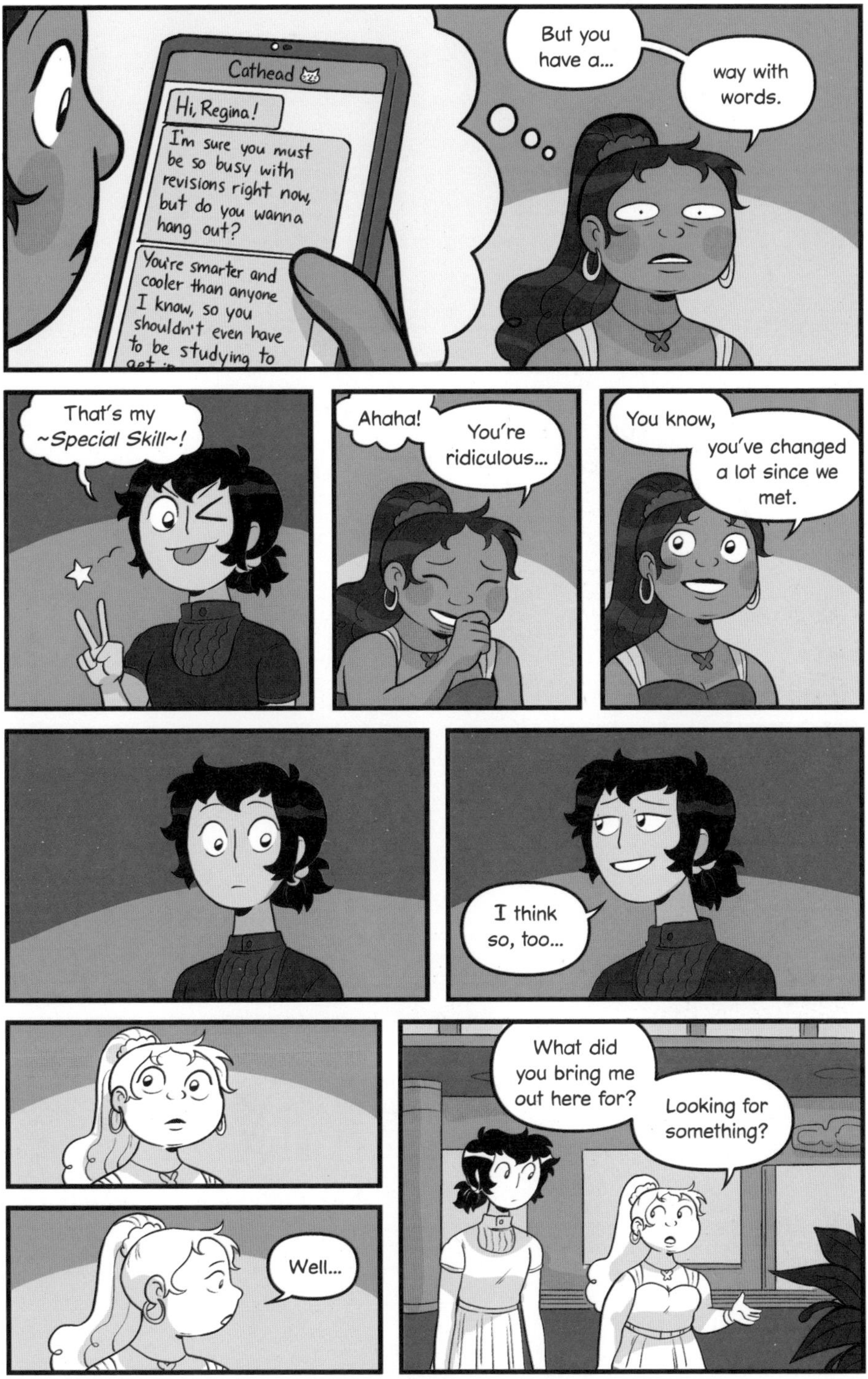
Cathead
Hi, Regina!
I'm sure you must be so busy with revisions right now, but do you wanna hang out?
You're smarter and cooler than anyone I know, so you shouldn't even have to be studying to
But you have a...
way with words.
That's my ~Special Skill~!
Ahaha!
You're ridiculous...
You know,
you've changed a lot since we met.
I think so, too...
Well...
What did you bring me out here for?
Looking for something?

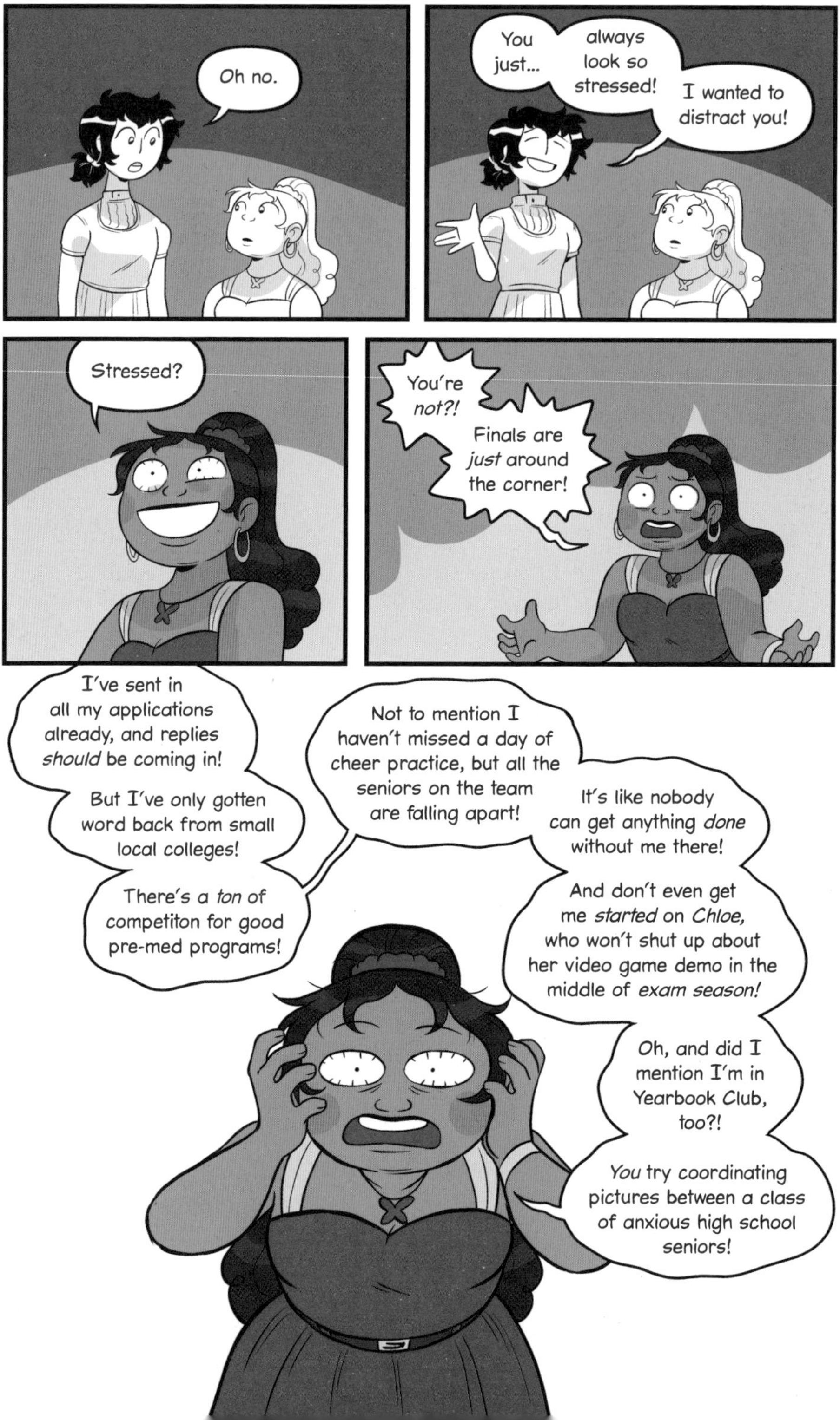
Oh no.
You just...
always look so stressed!
I wanted to distract you!
Stressed?
You're *not?!*
Finals are *just* around the corner!
I've sent in all my applications already, and replies *should* be coming in!
But I've only gotten word back from small local colleges!
There's a *ton* of competiton for good pre-med programs!
Not to mention I haven't missed a day of cheer practice, but all the seniors on the team are falling apart!
It's like nobody can get anything *done* without me there!
And don't even get me *started* on *Chloe,* who won't shut up about her video game demo in the middle of *exam season!*
Oh, and did I mention I'm in Yearbook Club, too?!
You try coordinating pictures between a class of anxious high school seniors!

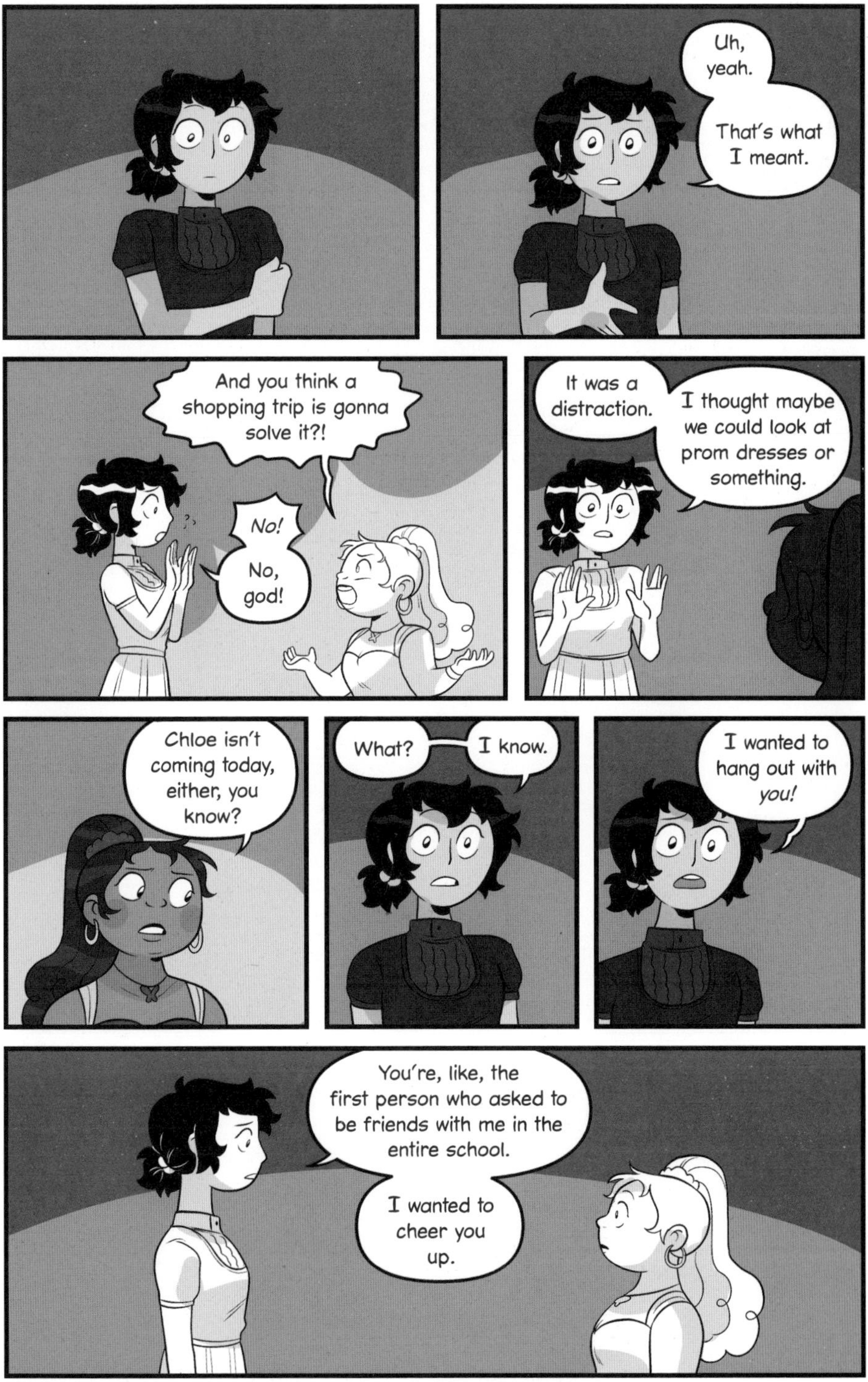
Uh,
yeah.
That's what
I meant.
And you think a shopping trip is gonna solve it?!
No!
No, god!
It was a distraction.
I thought maybe we could look at prom dresses or something.
Chloe isn't coming today, either, you know?
What?
I know.
I wanted to hang out with *you!*
You're, like, the first person who asked to be friends with me in the entire school.
I wanted to cheer you up.

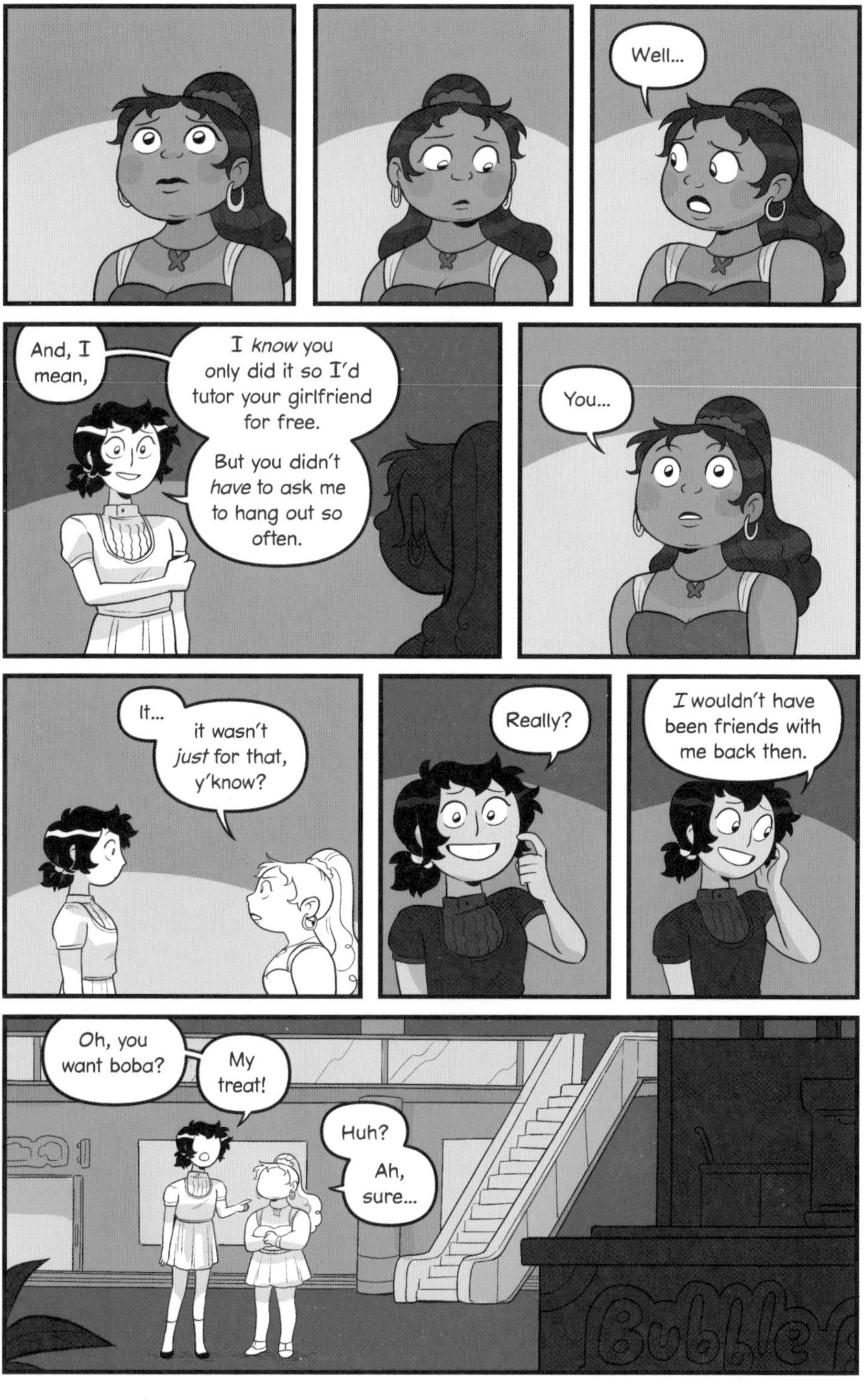
Well...
And, I mean,
I know you only did it so I'd tutor your girlfriend for free.
But you didn't have to ask me to hang out so often.
You...
It...
it wasn't just for that, y'know?
Really?
I wouldn't have been friends with me back then.
Oh, you want boba?
My treat!
Huh?
Ah, sure...
Bubble

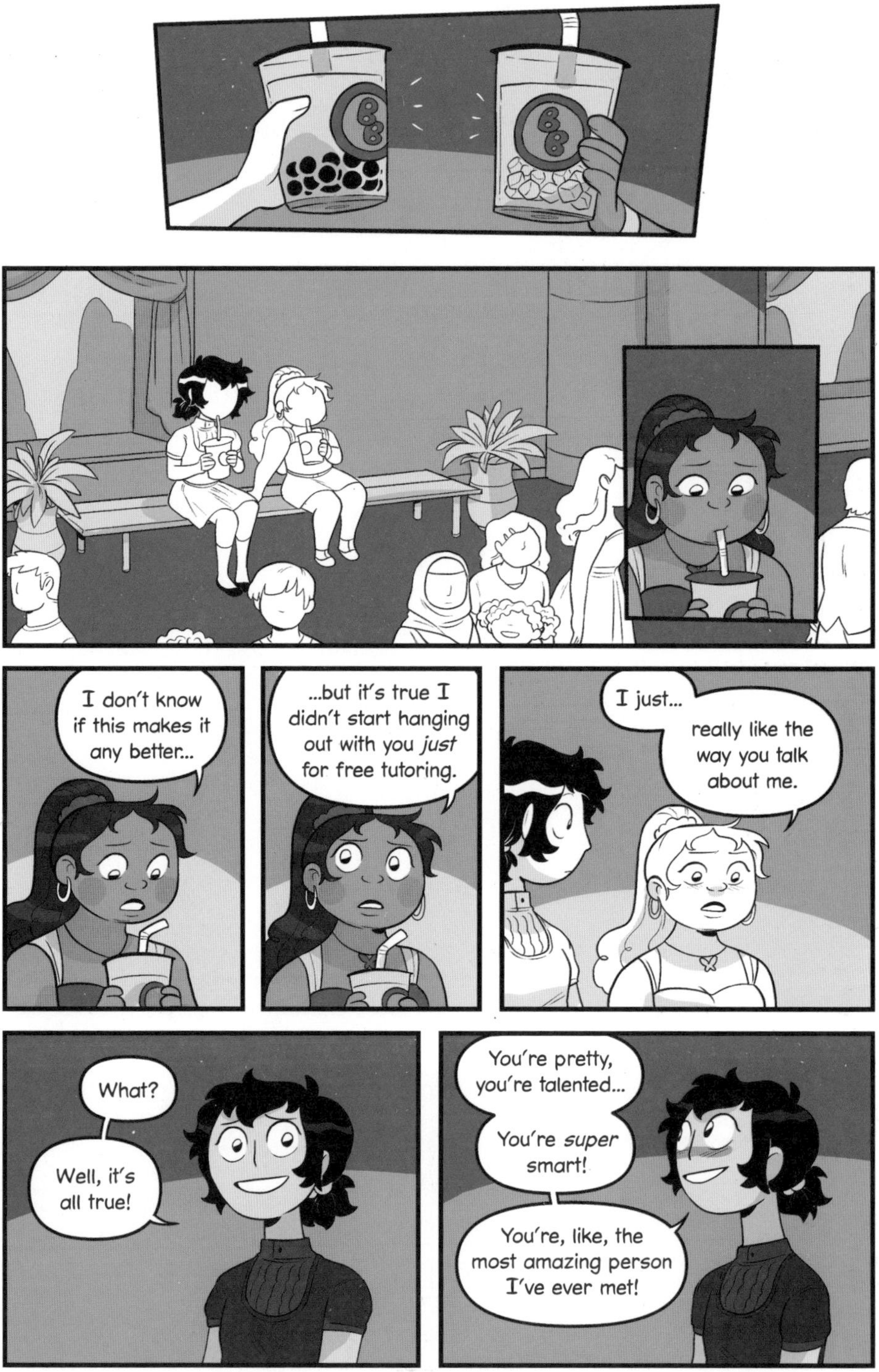

I don't know if this makes it any better...
...but it's true I didn't start hanging out with you *just* for free tutoring.
I just...
really like the way you talk about me.
What?
Well, it's all true!
You're pretty, you're talented...
You're *super* smart!
You're, like, the most amazing person I've ever met!

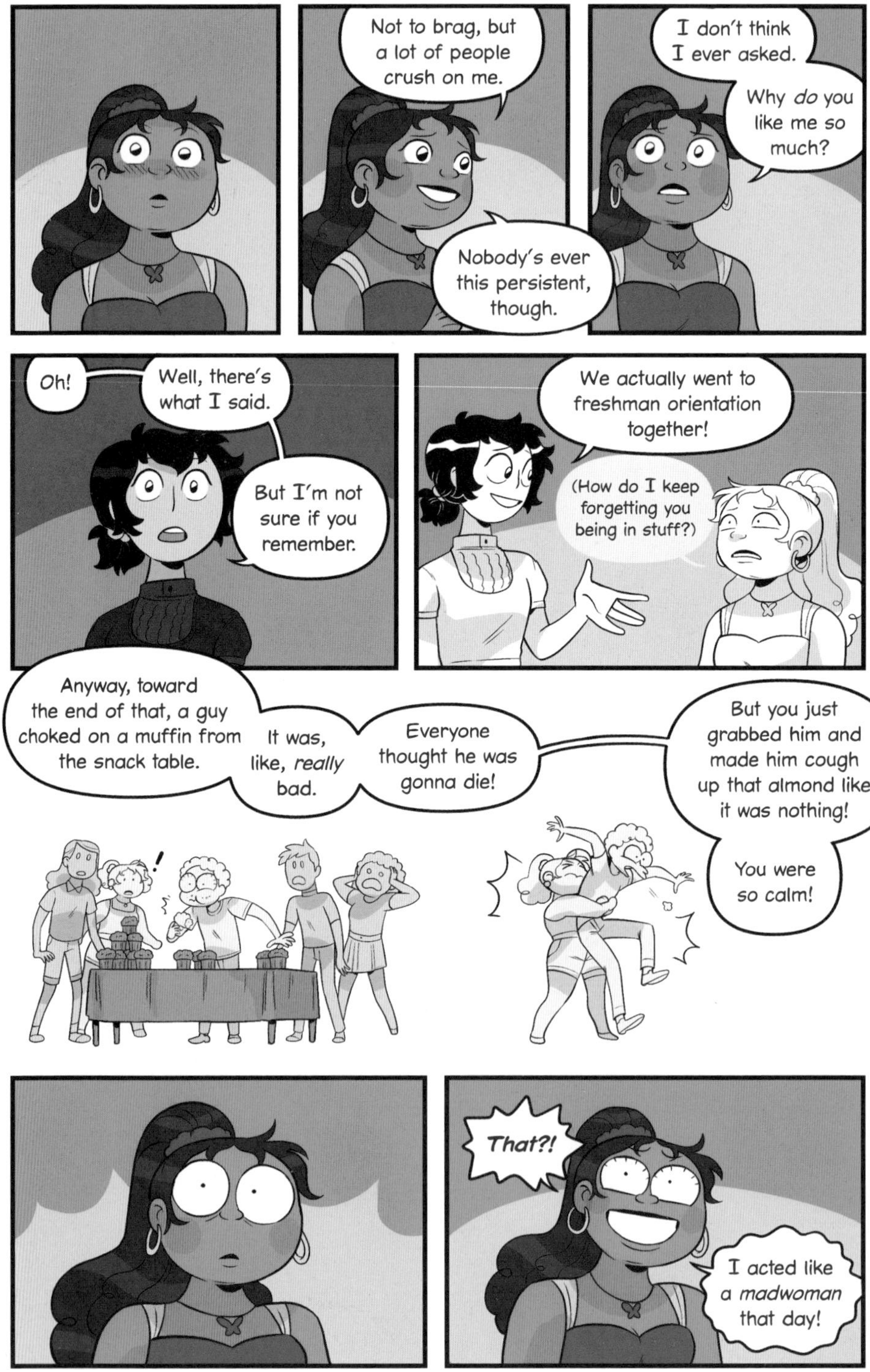
Not to brag, but a lot of people crush on me.
Nobody's ever this persistent, though.
I don't think I ever asked.
Why *do* you like me so much?
Oh!
Well, there's what I said.
But I'm not sure if you remember.
We actually went to freshman orientation together!
(How do I keep forgetting you being in stuff?)
Anyway, toward the end of that, a guy choked on a muffin from the snack table.
It was, like, *really* bad.
Everyone thought he was gonna die!
But you just grabbed him and made him cough up that almond like it was nothing!
You were so calm!
That?!
I acted like a *madwoman* that day!

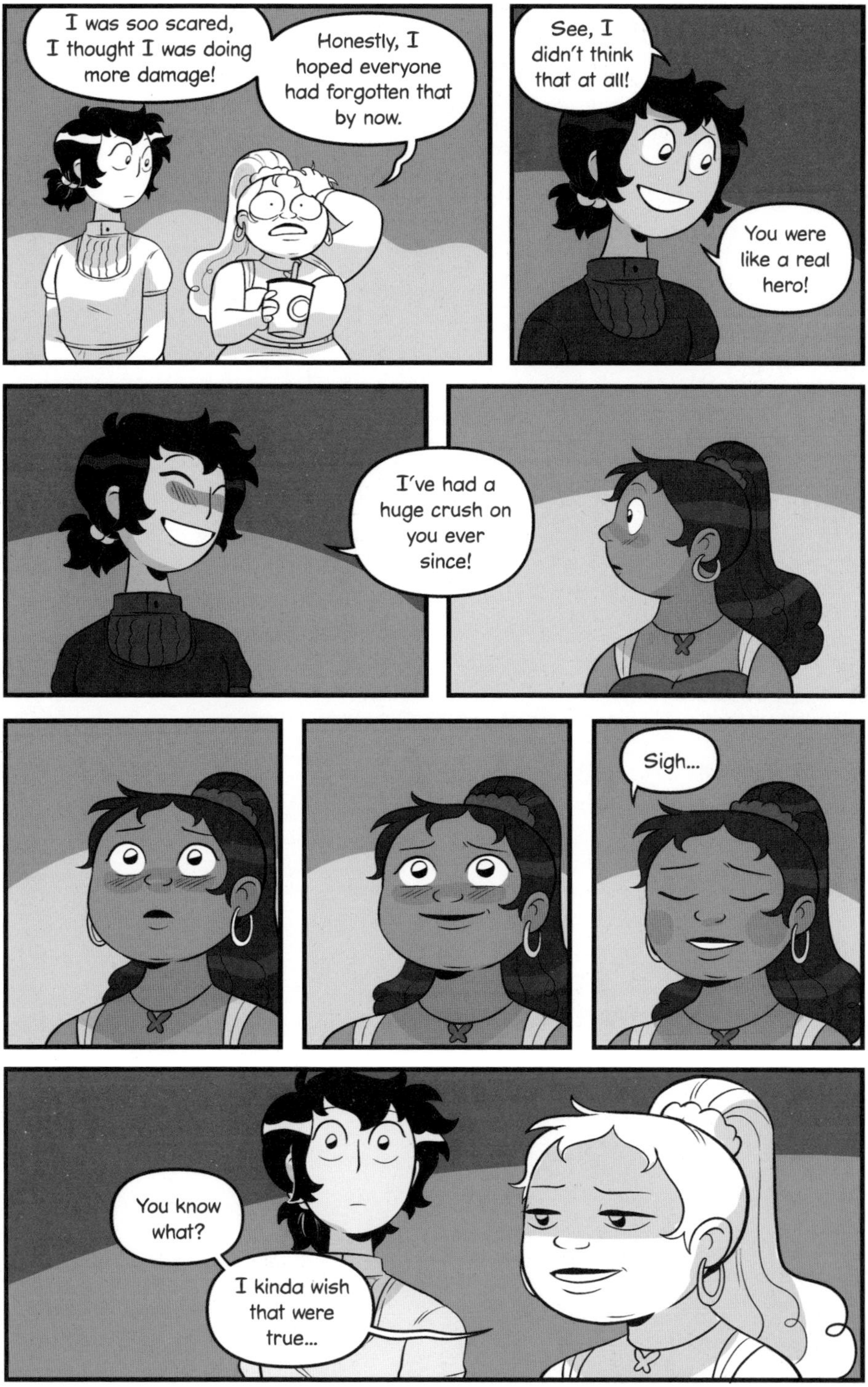
I was soo scared, I thought I was doing more damage!
Honestly, I hoped everyone had forgotten that by now.
See, I didn't think that at all!
You were like a real hero!
I've had a huge crush on you ever since!
Sigh...
You know what?
I kinda wish that were true...

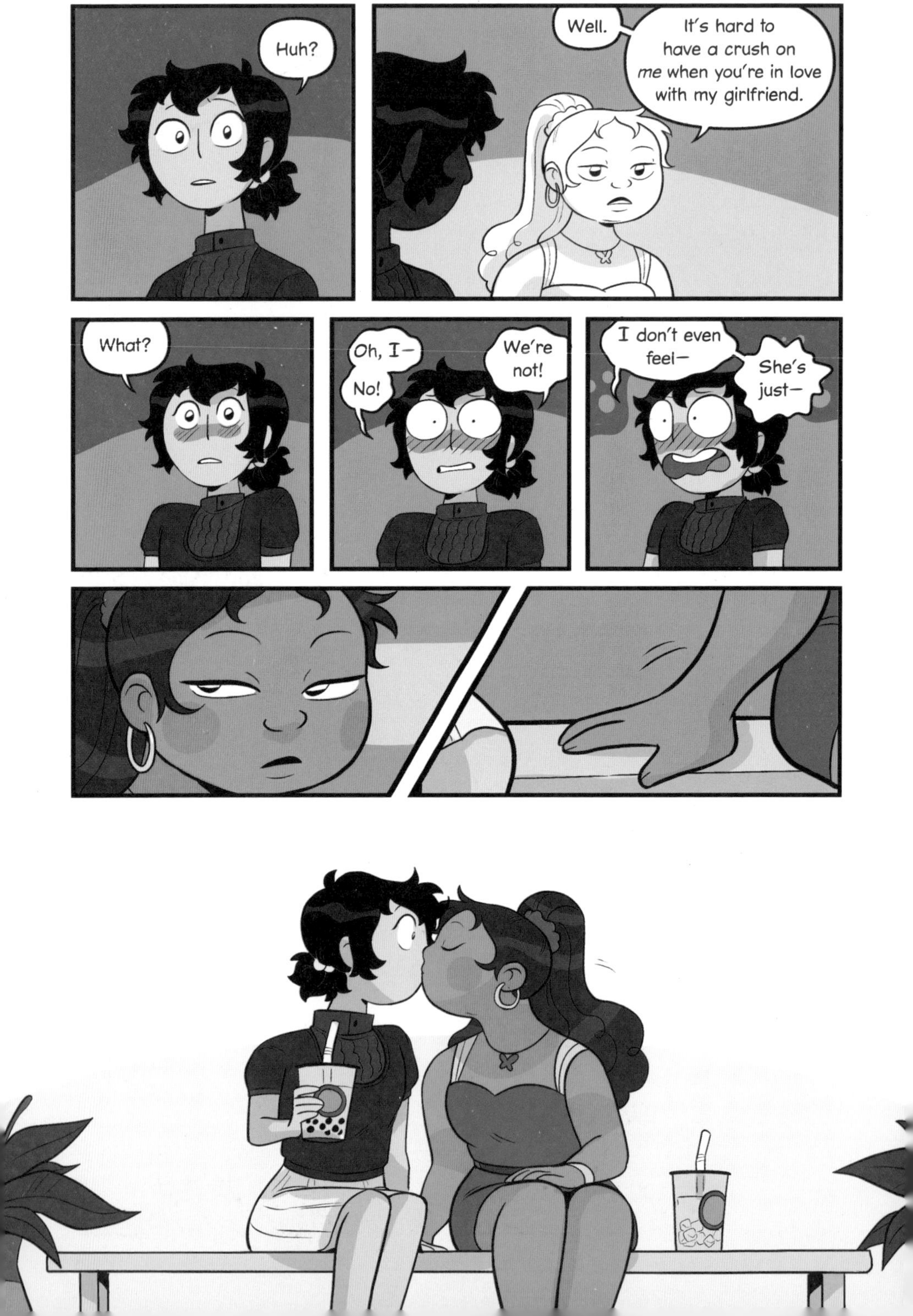
Huh?
Well.
It's hard to have a crush on *me* when you're in love with my girlfriend.
What?
Oh, I—
No!
We're not!
I don't even feel—
She's just—

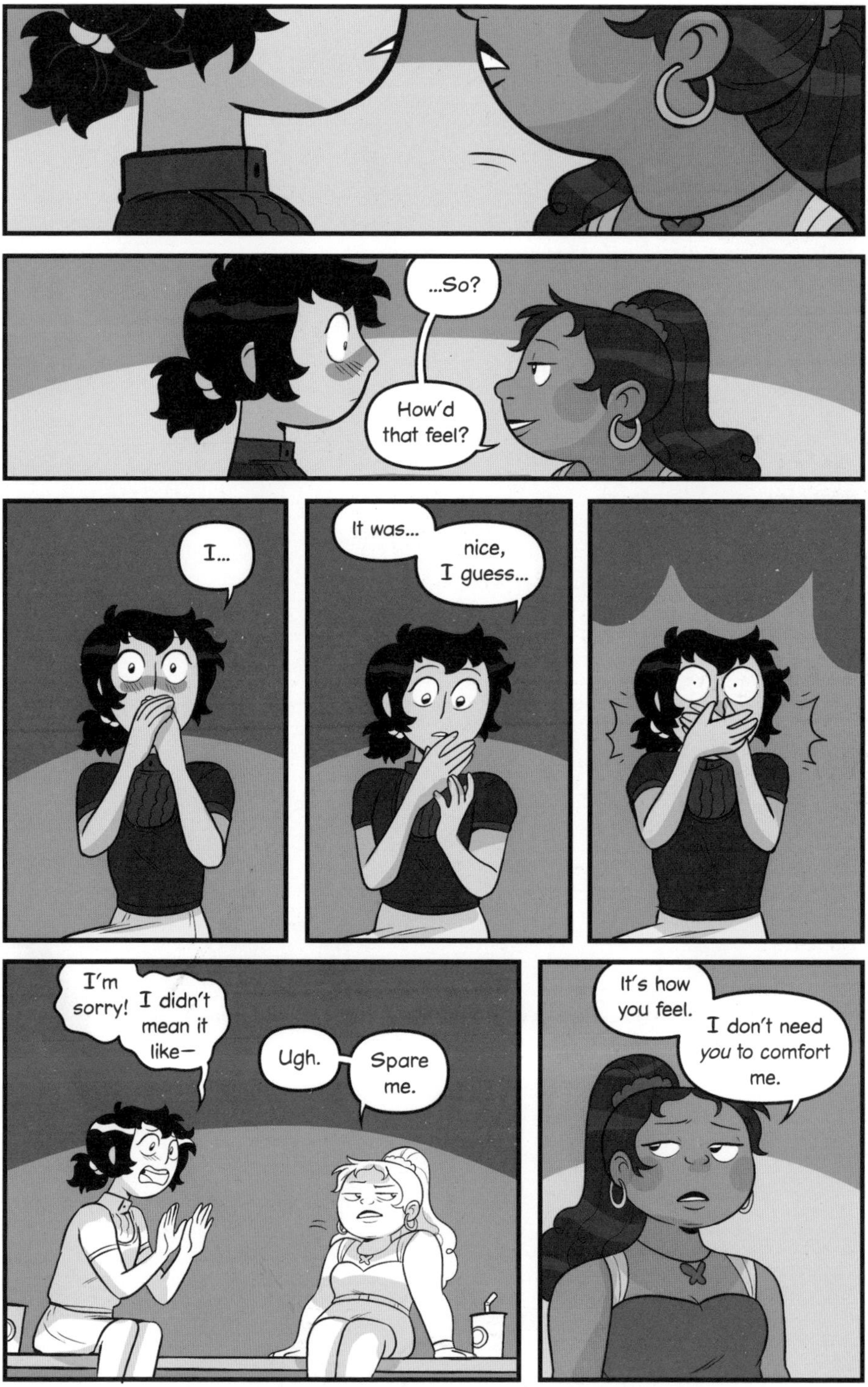
...So?
How'd that feel?
I...
It was...
nice, I guess...
I'm sorry!
I didn't mean it like—
Ugh.
Spare me.
It's how you feel.
I don't need *you* to comfort me.

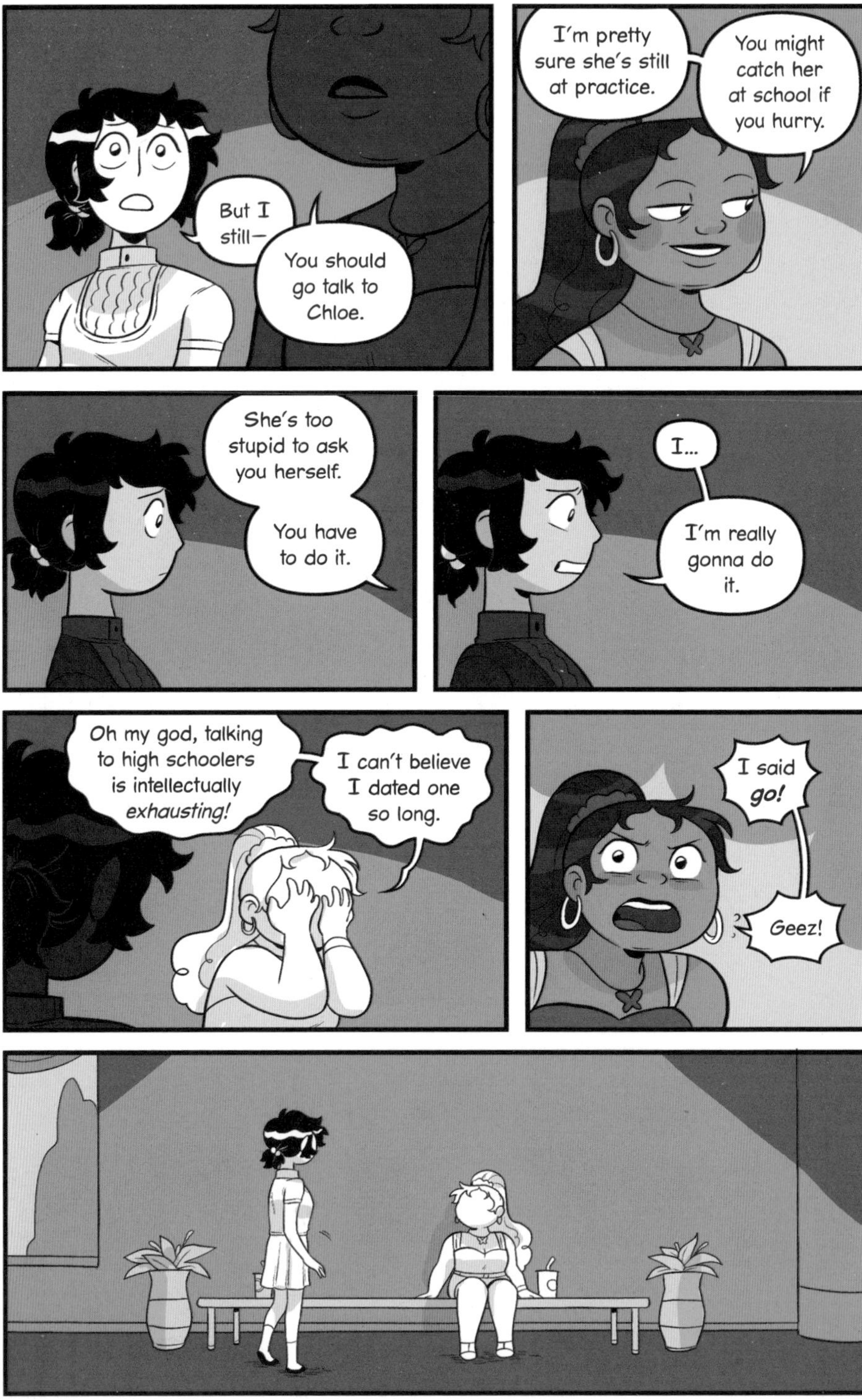
But I still—
You should go talk to Chloe.
I'm pretty sure she's still at practice.
You might catch her at school if you hurry.
She's too stupid to ask you herself.
You have to do it.
I...
I'm really gonna do it.
Oh my god, talking to high schoolers is intellectually *exhausting!*
I can't believe I dated one so long.
I said ***go!***
Geez!

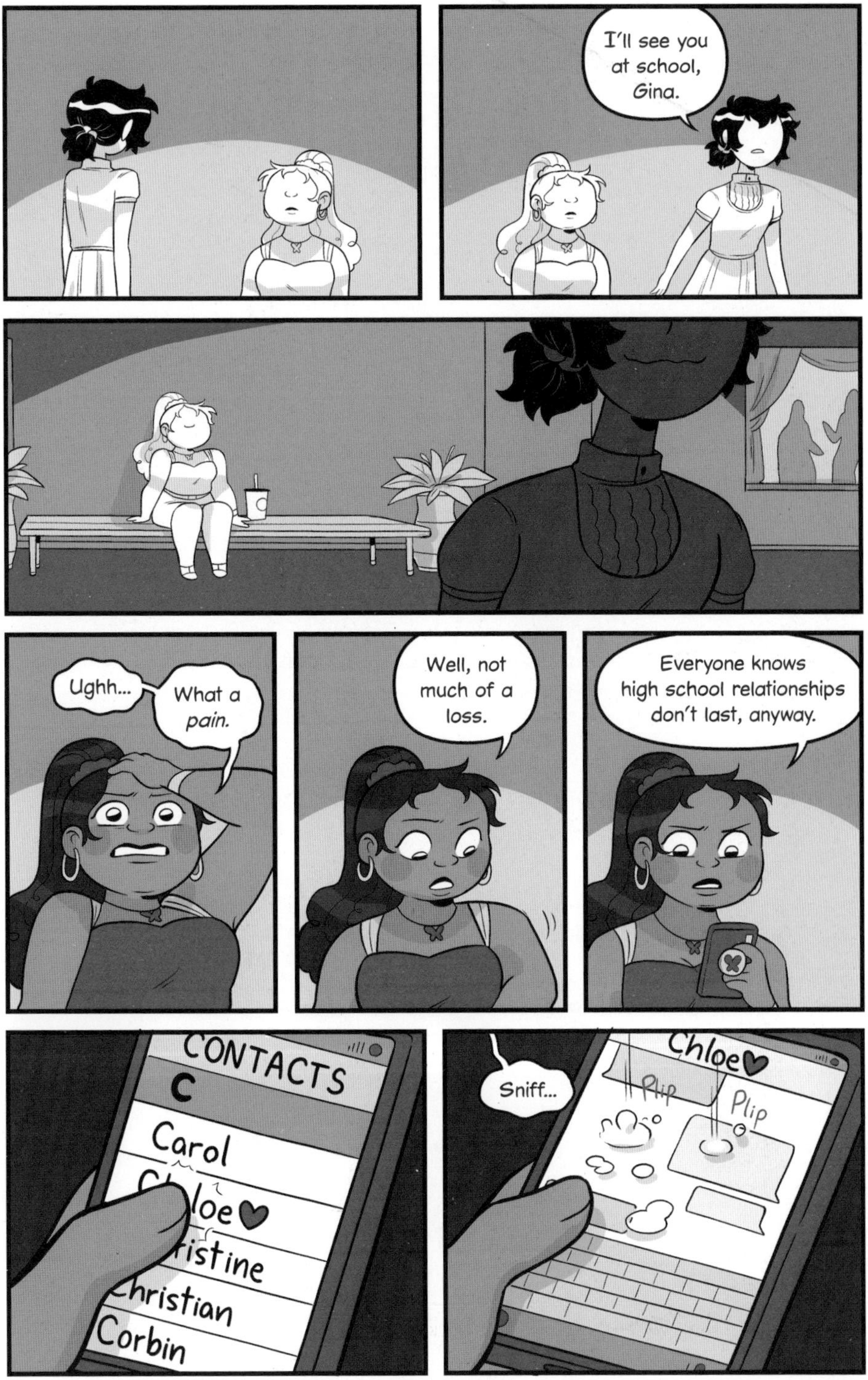
I'll see you at school, Gina.
Ughh...
What a *pain.*
Well, not much of a loss.
Everyone knows high school relationships don't last, anyway.
CONTACTS
C
Carol
Chloe
Christine
Christian
Corbin
Sniff...
Chloe
Plip
Plip

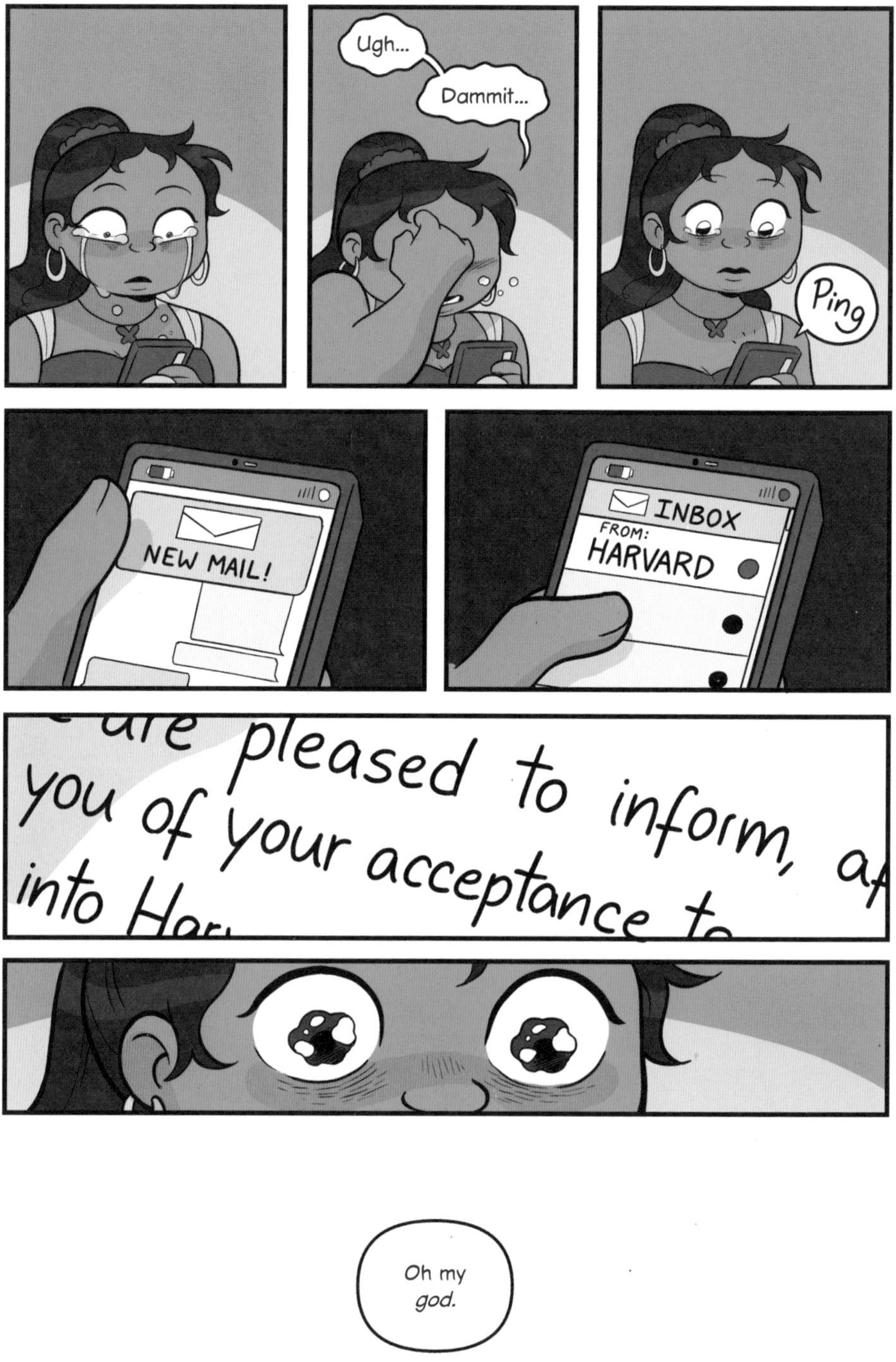
Ugh...
Dammit...
Ping
NEW MAIL!
INBOX
FROM:
HARVARD
pleased to inform,
you of your acceptance
into
Oh my god.

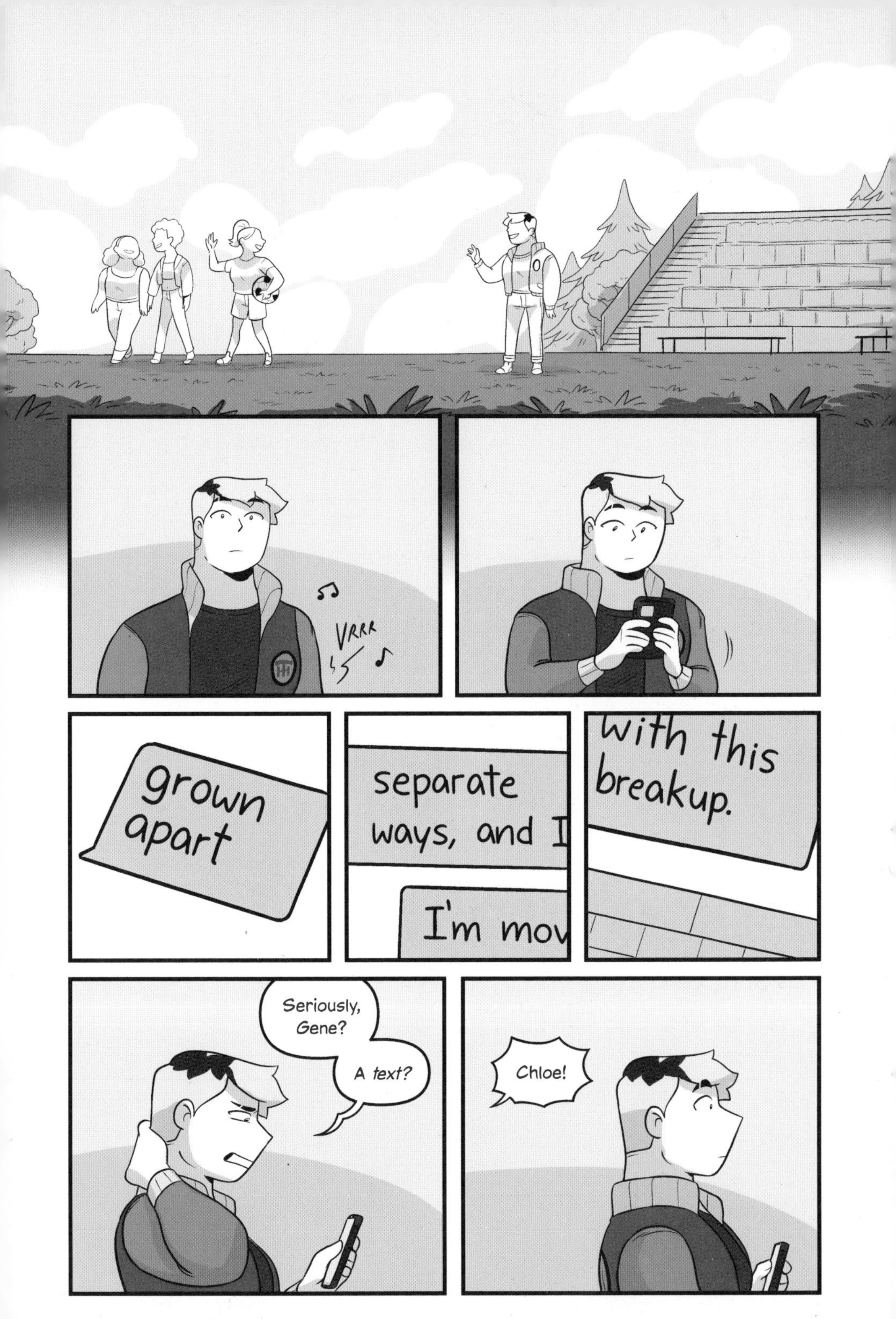
VRRR
grown apart
separate ways, and I
I'm mov
with this breakup.
Seriously, Gene?
A text?
Chloe!

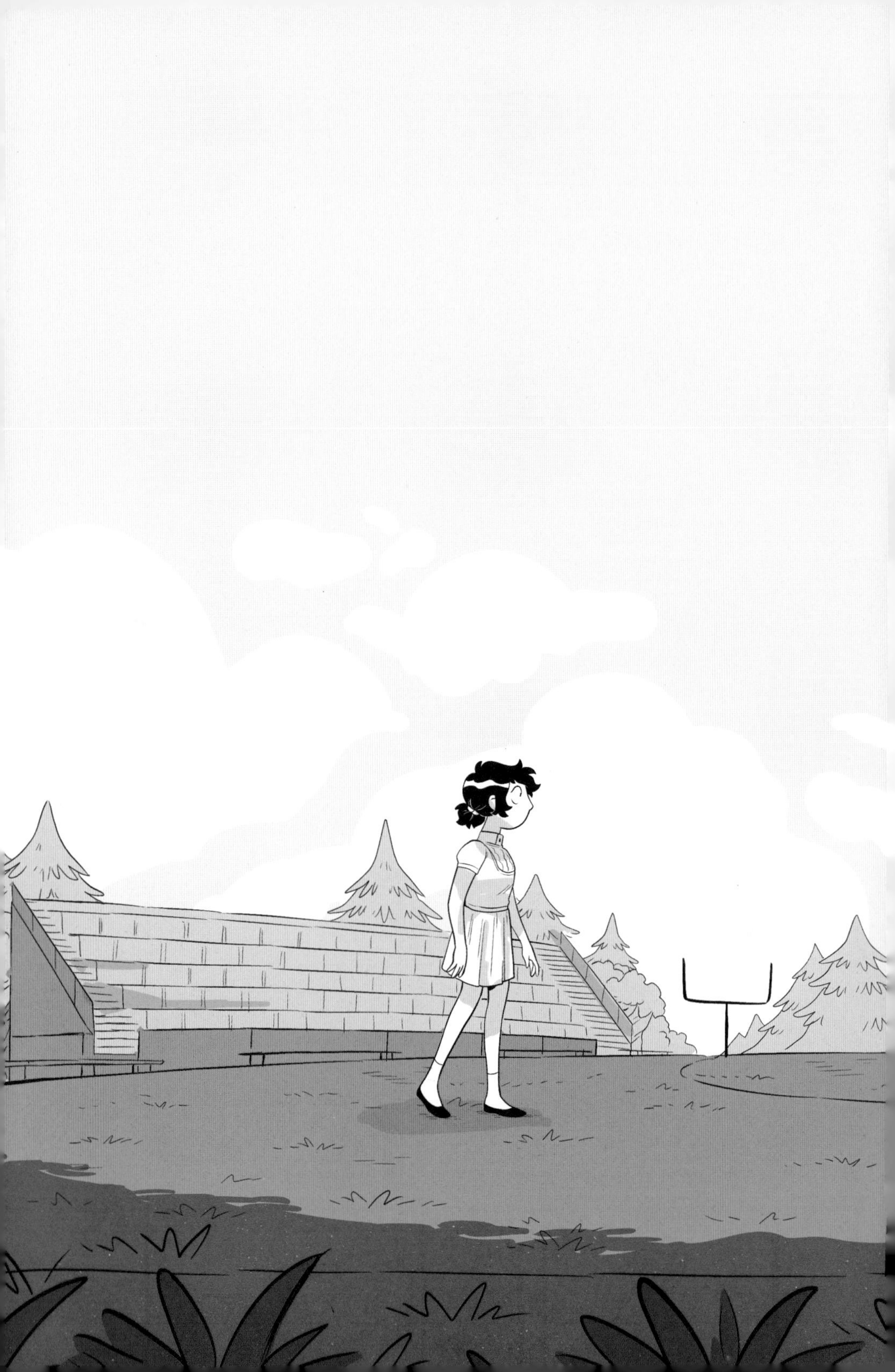

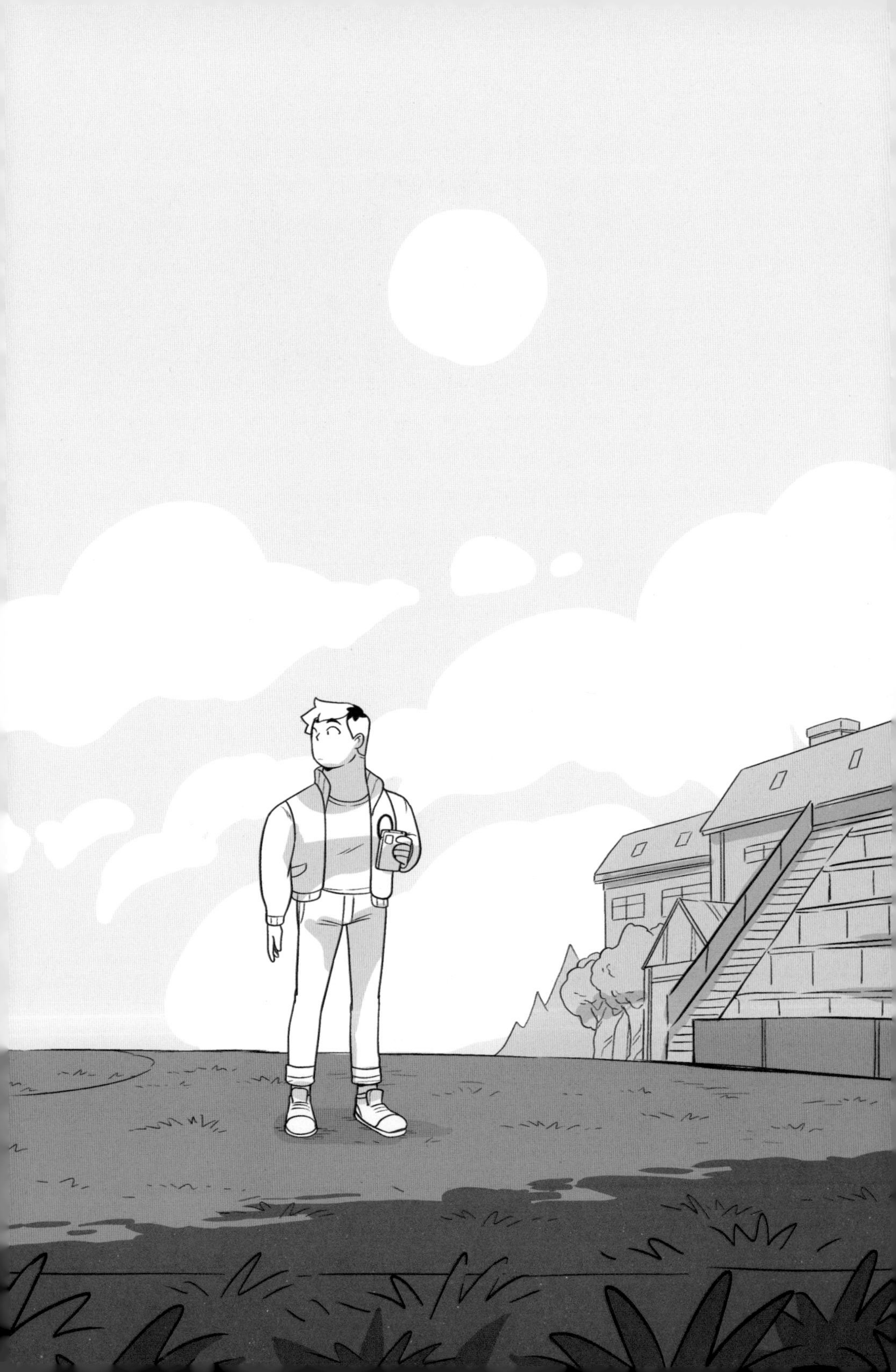

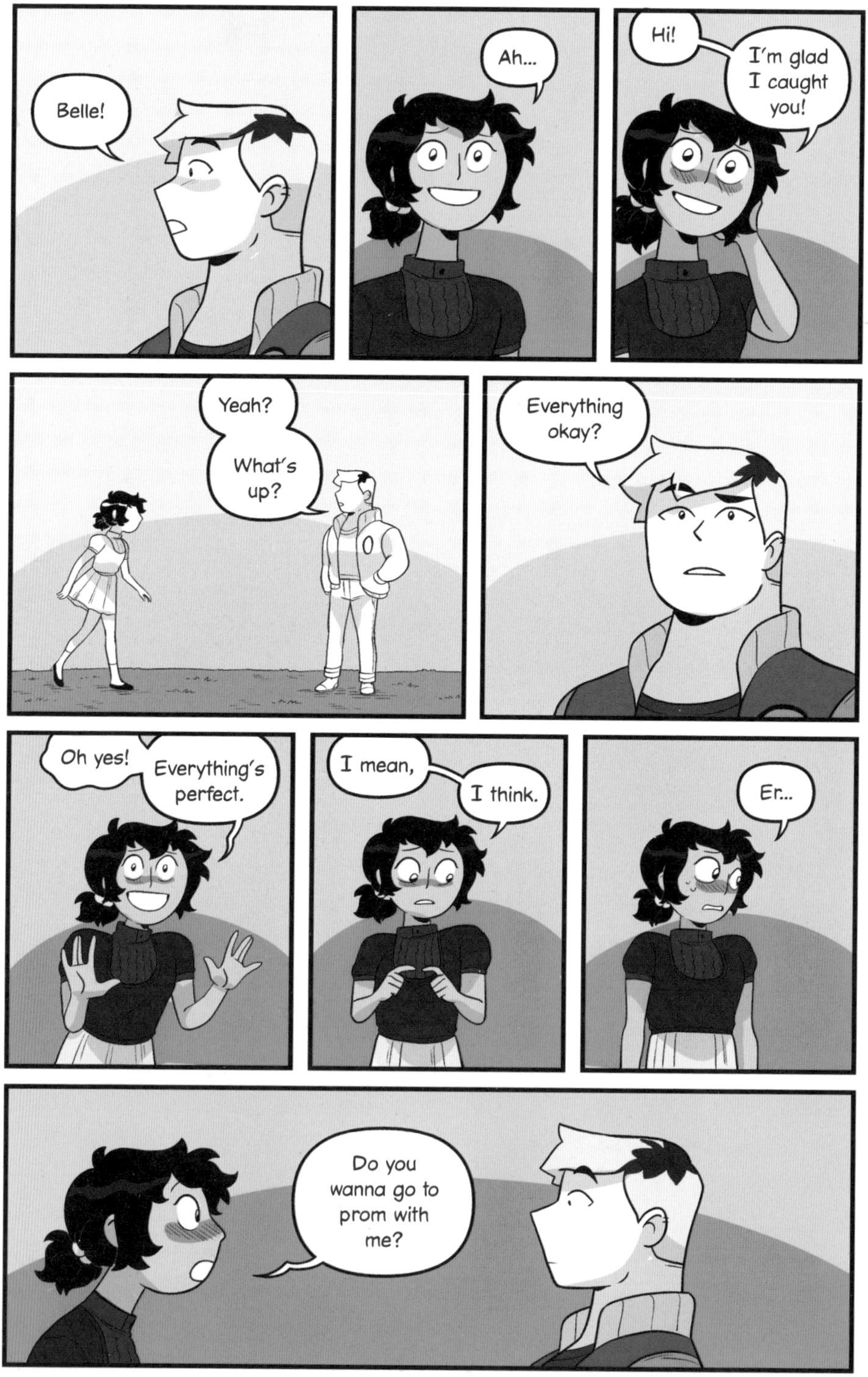
Belle!
Ah...
Hi!
I'm glad I caught you!
Yeah?
What's up?
Everything okay?
Oh yes!
Everything's perfect.
I mean,
I think.
Er...
Do you wanna go to prom with me?

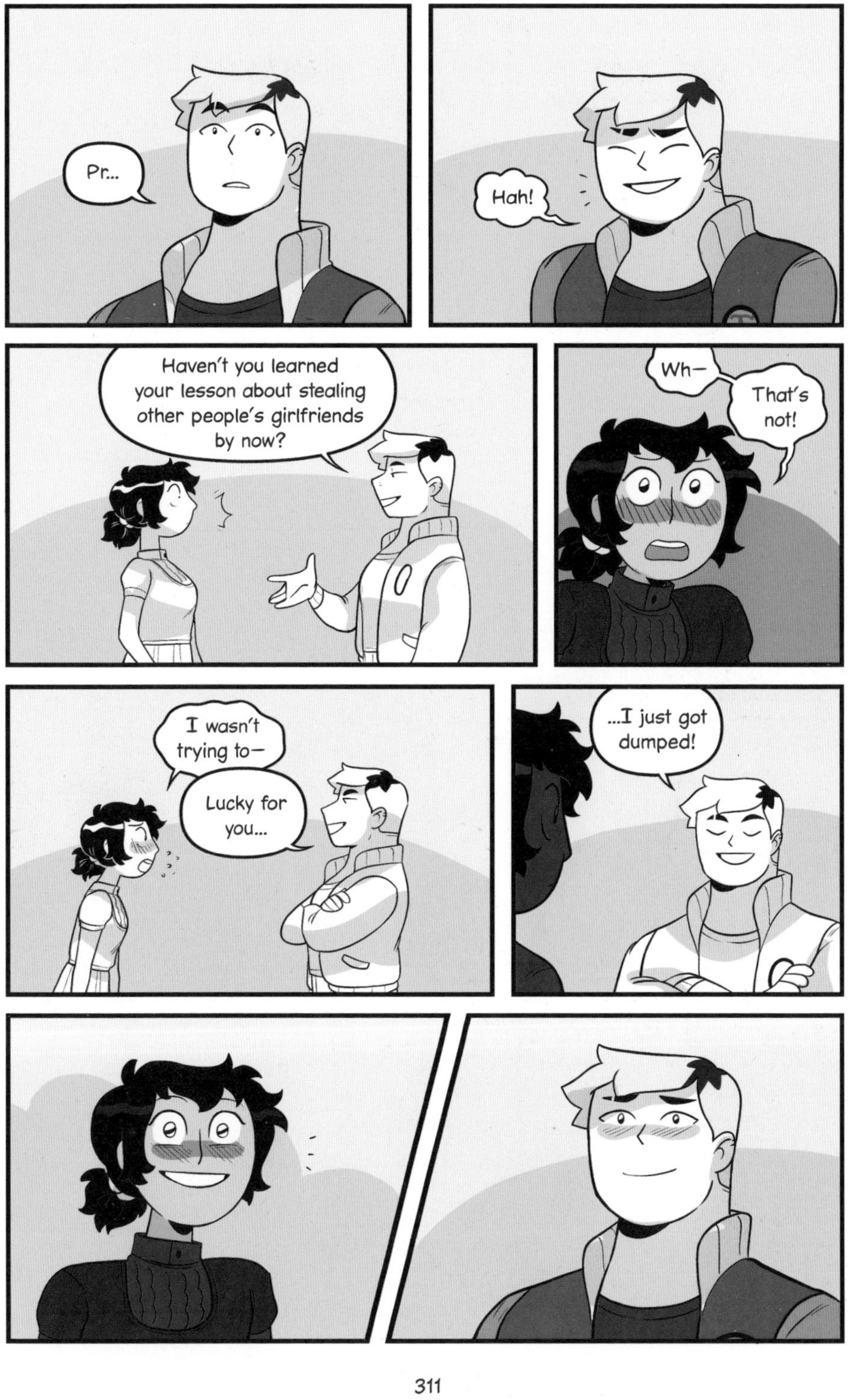
Pr...
Hah!
Haven't you learned your lesson about stealing other people's girlfriends by now?
Wh—
That's not!
I wasn't trying to—
Lucky for you...
...I just got dumped!

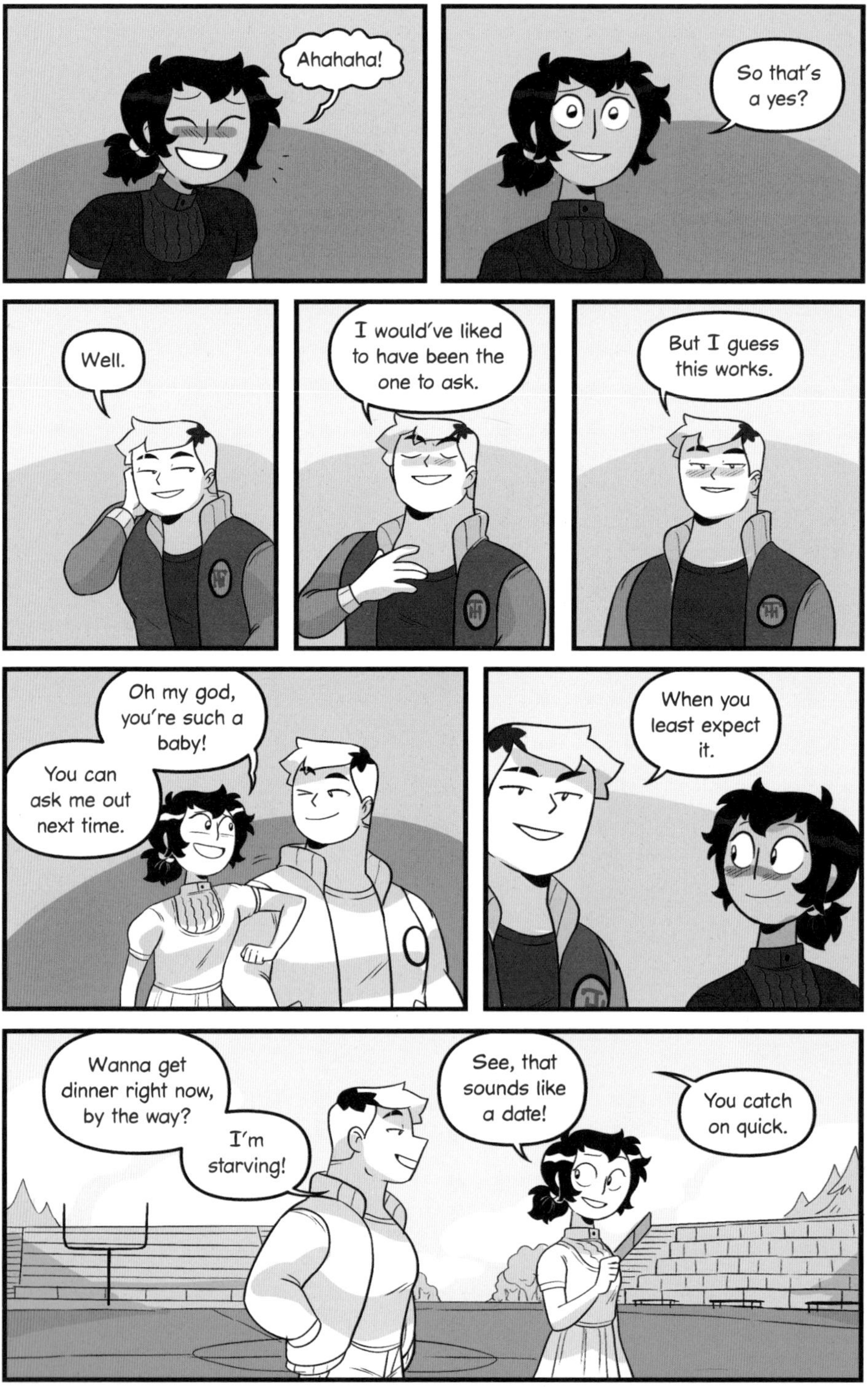
Ahahaha!
So that's a yes?
Well.
I would've liked to have been the one to ask.
But I guess this works.
Oh my god, you're such a baby!
You can ask me out next time.
When you least expect it.
Wanna get dinner right now, by the way?
I'm starving!
See, that sounds like a date!
You catch on quick.

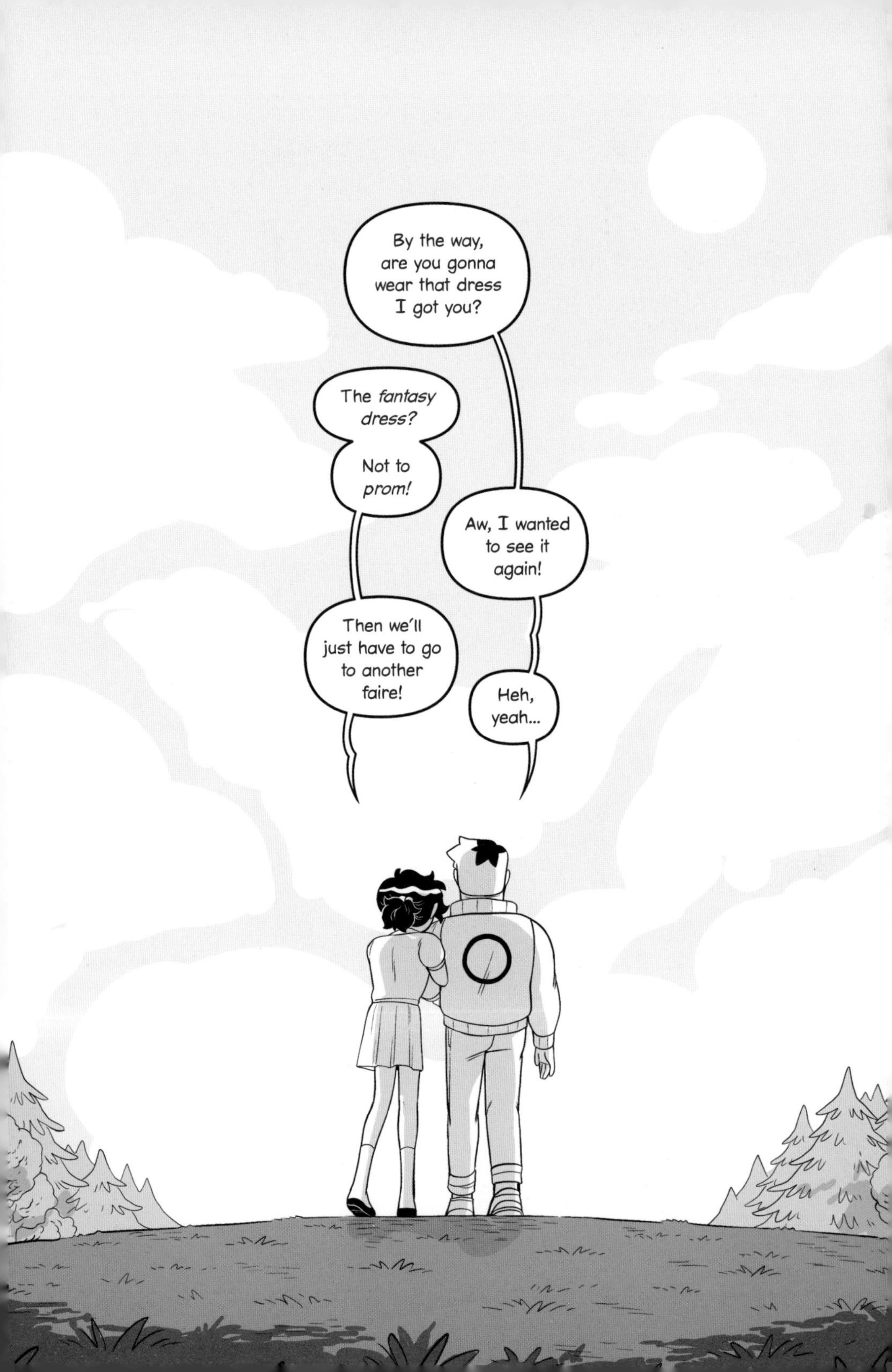

By the way, are you gonna wear that dress I got you?
The *fantasy* dress?
Not to *prom!*
Aw, I wanted to see it again!
Then we'll just have to go to another faire!
Heh, yeah...

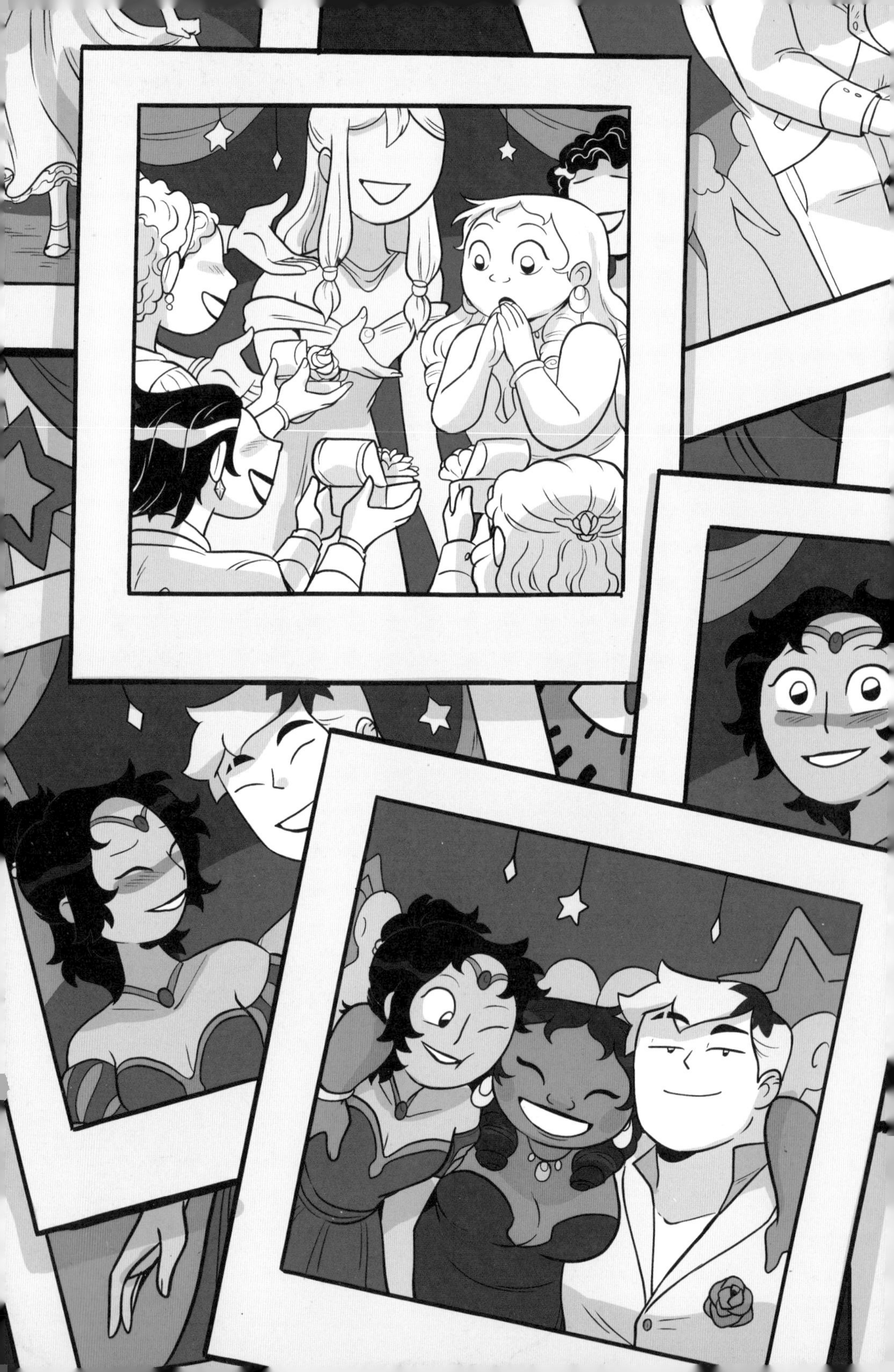

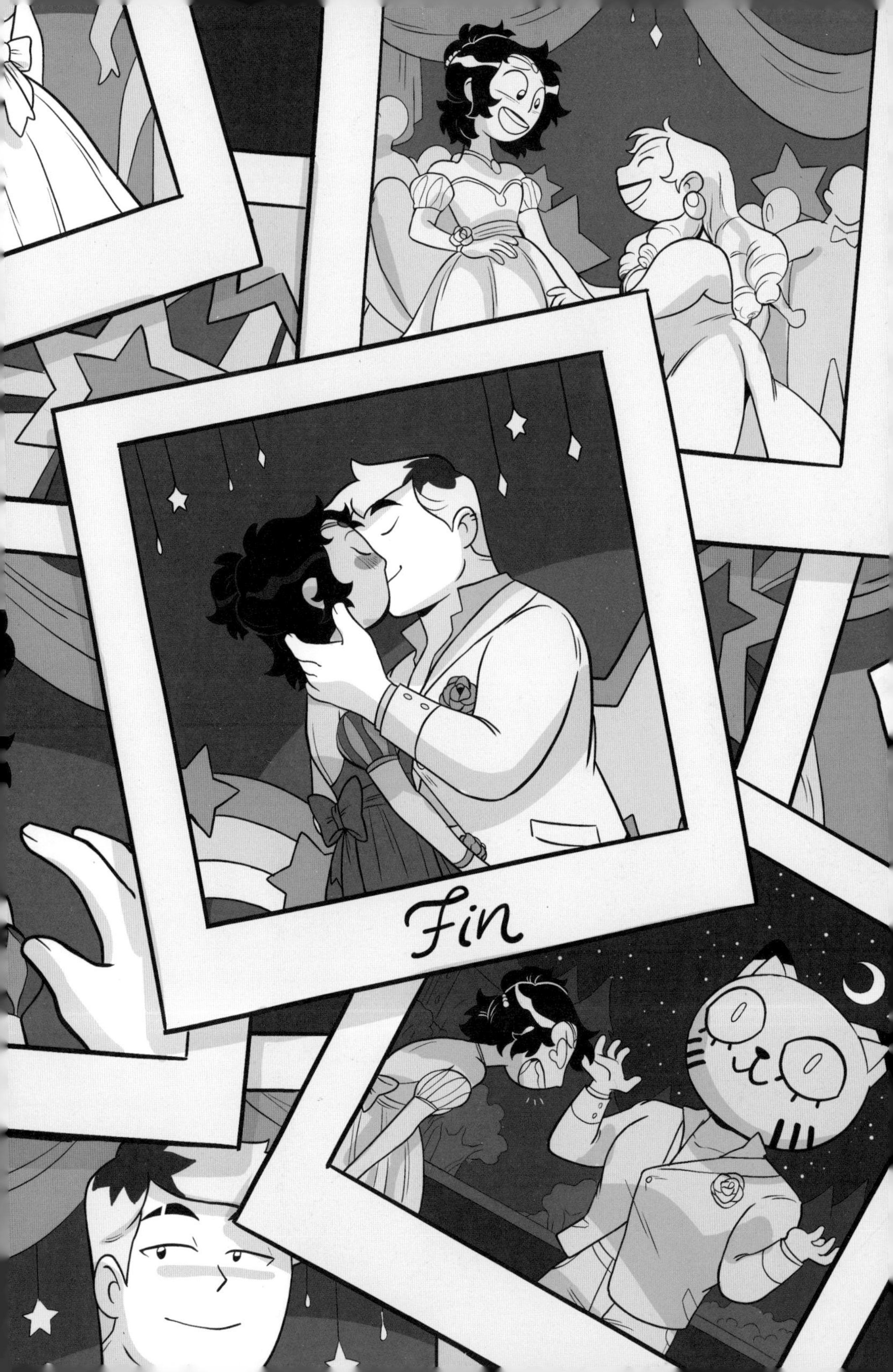
Fin

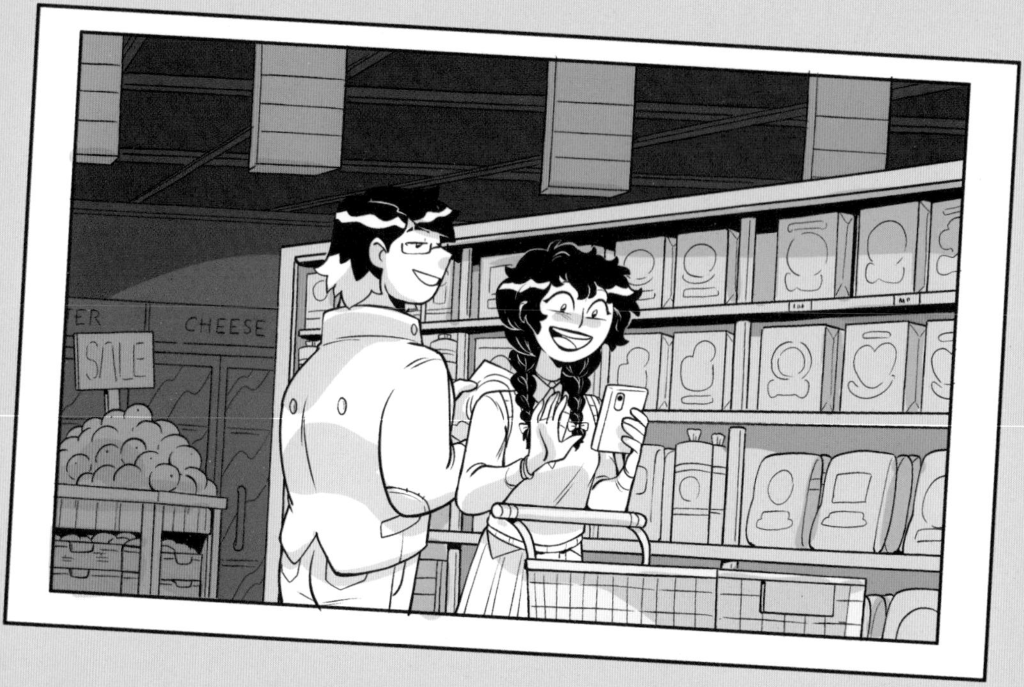
CHEESE
SALE

College Year 2

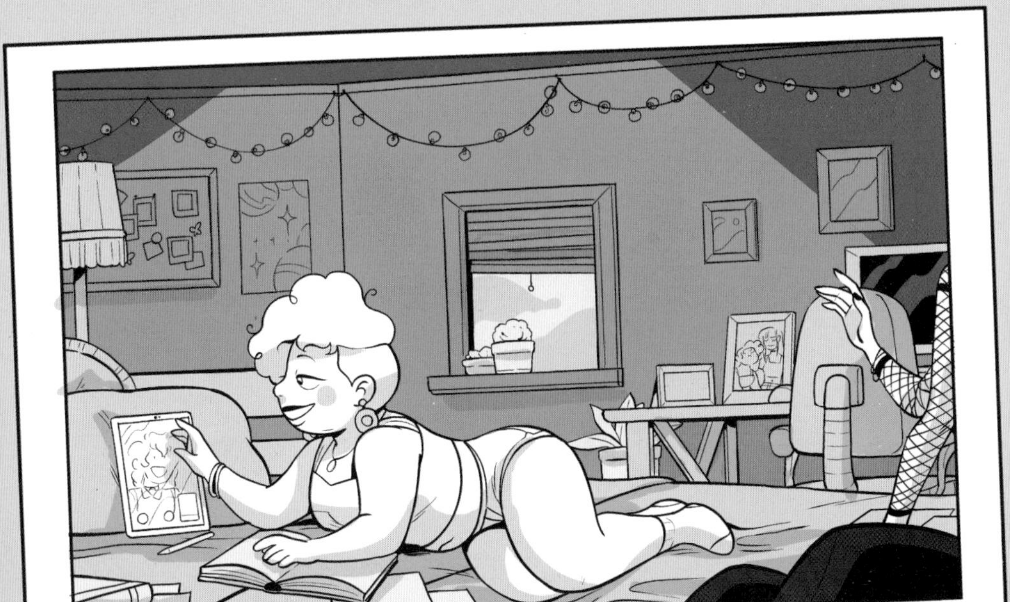

Acknowledgments

Once upon a time, there was a very weird little girl who went to preschool dressed like a princess when the occasion absolutely didn't call for it. As a woman, she still likes to feel like a princess, from time to time.

Once upon a time, there was a very weird teen who had an enormous amount of pressure put on her by her family of PhD graduates. She learned to be proud of that family while doing her own thing.

Once upon a time, there was a very weird young adult who chose an unconventional career path over something she knew she could excel at while also keeping with what was expected of her.

She's very happy she followed her dreams, or this little book might've never been made.

Thank you so much for reading *Belle of the Ball*. It was a labor of love, and I hope Belle's, Gina's, or Chloe's stories resonate with any young people out there the way I know they would've resonated with me.

Thank you Steve, Peter, Calista, Kirk, Molly, everyone at First Second, and all my friends who watched me shift into an absolute cave-dwelling witch crone while making this.

I hope you enjoy my future works. I'm just getting started.

XXOO,
Mari